T0059671

PRAISE FOR
The Book That Wouldn't Burn

"*The Book That Wouldn't Burn* combines extraordinary imagination with the expert craftsmanship of a writer at the top of his game. The power inherent in the written word provides the magical spine to an epic tale exploring the joys and dangers of human discovery."

—*New York Times* bestselling author Anthony Ryan

"This tale of knowledge and its cost flies by thanks to the gripping mystery and beautiful worldbuilding, ending on a devastating cliffhanger. Readers will be desperate for more." —*Publishers Weekly* (starred review)

"Reading Mark Lawrence's latest novel, *The Book That Wouldn't Burn*, feels like having your mind blown in slow motion." —Grimdark Magazine

"*The Book That Wouldn't Burn* was a fun ride from start to finish. . . . I simply can't wait to see what happens next." —Game Vortex

"Gripping, earnest, and impeccably plotted." —*Kirkus Reviews* (starred review)

"There is a lot to enjoy here, with a fantastic setting, a feisty heroine, and hints of a deeper mystery that calls to mind the depths of Frank Herbert's *Dune* and its intertwined cultural and religious issues." —*Library Journal*

"Pick this one up." —The Fantasy Review

PRAISE FOR THE NOVELS OF
Mark Lawrence

"An excellent writer."
—#1 *New York Times* bestselling author George R. R. Martin

"Different than anything I have ever read."
—*New York Times* bestselling author Terry Brooks

"An amazing series, and I eagerly anticipate Lawrence's next literary effort, whatever it may be." —*New York Times* bestselling author Peter V. Brett

"It's not like anything I've ever read before."
—#1 *New York Times* bestselling author Rick Riordan

"Dark and relentless. . . . A two-in-the-morning page-turner."
—*New York Times* bestselling author Robin Hobb

"Epic fantasy on a George R. R. Martin scale but on speed." —Fixed on Fantasy

"Mark Lawrence's growing army of fans will relish this rollicking new adventure
and look forward to the next one." —*Daily Mail*

THE
BOOK THAT
WOULDN'T BURN

THE LIBRARY TRILOGY:

BOOK ONE

MARK LAWRENCE

ACE
New York

ACE

Published by Berkley

An imprint of Penguin Random House LLC

penguinrandomhouse.com

Copyright © 2023 by Bobalinga Ltd.

Penguin Random House supports copyright. Copyright fuels creativity, encourages
diverse voices, promotes free speech, and creates a vibrant culture. Thank you for buying
an authorized edition of this book and for complying with copyright laws by not
reproducing, scanning, or distributing any part of it in any form without
permission. You are supporting writers and allowing Penguin Random House
to continue to publish books for every reader.

ACE is a registered trademark and the A colophon is a
trademark of Penguin Random House LLC.

ISBN: 9780593437926

Library of Congress Cataloging-in-Publication DataNames:
Lawrence, Mark, 1966– author.

Title: The book that wouldn't burn / Mark Lawrence.
Other titles: Book that would not burn
Description: New York: Ace, [2023] | Series: The Library trilogy; book one
Identifiers: LCCN 2022054527 (print) | LCCN 2022054528 (ebook) |
ISBN 9780593437919 (hardcover) | ISBN 9780593437933 (ebook)
Subjects: LCGFT: Fantasy fiction. | Novels.
Classification: LCC PS3612.A9484 B66 2023 (print) | LCC PS3612.A9484 (ebook) |
DDC 813/.6—dc23/eng/20221116
LC record available at https://lccn.loc.gov/2022054527
LC ebook record available at https://lccn.loc.gov/2022054528

Ace hardcover edition / May 2023
Ace trade paperback edition / March 2024

Printed in the United States of America
1st Printing

This is a work of fiction. Names, characters, places, and incidents either are the product of
the author's imagination or are used fictitiously, and any resemblance to actual persons,
living or dead, business establishments, events, or locales is entirely coincidental.

To my readers for sharing the journey

By book sixteen, I'm running out of targets . . . World peace next!

THE BOOK
THAT WOULDN'T BURN

PROLOGUE

The first arrow hit a child. That was the opening line.

. . . similarly impermanent. All books, no matter their binding, will fall to dust. The stories they carry may last longer. They might outlive the paper, the library, even the language in which they were first written. The greatest story can reach the stars . . .

The First Book of Irad

CHAPTER 1

Livira

They named Livira after a weed. You couldn't grow much in the Dust but that never stopped hungry people trying. They said livira would grow in places where rocks wouldn't. Which never made sense to Livira because rocks don't grow. Unfortunately, not even goats could eat the stuff and any farmer who watered a crop would find themselves spending most of their time fighting it. Spill a single drop of water in the Dust and, soon enough, strands of livira would come coiling out of the cracked ground for a taste.

Her parents had given her a different name but she hardly remembered it. People called her Livira because, like the weed, you couldn't keep her down.

"Come on then!" Livira picked herself up and wiped the blood from her nose. She raised her fists again. "Come on."

Acmar shook his head, looking embarrassed now that a ring of children had gathered. All of them were dusty but Livira was coated in the stuff, head to foot.

"Come on!" she shouted. She felt woozy and her head rang as if it were the summoning bell and someone kept beating it.

"You're twice her size." Benth broke into the circle and pushed Acmar aside.

"She won't stay down," Acmar complained, rubbing his knuckles.

"It's a draw then." Benth stepped between them, a broad-shouldered boy and handsome despite his broken nose. Seeing Livira's scowl he grabbed her hand and raised it above her head. "Livira wins again."

The others cheered and laughed then broke and ran before the advance of a tall figure, dark against the sun's white glare.

"Livy!" Her aunt's scolding voice. Fingers wrapped her wrist and she was being jerked away towards the black shadow of the family hut.

Aunt Teela shoved a cracked leather bucket at her. "The beans need watering."

"Yessum!" Livira had always loved the well. She spat a bloody mess into the dust then grinned up at her aunt before hurrying off with the bucket. Her aunt shook her head. You could put Livira down but you couldn't keep her there.

Livira's hurrying didn't last long. She slowed as she passed Ella's shack. The old woman collected wind-weed, or rather the kids chased and caught it for her, racing over the hardpan in pursuit of the tough, fibrous balls. The things were almost entirely empty space and Ella's cunning fingers could coax the randomness of their criss-crossed strands into meaning that pleased the eye. Deft twists could render a horse or man suspended in a network of threads within the outer sphere that was itself just a lattice of thicker strands.

Livira watched Ella work. "I wish I could do that."

Ella looked up from her task and held up her current piece on the palm of one wrinkled hand. "For you."

Livira picked it up, a small sphere of wind-weed just five or six inches across.

Immediately Ella took up a replacement and began anew.

Livira studied her unexpected prize. It looked half-finished, the mass of fibres compressed towards the middle seeming like just a clotting of many threads that wove nothing. But as she rotated the ball a shape emerged within it, still vague, like a man approaching through a dust storm, indistinct but definitely there. A young man or maybe a boy. Though if asked how she could tell his age or sex, Livira would have no answer. And it seemed to her that she knew him, or rather that she recognised him.

"I wish I could do that," she said again, cradling the ball in both hands.

"You have other talents, dear." Ella didn't look up from her task. Livira's past efforts with the wind-weed had been comically bad and part of her thanked Ella for not offering false hope that she would get much better.

"Talents?" Livira kicked at the dust. A memory like a steel trap seemed more of a curse than a blessing. A poorer memory, one that ran the dry glare of one day into the next, might stop the time weighing so heavily even on young shoulders. And she was pretty much unbeatable at the game of hollows and stones, but it seemed to make the old men angry rather than pleased. She also understood the odds when the younger men gambled on the game—better than any of them did—but none of them were interested in her advice. "All my skills are useless."

"There are no useless skills, girl. Only talents that have yet to find an application."

"Well . . . Acmar can fart a tune."

Ella looked up at that, lips pursed, dark eyes unreadable. Livira glanced down, noticed the bucket at her own feet, and, thus reminded of her task, opted to skip away.

THE WELL WAS a yard wide and a hundred yards deep. Livira had asked a thousand times how they ever managed to dig it. She'd scratched holes in the hardpan herself and never got deeper than the width of a hand. The well lay outside the settlement, beyond the bean rows. The scent of water attracts all sorts in the Dust, and rarely the sort you want wandering around your huts at night.

There was a wetness in the air above it, as if the well itself were a great throat. Livira could feel the dampness of its breath on her skin. She liked to lie on her belly with her head over the edge and stare down into the blackness. The children said Orrin had fallen in and that's where he went last month. But the water had stayed clear and sweet. Livira thought that a dust-bear had taken Orrin. The boy had never looked where he was going. And whilst that might lend credence to the idea that he could have walked into the well, there were, Livira said, many more dust-bears waiting just beneath the surface than wells.

Livira cranked the windlass, lowering the attached bucket towards the unseen water. She liked the well because it kept them all alive, but that wasn't the only reason. In her mind it was a connection to another world, out of reach but most definitely there. A world where what they needed most was commonplace, a world of darkness and flow, full of its own secrets, home to wet things that swam in blindness, tasting their way through unknown caverns.

"What you doing?"

Livira jumped, startled out of her daydreaming. She saw it was Katrin in her shapeless, dusty smock, hands crimson from shelling jarra beans. "I'm juggling elephants."

Katrin frowned, considering the statement. Katrin was loyal, kind, but really quite slow sometimes. "You're not ju—"

"It was a joke." Livira rolled her eyes and spun the windlass. "You can see what I'm doing."

"Oh." Katrin's frown deepened. "Why did you fight Acmar?"

Livira kept turning the handle. The rope spooling off the windlass was darker now—the new length that Old Kern had added so that the bucket would be able to reach the water again. The level had been sinking ever since Livira could remember. "He called me a weed."

"But . . . we all call you Livira."

"He called me *weed*." Livira shook her head. "It's not the same."

That had been part of the reason, the spark that had made her throw the first punch. But the real reason was that he had tried to snatch her scrap from her. That's what Aunt Teela had called it when Livira showed it to her. A scrap of paper. The wind had revealed this treasure to Livira months earlier, pushing aside the dust to expose a corner. A torn triangle, no larger than the palm of her hand and, like an old man's skin, thin, wrinkled, discoloured by age. Dark marks patterned it. Her aunt had shrugged when Livira showed her and had grown inexplicably angry when Livira persisted in asking about the marks, saying at last, "They're just scribbling. Tally marks for counting beans at market."

"But—" Livira had wanted to protest that there were so many different marks, they were too beautiful just to be counting, but Teela had cut her off and had set her to her least favourite chore: cleaning out the cookpot.

Livira shook off the memory. "See what Ella gave me!" She lifted the wind-weed that she had tied to her belt with a cord.

Katrin narrowed her eyes at it. "It looks like what we give Ella in the first place. Did it go wrong?"

"No!" Livira started to rotate the ball, searching for the best angle, but Katrin looked away.

"Did it hurt," Katrin asked, "when Acmar hit you?"

"Yes." Livira scowled and let the ball drop. "Lots." The windlass had run out of rope so she began to wind the bucket back up. After a few turns the reassuring resistance told her that the bucket had filled. Every time she carried out the task a small part of her held its breath, thinking that one day there would be no resistance. One day the water would simply not be there. An even smaller part of her hissed its disappointment when the turn of the handle revealed that new weight. When the water was gone there would be a change. Not a good change. But a change nonetheless. And sometimes, in the dark of the night with the hollow sounds of the Dust all around and the bright stars cold in their heaven, sometimes what scared Livira more than the water running out was that the water would *not* run out and that this would be her life. Dust, and beans, and dry-wheat, and the wind, and the little huddle of huts like stones gathered in the vastness of the empty plain, until *she* ran out rather than the water, and she joined the dust, and the wind carried her away as if she had never even drawn breath.

"I like Acmar," Katrin said.

Livira made a face and put her back into the winding. All the girls liked Acmar, at least to look at. Livira had never been able to put into words quite why he made her angry. It was to do with the way he didn't value any of the things she valued most. And all that lack of interest did was make him spokesman for the settlement, because none of them cared about those things really, not even Katrin or Neera, who said they were her best friends.

"You can have him," Livira grunted, her arms growing tired, her hands sore. "I'm going to the city soon. And you can all live in the dust while I . . . while I . . ." She didn't really know what they did in the city. She thought perhaps her scrap had come from there, stolen from the city folk by the wind. All she'd ever seen of the city were its walls, as a low smudge in the distance. She'd had to walk half a day even for that view, climbing the ridges to the west, returning to the settlement parched and dusty late at night to a frantic Aunt Teela. People said that the city was full of marvels with new ones added every week. But none of them had ever been there or even seemed interested in trying.

"I'm going to the city," Livira repeated.

"They won't let you in, silly." Katrin put out her tongue. "Even the dust doesn't get past their gates without permission."

She was just quoting what came out through Kern's grey beard, but it made Livira angry because she feared it might be true. "What I think is—"

Livira's hot reply faded from her lips and she rested against the windlass handle staring out to the east. There it was again, distant and dancing in the heat haze. A figure. "What I think . . . is that someone's coming!"

. . . and other doubters. The historian must ensure that all their work is plainly marked as such, for if it were presented as a work of fiction its readers would clamour that it lacked sense, the events too implausible, too random, and too cruel. Truth will set you free . . . from certainty, comfort, and the beliefs upon which we rely for sanity . . .

A History of Histories, *by William Ancrath*

CHAPTER 2

Livira

People never came to the settlement. Livira hadn't ever seen a visitor, had never met a single person who hadn't grown among the four dozen souls who sheltered in the huddled shacks. It was the sort of place that you went *from*, not to. Kern went from it to the dust markets. The patched waistcoat he was so proud of allegedly came from the city, purchased at great cost from a dust-market stall. What he bartered on his trips might then go on to bigger markets or to the city itself, but Livira had always had to take the existence of these places and people on faith. Now— someone was coming!

"Stranger!" Livira let the bucket fall and charged back through the bean rows, shouting her news, Katrin hard on her heels, eating dust. "Stranger!" She raced along the rows, rattling the drying beans in their pods. Only this morning she'd been watching the old men play stones and hollows, dreaming of an escape to something more, to a world that lay beyond the haze. Now that world was coming to her. "Stranger!"

"What are you saying?" Aunt Teela caught Livira's arm in a steel grip as she emerged from the crop.

"A stranger! Someone's coming!" Livira repeated at a lower, more comprehensible volume.

Teela's face stiffened as if a deadwasp had stung her. Her hand fell to her side. "Tell everyone."

Livira ran on, shouting. Something in her aunt's expression had put a chill into her and now fear edged her cries. The summoning bell took up the alarm.

"WHAT DO THEY want?" Livira stood with the others out by the well. Everyone she knew was there, except those few too old, too sick, or too small to emerge from their huts. Aunt Teela held her hand in a painful grip. Livira waited, still sweating from her run. The sun seemed brighter, the dust sharper on her lungs.

"You stay close to me, Livy. Do as you're told for once in your life." Her aunt pulled Livira's face around to hers, meeting her gaze with over-bright eyes. "I love you, child." Aunt Teela was not a woman given to displays of affection and this one filled Livira with a fear far greater than any that Acmar's approaching fist had instilled.

The figure was closer now, but still too far away for the shimmering heat to yield details. What the heat couldn't hide was that behind the lone traveller a larger band followed, perhaps half a mile back, raising enough dust for a dozen men or more.

"But what do they want?" Katrin repeated Livira's question. Neera pushed through the ranks to join them, easy for her with her too-skinny body. She coughed that dry cough which had got into her a while back and stared at the approaching stranger with fever-bright eyes.

Livira knew the answer to her own question. She just wanted an adult to give a different one. There wasn't anything they owned in the settlement that was worth walking across the Dust for. If someone had come here then there was only one thing they were interested in taking. "Us," she whispered. "They want us."

"Sabber."

Livira didn't know who'd muttered it first but soon the word was on a dozen tongues. She could see it now. The figure wasn't human. You could see it in their gait. And now, as it drew closer, something about the face. The sabber walked with a suppressed bounce as if holding back from some great leap at every step. Its legs bent too low down and were never fully straight; its shoulders rose as if beneath its hide armour there was a great ball of muscle at each joint. Closer still and she could make out the sharp angle of his cheekbones, and his mouth that was almost like Yaller's dog's: lipless, promising canines. Old Kern said the city folk called them dog-men these days and had new theories about their unclean origins.

The sabber's stiff, swept-back mane didn't end in a hairline but rather seemed to shorten into invisibility—as if, were she to stroke his face, Livira would feel the hairs there too, short and bristling. The seam of an old scar ran up across one brow, holding the eye beneath it wider than the other, creating a curiously unbalanced stare.

Livira's people stood in stunned silence, broken when Alica started to scream then ran for her hut and her new babies, dragging little Keer behind her. Others cried out and began to scatter. Five of the men stepped forward, Old Kern among them. Three had spears used to test the ground for dust-bears. The youngest of them, Acmar's older brother, carried Ma Esta's cleaver, and Robart had his ground-fork.

As the sabber closed the last twenty yards Livira finally understood its size. The creature stood at least eight feet tall. A scimitar hung from his belt. His hands were empty though, each sporting only three fingers, short-furred and ending in black talons.

"*T'loth criis'tyla loddotis!*" He had a deep, throaty voice and his words chained into one long growl.

The five men stopped their advance midway between the settlers and the sabber.

"Go!" Kern gestured with his spear. "Away!"

"You are all my property now." The sabber continued to pace towards them, empty-handed. "Resist and your lives are forfeit."

The man beside Kern launched his spear. The sabber didn't even flinch as the weapon sailed past him, a few feet wide of target. A second man let fly and, without breaking stride, the sabber batted the spear from the air. With ten yards between them Acmar's brother charged forward, screaming. He sounded terrified rather than fierce. He raised Ma Esta's cleaver above his head, flashing in the sun. The sabber backhanded him without apparent concern, connecting with a sick-making crunch. Blood sprayed, maybe teeth too, and the young man fell bonelessly into the dust.

The sabber passed by the body without a second glance and strode towards the four men still standing. The scrabble of their feet raised a dust cloud that hid the action. The sabber emerged from the drifting shroud at a walk, having taken no more time, Livira thought, than if there hadn't been anyone in his way. Nobody followed him out.

"You are all my property now."

This time his words were the cue for everyone to run, most of them shouting as if it might help somehow. Livira, her fear driven out by amazement, was dragged behind her aunt, choking as the dust rose around them.

It wasn't a planned response, just a general panic, but any panic out on the Dust soon devours itself in a great, blind cloud. Within moments, all of them were tripping over each other, over ropes, over hoes, and even over themselves. The dust made strangers of everyone. Neighbour screamed and clawed at neighbour as they collided.

Someone big crashed into Livira, tearing her free of Teela's grasp. She fell and her head hit the ground—harder than Acmar's punch. For a time she lay dazed, drooling into the dust, seeing nothing but the occasional foot stamping down close to her face. Later a hand snagged her and picked her up without effort. The confusion inside her head, and the maelstrom of dust and bodies outside it, combined into a blur from which Livira emerged only slowly, an unknown time after the sun had returned.

"My wrists hurt."

Someone had been saying that same thing over and over until it so irritated Livira that she lifted her head and realised that it had been her doing the complaining.

A rough rope bound her wrists together and a cord ran from the rope to a longer length to which a dozen other children were bound in a similar manner on alternating sides. Livira found that somehow she had been walking as part of this line of captives. Perhaps for miles. It was hard to get your bearings in the Dust and Livira recognised nothing save for the children around her. Katrin was three places ahead, Neera two places behind.

"My wrists hurt." Livira said it again. The rope had rubbed them raw. Perhaps she had been dragged part of the way. Her head ached too, as if a knife had been stuck through the top of her skull.

The lead end of the main rope dangled from the hand of a sabber. Maybe the one who had come first, on his own, maybe one of those in the group that had followed.

"Thirsty . . ." Acmar was two places ahead of her, limping.

"Where are they taking us?" The girl behind her, in a hopeless whisper. Blood had spattered her shift, leaving a tarry black pattern from shoulder to hip.

Looking left and right, Livira could see no other rope chains, not even dust clouds that might be rising from more distant captives. Where had the adults gone? The other children? Livira hoped they'd escaped but feared that their bodies were lying among the ruins of their homes. She'd heard that the sabbers ate people, but also that they didn't.

"Are you going to eat us?" she shouted at the sabber's back, her thoughts still loose in her skull and spilling out.

Her cry drew shocked gasps from the others.

"Ssshhh!" Acmar hissed.

"What?" Livira hissed back, feeling more like herself. "You think he'll only eat us if I give him the idea?" She bared her teeth at Acmar. The anger was helping to stop her imagining her aunt sprawled in the dust, neck broken or throat slashed. The anger was helping her not to wonder where Alica and her babies were.

The sabber walked on as if it hadn't heard. It had a scimitar at its hip like the one worn by the sabber that had stridden through the five men without raising a sweat or even breaking pace.

"Hey! You!" Livira shouted. "Are you going to eat us? I'd like to know."

The sabber turned its head and found her with yellow eyes. "Are you good to eat?" it rumbled, showing canines as long as her thumb.

"I taste like dung. Stringy dung." Livira tried to hold on to her courage under the creature's stare. She bolstered it with rage. "Where's my aunt?"

The sabber barked. Maybe it was a laugh. He turned his head back to face the direction of travel.

The march continued. Livira turned her attention to the rope around her wrists. She should be able to work her hands free, given time. Or chew her way through it, one strand at a time. Or . . . The other children's crying nagged at her, an irritant, but more than that, it came laden with the guilt that she, seemingly alone among them, had no tears to shed. It wasn't that she didn't care—simply that what she had lost was, right now, too big to fit within her thinking. Livira could see Aunt Teela's careworn face in the light of her mind's gaze, see the faded brown of her eyes, the crow's feet starting to show at the corners. But imagining her broken body, her blood in the dust, that was beyond Livira. Teela had been alive. She had been holding Livira's hand with that vital strength which had kept them alive all this time, despite the worst the Dust had to offer. She could not now be dead.

Livira glanced down at her torn and dirty feet. A loose cord caught her attention, dangling from her belt. The wind-weed that Ella had given her was gone, perhaps free once more, tumbling over the plains in the wind's grasp. Perhaps trampled flat in the ruins of the settlement. Either way it was gone, lost, lost with the lost boy trapped within it. Its absence pierced her, a cold knife thrust between her ribs, penetrating all her armour in a way that the larger tragedy could not. Her breath caught in her throat; another hitched in painfully, battling past a sob that demanded release. And over the loss of a toy the tears came in their own river.

THE SABBER LED them east for an hour, then another. The children walked in silence, their weeping exhausted. Four sabbers joined the one leading the children, the last of them shorter and older, a female with her grey mane in braids. This one wore many layers of tattered cloth despite the heat and walked with a staff that ended in a short tangle of thick roots polished by touch. Half a dozen cratalac claws hung from the root twists like black sickles. Livira imagined her to be some sort of sabber priest.

She puzzled over the whereabouts of the missing sabbers—surely there had been more than five. She hoped that there were other survivors who had escaped the raid. Perhaps the missing sabbers were hunting them.

From time to time Livira chewed at the knotted rope though her jaw was already sore with the work and it was hard to do while walking.

"Where would you run?" hissed Neera from behind.

Livira spat rope fibres from her parched mouth but didn't answer. She had no idea. But it felt good to be doing something. It helped stop her imagination filling the empty space with scenes of the dust settling on a corpse-strewn settlement. It clouded her visions of blood staining the thirsty ground and of Ella's wind-weed sculptures set free, carried away on the breeze. *Who'll water the beans now?* "Stop it," Livira hissed at herself and returned to her self-appointed task.

The sabber leading their rope proved watchful. He steered them past two dust-bears. Livira wasn't sure she'd have spotted the second one. It wasn't so much that they made a depression or a hump, though occasionally they did make the slightest dent; it was more that there was a difference in the quality of the hardpan where a dust-bear had buried itself, a slight variation in the granularity of the surface. Livira hoped he'd miss the next one and that the children could escape while it ate him. Perhaps she wouldn't even run, just stay and watch and scream her hatred. And she did hate them, Livira realised. The hate was in her belly, an unfamiliar sharp-angled lump of feeling that was at once both fire and ice, something heavy and uncomfortable and yet a thing that she wouldn't put down even if she were able to. She had thought before that she had known hatred, but those moments had been like shadows of passing clouds. And this, this was the night.

A thin wind blew up, stirring the dust to knee height. The landscape remained unchanged by passing miles, its flatness unchallenged. Livira had heard it was an ancient lakebed. That was hard to believe. Had fish swum through sparkling waters in the space before her eyes? Had boats floated far above her, their nets hanging fathoms deep? Even as these doubts assailed her something caught her eye. At first it seemed that the fingers of two great hands jutted from the ground, as if a buried giant were holding aloft some long-vanished bowl. But the fingers were wood. Ancient, brittle timbers, eroded into talons by the wind, the ribs of some vessel that might have trailed those imagined nets. The sabbers led them almost close enough to touch, and every child with more than half a breath left in them turned their heads to watch.

"I want my mother," Katrin croaked, her voice dried out by the wind.

Neera coughed for the hundredth time, a sharp, painful sound that seemed to stab at Livira's back. When Neera had started coughing nobody expected her to live long. Sour-lung took a lot of children out in the Dust. But she'd been coughing for a year already and right now it was the least of her worries. Livira hadn't any answer for Katrin. The girl wanted her mother; Livira wanted her aunt. It seemed impossible that the woman could be dead. But it was a day for impossibilities. Strangers, blood, and now a ship. They plodded on, leaving the ribs behind them, still reaching for an uncaring sky.

In the distance, low hills rose, barren rock challenging the wind to grind it into dust too. The sun sank to touch the distant ridges behind the children and still they hadn't reached the hills ahead. Another mile and the children started to follow their shadows up the first incline most of them had ever encountered, shuffling sore-foot across dusty stone. Livira knew about slopes; the year before she had scaled the western ridges to get a glimpse of the city, but her mouth was too dry to boast about it.

The first arrow hit a child.

. . . was said that no lock could defeat her. In later life Myra Hayes stepped away from her performances and earned a somewhat dubious reputation as a mystic. She returned to the stage after an absence of decades, promising the greatest escape of all. Disastrously, she drowned in a locked casket. The enquiry found no evidence that she had tried to free herself.

Music Hall Entertainers of the Eighteenth Century, *by Able Jons*

CHAPTER 3

Livira

For a moment after the arrow struck there was only silence. Even from Selly, who stood with the feathered shaft extending from beneath her collarbone. Another arrow hissed through the air, close to Livira, burying itself in the ground behind her. Then the air was full of them, and of shouting, and, inevitably, of dust.

In hindsight, the sabbers had been moving from almost before the first arrow arrived, but they did so without exclamation or alarm, leaving their prisoners in confusion.

For the second time in half a day Livira found herself being dragged this way and that, blind and terrified. It hurt more this time, for the ground beneath her lay thick with stones and ridges of rock slashed up through the hard-packed dust.

Screams rang out, shouts of pain and terror. Twice the guttural roar of a sabber shuddered through the air. In her extremity Livira managed to free both hands, proving Neera right: the rope had been an instruction to remain; the real cage had been the Dust.

An impact threw Livira to the ground and she curled up, shielding her head with both arms, waiting for the chaos to end.

The dust thinned. The screams became fewer and more scattered. And in time a rough hand knotted in the back of Livira's shift, hauling her to her feet. She blinked and spat, struggling to make sense of the scene before her through hazy air reddened by the remaining corner of the sun.

Children sat here and there, throwing long shadows to the east. Five were still bound to the main rope, Selly among them, face down in the dirt, the crimson arrowhead pointing skyward. Several others huddled close by. Uniformed men stalked here and there, sabres in their hands. The one who had pulled Livira from the ground dusted his hand off against his breastplate and took in the scene. He towered over her, broad-chested, his gleaming brass helm slightly askew and trailing a dusty plume. It was his bristling beard that Livira's eyes fixed on rather than his armour. The settler men rarely wore beards—dust traps, they called them.

"You're from the city," Livira said.

The man ignored her and strode away.

Neera sat two places up from the dead girl, still tied to the rope, coughing. Katrin had freed herself and edged silently towards Livira until the two of them were shoulder to shoulder. The girl might not be clever but she was always kind. Too kind to see what she'd seen today. Livira could feel her trembling.

As the dust cleared completely the soldiers cut the remaining children free. They stepped around Selly as if she weren't there, refusing to see what they'd done. There were twenty men in all, half a dozen bearing wounds. One had a broken arm, another bore three deep, bloody furrows running from forehead to chin, carved by a sabber's claws. Beneath the dirt their jackets were a bright red, more vivid than any cloth Livira had ever seen. The colour of fresh blood.

The soldiers lined the children up, ignoring questions or complaints, and marched them off into the dusk. They abandoned Selly still face down where she'd fallen, still tied to the rope.

"We can't leave her." Katrin tried to go back. "Her mother—"

Livira caught her friend's arm. "She's dead." She didn't know if she meant just Selly or her mother too. "Come. On." She tried to drag Katrin after the soldiers, though it wasn't until Neera lent her strength to the effort that the girl surrendered and the sobs that she'd been holding in came bursting out: ugly and startlingly loud.

Livira glanced back one more time at Selly, sprawled over the snaking length of rope. Katrin's grief shamed her. She wanted to feel as broken by the girl's death, but so much else filled her mind: fear for herself of course, but more than that—questions.

The rope was gone but apart from that Livira wasn't sure their situation had improved. She wasn't even entirely sure that the soldiers were less likely to eat them than the sabbers had been.

The bearded man seemed to be in charge. He was the only one with a breastplate and a helmet. He led the way into a gully about a quarter of a mile from the ambush. Here a score of dusty horses stood with their heads down. Livira could make out few details in the gloom but she'd heard enough stories to know a horse when she saw one.

Neera coughed her dry cough then asked in a parched whisper, "Are we going to ride home?"

Livira wasn't hopeful. She didn't know where their home was or how to describe the location. The idea that she might one day find herself so far from the settlement as to not know the way back had occurred to her before. The idea that she might be eager to return never had. Among the many ways she had dreamed of leaving her home and escaping into the wideness of the world, none had been as sudden, violent, real, and final as this.

The captain and his men mounted up. Livira found their conversation hard to follow. They employed the same words she used herself, not the sabbers' wholly new supply, but barked them out with such hard edges and strange emphasis that it stole away the meaning. From what she gathered, the captain was taking his soldiers to hunt down more sabber raiders. He ordered three of his men to stay with the children and take them . . . somewhere. Wherever the somewhere was it didn't sound like home. Livira got the impression that she and the others were an unwelcome discovery and that if the initial volley of arrows had killed them all, not just little Selly, then the captain would not have been too displeased.

The men chosen to stay were the two most badly wounded, plus the soldier with the clawed face. The ones mounting to depart gave this last man all manner of nods and cheers as they moved past, several clapping him on the back. Why so much respect should be aimed his way Livira couldn't tell, but she saw that it ran deeper than simple good will—there was an undercurrent to it, something between admiration and fear. None of those slapping at his shoulder let their hands linger. For his part the man just spat and shook his head.

The captain and his men rode off into the plains and the sun fell behind the hills, sealing the soldiers from sight. Livira would have warned them against riding the Dust at night. It was flat enough that their horses wouldn't lame themselves, but fear of breaking an ankle wasn't what kept the settlers in their homes after dark. Perhaps night terrors ran from men and horses and swords and bows. Or perhaps the night would stand its ground and make a fight of it.

"Where are you taking us?" Livira asked the clawed soldier. Of the three men left behind he was the shortest, though of solid build and bristling with a restless energy. His uniform was also the dirtiest and most torn of any of them. "Where are we going?" She spoke slowly and clearly in case her words were as odd to him as his to her.

He looked up from sharpening his sword, one of the thin curving blades that cavalry used, at least in the stories. "One thing I hate more than children . . ." Even in the dark his wounds looked ugly. They were deep and, Livira imagined, very painful. ". . . is fucking mouthy children."

"But wh—"

"Oh fuck my luck. Mouthy *and* fucking stupid. The city. You'll be allocated there."

"We're thirsty." Livira had heard swearing before but never quite so much of it in quite such a small space of time. Still, words were just words, and she'd had never been so dry.

"And yet again the gods shit on me." The man threw down his sword and whetstone then got to his feet with a groan. "You don't shut up after this and you're going to taste the back of my fucking hand." He limped to his horse and weighed the water-skin across its back. "Line them up," he growled. "A mouthful each."

It was the most precious mouthful ever, filling Livira's mind with thoughts of the well and its wet breath. She remembered the full bucket that she'd dropped at the sight of the first sabber—how she wanted its contents now, the whole lot. Even so, as she swallowed her single mouthful, she felt something uncoil within her as if she were her namesake, coming alive at the scent of water and seeking more. The others crowded in behind her and Livira went to stand by the soldier's horse while Katrin and then Acmar took their turns to drink. She liked the horse—it had a rich, pungent smell to it, and made slow movements of its heavy body, occasionally swishing its tail. When from time to time it snorted and rumbled it was a deeper and more resonant sound than even the sabbers made.

"What does 'allocation' mean? Will my aunt be there? How far is the city?"

"Kerod eat my fucking soul!" the soldier snarled, but Livira heard no malice in it and behind her Neera even sniggered. Where another might um and ah, or simply pause, this man filled the space with an obscenity. Even so, he shrugged off further questions as if they were grit in the wind. "All of you, lie the fuck down and sleep. Got a long fucking walk tomorrow."

And so they did; with dry mouths and rumbling bellies they shivered on the stony ground, whispering together beneath the stars, though less than children are wont to despite having more to discuss than on any day of their lives thus far. Some talked about the soldiers and some about the sabbers, both unheard-of developments. Livira guessed that one had brought the other rather than that lightning had struck her twice in one day. Her aunt always said that the city owned the Dust, even though nobody ever came from it to inspect their property. Perhaps they only wanted it when someone else did. Like small children quarrelling over a toy.

Livira huddled with Neera to one side and Katrin to the other. A hundred pieces of grit dug into her body, her wrists hurt, and her nose still ached where Acmar had hit her seemingly a thousand years ago. She watched the cold twinkle of the stars and thought that dawn would find her still awake. She wondered about her aunt and about the sabber that had walked into the settlement so unafraid. Was he scared when the soldiers attacked? Was he afraid now that they were hunting him in the dark? She hoped so. The anger that had been smouldering around the edges of her fears now kindled into flame and she wished the sabbers dead. All of them. And finally, she thought of Selly still lying in the dust a few yards from where the arrow had first struck the little girl and ended her story, and at last, dry as Livira was, a tear fell from her.

———

"Get up!"

There wasn't any food, just a smaller mouthful of water than the night before. The three soldiers were the man with the clawed face, the man with the broken arm, and a man bound about his middle with crimson-stained bandages. Unlike their commander, they sported stubble rather than beards, though they had the same pale skin and light eyes. The clawed man's limp seemed better, but it turned out that his horse also had a limp and so he walked, leading it and the column, while his two comrades brought up the rear, the bandaged man swaying in his saddle as if considering simply sliding to the ground when nobody was watching.

The soldiers turned their backs on the hills, leaving behind the first incline most of the children had faced, and set back out across the Dust. They headed west, in the direction of the distant city that Livira had once glimpsed from the ridges at the opposite shore of the long-vanished lake.

Watching the three men, it struck Livira that they were physically different from the people she had shared her life with: they had rounder heads, flatter faces, and were shorter than the settlement men, though better fed and sturdier. All of the horsemen from the night before had shared these same traits, though they varied one from the other in many other aspects.

"Why did all the soldiers cheer you before they left?" Livira had positioned herself behind the clawed man at the front of the group.

"Because they're fucking idiots." The man made to spit and then thought better of it, perhaps remembering how little water they had.

"But why—"

"Enough!" And he picked up the pace.

The walk back across the lakebed proved to be more wearying and almost as worrying as the previous day's expedition. All of them were parched. Even the soldiers complained. The bandaged man in particular muttered about his thirst and consumed more water on his own than all the children collectively. He fell off his horse around noon, hitting the ground like a sack of beans. The other two hefted him back on and tied him belly-first across the saddle, though that was where his wound was. Livira learned their names during these exchanges. Malar with the foul tongue and scarred face, Jons with the arm, Henton who might or might not now be dead.

Progress grew slower as the day wore on. Malar's limp returned and he looked flushed, dark eyes fever-bright. Jons hugged his broken arm. Some of the younger children began to stagger. Benth scooped up Breta who wasn't more than three and stumbled on grim-faced beneath the girl's weight. Katrin took hold of little Gevin's hand and made sure he kept up.

Once, in the distance, Livira saw a tree. She recognised it only from an image Ella had etched onto a piece of slate. Tall, staggeringly tall, and branching as it reached for the sky, a fluttering of dusty green at the very top of those stretching fingers. It stood alone and improbable in the vast flatness.

Ella had told her that the lakebed had once been home to a forest, but Livira hadn't been able to believe her. Her imagination scaled many heights but painting the Dust green had been a climb too far.

"Tapwood," she muttered.

Malar grunted.

Only a handful of the most ancient trees survived. As the water level sank, the younger trees had died, dried, and fallen apart before the wind's relentless assaults. But the thousand-year tapwoods had roots that reached down as far as the settlement's well and found water even now. The elders of a vanished tribe, standing sentinel over the desolation of all they had known. Livira felt a kind of kinship with them.

They drew no closer to the tree and soon it was lost in the haze behind them.

They approached the western ridges as the sun was sinking. The children were a uniform dusty shamble. Livira almost missed the rope. At least she could have lain down and let them drag her. Her feet were sore and cut and she eyed the soldiers' black boots with envy. She looked at her tattered leggings and the scabbed shins they exposed. Perhaps dragging wasn't a good long-term solution. Maybe she could ride with Henton. He hadn't complained about being thirsty since he fell off, not even once, and Livira was pretty sure he was dead.

It surprised Livira to find herself still at the head of the column just behind Malar despite her exhaustion. Anyone who felt as used up as her, she reasoned, should be stumbling at the rear, but here she was stumbling at the front. Perhaps the others were even more tired. Pride should have Acmar take the lead from her, but since his brother had gone down before the sabber he'd had nothing to say. In truth, though, Livira suspected that the difference was that while the rest of them felt they were being forced to go, she actually wanted to see this city, and had wanted to ever since she'd first learned that there was something in the world other than dust and beans.

Every mile or so Livira would find enough saliva to ask a question. She asked about the city, she asked how far it was, she asked what they did there, did they grow beans, was it true they didn't let the dust in? Malar, limping worse than his horse now, answered none of these questions, unless it was with a grunt that might mean yes or might mean no. But slowly it seemed that his fever was loosening his tongue, setting him to mumbling into the spaces between her questions.

"You should have had a helmet, like the captain," Livira said.

"Shut the fuck up or I'll find a helmet and make you eat it."

Livira shrugged. Malar wouldn't have got his face clawed if he'd had a brass hat with a front brim like the man who led him. His cuts must hurt like all the hells. And those jackets they wore—not a gleaming breastplate like the captain but thick cloth with a padded shirt—looked too hot and heavy for the Dust. It hadn't even saved Henton's belly, just allowed him to swap a quick death for a slow one.

"Why did they cheer you?" Livira returned to the first of her many unanswered questions.

"Because he killed a sabber," Jons croaked from behind her. "One on one. Men don't do that. It's like a dog taking down a lion."

Livira tried to picture it. Malar against a sabber. Something fierce burned inside her. Anger felt better than sorrow, and visualizing revenge better still. "I'm glad you killed one."

"I got lucky," Malar snarled.

"Luckiest soldier I know," Jons replied. "Sabbers are faster, bigger, stronger. But Malar here's been 'lucky' with a blade as long as I've known him."

"Shut it, Jons."

"If he was rich or good-looking or had an ounce of leadership in him, he'd be famous," Jons's dry monotone carried on. "Not that they'd ever make one of us an officer whatever we were. Need the right family for that. But Malar though . . . born killer. Twenty years back, on the Kerlo border, he cut down—"

"Stop!" Livira shouted. "Malar! Stop!"

The soldier paused, something angry on his lips, "Yo—"

But the dust-bear stole his words, erupting from the ground directly in front of him in a hail of grit, dust, and thrashing tentacles. To his credit Malar threw himself backwards without delay and it saved him from the rope-like coils that scythed through the space he'd occupied. He wasn't fast enough to stop the dust-bear snaring both ankles though, and it used his weight as an anchor to haul its quivering body from the pit it occupied.

The children screamed and ran. Henton's horse bolted; Jons cried out, struggling to control his own steed. The horror that was the dust-bear snaked out more tendrils, reaching for Malar. It dragged him feet-first towards the great dry, tooth-filled slit of its mouth that ran the whole length of its shapeless body. Somehow Malar had his sword in hand but with tendrils already snaring his arm the best he could do was drive the blade into the ground to keep from being drawn further in.

Livira should have run. Her nightmares had been filled with dust-bears for years, though she'd never seen one and had had to build her own in the pits of her imagination. The shock paralysed her in the moment. Before it was tugged free, Malar's sword bought the delay she needed to recover herself. She was terrified but suddenly her anger outweighed her fear. It was as if the dust-bear had declared itself responsible for everything that had happened to her. And more than that—it stood between her and the city— the only good thing that could possibly come out of all this disaster.

She'd watched the soldier for hours as he walked ahead of her. She knew where he kept everything. Most of all, she knew where he kept his water. But she'd also located his weapons long ago and mused on the possibility of snatching one. Now, as Malar roared, trying much too late to cut himself free, Livira threw herself to her knees beside him and pulled the larger of his two daggers from its sheath. His feet were inches from the first row of teeth, a hundred sharp yellow triangles.

Every settler knew how to deal with dust-bears. None of them in living memory had put the theory to the test. When a dust-bear attacks, you try to escape. When you can't escape, you thrash at it and it eats you, feet-first, its gelatinous flesh immune to spear thrusts owing to the stony hide that covers it. The way to deal with dust-bears is from the inside, and by the time the useful parts of Malar got inside he'd be very dead.

Livira dived in headfirst. The teeth, all inward pointing to prevent escape, offered no resistance. She got about rib deep before she could get no further, and in the damp, stinking, darkness she started slashing. She found a direction her arms could move in and hauled the dagger downwards in a long slicing motion, sawing at the obdurate flesh.

Dust-bears, it turned out, had mastered the art of projectile vomiting just for such occasions. Livira found herself back in the brightness of the day, with a brief sensation of flight. The dust-bear folded in on its injury, withdrawing all its tentacles in one swift motion, and scooping dust back over its pebbled hide.

Livira landed with a thud and rolled in the dirt, losing all the air in her lungs. She was still gasping for breath when Malar set her back on her feet.

"That was stupid." The anger in his voice didn't surprise her. She often heard the same tone when she solved a problem that was vexing the men at the settlement. Perhaps once they'd invested so much time hunting an answer they were aggrieved not to be the one to find it.

The soldier stared at the dust cloud around the pit as the 'bear reburied itself. He looked very much as if he'd like to take his sword and go back to finish it off. "Come on. Let's go." Swearing was, it seemed, saved for pleasantries.

Jons rounded up Henton's horse, and the motionless Henton, and the trek resumed. Half an hour later Malar shared out the last of the water, most of it with the horses. They climbed one ridge, then another higher one, then a third. In the distance a black fist showed itself, taking a first bite out of the reddening sun.

"The city's at the foot of the mountain," Malar said to nobody in particular. "The crowning jewel of the Amthane Empire, may it last ten thousand years." This last bit lacked sincerity.

On her expedition years earlier Livira hadn't seen any mountain. She realised with a shock that she must have seen just another ridge and let her childish imagination paint it as city walls. There was a lesson in there somewhere, but she was too tired and sore for lessons. All of her ached and her skin was burned everywhere the dust-bear's inner juices had touched her. She guessed her layers of dirt and immediate dust bath had saved her from further harm.

THE MOUNTAIN DEVOURED the sun and they walked on in growing darkness. The ground here was stony, studded with the occasional succulent, low to the ground and bristling with spines. The danger of ambush from below had passed.

The city first showed itself as a single light twinkling in the dusk, warmer than the starlight, as if being lower down it was more approachable. Within moments there was another. The children gasped in wonder as more lit up. In the settlement when the sun went down it was dark until dawn. They kept no light in the huts. What little they had to burn made too much smoke to use indoors.

The lights spread, picking out lines, some straight, some curved, the patterns making no sense to Livira. There was a beauty and a strangeness to it, enough to make her forget her aches and pains, even her thirst for a moment. Her other worries she had packaged away for later. She knew that, like many of the others who had cried for their parents until they were too dry for tears, she should be weeping over the loss of her aunt, and all the other adults who had been kind to her. Livira could feel that loss like a pit in her chest, but she had put it in a box of her own making. She planned to open it when she could do something about it.

"They're so yellow." The lights highest up the slopes didn't look like flames.

"Wisp-glows," Malar said. "A modern marvel." He sounded as if he preferred firelight himself.

Although they seemed close, the lights stubbornly refused to get closer as the children walked. They found themselves stumbling over rough ground and getting tangled in low shrubs with vicious thorns.

"Hold up, you little shits. We'll make camp here." Malar's weary voice reached them through the darkness.

Making camp consisted of lying on the ground and trying to sleep. Malar and Jons didn't untie Henton from his horse, so Livira decided that he was dead.

"Why did the sabbers want us?" She aimed her question in the soldiers' direction.

"Why do the dog-men want anything?" Jons's voice came out of the night. "We're driving them back. That's what matters."

Malar snorted.

"That's what the criers say." Jons sounded defensive.

"The criers didn't even report it when sabbers got over the walls last month. We both know it happened. We saw the bodies," Malar said. "Anyone with half a brain who's ridden out knows they're massing. And if we're not losing now, we're going to be in ten years. They breed faster than we do and there were more of them to start with. Plus, they keep coming from the east. It's more of a tide than a migration."

"They're animals," Jons snarled.

"Aren't we all?" Malar sounded sleepy, and silence followed.

Livira lay down between Neera and Katrin, both of them too exhausted for questions. Tired as she was, she thought that she would fall asleep in moments, but thirst tortured her for an age and when dawn rolled over her she was sure she had only just begun to dream.

In the daylight, Livira could see the mountain clearly, the first and seemingly the largest in a series of peaks that burst from the plain without the preamble of foothills. The city scaled the lower slopes like a wave washing up as far as its momentum would carry it. A great curtain wall sealed the city into its valley, bordered by two of the mountain's vast roots.

There was no breakfast or even breakthirst: the water had gone. Malar had spent much of the night muttering and shivering beneath his blanket, but his fever seemed to have broken and the black crusts over his wounds looked healthy if ugly. He got the children up, urging the weakest to their feet with curses and threats, then led off.

Three roads cut across the scrub, all aimed at the city gates, one from the north, one from the south, and the smallest trailing east. Malar led them to join this trail. Livira saw her first cart, creaking up behind them to overtake the shambling children. She'd heard of carts, of course, but the settlers carried their beans and their corn to the trade meet in sacks hefted onto sweating backs. Seeing so many fat sacks heaped on the cart and pulled so easily by one small horse amazed her.

"How many people have you killed?" Livira hadn't known she was going to ask the question until it popped out of her mouth. She flinched, expecting to be slapped, as Malar's head snapped round to fix her with a dark glare. But instead, he returned his gaze to the way ahead, answering only after a pause long enough to make her think she would be ignored again.

"Lots."

"You must be very brave." Neera spoke timidly from his other side. "Fighting a sabber like that."

Malar answered but it seemed to Livira that he wasn't really talking to either of them. "There's nothing brave in committing to a fight—you just need to understand that there's a scarier outcome waiting for you if you don't. Hesitation's the killer. They try to train hesitation out of you, but most people have it in their bones. Only thing that makes me different is: I see—I do. It's not a matter of heart and soul."

"Why aren't you in charge?" Livira asked. "If you're so good at killing people? Why aren't you the captain?"

Jons snorted from behind them. "Captain Malar!"

"Leading's a different game," Malar growled to himself. "A good leader's worth ten good killers. Not that our captain's good at either. Got the job on his father's coin. But killing's cheap, girl. Today's bows make it a game of chance. And they say they're working on new stuff in the city. Fiery death you can hold in your hand and throw leaving a dozen dead. Bows without strings—just point at someone and . . . zip . . . they're dead. Times are changing and I'm getting old."

"Something new every time we come back," Jons said. "My father says he hardly recognises the place from when he was a child."

The way thickened as it went. As if carts and wagons joined it from all angles until, together, they made such a flow as to clear the stones and carve a single great rut. Livira saw wagons ahead, and more traffic in the distance on the north and south roads, heading in both directions. No homes though, no settler shacks, nothing but the vast stone wall and the distant rooftops clothing the slopes.

With several miles left to reach the gates, Acmar, carrying Gevin again, collapsed under the boy's weight. With a curse Malar strode over and yanked the small child from the dust, setting him beside Henton's body on the soldier's horse.

"Fucked if I'm leaving the sabbers anything to eat. Don't fall off!"

Half a mile later Benth sank to his knees, dropping little Breta to the ground before him. Malar offered the same excuse as before, only with even less grace, and set the girl on his horse. With a mile to go there were two more of the little ones behind her.

The traffic was building now, the rumble of wheels both before and behind them.

"What's going to happen to us here?" Livira's tongue was so dry it felt stiff.

"You'll be allocated."

"Wh—"

But Malar saved her the struggle of asking what that meant. "You'll be allocated tasks within the city and in return you'll be fed, watered, housed, and protected." He glanced back at her, frowning. "Don't get too excited though—dust-rats get the shit jobs."

Livira trudged on for a while, mulling over what might constitute a shit job. A new thought occurred to her.

"How do they eat?"

"With their fucking mouths, just like everyone else."

"I mean, there's no fields," Livira said. The settlement had fifty times the area dedicated to its huts given over to growing the food for those who lived in them.

"You didn't notice the thousand fucking wagons, little rat?" Malar made an exaggerated gesture towards the north and south roads, the dust from a host of wheels drifting from both.

Livira frowned. "But why bring the city people food? How do they pay?"

"You're too clever for your own fucking good, girl. Get you into trouble, that will." Malar shook his head. The flesh around the furrows the sabber had carved across his face was still an angry red. Sweat ran from beneath hair streaked with the first touch of grey. He looked as tired as Livira felt. "Knowledge. That's what they pay with. Whole city's here for one reason. This is where King Oanold's great-grandfather built the library."

Without guilt we would all be monsters. And memory is the ink with which we list our crimes.

Notes from the trial of Edris Dean

CHAPTER 4

Evar

"What are you doing?"

Evar turned with a start to find Starval standing behind him. Nobody ever heard Starval coming. The smallest and darkest of his brothers, Starval had been lost in the Mechanism while carrying a book concerned with the arts of assassination. Strange reading material for a child, Evar thought. Many decades later, the Mechanism had spat out all five of the lost children it had inadvertently swallowed. It had vomited them up together, none of them seeming a day older than when they were taken. None of them were the same though. In Starval's case, the contents of that book and more beyond had been printed on his soul.

"Me? Doing?" Evar swallowed. With Starval there was always that moment of terror when you were certain you were going to die. Then he'd smile and you'd remember he was your brother. "I'm building a staircase."

Starval cast a critical eye at the ramp of books Evar had piled up. Along its side the ramp was braced against a wall, and at the end by a second wall where the two formed one of the chamber's corners. "You've got a way to go . . ."

"I'll get there." Evar wiped the sweat from his brow and craned his neck to take in the scale of the task. Although the ramp reached well above his head it wasn't yet one-twentieth of the way to the ceiling.

"Dare I ask the reason for this . . . staircase to heaven?" Starval frowned at the structure. "You know it's going to collapse with you on it, right?"

"I'm going to check the ceiling."

An uncharacteristic concern creased Starval's brow. "Is it time for Kerrol to give you the talk again?"

"I don't care about the talk." Kerrol would ask what he thought he was escaping from. He would remind Evar that wherever he went he would take himself with him. "I need to find—" He stopped himself. None of the others believed in her. The books they were lost with in the Mechanism had tutored them, left them with skills honed to the sharpest possible edge. Clovis the warrior, Kerrol with access to the levers of the mind, Mayland with his histories. Evar had emerged with nothing, just the sense that something had been torn from his memory, leaving a chasm so wide he could fall into it and never be found. *Someone* had been torn away, not *something*. She was out there. He knew that. And she needed him. He'd left her in danger, and he had to get back to her before it was too late.

"Well, have fun. I'm going to the Mechanism. I'm late for my turn." Starval set a hand to Evar's shoulder. "Don't die here, brother. We need you." With that he turned away and walked off towards the distant reading room, whistling a jaunty tune to challenge the library's overwhelming silence.

Left on his own again, Evar paused to contemplate his stairway before wiping his brow once more and bending to the work. The ceiling would offer a way out. Why else would they have built it so very far from the floor?

Evar's brother Mayland had always said that the fact they could see the walls of their prison was a blessing afforded to very few. Their cell was larger than those enjoyed by most inmates, approximately two miles on each side with a ceiling that was more of a stone sky, too high for them to be able to hit it with anything they could find to throw. There were even four doors rather than the traditional singular exit. Each of which Evar had tried ten thousand times, even the one that lay behind a hundred yards of char and ash. But he'd never examined the ceiling. None of them had.

SINCE THE LIBRARY offered no measure of time, its light unwavering, it was exhaustion that reeled Evar back to the pool and its green halo of crops. Save for the crop circle around the pool, the entirety of the chamber's floor space, some two and a half thousand acres, lay covered with stacks of books. A forest in which, even now, it was easy to become lost.

He followed the chamber wall for a mile before passing the short corridor to the north door. A half mile after that he reached the corridor to the north-east reading room. The chamber boasted one more reading room, west of the south door, but this one held the Mechanism and it was to this one that Starval had gone many hours earlier.

Before striking out among the book stacks, aiming for the pool, Evar took a long look at the Mechanism. A hundred yards of corridor led to the reading room, and down it, across a sea of reading desks in tumbled disarray, Evar had a clear if distant view of the Mechanism, a grey lump large enough for all the siblings to fit inside together with room to spare, though the rules allowed only one person and one book at a time.

The Mechanism's pull was that while a reader's imagination could animate a book inside their head, the Mechanism would build that world around you. It offered the contents of each book as something to be physically experienced, walked through, partaken in, interrogated, shared. You could immerse yourself in the book in whatever way you might desire.

Over the centuries that Evar's people had been trapped within the chamber the Mechanism had been their escape. Every generation or so someone who went in didn't come out again. And even though on each of the five occasions on which such a tragedy had occurred, the victim had been a child of maybe eight or nine years, it seemed that the draw of the Mechanism was such that this was considered a price worth paying.

Evar had been the second child lost, Clovis the last. Evar had been the only one of them not to return to it after their eventual release.

He stood for a while, resting his eyes on the grey structure, wondering what adventures Starval might be experiencing within it. Typically, he spent his time honing his skills with blade, poison, or one of a score of other ways to take a life. It must be hard, Evar thought, to see real people as having value after taking the lives of so many pretend ones.

EVAR FOUND ONLY Kerrol, lounging on his preferred book pile while reading a more favoured volume.

Evar had three brothers: Mayland, the historian; Starval, the murderer; and Kerrol, whose speciality they all had their own unflattering names for. Kerrol chose to refer to his calling as psychology. Kerrol said that it was in people's nature to feel trapped, and that being unable to see what had hold of them was what led so many into dark places within their own minds. Evar, at least, knew what was holding him back. But knowing had never felt as if it helped.

Evar went to his own pile, ready for sleep, glad that his brother had nothing to say to him. He was still yawning and searching for his dreams when Clovis came through the gate in the book-built wall that served as a perimeter for their settlement. She rounded the corner sharply, all the angles of her body pointing towards trouble. Evar got to his feet with a groan, braced for the storm. Kerrol, lounging nearby, looked up from his book.

"Defend yourself, little brother." Clovis came on without pause.

Evar was taller than Clovis and technically older since he'd been lost in the Mechanism decades before she was. Clovis, however, had been a year or two older when the Mechanism took her. When it spat them all out together, none of them had aged, so he was the little brother. Now twenty years old, he was still the little brother, apparently.

Evar took the first blow on his shoulder, blocked the second, and found himself falling, legs swept from under him. He hit the ground hard and rolled away from the heel descending towards his face. The kick he aimed at his sister's ankle somehow missed but gave him space to get back up. Or so he thought. Clovis closed the distance with remarkable speed, slamming her knee into his stomach.

"Get up!"

Evar lay gasping.

"Get up!" Clovis raged.

"Could you kill him a little more quietly?" Kerrol got to his feet, yawning, and stretched to his full height.

Clovis spun away from Evar to round on Kerrol. Their oldest brother was a good head taller than either of them, and wouldn't last five heartbeats in a fight against Evar. Clovis would fell him with her first punch. Neither of them had ever laid a finger on him though. Words were Kerrol's weapons, and he wielded them to devastating effect even in gentle conversation.

After a long moment of eye contact, Clovis looked away and spat to the side. "I've got an Escape to hunt down. We'll train again tomorrow, Evar. Try not to be so pathetic next time." She stalked away.

"I wouldn't follow her," Kerrol advised. "Starval says this Escape's a big one. Particularly sneaky too."

Evar watched Clovis walk away into the book stacks that surrounded them on every side. She wasn't his true sister any more than Kerrol or Starval shared his blood. The only thing that made them siblings was that the Mechanism had returned them together, stumbling back into the library, wrapped in confusion. Of all of them only Evar had emerged from that grey womb without a gift of knowledge, and only Clovis had come out blood-stained and screaming.

"I worry about her," Evar wheezed. He clutched his ribs and hobbled over to Kerrol.

"Of course you do." Kerrol rolled his eyes.

He had once described Evar as burdened by kindness. If the library were to start to collapse, Evar, Kerrol said, would be too busy trying to mend whatever the world put in front of him to even notice the ceiling falling, let alone run for safety. It wasn't a portrait of himself that Evar recognised—if the library started to fall, he'd be out through the first crack—but he had to admit that Kerrol's assessments cut to the quick when it came to their surviving siblings.

Clovis had sheltered in the Mechanism to escape the massacre that had killed the rest of her people. While the sabbers had gone about their slaughter, the Mechanism had swallowed Clovis away. Untold years later it had returned her and the four boys it had taken earlier, spitting them out into a chamber populated only by bones and books. Kerrol said the attack might not have left scars on Clovis's body, but it had left scars on her life, criss-crossing all her years, marked by the black days when she lay wounded, too dangerous to approach, beyond the reach of words. For all the sharpness of her combat skills she was, in conversation, a blunt weapon, and immune to the delicacy her injuries required if they were ever to heal.

Starval, who had emerged from the Mechanism as deft in matters of murder as Clovis was in combat or Kerrol in manipulation, mistrusted their brother's skills. Kerrol, in turn, described Starval as hungry for meaning, looking for it in all the wrong places, thinking he might cut it from the world if only his knife bore a keen enough edge.

Evar had long since learned to keep interactions with Kerrol to a minimum. Anything you gave him could be ammunition, rope to hang you with later. He'd learned it from Kerrol's own teaching. All of Evar's siblings had spent years training him in their particular field of expertise. Evar had come to understand it as ultimately a selfish act. Each had honed their talent to an extraordinarily keen edge and had no audience for their skill other than the siblings with whom they were trapped. And the truth is that nobody can truly appreciate world-class talent unless they themselves have spent a great deal of time trying to be even a fraction as good. Evar claimed boredom led him to letting his siblings train him. The truth was that he enjoyed their company.

In any event, along with a considerable wealth of psychology, the main thing Evar had learned from Kerrol was not to underestimate his reach. His brother was flexible as water, capable of filling any hole in a conversation, flowing on, carrying nothing of it with him save for useful information, no more touched by passion or honesty than a river remembers its course.

Evar abandoned Kerrol to his reading and carried his exhaustion into the stacks. Clovis had left him too sore for sleeping. And besides, she might need help.

At the back of his mind Evar had the suspicion that Kerrol had sent him after Clovis. It was always hard to know with Kerrol. Evar shrugged it off and carried on, following the signs of his sister's trail. She'd left faint hints at footprints in the thin layer of sooty dust that drifted here and there against the book towers.

Starval had taught him to track, though Evar could never track Starval. Second-best at everything. That was Evar. And a distant second place at that. Evar didn't even know what book he had taken into the Mechanism on that fateful day, but it hadn't given him a skill. He'd even proven himself to be bad at escaping.

The task of escaping the chamber was one that Evar had set himself very early on, and it had occupied him wholly for years despite the others calling it an exercise in futility.

He had read many books about people who had escaped from prisons, each prison more terrible and impenetrable than the next. It seemed to him that what had set apart those remarkable individuals who did indeed win free was that they all had something to escape for rather than from. A reason to aim themselves at. Unlike his three brothers and one sister, Evar had a reason. A better one than simply an unquenchable desire to know what lay behind each of the four white doors that confined them. A better one than the ache for new horizons or the need for any company other than that of his siblings. Evar had someone to save.

The library's silence and the solitude of his walk polished the stone of Evar's ever-present loneliness, burnishing it until it gleamed with a high shine. Evar's parents, everyone he had known as a child, were long dead. Time's tide had carried them off while Evar passed the decades away in whatever place the Mechanism had held him. He had few memories of the time before. The Mechanism had reduced that to a blur.

Of all of them only Clovis properly remembered the childhood she'd had before the Mechanism took her. She had been the last child the Mechanism took. The four brothers had been lost inside it years before, on separate occasions, separated by decades. Their disappearances had been random, unfortunate accidents that their people either forgot or considered a risk worth taking for the delights offered within.

Clovis's final day had been written too deeply to be erased. The slaughter that she'd run from was the anvil on which she had been formed and she carried the weight of it about her neck everywhere she went. It would never bow her—not Clovis—but it left her too hard for kinship, unable to bend in the ways that mattered when living among others.

EVAR WALKED ON, trying to stay focused on Clovis's trail and on the danger posed by the Escape that could be lurking behind any of the thousands of book stacks. Despite his efforts, his thoughts kept straying to his unfinished ramp, his probably doomed attempt to reach the distant ceiling. Of late, his struggles to find a way out of the chamber had grown steadily more intense. The Escape, clothed in whatever nightmare form it could find to steal, would be scary enough, but what Evar truly feared was that he would die here in this chamber, not beneath the talons of a monster but of old age. That he would wither and die within a stone's throw of the place he had been born, and in the company of the same three faces he saw every day. That he would see nothing, do nothing, spend his days in the same cage, and even his remains would wait out eternity in the same chamber. Lately though, something had changed, something ineffable, a wind that moved not even the smallest mote of dust had blown through the room, and Evar knew it was time to go. If not now, then never.

As a child, Evar had found a book that claimed a circle of blood could open a door. He had nearly bled himself dry drawing crimson loops on the white expanse of each of the doors that held them in. But what ran in his veins proved unequal to the task. Undaunted, he continued to hunt the walls and floor in search of secret exits. It stood to reason that amid the thousands of acres, almost all of it covered with books in columns and towers stacked to precarious heights, there might be a dozen hidden ways that had not only eluded his small family, but the many generations that had dwelt in the same prison before them.

Since Mayland's death, Evar's efforts had taken on a new tone that even he acknowledged carried a note of desperation. All of them believed that Mayland was dead, though his body still lay hidden out among the stacks. Kerrol and Clovis seemed to think that Starval had murdered him. Starval thought there was a good chance that Clovis had cut Mayland down in one of her black moods. Evar felt it more likely that an Escape had killed Mayland, or perhaps he had simply been the unfortunate victim of a tower collapse and they would one day find his bones beneath a drift of books.

Evar had been on Clovis's trail for an hour or so, winding back and forth through the stacks, before he realised he was being stalked. Book towers rose around him on all sides. The stacks extended from wall to distant wall. In some areas the towers stood no higher than Evar's knees, like a shallow sea, its waves frozen in place. Here, though, they were five books thick and twice or even three times his height, sometimes with barely enough room between their bases for him to squeeze through. Few places in the chamber offered much of a view. Despite the many acres, the sight line in most of it extended only a few yards, wrapping any venture into the interior in a sense of growing claustrophobia.

Evar had fought Escapes before with his siblings. The things leaked from the Mechanism, black ghosts seeking form among the richness of the book stacks, feeding on old ideas. Kerrol said age had finally reached into the device and cracked it.

The first Escape had emerged several years ago and whilst the frequency with which they had appeared seemed to grow, still they had been a rarity. This year, however, there had been six.

Twice, Evar had faced one alone and emerged victorious. Something was different here though. Here the library's habitual stillness had grown brittle. The light that bled from everywhere and cast no shadows seemed . . . changed. Challenged. The hairs across the back of Evar's arms prickled and a primal terror constricted his throat. Suddenly being out alone, against Kerrol's advice, seemed less a righteous act of defiance, and more of a mistake. A potentially fatal one.

Evar moved on, glancing behind him at regular intervals. In a place where shadows held no sway the eye couldn't take comfort in self-delusion. The blackness that flitted from behind one stack to hide behind another could have no source other than the Escape. Evar had come out among the stacks as the hunter and in some manner he didn't fully understand had become the prey. Fear filled him from toe to head, as if he were an empty glass into which the Escape had poured all its terror in one swift action.

He started to run.

He sped between the towering book stacks of the east corner, chased by a dark malignance that meant to eat him whole. And as the Escape steadily gained on him—despite the great hurt that the Mechanism had done him—had the grey structure stood before him, door open wide, he would have dived right back in to win free.

In the third age of the Arcadian Federation, man's mastery of nature reached such heights that disease was undone, age defeated, and even the stars were claimed as jewels in humanity's crown. In short, any dream might be made real. But some dreams are dark.

The Dust of Arcadia. *A fragment. Author unknown.*

CHAPTER 5

Evar

Evar sucked in a breath, pushed through a narrow gap, raced on. He turned in time to see the Escape flicker from the concealment of one stack to the next, a black insinuation, half-seen tendrils ghosting across the spines of a dozen books. Given time, it would drain them, leaving blank pages, constructing itself from fragments of stolen thought, old ideas repurposed to the business of death. In its pursuit of Evar, though, the Escape hadn't time to empty whole chapters, and the stories beneath those covers left only unquiet ripples across its many surfaces.

Breath ragged, heart hammering, Evar tore through the stacks, ricocheting from one to the next, leaving them rocking behind him. The Escape wove a cleaner path, following his fear, reaching for him with thin, dark hands. The faster he ran, the more quickly it gained on him.

Think.

He was too far from home. Too far from the safety of the others. It would catch him long before he could make it back to the pool. It would catch him, kill him, and hide his corpse. They hadn't found Mayland's body yet and it had been a whole year.

Evar glanced left and right, sucking his breath past bared teeth. The Escape had hidden itself again, but he could feel it out there, feel its hunger pulsating in the unseen spaces beyond his vision. This one was worse than the others had been. Evar had fought Escapes before, but he could tell this one was something new. Something awful.

The air lay thick with must, the lazy drift of dust motes bright with light, oblivious to the tension. The dust underfoot here was gritty and red, untouched by soot. Evar shot through, pursued by the pounding tattoo of his own feet.

A misstep and Evar's shoulder hit a tower. The impact spun him half around—long enough to see the tower sway and begin to topple in his wake. Behind it the Escape boiled towards him, a black flood . . . with legs. Evar's next crash was into something more solid, without even a hint of give in it. The collision threw him to the ground and broke his vision into bright fragments.

Evar lay curled around his pain, lungs emptied and unable to haul in much-needed air. The Escape, contrary to expectation, shuddered to a halt against the nearest stack. The breath that might keep Evar from blacking out hissed into his throat with agonising slowness. Evar imagined that he heard the creak of his ribs as his chest rose by fractions.

The Escape sunk its tendrils into the book stack like roots hunting moisture. It found a form and began to grow, elongating, painting in the details as wisps and hints hardened into sharp-edged fact. Long, painfully thin limbs encased in a gleaming black carapace ended in scythe-like appendages. The Escape watched him through multi-faceted eyes set into a small triangular head atop a tall body. Evar levered himself upright using the colossal book tower he'd crashed into. He'd been right—this Escape was different, larger, carrying its own weapons.

The Escape choked a noise past the complication of its mouth plates, a weird combination of dry rattle and, further back, a thick spluttering. It made the noise again, then once more, coming unnervingly closer to a word each time. "Evar."

Evar had been foolish, coming out to search the stacks. He'd known it from the start, though back then the knowledge had made him angry. Now it terrified him.

"What are you?" Even now, with a bloody death moments away, more than anything Evar wanted answers. He'd lived his whole life surrounded by knowledge, piled high, heaped on every side, and still questions defined him.

"Evar." His name sounded dirty in that mouth.

"Stay back!" Evar drew his knife, which was really a sharpened piece of an iron book hinge, and held it up. It was an unequal contest; his opponent had a much longer reach—one swing of the creature's scythes would leave him with a bloody stump. The Escape already had his name. Soon it would have the portal to his mind fully open and be rooting around his childhood memories for the form best suited to horrifying him. Evar was tempted to let it in. The Escape would find slim pickings among the wreckage.

Evar gathered himself. He was done with running. He raised his blade. "Come on then."

The Escape tensed to launch itself. Evar moved to attack first, but the creature jolted forward, unexpectedly throwing its scythe-arms wide with a crackling hiss. It spun around, turning away from him. A shard of iron had bedded itself deeply in the creature's narrow back, cracking the armour plating. Ichor leaked out around the cutting edges.

The Escape swayed, hissing, hunting for its attacker. Clovis came from the side, stepping out from behind a book pillar. The Escape managed to swing for her, but she leaned back, letting the blade pass an inch before her chest, then spun in to drive her knife into the creature's neck, twice, then twice into its head. Evar stabbed its back, hammering his blade in deep. Ichor spattered across his face—unpleasantly cold—and he lost his weapon as the Escape collapsed.

The Escape hit the ground with the clack of dry bones. Its dissipation began almost immediately, the dark stuff of its interior smoking off Clovis's blade, leaving the steel bright.

Clovis always fought with dispassion. The hatred only showed once the killing was over. For a long moment, with her lips twisted back to expose both canines, she stared at the fading stain where the Escape had fallen, her naked want on show, her bare hunger for something more to fight. Over the course of five deep breaths, she drew herself back, hiding from Evar's sight, a book closing its covers, story hidden once more.

Evar picked up his knife, hands still trembling. He'd never seen Clovis scared. Nothing frightened her. Nothing, except that the war for which she'd been training all her life might not happen—the one with the sabbers who had killed her first family. Her unspoken fear had always been that the enemy would not return and that she would grow old here, trapped in a forgotten corner of the library. That she would die ancient and feeble having tested herself against nothing but the occasional Escape.

"What have you found, little brother?" Clovis turned curious eyes on the book tower that had stopped him dead. It was, by some considerable margin, the thickest and tallest he had ever seen.

Clovis picked up her other knife and slid both into their sheaths. The Escape had seemingly gone from her mind as swiftly as its body had evanesced. The weapons and their housing had been fashioned from books, the blades, like Evar's, from the hinge of some great tome. She had armour made from the same raw material though she'd not worn it on this occasion: a weight of leather covers stitched together and overlaid with metal plates.

Clovis ran a hand across the wall of the colossal book tower. "How has this been here all our lives and not been discovered?"

Evar, still trembling, wiped at his face. The ichor had undoubtedly evaporated by now, but he could still feel it there, cold and penetrating. "What are you doing here?"

"Saving your life." Grey eyes continued their study of the structure, not so much as flickering his way.

"Right here? Right now?" Evar understood and slumped. "You used me! Both of you used me!" Kerrol had suggested that he stay close to the pool until the Escape had been dealt with, but what Kerrol wanted and what Kerrol said were rarely directly related.

"You'd have made lousy bait if you'd come out here knowing I had your back. Kerrol sent you after me." Clovis shrugged. "It was a sneaky one. I needed someone to lure it out."

She meant she'd needed someone scared to lure it out with the scent of their fear. To embolden and distract it. Evar showed his teeth. "You used me!"

"Why didn't you call for help?" Clovis cocked her head, regarding him with narrow eyes. "I was almost too late."

Evar's anger blew itself out. "I was stupid." The answer was more complex than that, but Evar had little time for his own excuses at the best of times, and stupidity did seem to be the core of it. "Dumb."

Clovis ignored his statement of the obvious. She shook the red mane of her hair and craned her neck to look up the tower. The tumbling book would have hit her full in the face but for the speed of her reflexes. Several others crashed down in its wake, but she sidestepped them.

"Damn! How hard did you hit this thing?"

"Very." Evar rubbed his shoulder and stepped back. Some of the towers would topple at a touch. With no weather to bother them they could stand on the edge of collapse for centuries. This one had felt as solid as the chamber wall when he hit it, but sometimes the effects of a blow are not immediate. Clovis had taught him that.

More books fell from on high, and though it might have been a trick of the eye, the whole thirty-yard height of the tower seemed to sway. Evar felt guilty. He'd knocked down dozens of smaller towers in his youth, but suddenly this one felt worth saving.

"Help me!" He threw his weight against the far side, seeking to counteract the lean.

Clovis lent her shoulder to the effort. She lacked a couple of inches on him in height and her limbs, though corded with muscle, were hardly thicker than his, but she always knew how to apply her strength in exactly the right way.

It made no difference. Some things when set in motion by the lightest touch cannot be stopped by a whole army. Somewhere within the tower's inner architecture something vital had slipped. More books fell. One bounced off Evar's shoulder. He managed to shout "Run!" before the whole thing came crashing down.

Thunder swallowed them. Confusion followed. Silence—the library's undertaker—re-established itself in the wake of the collapse.

Evar found himself entombed. He struggled to find which way was up, and then to follow it. He emerged panting and sweaty, and slumped forward, still half-buried in the heap of books. For a moment he wondered if Mayland's bones lay beneath a heap like this somewhere out among the stacks. Then he remembered his sister.

"Clo!" He crawled free. "Clo! Where are you?"

A groan behind him drew his eye to a heaving patch. A moment later, her hand emerged, and by the time he reached her she had her head and shoulders free. He grabbed her arm and hauled her clear.

They stood together on the uneven surface, heads bowed, breathing hard, his hand still on her shoulder. For a moment it felt almost as if they were back five years ago when for a brief but glorious time Evar had thought they were in love. The fiction that they were truly siblings had been cast aside and for weeks or perhaps months Clovis had been his world. She'd broken his heart, of course. Evar didn't need Kerrol's skills to tell him that Clovis couldn't allow her armour to be breached. Even so, it had hurt. But not so badly that he regretted it. Not even when she took the anger at what she thought was her weakness and turned it on him. Evar couldn't be sorry for the only moments of tenderness he'd ever known. Not even when she mocked him and took Mayland to her bed.

"Idiot." Clovis shook his hand off. "You nearly got us both killed."

Evar's reply stayed on his tongue. Among the thousands of books mounded around them, one had somehow drawn his eye. He walked towards it, slipping on the shifting surface. A thin, flexible book with a plain brown cover, time-smoothed and free of any markings.

Evar could neither understand nor resist whatever force it was that drew him to the unremarkable book. It almost felt like memory. Perhaps something had been broken free when the Escape tried to invade his mind. He bent to pick it up. A shock ran through him as he touched it. Recognition.

There are moments in life when you know with a great and unshakeable certainty that everything will change. Evar straightened, book in hand. He knew that he had set his foot upon some great new path, though he had no notion of what it might be or what reason he might have for feeling this way. But, blood to bone, he knew it.

"Let's see." Clovis had followed him.

"It's mine. Find your own." He waved his arm at the heap and at the dozens of lesser towers toppled by the giant's fall.

Clovis shrugged and turned away. Her rotation flowed into a blur, dropping and sweeping his legs. A moment later Evar hit the pile hard. His vision cleared in time to see Clovis heading away with his prize in her hand.

Evar rolled, rose from all fours, and ran after her, scattering pages. Clovis swayed aside as he charged at her back and somehow left enough of her leg in his path to trip him. He went sprawling into a book drift, rolling back to his feet with a snarl.

"Here." Clovis tossed the book at him. "Good luck reading it without the Mechanism."

Evar caught the flutter of pages and covers awkwardly. It hit him as if she'd thrown a reading desk rather than a book, still weighted with that shock of revelation—of recognition. His excitement collapsed, though. If Clovis couldn't read the language it was written in, then he wouldn't be able to either. The Assistant had taught them to read well in several languages and had handed over the rudiments of a dozen more, but still, without the Mechanism the great majority of the library's tomes were closed to their understanding, however easily the covers might be opened.

"Come on." Clovis walked on at pace.

Evar followed, resenting her tone of command. He'd vanished into the Mechanism long before Clovis had been born. Mayland had been first, then Evar, then Kerrol, Starval, and finally Clovis, the only survivor of the sabber attack that left the five of them as the last of their kind. The four brothers had already been lost within the Mechanism, generations apart and a generation before Clovis had somehow fled into it.

Years later they had been disgorged together, vomited up from the unknown, reborn. None of them had aged and the Assistant—who had been created for duties very different to those of raising children—became mother to them all.

The resentment slid from him as they walked. Evar had never been able to hold on to anger or bitterness for long, perhaps encouraged to let them go by witnessing their corrosive effects on both Clovis and Starval. He turned his attention to the book tingling in his hands.

The book had no title. Its thin leather covers were smooth with touching, its flexible contents loosely bound. The pages seemed oddly matched and sized for some fatter volume, being maybe two handspans wide and three tall. Ahead of him Clovis broke into a jog, news—at least of the kind not discovered between the covers of a book—was a great rarity and although her audience was small, Clovis clearly burned with the need to report it.

On any other day Evar would have raced her to be first with the news. Today curiosity won before the race had started. He slowed and, at the risk of an embarrassing collision with one of the many pillars, he lifted the new book and turned the cover.

He stopped dead in his tracks. Clovis had been right—the Assistant had never taught them this language. She'd never even shown them this alphabet, a flowing fourteen-letter script reminiscent of old Etrusian. The first page was blank save for a single line slanted across the middle, written in haste by a careless hand, seemingly terminated in mid flow. Evar had never seen another example. And yet he understood it perfectly.

Evar! Don't turn the page. I'm in the Exchange. Find me at the bottom

It seems clear that, like archetypes in works of fiction, certain cities spring up wherever the conditions allow—though from what spores, I cannot say. The origins of the name remain unknown, lost amid dozens of theories. Like children's names, falling in and out of common use, the names of great cities can recur after long periods of dormancy and be passed from ruin to building site in quick succession, creating dynasties in stone to rival any royal house.

A History of Crath City, *by Kerra Brews*

CHAPTER 6

Livira

L ivira had been dirty her whole life, but she had never *felt* dirty until she stepped through the vast gates of the city. She had been dwarfed by the great expanse of the Dust but never felt small until the sandstone walls of Crath rose above her.

The sabbers, and then Malar and his comrades, had been the first strangers she'd ever met. She was still getting used to that idea when the city crowds closed around them, allowing no space even for Henton's pungent corpse. A babble of voices, the shouts of wagoneers, men and women crying out seemingly just for the hell of it. Booted feet, sharp elbows, incurious eyes, a seething mass of people hardly touched by the dust, their clothes unpatched, untorn, and sporting colours other than that of the dirt from which Livira and her fellow settlers had been born. Here and there some wore the smocks and shifts and jerkins that you'd see at the settlement, only cleaner and more colourful. But the majority wore a bewildering variety of garments, many of which Livira had no name for. Coats of many designs, some sweeping to the back of the knee, waistcoats, dresses that billowed out as if the women beneath them had hips a yard across, jackets with silver buttons, hats of a hundred designs . . . Some of the most richly dressed men and women even had hair unlike anything she'd seen, hanging in unnatural curls and such a uniform shade of grey that it might have been painted.

Malar started to haul the smaller children off the horses and set them on the ground where they clung to each other and to the bigger ones—an almost singular knot of dirty rags amid the bustling crowds.

"Godsake!" Malar deposited Breta, the smallest of them, on the cobbles. She stood with her fear trembling through every limb, unable to walk. "Stop with the snivelling." He pointed to the gates still visible behind them. "No sabber ever got through those gates 'less it was wearing chains. We made it. You're safe."

Malar led off, forging a path through the press of people. Livira stuck to the soldiers' heels, sandwiched between their horses.

"How long before they do?" muttered Jons, now dismounted.

"Do what?" Malar didn't look at him.

"Come through those gates." Jons said it so quietly that Livira almost didn't hear him over the clatter of hooves and voice of the crowd.

"Ten years?" Malar shrugged and spat. "Tops."

An old woman in black elbowed past Livira in the throng, spitting at her as she went. No anger in it, the casual hostility the more shocking for that fact. Livira wiped the saliva from her shift. She'd have spat back if she'd been less surprised and less dry.

For a while all questions deserted Livira, her curiosity voiced only by eyes that blinked and grew wide and flitted from one astonishment to the next. She almost missed Jons leading his and Henton's horse off down a side road as the thoroughfare Malar was following started to climb the slope. Only Malar led them now, and with nobody guarding the rear it would be easy to slip away. Livira could smell food and water, though she could see neither, and the scent was driving her mad. The stone houses lining the street were several storeys high with dozens of windows both shuttered and unshuttered. She could be through one of those openings and hunting the source of those tantalising odours. Water first, then something to fill her belly. Malar wouldn't even know she was gone until he got where he was taking them.

First it had been the vastness of the Dust holding her where she was. It had never been her aunt's expectations, or the sabbers' rope, or the unvoiced threat of the soldiers that had imprisoned her. It had been the fact that she was lost—she'd been lost her whole life, bound to the one point that she understood. And now? Ignorance still held her captive. She knew too little to stray from the path and the knowledge chafed her worse than the rope had. Malar knew it too. He didn't even glance back to see that they were following. In the end it was his indifference that kept Livira at his heels. It might please him if she ran. Relieve him of a responsibility he hadn't ever wanted.

"Dusters!" A small boy threw a stone, missing all of them, and ran away with two friends, laughing.

"Your kind aren't liked here," Malar said matter-of-factly, without looking back.

Livira hadn't known she had a kind. "Why?"

"The criers say your lot don't do anything to keep the sabbers at bay." Malar shrugged as if he knew how ridiculous that was. "There's even rumours the settlements are in league with them."

They climbed higher and her legs complained. The buildings grew higher too, reaching for the sky's pitiless blue. The crowds thinned enough for the children to gain the space to breathe. Livira noticed that up here the looks thrown her way grew even more disdainful. They passed through a long street so steep that anything you dropped might roll away and whose sides were crowded with carved entrances, the doors open wide, the faces of gods and demons set into the stone above them. Incense flavoured the air and from gloomy interiors the sounds of bells and chanting and gongs reached out.

"What gods do the city people have?" Livira hadn't considered that they might not honour the same collection of wind spirits and roaming godlings that the settlers did.

"Too many to fucking count." Malar spat outside the door of one narrow building whose pillars were carved with bones and skulls. "The library's the real religion in Crath though. It's given the people more than this lot ever have." He waved an arm up the street. "Folks these days don't have time for gods. Progress is the new deity."

Still the city rose before them, an endless tide of stone, until at last, far above them, it did finally end and hand over the climb to the mountain, which took the challenge and ran with it, making it nearly all the way to the heavens. They'd only just left the temples and shrines behind them when little Gevin collapsed. Acmar, prompted by Benth who was labouring once again beneath Breta's weight, picked the boy up and carried him, a grimace of effort on his broad face. Livira noticed that Malar's scowl deepened but he didn't offer any more rides on his horse, as if that were something that could only happen outside the walls with nobody to see.

"Where's he taking us?" Katrin wanted to know, even though she'd been told.

"Allocation." Neera puffed and wheezed as if she still had dust in her lungs.

Livira wanted to know who decided their fate and what they'd done to be allowed to make such decisions. She found herself amazed that all this had sat here her entire life, just beyond the horizon, ignoring her existence completely. And now, suddenly, this mass of stone and people had decided it owned her and had the right to set her to a purpose.

"This way, dust-rats." For the first time Malar turned away from the main street into the shade of a side road. And there, rippling and glistening in a great stone trough, was more water than Livira had ever seen in one place. "Slow down, you little fucks!" Malar roared, catching Neera by the neck as she rushed at the water with new-found energy. "Sips! Sip it! I don't want you throwing up over my nice clean city."

Livira tried to take his advice. She knew he was right. But the water tasted so damn good. Even when Malar's horse stuck its great head beside hers and began to guzzle noisily, she couldn't find it in her to stop.

Finally with a heavy stomach she rolled to the side, fighting off sudden nausea. She stretched her legs out across the cool flagstones. Malar stood and watched, shaking his head in disgust. "Dust-rats." He drank, then took a double handful of water and splashed it over his face. His skin beneath the dirt was paler than Livira had realised. He took another mouthful, swished it around, and spat it against the wall.

"Damn, but it's good to get the taste of the Dust off my tongue."

"The dust has a taste?" Livira blinked.

"It's sour!" Malar stared at her. "By the gates, if someone puts an apple pie on the windowsill to cool, they cover it. If the dust gets at it nobody wants any."

"What's an apple?" But what she was really thinking of was when Jons said "twenty years back, on the Kerlo border." Malar was *old*. Just a few years shy of Old Kern, but Kern had been hollow-chested and milky-eyed, no match for a sabber even with four others at his side. Perhaps the dust turned people sour too—old before their time.

Malar had already turned away, leaving her question about apples unanswered. He went to his saddlebags and drew out a bundle of black cloth.

"There's so much!" Katrin had both arms in the water, past her elbows. "How did it get here?"

The question distracted Livira from Malar's activities. How *had* it got there? A hundred buckets' worth. More, perhaps. Just standing there with none of the passers-by taking a second look except to frown at the children.

Lacking an answer, Livira turned back to Malar. "How—"

The soldier shoved her, one hand flat to her chest. The wall of the trough met the back of her knees, and in the next moment she was floundering in the water, the cold shock of it stealing her breath. She flailed in terror, crying out only to find water flooding her mouth. Somehow, she caught hold of an edge and hauled herself out, blind and coughing. Strong hands seized her. For a moment she thought she was being pushed back in and used her teeth.

"Fuck that, you biting little shit-bag!" Malar set her on her feet. "That bath's for all your questions. Ask some more if you want another." He shook his head. "Let's see if you can keep your fucking mouth shut longer than you take to dry."

Livira coughed and spat. Some of the children were laughing nervously. A woman passing by snorted her amusement. The horse snorted too. She found herself angry. Furious. "I should have let the dust-bear have you!"

"Yes." Malar nodded. "Yes, you fucking should have." A wooden post stood beside the trough and the soldier tied his horse to it. "Come on then, rats. Time to get rid of you. You're lucky we got in on a Wodesday or you'd be bedding down in the stables till it was one."

He waited for them to rise, patient for once, then led them back to the main street. It climbed sharply though the gradient no longer seemed so taxing to Livira, thirst quenched, muscles fired up with rage. By the time it levelled out in an enormous square she was no longer leaving a trail of wet footprints. At the square's centre stood a round, stone-sided pond,

dwarfing the trough they'd just drunk from. It had a stone . . . creature . . .
at the middle, spouting streams of sparkling water into the air. Buildings
far grander than any yet seen bordered the square, each fronted by carved
pillars and with steps that all the children could climb shoulder to shoulder
and have room to spare. Livira found it hard to believe that people could
have built it all. Maybe the gods that they no longer believed in had done
the work.

Malar marched the children towards the smallest of the buildings,
though it still seemed far too large and important to want anything to do
with anyone from the Dust. The square's stone acreage lay almost empty, at
least compared to the city streets. Perhaps the inhabitants preferred the
shade. The sun and the hungry air had already stolen most of the water
from Livira's rags and it was no place to linger when you had an alternative.

A crowd of perhaps a hundred people milled before the steps of the
building Malar was aiming at, their number distributed along the narrow
strip of shade cast by the portico. Higher up, near five large doors, stood
white-robed figures, one at each entrance.

"Five," Malar muttered unhappily.

"Five is bad?" Livira asked.

"Just rare. You get a crowd. The first door's open every Wodesday. The
second every other Wodesday, and so on. The fifth is open every five
Wodesdays. So having them all open together . . . that happens once
every . . ."

"Sixty Wodesdays." Livira had no idea how often a Wodesday happened, but she could count.

Malar brought them to the base of the leftmost of the pillars that supported the roof above the stairs. He snaked out a rough hand and grabbed
Livira's shoulder. "You, stand behind me, right be-fucking-hind me." He
sounded curiously anxious. He shoved her into the position he'd indicated.
"Get a move on!" He waved the rest of the children ahead of him.

Livira stalked behind the soldier, rubbing her shoulder and fuming.
Snatching a glimpse past him she could see that the white-robe at the leftmost door had marked their approach and was descending the steps to
meet them. Malar herded the children ahead of him, snarling at them to
go towards the woman in white.

"Go on," Malar growled. "Up!" He gave Acmar a shove, encouraging him to take the steps. Like Livira, none of them had actually seen or used a step before. "Not you!" As Livira tried to join the others Malar dragged her from his shadow and pinned her to the pillar so she couldn't even see the others. "You stay here!"

"But—"

The back of Malar's hand met with Livira's mouth so unexpectedly that she nearly fell down. It wasn't the pain but the shock of it that silenced her. She thought she'd understood him but, clearly, she'd been wrong. It was that sense of amazement and outrage which kept her there in the shadow of the pillar despite the unfairness of it all while Malar went to speak with the white-robe. Only the sudden humility in his tone reached back to her, lacking meaning. Livira pressed her hand to her throbbing lips—he hadn't struck as hard as Acmar had, but still she cursed herself for thinking that perhaps the man's bark was worse than his bite. His bite had killed a full-grown sabber.

And then he was in front of her again, shoving something black at her while the others trailed up the steps after the woman in the white robe.

"Put it on."

"What?" Livira scowled at him and blinked at the bundle of cloth pressed against her.

"Quickly! Put it on. Dust-rats get the bad jobs. You want to be crawling about in the sewers for the next twenty years?"

"I . . ." She took the bundle. It was a cloak, like the one he was wearing but without the dust and the rips.

"You're clean for the first time in your life. Cleanish anyhow. Put that on and I can blag you through the middle door. You'll be serving dinner to rich bastards. Easy life. Get to pick at what they leave. This time next year those other rats'd kill to swap with you."

"I don't—"

"I pay my debts. Now follow me and button that fucking mouth. They're big on tradition here. All those old-fashioned robes and such. It's all about putting you in your place. So, know yours!"

With that he set off up the steps towards the middle door of the five.

After a pause, perhaps the longest moment of indecision in her life,

Livira followed, wrapping the cloak around her as she went. It was too long of course, but Neera had been right about the city not allowing the dust past its gates, and the cloak swept the steps behind her without raising a cloud. Malar glanced back and motioned for her to pull it tight at the front. "Don't let them see you're barefoot."

Climbing steps was a new experience for her, but not so new or absorbing that it stopped her looking around. Here and there along the broadness of the bottom step other children were breaking away from the groups of adults she'd seen milling around. Breaking away or being pushed, some parting with hugs and kisses, others hanging their heads beneath the stern command of an extended arm and pointing finger.

She could see now that there were strata in the groups at the base of the steps, just like the layers the well cut through out in the Dust. At one end the people were ragged, smaller, nervous. At the other they stood tall, proud, magnificent in the finest of clothes, adorned with curious, elaborate hats, their bodies sparkling with jewelled brooches and gold chains. These last few were the people who owned the world, without shame. A boy marched from their ranks, climbing the steps towards the fifth door, head high, his hair a buoyant golden cloud that made Livira wonder how much filth her own damp mane still harboured.

Two children in sky-blue cloaks glanced her way, only briefly, as if letting their gaze linger might dirty their finery. They were climbing towards the fourth door, which looked no different from the rest—a huge dark slab of wood, round-topped and studded with square-headed iron bolts.

"What's behind those other doors?" Livira called after Malar.

"None of your gods-damned business is what." Malar turned and beckoned her to close the gap between them. "Fourth's for merchants' sons and daughters. Fifth's for the fuckers that got fed with a gold spoon." He shook his head and stomped on up towards the third door. "They'll probably kick you out of here but I'm giving you the chance, and you'll definitely get into second after. Now shut it and let me do the talking when we get to the robe."

A girl heading towards the fourth door caught Livira's eye. She looked magnificent in a crimson tunic that seemed to flow around her, a silver necklace of interlocking leaves around her neck, red hair coiled artfully atop her head. Livira had never seen red hair before—in the settlement nearly everyone had black hair like hers. She wondered if it was real. The girl caught her looking and sneered. Livira held her gaze and the girl stuck out her tongue, though she looked too old for such silliness. She was taller than Livira. Old enough to have her blood for sure.

Livira looked away and promptly tripped on the next step. The girl's laughter proved to be as refined as the rest of her, a delicate trill, like music rather than something honest from the belly, something you could trust. Despite herself, Livira looked again as she picked herself up, big toe and shin hurting. Livira had seen the girl's current expression before. Acmar had worn it two days ago when he called her "weed." Back then she'd punched the look off his face. This time another impulse seized her. Not a sensible one. Not one that had been thought out, but something born from two days of loss and pain and growing anger. Livira began to walk towards the girl.

The girl gave a genteel shriek and hurried up the steps after the pair in blue. Livira didn't alter her course.

"Hey!" Malar hissed after her. Livira kept walking. She passed the spot where the girl had stood and kept going.

"Hey!" Malar struggled to shout without shouting, a touch of unaccustomed fear mixed with the fury. Livira heard him come after her then falter a few paces on.

"Little fucker . . ."

A man had been sitting on the steps between the third and fourth door, up near the top, the only person seated. Livira hadn't seen him until he stood, for his robe was the same dark grey as the stone, and although he didn't look old, his hair was white as bone. Now he was descending in her direction.

She kept going, angling across the steps rather than up them, stopping only when level with the fifth door. The golden-haired boy was already at the entrance, being spoken to by the white-robe on duty there. Back at the base of the pillars, brows were elevating among the lords and ladies preparing to send forth their progeny. Livira, about halfway up the fifty-yard flight of steps, scowled back at them. She'd heard about kings and emperors in the dark-time stories of course. The bit she never understood was why anyone did what they said. Soldiers, her aunt would say. The king has soldiers. But why, Livira asked, did the soldiers do what he said? None of it made sense to her. Her aunt would tell her not to spoil the story with all her questions. Malar was the only soldier here, and it didn't seem as if he was going to stop her.

Livira looked down on the princess in green and gold emerging from the velvet ranks at the foot of the steps. The city had thrust a sense of smallness and dirtiness upon Livira as she entered it, but the anger she'd carried with her from the Dust had started to burn through. The girl now climbing towards her might look like a king's daughter plucked from the tales, and perhaps her garden did have silver trees with golden fruit. But none of that made Livira think she should get out of her way. Instead Livira turned resolutely towards the fifth door, ignoring Malar's wide-eyed silent entreaties, and climbed towards it, increasing her pace slightly to prevent the man in grey from catching up.

The boy had already gone in by the time Livira presented herself at the door. The guardian in the white robe was tall, hunched, and old—older than anyone Livira knew. His hair was as white as his garment, his face as crumpled as the triangle of parchment Livira kept in her pocket. He squinted down at her with faded blue eyes and a puzzled frown.

"And what can I do for you, young lady?" Like Malar he spoke his words with strange edges on them that tried to hide the meaning, though they were not the same edges.

Livira had been planning to say that she wanted to be allocated. Now she realised that even if the ancient's eyesight wasn't sharp enough for him to be entirely certain that she didn't fit, his ears would tell him so as soon as she spoke. She could say whatever she liked: what he would hear was "dust-rat."

The old man cocked his head to the side, inviting her answer.

Livira drew a deep breath, her heart pounding. She would rather dive into another dust-bear than be turned away with the princess behind her watching, and to have to trudge shame-footed past the sneering girl in red to face Malar's wrath. She'd done it to herself. Everything else since the sabbers came had been done to her—but this, this she had done to herself. She growled.

"Your pardon?" The white-robe frowned, adding more wrinkles to his already impressive array.

Livira snarled, growled deep in her throat and released it. "*T'loth criis'tyla loddotis.*"

Two white eyebrows shot up and a strange delight lit the ancient's face. He clapped his hands together gently. "Have you indeed?" He glanced away towards the approaching man in grey, decades his junior but with hair even whiter. He frowned and pressed his lips into a flat line. "I'm afraid, young lady, that I must respectfully—"

"Wait." The man in grey reached them. His skin was as pale as milk and he watched Livira unsmiling, from beneath white eyebrows. He carried a peculiar, bulky walking cane, though he didn't use it for support. "Why not let her in, Hendron? I want to see what they make of her."

Hendron's own smile returned. He turned and reached for the black iron knocker at the centre of the door, banging it three times.

"Good luck, child," the man in grey said seriously. "You'll need it." He inclined his head towards Livira. She saw now that even his eyelashes were white, guarding pink eyes that studied her with a consuming intensity. Nobody had ever shown even a fraction of the interest in Livira that this stranger did right now. Except perhaps Ella, on the rare occasions when the old woman wasn't busy with her wind-weed or the necessities of scratching a life from the Dust. With his unworldly eyes, the man seemed somehow stranger to her than the sabbers had. And almost as unnerving.

As the door swung open the princess in green and gold arrived. Livira was pleased to see that close up the girl's face was less perfect than she had imagined and a sheen of sweat glistened on her brow.

"You may go through too, Serra Leetar." The white-robe made the smallest of bows in the girl's direction and held the door for both of them. As Livira passed him he offered a small smile. "Those were big words for a young girl. I hope you can live up to them."

The guard who had opened the door from the inside gestured with his large-knuckled hand, indicating Livira and the princess should move on. A corridor stretched before them, lit by lanterns, with no side doors to worry about. Livira strode down it, her overlong cloak swishing behind her, the stone cold beneath bare feet. Serra Leetar followed. Livira could almost hear the girl's curiosity battling her distaste.

Finally, halfway down the corridor, the girl snapped, "What did you say to him?"

Rather than admit that she had no idea what the words meant, and that she had just repeated the sounds the sabber made, Livira gave her own translation.

"I declared war."

. . . debate of carrot or stick. And for many children these are valid considerations. Marquart, however, reminds us that for some few, a stick would be required to keep them from such knowledge rather than drive them to it. It is important to investigate the origin and breeding of these outliers. Such a child is a spark, and only a fool invites fire into their library.

On the Education of the Lower Classes, *by Einald, Duke of Ferra*

CHAPTER 7

Livira

Livira emerged from the corridor into a large chamber taller than it was wide. Sunlight decorated the wall to her left and half the black floor, streaming down through the perforated ceiling far above them. Livira looked up to see the blue sky divided into a thousand shapes and when she returned her gaze to the room she saw only after-images.

For a long moment she stood swaying, dizzy with more than just hunger now, teetering on the edge of a faint. Too little sleep, too much stress, and plenty of exhaustion all chose this moment to catch up with her.

"You're first." Serra Leetar pushed her shoulder. "Gods know what they'll do with you! I'm to be allocated to the university. Embassy service wouldn't suit me, and the laboratory is right out." She said this last one with a shiver.

Blinking, Livira noted that the girl's sleeve of green slashed with gold was further decorated with minute embroidery picking out the same kind of geometric patterns that pierced the roof. Malar's cloak, which was by far the finest garment she had ever owned or even touched, seemed suddenly shabby. She shook the fuzziness from her head and looked to see what the princess was pushing her towards.

Four tables stood by the light-dappled wall. A figure seated at each. And behind them three corridors led off. The golden-haired boy was leaving the first table and walking towards the second, a tall, raven-haired girl was at the fourth. A small group of children had collected by the leftmost of the three exits, two others stood at the exit to the right, none at the middle one. Livira had no idea what a laboratory was, but it sounded bad.

Serra Leetar sighed. "Go on. Don't you know anything? First table."

The princess didn't seem the sort to let others go in front of her. Livira guessed she wanted to see what would happen. Perhaps Serra Leetar didn't know as much as she'd like others to think. Perhaps even she was nervous.

Livira went forward, suppressing a shiver of her own. The room was much cooler than the square and under her cloak her rags were still damp. She straightened herself up, reaching for her old fire. The defiance that defined her uncoiled in her chest. The same anger that had seen her take Acmar on in a fist fight, the resilience that had had her demand to know if the sabber was going to eat her. She was Livira. Give her an inch and she would take all the miles you owned. She had chosen this door and win or lose she was going to fight for her place.

The first table was bare save for a small wooden frame with five wires stretched left to right, each strung with black beads. A bald, heavyset man sat behind the table, small eyes tracking her progress, mouth puckered as if he'd just bitten a wormy bean. Like the man at the door and the figures behind the other desks, he wore a white robe, though his bore several faint stains on the chest and belly.

Livira came to a halt in front of the table.

"Recite your thirteen times table."

Livira looked to the other tables. There were only four of them and the man's words made no sense. She looked past him to the children by the exits. They might be dressed in silks and gold, but their expressions could have been taken from the ring of children who watched Acmar beat her. They could smell the blood to come.

"Divide a hundred and sixty-five by eleven." The man sounded bored.

"Divide?" Livira knew what the numbers meant.

"Twelve times twenty?"

"Times?"

One of the boys laughed. Not a kind laugh. Livira took it like Acmar's punch—it hurt—she knew she deserved it—she'd bitten off more than she could chew—but she wasn't going down without a fight. "Explain."

The bald man showed a flash of interest at that, leaning forward so his belly folded over the desk. "I'm the one who asks the questions, girl, and you are clearly in the wrong place. I can see the dust behind your ears."

"Explain what you mean." Livira stood her ground. "Then we'll see if I'm in the right place or not." At any moment she expected someone to take her by the shoulders and turn her back the way she'd come. "I don't know what this *divide* means, or this *times*."

"Tell it to her in beans!" laughed one of the girls who seemed to have passed all the tests.

"Dusters know all about beans." A blond boy whose sneer seemed a permanent fixture.

The fat man frowned, pursing his lips in annoyance. "Very well . . ." He rolled his eyes and made an exasperated gesture with his hand. "If I had thirty-six sacks, each with two hundred and eleven beans in, how many—"

"Seven thousand and five hundred and ninety-six," Livira said.

The girl who had laughed now snorted.

The white-robe peered at Livira, then with a sigh, picked up the frame with the beads. "You were supposed to use this." Quicker than the eye he flicked a few of the beads back and forth.

"Ask me another," Livira said,

"Don't you want to know if you were right?"

Livira blinked. "How could I be wrong?"

"Share three hundred and seventy-three beans fairly among eight people. How—"

"Forty-six each with five left over."

"You're sure?"

"Yes." The question puzzled her. They were just numbers. It was like being asked which stone was on top of the other. How could you get it wrong?

The man waved her towards the next table.

A woman of middling years sat behind this one, sandy hair tied back in a severe bun, and eyes that suggested her mind might also be tied back in that same no-nonsense manner. A roll of parchment lay on the polished wood before her, next to it a small pot filled with black liquid. A large feather lay beside the pot. To one side four rectangular objects were stacked in a small pile, each the size of two spread hands and an inch or so thick.

"Pick any of the books and start reading."

Livira's gaze darted wildly between the objects on the table.

"Do you need me to explain 'book' to you?" the woman asked, and the giggles that had died away when Livira started answering the questions about beans now surfaced again.

The old woman at the next table looked at Livira sympathetically from behind the curios arrayed before her. She offered a nod of encouragement.

Livira reached for one of the rectangular things. The woman had said "any of the books" and these were the only things of which there was more than one. It seemed to be a box of some sort, but as she opened it, she saw that it was full of paper, and that every part of the paper was covered with markings. She looked up from the page, met the woman's level stare, and returned her eyes to their study. The markings meant something. Her aunt had told her they did. Was reading the business of saying what they meant?

The sniggering grew.

"You're in the wrong place, child," the woman said heavily. "The trick with the numbers was impressive but you're in the wrong place. Go down to the second door. A merchant would be happy to have you tally his warehouse goods."

"I bet she can't even write her name!" a boy called.

The white-robe cocked an eyebrow at her. "If you can use a quill you can allocate at door three." She took the feather, dipped the pointed end in the black liquid and unrolled part of the parchment, placing a smooth, flat stone to hold it. "Here." She offered Livira the quill, not unkindly.

Livira took it.

"Write your name." She might as well have asked for one of the moons.

Livira leaned over the table, holding the quill trembling above the yellowed expanse of the parchment. A drop of glistening blackness fell from the tip and hit, spattering smaller droplets in all directions. More laughter.

My name? Livira tried to imagine what that might look like. She closed her eyes, lowered her hand to the parchment, and began to move the tip in small, precise motions. Time passed. Sweat crowded her brow. Twice she had to dip the quill again. Three times. Finally, she straightened up.

The woman looked at her with narrow, angry eyes. Gone was any of the kindness on display when encouraging her to write her name. "This is Cru-nian. How do *you* possibly know Crunian?"

"Crunian Four, if I'm not mistaken," said a softer voice. A tall, impos-sibly thin man had come to stand behind the woman. Livira had seen him from the corner of her eye as he entered the hall through one of the corri-dors at the back. He wore a deep-red patch over his right eye, which left Livira with the unsettling impression that she was staring into the recently vacated bloody socket. He wasn't wearing robes like the others—his clothes lacked the ostentation of the parents at the foot of the stairs: black jacket, charcoal waistcoat with a silver chain looped from one pocket to a button-hole. His hair rose around his head in unnatural grey curls and seemed as if it were something he wore like a hat. "Yes, Crunian Four. Holy text. Strangely incomplete. Clearly copied. I doubt she knows what any of it means. Someone's coached her."

The word "cheat" reached Livira, an overly loud whisper from the group at the corridor. Her face burned both with a shame that she didn't feel she deserved and an anger that she didn't fully understand.

"Enough of this farce." The old woman from the third table got up from behind the collection of strange objects scattered before her. "Send her back where she belongs and find out why Hendron let her in in the first place." It seemed that the arrival of the man with the eyepatch had swept away any sympathies she might have had, infecting her with his disap-proval. A powerful man then. One who even these people feared.

A large-knuckled hand descended, taking a grip on Livira's shoulder. "Come with me, serra." Livira was about to protest that she wasn't Serra, that was the other girl, then realised it was some kind of title. A title not meant for her, though there was no mockery in the guardsman's voice.

"And send Hendron in to explain himself!" the thin man told the guard.

"I asked Hendron to let her through." The speaker came from the same direction as the guard had come. He passed them both, with a swish of grey robes. The assessors watched the white-skinned man with guarded expressions. Eyepatch's single eye held only distaste.

"Master Yute." The woman with the books inclined her head.

"She speaks the sabbers' tongue too." Yute came to peer at the parchment on which Livira had made the marks that her memory had stolen from the torn scrap in her pocket. "Curious."

"A parlour trick." The thin man dismissed it with a wave of one narrow hand.

Yute leaned in closer. "It looks as if she's never held a quill before—see how the lettering improves as she goes. And did you notice that she's written it upside down? You didn't need to rotate the scroll to read it." He turned to face Livira. "She came in from the Dust with a soldier. Not an hour through the gates to look at them. He wouldn't let her go with the rest. Clearly his judgement was that she's destined for better things." He looked at the thin man with the eyepatch. "You disagree, Algar?"

"Soldiers get paid to fight the king's enemies, not to allocate his subjects." Algar glared at the guardsman as if it was his fault. "After you've brought Hendron in find this soldier too. I want to know his captain's name." He returned his sour gaze to Livira. "The child's learned a few things off by heart. Parroting some sabber yapping, scrawling a paragraph of Crunian Four . . ."

"Her mental arithmetic was impressive," Yute countered.

Algar waved the words away. "I'm sure any of the others could do better." He swivelled his singular gaze towards the bald man at the first table. "Botan, pose one of her questions to Serra Leetar."

Botan gave a heavy shrug and picked the first and easiest. "Thirty-six two hundred and elevens."

Livira would have protested that the girl had already heard the answer but the fact that it was so simple combined with the weight of hostility in the room made her hold her tongue for once.

"I . . . ah." Serra Leetar coloured beneath the chestnut sweep of her hair. She licked her lips, eyes focused on something that wasn't there.

Livira frowned. If she'd forgotten the answer given shortly before then surely she could just see it anew?

After a painfully long pause the girl started to stammer out her answer. "Six thousand . . . and . . ."

"A difficult one." Master Yute came to Serra Leetar's rescue. "But young . . ." He circled his hand as if trying to draw forth a memory.

"Livira," Livira said.

"But young Livira didn't learn thirty-six two hundred and elevens by rote." Master Yute had clearly followed Livira and the princess in within moments of their admission to watch her assessment. "Wouldn't the laboratory benefit from someone with such arithmetics spilling from her tongue?" He turned towards the bald man, Botan, who had asked the number questions.

Botan shrugged heavily. "There's a baker's son in Quell Quarter who can spit out prime numbers all day long. Can't dress himself though. Such things are the side effects of broken minds. And that's the last thing we want amid vats of corrosive and barrels of detonator."

"She's bold." Yute returned his attention to Algar. "And she's survived an encounter with a sabber warrior—her pronunciation could only have been learned first-hand. Wouldn't she be an asset in the embassy service, my lord? Or the missions, at the very least?"

Algar brushed at the sleeves of his jacket as if he imagined that even talking about Livira might sully them. "She's a blunt instrument. We require finesse in the diplomatic service. She's a parrot. We require the clear sight of eagles." His dark eye flickered towards Serra Leetar in her green and gold. "Besides, you know the king's views on . . . these people."

"The university could make a marvel of her." Yute looked towards the two women occupying the middle tables, one with her books and the other with her curios. He spread a hand towards the man at the last table, inviting his thoughts. "This diamond in the rough!" He gestured expansively towards Livira.

"You know that won't fly, Yute." The book woman's refusal carried the slightest edge of apology. "Even if she survived the students . . . how long would their fathers and mothers tolerate it?"

"And with good reason!" The other woman raised her voice. "Rejected."

The last man, small and bearded, shook his head.

"Rejected," Lord Algar repeated with a thin smile. "Why are you wasting our time with this, Yute? Upsetting quality candidates." He flicked another glance towards Serra Leetar, who scowled, clearly unhappy at her failure being singled out. "You think you can make a house reader out of a child that doesn't even know her letters at allocation? I'd wager ten golden royals you can't get her placed."

Master Yute shook his head as if humouring the man. "I don't gamble, Algar."

Botan, the numbers man, flapped his fingers at Livira in a shooing motion. The book woman rolled her scroll back up with an air of finality. And the guard, taking hold of Livira's other shoulder, steered her around until she was facing the long corridor down which she had first come. He released her, not ungently, and the pressure of so many eyes, combined with a growing wave of children's laughter, set her walking.

The guard followed. He opened the door to the outside world, and she stepped out to find the old white-robe waiting. He offered her a commiserating look. "I'm sorry. Sometimes Master Yute's experiments can be a bit harsh. Go down to the third door and tell the woman there that Hendron sent you." With that he turned to greet a boy with shining hair and a jacket of silver and scarlet whose buttons looked like bits of midnight.

Seething with conflicting emotions, and acutely aware of the scrutiny from the scores gathered at the bottom step, Livira stalked back towards the place where Malar had been standing. She could see that the soldier was no longer there. She hoped he was long gone, out of range of Lord Algar's spite.

"Wait!" someone called after her.

Livira walked with her arms stiff at her sides, rigid fingers spread wide, and kept her eyes resolutely on her destination, refusing even the chance of meeting someone else's gaze.

"Slow down." Someone strode after her. Master Yute, spinning his strange cane in a vertical circle about its curved handle.

Livira kept walking until he finally drew level, at which point she turned on him sharply. She knew her anger should be directed at her own failure but was unable to stop it flooding out even so. "I'm so sorry," she snarled, "that I failed your tests."

Yute smiled for the first time, his pink eyes suddenly no longer sinister. "My dear child, I wasn't testing you—I was testing them. You had me at *t'loth*."

Livira found herself smiling back uncertainly. Something about a grin on such a serious face demanded an echo. "What . . . what did I say?"

"*T'loth criis'tyla loddotis*," Yute growled. "You told Hendron that all of this"—he waved his arm at the building—"was yours now and that you would accept his surrender."

Livira frowned thoughtfully. "Well, I gave them the chance. They should have taken it." She turned and started to climb towards the third door.

"Where are you going?" Yute asked.

"Allocation."

"I can't allow that," he called after her.

Livira spun back around, fists balled, tired of being told what to do.

Yute shrugged. "The system's broken. Always has been. I get my recruits direct. Come on." And he turned and started down the steps.

"Come on where?" Livira didn't hide her suspicion. For all she knew the man wanted her for that sewer-work Malar had warned her about.

"I've got a job for you," Yute said over his shoulder. "At the library."

Some words are so suited to their task that they keep their role within scores of tongues. Some sentiments transcend language. When spoken, expressions of love or hate rarely require translation for the meaning to penetrate.
The Common Roots of Etruscan and Old Miscenren, *by Axit Orentooroo*

CHAPTER 8

Evar

To discover that you can read a language you never knew existed is a surprise. To be instructed to stop reading, in person, in that language, on the first page of a book, is perhaps an even greater one. Evar attempted to stifle any reaction and, holding the volume at his side, followed Clovis as she led the way through the book towers. Evar had few secrets. It was hard to keep them from his siblings given their respective talents for violence, espionage, and manipulation. This particular piece of strangeness he wanted to have for himself for a while. It wasn't just the revelation of his unsuspected skill or the fact that the book had addressed him by name. It was that when he had first set a finger to the cover something had struck him.

But it hadn't ended there. Instead, as if some object had fallen from a great height into the centre of his being, waves had spread through Evar, moving through the unknown reaches of his self, lifting and rearranging as they passed. Even now he could feel the outer ripples, still running through the shallows of his dreaming.

"Keep up!" Clovis barked, accelerating into the Narrow Forest. The stacks here were all a single book thick, stretching yards above their heads. Evar focused on his path, weaving after his sister. The towers were easy to topple and as children they'd felled hundreds just for the fun of it, competing to see how many might fall as a result of a single well-judged push, one tower bringing down another, which in turn might knock over two more and so on. As he'd grown older, though, Evar had made the effort to preserve them. Not because they were in any danger of running out of book towers to fell, but out of respect for the effort that their construction had taken. And because the mystery of why his ancestors had invested their labour in such a manner remained unsolved. Even Mayland, who'd had intimate knowledge of the history of more civilisations than Evar could list, had had little to say on the subject of the centuries his own people had spent trapped within the library. It was, he declared, an irony of the greatest order that their ancestors had lived and died hemmed in by books and yet made no record of their own lives. Perhaps their surroundings had brought home to them how such an act would be the addition of a teardrop to an ocean. Hardly anything remained of them: no bones, and no artefacts that were not fashioned from what could be taken from the book stacks—save for three curved swords, one broken, all of them rusted beyond use, and a broken staff polished by the touch of innumerable hands.

Clovis drew close to the north wall and followed it east, breaking free of the stacks after a hundred yards. If Evar were to set his back to the wall and walk until he met the opposite one it would be a journey of around two miles. The prison that held them was large enough to contain a city but it was still a prison for all that, and one from which he had vowed to escape.

The area around the pool was already clear when, over a decade ago, and an age after the slaughter of their people, the Mechanism had spat out the five children who had for so long been lost within it. They had emerged with empty bellies and full minds, all save Evar who had no memory of his lost time.

Clovis had overseen the effort to enlarge the book-free area—exposing the lines of sight, she called it—and now the clearing lay a good two hundred yards across, surrounded by a chest-high bank of books. The pool lay at the centre, only two yards wide, easy enough to leap, but unknowably deep. A green halo of crops surrounded it, rooted in their beds of paper-mulch.

Mayland had always said that he considered the greatest mystery of the library to be the presence of a pool amid all these books, and the greatest mystery of their people to be not how they became trapped within the library but how they happened to be in fortunate possession of the seeds that would sustain them for generations. Clovis was more interested in what they had eaten before the first squashes ripened. Evar preferred not to know.

Kerrol rose to meet them, putting aside the great scroll he'd been working through, on and off, all week. He was the tallest of them, always well groomed though there was nobody to impress. The rest of them were prisoners of the chamber but Kerrol managed to give the impression that he was simply a guest, free to depart whenever he chose to. "What's the excitement?"

Clovis shot Evar a rare conspiratorial glance. "There's no hiding anything from our brother, always so perceptive!"

Evar managed a grin. Kerrol's ability to read his siblings as easily as he deciphered the scroll before him irked them all—perhaps Starval the most. Secrets were his business, after all. And although Clovis mocked Kerrol, the fact was that no matter the manner of their return he would have known they had news. It might take him a while to get the detail out of them if they tried to hold on to it, but he'd have them talking soon enough. Kerrol knew exactly which strings to pull. How his methods might work on a stranger Evar didn't know, but he'd been practising on his brothers and sister most of his life and played them with a virtuoso's touch.

"The plan worked," Clovis said. "I killed the Escape."

Kerrol raised a brow. "And the other thing?"

Clovis hesitated, but Evar jumped in with all the enthusiasm he could muster. "We found the tallest tower ever. A giant! I knocked it down with my face."

Kerrol's other brow lifted to join the first. "Remarkable." He frowned, as if sensing Evar's ploy to bury news of the book beneath that of the Escape and the giant tower. His blue gaze found the volume held at Evar's side. Perhaps he noticed the tightness with which Evar gripped it or maybe it was as his attention returned to Evar's face that he found his clue as to its importance. "What's the book about?"

Evar turned away without replying. The best defence against Kerrol was to be out of earshot. Failing that all you could do was refuse to reply for as long as you could manage and hope that his boredom found a new focus. He walked off towards the field where the Soldier was making his patrol, ever vigilant for weeds.

"Did you find it in this tower of yours?" Kerrol called after him.

With Kerrol it was always boredom rather than malice. With Starval it was harder to tell. The Soldier had a quote: *Steel demands to be used.* Which, according to him, meant that any weapon aches for violence and sooner or later that ache will pervade the one who owns it, until at last the weapon owns them. It seemed to Evar that it wouldn't be until there were other targets beside himself that he would know where his siblings truly preferred to aim.

The Soldier paused his rounds hip-deep in new corn as Evar approached. The Soldier and the Assistant had raised Evar and his siblings. They had been all that was left when the Mechanism had regurgitated the children. Only Clovis—who had spent the least number of "outside years" lost within the Mechanism—held any substantial memories of the time before, and she claimed that neither the Assistant nor the Soldier had been part of the community she'd been born into.

The Soldier and the Assistant did not closely resemble the children. Even Starval was a head taller than their replacement parents, and although the essentials were there—two arms, two legs, a head, and so on—the details diverged. More importantly the Assistant and the Soldier were hairless, impossibly smooth, and their flesh-that-was-not-flesh had the colour of old ivory, yellowed with age, veins of grey running through them here and there. Their bodies were hard and cold, lacking pulse or heartbeat. Mayland had surmised that they were made things. Both of them not crudely carved but simply modelled on some idealised form, lacking detail or individuality, with only faint hints at gender to distinguish between them. That and the white sword the Soldier always carried.

Mayland's suggestion was that they had been fashioned from the same stuff that had been used to construct the Mechanism itself—smooth, cold, and indestructible. That said, the Assistant did sport a puckered crater on the left side of her forehead, about the same size as a thumbprint, and slice marks across both palms. The Soldier was scorched across much of his right side, his flesh holding a melted look. On his face a narrow groove had been carved across his brow, cheekbone, and chin.

Given how much punishment Evar had seen the Soldier absorb without so much as a scratch when sparring with Clovis, he found his imagination failed him when it came to the forces that must have been used to inflict such visible damage.

"Evar Eventari." The Soldier inclined his head, one ivory hand on the hilt of his sword. The Soldier was rarely anything but reserved, though it seemed to Evar that another personality would occasionally surface. Once or twice, when pushed particularly hard by Clovis in combat, he had seemed to come to life, something wilder and more raw taking possession of him, as if a fire had lit behind those white eyes. "You have a new book."

"I do." Evar blinked. The Soldier didn't make small talk. Evar doubted the Soldier would comment if he arrived with the severed head of a sibling under one arm. But here he was, commenting on a book, in the library. Evar waited to see if there was more, but the Soldier simply watched him. The Soldier never told any of them to go away but somehow despite the lack of expression on his moulded features he managed to convey the sentiment with sufficient volume to stop even bored children from following him for very long. "I . . . uh . . . Clovis got the Escape."

The Soldier turned his head to face the Mechanism even though it lay beyond sight a thousand yards off behind a great thickness of stone. "I will adjust my rounds accordingly." He rotated and began to walk away, stepping between the rows of corn with unerring precision.

Evar hesitated, his eyes drawn to the black, unrippled waters of the pool. He shivered, the memory of its coldness somehow combining with that of the Escape attempting to speak his name.

"I'll come too." Evar turned away from the pool. The days following the destruction of an Escape were the ones when another Escape was most likely to free itself from the Mechanism. The Soldier would stand guard.

"Wait for me." And, knowing that the Soldier would not wait, Evar gave chase.

. . . scattered in the streets, the bodies of the smaller children already carried away by wild dogs. The town of Lakehome was younger than its oldest resident, Kanna Gelt, who first built a log home on Shimere's shore. In a scant fifty years its population had grown to over five hundred souls. Fewer than twenty made it to the gates of Crath City. Most of those who survived the sabbers' raid succumbed to the hardships of the Dust. Cratalacs alone accounted for nearly forty disappearances. Not a single night passed without . . .

Eyewitness Accounts of the Lakehome Incident, *collated by Algar Omesta*

———————

CHAPTER 9

Evar

Evar followed the Soldier down the corridor leading to the reading room. The destruction of one Escape often presaged the appearance of another, and this was the place they'd appear.

The ceiling of the passage was far lower than that of the stack room. Even so, a giant as tall as Evar and his siblings all standing on each other's shoulders wouldn't have had to stoop. A similar passage led from the far side of the stacks to the second reading room, identical save it lacked the Mechanism.

The Mechanism lay at the centre of the room, surrounded by nearly a thousand reading desks. Presumably they had once been arranged in neat rows, but Evar had never seen anything except the current chaos—a chaos that he had actively worsened when playing endless games of "the floor is lava" while growing up. With his brothers and sister, he'd created innumerable desk-islands linked by weaving bridges of desks where the gaps grew progressively wider. In other places the tables had been upended and stacked to make walls, tunnels, and forts . . . Battles had played out here. Blood, both imaginary and real, had been spilled aplenty. But even with all four brothers against her Clovis had only ever been defeated by falling unaided—generally in pursuit of Starval whose acrobatic prowess exceeded even hers.

Once, smarting from yet another Clovis-related tumble into the "lava,"
Evar had snarled from the ground that she might win every fight, but Starval could kill her in her sleep.

"So, if I fall out with Starval I'll remember to deal with him before
bedtime," she'd replied.

"You'd only know you'd fallen out with him if he wanted you to know."
Starval was hard to read, a sunny liar on the surface but with darker waters
swirling beneath.

Clovis had shrugged. "At least you're an open book—you want to
punch me in the face. Come and try it!" She'd showed her teeth in a fierce
grin. "Anyway, Kerrol would tell me if Starval meant me harm. Kerrol
knows how everyone's feeling." She had frowned at that, glancing towards
the brother in question as if thinking that perhaps he knew too much for
his own good.

As THEY HAD grown, those tensions had only worsened. They were young,
overburdened with talent, and trapped with no target for their frustration
but each other. Clovis believed Starval had murdered Mayland. Kerrol said
maybe, but Kerrol said what was needed to achieve his unknown aims.
Evar didn't think Starval capable of killing any of them, whether they were
true siblings or not.

Kerrol said that Evar was the drop of oil that kept the cogs and gears of
their family from seizing. He called him the peacemaker and said that
without Evar, Starval would have murdered him and Clovis in their sleep.
He said without Evar Clovis would have butchered one of them in a moment of anger, and that he—Kerrol—would surely have tormented any
survivors into madness just for the diversion it offered.

Evar did not enjoy that weight upon his shoulders, though he sensed
the truth of it. Most often, the others spoke to each other through him
these days. The Assistant had been sufficient to keep order among children,
but she lacked the subtlety, or perhaps interest, to untangle the dysfunction
of their adult lives.

The Soldier plotted an efficient path through the scattered desks. The

Assistant waited by the Mechanism's single door, perfectly still, her ivory eyes invisible in an ivory face.

Despite her emotional distance, the Assistant had been the closest thing to a mother that they'd had growing up. Each of them had projected the fading memories of their own mothers, lost generations ago, onto the Assistant's ivory symmetry, until in time one became the other.

Like the Soldier, the Assistant's flesh was as impervious as enamel, the only difference between them being that her sculpting leaned towards the female form, and where the Soldier's eyes were no different from the rest of him, hers held a bluish glow from time to time. The glow came when a question required special thought, though Evar could never seem to guess which question might trigger it.

Also, sometimes when nobody was nearby, the Assistant could occasionally be observed acting as if she were seeing things, perhaps people, that weren't there. At such times her eyes shone brightest.

As a mother the Assistant left a lot to be desired. She was like a tool designed specifically for one job being used for something to which it was poorly suited. A claw hammer used to arrange flowers, perhaps. But still, whatever force had compelled her to the task carried with it an innate if crudely realised kind of love that each child had in their own way reciprocated.

She had always been hardest on Evar when the siblings were children: even the others admitted it. He felt her judgement now as he approached. As a boy he'd protested the unfairness of her expectations: Clovis hadn't known how to decline the verb either; Kerrol had also started the fight; Mayland had cheated on the test too; Starval had stolen the rolls and given him one.

"It isn't fair," he'd said, time and again, smarting beneath her sharp, non-physical discipline.

She'd replied only once but the words had stuck with him. She'd caught Evar and Starval trying to steal the Soldier's sword while Mayland sought to distract him with questions about ancient wars. Mayland had scurried off with the Soldier in pursuit, leaving the other two brothers in the grip of two white hands, both boys dangling from an ankle. Starval had been sent on his way without his favourite knife. Evar had been told to translate, from Eleayan to Truc, a thick and dull tome on the gods of a long-vanished people. "But Starval only—"

"You should know better. Do better. Their minds are overfull. Each of them crammed with not just the words but the deepest meaning of the book they vanished into the Mechanism with. Those texts and the wisdom and knowledge of their authors are grafted to their souls. You, Evar Eventari, appear to have returned with nothing tangible, and thus I expect more of you."

And so, he'd learned more, read more, studied more, tried to understand the expertise of his siblings in the hope that some might rub off and infect him with their particular competencies.

He did, however, remember how she had sat with him as a child when he caught a fever from some tainted book. The dedication with which she had mopped his brow, and watched over him while he shivered, had remained with him years after the fever broke.

And once, only once, when Clovis had broken his teenage heart, the Assistant had wrapped her ivory arms about him and held him close until his pride left him, and his tears flowed.

"Oh, Evar," she had said, not sounding like herself at all. "Oh, Evar Eventari, she was never the one for you. That girl's still waiting."

That had been an unprecedented event though. And the mothering, such as it was, had ended along with the lessons a few years ago when she announced that they were all eighteen and old enough to plot their own course.

"You have a new book," she observed as he reached her. The Assistant at least had a consuming interest in books and, unlike the Soldier, would be expected to note Evar's acquisition. Her eyes lit with that pulsing glow which normally only came when she stood lost in the search for an answer to some difficult question.

"I do." Evar held the slim volume up. "What can you tell me about it?" He turned the worn cover towards her. The lack of a title wasn't important. The Assistant knew everything about every book. Whether she would answer any particular enquiry, though, was another matter. And quite why she offered only silence in response to so many questions was in itself a question that would elicit only more silence from her. "Who wrote it?"

The Assistant's eyes burned blue, so bright it almost hurt to meet her gaze, and she stood without motion, considering the question for longer than Evar had known her to pause on any previous occasion. At last, she spoke. "The person who finished writing it was very different from the one who started it."

Evar blinked and looked down at the book in his hand. When they were growing up, instead of knowledge, the Assistant had handed them the keys to knowledge. She taught them the languages that would unlock a million books. Before he vanished, Mayland had accused her to her face of being a mechanical, a made thing, and a broken one at that. The words had brought a different glow to her eyes—but his accusations provoked only a new kind of silence.

Evar tried again: "Who—"

But behind the Assistant the Mechanism shuddered, seizing all their attention.

"What's going on?" Evar stepped past the Assistant to set his hand to the grey wall at her back. In defiance of its name, the Mechanism showed no complexity, sporting neither levers nor gears nor the cogged wheels that Evar had read were essential for making clocks work. It was instead a monument to simplicity, a block as tall as he could reach, built from grey . . . grey something. Built from greyness. An odd choice for a device that could generate the whole spectrum of colour into which light could be broken, and more beyond. "It's never done that before!"

"Not since the day you children returned," the Assistant corrected. "That was the first time."

Beneath his fingertips Evar felt a faint trembling.

"Is Starval in there?" Evar went to the door. The door was the only thing about the Mechanism that was subject to change. Some days it appeared as weathered planks on rusted hinges, on others a gleaming circular weight of steel. Yesterday it had been a perfectly round wooden door painted green with a yellow brass knob in the middle. Today it was plasteek, white panels with a small window high up, and, oddly, a button set dead centre above a metal slot that was covered by a flap and perhaps wide enough for Evar to push both his hands through together.

"I'm calling him back now." The Assistant set ivory fingers to the door, but as she did so it seemed that another reality tried to push its way into the space currently occupied by the one Evar inhabited. Stone pillars interspersed themselves among the scattered desks, rows of them marching across the hall in a gloom all their own, vaulting upwards to support a half-seen spectral roof. Evar caught a whiff of moist decay. Bales and barrels were heaped all around. This, he realised, was the Mechanism's work—an echo of the world it had created for Starval from the book he'd taken in with him. But the world had escaped the boundaries of the Mechanism . . .

Even as the word "escape" crossed Evar's mind he saw a clot of shadow had started to coalesce into a thicker darkness. *An Escape!* This was how it happened. He'd never been present to see it before. While Evar stood, wrapped in his amazement, the Escape took form, a knife-handed assassin carved from jet, hurling itself at him.

Black blades sought Evar's flesh, but fast as the thing was, the Soldier was quicker. His white sword sheared through the Escape's torso and the closest of the knives dissolved into smoke even as Evar tried to block it from reaching his ribs. The second Escape made the mistake of attacking the Soldier. It leapt onto his back. Knives skittered across his shoulders and, as the creature wrapped its legs about his waist for greater leverage, the Soldier drove his sword under his left arm to impale his enemy.

"Two?" Evar had ended up on his backside and was still wrestling with the idea that there had been more than one Escape—there was never more than one—when the third shot past him, aiming for the passage.

"Get Starval out of there!" the Soldier shouted and set off in pursuit of the last Escape, smashing a path through the desks where his prey had vaulted them with barely a touch.

EVAR STARED, DUMBFOUNDED, at the trail of wreckage left behind the Soldier. The world that had leaked from the Mechanism was fading, as if the third Escape had carried the last of its strength away. Evar turned back to the grey block and to the white door which the Assistant appeared to be having trouble opening. Evar had watched before and the process was almost instant. She would set her hand to the door, and it would open.

"Starval!" Evar got to his feet. He didn't know if his brother would hear him. There was a whole world inside the Mechanism. Depending on the nature of the book he'd taken in with him, Starval could be streets away or on a different continent. "Starval!" Evar hurried to the Assistant's side and wrapped his hands around hers on the door handle. He'd never found a limit to her strength so he didn't know what help adding his own might offer.

Immediately he started to pull, the Mechanism gave a second even greater shudder, and the door flew open with such force it threw both Evar and the Assistant to the floor.

Starval shot out, carrying a book. His lead foot hammered the ground between Evar's head and the Assistant's. Behind him a dark maelstrom rapidly consumed the long road down which he'd been racing. The tall houses lining either side fell to pieces in sequence—the destruction advancing with terrifying speed.

The Assistant was swiftly on her feet, slamming the door shut some small fraction before the storm hit. The impact came like a giant's fist striking the other side. For a moment the Assistant skidded back, and blackness sprayed from the gap like water under pressure. A heartbeat later she threw her weight at the door again, this time seeming to seal it properly.

Evar slumped with a sigh of relief only for Starval to cry out a warning. Behind them, still forming as the last of the blackness flowed across the stone floor to join it, a nightmarish insect had risen. It loomed above them, as big as the Mechanism itself. By far the largest Escape Evar had ever seen.

The Assistant rose to her feet between Evar and the monstrosity.

"Run," she said, not looking his way.

The Escape resembled a black wingless hornet, its hulking thorax raised on six barbed and articulated legs to a level where its great head could look down on both brothers. The span of its snipping jaw was wide enough to encompass the Assistant's whole body. The shearing plates gleamed with ichor that dripped but never hit the ground, smoking away into darkness mid-air.

Evar ran. He threw himself behind the nearest clump of reading desks and began to scramble deeper into the maze on hands and knees. Glancing back through a forest of table legs Evar saw the Assistant lifted in the Escape's jaws.

"Hey!" Evar hollered at it. "Over here!"

The Assistant had almost never been a loving mother, providing information rather than hugs, lessons in place of comfort. But "almost never" is not "never" and seeing her in peril pulled on a hook set deep in Evar's heart, a hook he'd never been aware of before, and without hesitation he turned to go back.

A hand gripped his shoulder and hauled him down into cover once more. "Idiot."

The Escape bowed its head, straining its jaws as it tried to divide its prey into two. A thin hiss of rage leaked from the insect as unknown pressures failed to achieve its goal. With a toss of its head, it threw the Assistant a good fifty yards across the room then zeroed its black gaze on the spot where Evar had shown himself.

"We've got to move." Starval released his brother and scurried away. "Stick with me."

Evar was no stranger to playing hide-and-seek among the jumbled desks of the reading room, and Starval's skills at both the hiding and the seeking parts were unsurpassed, but the Escape covered the ground with frightening speed, stepping over rows of double-stacked desks and staring down into the valleys between. Evar hadn't ever had to consider such a high vantage point when concealing himself.

"Here!" Starval hauled him under a table. Despite being the smallest of the siblings, he had a wiry strength that Evar constantly underestimated.

The Escape hunted them through the desk maze, in some places crashing through walls and toppling stacks, in others picking its way delicately in an almost-silence broken only by the soft clicking of its armour. Starval led the way through tunnels they'd made long ago, back when they'd thought Clovis the scariest thing that would ever stalk them here.

"Can you kill it?" Evar whispered at Starval's shoulder, crouched amidst a thicket of table legs beneath a thin wooden sky.

Starval produced one of his throwing stars with a flourish, a wicked piece of sharp iron fashioned laboriously from two book hinges. He had others that were cogwheels with sharpened teeth—source unknown. "Maybe." He sounded doubtful. "But definitely not while keeping you alive at the same time."

"Since when has that bothered you?"

Starval turned his head sharply and looked at Evar with genuine surprise. "You're the only one I can stand to be around. I'd miss you."

A black leg crashed through a desktop ten yards to their left. The Escape freed the limb with an irritated shake that sent half a dozen other desks tumbling away and rattled the brothers' cover.

"This way." As he crawled away Starval tugged on a cord. Evar hadn't seen him do it but somewhere along their journey Starval must have tied the other end to a desk leg. The tug set off a collapse way off to their left and the Escape raced in that direction, scattering desks with such ferocity that they came raining down on all sides.

"We can't do this forever." Evar caught up with his brother. "And there's no way we'll make it down the passage without it seeing us."

Starval was looking at his hands, both flat to the floor. "We may not need forever."

Evar realised for the first time in all the panic of running and hiding that it was unusually gloomy beneath the desks. Normally the library's light would be as bright in their current hiding place as everywhere else, but now there were mist-like shadows. More than that, they seemed to be moving, a slow tidal flow, most visible around Starval's fingers. "It's being drawn back in?"

Starval nodded. "With luck we can just wait it out."

Evar frowned. It was certainly true that Escapes always liked to put a lot of distance between themselves and the Mechanism as soon as they got free of it. And Starval was pretty much an authority on creatures of the night.

"Where is it now?" Everything had gone worryingly quiet. Evar lifted his eyes above the fallen desk to his right.

"Idiot." Starval hauled him down almost immediately.

In his brief glimpse across the reading room Evar's gaze had followed the trail of scattered desks and fixed for a moment on the midnight mass of the Escape, blacker than a hole cut into the world, its prey all the more clear for that blackness. It had the Assistant in its jaws again. The sound of the first impact came as soon as Evar lost sight of the scene. A concussive blow like Clovis hammering her armour too close to his ears.

The sound echoed through him. For all that she seemed impervious, the Assistant gave him the distinct impression that if her limit of endurance was ever reached it would be sudden. There wasn't any give in her, nothing left a mark, except for that one wound on her temple and the old cuts on her palms. The Escape smashed her into the floor a second time and Evar had a vision of the Assistant shattering like cast iron driven beyond its strength.

Evar found himself running towards her. What he might achieve he had no idea but staying put and watching apparently wasn't an option. The library had given him few opportunities to test his bravery. In the stacks earlier he'd been terrified and had run to save himself. But here, with the Assistant at risk, it wasn't even a choice, and he flung his own fragile body towards her seemingly indestructible one.

Starval's shoulder hit the backs of Evar's knees, taking him to the floor mid-stride. "You're going to get us both killed." Starval sent two throwing stars slicing through the air as the Escape's head turned their way. One hit an eye and the other bedded into its jaw, but the thing lurched towards them even so, abandoning the Assistant. Starval threw again, exhausting his supply, and still the Escape came on, gaining momentum, desks hurled into the air on both sides as it rushed them.

"Run!" Starval slithered into the nearest cluster of desks. "Evar—"

The Escape came crashing on, the thunder of its approach drowning out anything else Starval might have had to say. The smoke from its wounds bled away in horizontal lines as if caught by a strong wind. Wherever Evar hid, the Escape would scatter his cover and devour him. With sudden inspiration he turned and ran across the clear ground, aimed directly for the Mechanism. The door was still closed but somehow the structure was sucking the Escape back in.

Evar sprinted, unable to look behind him, expecting jaws to close in on both sides at any moment. He felt the Escape's cold malice focused on his back, aching between his shoulders. The din of its charge overwrote his booming heart and the labour of his lungs. Unwilling to check his speed Evar hammered into the Mechanism's grey wall, taking the impact on his shoulder and hip as he turned to meet his fate.

The Escape had skidded to its own halt and stood about thirty yards back, legs rigid, slanted to resist the pressure that had darkness streaming from every surface, to be sucked into the Mechanism's vortex. The creature trembled, the vibration fierce enough to blur its outlines. One foot—a hook bristling with black spines—slipped, only to regain traction a yard further forward. The smoke billowed from it, pieces of its exoskeleton ripping free and hurtling towards the grey wall at Evar's back. Even as he ducked a large plate, the whole Escape disintegrated, the bulk of it sucked in on the Mechanism's endless inhalation while some dark core found new form and fled towards the passage, aiming for the freedom of the stacks.

Evar shuddered as the wash of darkness flooded over him and was drawn away.

He was still trying to brush the invisible filth from his chest and arms when Starval reached him. "Are you insane?"

"I had to save her," Evar said, feeling foolish.

"How? By temporarily blocking its mouth with your body?" Starval gestured towards the Assistant, now on her feet again and walking unhurriedly towards them. "It's not as if she needed your help. Clovis couldn't put so much as a dent in her even if she had all day and a big hammer . . ."

It wasn't until she drew near that Evar saw the damage. Part of her shoulder was gone, fractured away along one of the grey seams that ran through her. Not a large chunk but noticeable to eyes that had watched her for most of twenty years. A rough-edged wound showing only more of the same flesh beneath. To Evar it felt disproportionate, like a chip from a tooth, the damage magnified by the tongue's exploration and ability to lie. The Assistant was part of their foundation. And she had cracked. He had let it happen.

"Come back with me." She turned and walked away.

The brothers shared a look. Evar wondered if his was as unreadable as Starval's or if the lost feeling welling up inside him were written there as plainly as he felt it was.

Starval frowned and looked away. He hunched as though cold, scratching at his arms. "Come on." He moved away from the Mechanism and followed the Assistant.

Evar shivered, glanced back at the Mechanism, then followed too. He felt something else, something not related to the Assistant's sudden hints at mortality. Evar shivered and knew that Starval had felt it as well. The force that had sucked the armour off the Escape—it had also pulled at the brothers. Not with the same fierce insistence, but it had been there, and a ghost of it was still there, maybe it had always been there, only understood now after all these years. The Mechanism wanted them back as well. After all, Evar and his siblings had escaped it too.

. . . sorting hat! But even the most sober of systems must admit the possibility that the judgements levelled against the young, no matter how exhaustive the testing on which they might be based, must allow some "wiggle room." On the forest floor certain blooms unfurl long after snowdrops and crocuses have tested the icy crust . . .

Career Advice for Mid-Ranking Civil Servants, *by R. I. Perrin*

CHAPTER 10

Livira

As Yute led Livira out of the shadow of the Allocation Hall's portico, he raised his cane and slid his other hand inside the cloth cover. Miraculously an array of spokes spread out, stretching the fabric between them into a circle that cast him into shadow once more.

"It's a parasol," he said, seeing Livira's amazement. "The sun is unkind to skin as pale as mine. Ironic that a world as ancient and used up as ours basks in the fierce regard of such a youthful star." He led on, across the plaza.

Livira could barely understand half the man's words, and it was nothing to do with his accent this time. She opted for silence and followed in his wake, wondering what kind of job he might have for her at the library and what a library was. Like Malar, Yute didn't check to see if she was with him. It was as if, without even meeting, the two men had exchanged the set of invisible chains by which she was bound, links forged from the certainty that alone she would be more lost on the crowded streets of the city than she ever could be in the featureless wastes of the Dust.

"Your parents were killed by sabbers." It didn't sound like a question.

"No." The Dust had killed them. That's what Aunt Teela had said. And though it had been a storm that took her mother and a septic cut that had taken her father, Livira was minded to agree. These were among the many weapons that the Dust wielded against flesh.

"No? But you came in from the Dust in the care of a soldier." Yute glanced back at her for the first time.

Livira had started to curl her lip at the word "care," but it was true at least that the soldiers had not left them to die, and Malar had paid out the debt he thought he owed her. "Sabbers killed my aunt and took us from the village." She had wondered about that. "Why did they want the children?"

Yute frowned and turned away. "I don't know. They don't normally treat children any differently to anyone else."

He led Livira across the vast square, passing the central fountain. She found herself staring at everything and everyone. The variety among the people astonished her.

"That man has hair like Lord Algar. That one too!" She pointed at a fat man with red cheeks, the grey coils of his hair unmoving despite the breeze.

Yute gave an amused snort and pressed down her pointing arm. "Those are wigs. People with an abundance of money and spare time turn to fashion. A librarian's robes offer an escape from such vices."

He led on, aiming for the gap between two of the halls fronting the square's far edge. Behind the largest of these halls the mountain's gradient, which had been arrested by the plaza, now reasserted itself and, in a hurry to catch up, a flight of steps wound its way back and forth across what was essentially a cliff face that Livira doubted her ability to climb.

Master Yute set a steady pace, though he paused to gather himself at each of the turns where a small level area had been cut into the rock to allow people to pass without danger on the narrow stair. As they gained elevation, he began to look more and more weary, sweat sticking his white hair to his skull. The wind grew stronger and occasionally tried to wrestle the man's portable shade from his grip, straining the spars supporting the cloth. On the third such occasion Yute gave up and folded his parasol back into its original form.

"Not so far now." He sighed, looking up at the steps zigzagging across the elevations still to come.

Livira followed. The ache burned in her calves and thighs, but she could have overtaken Yute—the age promised by his white hair was a lie but perhaps some illness had weakened him. By the time they reached the top his breath was laboured, and the parasol was serving as the cane Livira had first taken it for. The fact he didn't try to hide his weakness made her trust him more. Not much, but more.

"What's the library?" Livira could only go for so long without asking a question. On the Dust she had learned to answer them for herself, but they had never ceased to bubble from the depths of her mind and sit behind her tongue, building pressure.

"A library is a place where books are kept and made available," Yute said. "*The* library, the particular library to which we are ascending, is the greatest of all libraries by a similar margin to that by which this mountain is greater than your nose."

Livira nodded to herself. Malar had said the city thrived by trading knowledge, and she now knew that knowledge could be trapped in ink. It could be snared in words and locked to the pages of a book such as those she'd been shown in the Allocation Hall.

The stairs brought Yute and Livira to the top of the cliff, and a steep path led them to join a paved road that snaked its way still higher up the mountain's flanks. Houses crowded the road's margins wherever there had been space to carve a platform for them, and in other places they clung to the rock face like sweat-bugs, some on alarming arrays of wooden beams, stilts that stepped up the slope and looked too frail to support the teetering edifices they bore. The houses here were far less grand than those around the plaza, but to Livira's eye they had much more character and variety, seeming as individual as faces, and not just human faces. Yute paused to gather himself outside a house of perhaps five or six storeys, each of which was not much larger in area than Aunt Teela's house and none of which seemed to be set quite squarely atop the one below. Unlike the dwellings to either side, no two windows in the tower were the same, and at the very top the structure sported an unlikely number of turrets, none of which seemed large enough for a person to enter.

"Yute!" A woman of middling age and considerable girth came from the front door of the tall house and out into the street, skirts swishing as she swept past a man and his slate-laden donkey. "You'll burn up!" She snatched the parasol from his grasp and opened it above him.

"Ah, yes." Yute spread a white hand before him, studying it with a frown as if expecting to see tiny flames licking around the fingers. Livira noticed for the first time that the man wore a single piece of jewellery, a silver ring set with a small moonstone of the sort that might very occasionally be found out on the Dust. The tears of god, Ella had called them, scattered across the world in the long ago.

"Honestly! Get inside." The woman took his arm and tried to steer him across the road to the open door behind her, only noticing Livira at this point. "Another one, Yute?" Her voice somewhere between disapproving and disappointed.

Yute tore his gaze from his hand. "Livira, meet Salamonda. Salamonda, Livira."

"She looks like she's been through a thorn bush backwards," Salamonda said, not unkindly. "And she could do with a bath."

"I've ha—" But Salamonda didn't give Livira a chance to protest that she had already had a bath. She fastened a meaty hand around Livira's forearm and began to pull her towards the doorway, abandoning Yute in the street.

The ground floor was a kitchen, crowded with cupboards, hung with hams and links of sausage, strings of garlic, onions, and other unknown but surely edible objects, the air thickened by heat and by an array of scents that filled Livira's mouth with saliva. A whole meal dangled just out of her reach!

A large iron stove poured warmth into the room. A table took up half the free space, its scarred surface scattered with knives, pots, onions here, a carrot there, bottles of unknown liquids standing sentinel dangerously close to the edge. Three small windows, one arched, one square, one round, pierced the rear wall overlooking a precipitous drop to the city below, and through these light streamed, hurling shadows across the floor, turning dust motes to golden dancers, and gilding every curl of smoke that escaped the stove.

"No dawdling." Salamonda drew Livira on behind her as if fearful that Yute, now coming in through the front door, would catch them and wrest his charge free of her grip.

"More climbing," Livira muttered as they began to ascend a wooden staircase that wrapped tightly back and forth across the inner left-hand side of the tower. The steps were barely wide enough to accommodate Salamonda's girth and creaked alarmingly the whole way up. Yute followed behind as they passed room after room, all comfortably cluttered and filled with a diversity of wonders, few of which Livira felt equipped to name.

The third floor was lined with shelves, dark wood polished to a high shine, and every shelf, floor to ceiling, groaned with books. In sections, runs of similar books made bands of colour: ochre, warm brown, dark crimson; other shelves were more chaotic, with additional books laid lengthways across the tops of others. A large table was mostly hidden beneath a jumble of leather-bound tomes, many left sprawled open with their pages fanning like the plumes of strange birds.

"Is this . . . is this the library?" Livira stared in awe.

Salamonda's laughter was loud and deep and left no sting in its wake. "It's 'a' library, child. Not 'the' library. A very small private library." She carried on up the stairs.

The warmth and smell of the kitchen pursued them for several storeys, gradually surrendering to a mustier aroma that reminded Livira of the books that had been briefly thrust towards her in the Hall of Allocation. Other scents wrapped around the book-musk, many she didn't recognise but one that made her think of the shack where Ella had wrought marvels out of balls of wind-weed, the calming scent of the oil that lurked in the core of those tough fibres.

"You stay down here," Salamonda said as they reached the penultimate level.

Livira paused but the instruction was for Yute, and a tug had her climbing the remaining stairs.

The room at the top had windows facing in all directions, the wind kept out by many small panes of glass leaded together to fill the frames. Five poles studded with footplates ran up into the various turrets Livira had seen from the ground.

The room boasted a bed, a thick rug, two wardrobes, a chest of drawers, and a desk on which were scattered papers and round-bellied bottles of ink in several colours. It looked as if someone had left it moments before they arrived, and yet Livira had the sense that nobody had entered here for quite a while. She couldn't put her finger on the reason she felt that way but even as she questioned it the impression hardened towards certainty. Her fingers itched with the desire to touch everything, pick it up, put the best objects in her pockets. But something in that air of quiet abandonment kept her hands at her sides.

Salamonda turned to look Livira up and down with a critical eye. Livira returned the scrutiny. She'd never seen anyone remotely as fat as the woman before her. Salamonda's dark eyes were sunk within a face that seemed ready to burst, only barely contained by the rosy skin stretched over bulging cheeks. It wasn't an unfriendly face, though, even now when furrowed in consideration.

Salamonda crossed the room, navigating between the poles—a tight squeeze in places. She opened the smaller of the two wardrobes. "These, I think." She nodded and plucked out a blue dress, which while a world away from the finery that Serra Leetar had worn in the Allocation Hall was also a world away from anything Livira had ever owned, both in terms of quality and cleanliness. Salamonda motioned for Livira to open her cloak. The woman's face fell when she did so.

"Gods below! We'll have to burn those! And where are your shoes?"

"In the future." Livira was tired of being judged.

Salamonda frowned then pressed away a smile before it could take command of her lips. She held the dress towards Livira, taking care not to make contact. "A little big . . ." She shrugged. "Choose three and bring them down. Find some shoes too. You'll grow into them. I'll be heating up the water."

Livira said nothing, wondering both about the heating of water and about where the catch in all this might lie. Her Aunt Teela had offered little by way of wisdom about the world but one maxim she often repeated was: *There's always a price.* She looked around again. She'd been aching to help herself, to fill her pockets in this place of plenty. The unexpected instruction to take what she needed had removed the wind from the sails of her imagined thefts.

Salamonda creaked away down the stairs, leaving her alone. Livira stood, tingling with an emotion she only half recognised. Kindness carries a weight; it's a burden all its own when you have nothing. Some undeniable part of Livira wanted to bite the hands that offered so much so freely. Pride is stupid, pride is blind, but pride is also the backbone that runs through us:

without pride there's no spring-back, no resilience. Malar had been precise with his kindness as only those who've been hurt and humbled themselves can be. Livira's lips were bruised where the back of his hand had caught her, but it was a different quality of sting to the one that ran through the salvation Yute offered. There would be a weight to these dresses that she hadn't felt beneath Malar's best cloak. And though the soldier could probably never explain all that, Livira felt that in his bones he understood it.

Ignoring the clothes, Livira inspected the nearest pole instead. A thin layer of dust covered each footplate. She climbed up, into the turret above, stopping only when her eyes were level with the observation slits and the cone-shaped roof lay inches above her head—ready to become her hat should she climb just a little higher. Both her shoulders nearly touched the wall. This was a view no adult could share.

From the slits Livira could see out across the city, from where it washed against the mountain's roots all the way to the outer wall and beyond into the hazy infinities of the Dust. That same haze had swallowed her horizons every day of her life until this one. Turning her head, she could look out over the road they had been following. The road itself wasn't visible—she would have to be able to lean out and look down to see it—but she *could* see the houses opposite the one she occupied. The building directly across the road was also a tower, but a wider one and built against the cliff like a drunk man leaning on his friend for support. A patch of faded colour caught Livira's eye. Not on the building but on the rock some fifty feet above it. Protected from the weather by an overhang. Symbols had been daubed there in red paint, now faded with age, symbols not unlike those she had memorised from her scrap, but each of them half a yard tall. It seemed to Livira that this "writing" which Yute and his friends kept hoarded between the covers of their books was eager to escape. The scrap had found her out in the depths of the Dust, and here was more of it, in unexpected circumstances. Someone had risked their neck to set it there, high on the rock. Indeed, as Livira started her descent into the room, she found yet more writing, this time scored into the wood of the turret's inner frame with a knife or some sharp edge. She ran her finger over the neatly executed letters, repeated the action more slowly, and then returned to the room to choose her garments.

Livira picked three smocks and a pair of leather shoes, the first she'd

ever worn. She took the shoes off again—not understanding the laces—
and then carried them down the creaking stairs.

"THAT WAS QUICK." Yute was sitting in the shadowed corner of the room
below, perched on the edge of a wooden chair as if ready to leave at a moment's notice. Beside him, its head level with his elbow, sat a creature that
seemed to be mostly fur.

Livira took a step back up the stairs and hugged the bundled clothing
protectively to her chest. "What's that?"

Yute looked surprised. "Wentworth is a cat. I doubt you've seen a bigger one."

"I've never seen a smaller one." Livira cocked her head, considering the
beast. "Are you going to eat it?"

"What?" Both Yute's white eyebrows lifted. "No!" He stroked Wentworth's furry head. "Are there no animals you don't eat out on the Dust?"

Livira considered. "The ones that are too fast to catch. And there might
be ones that are too good at hiding for us to know about. Also, scargs because they're poisonous *all* the way through. And cratalacs, because they'll
eat you first, every time."

"Well, nobody's eating Wentworth. He's a type of Cornelian Mountain
Cat, though I suspect that line was established when someone carried a
distant ancestor of theirs up the mountain and all subsequent generations
have been too lazy to walk back down."

"Is he friendly?" Livira frowned at the cat. His deep-green eyes didn't
promise friendship.

"Not in the slightest. Except when he's hungry," Yute replied. "He dis-
likes Salamonda the least—probably saving her for lean times—the rest of
us get bitten if we turn our backs. If you start stroking him it's important
to have an exit strategy. He doesn't like it when you stop."

Livira was about to ask why Salamonda shared her house with the beast
but a glimpse of the rock face rising behind the houses opposite reminded
her of what she'd seen above. "There's writing on the cliff. High up. What
does it say?"

Yute glanced out of the window then shook his head. "It's a name.

Meaningless graffiti written at great risk for an audience of dozens. Some people strive so hard for centre stage—bleed themselves dry for your attention—and when they finally get there and the lights find them, they discover that all they had to say is 'I was here.'" He frowned. "Though in truth, that might be an accurate precis of much of our great literature."

Livira thought about the effort that unknown person must have put in and the danger they'd endured just to set their name there. "There's a place in the Dust where someone made a picture out of stones. Only you can't see what it is because it's miles across. You just see lines of rocks, and mostly it's covered up. But when the Sirral wind blows hard, every few years, it's exposed for a week or two and if you were in the sky, you could see what it is. My aunt said it was made for the gods to look at. Maybe it's the same thing."

"Maybe . . ." Yute nodded. "None of us really know what we're here for or what we're supposed to be doing. So, we shout out, hoping someone will hear, hoping someone will see us and reveal the great secret."

Livira stared at the man, this curious pale man, both young and old, perched in his chair with his great furry attendant. She was used to being told not to ask questions. Adults didn't like it. But she had always thought that they knew the answers and that they simply found it too irritating to supply them to a child on demand. And yet here was a man who dwelt in a city built on selling knowledge, a man with direct access to the library from which that wisdom came, and rather than deflecting questions with angry denials he admitted his ignorance with weary acceptance.

Yute made to stand from the chair then kept his place. "You should go down and let Salamonda have her way with you. I'll wait here."

THE SUN HAD passed its zenith by the time Yute and Livira returned to the street. Livira wore one of the smocks and clumped along awkwardly in the shoes, feeling as if she had a box on each foot. Salamonda had expressed dismay at her choice of dresses.

"These are all the colour of dirt! Didn't you want the nice red one? Or the green one with the blue sleeves?"

Livira hadn't given the selection much thought, instinct directing her towards camouflage. Life on the Dust had taught her that it doesn't pay to stand out against the background. In truth she'd been distracted by the scent of food, even in the topmost room of the house. Back down in the kitchen it had filled her mouth with saliva to the point that it became hard to talk.

It wasn't until Salamonda insisted that Livira remove Malar's cloak as a necessary first step in trying on one of the "mud dresses" that the woman had offered her anything to eat.

"God's teeth, girl! You're nothing but bones and dirt!" She threw the dresses onto a chair in the corner. "You're having a meal and a bath, in that order."

The meal was a swift affair. Salamonda ladled out a bowlful from the pot simmering on the stove. Livira devoured it at mouth-burning pace. Not even the fact that it was by far the most delicious thing ever to pass her lips could slow her down enough to savour it. Beyond the vegetables scattered across the table Livira couldn't guess what was in the stew—the complexity and richness of the flavours denied analysis and overflowed her limited experience. But as she scraped her spoon across the bottom of the bowl, she resolved that if Yute didn't bring her back she would one day have to break in during the dead of night and hunt for more.

"You should let that settle." Salamonda folded her arms, still frowning at the Livira revealed beneath the black volume of Malar's cloak. "Too much too soon and we'll be seeing it all again. Bath time."

Salamonda's bath proved to be a slower and warmer affair than the one Malar had given her. The notion of water in such quantities that it could be directed to ends other than quenching thirst and irrigating beans had been a revelation that morning but the sudden introduction of that concept via the horse trough hadn't been welcome. The idea of warming water for comfort was a different matter and Livira wallowed in the tin tub that Salamonda set beside the kitchen table. She closed her eyes and imagined that she had finally reached the secret watery heart of the well and now floated in another world from which she was unwilling to return.

When Salamonda had hauled Livira from the tub the water left behind had been grey and she had wondered how many baths it might take before she was truly rid of the dust.

"I like her." Livira aimed her remarks at Yute's back as he led the way onwards up the road. "Does she live alone in that tower?"

"Well . . . there's Wentworth," Yute replied.

"But it's so big!" Livira glanced back. The house wasn't actually the biggest or the grandest of those crowding along the road, but, in her view, it was certainly the nicest. "How did she come to own all that? Is she terribly rich?"

Yute snorted. "Well, I do pay her quite handsomely for a housekeeper. But it's my house."

And suddenly of all the many mysteries crowding her day Livira found the strangest to be that a man would seem so out of place in his own home.

We humans are herd animals. When several gather to browse in one spot, more will come. Few places offer more eloquent testimony to this fact than does a library, wherein our focus ensures some few books scarcely touch the shelves from the moment of their binding until the day they fall apart from overuse. Whilst all around, in sullen silence, the unloved show their spines in endless rows, aching for the touch that never comes.

The Art of the Index, *by Dr. H. Worblehood*

CHAPTER 11

Livira

For the last and steepest two hundred yards no houses bordered the road. A yawning cave mouth loomed ahead. Rubble strewed the slopes, broken rock and shattered masonry, not the weathered crags and boulders Livira could see further out.

"This is the entrance to the library?" Livira asked.

"One of them," Yute panted. "It's had different gatehouses over the centuries but they've each been pulled down in their turn. The mountainside was once carved to look like the face of a god, with the entrance as his roaring mouth." He drew a few deep breaths. "It was a very unsettling sight . . . I imagine."

"It looks like a mine." Livira had never seen a mine, but Old Kern had once described the slate mine at Cernow to the settlement, and this fitted the picture his words had drawn for her.

"I suppose it does a bit." Yute paused and leaned on his cane. "And we librarians are not unlike miners, given that we spend so much of our time digging and burrowing in the depths, hunting valuable nuggets."

They passed several people coming down the path: two young men, a woman of middling years, a thickset man with greying temples, all of them wearing similar robes of light-blue wool. Yute returned their nods and Livira held the young men's stares until they had the grace to look away.

"I thought there'd be more people . . ."

"The public entrance is further down the mountain. The foyer there is always crowded, and the front counter stretches for a hundred yards. People can request books there and once a librarian has recovered the tome in question it's sent there to wait for them. This entrance is the one for staff."

A guard stood to either side of the cave mouth, each wearing a steel breastplate chased with gold, far finer than Malar's captain had worn. Both sported a cloak sewn with feathers, and their helms resembled owls' heads, eyes circled in iron. The men had swords at their hips, but each held a long steel tube across his chest in both hands. They watched Livira's approach and made no move to stop her entering. Livira stared back, widening her eyes in mimicry of their helms. Even as Yute led her between the guards she wasn't sure why she'd stared them down—just that she always did it, she always fought back, and that all this newness, all this grandeur, seemed to scream that the place and everyone in it was better than her.

The paved path continued into the cave and led to a corridor at the back, precisely cut through the stone.

"That was a pair of the Library Guard," Yute said as they left earshot. "A curious mix of the ceremonial"—he made ovals with finger and thumb and held them briefly to his eyes—"and the very latest innovations." He mimed as if he were pointing one of the tubes down the corridor ahead of them. Livira liked that Yute didn't take the guards as seriously as they appeared to take themselves.

In the stories caves were damp and dripping, or else filled with a charnel reek and the fumes of dragon breath. This one, however, was dry and smelled of nothing. Once in the corridor Livira could easily imagine herself back in the Allocation Hall. Yute led the way to a junction and from there through an increasingly complex maze of passages, with steps variously ascending and descending. They encountered more and more staff: a mix of men and women, some in blue robes, others in white, almost all of them in a hurry to get somewhere. Some were carrying a single book, others hefting whole piles of them. One woman in blue, hardly taller than Livira, pushed a wheeled set of angled shelves on which maybe fifty leatherbound volumes were supported. Livira pressed herself to the wall and the woman puffed past before spotting Yute and trying to arrest her progress.

She dug in her heels and brought the cart to a white-knuckled stop inches before it would have hit Yute had he not already heard the squeak of her wheels and moved.

"I'm so sor—"

Yute halted her apology with a raised hand, gave a puzzled smile, and gestured that she should proceed.

Livira watched the woman hurry away. "Why are they all in blue or white and you're in grey?"

"Blue is for general staff and trainees. More senior staff shade from white at the librarian level to black for the head librarian." He took an unexpected left down the next side corridor and Livira swerved to follow.

"And if she'd hit you just then?" The woman had seemed genuinely worried.

"Well, then I might have been forced to reach for the sharpest weapon at my disposal." Yute continued to stride forward and raised his arms as if he might be summoning a thunderbolt. "Sarcasm."

Livira wasn't sure what sarcasm was, but it sounded pretty bad.

She stared at his arms as he lowered them. Salt-white, the same as the rest of him. She would have thought in flesh so pale the veins would stand out like the city streets seen from the mountain, but none showed.

"Here we are." The librarian stopped before a large oak door and rapped on it with the handle of his cane. "I'm going to leave you in the tender care of Heeth Logaris. I expect only to hear good reports about your behaviour."

Livira looked up at him from beneath furrowed brows. "Really? Because I'll try but—"

"Gods no!" Yute laughed, a surprisingly deep sound that didn't seem possible from so narrow a chest. "That was sarcasm. Give him hell!"

The door opened enough for a man to poke his head out, a blunt bald head in this case, fringed with greying hair. The man's gaze flitted towards Yute, and the door opened wide. "Master Yute, I wasn't expecting . . ."

"Apologies for the interruption, Heeth. I've brought you a new trainee."

The man before them was taller than Yute and remarkably broad in the shoulder. Had the fates not brought him to the library, Livira thought that he might have made a good wrestler. The robe stretched across those shoulders was a lighter grey than Yute's, which Livira now understood to indicate lesser status.

Broad as he was, Heeth Logaris was not wide enough to block the doorway entirely and behind him Livira could see a large room in which children ranging considerably in age and all wearing blue tunics sat at desks heaped with books. Their work lay abandoned before them now as all had swivelled to try to glimpse the newcomer past their teacher.

Yute stepped aside, revealing Livira more thoroughly. "Here she is."

The man's pale eyes studied Livira, his bushy eyebrows elevated. "Another." Something about the intensity of his stare betrayed the effort required to keep the word wholly neutral. "And this one is from the Dust . . ."

"Indeed." Yute nodded and pressed a hand between Livira's shoulder blades, propelling her gently into the room. "I'm leaving you in Master Logaris's care, Livira." He smiled brightly at the teacher. "I'm sure she'll do great things."

Master Logaris nodded slowly. "I fear she will need to."

"Good. Good." Yute dusted his palms as if ridding himself of further responsibility. "I'll come back to check on her in . . . a while." He stepped back, starting to draw the door closed as he did so.

"I trust she's been trained in the basics." Logaris raised his voice. "This year's trainees have been lacking in their scientific education, and barely adequate at penmanship. And—"

Through the narrowing gap Yute called, "She'll need to be taught to read. And to write. And . . . all the other stuff." The door closed on his last words. "Consider her a blank slate."

"BACK TO YOUR texts!" Master Logaris stamped his foot and nearly two dozen heads snapped towards the pages that had held their attention until Livira's arrival. The teacher set a large hand to Livira's shoulder and steered her towards the back of the room. "This way, Yuteling."

"My name's Livira."

"You're a Yuteling until I say otherwise."

"Why—"

"Yutelings always have too many questions." Logaris brought her to a long table where four children were poring over their books, moving only their eyes when they sneaked swift looks at the new arrival. They seemed to be the youngest in the room and approximately Livira's age, two boys and two girls.

"Language is like a tree," Logaris said apropos of nothing, his deep voice descending from on high as if declaiming a favourite poem. "It grows and changes too slowly for us to see, and yet we know that it was once a seed small enough to be lost in the breadth of our palm, and we know that one day it will topple and die and rot away."

Livira had only ever seen one tree, but she was familiar with the concept. She had questions but she bit her tongue, not wishing to prove the master correct about Yutelings so hard on the heels of his pronouncement.

"Language changes as it ages, becoming unrecognisable to itself in just ten generations. Our library is old. Not old like cities and civilisations but old like this mountain. Vanishingly few of its works have been written in living memory. Expect to wrestle with change. The books before you are fossils. Relics of an earlier age that have survived against all odds and in the face of common sense itself.

"And like the branches of a tree, language forks and forks again until the common root is barely a whisper. Those branches spread and touch distant lands where strange tongues reshape both words and grammar, and where strange hands find new alphabets in which to trap new sounds. And that's just for books from our world."

"There are other worlds?" Livira felt her eyes widening as if trying to see where such things might be kept.

"Hush, Yuteling." Logaris reached out one of his overly huge hands and covered her entire face with it, curling his fingers over the top of her head. "There are worlds upon worlds upon worlds. An infinity of languages so opaque to us that we can see no further than the ink upon the page. Languages we must chip away at for each scintilla of understanding. Others that we must sidle up to via unsuspected connections and take by surprise. Others still that might suddenly unfold to us at the discovery of text duplicated in a tongue we comprehend.

"I teach you what I know not so that you can translate whole volumes—though that will be required when books of sufficient value are identified—but so you can hunt through the vastness of what we have in order to find what we need." He took his hand, now wet with Livira's breath, from her face. "This girl"—he fixed his gaze on Livira—"this Yuteling, can neither read nor write in the tongue in which she so eagerly frames her over-many questions. As our newest recruits I am charging you four trainees to change that unacceptable fact into a slightly more palatable one. If this does not happen swiftly my displeasure will be . . . considerable, and it will fall upon the heads of all those at this table." He clapped his hands. It sounded like two rocks being banged together. "Begin!"

With that, Master Logaris turned his back on Livira, discharging her into the care of underlings, much as Yute had done to him only minutes earlier. Livira glanced at the accusing faces turned her way and wondered who they in turn might try to abandon her to.

Perhaps the sewers that Malar had talked of so ominously really were unpleasant, but at least she would have been with people she knew there and not expected to do the impossible six times before breakfast.

A prism can divide white light into an infinity of shades. The colours of the rainbow are simply a taxonomy applied reductively for convenience of use. Where indigo ends and violet begins is a debate that might be substituted for any shelving argument amongst librarians seeking to place a novel. Even fact and fiction can bleed into one another.

Compromise: A Librarian's Tale, *by Davris Yute*

———————

CHAPTER 12

Livira

"Where has my shadow gone?" Livira glanced around for it.

"Most people ask where the light is coming from." Arpix was one of the four newest trainees who had been charged with teaching Livira to read and write. He was a year or so older than her, tall for his age, narrow-shouldered, and the most intensely serious child Livira had ever met. Livira immediately made it her mission to make him laugh and had so far failed to elicit even a smile.

Arpix made a fair point about the light though. Livira blinked and lifted her gaze, hunting for windows or lamps. Where *was* the light coming from?

"It comes from everywhere." Carlotte held her books against her chest behind crossed arms as if in constant fear of theft. "It's library magic."

"There's no magic," Arpix said. "Anyone could light their homes the same way if they knew the secret to it."

Carlotte, out of Arpix's eyeline, mouthed the word *magic* at Livira. Livira had liked Carlotte immediately; they were of an age and Carlotte was almost scrawny enough to be from the settlement—only her wiry blonde hair and blade of a nose would have marked her as an outsider.

The five of them were now among the last remaining at the tables of the great dining hall. Livira had thought herself too tired to eat despite her hunger, but once they'd entered the crowded refectory the aroma had swiftly reversed the balance between exhaustion and starvation. After three bowls of thick meaty soup and four warm crusty rolls the tiredness had returned in force and her thoughts had turned to sleep.

"So, the library never gets dark?" Livira asked, thinking of her nights out on the Dust when so often the stars lay hidden, and you might as well have plucked out both eyes for all the difference it would make to what could be seen.

"Oh, it's dark," Meelan said. "In places." Meelan was the oldest of the four, though shorter than Livira and skinny with it. From what Livira had seen he rarely spoke, and when he did it was usually to say something unsettling. If he'd been speaking a different language earlier when he had asked Arpix to pass the ink Livira could have believed he was making a death threat, such was his intensity and the black focus of his stare.

"Dark in places?" Livira asked. "Which places?" But none of them seemed interested in supplying an answer to that.

"What happened to your face?" Carlotte touched her lip and then her cheek as if Livira might not be aware of the swelling and the bruise.

"Fist fight." Livira hoped Acmar was fed and sheltered now. She hoped the same for Neera and Katrin and Benth and the little ones: Gevin and Breta and the others. She felt as if they were watching her gorging, silent and reproachful at her shoulder—ghosts already. She pushed her bowl away.

"And here?" Jella winced and circled her own thick wrist with her fingers while looking at the raw flesh around Livira's.

"A different fight." Livira pulled back her sleeve to hide the rope marks. "That one I didn't win."

Meelan studied her critically. "Your hair has holes burned in it."

"And you have cuts on your neck," Arpix added.

Livira shrugged. "A dust-bear swallowed me and spat me out."

Arpix raised his eyebrows. Any of the boys from the settlement would have called her a liar. And Livira would have fought them. But she was too full and too tired and suddenly too sad even to stare him down. "That was my yesterday."

It had been a long day. Heeth Logaris had finished his lesson and sent the trainees on their way. Livira wasn't sure how long she'd spent in the classroom. Long enough for her to grow thirsty and for her stomach to rumble its desire for more of Salamonda's stew. She had left the classroom with her mind buzzing, overflowing with the information that her four table-companions had hurled at her. The shapes and sounds of letters, the combination of them into words, the stringing of words into sentences. For the first time in her life, she found herself overwhelmed. Too many new things at once to find a place for. Too much chaos to organise. Her dreams tonight would be full of letters, fighting for her attention, calling out their names, singing their sounds, dancing in rows. And still the day that had started outside the city gates wasn't over. In fact, within the library's unfading light she'd had no idea whether the sun had already set. After the lesson the others had led her to the dining hall.

"Come on." Arpix pushed back his chair and stood.

"Don't we . . ." Livira gestured at the cluttered debris scattering the length of the table.

"The kitchen staff do that," Meelan growled.

"Kitchen staff?" Livira blinked. At home she was happy to skip out on tasks she knew she should do in favour of mischief she shouldn't. After such a feast, though, she felt a sense of obligation to help. But the others were already making for the exit and, fearful of being left behind, she followed. Carlotte led the way, taking lefts and rights. There were fewer people now, their pace more relaxed, as if whatever the light said, their bodies knew that it was time for bed.

"Here we are." Carlotte turned from the main corridor into a narrower passage sporting a doorway every few yards on both sides, dozens of them. "These are the trainee rooms. We're at the end. There are plenty empty. The one next to mine is free."

"I get a room?" Livira asked, amazed. One of the many bread rolls she had stolen from the dining table chose that moment to fall from inside her dress and run across the floor. Nobody said anything as she recovered it.

"You get a room," Carlotte agreed.

"It's not much," said Jella from behind them. Jella had been mostly silent ever since the lesson but had talked at every opportunity during it when they were supposed to be working. She was built on the same generous lines as Salamonda, something never seen on the Dust where nobody carried a spare ounce of fat. "Just a bed and a desk and shelves to keep any books you're working on."

"And a pot to pee in," Carlotte added. "Don't forget that."

They walked on past door after door. Arpix explained that the most senior trainees had the rooms closest to the main corridor, which gave them easiest access to the dining hall, scriptorium, binding workshops, stores, and—as Carlotte interjected—the toilets.

"King Oanold's great-grandfather built all this?" Livira asked, quoting Malar. She'd already known that the king existed but until that morning she'd never known his name or quite how close his palace lay to her aunt's hovel. "It's not *that* old then?"

Arpix and Meelan exchanged glances at that, the tall boy and the short one, one sandy-haired, one dark.

"The library is only books and reading rooms," Arpix said. "It's not like this place. These corridors and chambers were dug out much later for the librarians. And the library light filled them."

"So, the king's father built—"

"Here's your room," Carlotte said brightly, pushing one of the heavy wooden doors. It was marked with what Livira knew were numbers but couldn't quite identify.

The space beyond was bright and clean. The bed had grey woollen blankets. The desk and chair were finer pieces of furniture than anyone in the settlement had ever owned. The walls were flat, and hardly rippled by the marks of the tools that had been used to excavate the rock.

"Do you need anything?" Jella asked.

Livira discovered that more than anything she wanted to be alone. Grief had been stalking her all day, dogging her trail in from the Dust, and now, though she feared it, she knew it was time to set aside her protective ring of strangers and their strangeness and to let the sorrow have its way with her. She shook her head.

"I'll wake you in the morning," Jella said. "Simpax rings a bell, but I always slept through it the first month I was here."

Livira nodded.

"There's ink on your desk and paper in the—"

"Come on." Arpix plucked at Jella's arm as if sensing Livira's sudden need to see them gone. "Good night, Livira."

And with that the four of them left, Carlotte last out, offering a brief smile and closing the door behind her.

LIKE ALL HUNTERS, sorrow advances on slow, silent feet, until the last moment when it attacks from cover, springing with such speed that the impact rocks its victim on their heels. The first sob broke from Livira violently, as if her chest had been punched from the inside. She reached for the wall, seeking support, unable to haul her breath back in. Her legs gave way, incapable of bearing the weight of it all, and she slid to the floor. It had taken murder, death, blood in the dirt, the destruction and upheaval of everyone she had ever known, but the world had given her exactly what she had always wanted and never been able to name. Unknown gods had heard and answered the wordless prayer of her life. She had left the Dust behind her. She was clean, fed, chosen, and special. And it was all her fault.

And even if the library contained a million books and each book a million words, there couldn't be among all that wisdom a single line that would convince her otherwise.

The larger a ship, the more consideration must be given to its course. Any turn must be plotted well in advance. Indeed, for the largest of vessels, it is advisable to set the rudder in the desired direction before casting off at the port of origin.
Great Sailing Ships of History: An Architectural Comparison,
by A. E. Canulus

CHAPTER 13

Evar

Evar and Starval made their way slowly through the ruin of reading desks. Splinters and shards of ancient wood littered the floor beneath their feet. The enormous Escape had left a trail of destruction before the Mechanism sucked most of it back in. Only now, with the Assistant walking away from them, carrying her new wound, could Evar even start to wrestle with the scale of what had just happened. Instead, he chose something smaller to tackle.

"I'm the only one you can stand to be around?" Evar looked back at his brother, repeating what Starval had said after he'd hauled him into cover. "When are you even around me?"

Starval shrugged and took the lead.

Sometimes whole months passed when the two of them hardly exchanged three words. Conversations of any worth only seemed to happen on the sharp edge of things, and the library didn't offer many such times.

Evar wasn't expecting his brother to say more, but the silence only stretched as far as the mouth of the corridor.

"You're the glue that keeps us together. You must know that." Starval didn't look back. "The walls stop us leaving—but you're what keeps us together. Unlike me, you actually like people, or would if you had the chance. You spend ten times longer with me and Clovis and Kerrol than we spend with each other. You're the overlap. Clovis likes you—"

Evar snorted at that.

"She pretends not to," Starval said.

"Well, she has me fooled." Evar rubbed his ribs, feeling the ache from the kick that finished his most recent training session with his sister.

"She likes you. And I don't mean all that fucking when you were kids. She'd die for you."

"She'd die for a chance at dying," Evar said.

"It's more than that." Starval shook his head. "Even Kerrol likes you—if he can like anyone. You have that memory hole. It means he can't read you as well as the rest of us. Means he can be more real around you. You can still surprise him. He can't unlock you, which makes you the closest thing he'll ever have to a proper person to talk to." He paused. "You're the only one of us that's . . . real."

Evar snorted again. "The weakest link, more like. I'm the broken one."

Starval grinned. "I kill pretend people in pretend places, recreationally. What does that make me? Clovis is wrapped around a war that will never happen. Kerrol sees us all as equations . . . You're the only one of us who cried for Mayland. I can guarantee you that."

"That was weakness—Clovis said so."

"It's strength," Starval said. "You're sure as hell the only person who might cry if I were killed. That's worth something. You escaped the Mechanism with a superpower—it's called being nice."

"I don't feel nice . . ." Starval had called him their glue, yet Evar had spent most of his life trying to escape, and not just from the chamber but from everything and everyone in it. If one of those doors ever opened, he'd be through it in a heartbeat, dragging his guilt behind him.

Evar felt like someone who'd been waiting his whole life for something to happen, constantly worried by the fear that it already had, and that he had missed it. The book—that was something, something that was happening to him, and as his fingers tightened around the covers, he swore that, whatever it was, he wouldn't let it slip his grasp.

BY THE TIME Evar and Starval made it back to the pool the two surviving Escapes had already lost themselves among the stacks. Clovis and Kerrol were waiting for them with the Assistant and the Soldier. A council of war. Although there were only six of them now, they were rarely all in the same place at the same time. Somehow the depth of the siblings' loneliness seemed to have made the company of a brother or sister hard to bear. The knowledge that each had years ago sucked the other dry of entertainment was a burden that made the silences uncomfortable.

Each knew the other so well that they might as well talk to their own foot for all the novelty they would get out of conversation. Besides, one of them was always in the Mechanism. It was their drug of choice, and even if the narcotics that Evar had read of were available in the library, he found it hard to believe any of them would have the potency to break the addiction that drew Starval, Clovis, and Kerrol back to the Mechanism the moment it was their turn.

"The wise move would be to stop using the Mechanism." Evar said it just so that it had been said.

Clovis barked a harsh laugh. "Quitting the battlefield can sometimes be a step towards winning the war. But here, for us, the Mechanism *is* the war! What else is there for us except to grow old and die among these rotting books?"

Evar looked away, out across the border wall to the forest of stacks beyond. Clovis wasn't alone in her swiftness to forget that these "rotting books" were all he had. The Mechanism had given him a blur where his first eight years had been, followed by a gaping hole where the others held memories of training and study decades deep. He'd refused any and all suggestions that he might return to it. For all he knew the next time it might spit him out ancient and alone, with his memory so blank that he wouldn't even know that he'd lost anything. If nothing else, he worried that if he spent a day in it without incident, he might emerge to find that the others had killed each other. Sometimes the burden of holding together his randomly assembled family felt too much. Other days it felt like all he had—which was also too much.

Kerrol set a hand to his chin, perhaps seeking gravitas amid the stubble. He looked slowly around at them all as if being the tallest somehow made him their leader. "I've conducted a study into the matter. The Assistant was good enough to locate some relevant texts . . ."

Heads turned towards the Assistant. Despite her name, getting assistance from her was extremely rare. She'd fed and raised them, equipped them to read in a considerable number of languages, and protected them from hurting each other and themselves. Beyond that she seemed bound by constraints that allowed her to be of very little help either in the locating of books or in the business of finding a way out of the library. She wouldn't even say how far beyond the doors the library extended. Starval maintained that the outside world lay behind one of the four exits. Mayland had thought it unlikely, saying that the few books that mentioned the library directly claimed that it had many chambers.

"The tomes I've been reading concern devices from antiquity that seem related to the Mechanism." Kerrol reclaimed his siblings' attention. "What's leaking from the Mechanism appears to be excess creative energy—the fuel that powers its proper function and which, when used correctly, draws on the book brought into the Mechanism, taking its form and direction from the pages we wish to experience. When outside the Mechanism the stuff is, as we've seen, dangerous. It can take passing form from the books in the stacks but to be properly sustained it needs a person."

"But why's it always so aggressive?" Evar could still see the insectoid looming over the desks, jaws wide as it hunted them. "So destructive?"

"Perhaps that's what's inside us." Clovis looked up from inspecting one of her knives. "We hate our lives and hence ourselves."

Evar bit back on his reply. Clovis wanted war. If none came, then war against herself might be the logical alternative. But the rest of them? He wasn't particularly impressed with himself—but "hate" felt like too strong a word. "Disappointment" was closer.

"Who's doing it? That's the important question," Starval said.

"Does there have to be a who?" Evar asked. "Can't it just be broken? Things break. Things wear out."

"In the library?" Starval shook his head. "Has the light ever so much as flickered? The texts talk about the library's age in geological terms. It's built to last."

Evar frowned. "We have a Soldier and an Assistant. Perhaps there are others whose job is to maintain things, to fix them if they go wrong. Only, the Mechanism is in here and they're out there." He pointed in the direction of the char wall. The char wall's corridor was identical to those that led to the other three doors, except this corridor was crammed to the ceiling with books, all of them roasted into charcoal by some immense heat. When they were children the Soldier had forbidden any attempt to try to dig a way through but, when the Assistant had said they were grown, Evar had begun his tunnel immediately. He'd almost died three times in three separate collapses, but in the end, utterly filthy and after weeks of labour, he'd reached the door, to find it white and unsullied. And, like the others, this fourth door had resisted him. He'd beaten on it, wept against it, even cut himself once more and made a circle of his soot-stained blood. Finally, black as any Escape, he had crawled from his hundred-yard tunnel in defeat. Still trapped.

"Someone's doing it," Starval insisted. "Trust me. The Mechanism didn't just break. I know murder. Someone is trying to kill us all."

"Sabbers." Clovis slammed her knife back into its sheath with an energy that suggested she was imagining driving it into an enemy's neck.

"They came themselves," Starval said. "Last time. So why not again?"

"If we knew how they came here then we might have an answer to that question." Kerrol didn't look at Clovis, but they all knew she was there when the sabbers came, there when they slaughtered everyone, saved only because her mother threw her into the Mechanism. Whether the book of war that had accompanied her had been chosen at random Clovis was unable to say, any more than she could explain the sudden appearance of hundreds of sabbers in the encampment among the stacks.

Evar had seen Kerrol remind her of these facts before. It seemed to be a goad he used to steer her in the direction he chose. It was easier to see when he did it to the others. Harder to understand how he got under Evar's own skin so effortlessly and aimed him towards ends he would not otherwise have chosen. All Evar knew was that when he thought he saw it—when he fought against it—that had always seemed to be part of Kerrol's plan all along and he still found himself doing his brother's will and not even hating him for the offence. At least not enough to do anything about it.

Starval turned to Evar. "What do the histories teach us? You're our Mayland now."

Mayland had always liked to say there was nothing new under the sun—whatever anyone said, or did, he'd tell the others that history had seen it before and that the answer to any current dilemma was written somewhere, and had been waiting for them all their lives and more down among the dust and must of the stacks.

"I'm not—" Evar began his usual denial.

"You don't know half what he did about the past." Starval waved Evar's objection away. "You don't know half what I know about murder, or Clovis knows about war, or Kerrol knows about changing someone's mind. But you're still our second-best historian, assassin, warrior, and whatever it is that Kerrol is."

"Psychologist," Kerrol said.

"Too short a word for that shit," Clovis grunted.

Evar knew it was true though he didn't like to admit it. You can't grow up in such a sterile environment alongside masters like his siblings and not pick up anything. In fact, they'd all tried to make him their apprentice at some point or other. He'd thought at the time they were just looking for an audience for their skill. But looking back he'd realised that perhaps they'd all felt a little guilty in their own ways. Guilty that they'd emerged from the Mechanism with gifts and he with only the wound where something had been ripped away.

"What do the histories say?" Starval asked again.

It was hardly the first time Evar's siblings had asked for answers to the fundamental unknowns of their captivity. None of them really expected anything new from him this time, but Starval liked to be told things several times—perhaps looking for inconsistencies that might reveal a lie.

"The histories say a lot of things. Some of it contradictory. They say things about different empires, and we don't know which empire surrounds us. They say things about different worlds, and we don't know which world we're on. They say things about different times, and we don't know when our kind became trapped here. They say things about different species . . . and we don't even know which species we are. We know we're not icthid because they live beneath the waves. We know we're not ganar or skeer because they have fur and armour-plates respectively. But what we don't know vastly outweighs what we do know."

Clovis spat. "I'd know a sabber if I saw one again." Her eyes clouded with memory. "Two of everything we have two of. Nose and mouth not so very different. It's how their legs bend. I'll never forget that." A shudder.

"The only relevant lesson I can find in the past," Evar said, reclaiming the conversation, "is that when things start to break, they get worse not better. A leak becomes a flood. So, expect the trickle of Escapes from that Mechanism that you refuse to leave alone to become a deluge until the stacks are thick with them and we're fighting this battle at the wall."

"All the more reason we should end the ones that got away." Clovis spat again. "Two at once!" She shook her head in disbelief. "And how big was the one that got sucked back in?" Her stare challenged him to repeat his claims.

"Four," Evar said.

"What?" Clovis darkened.

"Four Escapes." He realised that he had been the only one to see the full horror of the situation and that he had mentioned neither of the miracles. "Three regular ones, but the Soldier destroyed two of them."

"Four?" Kerrol asked, horrified.

"The Soldier?" Starval frowned, glancing towards the enamel warrior. "The Soldier fought Escapes?"

Quite what the Soldier's function was Evar had never fully established, but the Assistant had barely acknowledged the Escapes before today. It had been as if they didn't exist. One part of the library incapable of opposing another. The Soldier had watched for them, but only to direct the siblings. He hadn't intervened until now.

"He attacked the first and then the second attacked him." Now Evar thought back on it, it had been as if the Soldier had declared war and the Escapes had responded—the truce between them suddenly void. "It might have been because the first one was going to kill me." Evar turned towards the Soldier, who had stood statue-still this whole time, the ivory mask of his face devoid of expression. "You did it to save me?"

The Soldier snorted. Evar had never heard him sound more like a person. "I did it to save the book."

"What book?" Starval looked confused.

Clovis stalked towards them, small but bristling with the potential for violence. "Not that tatty thing from the tower?"

Kerrol leaned in, blue eyes fixing on the corner of the book where it protruded from Evar's jerkin. "What's it about?"

"Evar doesn't know. Ask her." Clovis pointed to the Assistant. "It's a language she never taught us. But she knows. Don't you?"

The Assistant's eyes glowed a pale violet but her only answer was the same silence that most questions received.

"Let me see the book," Kerrol said.

Evar didn't want that. Even if Kerrol couldn't read it, it was still Evar's name that was written on the first page. It had been intended for him, Evar; the line began: *Evar! Don't turn the page. I'm in the Exchange. Find me at the bottom—* He didn't want Kerrol turning that page any more than he would want his brother rummaging about among the secret thoughts within his head. And yet this was Kerrol. If he wanted the book, he would get it. He wouldn't even have to steal it like Starval, or take it like Clovis: in time, a much shorter time than Evar liked to admit, he would steer Evar into giving it to him, and when he did so he would think it for the best.

Slowly, Evar eased the book from its place tight against his chest. The more he resisted sharing it the more the others would understand its importance to him, the more likely it would become a stick to beat him with. Kerrol would know that already, of course, but despite his brother's insights into the rest of them, the depth of Kerrol's vision seemed unable to penetrate his own skin, leaving him as afloat on the sea of his own emotions, prejudice, and desire as the rest of them. Giving him this victory would lessen the advantage he would take from it.

"Here." Evar reached out, offering the book.

But a pale hand took it. The Assistant plucked the book from his grasp and studied it with eyes so bright that their hot blue light cast the shadow of her other hand across the leather. She ran her gleaming fingers over the worn cover as if reading a tactile story all her own among the tiny bumps and indentations.

"It's Evar's book," she said, her eyes dimming. "Let him keep it."

And as she handed it back it seemed that she had uncovered something. For there, where there had been no title or decoration, ghostly lines held the remnants of the light that had spilled from her eyes. Within the faint outline of a circle lay a thousand barely visible lines, scrawled without purpose, a tangle, the mass of them growing denser towards the centre. And out of that chaos a shape might be imagined, a figure, a person walking towards Evar as if emerging from the smoke of some unseen fire.

Cavers are, for many, the very definition of bravery. For a non-subterranean spe-cies to face the fear of tight spaces in depths where light has never ventured requires courage. But ask the caver who they admire, and without fail they will name the divers. Those who practise that same madness, but through flooded caverns and flowing tunnels.

Secrets of the Deep, *by Miles Stanton*

CHAPTER 14

Evar

Evar's lost brother, Mayland, had had intimate knowledge of an end-less number of mythologies. Mythology was, he said, the product of history. Just as the trees of ancient forests fell and became buried and compacted by each subsequent generation, covered over, buried ever deeper until the crushing pressure of untold fathoms changed their structure into coal, history itself became buried by the flood of years and crystallised into myth. He knew so many tales concerning the origin of all things, and told them with such gusto, that after his disappearance the others had perhaps missed the entertainment of his storytelling even more than they had missed their brother.

But the mythology Mayland had liked best was told in the book that he had taken with him into the Mechanism as a child and vanished with. That had been his first disappearance and, so far, the longest. A decade from his perspective, lifetimes from the perspective of his parents and all those others he had left behind. His second—ongoing—disappearance was still a little shy of a year. And, whilst Starval blamed it on an Escape and was confident their brother's bones would be found in time, Evar often wondered if perhaps Mayland hadn't returned to the Mechanism and sim-ply disappeared into it again with a new book, leaving his siblings to their own devices for the rest of their lives just as he had once left his true family behind.

Mayland's favourite mythology was, like so many others, an origin story for existence. It told of the first two people. This original generation was the first to sin against the god who had made them. The first crime to be committed was the pursuit of knowledge. For the first murder one had to wait until the second generation when the couple's children grew to adulthood and one brother murdered another. The first murderer had a son, Enoch, who founded the first city. And within that city, in the fourth generation, Enoch's son, Irad, had founded the first library—the athenaeum.

Mayland liked to say that after the original woman's sin—that of seeking knowledge—it took three generations until her great-grandson cleaned up the mess and formalised the process. Mayland tracked the library myth through a thousand books and found a common thread spun from sources far apart in space and time. So disparate were these sources that Mayland claimed to have found a truth. Namely that the first library echoed itself on many worlds across many aeons, and that whether or not it truly was founded in Enoch's city by the grandson of the first murderer it certainly grew with an ancient species, taking root at the time of their very earliest records. And in his view the library which had held them captive their whole lives was an echo of the first, the foundational, original library, and he considered it as valid an expression of that primal library as any other.

Evar sat facing the border wall that Clovis had had them build around the pool and its crops long ago. Borders, Clovis said, were important. Something to be defended. Something that defined territory, declared ownership. Evar knew from personal experience that Clovis had her own walls and defended them fiercely. Theirs had been a rough courtship, almost a battle at times, the fierceness all hers. He had been allowed through one gate only to be confronted with a second wall, and later a third. And finally, when he thought he might just be close enough to hear her heart and see whatever final castle lay amid so many concentric defences, she had thrown him out without ceremony and shot her arrows from the battlements.

Kerrol, in a rare moment of concern, said she had taken fright and acted to protect herself. Evar, in the midst of his own pain, could only see that she had drawn him close enough for her to see the true content of his soul, and that what she had seen there she had found wanting. Like the chamber doors that his blood had failed to open, Clovis had closed herself to him, and they had retreated to their own islands.

And alone on his own shores, Evar had considered that he deserved everything that had happened. He had pretended to himself that Clovis might have been the one who haunted him—the reason he'd been trying to escape the chamber for so long—that the one who needed his help had been in front of him all along, and it was her. For those months he had given up his search for an exit. But Clovis had seen it in him. Seen that his search wasn't over. And had rightly tossed him aside. She'd called him soft, and perhaps he was, but he thought that it hadn't been disdain for his gentleness that had put the walls back between them—more the fear that he might in turn make her soft too.

Evar scanned the book-made ramparts around him. The wall might only be chest-height, no significant deterrent even to the scarce rats and scarcer cats that hunted them among the stacks, but it represented, in Clovis's mind, a decision made solid: *This is our line, cross it and you have passed the point of no return.* Cross it and Clovis would have her war.

In his mind's eye Evar saw the moments when Clovis had driven her knife into the Escape again and again. He'd glimpsed once more the awful anger that ran through her core. She might rage against the Escapes but her true hatred was reserved for the sabbers and over the years an echo of it had infected her brothers. Evar, Starval, and Kerrol had, however, not lost their own families to the sabber raid. That attack had killed the last of their kind and had left them alone on their return, but the brothers' parents had been killed by time, their deaths as peaceful as nature permitted. The true villain for the brothers had been the Mechanism and Evar had been the only one of the three not to forgive the crime. Only Clovis had lost her people to the sabbers' blades. Only she had had to watch. Only she ached for their return. And often Evar thought that her strongest yearning was not for the return of her parents or her people but for the sabbers to come back so that she might at last give full voice to her outrage and take from them the blood price for which she had trained her whole life.

At Evar's back the corn stood silent with no wind to rustle it, and at the centre lay the unrippled eye of the pool. He sighed and turned his thoughts away from his brothers and his sister. On his knees he balanced the book that he had recovered from the tower. It might have rested at the very top, high above him his whole life long, like a bird with its wings pressed to the sky.

The book's cover now bore an image of a person bound by a thousand threads—defined by those threads. Possibly it was one unbroken line, a single string that could be straightened out leaving no trace of the figure it seemed to reveal. He lifted the cover as he had raised it so many times before and stared at the single, unfinished sentence on the first page.

Evar! Don't turn the page. I'm in the Exchange. Find me at the bottom

The Exchange? Evar had no idea what that was. Questions had revealed no answers. He resisted yet another sudden urge to turn the page despite the instruction, to rifle through the contents demanding satisfaction. His fingers rested at the bottom of the page, feeling the texture of the paper as if the author's intent might reveal itself to touch where sight failed. He held the book and let its thrill echo through him—let it echo in the void where his lost years should be, the years the Mechanism had stolen from him. And gradually, as it had been doing with aching slowness since the first day he brought the book back, the void began to take on shape, until the emptiness was no longer a smear in the back of his mind, but an absence confined within a border. And its outline was the outline of a girl, a woman.

Find me at the bottom

The bottom of what? Evar gazed out across the stacks rising in their silent forest beyond the wall. At the bottom of a book tower? Which one? The tallest? At the bottom of the library? If it had lower levels Evar and his siblings had never found them.

Evar looked around. Clovis had gone off to use the Mechanism, ignoring the risk of more Escapes. Her addiction to her own escape from the dusty sameness of their lives outweighed any danger. Kerrol and Starval were out among the book towers, hunting the most recent Escapes. The Assistant stood near the pool, looking across the crops, more still than the plants themselves, her eyes blank. She could stand like that for days, moving only when called upon.

Evar closed his eyes and listened. Some silences stretch, the tension builds and builds again until the suddenness of the inevitable snap. That's the quiet which lies between people. Other silences fall like a heavy blanket, enduring so long that they become a second skin which can be punctured but never broken. Words are like wounds to such a silence, quickly healed over, quickly forgotten, leaving no scar. The library's silence was like that. Thick, ancient, the sediment of centuries, settling back swiftly after any disturbance. He opened his eyes and decided that it was time to make some noise.

He stood slowly, closing his book. He approached the ring wall, glanced around once more, and vaulted it in a single fluid motion. Within moments he was among the stacks, advancing with purpose and moving with a stealth that only Starval could better.

EVAR SMELLED THE char wall before the thinning book towers revealed it. After two centuries the stink of burning still tainted the air. Evar had never seen a flame. The Assistant could generate sufficient heat to boil water around her hands and make edible what otherwise would not be. But for obvious reasons she would not, or perhaps could not, make fire. Evar had read about it though. He'd even seen drawings of great cities ablaze, and in his mind's eye the ghosts of ancient flames flickered here even now.

In a rare moment of sharing, the Assistant had once told the siblings that there had been char walls before each of the three doors now exposed. That was the source of the black dust that coated the chamber. Their ancestors had dug out those corridors to confirm that the doors there could not be opened. They had never put the same effort into the last corridor since that had been the route by which they had entered the chamber and they knew that without help they would be unable to open the fourth door again. Evar had only exposed a small patch of the door. Now he meant to clear the whole of the base. *Find me at the bottom—*

Drifts of powdered charcoal swamped the feet of the last few book towers, and by the time Evar reached the char wall itself he was wading in the stuff, the memory of the long-vanished fire even sharper in his nostrils. The shape of the carbonised books persisted in the black wall that stretched twenty yards above his head, filling the corridor. About a hundred yards in, behind an unknown tonnage of roasted books, stood a white door, just as in the other three exits from the chamber.

Evar eyed the mouth of the tunnel that he'd dug into the char long ago.

"Evar Eventari."

Evar turned to see the Soldier standing behind him. Irritatingly, the Soldier was spotless, not a single particle of soot finding purchase on the enamel smoothness of his skin. The Soldier's eyes were the same gleaming ivory as the rest of him, without iris or pupil, yet somehow they managed to convey a measure of his disapproval.

"You should not dig here, Evar Eventari. It would be a foolish way to die."

"How did you even know I'd come out here?" Evar spat black saliva into the black drifts around his calves.

"Protecting you is one of my directives," the Soldier replied as if that somehow answered the question.

"I need to get out of here." Evar stalked towards the tunnel mouth.

"Need?" the Soldier asked. "Or want?"

Evar tried again. "You're protecting my life but what's my life worth if it's spent in this cell?" He waved an arm at the stacks.

"Come away, Evar Eventari." A white hand reached for him.

He wanted to rage but that would wash over the Soldier without trace. Instead, he drew the book from inside his jerkin and held it out, cover forward. "Her. I need to find her." There was more to say. Much more. But none of the many languages at his disposal had the words for it. "I need to find her. She's in danger. She needs help. What's the Exchange? Where is it?"

The white hand stopped, inches from closing around Evar's upper arm. For the longest moment the Soldier stayed frozen in mid-step. Slowly he lowered his foot but not his hand. The Soldier's eyes darkened, the irises shading to grey, the pupils black as the char wall. Evar had never seen them anything but white before and the effect was alarming, changing what had always seemed more of an animate statue into someone very definitely alive, a mask that had become a face. More surprising than any variation in colour, though, was that for the first time ever the Soldier looked confused.

"I . . . also want . . . to find her." The ivory hand changed course, grasping the front of Evar's jerkin and dragging him down until his face was level with the Soldier's. "I've lost her. I've lost myself . . ." He looked into Evar's eyes, his own shading darker still. His voice, which had been sterile and without inflection Evar's whole life, now took on tone and character. "Know this . . . if you hurt her, no army will save you from me."

Evar tugged free, amazed. "I just want to help her. That's why I need to leave. There might be a way out at the bottom of this door. Or . . . I don't know . . . I've got to get lower. To the bottom. I think she's in a basement somewhere . . ."

"You won't find her out there, boy." The Soldier took a step back. "Any idiot can see that. It's fuc—" Without warning the colour fled from his eyes and his voice became its calm, implacable self once more. "Come away, Evar Eventari." And he turned and walked back among the book towers.

For all but the most damaged of us, doubt is the other side of that coin. Success, even if earned through hard toil, comes hand in hand with the belief that one is an impostor, admitted to an inner sanctum by mistake and without invitation. The performer watches that sea of adoring faces with the firm belief that at any moment one among the crowd will voice their doubt, and as the tide must turn, so must their audience.

Limelight and Grease Paint: An Autobiography, *by Sir John Good*

CHAPTER 15

Livira

What's a house reader?" Livira asked. She'd been at the library for a week. The question had burned behind her lips all that time but unlike a thousand others she had kept it there, unsure that she would like the answer.

"You really are from the Dust." Meelan tore his bread in two and put half the roll in his mouth.

"Every grand house has a house reader." Carlotte raised her voice above the clatter and din of the dining hall. "A house reader reads aloud to the family when asked to. They will translate from texts not in the empire tongue. They—"

"They summarise books for lazy rich people," Arpix said. "Primarily the books that the king says we should read."

"But why would the king care what books people read?" Livira had been told anyone could come and request any book they chose.

"The library is the source of truth. The king is sometimes called the Voice of the Library. The authority of his line has been built on revealing its truth," Arpix said. "The king is the source of our law, but his decisions and opinions must stand on truth if he's to sway the nobility and win their support. Among the gentry, and among our neighbouring kingdoms, opinions gather the most weight most swiftly if you can point at the ancient text that backs you up. It is the duty of the nobility to confirm this sacred connection. But riches make you idle and if you can pay someone else to do it for you . . ."

Livira frowned. "That sounds stupid."

Meelan barked a rare laugh.

"It's from history," Carlotte said, as if that explained everything.

Jella wasn't normally interested in conversations that weren't about people, but she jumped in now. "The library's why this city is here. The place is holy to us."

Arpix nodded. "The library lifted us from the dust to what we have now in a handful of generations, and it can take us to the stars in a handful more. The power we have now came from the library and that power is wrapped in tradition. In statues, the rulers of other nations carry swords—ours carry a book in hand and are more feared for it. The empire—"

"Wait," Livira said. "Is it an empire or a kingdom? We have a king not an emperor. And"—she raised a finger to forestall any answers and lowered her voice to a stage whisper—"who's that woman with the red hair?"

Livira had felt the librarian in question's disapproving gaze sliding over her on several occasions in the past few days, but now the woman's stare needled across the dining hall with a sharpness that was hard to ignore. The robe she wore was darker than Master Logaris's—indicating seniority though she was half his age. The frown she aimed at Livira felt more suited to some misshelved book, one perhaps that would be better given to the hearth than left in the company of its current neighbours.

"That's Master Jost," Carlotte hissed back in a lower voice. "Do *not* get on her bad side."

"She leads trainee expeditions into the library sometimes," Meelan said. "Likes climbing ladders, but not to reach books." At Livira's puzzlement he elaborated. "Mostly social ones in the city. You're more likely to see her dining in some lord's home than here with us lot."

Livira stared back at Jost, aiming her own frown. The woman's luxuriant hair marked her out among her fellow librarians, who tended towards short and practical cuts. Meelan's comments on mixing with society down in the city explained that part at least.

"To answer your other question . . ." Arpix steered them back onto safer ground. "It was an empire. But it fractured as it spread, and now it's a collection of kingdoms. But our kingdom is the largest and King Oanold has circulated historical accounts that show it's always the emperor who controls the library, by ancient law. So, all the kingdoms should pay fealty to him. And they might grumble about it but all the alliances balance in our favour because without us, without the library, the other kingdoms would still be fighting sabbers with clubs and rocks."

"Come on." Jella, uninterested in Arpix's lesson, had been brushing her thin brown hair, which, given that it was no longer than Meelan's, seemed a waste of time to Livira. Putting her brush away, Jella stood up from the table. "Don't want to be late back to class. Master Logaris is already in a bad mood." The dining hall had all but emptied, and those that were still coming in were white-robed librarians planning to enjoy a late lunch. Arpix, Meelan, and Carlotte pushed back their chairs then followed Jella out.

Livira paused to cram a few bread rolls into her pockets. Her room already had a store of stale bread, threatening to moulder, but the instinct to hoard in times of plenty ran deep. Plenty never lasts—that was the lesson of the Dust—not that they had known what plenty was out there on their dried-up lake. For a moment she saw blood spattered on cracked ground, and the anger that never left her flared. With an effort she shook the image of the sabbers from her head, unclenched her fists, and got herself moving.

She sped after the others, emerging from the dining hall into a glancing collision with someone hurrying the opposite way. Books hit the floor with half a dozen thuds.

"Sorry! Sorry!" Reluctantly, Livira tore her gaze from Meelan and Carlotte's retreating backs and looked to see what harm had been done. To listen to some of her older classmates, if a spine got broken the librarians would rather it belonged to a trainee than to a book.

For a moment the preponderance of grey made Livira think she'd felled someone senior, but it was a girl on her knees collecting the fallen volumes. She wasn't library staff—no robes but was dressed instead in a jacket and blouse, pleated skirts spread around her, an odd wedge of a hat crowning luxuriant chestnut hair.

Livira shot another look after the others, now vanishing around a corner. She considered running after them and abandoning the girl before her.

With a sigh she crouched down and reached for the nearest volume. "Let me help."

Something about the lettering on the first book's cover caught Livira's attention. Not the title—something dull about ethics—but the author's name. She began to spell out the sounds. "Dah-Vris-Yu—"

"Oh gods! The librarian really is trying to make a house reader out of you!"

Livira looked up and found herself staring into the blue eyes of Serra Leetar, her fine gown replaced with this symphony of greys, her jewellery traded for a single golden circle pinned to the lapel of her charcoal jacket.

"I'm training to be a librarian." Livira thrust the recovered book at her.

Serra Leetar put a hand to her mouth, almost hiding the incredulous smile. "Did he tell you that?"

"Yes." Though in that moment Livira couldn't remember if those words had actually passed Yute's pale lips.

"Well, Lord Algar will be delighted to hear that his bet's been taken up." Serra Leetar collected the last of her fallen volumes.

"What are you doing here?" Livira stood up, brushing at her knees. "University students go to the front desk." Serra Leetar had said she'd set her sights on the university.

The girl got up, scowling over her armful of books. "Lord Algar has direct access. I don't need to use the front desk." And with that she stalked off.

Livira was left with the strange impression that her last question had caused more upset than their collision had. Any pondering on the subject ended abruptly, though, as the last part of the name on the book she'd picked up settled into place. "Dah-Vris-Yu-Te . . . Davris Yute." She knew why the combination of letters was familiar. Not because of what they spelled but because she had seen the last part before. In faded letters high upon the rock opposite Yute's house. Had the librarian been deriding his own attention-seeking when he talked about the writing? Or had some relative of his climbed so high and set their name for the birds to see?

LIVIRA WAS THE last into the classroom, running past Master Logaris and blurting apologies on her way to the table where the others already sat. A quill, ink, and a brownish sheet of the lowest quality paper awaited her.

Arpix nodded to the open book she was to copy from. Livira flexed her writing hand and settled to her work.

The business of learning to read and write was both an immense frustration and at the same time the most wonderful thing that Livira had ever done. For the first week her head ached, as if threatening to burst under the pressure of all the new information being crammed into it. Sleep didn't happen. She lay in the unwavering light, staring at the ceiling where letters arranged themselves into one word after another. Her lips moved soundlessly as the words ran across the stone like a river, whole sentences streaming by. There was so much that was new, so much to learn, that for a time even Livira's irrepressible urge to explore, investigate, break rules, and get into trouble was overwhelmed. It turned out that all she'd ever needed in order to behave herself was a total absence of boredom.

Jella said the dark circles around Livira's eyes made her look like a coot-rat. She said Livira needed to eat more, sleep more, spend less time at her books.

Meelan said Jella was the worst teacher ever and criticised Livira's quill work. But even he expressed muted amazement at how swiftly she was learning.

Carlotte was the best teacher to start with. She had a little sister and had taught her the basics the year before coming to the library. Arpix was the best teacher now. He had the sharpest mind and was quickest to understand Livira's confusions. Her main frustration concerned the constant inconsistencies.

Arpix sympathised. "I've learned three languages so far and all of them have rules that make no sense and are broken almost as many times as they're followed. The thing to remember is that it's nobody's fault. No one sat down and said, 'Right, I'm going to invent a language.' Languages bubbled up out of animal grunting and shaped themselves over a thousand lifetimes, and, like streams cutting their course across a plain, they're always changing."

"Languages change?" Livira had been aghast, part of her had wanted to believe Master Logaris was joking when he'd said as much on the day of her arrival. She was having enough difficulty hitting the target without being told it was moving.

"Not swiftly, but pick three books in Charn tongue spaced a few centuries apart and you'll see it. At first sight you might think the youngest and the oldest were written by authors of different nations."

"Where did they keep the books before the library was built?" Livira wanted to know.

"We don't have any books that old." Carlotte joined them. "I'm not sure there are books that ancient."

"But . . ." Livira frowned. "Then how old is the king? If his great-grandfather built this—"

Meelan rose from the other side of the classroom table and without a word set his finger across Livira's lips, dark eyes boring into hers from beneath his low, black fringe. "Enough."

That night Jella lingered at the door to Livira's room, and when the others were gone, she spoke in a low voice. "Some questions about the king . . ." She took a deep breath. "Didn't your mother ever tell you that if you don't have anything nice to say then don't say anything at all?"

Livira shook her head. "She died when I was little, but I'd remember if she'd said something that stupid."

Jella pursed her lips. "Well, it's not stupid when it's about the king. It can get you in trouble. And that's why people don't want to answer you. Get some sleep." And she left Livira to her thoughts.

Livira eyed the bed then went to sit at her desk. The quill, the ink, and the blankness of the paper called to her as they had called every evening. The light's constancy seemed to exhort her to stay awake, as if the unsleeping library wanted company through the solitude of the night. She took the feather and dipped the split end. Her lettering was still crude. Meelan called it a child's writing—which wasn't a particularly cutting insult given that they were all children. L-I-V-I-R-A. She wrote her name. Names were all well and good but what fascinated her was that her thoughts could spill out onto the page and somehow be trapped in these marks, like frozen speech, waiting as long as you liked for someone to release it with their eyes. Arpix had told her there were books in the library that were thousands of years old. And not just one or two, but legions of them. So many that there must, Livira thought, be pages within their covers that had waited a thousand years to be seen again. And the magic was that just by running her eyes over those squiggled letters the thoughts of some long-dead author would wake within her head.

Livira laboriously spelled out k-i-n-g and then e-m-p-e-r-o-r and drew a box around both of them. Then she wrote b-o-x and drew a box around that too.

She woke to Jella's knocking, finding her face on the desk. Levering herself up she detached the sheet of paper that had glued itself to her cheek, and found it covered in words and boxes. Boxes within boxes. The largest one the same shape as her room.

LIVIRA WATCHED MASTER Logaris prowl between the tables of the more senior trainees, dispensing advice and admonishment in equal measure. In the weeks since her arrival he had seldom strayed near the table she shared with the four newest trainees. From time to time he would cast a suspicious glance their way. Occasionally he would throw a tightly crumpled ball of paper at Jella's head—he had yet to miss—and indicate by aiming a scowl from beneath bushy eyebrows that she was to close her mouth and open her book. The paper balls themselves bore meditations on silence in Triestan, the language Jella was supposed to be learning, and a translation was expected by the close of day.

When not teaching Livira, the others worked on their second, third, or—in Arpix's case—fourth language. Jella said that teachers fluent in the tongues came in from time to time to improve the trainee's skills, but none had visited since Livira's arrival.

In fact, the classroom received almost no visitors at all. Perhaps once or twice a week someone would come with papers for Master Logaris to sign, or a boy would bring fresh writing supplies, or a messenger would arrive to summon away one of the most senior trainees for some task. Once an elderly woman in a light grey robe arrived from the scriptorium with a newly bound book for Logaris's inspection.

When, at the very end of a long day, the door opened—this time without the customary knock—Livira looked up expecting another such interruption and was instead surprised to find herself looking at a man she recognised. A man nearly as tall as Heeth Logaris though with barely half his width. A man whose frock coat, waistcoat, and trousers were all the darkest grey, offset by the whiteness of his wig, and whose lapel sported a gold disc. A single dark eye scanned the room, the other covered by a crimson eyepatch.

"Algar." Livira muttered his name. The man who had called her a blunt instrument, laughed at her talents, and refused her when Yute had suggested her for the diplomatic service. The man who had wagered against her becoming a house reader when her ambitions were far more lofty. "I hate him."

The four closest heads swivelled her way.

"How do you know Lord Algar?" Jella hissed, amazed.

"From the Allocation Hall."

Meelan, who had said nothing all day, now snorted. "The only hall you might see Algar in is the fifth."

Livira said nothing, straining and failing to hear any word of the conversation between Algar and Master Logaris, both standing by the door, heads bowed together.

"*You* were tested in the fifth hall?" Meelan persisted.

Master Logaris glanced their way then returned his attention to Algar, his face grim.

"Who is this Algar then?" Livira muttered.

"*Lord* Algar," Arpix said, "is old money. Part of the king's household. Albeit a rather minor member. His father spoke for the king in foreign courts and Algar has inherited the position. Some notable wars both started and ended in such discourse during his father's tenure."

"All Algar's done is find out what happens when you use figures of speech with Gathians," Carlotte said.

"Carlotte!" Arpix admonished her.

Carlotte spread her hands. "I heard he told a Gathian prince that he'd rather be poked in the eye with a sharp stick than sign the trade deal as it stood."

"That's not true," Jella said.

"Well, it's what I heard."

Arpix re-established control. "The point is that he's a big deal and rarely attends anyone's allocation. If he was there, it must have been for someone special." For some reason he looked at Meelan.

Meelan, who tended to glare most of the time, narrowed his eyes, re-doubling his normal intensity, and turned away to study his work. Livira half expected the parchment to curl up and start smoking.

Algar swept from the room and ribbons of muted conversation fluttered among the trainees. Master Logaris looked at Livira and her companions, contemplating, and then with a weight of purpose on his broad shoulders he strode towards them.

"This is bad," hissed Jella, saying out loud what Livira was already thinking, although she had no real grounds for her conclusion. "He looks like—" Jella's mouth closed with a snap as the master drew near.

Master Logaris loomed above them and set both skull-crushing hands on the table. Livira found herself marvelling at the smooth baldness of the man's scalp in contrast to the explosive bushiness of his eyebrows. Some-where in the library would be a book that explained why baldness never seemed to claim eyebrows. She shook her head, forcing herself to concen-trate on what he was saying. The lack of sleep had set her mind to wander-ing of late and she resolved that tonight she would go straight to her bed after the evening meal.

"Well, little Yuteling, have these brats taught you anything?" Logaris fixed his pale eyes on Livira.

"Yes."

The man furrowed his brow. "And what's the most important thing you've learned?"

"Brevity." Livira had many new words like this one that she was eager to try out. She'd been working slowly through the first chapter of one of Meelan's books written long ago and far away and concerning the arts of armed combat. According to the author, presenting a small target was of prime importance. Livira had decided to opt for the same tactic with her current opponent.

Logaris snorted his disapproval but was unable to suppress an under-current of amusement. "Brevity is a desirable quality in those with nothing to say, and it generally takes me a good four years to hammer any worthwhile opinions into new trainees." He turned to Arpix, whose height and serious demeanour marked him as the group's leader—certainly to outsiders. "I want this book." He held up a slip of paper between massive thumb and massive forefinger.

Arpix paled and nodded. "Yes, sir."

"You have two days."

Arpix's eyes widened but he kept his mouth tight shut and took the slip.

Master Logaris frowned. Regarding them all with an unreadable expression. "Fail me and one of you will be leaving the library."

The five of them watched as their teacher returned to the front of the classroom and to his favoured senior pupils. Livira wondered if the paper Arpix now held had passed between Algar and Logaris. Algar's reappearance in her life seemed suspicious, coming as it did so hard on the heels of her encounter with Serra Leetar the previous day.

"What does that gold disc mean?" Livira asked.

"What?" Arpix looked up distractedly from his contemplation of the slip.

"The disc that Algar—Lord Algar—was wearing."

"It's the symbol of envoys, and negotiators." Carlotte answered for Arpix. She looked frightened. "In his case it shows he's the king's mouth."

Serra Leetar had worn it too. She hadn't wanted to become a diplomat though. Algar had taken her into his service and killed her hopes of joining the university. Livira wondered if that had always been going to happen—something arranged between him and the girl's parents—or if it had been a spur-of-the-moment thing, somehow connected to her own appearance at the allocation in Serra Leetar's company.

Meelan took the paper from Arpix. "This is bad."

"Two days to bring him a book?" Livira asked. "How hard can that be? We should be able to look it up in the index. If it's not there and we know what type of book it is then we can narrow it to a section. And even if it's not in the index and we don't know what it's about we still have time to hunt it down. You and Arpix start at the far end of the hall and we three start at the other. We can check every damn book in two days if we work fast." At least if they worked fast and didn't sleep.

"What are you talking about?" Meelan flashed her an irritated look.

"I said we should start at opposite—"

"She thinks she's seen the library." Carlotte laughed nervously.

"I have seen the library . . ." The hall was huge. Twice as long as Yute's house if you laid it down on its side and many times as wide. The shelves that ran from floor to ceiling were so tightly packed that a man like Master Logaris would have to edge between them facing the books.

"That's the trainee library." Arpix sighed. "It's just for projects and learning the trade."

"Oh." Livira deflated. "How big is the other library?"

Arpix spread his hands. And kept on spreading them until his arms were stretched out to their limits. ". . . Nobody knows."

Many sources report that Irad's great-grandmother was tricked into an education by a smooth-talking serpent. Whilst the records agree that she and her husband were evicted by their landlord shortly afterwards, the exact reasons remain an area of academic dispute. It is known with more certainty that once Irad founded the first library—the athenaeum—the serpent became a regular visitor, being credited with controlling the rat population.

Shadows of the Athenaeum, *by Methuselah Deusson*

CHAPTER 16

Livira

I'd like to be able to explain the library to you," Arpix said.

They had been served a breakfast of seed-crusted black bread and white goat cheese, with apples piled at the centre of the table. Each of them had immediately scooped up a plentiful supply and followed Arpix from the refectory.

"Go on then," Livira said, biting into a crisp red apple. The explosion of taste and wetness in her mouth was still a delicious astonishment to her. The only fruit she'd ever eaten out on the Dust was dried strips of pear with the ghost of flavour still clinging to them. "Explain it."

"I'd like to be able to," Arpix repeated. "But I can't."

"You have to see it for yourself," Jella said from behind them, puffing to keep up with Arpix's strides. They had two days to find Algar's book and Arpix had warned against wasting any of it. All of them were eating as they went, leaving a trail of crumbs. The water-skins that Arpix had filled and handed out hung from their belts and bumped annoyingly against their thighs.

The corridor was not one that Livira had followed before. It turned and turned again with flights of steps on each stretch. Livira's thigh muscles told her that she was climbing the mountain from the inside.

"Keep up," Arpix called back at Carlotte, bringing up the rear.

Livira paused to walk beside the girl. Carlotte had been quiet since they woke and Livira now saw the dark circles of a sleepless night around her eyes. The bread in her hand was untouched. "Are you all right?"

"Fine." Carlotte kept her gaze on the steps ahead of them. Her hair, which was always a wild, wiry mess, now stood in random tufts and clumps that made the normal chaos look like order.

Jella laboured ahead of them, puffing and red. The day before, an older trainee, Marta, had called the three of them the ugly sisters and her table had laughed even though it made no sense. Livira thought that she, Carlotte, and Jella were about as unlike as three girls could get. Later, after class, Jella had said Marta was wrong about Livira and Carlotte but right about her: she *was* ugly. And her normally smiling face had taken on a closed, tight look. Livira hadn't known what to say. She seldom thought about people in such terms, though she supposed she had agreed with her settlement that her friend Katrin had a face which made all the boys look twice.

She'd never really given thought to her own appearance, and it seemed that in the city everyone held the opinion that dusters were ugly in general. Meelan had told her that most city folk, when they weren't calling her people dusters, called them dogfaces and claimed they were cousins to the sabbers. He also told her that most city folk were idiots who should be pushed off the wall. He said that over the Remmis Sea lived a people with skin as dark as old leather and without a single hair on their body from head to toe. Those people, he suggested, would have trouble telling the people from the Dust and from the city apart.

Unexpectedly the sound of their footsteps took on a new hollow tone and within a few dozen more paces the corridor ended, releasing them into a natural cavern large enough to hold all the rooms that Livira had encountered so far. Arpix led across it. The uneven floor had been tamed with steps carved into the rock and wooden bridges to cross ravines. The far wall of the cavern was clearly different to the raw rock on all other sides. It was a uniform grey and so smooth that the directionless light gleamed from it as if it were the surface of still water.

"Why haven't we seen anyone?" Livira was used to the bustle of activity around the sleeping chambers, refectory hall, classroom, and other departments.

"A visit to the library is an expedition," Meelan growled.

"You don't just pop in for a book," Jella expanded. "So, people spend a lot of time in there. And a lot of time in the work areas when they return. But not much time trekking between here and there."

Livira frowned. "So why don't we just live inside the library? Until yesterday I thought we were."

"Not allowed to bring in food." Jella spoke around the bread and cheese she'd just crammed into her mouth.

"That's a silly rule." Livira took another bite of her apple. "They should just change it."

"That's where we're going." Carlotte pointed at some distant spot, her face still drawn and tense.

At first Livira couldn't make out their destination, but there it was, an opening in the wall and, set some way back into it, a white door. The corridor and the door looked tiny in the vast grey expanse of the wall that sealed the far side of the cavern. They grew larger as the children approached, until at last what was tiny became something that dwarfed them. Livira found herself staring up at the mouth of a corridor over twenty yards high. A hundred yards back what she had taken for a door now looked like a white wall sealing the corridor. If it was a door then it was one without handle or window or any feature whatsoever.

A pair of library guards stood watch at the base of the door, looking like toy soldiers. Both wore the traditional owl-eyed helms and carried the weapons Meelan called arrow-sticks. Arpix respectfully handed over the permission form that Master Logaris had given him. The others hurriedly ate the remnants of their breakfast while the guard studied the paper.

"Paper's in order. Ready to go in?" the guard asked.

"How does your arrow-stick work?" Livira resisted the urge to reach for it. "And where are your spare arrows?"

The man's eyes widened within the owl eyes of his helm and Livira suppressed a snort of amusement at his sudden similarity to the bird on which the helm was modelled. Her four classmates focused the kind of intense stares on her that said trainees don't interrogate library guards.

"It fires small lead balls." The other guard unslung her weapon. "It uses compressed gas. The laboratory knows of explosives that will throw the ball harder, but the ingredients are difficult to come by."

"We'll be needing that sort soon enough," the first guard growled cryptically.

Livira ran her gaze up and down the length of the gleaming barrel, wondering what they might find to shoot so far inside the mountain. "Thank you." She pushed the remainder of her apple core into her mouth. The others threw the cores away, but Livira could never bring herself to do so even though there were plenty more apples and the core was the least pleasant part.

"Ready?" the other guard repeated.

"We are." Arpix nodded.

The guard tugged on a pure white glove and set his hand to the door. Livira had expected it to open and that some considerable effort would be required. Instead, the white surface simply melted away. The man gestured them through. "Happy hunting!"

Livira hadn't known what to expect but she'd thought there would be some kind of preamble, some lead-up to the books. She'd been wrong. The doorway opened into a chamber that dwarfed the cavern they'd taken several minutes to cross. The ceiling vaulted a hundred yards and more above their heads and bookshelves divided the acreage of the floor into a sprawling labyrinth. The floor plan reminded her of both the city outside and of the confusion of worm-tracks in the mud after one of the eight or nine rains that had fallen in her lifetime. It was possible to observe these similarities because the door that had just vanished wasn't at ground level but rather halfway up the chamber wall at the top of a long, wide flight of steps leading down to the left. And whilst the shelves were extremely tall, none of them reached as high as fifty yards.

"Oh." Livira stayed rooted to the spot, gazing out towards walls so distant that they became part of the light. She was surprised that the mountain was big enough to hold the room. Just to walk along every aisle would require weeks. There might be five hundred miles of shelving, all of it reaching up far higher than a man.

The scent of the place hit her immediately, infinitely complex. Like

most smells, the aroma of books was neither good nor bad. Scent is a peg
on which memories are hung. When Livira had opened her first book in
the Allocation Hall its odour was simply the way it smelled. And afterwards it might have remained the scent of failure and rejection. But Yute
had overwritten those memories and now whenever she breathed in a book
it took her back to his narrow house and the crowded little library on the
fifth floor, stuffed with curios. It came freighted with salvation—with
someone seeing past dirt and ignorance and finding value. Livira took a
deep breath. "I never imagined it would be so . . . big."

"That's just the first chamber," Carlotte said tightly. "There are hundreds of others that we know of. And if we don't find this damn book in
two days Logaris is going to send one of us home and it's going to be me: I
know it. I'm the worst at Tracian and I hardly understand a word of Linear
and I—"

"Idiot." Livira whirled round to face her. "This is all for me. I thought
you knew that!"

"What . . . ?" Carlotte blinked. "You learn so fast. They'd never get rid
of you!"

"Algar wants me gone. When that girl, Serra Leetar, told him I was here
even though Yute didn't take his bet . . . well, he came to the library himself and pressed Master Logaris, and here we are."

"The bastard." Of her four companions Livira would have picked Meelan as the last to stand up for her, but instead he looked ready to do murder
on her behalf.

A meaningful cough to one side reminded them that they were criticis-
ing a relative of the king within earshot of the Library Guard. Arpix put a
hand to Livira's back and propelled her gently but firmly into the vast
room.

He steered her towards the stairs on their left. "Careful. There's no rail."

The steps were broad, a good three yards wide, so by sticking close to
the wall the group could pretend the undefended drop wasn't there. The
steps were also rather too big, so that each one turned into more of a jolt
than anticipated.

"Why does he hate me?" Livira jumped down another step, landing
heavily on tired legs. She'd been thinking about it for the whole descent. A

lord who must live in a great house and have bags filled with gold. Why had he taken the time to hate her and to pursue that hatred? It made no sense. His wealth could purchase endless pleasures to divert him. Had their roles been reversed Livira imagined she would have forgotten about the girl in the black cloak even before she reached the streets again.

"Politics." Arpix dropped beside her.

"Because you're not doing what you're supposed to." Jella thumped down with a gasp. "I hate these steps!"

"Because you're a duster and he's a bastard." Meelan jumped down on her other side, took two strides and dropped off the next edge.

Duster. Livira had first heard the expression on the day she entered the city, and it had haunted her ever since. She understood when people in the streets had called the children dusters as they followed behind Malar in their rags, fresh through the gates. They were literally dusty. But by the time she'd entered allocation she'd had her first bath and was wrapped in Malar's cloak. "So, whatever I do, I'm a duster? It never washes off?"

Arpix, Jella, and Carlotte exchanged glances.

"Well?" Livira demanded as their silence dragged out.

"You look different," Meelan called up from two steps below. "Black hair with a reddish sheen. Most of you have it. And something in the shape of the faces. You can just tell."

"They say your people aren't the same as us." Arpix found his tongue. "Not as clever."

"They say you're a breed." Jella nodded. "Coyoye blood in you."

Livira laughed out loud. "Coyoye? Coyoye are a kind of dog . . . how could—" Suddenly she was furious. First dogfaces, now dog-fuckers. "Who says? Who's saying it?"

Carlotte pointed up with one finger held close to her chest.

"The king, his brothers, his cousins, all of them," Meelan said. "If you're not properly human then we shouldn't have to risk soldiers to defend you from the sabbers."

"And why would anyone believe them? I mean, you don't. Do you? It's stupid talk!" Livira looked around at the others, seeking any challenge.

"It's written." Carlotte dropped her gaze. "There are books . . . The house readers have them on their lists."

"Books from this library?" Livira blinked, aghast.

"Yes."

"So, you being here and learning to read and write better in one month than most manage in their first three years at school . . ." Arpix shook his head. "That's reason enough for Lord Algar to want you to fail. As far as he's concerned, you'll serve the king's aims far better in the sewers or the mines than you will in the library, no matter how clever you are."

When asked to pick from the treasure chest of the divine and take just one power, it is often that of flight or of invisibility that prove to be the most popular choice. The power to find that which has been lost is commonly overlooked. But when one considers just how much our kind have lost, and how often, then the wisdom of such a path is . . .

Dewey Decimal Classification, *by Henry M. Stanley*

CHAPTER 17

Livira

"Tell me there's an index."

They were down among the shelves now and if the light had been overhead like the sun instead of bleeding from every cubic inch of air, then they would be mired in shadows. The space between shelves was a small fraction of the heights they scaled, and to walk among them was to find oneself at the bottom of a deep book-lined gully. The shelves themselves were wooden, dark with age, pitted and stained by unknown calamities. Livira had no idea that the world held so much wood. Perhaps it no longer did now that these forests had been felled to serve the needs of the library. Without an index their hunt would be simply impossible. A lifetime would likely not suffice even if the book they were hunting could be guaranteed to lie within this first chamber.

With an index they stood a chance, depending on how precise it was and how well order was maintained when returning books. Livira stared up at the dizzying heights to either side of her. Shelf upon shelf upon shelf. She took a deep breath of the book-scented air. "Tell me there's an index. Also, a ladder."

"There's an index," Jella said. Something in her tone didn't alleviate Livira's concern.

Meelan snorted. He pulled a book from the nearest shelf and began leafing through it. He looked up and pulled out the next book, fatter and taller than the first. "Here's an index." He handed it to Livira. "There are lots of them."

"What? Why?" Livira wrapped the heavy tome to her chest.

"This place built the city," Arpix said. "It built the nation. The empire. All of it. But those guards we passed don't work for King Oanold. The head librarian doesn't work for the king, whatever the people in the streets think." He waved an arm at the aisle stretching away from them. "This is power. This is where the histories are. This is where the great philosophers are. This is where the secrets that arm our soldiers with arrow-sticks are written. This is where the next secrets will be found. You think our people would have even a fraction of what they have now without the library? It wasn't many generations ago we were fighting each other with bones and rocks, and we thought fire was a great magic . . ."

"What does any of that have to do with indexes?" Livira asked helplessly. She noticed the book she'd been handed was numbered volume thirty-six.

"Why doesn't the king have the head librarian killed and replaced by someone who'll do exactly what he says? Why doesn't Yute stab the head librarian in the back and take the job for himself?"

"Because he's not a murderer." Livira couldn't imagine Yute raising his voice against someone, let alone a knife.

"Well, Yute might not be . . ." Arpix agreed. "But in general, it's because without the index the library becomes unusable, and progress would stall for however many decades were needed to create a new one. And the thing is that each new librarian who gets control knows that in order to keep it they need to change the index so that their knowledge becomes indispensable."

Livira started to walk down the aisle, running her fingertips over the spines of the books at hand level. Many were not actually books but narrow boxes packed with yellowing index cards like in the trainee library. She spotted a ladder ahead of her, leaning against the shelves and reaching several yards over the very topmost. "They move all these books around every time someone new takes over?" She was aghast at the effort that would involve.

"Not all of them." Arpix followed her. "Just the ones thought to be most important at the time in question. And that's the problem. There are lots of different systems at work here at the same time, lots of categorisations." He caught Livira's wrist and pulled her fingers down to the wooden edge of the shelf beneath the books she'd been touching. The edge was scarred by innumerable cuts. At first it looked like random damage, the work of hungry rats with a taste for oak perhaps. But now she could see that there were numbers there, letters, codes of dots and slashes, all intermingled, overwritten, competing for space. "Depending where you're standing a different system will be in use, and the boundaries between those systems are not well defined. Our current head librarian's system is employed on the outer boundaries—"

"Of the library?"

"Of the area that has been catalogued."

"But . . ." Livira struggled to frame her question. "How can there be areas that aren't catalogued? Surely when the books were put out—"

"The books were all here when the library was discovered—"

"Rediscovered," Meelan interrupted Arpix's interruption.

"Rediscovered," the taller boy agreed. "Don't say that outside though—only in here. But yes, some savage wrapped in animal skins rediscovered this place less time ago than you might think, and all the books were here already, waiting on the shelves, without any apparent order to them. And we've been working at cataloguing and organising ever since. Spreading out from where we're standing while a city grew up outside." He waved a hand down the aisle. "And somewhere out there is the 'edge,' the limit of our progress. And if we needed to find a book close to that boundary, we'd have to have someone very senior with access to the current card-based index to come and help us. And if we were in the very outermost sections, right on the edge, then only the head librarian herself would be able to help."

"Dear gods." Livira turned round and started heading back to where Meelan was still leafing through the first index he'd taken from the shelf. Jella and Carlotte had joined him, looking through other indexes taken from beside his.

"Where are you going?" Arpix called after her.

Livira looked around at him. "Back to the indexes of course."

Arpix pulled a slim volume from the shelf before him. "Try this one." He held it out towards her. "This whole aisle is indexes."

IN THE FACE of Livira's despair, Arpix had explained that the situation wasn't as dire as it might seem, though it was dire. They knew what language the book was written in, and many indexes specified different sections for different languages. Arpix also said they had a fair chance that *Reflections on Solitude* was a book of poetry or philosophy, which would place it in a limited number of sections. And finally, the author's name would position it in an alphabetic ordering within whatever section it lay in.

For someone who had reached the lofty station of librarian, generally with over a decade of training beneath their belt, the black art of finding a book via the sprawling system of index systems was one that could usually be accomplished within hours rather than days.

"There should be an index of indexes," Livira declared, hefting another heavy volume from the pile to her right and balancing it on her knees as she sat with her back against the shelves.

"There are lots of them," Meelan grumbled from the other side of the pile.

"And indexes of indexes of indexes," Arpix added. "A pyramid of them with the mythical master index perched at the very top!"

"How do we know this book even exists?" Livira held up the paper that Master Logaris had given them. She puzzled through the words and then the name. "*Reflections on Solitude*, by Arqnaxis Lox. Relquian." Arpix had explained that the title and name were translated from Relquian, a language none of them knew and which used a totally different alphabet. He'd had the foresight to equip himself with a Relquian dictionary from the trainee library.

"It would reflect poorly on Lord Algar if it were later found not to exist," Arpix said.

"How would anyone know?" Livira slumped against the shelves. Her legs were tired, her throat was dry, and they hadn't moved more than two yards from the place where Meelan had pulled out the first index.

"They would ask an assistant," Arpix said. "Assistants are rarely helpful, but they will confirm the existence of a book if asked."

Livira tilted her head, intrigued. "An assistant? Where would we find one and why wouldn't they just tell us where our book is? And how do they know anyway?" She knew her memory was much better than most people's, but to memorise the title of every book in the library was surely impossible.

"You find them wandering," Jella answered her first question.

"Not often," Carlotte said. "It's a big place and there aren't many."

"How do they know?" Meelan repeated Livira's question, looking up from his book. He'd seated himself on the ground and had a sheaf of paper beside him, the top sheet covered in untidy notes. "Assistants know everything because they're part of the library. The master index may or may not be out there somewhere but it's definitely in their heads."

"The assistants aren't the only thing wandering out there," Carlotte said. "There are helpers that were built by librarians long ago. But most of them are broken."

"They're not safe to use even when they're not broken." Arpix shot Carlotte a warning look. "If you use the wrong index the worst thing that can happen is that you won't find the book you're after. Use the wrong helper and you might not survive the experience."

Meelan nodded his dark head. "The library business was cutthroat back in the old days. There were guardians too, made by librarians from way way back, though the last of those were dealt with a century ago. A bloody business, by all accounts."

"Some were *huge*!" Carlotte raised both hands above her head. "It took hundreds of soldiers to drive them off or break them. They say they were hunting something. Maybe just people or perhaps for someone in particular. Other, smaller ones, like the Black Knight, were set to guard particular aisles or doors. But most were guides to help you find things. There was one like an owl that the previous head librarian had. But that stopped working—"

"I vote we go and find one of these assistants." Livira had enjoyed learning to read and loved using the skill to unlock the contents of books. On the other hand, this whole business of indexes and categorisations and hunting through ancient lists to find a particular book in a system designed specifically to be opaque . . . well, that could go drown itself in a hole.

Arpix shook his head. "Absolutely not."

"Not the helper things city people made—the proper ones, the assistants." Livira looked at the others for support but all three seemed suddenly very interested in their books.

"We need to spend our time wisely," Arpix insisted. "The chances are you wouldn't find one in two days, and they almost certainly wouldn't help you even if you did. Don't be misled by the name. They rarely assist. You'd probably just get lost. Without instruction people can get lost and die of thirst in the aisles. We stay here and do this the proper way." He folded his arms across his chest, regarding her from his height.

"Maybe I'll go and have a little look." Livira pushed away from the shelf she was leaning on and stretched her stiff legs. It seemed that the grand punishment for not being able to dig through this tedious mess was to not be allowed to do it anymore. Apart from natural stubbornness making her want to thwart Lord Algar, she wasn't sure she wouldn't enjoy life outside the library more than life inside. Especially now she could read, more or less.

"We need you here," Arpix said. "You're not to go wandering."

Livira frowned. "Do you though? Need me? I mean, I only speak one language. I'm the slowest reader here. I've only ever seen one index before in my life. What use am I?"

"You'll get lost." Jella looked worried.

"You should listen to Arpix," Carlotte said, while making shooing gestures with her hands where Arpix couldn't see them.

"You wouldn't be the first trainee to get lost out there and die of thirst," Meelan said.

Arpix nodded. "Senior librarians come back with bones sometimes. Along with their books."

"You're just trying to scare me." It did sound to Livira like the sort of thing they'd make up to keep her in line.

"You're staying here. I promised Master Logaris I'd keep an eye on you." Arpix took a tiny bottle of ink and a quill from inside his robe and handed them to her. "You can help Meelan with his map." He walked off with the index he was studying and positioned himself at the end of the aisle to block her escape.

LIVIRA ESCAPED AN hour later. The irrepressible nature for which she had been named, called rebellion by some, irresponsibility and recklessness by others, had been stomped further down than ever before by the tragedy at the settlement and the total upheaval of her existence. Quiet weeks of study had, however, watered the ground and the hardy strands of her disobedience had begun to re-emerge.

She spent an hour searching out information for Meelan to add to his maps and lists, all the while edging closer to the ladder. As she set her hand to the rungs Carlotte started talking.

"If Lord Algar truly has engineered this to get rid of you, then the real question is how badly he wants you gone. I mean, he could have made it impossible. Hidden it in the wrong place."

Arpix shook his head. "Only librarians and trainees are allowed in the library proper."

"He could have paid a librarian to do it," Carlotte muttered.

Arpix looked scandalised at the idea.

Livira began to climb slowly. "He'd have to get all the copies hidden," she said.

Meelan rolled his eyes but corrected her without malice. "There's only one copy of each book held in the library. That's a lot of what we do—making copies of the books the king approves of so the house readers can spread the word."

Livira looked at the expanse of shelving all around her with fresh wonder as she climbed. One copy. Every book unique!

Livira continued upwards, a good six feet off the ground now. She wasn't sure how far Arpix's sense of duty would go when it came to confining her, but the boy seemed really quite conscientious, and she'd rather not have to punch him on the nose to get past him. On the other hand, she'd welcome a punch to her own nose if it meant she could abandon the search for Lord Algar's book.

"Livira!" Arpix realised what she was doing.

"Just getting a book." She kept to the same pace. Speeding up would be an admission of guilt.

"Get down here!"

"I've seen the one we're looking for," Livira lied. A good lie can sow confusion and win vital moments of freedom.

"Get her!" Arpix began to run for the ladder. Clearly on this occasion her lie had been a bit rubbish.

Livira accelerated, climbing as fast as she could. She was five yards shy of the top when she felt the jolt of Arpix grabbing the ladder's base.

"Damn." She'd been planning to lift the ladder up behind her and use it to descend the far side.

"Come down!" Arpix called. "You're not going anywhere."

The certainty in his voice, hinting at smugness, convinced her to keep climbing. She passed row after row of leathered spines, all marked with numerals. Astonishingly, even up here, far above the rooftops of any normal town, the books stretching left and right weren't library books but merely volumes concerned with the organisation of those books.

Moments later she clambered onto the shelf top and peered down into the chasm of the next aisle. Around her, shelf tops marched away in all directions. From this level the variation in heights made it look like a landscape of rolling hills with the occasional cliff face interrupting. From on high it had seemed a labyrinth.

The nearest row of shelving stood little more than six feet away, not far but a misjudged leap would spill her into the depths below amid a fluttering torrent of pages. Even as Livira considered it, vertigo reached up for her, twisting her stomach and turning the muscles of her legs to water. She fell to her hands and knees, fighting dizziness.

"Get down! Right now!" Arpix shouted up at her. Jella and Meelan added their calls to Arpix's.

"I'm fine." Livira tried to keep the tremble from her voice. She hoped she was fine. She considered hanging over the opposite side and descending shelf by shelf but hanging from the tops of books while questing for the tops of other books below her with the toes of her shoes seemed like a recipe for disaster.

Retreating back down the ladder to the others was more than her pride could bear though. She began to crawl doggedly along the top, keeping away from the edge so that her progress could not be tracked from below. Her speed grew along with her confidence, and she found herself rather liking this new, forbidden perspective.

If Lord Algar's plan to have her evicted from the library was going to work, then she'd rather her last memories of the place be of exploration and adventure than of being the least useful member of a team poring over dusty indexes in a futile attempt to master the librarian's craft in two days.

"Come back!" Already the voices sounded more distant. It might not be long before one of them thought to climb up after her though. She sped up.

She felt as if she'd crawled a mile before she spotted her first ladder, and the damn thing was leaning against the shelves on the other side of the aisle. She couldn't hear the others anymore. They'd lost her or let her go. She stood, rubbed her sore knees, and cursed. She had four choices, and since one of them was "to go back" that left three choices. To go on, to jump for the ladder, or to climb down this side, which she could have done immediately.

Livira got ready to jump.

"It's not far. It's not far. It's not far." Somehow the repetition—even though true—did nothing to shrink her perception of the six-foot gap. The drop beneath her managed to magnify the width of the aisle into something that she'd be hard pressed to throw a rock across, let alone her whole body. The floor seemed to reach up for her with invisible fingers, seeking to haul her from her perch.

With watery muscles, a racing heart, and a despairing scream, Livira made the leap. A moment of falling and of utter terror, and she hit the ladder. She had overestimated the gap and underestimated the difficulty of holding on once she got there. She hit far harder than anticipated, smacking her face into one of the higher rungs whilst missing her footing on the lower ones.

For a few heartbeats everything was pain and dancing stars and confusion about which way was up. She wasn't even sure that the falling had stopped. Livira's senses returned to inform her that she was hanging at a back-breaking angle over the drop, both legs painfully threaded through the rungs. The ladder itself must have bounced around a bit and was now worryingly less vertical than it had been. Only the considerable weight of the wood and Livira's comparative lightness had prevented a fatal sideways slide and a sharp reunion with the library floor. Gingerly Livira straightened and reached for the rungs. Her face felt twice its proper size and her nose was bleeding, spattering the blue of her robe with scarlet. Taking considerable care, she extricated her legs and began a slow descent, trusting the ladder not to tilt further to the side.

By the time she reached the ground her nosebleed had stopped but her robe looked as if she'd slaughtered a pig on her lap. She looked up at the narrow slice of ceiling far above her, gazing left along the aisle, then right. With a shrug she chose left and started to walk before pausing and pulling a book at random from the nearest shelf. She set it on the floor at the base of the ladder. Her memory was good, but a trail of books placed at key points might prove useful if she were in a hurry.

She felt a small pang of guilt at leaving the others behind, but only a small one. It was she who would suffer the consequences of failure and she who could do least to avert it. She touched her aching face delicately. There'd be a fine set of bruises along that side in due course. She shrugged again and, with a heart lighter than it had a right to be, she set off towards the seeming infinity where the left-hand and right-hand set of shelves appeared to converge.

There is a scurrilous but persistent rumour that, under pressure from King Dubya and later from his son, Oanold, a great many books written in sabbertine were removed from the shelves, leaving the catalogue free of any works by their kind. These days, the suggestion that a sabber can reason, let alone read and write, is apt to earn a beating from the king's justices.

The Purge, *by Anon*

CHAPTER 18

Evar

E var shook the char wall's soot from the mane of his hair as best he could. He allowed the Soldier to lead him back within the wall of books that formed a perimeter around the pool. The Soldier didn't physically keep Evar from the char-wall tunnel now that he was grown, but the Soldier's passion had shocked Evar. The Soldier's distance and silence had always presented him as closer to a thing than to a person. Today's revelation deserved respect: Evar owed him that much and had allowed himself to be led away.

"I was charged to keep you all safe, Evar Eventari." The Soldier stopped halfway between the book wall and the start of the crops that surrounded the pool. "All of you."

"By who?" Evar couldn't keep the exasperation from his voice. He already knew there would be no answer to that question.

The Soldier bowed his ivory head.

"Whoever it was never met me. They never met any of us." Evar waved his arm in the direction his brothers had left hours earlier. "The people you should have guarded are two centuries dead. You couldn't protect them against time, and they're dust now. Soil!" He kicked at the earth at the rim of the crop circle. "Your duty is done. Gone. You've no authority over us."

The Soldier remained statue-still and made no response. Fifty yards away, not far from the edge of the pool, the Assistant stood similarly immobile among a curling riot of melon leaves in exactly the place Evar had last seen her.

Evar's frustrations marched him around the perimeter a dozen times, part of him wanting to vault the wall and join his brothers in their hunt. Clovis would return from the Mechanism soon and some instinct had started to prod him to move on. The siblings had spent so long in each other's company that they moved through most days in an unacknowledged dance of avoidance, one sliding past another, sidestepping friction. With Clovis the necessary steps were intricate and performed on eggshells, any error running the risk of snagging on her many hooks and pulling loose one of the host of grievances that, even without Kerrol's skill, Evar could see all sprang from the same deep root.

In the end the pace of his circling diminished, and he meandered towards the pool and the Assistant, carefully plotting a path through the greenery that sustained his family.

The Assistant tilted her head at his approach, a faint blue glow reaching her eyes. "Evar."

He sat himself at the pool's edge, legs drawn up, heels resting at the edge of the water which came right to the very lip no matter how much was taken for irrigation. The library's light didn't penetrate the depths, and darkness waited beneath his toes. He'd been scared of those blind fathoms as a child. They all had. Even Clovis. The Assistant insisted that they learn to swim in case any of them should ever fall in, but none of them had enjoyed it and at barely more than two yards the diameter of the pool didn't allow for any of the strokes illustrated in the texts. Treading water was the most that any of them could do and they'd avoided doing even that as soon as the Assistant was convinced that if they fell in, they could get out again.

There was something about being wet that just made Evar want to shake himself dry. Besides, the stuff was always icy cold.

He took the book from inside his jerkin.

"Careful." The Assistant spoke from behind him. She never liked books to be taken to the pool. As children it had been utterly forbidden, but orders had mellowed to strong advice now that the siblings were older.

Evar, still gnawed at by frustration, held the book out over the water, ashamed of his childish pique even as he did so. What would she do if he dropped it? Jump in after it? She would sink to the bottom like a lump of iron—if there even was a bottom . . .

Instantly, before the Assistant could move or protest, Evar jerked the book back to his chest. A thought had struck him. It hit home hard enough to leave his head echoing with shock at his own stupidity. *Find me at the bottom.* The line read: "Find me at the bottom." Could it be so simple? In the great acreage of library to which he had access, everything was level. Except here.

Doubt followed hard on the heels of certainty. How could he find her at the bottom of the pool? Had she drowned herself? And what good would it do to dredge up her bones from the murk?

"How deep is the pool? What's at the bottom?" He turned to face the Assistant.

"Those aren't meaningful questions." She began to walk away.

"How can they not be meaningful?" Evar got to his feet, glancing between the pool and the Assistant's retreating back. "How deep is it?" He watched her go.

"I REALLY DON'T want to do this." Evar spoke the words to himself. The lightless depths of the pool somehow scared him in ways that the tunnel into the char wall had not. None of them had ever spent much time by the pool, steered away by an instinctive mistrust and by unpleasant memories of enforced immersion. Despite it being the dark eye at the centre of their existence, the literal giver of life for their community, and that of their ancestors down the span of two centuries, it somehow evaded their imagination. Any sense of enquiry had never reached much past the surface, going no deeper than the scoop of a bucket or the limits of kicking feet.

Evar still had nightmares from the times he had jumped in as a child under the Assistant's direction, the plunge, the bubble-chasing struggle to regain the surface—these things had yanked him from the depths of his dreaming on many occasions. "I *really* don't want to do this . . ."

He jumped in, arms raised, making an arrow of his body, feet pointed towards his destination. The splash, the cold thrill of immersion, the terror of sinking, and then—finding nothing but space with his questing toes—

the sudden panicked thrashing towards the sparkling surface a yard or two above his fingertips.

Evar hauled himself out on the edge and lay there with the water streaming from him. He was panting, more from the urgency of his escape than because of air-starved lungs. The whole thing had taken only a fraction of the time he knew he could hold his breath for.

"Hell." He was glad that his only witness was the Soldier and even he didn't appear to be paying any attention. He wanted to say that that was the end of it, he had tried, and the idea was a stupid one. *At the bottom.* How deep did he have to go? He could make a long thread from endless book bindings and lower something in to gauge the depth to the bottom. But in the end, all that mattered was could he reach it or not? With a sigh he got up and went to gather what he needed.

EVAR RETURNED WITH a double armful of loose iron. With limited breath in his lungs, he would have to descend as swiftly as possible. He could sink faster than he could swim, but only if he carried sufficient weight. His burden would have to be released to allow him to return, and such a collection of iron could not be discarded lightly. The others would be furious with him. He had gathered up most of the iron book hinges that had been salvaged over the years, along with some mysterious plates and rods and toothed wheels whose origin and purpose remained unknown. Some of these had been part of their heritage, collected by Evar's ancestors over many lifetimes. Two of the loose metal plates Mayland had found discarded among the stacks. The rods and wheels were not even iron but some other metal that Starval said was probably brass.

Evar stood at the edge of the pool, staring at the sparkling surface. He clutched the angular mass of his burden tightly to his chest, gritting his teeth against the pain of sharp corners digging in. He felt the weight of it in his arms. He would have to descend close to the side to prevent the load tipping and spilling before he wanted to rise.

A sensible plan would be to recruit one of the others. To make two leather ropes and a leather bag so that both he and the precious weight he had gathered could be recovered. That would be the sensible path. But common sense seemed somehow less important than speed. And some selfish part of him wanted this for himself, the definite danger, the likely disappointment, the remote chance of escape.

The library had always been timeless, at least on the scale of Evar's existence. He and his siblings were the only clock, the only things to notice the passage of the years and give them meaning. Without Evar and his kind the library would simply step outside the domain of years, decades, and even centuries, taking the Soldier and the Assistant with it, paying only scant heed to the passage of millennia as its books fell into soft decay.

Recently though, starting before the discovery of the book, but increasing swiftly since then, there had been a sense of acceleration, some impression of rapidly building change. And with it also came a swelling fragility, a futility, as if should the demand and potential not be met then the chance would not ever come again and time would grind their lives back into the dust, unmarked.

An acceleration—that was the word for it. The Escapes, coming more often, faster, bigger, stranger. The Soldier and the Assistant, both as unchanging as the very floor, now showing flashes of some internal conflict, an awakening perhaps. The book and the woman who lay behind it. The woman whose outline had become the perimeter of the void that the Mechanism had left inside him. The woman whose name his tongue wouldn't form but whose scent seemed to find him now in quiet moments. He found that although he knew nothing about her, remembered nothing . . . he needed her. Perhaps more than he needed to draw breath. The pool would decide that one.

All of it was rushing at him. All of it could so easily pass him by. And that one line. A riddle or a challenge: *Find me.* It was not a time for waiting. *"I don't want to do this."*

Evar took one step forward and sank like a stone.

It was Jaspeth's and Irad's grandfather who invented fratricide, and at an early age the brothers resolved to use other means to settle their differences. When Irad raised the first library, a temple to the sin of knowledge, a stone house in which his great-grandmother's original crime could shelter, Jaspeth resolved to tear it down. In previous generations a death would have followed. Instead, they found an uneasy compromise and the echoes of their bickering have rattled down eternity's corridors.

The Library Myth, *by Mayland Shelfborn*

CHAPTER 19

Livira

Livira felt that her life until the sabbers came had been spent running in circles, covering great distances all while remaining within sight of Aunt Teela's shack. The soldier, Malar, had led her on the longest journey of her life, crossing the Dust to reach the gates of the city. Within the library, though, she felt that perhaps she had travelled still more miles.

The aisles turned her back on herself countless times and it proved almost impossible to keep a sense of direction with just a slice of the distant stone sky visible above her. The square miles of the chamber had been divided into regions and, although it was clearly not a deliberate maze, finding the exit from one to another proved to be a dark art.

The scale of the place put Livira's meagre knowledge into perspective. She'd been a trainee for just over a month and she didn't even know the name of the mysterious head librarian yet, let alone have any handle on the many mysteries of the library itself. Back at the entrance, Jella had spoken of all manner of marvels lying deep among the untold miles of distant chambers. She had mentioned a chamber that lay permanently dark and haunted. In another she said that each "book" was in fact just a curtain of thin cords, each cord serving as a page where the knots bound into them constituted individual letters and words. Clearly, a landscape of wonder waited for Livira, and here she was, lost in the first room. Livira considered her travel plans. It seemed to her that however large the library might be there was an effective limit on it set by how far a person could get without food and with only the water they could carry. She wasn't yet sure if she intended to test that limit or to turn back after what she guessed was a day's travel. Part of her worried that the others might find the damn book within the two days Master Logaris had allocated, leaving her as the only impediment to success.

Livira took a swig of water and jogged on.

Finding the book herself was out of the question. Simply to examine the spines of the volumes to her left and right would require a ladder, preferably one for each side, and would slow her advance down to about a yard per hour. She was looking for something else. She didn't know what, but something to hold on to and to remember long after Master Logaris had booted out the first and probably last duster ever to sully his classroom.

So far all she'd found, and the lasting memory that would fill her dreams next time she slept, were the endlessly stretching aisles, the deep book-lined trenches that went on and on relentlessly, each one unique but somehow the same.

The further Livira travelled into the library the stronger grew her impression that the place had not been built by or for people. The shelves might have been crafted by human hands, the ladders too. Perhaps not all of the books, but many of them, had been written by men and women. But the library itself made no concession to human architecture, or scale. Even human frailties were overlooked. There wasn't so much as a corner for Livira to relieve herself in. The only privacy was the vast, aching solitude.

Livira had to imagine that unseen and possibly invisible servants of the library must clean the floors periodically. Or maybe it was just so large, with each part so seldom visited, that such befoulments were simply erased by the passage of time. Time itself was, perhaps, that invisible servant she had surmised. Time itself in thrall to the library. She carried on, feeling small, smaller even than when standing beneath the star-scattered arch of the sky.

In places a book bound in gleaming metal might catch her eye, or one whose lettering along the spine glowed with an unnatural sheen. On rest breaks she would pull random volumes from their place and leaf through them, marvelling at the strangeness of their alphabets and the dense packed lettering that might take days or weeks to read from cover to cover.

Shelf upon shelf, aisle upon aisle. The weight of it all, the sheer physical weight of it, felt like a burden on her soul. All these words screaming silently to be read. She hurried on with no clear destination, passing lifetimes of endeavour with each step.

She had been exploring for hours when something caught her eye. A thing rarer than a golden cover or the bejewelled spine of an ancient tome or a book too large for her to lift. It was a gap. As stark as a missing tooth in an otherwise perfect smile. A black slot, a gaping socket. It was the first time in all her travelling that she had seen a gap in the shelves that wasn't made by her or her friends.

Livira stretched her fingers into the space as if trying to feel the ghost of the missing book. This, more than anything else she'd seen so far, was eloquent testimony to the sheer size of the library. She had needed to travel this far to find any evidence that the community of librarians she lived among and the city beyond them existed at all.

Livira found a claw at a T-junction in a section where the books all had red covers as if the librarians, tiring of organising by author in alphabetical order, or by subject according to some taxonomy agreed in ancient times, had simply opted to work their way through the spectrum. The aisle looked like a trench whose walls were covered in blood.

The claw itself was a scimitar of yellowish metal that barely fit into Livira's palm, a sharp edge on its inner curve. It had lain on top of the books on the first shelf, at shin level. She'd almost missed it entirely. She tucked it into her belt and carried on, trying not to worry about where the owner was.

Three more aisles brought her to a clearing—empty space! A wide semicircle clear of shelving and of books. And—as if empty space wasn't shocking enough after so long with shelving pressing on both sides—the clearing ran to the base of the wall that had been looming above the tops of the towering shelves for so long.

Livira stumbled forward on weary feet. A corridor was set into the wall at ground level, fully as tall and wide as the one through which she had entered the library, and like that one it was sealed by a white door about a hundred yards in.

The guard back at the entrance hadn't used a key, he'd worn a special white glove and the white wall had melted away before it. She pressed her lips into a flat line and stood staring at the door. The folk of the king's city liked their doors. Right from the mighty gates that were said to keep out even the dust, to the front doors of even the humblest homes where iron locks made it clear you weren't welcome to come in. The library though . . . what purpose did it serve if people weren't allowed in to read the books?

Livira marched up to knock on the door. She didn't have any magic glove, but she would hammer on that perfect white surface and stain it with her sweat and demand entrance.

"Let me . . ." Before her knuckles could register contact the whole door melted away just as it had for the guard. ". . . in . . ."

THE CORRIDOR OPENED onto a second chamber of similarly titanic dimensions to the one Livira had just escaped. A semicircle of clear ground some thirty yards in diameter lay beyond the door, after which the towering shelves re-established themselves, offering a score of aisles down which she could travel.

Out in the clear area, a little off-centre, stood the first thing Livira had seen in an age that wasn't shelf or book or ladder. A strange humanoid fashioned in dull brown metal, his articulated limbs polished as if by the touch of countless passing hands. He might once have had wings, but just a metal skeleton of them remained.

Livira went to study the man. His empty sockets gazed out at the looming shelves, head tilted slightly as if in enquiry. She grasped his arm, finding it cold to the touch, and tried to move it. It gave a fraction then locked with a grating sound.

"Hello." Livira felt a little foolish despite having talked to herself many times in the aching solitude of her journey to this place. She'd even talked to several books. And one ladder.

The metal man made no reply. He was, she assumed, one of the helpers the others had warned her of. The work of earlier librarians—though how they'd been able to accomplish such wonders when Yute and his fellows could not she didn't know.

"I'm looking for a book," Livira told him, then immediately felt foolish. What else would she be looking for in the library? "You're not going to help me, are you?"

Livira released the man's arm and wondered how long he had stood waiting, how many people had passed by him. The mechanism must have died long ago, and this was his immutable corpse, standing down the long march of years as a marker of his demise.

"Goodbye, metal man."

Livira didn't waste any time choosing which aisle to take. Since she had no destination in mind, she struck out straight ahead, aiming for the door that would lie opposite hers. An hour of back and forth among the aisles brought her to her first dead end. Shortly after the dead end she discovered her first curve. It came as a relief after what seemed like a lifetime of straight lines, though why anyone had gone to the trouble of manufacturing shelves that not only snaked gently from side to side but doubled around on themselves in tight turns she couldn't fathom.

It took another hour and a dozen dead ends for her to understand that she had exchanged a labyrinth that would lose a person by virtue of its sheer scale and repetition for a more deliberate maze. Here she was constantly returned to the same circular clearing in which eight aisles met. The junction was a clear space scarcely larger than the room the librarians had given her to sleep in. A room for whose comforts both her body and mind ached. The certainty that she would never return to this place of wonder kept her going. She could rest after they threw her out.

Livira stood and studied her choices for what seemed the hundredth time. Her gaze returned to the off-centre stain that marked the ground in the circle. It was the first blemish Livira had seen on the stone flooring in all her journeying. The stain had a vague symmetry, and her tired mind made all manner of images from the blackness of it.

"Enough." Livira forced herself to look away, gathered energy, and set off again. She began to memorise the names on the books she left out on the floor as markers, by this means allowing herself to understand which places she had been returned to by the maze's dead ends and turns.

Livira was already flagging when she found herself unexpectedly back at the circle for what now felt like the thousandth time.

"Not possible." She spun around. "Someone's putting my books back on the shelves!"

In her confusion and frustration, she nearly left the place without noticing that the stain on the floor had gone. She wondered how many adventurers in antiquity had gone mad and died in the labyrinth without understanding that there was more than one clearing in it. She took a book and set it on the floor to label this place as distinct from the other.

Much later she returned to a fork in the aisles that memory told her she had visited before. "There's no book . . ." Livira crouched, touching the cold stone in the exact spot she was sure she had placed the book. She walked the shelves, trailing her fingers across the books at shoulder height, looking for the title, *Tales from the Unterworld, Volume Six*. "There's no book . . ."

Was someone returning them to the shelves? In so vast a place several people could wander for days without ever encountering each other. The maze though, the maze concentrated people. It trapped them. It turned them in on each other and made them pass through the same spaces over and over. If she were ever to meet a fellow trainee or librarian, it would be here. If she were to find a bleached skull and neat collection of bones—this would be the place.

Livira shook her head. She was simply lost. Confused by the maze's convolutions.

Livira had no problem remembering the lefts and rights she'd taken, but to see a way through the maze that confined her she really needed to make a map, something she could look at. She selected a large book from the shelves, one that reached her knee when set with the edge of its deep turquoise cover to the ground. The tome was written in the empire tongue, its title *Great Sailing Ships of History: An Architectural Comparison* stamped in black along the spine and surrounded by geometric patterns.

Livira had been hoping to find a blank flyleaf, but the closest *Great Sailing Ships of History* had to offer was the dedication page, blank on one side and on the other bearing only the legend "To Captain Elias with my deepest apologies for the wreck."

With a murmured further apology to Captain Elias, and a second one to the author, A. E. Canulus, Livira tore the page free. The time-foxed sheet dangled from her fingers with all the grace of a severed limb.

There are moments in life when you know with a great and unshakeable certainty that everything will change. When Livira had stood beside the well and looked out to see the sabber approaching through the dancing heat, she had known herself at such a tipping point. Now, with the torn page trembling in her grip, she knew again that she had set her foot upon some portentous new path, though she had no notion of what it might be or what reason she might possibly have for feeling this way. But, blood to bone, she knew it.

Livira felt a weight descend upon her shoulders, the cold disapproval of librarians in untold numbers, generations of them, packing the aisle in ghostly outrage. The library's silence, which she could have sworn could grow no deeper and no thicker, congealed about her, as if the whole chamber, and however many others lay beyond like the alveoli of some great lung, held its breath.

The moment passed. Livira would never have dreamed of such vandalism when introduced to her first book, not even when faced with those arrayed in their tens of thousands upon the shelves of the trainees' library. For weeks each book had seemed a temple, a holy space in which the author became the priest, celebrating something greater even than the work of their own intellect or imagination, each opus a prayer to the infinite that had delivered such wonder into the realms of possibility, placing it in reach of a quill, ink, and a small collection of letters.

That had been last week, that had been yesterday, that had been this morning. Familiarity breeds contempt and Livira was quite certain that when nature next moved her, if the makers of the library still hadn't put in place provision for her to answer its call, she would be wiping herself with another author's heartfelt dedication.

Without the quill and bottle of ink that Arpix had given her, Livira might have had to smear her map in blood. Instead, she executed a decent attempt at capturing the labyrinth on the page. She struggled mainly when it came to cramming all the passages into the too-cramped space. But logic dictated the paths she must have travelled in order to reconnect to the aisles that eventually returned her to the two circles that stared at her like a pair of eyes at the heart of it all.

Livira sat back and considered her work. A possible exit suggested itself quite swiftly. The radical change of perspective from a burrower to a soarer who shared the gods' view made the problem an easy one. She took a swig from her sagging water-skin and got back onto her feet, flexing first one then the other against the ache of so many unaccustomed miles.

With map in hand, Livira set off once more. She had advanced no further than a hundred yards when a distant but terrifying screech tore the silence and left it quivering. Livira clutched her map to her chest as if it might shield her. On the Dust there were many frightening sounds you could hear in the darkness: the triumph of a cratalac on making another kill; the dry scrape of a dust-bear relocating itself in the hope of a morning ambush; the clickety-click of a shell-spider column on the march. But nothing like this broken rage which set her teeth on edge.

Livira held still, listening, hearing nothing but the rapid thump of her heart. In the library's endless quietude the shriek had struck like a hammer. Her ears still rang with it and her mind echoed with its wrongness. It felt like a crime. She was about to move on when it happened again. Several screeches this time, the gaps between them somehow judged to the length where she was almost certain there would not be another. The final one seemed the closest of all. At last, an uncertain quiet crept back and she picked up her map. The route she was following would return her to the circle clearing. Was the thing that seemed to be closing the distance between them with each passing minute tracking her through the aisles . . . or simply waiting for her to arrive?

Approaching the stained circle, Livira was shaken by the loudest screech so far, a sound that made her want to hide her own scream inside it. A sound so loud that it seemed impossible to have come from any creature that might fit between one wall of books and the next. Terror trembled in her limbs like an echo. Still, she had nowhere else to go—if she didn't pass through the circle, she would forever be trapped within a lobe of the maze that, whilst it covered a significant acreage of stone, led nowhere but here.

Livira crept towards the clearing. The more she heard it the more the screeching sounded like the voice of some great raptor. Perhaps one of the rocs that Ella used to tell tales of in her workshop out on the Dust. Birds whose wingspan was so vast it turned day into night and who in the days of forests could uproot half a hundred trees in one taloned foot.

Livira inched her head around the final corner. Nothing. The book-lined circle lay empty. No horror waited for her. Relief filled her lungs only to explode from them in a shriek that was wholly drowned out by the shattering cry rising before her. A creature, which she had mistaken for the stained floor, lifted from the ground. A creature too small for the volume that issued from its midnight beak. A creature that looked for all the world like a battered crow that had barely survived the hailstorm which took most of its feathers.

It hopped awkwardly towards her, trailing a damaged wing. It was scarcely larger than the crows that Livira chased from the bean rows. With her hands clamped over ringing ears Livira stepped forward to meet its advance. The crow or perhaps raven issued its cry once more and, even with her ears covered, the fist of sound shook her so badly that the map came tumbling from her fingers.

Immediately the bird launched forward in an explosion of flapping and clawing. It snagged the map in its beak. Before Livira could stop it, the thief was past her and off down the aisle she'd just left.

"Hey!" Livira gave chase. "Come back!"

Ravens. Always the ravens. When Abel fell to Cain, a raven watched, hungry for the dead man's eyes. When Cain's son laid the foundation stone of Enoch, a raven watched, hungry for shelter. And when Irad raised the first library, a raven settled on the capstone, hungry for knowledge.

Birds of a Feather, *by Robert J. N. Adams*

CHAPTER 20

Livira

Livira gave chase as the raven fled with its prize, the map on which she'd laboured so hard. She'd no desire to have the thing scream at her again but she wasn't going to let it abandon her in the maze either.

The bird wasn't overly fast, what with its broken wing and scarcity of feathers, but it possessed a manic energy and threw itself into fluttering leaps in which it almost flew and managed to cover considerable ground. Livira's exhaustion kept her behind it, as did her curiosity regarding where it might lead her. It seemed reasonable to assume that, like the metal man by the entrance, the bird was one of the guides manufactured by librarians in past ages. Quite why it had turned from helping in the search for books to theft from strangers she couldn't say. Perhaps it was merely broken. Livira knew that people could become very strange as they got old. Neera's grandmother had first forgotten her grandchildren's names, then her daughters', and finally her own. She would wander off into the dust looking for her husband who had died before Neera was even born. The years might have turned this pretend raven strange too.

In the end it led her to a place she'd been before and danced an angry jig at the base of the shelves.

"Why here?" Livira arrived and stood, leaning forwards, hands on her thighs to prevent her from folding.

The bird regarded her with the bright black stones of its eyes. It shook the map in its beak at her, all belligerence and intensity.

Livira lunged for it. "That's mine."

The bird hopped out of reach and stopped. It glanced from her to the shelves, repeated the action, repeated it again, the map flapping. Slowly Livira went to the shelf, arm raised, fingers questing as she tried to gauge where the bird was staring.

"Oh." Her fingers came to rest on the spine of a large book. *Great Sailing Ships of History*, by A. E. Canulus. The volume from which she had torn the dedication page that she had drawn her map on.

The raven dropped the map and opened its beak for one of its ear-shattering screeches.

"No!" Livira raised an open hand while ducking to snatch up the map. "No, wait, I'll put it back!"

The bird held its breath, watching her with glittering eyes.

With some effort Livira pulled the book back out of the shelf and opened it to the place she'd ripped the page from. She eyed her map with a frown, biting her lip as if the pain would help imprint it on her memory. The bird opened its beak, impatient at the delay.

"Shush, you. It's done." Livira smoothed the dedication page into place, the apology to Captain Elias restored, and closed the book. "There. All good." She hefted it back onto the shelf. "Now what can you—"

The raven launched itself at her, a black squall of beating wings. She felt a sharp pain at her hip.

"Ouch!" She threw the bird back. "That hurt! You pecked me!"

The raven screamed at her from where it lay in disarray on the floor, though slightly less loudly, perhaps needing to gather itself for full effect.

Livira patted her thigh, looking for any blood seeping through her robe. The raven had torn a small hole in the blue wool. Reaching inside she found that the hole aligned with an internal pocket, from which, with some surprise, she withdrew her scrap, the text-covered corner that she'd found long ago in the Dust, and which had been somewhat forgotten during these past few weeks, surrounded as she was by whole pages covered with writing and bound into whole books.

"SQUAAAAAARK!"

The raven righted itself and looked at her expectantly before stalking off up the aisle, back the way they'd come. Livira stood holding her scrap and watched the bird go, until the point it looked back over its shoulder at her and repeated its call a fraction louder—then she followed it.

"What? I've got to put this back too?" Livira didn't want to part with her scrap despite feeling that holding on to it was like clutching a grain of sand while surrounded by a desert. "Who put you in charge?" Even so, she followed the raven. At least it had a destination in mind, and she was curious to see the book from which her corner had been torn. Also, she didn't want the bird to yell at her anymore.

The raven led her back to the clearing with the stain, its pace more sedate now that it knew she was cooperating, or perhaps it too was tired. The path it took out of the labyrinth was the one that Livira had plotted out and she took some satisfaction in the fact.

Once they reached new territory, she resumed her placing of books to mark the way. The raven watched her with evident disapproval but didn't choose to make a fight of it. It seemed prepared to tolerate disruption but not damage.

A few dozen more twists and turns brought them back to the straight lines and right-angled corners that dominated the library. Livira found herself relieved, even though she was really just exchanging one kind of lost for another.

The raven led with a sense of purpose, taking her across the chamber towards the door opposite the one she entered by. After a near infinity of narrow aisles they broke into a clearing before the corridor.

Momentarily filled with the energy that change can infuse, Livira overtook the bird's hopping and raced ahead to the door, arriving breathless. She slapped both hands to the white surface, pulled them back and slapped them down again. The door, which was supposed to melt into mist, didn't register the impact of Livira's hands in any way.

"It's not working!" Livira spun around to fix the raven with an accusing stare. A sudden fear seized her. What if the door she'd come in by no longer melted away at her touch? What if she were trapped in this second chamber, locked away from her classmates through simple ignorance of some small trick required for returning?

The raven continued its jerky advance, paying her no attention.

"It's locked," Livira repeated. But as the bird tapped the blackness of its beak to the pristine white of the door the whole thing melted away like well-mist before the sun's glare. Livira frowned critically at her hand and cast a side-eyed glance at the raven's beak. "It was locked . . ."

The raven carried on, paying Livira no heed, and after a pause, she followed it. A hundred yards of corridor led to a third chamber, seeming just as huge as the previous two. The clearing before the door was rectangular. The shelves were taller, fashioned from what looked like black wood, the gaps between them wider. It was still the library but somehow, although so much was exactly the same, it managed at the same time to seem utterly alien.

Livira took a deep breath. The place even smelled different. The smell of books was something she had come to appreciate over her weeks in the outer library. The scent of old glue, of polished leather, dry parchment, the mustiness in the air as the spores of a thousand moulds and fungi sought purchase: it was the aroma of time itself, the scent of passing years. And when you opened a book, especially one that had waited lifetimes for someone to turn its cover, that first breath was of something new, almost individual.

The foxing that marked almost every page had a sourness to it. Sometimes Livira would stare at the brownish patination instead of the text, wondering what alternate story might be read there if she only knew the language. She thought of it as time's fingerprints left on the whiteness of the page, or the marks of water that never was, tears that never fell.

The Dust had been haunted by the ghost of the water which once filled the vanished lake. The phantoms of long-departed waves still rippled the light, and their whispering mocked the last of the dying trees. That same invisible ocean seemed to have flooded the library and left its touch on every page.

"Something's different here." Livira followed the raven, whose progress hadn't slowed one iota. It chose an aisle and wove its erratic path between the opposing shelves. Livira paused to check the spines of the first books. She was used to not understanding the language, and often not recognising it. Most of the alphabets in the first chamber had been ones she was now acquainted with, thanks to what Meelan had called the steel trap of her memory. Less so in the second chamber. But here, in the third of the chambers she'd entered, the writing on the spines seemed like something different entirely, scattered dots and ridges, some raised, some indented. The bird squawked at her, and she hurried after it.

DIFFERENCES ASIDE, THE chamber, like the others, demonstrated a patchwork of approaches. As if the shelf-builders started by one door and built outwards over many generations, using different materials, different designs, stamping the spirit of their age onto the effort, eschewing tradition. Did the first to come here simply find vast empty rooms? And if so . . . who decreed that books be stored here?

Exhaustion began to sink its teeth again and Livira longed for sleep— but what she saw around the next corner woke her up. Something she hadn't seen for over a month and had never expected to find in this place.

"It's dark . . ."

It was either darkness she saw before her, or a black mist filling the space between the two walls of the aisle and reaching a good two yards up them. A black mist would make more sense, for surely darkness didn't behave like this, standing shoulder to shoulder with the light and separated by a sharp divisor. But it looked like darkness as the raven hopped into it without pause.

Meelan had said something ominous when she'd asked if it ever got dark in the library. She remembered his unsettling growl as he'd said, "In places." Livira gathered her scattered courage. She tightened her jaw. Had Meelan ever really seen it himself? Had he been *this* far out before? She stepped closer to the black wall barring her way. It didn't look like mist. It seemed like darkness as she reached in tentatively, pulling her fingers swiftly back for examination. If it were a black mist then it was one that couldn't be felt or disturbed. The bird had been worryingly silent since it went in . . . "Dung on it!" Livira plunged forward and immediately found herself in darkest night. She pulled back and blinked in the light.

"SQUAWK!"

The bird's cry, like nails scraped down Master Logaris's chalkboard,

summoned her on, and thus commanded she followed, arms questing before her.

Livira inched forward, listening hard for the scrapes and stutters of the
raven ahead of her. The library had still to show her any horrors, and yet all
it took to summon monsters from her imagination was to veil her sight.
She pictured huge and silent spiders clinging to the shelves above her,
watching with too many eyes as she walked blindly towards their webs. She
imagined her double, walking noiselessly behind her, identical in every
detail save for the void of its eyes and the murder twitching in its fingertips.
She imagined—

"Oh." The darkness vanished as suddenly as if she had just opened her
eyes.

The raven raised its head from pecking at the cover of a small black
book that lay on the floor a yard ahead of Livira. It eyed the misplaced
tome with that same air of agitation it had when seeing Livira set the
marker books she hoped would lead her home. Livira scooped the book up,
planning to replace it and thereby win some measure of approval from her
guide. She looked around for the slot that would reveal where it had come
from. There wasn't one.

She turned the book over in her hands. The edges of the pages were also
black, and the title proved impossible to see, only revealing itself under her
fingers as an unintelligible series of bumps and dents in whatever hide
had been used to bind the covers. Wondering if the pages were similarly
indented Livira opened the book. A shriek escaped her, and she nearly
dropped it. She'd gone blind! *She'd gone blind!* Panic subsided as she
realised that it must just be that the darkness had returned after a brief
respite.

"Bird?"

Silence.

"Bird!" Livira called more loudly. Silence answered. She drew a breath
and shouted. "Hey! You! Get me out of here." She was about to add something about the noisiest thing in the whole library picking a fine time to go
quiet when it squawked again. With a sigh she advanced towards it, arms
out once more, one hand clutching the open book.

At a snail's pace she followed the raven for several hundred yards before another squawk indicated that it had changed direction. She made the turn, brushing rows of spines with an outstretched hand. "How far does this dark go?"

"SQUAWK!" This call somehow managed to sound both disdainful and slightly mocking despite the raucous volume.

Livira realised with some horror that there was no reason it shouldn't go on for mile after mile. She had only a sense of optimism to armour her against the idea. There was no particular reason why half the library couldn't be in this strange night while the other half existed in its equally strange day. No reason except that people needed to see to choose and read books. But Livira had already speculated that the library wasn't necessarily built by or for people. Certainly not people like her.

The blind march continued for what seemed an age, followed by another age. What if she actually had gone blind? What if the light was still there and her eyes had simply ceased to work? She plodded on, haunted by strange thoughts, led by the raven's scratch and flutter.

Livira stumbled time and again, bumping into the shelves. Eventually she walked headlong into the shelving at a T-junction, bruising her hands and dropping the small black book she'd been carrying all this while.

"Dammit to the hells. All the hells!" She wanted to swear like Malar had done, but the soldier's words didn't fit in her mouth, and she knew she would sound and feel silly. She fell to her knees, patting the ground for the book. "There you are." Her fingers found the open cover. She picked the book back up, closing it. Suddenly she could see. The light stung her eyes, making her shield them. "How . . ." A strange suspicion sank its teeth. "No?" She opened the book. Darkness. She closed it. Light. She opened the book, set it down, and backed away through the darkness. After just a handful of paces she broke into the light again with no warning. Darkness surrounded the open book in a dome maybe five yards across.

Livira spun around, fixing the raven with an accusing stare. "You let me walk around in that . . . FOR HOURS!"

The raven shrugged. Livira hadn't known birds could shrug. She hadn't known this one would close open books either, but that's what it must have done when she thought it was just pecking idly at the cover.

Livira scowled and then retraced her steps into the darkness. Outside the bird squawked at her. "And aren't ravens supposed to caw?" Livira shouted back. The criticism seemed to strike home as her guide held its voice long enough for her to find the book once more, close it, and put it into an inner pocket. "What?" She returned the raven's stare. "I'm borrowing it. It's all right if I borrow *all* of a book. It's just borrowing pieces that you object to." She strode on and the raven scuttled ahead, fighting to keep its lead.

Understandably, the vast majority of literature on childbirth describes the process from the mother's perspective or that of the physician in attendance. Occasionally, the father's point of view is covered, be it striding the corridors whilst puffing furiously on cigars, or hip-deep in the birthing pool shouting misguided encouragement. The person being thrust into a new world through a wet tunnel is generally overlooked.

The Three Hundred Lives of Jemimah Button, *by Jemimah Button*

CHAPTER 21

Evar

E var sank into the pool. He clutched to his chest the weight of iron book hinges, cogwheels, and other scrap scavenged from the floor of the library. The coldness of the water was always a shock. He'd lived a life where the temperature never changed, where the light never changed, a life without any sound other than that they made themselves. Now everything was change. The water pressed on him from all sides, darkness too, far above him the circle where the light still sparkled and danced was rapidly diminishing. A strange, muted rush filled his ears, emptiness beneath his questing feet.

If he let go of his burden, he might still regain the surface, he might fill his lungs once more. He'd never gone much deeper than the length of his arms, and whether even now he could survive the return he didn't know. His chest ached with the demand for air. Every part of him screamed that he should abandon his precious burden to the depths and strike for the light. He was being stupid. He was going to die—to kill himself—and for what? For a misunderstood line scrawled in a random book. And still Evar clutched his arms to him and yet another fathom passed as the light dimmed both outside him and within.

He had spent his whole life searching for a way out. His brothers, his sister, their people before them, the hundreds who had lived in this chamber for centuries, all of them had tried and failed. Finding the way wasn't going to be a matter of half measures. Maybe he would pay for this attempt with his last breath, but a life trapped among the stacks had become a coin he was prepared to spend.

The darkness grew, within and without.

Suddenly Evar was spluttering, gasping for breath, hauling himself out of the water, back in the light. He collapsed, eyes tight shut, face down, panting. The weights he'd held in his arms were gone, replaced by the crushing burden of his failure. The life he hadn't *wanted* to sacrifice but was prepared to give now stretched before him, feeling like a burden too. A life that in this place promised just the long march of years, across which the only change would be him and his siblings growing old, together and alone.

He stopped halfway through another much-needed breath. He wasn't in the library. Things towered all around him, but they were not book towers. The ground beneath his hands was soft and furry and green. Green strands reached up between his spread fingers. Grass! It had to be grass. And trees. He'd seen illustrations—of trees just like these—but somehow it hadn't prepared him for the greenness of their leaves, the complexity of their branches, the slow, heavy life right there beneath gnarled bark, the thick and tangled roots questing into the soil. A forest! The very thing that the stacks now seemed a sad parody of. And pools! Pools everywhere, spaced between the trees, marching away in all directions, rows of them stretching away into a verdant, emerald infinity.

Evar levered himself up. The softness of the ground was a marvel. He realised with a start that he wasn't wet. The trees caught his attention again, branches just out of reach, and the pools, reflecting the greenness. To rest his eyes on such difference, the colours, the textures . . . It wouldn't have such an impact on the others: to hear them speak they wandered strange new worlds every time their turn in the Mechanism came, but to Evar, who remembered nothing except the stacks, it was as if a dream had come to life and swallowed him whole.

The others . . . Clovis would be furious. She'd searched for exits with the rest of course, but only to barricade them and then plan her assault on the sabbers.

Evar got to his feet: a gentle motion that turned into a sudden lunge as he realised that something dark was following him. He spun with a harsh cry, lashing out at his attacker, only to stand confused and staring. The black shape on the grass twitched with pent-up energy as if about to strike. He changed to a better defensive stance and his opponent moved too, twisting itself across the ground. He saw with a start that it had already reached all the way to his feet. But it had no substance to it. The thing lay flat on the ground. He could see the grass through it . . .

Shadow . . . Evar had read about the concept many times. He raised his hand and a shadow hand aped him, though its shape was hard to pick out amongst the latticework shadow of branch and leaf. He laughed. Amused, embarrassed, fascinated. "I have a shadow!" The library had never given him one. For a long while Evar did nothing but play with his new friend.

The place was silent, but it was a different kind of silence to that of the library. This was the peace of green things growing. Taking his gaze away from the fascination of his shadow, Evar made a slow rotation, taking it all in. The pool was circular, two yards across, just like the one he had jumped into, save that this one sat in a gentle incline with short-cropped grass growing to the water's edge and the roots of trees reaching in to drink. All of the pools were identical and the regularity of their spacing made it clear that whatever this place was, it had been designed rather than being thrown up at nature's whim. The trees joined arms above the pools, affording a thousand glimpses of blue between the still leaves, a broken mosaic of what Evar had to assume was open sky.

He ran a hand over his chest, still surprised to find himself dry. How long had he lain there? If he'd passed out and dried while he lay there then why was he gasping for breath when he came to? He completed his slow turn and, having seen nothing save trees and grass and pools he went to set his hand to the trunk of the nearest tree. He knew that the wood from which the reading desks were made was once a living thing, but he had never expected to meet the source. Paper too could be made from wood, so the stacks not only mimicked a forest but were in part made from one. The roughness beneath his fingertips was as strange as the softness of the ground and the tickle of grass. For a moment these wholly new sensations stopped the flow of questions. But that flow could only be dammed for so long before one burst out.

"What is this place?" He stared at the countless pools. The one by his feet was a gateway to the pool—the only pool he'd ever known—and by extension it was a gateway to the library. Were these others also gateways to the library? Different parts of it? Or different libraries, or entirely new places—wild forests, dune-rippled deserts, cities thronging with people? He took a step towards the nearest of the other pools, then another, before turning and taking out his knife from the sheath at his hip. He stuck it into the ground to signify that this pool among all the others was the one from which he had emerged and through which he hoped a return was possible. He could have marked it without leaving something of such great value but to carve a symbol upon the ground or to break a branch from the tree and set it as a flagstaff seemed too great an act of vandalism for one so newly arrived.

"One thing's for sure, I'm not in kansas anymore." It was a phrase in half the languages he knew and one that had led to a saying almost as ancient: "We don't even know what kansas is anymore." Mayland said that in the histories some held it to be a real place, some a mythical city, and others still an enlightened state of being. Evar leaned towards agreeing with those who thought it was a state.

Still in a daze of newness he went to the next pool. There were, he noted, four pools equidistant from his, since they appeared to be laid out on a grid, but this one was nearest to where he had emerged from his pool.

In a sudden panic he remembered the book inside his jerkin and pulled it out, hoping that the water hadn't ruined it. Taking it with him had been a calculated risk. He had determined to find the exit and given no consideration to a return.

He turned to the first page, relieved to find the paper dry and the line of text undamaged. He closed it and approached the pool. Its surface showed only a reflection of sky and leaves, broken apart by ripples when he touched the water with a tentative toe. He circled the edge, hoping that he wasn't required to nearly drown himself again to leave the wood.

If there had been only one other pool Evar would probably have jumped into it after just a short while to appreciate the strangeness of his surroundings. But there was something about the number of choices that paralysed him. Rather like when it came to choosing a new book from the stacks. The knowledge that he couldn't possibly read all the books on offer put a peculiar pressure on choosing his next read. There must be diamonds out there, the best book in a thousand, the best book in a million, and surely he didn't want to waste his time reading one that was merely adequate when he could be reading one of those diamonds? So instead, he often wasted his time hunting for a read instead of reading.

Here the problem was similar. With so many places he could go, how did he decide? The total lack of information might make a random decision the obvious way forward, but for now Evar decided to explore a little and see if there might be some clues on which to base a choice. After all, he had marked his pool with a knife. Might there not be other markers out there along the rows?

Evar passed the pool by and moved on to the next. He studied the ground, the tree trunks, and even the pattern of their branches for clues. It still felt like a dream to be here, somewhere different. He breathed in the air, rich with strange aromas and absent the scent of mouldering books that had dominated every breath he'd ever taken to this point.

It would be beautiful just for its difference, but the place truly held a peace to it that Evar hadn't known he needed. It was somewhere you could lie down and sleep, perhaps for years, and wake up a new person.

He moved on to examine the tree beside another pool. The fifth along from his. The rough whorls in the bark put him in mind of a face, and for some small fraction of a second he saw her, there in the shadows of his imagination. He glimpsed a woman's eyes, the curve of her cheek, and he knew it was her. The book in his hand seemed to pulse. He held it up, and for a moment the shape on its cover, the figure of a young woman, described by so many interwoven threads . . . held a shadowed face.

She had been there with him, in whatever world the Mechanism had stolen him away into. She had been there through those missing years. She was the core of it. Important to him in ways he couldn't explain or properly remember. But for a moment he had held her face in his memory like a dissolving fragment of a waking dream.

Evar studied the water. Leaves and sky: reflections patterned the still surface. Was this the pool he should try to leave by? Or was his stirring memory a coincidence, driven by this place rather than by this specific pool? He decided to walk on down the row. If he found nothing better, he could return to this one, five down from where he started.

Tantalising wisps of memory continued to tease him as he walked between pools and as he paused to study them. Sensations of places, of open skies, of wind on his face. The feel of her hand in his. He walked on, hardly looking now, past ten pools, twenty, maybe more, enthralled in this slow awakening.

"What?" Evar stopped dead, shaken from his reverie. The pool before him didn't reflect the leaves above, or anything else. It was as black as the tunnel into the char wall. He couldn't tell if there was even any water there, or just a midnight void, a shaft straight down into the under-world. Disturbingly, he had almost stepped into it, and he had no idea if it had been black all along or if it had darkened at his approach. Surely he would have noticed it as he walked the row had it been a tar pit all along?

A white hand suddenly emerged from the blackness near the edge of the pool and pressed itself to the underside of the surface. Evar stepped back sharply, shocked by the suddenness of it. He tensed, waiting for something to emerge, but the water didn't so much as ripple. Just a hand, the palm pressed to the surface as if it were unable to pass through, fingers splayed, the rest lost in the darkness beneath. The hand slid to the side, tearing at the barrier, seeking a way through and finding none.

Evar's momentary fear for himself turned to fear for the person lost beneath. He had nearly drowned getting to this place himself. The mem-ory of that desperation for air made him gasp. He hurried forward, falling to his knees, and reached towards the hand. He stopped short, fingers hesitating, seized by a host of fears. The only strangers he'd ever met had been Escapes that wanted to destroy him, to drink his soul and wear his skin. What any of them wouldn't have given to have him take their hand in his he couldn't say.

And there it was again, that flash of memory haunting the recesses of his mind, her face seen and yet not seen. The woman whose name his lips knew but couldn't speak . . . surely this was her . . . and he knew, in that moment, that even if the pool had been a pit of burning coals he would have reached in to save her.

The importance of "between" is often overlooked in the hurry of getting from one place to another. In truth it is these interstitial spaces which, in their linking of this to that and of now to then, might be considered a more fundamental layer in reality's manifold.

Connective Tissue, *by C. S. Leylandii*

CHAPTER 22

Livira

The raven seemed to be tiring. It had entirely stopped making attempts to launch itself into the air and its hopping gait had become more of a plod, both wings trailing on the floor, several of its sparse feathers looking as if they might be abandoned in its wake. Livira wondered if it would recover its strength by resting—did it need to eat like a real bird? She thought it unlikely that it had endured for many lifetimes only to expire during its bullying of her. Though perhaps it had spent decades perched atop a shelf deep in the chamber waiting for some book crime sufficiently heinous to bring it down to ground level. Making such an ear-splitting cry had to take something out of it, surely?

Livira was considering offering to carry the guide when without warning it stopped and directed its beady gaze upwards.

"What?" Livira gazed up at the shelves.

The raven made a sound that was actually closer to a caw than a squawk.

"We're here?" Livira looked around. "Really?"

The raven refused to look at her, keeping its stare on what she realised must be the book from which her scrap was torn.

"This one?" She reached up to touch the ridged spine of a fat tome on the shelf. Silence. She moved to the next. "This one?" She waited then reached for the next. "This—"

"SQUAWK!" The sound nearly made her wet herself.

"Gods dammit!" She pulled the book out and staggered beneath its weight. The thing was as heavy as a small child. A big small child.

She set it on the floor before the raven, rubbing her aching arms. The book was a good two feet tall, covered with a hide that still bore the pebbly texture of whatever beast originally wore the skin. The legend indented into the cover and gold-foiled was presumably the title and author. The unreadable text matched the alphabet on Livira's scrap. Metal hinges reinforced the structure, dark and time-polished.

"A lock!" Livira spread her hands in exasperation. "Who puts a lock on a book?" She knelt and put her finger to the keyhole. A lock had to mean that some books should not be read by some people. She wondered who got to decide such things and why. Was the book being protected against the wrong people, or were people being protected from the knowledge it held? She would have complained that if books needed locks, then didn't the whole library—but she remembered that the white door had refused her. She was only standing here because the bird at her feet could go where she could not.

Livira fished her scrap from her pocket. "This really came from here?" She stroked her fingers across the cover in front of her. The lettering in dark grey on black was hard to see but it was the same alphabet as her scrap bore. What had they called it? "Crunian," Livira spoke the name out loud. "Crunian Four." Lord Algar had been the one to narrow it to a particular dialect. "You're not much of a guide really," Livira complained. "Couldn't they have made one that could answer questions?" She raised her hand as the bird opened its beak. "With words!"

The bird closed its beak.

"Well, look, I can't put this back"—Livira pushed her scrap against the edges of the pages—"if the book won't open." She was fond of her scrap and despite the distance she'd had to walk she didn't feel too bad about not being able to return it. She looked at the familiar markings. It was something she'd brought with her from the Dust. The only thing she still had. Even the clothes she'd worn were gone. She'd found it and it was hers. Livira stood up. "It's really time I should be getting back." It was past time, in fact. She was sure of it. There was no way her exploration had taken less than a day and in her current state of exhaustion the return would take longer. She regarded the raven and it looked back at her with its head cocked to one side. "This has been . . ." Livira hunted through her recently expanded vocabulary for a word that fitted. ". . . educational." It was the kindest thing she could find to say that wasn't all lie. "Can I . . ." She looked around to see if there were somewhere she could set the raven that was more dignified than the floor. There wasn't. "Goodbye then." She gave a small bow like the ones she'd seen city people do outside the Allocation Hall, then turned to go.

"SQUAWK!" The cry hit her between the shoulder blades, setting her teeth on edge and making her stumble.

"What!" She spun around. "I can't open the damn book!"

The bird just watched her.

"All right. All right." Livira set the scrap down on the book's cover, not sure that she would leave it but prepared to test herself and see how it felt. Actually, it felt a lot better than being pursued by a screeching raven for the next few miles. "There! Happy?"

Livira turned to go.

"SQUAWK!"

"Oh, come on!" Livira turned back slowly. "I can't leave with the corner. I can't leave without it. I can't open the book . . ."

With a grunt of effort, she picked up the book and the scrap together. She walked away, already feeling the strain in her arms. The raven followed. "Really? This is what you want?"

With a burst of energy, the bird got ahead of her, a guide once more. At the next turning it veered to the left.

"It's this way back." Livira nodded to the book she'd set on the floor to indicate the way. "You're just going to yell at me if I go that way, aren't you?"

Livira followed the bird, abandoning the return path. An image of raven wings poking out from beneath the heavy tome bubbled up unbidden from the undercurrent of her thoughts. It wasn't something she wanted to do. But then again neither were any of the alternatives. She followed, labouring beneath her burden, pushing the ethics of the situation around in her mind. She had to admit that if a crow had landed among the bean rows at the settlement, she would have immediately taken any opportunity to kill it. A crow livened up bean soup considerably. Most things did.

She'd kill a crow if she were hungry. This thing wasn't even properly alive. It was cogs and wire or some such cleverness. But it was also more than a regular crow or raven. And not only was it possessed of the intelligence to navigate the library with purpose, it was old beyond knowing, something precious, made with lost lore, bound with secrets. Flattening it beneath a book merely to escape the irritation of its scolding seemed . . . Livira couldn't find the word, but whatever the word was it was slowly turning into "necessary" with each passing step.

"I can't do this." Livira dropped the book. It hit the floor flat with a shockingly loud slap. She stuffed the scrap in her pocket and rubbed her aching biceps. She looked to see what her guide would do, but something further down the aisle caught her eye. Some object on the floor a hundred yards past the raven. A thing that wasn't a book. And more than that, there was an oddness going on with the shelves beside it. Something her eyes couldn't make sense of. She started forward.

"SQUAWK!"

"Gods DAMN you, bird!" Livira picked up the book and hurried forward with it hugged to her chest once more.

The object on the ground was a person, or rather something made in the shape of a person. She was, like the metal man at the second door, an imitation, but this time in grey stone, the same grey stone that the floor and walls were made of. There were no indications of joints—she could be a statue, if the sculptor had chosen to carve her face down to the floor as if she had collapsed, head to one side, one arm outstretched. The outstretched arm led to the second thing that was perhaps still more strange. A circle of shimmering light that stood almost as if it were a doorway into the shelves. It was taller than Livira could reach but not much. The grey woman's hand stretched towards the light, her fingers not quite making contact.

Livira knelt and set her book down. She touched the woman. Hard as stone, smooth, slightly cold. She had been made, or carved, with insufficient detail to convince anyone that she was real. She wore no clothes but didn't appear to have anything to hide. Her hair wasn't hair, just the shape of it around her head, ignoring gravity's pull. She appeared to be perfect in all regards save for a curious cratered wound to the side of her forehead not pressed to the ground. The indentation was no bigger than a thumbprint and maybe a third of an inch deep.

"Who is she?" Livira turned to the raven as it caught her up.

The raven hopped around the fallen woman cautiously, observing her from all angles. It made a soft cawing sound at the back of its throat. A mournful noise. And pecked gently at the figure's shoulder.

"Was this where you were leading me? Can you wake her up?" Livira thought that the raven's cry might, at full volume, wake the dead.

The raven repeated its sorrowful cawing.

Livira pursed her lips. She looked at the circle of light. The shimmers reminded her of water in a pail and the sunlight dancing across it. She knelt and studied the woman's hand. Her fingers stretched towards the light. The circle stood flush against the shelves. What had she been reaching for? It didn't make sense unless there was a gap behind the curtain of shimmers. Was it placed here to hide something? Perhaps a doorway had been cut through the shelves allowing access to the next aisle. Was there some secret hidden here?

Although she wasn't generally given to caution, Livira felt that a measure of it might be called for. The woman appeared to have been felled by a blow to the head. And given that she was made of stone it must have been a remarkably hard blow. Even so, walking away from a mystery wasn't something Livira could do. Certainly not when it had taken the breaking of many rules and the expenditure of all her stamina to find this particular mystery. She reached a hand towards the circle of light, then pulled it back. She looked at the bird.

"We should be clever about this. Use our advantages." She withdrew the small black book from her inner pocket. "If I go through there and something chases me out it's going to run smack into the shelves if it can't see . . . But I'll know to turn left and run." She opened the book, and everything went black. She placed the volume on the floor. "You should stay here, bird. With her. I don't think you're very fast anymore. Just be careful and hide if there's trouble."

Now that it came to it, Livira didn't feel like going into the light at all. She couldn't even see it, but she knew it was there. She reached towards it.

"I'll just feel around a bit." She let the woman's arm guide her own, sliding her fingers along the back of the cold stone hand. She touched the light.

"Oh." Her fingertips met resistance. She pushed but made no progress. Setting her palm flat against the surface she began to quest for some gap in it, pushing and feeling only the slightest give. "I don't think—" And without warning a stranger's hand closed around hers and yanked her forwards.

. . . from Ectran, primarily boats fishing close to the Broken Shore. All of which suggests that rather than an invasion, what we are seeing is in fact a migration. Reliable sources west of the Thellion Confederacy are rare, but the names skour, scare, scar, and, most commonly, skeer, crop up time and again. We don't know the nature of this foe that has driven such a vast horde of sabbers from their ancestral lands. But one can be sure that—even when we discard fanciful tales of vast white spiders devouring all they encounter—they must be implacable to make the sabbers know fear.

Intelligence report XXVI-CXX, *from the desk of Lord Algar Omesta*

CHAPTER 23

Evar

Evar's fingers closed around the hand in the black pool and in a confusion of flying water he found himself on his back at the pool's edge with a stranger on all fours beside him. A dark-maned girl, in a blue robe, gasping for air.

"You're not her." Evar had often imagined meeting someone new, usually a character from the pages of one of the books he so regularly consumed, someone—*anyone*—other than the three people he spent all his days with. He had never imagined that the first words out of his mouth would be a complaint that the stranger was the wrong person. He sat up and shuffled back to create some space between them.

The girl raised her head and gave him a withering look. She got to her knees. She was a child. A skinny, ink-stained child with a bruised face. Strangely, the blue robe she wore was dry, not even splashed, though it *was* spattered with dark stains that were not ink.

"Who are you?" Evar asked, but at that point she noticed her surroundings for the first time and stood, turning in a slow circle, drinking it all in. Evar stood too.

Eventually the girl's dark eyes returned to him. "You're very tall."

"I . . ." The unexpected observation caught him off balance. "You're quite short." He frowned and tried to get the conversation back on track. "Where did you come from?"

The girl elevated one eyebrow at that and glanced meaningfully back at the pool's black water, still dancing from her sudden emergence.

"I mean, what's down there?"

"Down?" The girl echoed his frown. "I came from the library. I'm Livira. Who are you?"

"Evar Eventari." The Assistant had always called him that. Whether it was his name when he first stepped into the Mechanism, he wasn't sure. He opened his mouth and found he'd run out of words. A stranger. An actual stranger. How did you speak to people you didn't know?

"What is this place?" Livira wandered over to the next pool.

"I . . ." Evar watched the child go. She was very bold for someone so small. "I don't know." And then, because it seemed an insufficient answer: "I was looking for someone."

Livira turned round and offered a lopsided grin, the side of her mouth swollen from some recent impact. "You found someone."

"A woman," he said.

"Oh." She looked back at the pool she stood beside. "Each of these must go somewhere else. This is an in-between kind of place. How many have you tried?"

"Uh, none."

"None!" Livira peered at him. "Have you only just got here?"

"I was choosing," he said defensively. "There are a lot of them."

"You came from the library too?"

He nodded. "But this was the only way out from my part. We've been trapped for years, centuries. We—"

"What's her name?"

"Whose?" For a moment Evar could only think of Clovis.

Livira rolled her eyes and came back to the black pool. "The woman you're looking for." She reached into her pocket and pulled out a gleaming brass claw. Kneeling she began to cut a mark into the turf beside the water.

"I, uh, I don't know her name."

Livira stood up to admire her handiwork. The torn corner of a page lay on the grass beside her foot. "You don't know where you are or who you're looking for?" She glanced his way, perhaps impressed by him for the first time. "I'm doing the same sort of thing myself. Only I'm after a book I can't read for someone I hate."

"Which book do you want?" It didn't seem important, but Evar felt it steered the conversation away from the fact he didn't even know who he was searching for.

"*Reflections on Solitude*, by Arqnaxis Lox," the girl said. "It's written in Relquian."

Evar furrowed his brow. He'd never even heard of Relquian, let alone the book. "I—" But a figure glimpsed between the trees stole whatever he'd been about to say. "The Assistant!" He started to run.

He could see her more clearly now, putting something down beside a distant pool. "Hey! It's me!"

He leapt a pool in one bound and wove his path between two trees, ducking where the boughs hung low. The Assistant turned away, dappled sunlight gleaming on white enamel shoulders.

"Wait!"

But between one moment and the next, in the briefest of gaps as intervening trees interrupted his line of sight, she was gone. He arrived at the pool seconds later to find it still dancing. A book lay on the grass at the edge. He picked it up. A small thing bound in creamy leather. He couldn't read the title.

"You . . ." Livira arrived, panting. She leaned against a tree and caught her breath. "You're so fast!"

"You should see my brother Starval. And my sister." Kerrol was the only one he could outrun now that Mayland was gone. He looked at the pool again. "I saw the Assistant. I don't know why she left." He stared, trying to see past the surface and the sunlight. "I think maybe she wants me to follow."

"That was an assistant?" Livira blinked and pushed away from the tree, looking around as if the Assistant might still be there, hiding behind another trunk.

"An Assistant?" Evar repeated the girl's strange phraseology.

"I saw one too." She waved her hand in the direction they'd come from. "Back there. But she was grey. I think someone broke her."

Evar's eyes widened. "There's more than one?"

She didn't seem certain now. "That's what Arpix told me . . ."

"Who?"

"Arpix. He's a friend. Well. I think . . ." She frowned. "He *is* a friend. And Jella and Carlotte and Meelan. I had other friends but—"

Evar raised a hand to cut her off. More strangers. One was overwhelming. His thoughts returned to the Assistant by the pool. She had been very white, now he thought about it, not the old ivory he was used to. "Did they say how many there are?"

"No. Just that there weren't a lot, and you sometimes find one in the aisles." Livira squinted at the book in his hand. "Did she leave that?"

Evar offered it to her. "It was by the pool."

The girl frowned at him and opened her mouth to speak but something about the book caught her attention. "This is it!" She shook her head. "I don't believe this . . ."

"It?"

"*Reflections on Solitude.*" She shook the book at him. "This is crazy! How is it here? What is this place?"

"I don't know." Evar was still struggling with the idea that there might be more than one assistant. Common sense told him that if there were many people then there could equally well be more than one assistant. But emotionally he couldn't quite wrap himself around the concept. "Do you have soldiers too?"

"Yes, lots." She waved the question away, still fixated on the book in her hand. "I don't understand . . . The library is only supposed to have one copy of each."

"Maybe these don't all lead to the same library," Evar said.

"There's more than one library?" Livira, who had been wrestling with the idea of many copies of a book, seemed to find the notion of multiple libraries as outlandish as Evar found the notion of multiple assistants.

Evar shrugged. "My brother thought so. There are mythologies about the first library and the shadows it casts. He liked the one about Irad who made the library and Jaspeth who wanted to unmake it—warring brothers who—" A sudden fear seized him. "We should go back. Before we lose the pool." Having raced past so many pools and trees the place seemed much bigger now.

Livira appeared unconcerned. "I know the way." But she turned round and started walking back. "Why do you want to find this woman whose name you don't know?"

The question caught Evar off guard. He'd told this strange child more than he'd told any of his family. "She . . ." He could almost see her behind his eyes. "She's part of me." It was the truth—he knew that now he'd spoken the words. "She's been with me my whole life—or since I was younger than you, at least." The woods were warmer than the library. Patches of sunlight slid across Evar as he walked; he couldn't feel them, but they were there, and if he closed his eyes they would still be there, warming him. The woman was like that. The wood wasn't completely silent, not like the library. There were sounds beneath hearing, sounds that he knew were there, like the sliding sunlight. Trees drinking, slaking their slow thirst. Grass growing. And above them, despite the lack of wind, the occasional creak, the slight flutter of leaves. And somewhere . . . somewhere . . . a distant song, the high, sweet, heartbreak that must be birdsong. "There's a hole through the heart of me," Evar said. "And it won't be gone until I find her." The hurt, which had lived in his bones, so deep that he'd grown around it without recognition, trembled now in his voice, threatening to crack it.

"I'll help you."

She said it so lightly that Evar took a moment to understand her. He realised that they were back at the very edge of the black pool. One more step and he'd be swimming. "You will?"

"You helped me find my book." She smiled and the smile lit her up. Beneath the dirt and bruises she had an open face, strong-featured, dark eyes full of intelligence and mischief. "I'll help you find your girlfriend."

Evar looked down at the grass. "She's not my . . ." But maybe she was? The others had spent ten years in the Mechanism. They'd all emerged the same age as when they went in but carrying ten years in their heads—ten years of war in Clovis's, ten years of murder and secrets for Starval, and for

Evar a wound a decade deep. "Thank you." He turned to meet Livira's gaze. A startled expression seized her face. They both looked down. A grey hand had reached from the pool and closed around her ankle.

Fast as he was Evar couldn't catch her. In a broken moment she was gone.

Strong arms propelled him through the door, and the wet pavement received him. He railed first against the bouncers who had identified his interloping and had ejected him without ceremony. When his ire had been spent, he declared to passing strangers that the party had been a terrible bore. And when his audience had gone beyond hearing, he studied his shoes, wondering what failing had marked him out, and how he might sneak back into the warmth, the light, the music, but most of all the company of others.

Pygmalion's Progress, *by Anneta Drew*

CHAPTER 24

Livira

N o!" Livira thrashed blindly. "Help!"

The hand that had snared her ankle was gone now but the shock still trembled through her and for some terrifying seconds she failed entirely to remember that the pitch-darkness was wholly of her own making. Cursing and sweeping the floor with her hands she finally found the book and closed it. As the covers came together the light re-asserted itself.

She rolled over and sat up. The assistant lay where she had been, but the reaching hand now touched the circle of light through which Livira had travelled. The other arm had moved too, and on her shoulder lay the raven, not perched but slumped with its wings an untidy sprawl across grey flesh.

Livira threw herself at the circle of light, and bounced off, coming to rest back on the floor. She surged forward, pressing both hands to the tingling shimmering surface. She found no way through and, unlike before, Evar did not reach to pull her in.

"Why?" Livira scrambled over to the assistant and grabbed the hand that had snatched her from the world beyond. "I was going to help him! I was somewhere new! I could have got back here when I wanted to, without help!" She tried to shake the arm in her frustration, but it was as if the assistant were carved from the same stuff as the floor, and either bonded to the ground or unexpectedly heavy, even for stone. "Why?"

". . . the Exchange . . . is for . . . bidden . . ." Her grey lips barely moved and no other part of her even twitched.

"The Exchange?" Livira lowered herself to the floor, so their faces were level. "Is that where I was, with all the round doors? That wood between the worlds is the Exchange?" Livira had been astonished by the towering tapwood trees, their rows stretching out beyond sight. There had been ravens flying between their branches, and everywhere doors of light like the one before her, standing in ordered rows. She'd been fascinated by the way the doors always faced her, whichever way she went, so that she had seemed the centre of that strange and endless wood, with a million shimmering eyes turned to watch her.

". . . not meant . . . for . . . you . . ."

Livira frowned and sat up. "I'll go back if I want. I said I'd help him." She watched the circle of light, expecting Evar to follow her through any moment. She was rather disappointed that he hadn't already. He must have seen that she was yanked through unceremoniously. Livira glanced between the doorway and the new book she was still clutching. *Reflections on Solitude* could save her in more ways than one. The others would forgive her running off. Master Logaris would have no reason to punish them. Lord Algar's plan would fail. But she'd need to get it back, and fast. She stood and found that for reasons beyond her understanding she felt re-energised, as if she'd had several good meals and a week of sleep. She felt better now than she had at breakfast.

"I need to tell Evar I have to go back with the book." Livira got to her feet. "I can come back here later and help him if he still hasn't found this woman of his." She approached the circle of light and tried to reach in again.

"Let me through!" Livira pushed harder. She looked down at the grey assistant, unmoving at her feet. "I don't care if it's forbidden! You let me through once. Open it!" If Evar could see her he would have pulled her to him by now. "Help me."

But the assistant neither moved nor spoke.

"Please!" Livira dropped to her knees beside the creature. "At least let me speak to him. Let me explain . . ." She'd only spent a few minutes with Evar, but she didn't want to abandon him like that. He'd seemed more lost than she was. Even a goodbye would have seemed uncomfortably final, but to have been torn away mid-sentence was intolerable. She hauled on the assistant's outstretched arm without result. She may as well have tried to dig a hole in the floor with her bare hands. Livira smashed her fist on the ground in frustration.

"How about you?" She turned her attention to the raven. "Can you do anything?"

The raven seemed as lifeless as the assistant. Its pitch-black feathers even appeared to have taken on some of the assistant's greyness. Tentatively, since the raven had always seemed a skittish thing on the edge of a frenzied attack, and since she didn't want to shock it into one of its ridiculously loud cries, she picked the bird up. For something that had, on many occasions, almost flown, it was surprisingly heavy. Its feathers were stiffer than those the wind had sometimes brought to her back on the Dust, and their edges were sharp enough to cut skin.

"If I leave you here you might turn just like her." Livira even suspected the assistant of having drained the life from the raven to fuel her own modest burst of activity. The bird might have bullied her across what felt like half the library, but it had also been her only companion in the vast solitude of the place. If the book in her hand in any way lived up to its title, then it would have something to say about the bonds that companionship under such conditions could form. In any case, having been forced to abandon one new friend, she wasn't about to abandon the only acquaintance that she might be able to help.

With both books, the dark one and *Reflections*, secured in the capacious book-pockets of her trainee robe, and the bird under one arm, Livira started back the way she'd come. The strange rejuvenating effects of the Exchange stayed with her, putting a spring in her step. In addition, there's a certain measure of speed added to any journey when both your route and destination are known. The outward journey was a meander—the return was a race against an uncertain time limit.

On the way here she had been exploring, already resigned to failure, and so soured by the dull complexity of secretive and ever-changing index systems that she hardly cared if Algar's plan to remove her from the library succeeded. Now, with the book in her hand, she understood that the wonder of the place wasn't in the order that the librarians had forced upon one small corner of it but in the mysterious chaos of the unknowably huge remainder. Each book contained a world of its own, and the minds and times behind those worlds were infinitely fascinating.

Underlying it all was the mystery of the library itself, and the inhuman guardians who operated it. That some petty-minded lord should seek to keep her from all this was intolerable. So intolerable that, even knowing the distance ahead of her, Livira began to run. After all, in a straight line, if such a line could be found, it wasn't much more than four miles.

Livira was still feeling relatively fresh by the time she reached the chamber door, though her initial run had devolved into something only slightly faster than a brisk walk. She approached it with hesitation, aware that the door might refuse her. "You let me in—so if I'm in the wrong place then you should let me out. If you make a mistake, you should always try to fix it." Livira didn't believe that last part, but Aunt Teela had been fond of saying it. Especially to her.

She reached out to touch the door and found it no different to the wall or the floor. Fighting back the panic that took hold of her heart, Livira got the raven out from under her other arm and held the bird up to the white surface.

On previous occasions the library's doors had either remained unmoved or had departed swiftly. This time the one before her slowly began to fade around the area that the raven was touching, as if uncertain of the bird's credentials. The effect spread like the ripples of a stone dropped into water. At last, a hole appeared, an irregular hole with smooth edges, yawning around the bird. It was as if the door were debating if the Raven was still the Raven or simply a collection of its pieces, devoid of the feisty, argumentative spirit that had previously animated it.

The moment that the hole was wide enough for Livira to slip through she did so and hurried on, worried that the process might reverse if the door finally decided the Raven had died.

Crossing the second chamber was a lengthier process but Livira was at least able to avoid all the time she wasted in the labyrinth on the way out. By the time she reached the first of the maze's two focus points, the place where the floor had been stained by some ancient calamity, both her arms were aching. The Exchange's energy was leaving her and, no matter how often she swapped the side on which she carried the Raven, its weight was beginning to tell on her.

"This is where I found you." Livira sat in the cleared circle for a rest, placing the Raven on her lap. It hadn't stirred the whole time she'd been carrying it, and its body felt stiff, its limbs and neck resisting any attempt to move them. "I could leave you here?" It had been on the stain when it first saw her, hidden from casual inspection. Perhaps the blackness would regenerate it. Maybe that, rather than camouflage, was why it had been there.

"How about this?" Livira hefted the bird from her onto the darkly stained floor.

She massaged her arms as she watched it. Her helper. Her guide. It looked untidy, as if it had fallen from its nest, a broken sprawl. Still no movement. At last, she stood to go. She walked halfway to the edge of the clearing and looked up, craning her neck to fix her gaze on the top of the shelves. "Would you rather be up there?" She looked back. "Birds like to be high up, don't they?" She remembered the ravens flying among the branches of the tap-woods in the Exchange. She should have taken her raven there and set it among its fellows. Or would they have mobbed it, sensing its strangeness and seeing its injuries? "I could carry you to the next ladder and put you up some-where you can . . . perch."

The bird simply lay there so Livira decided for it. She hefted it onto her hip once more and set off, pausing only to replace the books that she'd left as markers.

"If you laid ladders across the tops of the shelves it would give a whole new way to access the aisles." Livira told the Raven about her theories as they walked. "If I were head librarian I'd have walkways over the top and ropes you could swing on or slide along. And horses. Horses would be good. You could get along much better like that. Malar had a good horse. Malar's this man who— Well, we've found a ladder . . ."

They'd left the labyrinth behind them. Livira wondered if ladders were rarer in this chamber or perhaps there was a cluster of them somewhere where hundreds of them had gathered, seeking safety in numbers.

Livira's arms were pleased at the prospect of being able to put the Raven down at last, but the rest of her was less happy about the idea. She climbed awkwardly with her burden, still discussing the matter.

"I think you'll be happy up here. You'll be able to see for miles. Well, to the walls at least. And I guess you've not been up high for a while . . . Since you . . . broke your wing."

She got to the top and heaved the bird up. "This will be all right, won't it?" The bird looked dead. It reminded her of Henton, the soldier with Malar and Jons. He'd died on the journey from the Dust. She wasn't sure when. Like the Raven he'd died when no one was looking at him. People seemed to choose those moments. It seemed a lonely thing, dying.

"I'll sit with you a bit." Livira left her hand on the bird's back and gazed out across the shelf tops, her eyes prickling. The urgency of her mission slipped away from her. She got out the last of the apples she'd brought into the library against the rules and took a half-hearted bite. Without thinking about it she started to stroke the Raven.

Later—she couldn't say how long had passed—a flash of white at the corner of her vision caught her attention. She turned and saw nothing. But something had crossed the small patch of floor she could see in the aisle below her, far to her left. She was sure of it. Something white. She stood, and immediately the drops to either side reached up for her, filling her with dizziness.

"Hey!" She began to run, hunched low so that if she started to fall, she could throw herself at the wooden floor beneath her feet. In one hand she still had the uneaten half of her last apple. "Hey, you!"

Straying closer to the edge allowed her to see more of the aisle floor twenty yards below her. A pure white figure was walking away. Another assistant. "Hey! Stop!"

The assistant stopped and turned around slowly while Livira closed on it as swiftly as her courage would allow. She came to a breathless halt directly above it. The assistant looked up. Like the one at the portal to the

Exchange it was sexless, but the shape of this one in the chest and hips suggested male rather than female. Looking down at him redoubled the dizziness already making her sway.

"Yes?" A faint blue light flickered in his eyes, and his voice, though soft, reached her without effort. If seeing a young girl hurrying along the shelf tops surprised him in any way, none of it showed on the white enamel of his face or ruffled the calmness of his tone. Before she could speak the assistant seemed to notice something, tilting its head to the side as he stared at her. Livira's fingers closed on air. Something rattled softly around her feet. She looked at her hand. The half-eaten apple was gone. A few pips lay scattered on the shelf top below her hand. The assistant spoke again: "You are not permitted to bring food into the library."

"Well, that's a stupid rule for a start!" Livira had more to say but looking down at the pips and the edge of the shelf with the too-distant floor beyond it had been a mistake. She shuffled her feet to keep upright. "Why don't you—" And she fell into the empty space below.

Humpty Dumpty sat on a wall.
Humpty Dumpty had a great fall.
Four-score men and four-score more,
Could not make Humpty Dumpty where he was before.
Juvenile Amusements, *by Samuel Arnold*

CHAPTER 25

Livira

L
ivira jolted awake from a dream of falling where she hit the ground
with just enough force to emerge into a mirror world on the other
side of it.

The scream died on her lips as she sat up. She was in a circular clearing
larger than those in the labyrinth. The shelves that terminated at its edge
were the shortest she'd seen, just five yards tall, and those behind them
increased in height steadily, giving the feeling that she was in the bottom
of a vast bowl.

Her body was a single dull ache. "I fell!" She remembered all of it. Still
sitting, she looked left then right and found the assistant standing close by.
In one hand he held *Reflections on Solitude*, his fingers whiter than the
creamy leather of its cover. "Yute." Livira coughed out a laugh. "You're
whiter than Yute even." Her thoughts felt fragmented as if her fall had
broken them along with her bones.

"This is an unusual book." The assistant held it up.

"It was hard to find." Livira tried to get to her feet and found herself
incapable, limbs making only token efforts to obey. "Very hard."

"By some measures it should be the easiest book to locate in the whole
library," the assistant said. "Given that it is the only book we have two copies of."

"I couldn't find the other one." Livira coughed. Her chest hurt. "Where is it? Where am I for that matter? And where's my bird?" Arpix had said that assistants were rarely helpful, but Livira had too many questions not to try for some answers.

"The second copy is concealed behind other books. Your predecessors have organised many volumes in a hidden index that exists behind the rows displayed on the shelves. It seems an unhelpful system." He lifted the book in his hand, regarding it with blank eyes. "This should be returned."

"Wait!" Panic managed to get Livira to her feet. "Can't you return the other one?"

"Why would I?"

Livira thought fast and talked faster. "An assistant brought that one to me. Someone wants to read it. The other one is lost. My friends have been looking for it for days and haven't found it. Isn't this place here so we can read what we want?"

"*Isn't this place here so we can read what we want?*" The assistant paused. "That is perhaps the biggest question I have ever been asked." He handed her the book and she quickly stashed it with the black volume that had remained in her book-pocket. "However large the answer may be, I will return the other one."

"Why do I hurt?"

"You fell."

"You didn't catch me?"

"I brought you to the centre. At the centre of each chamber is an area that nourishes and that, as a secondary effect, will reverse recent damage."

Livira rubbed at her arms. She wondered quite how much damage she had sustained. All she remembered after she began to fall was a crunching sound. Had that been her? She touched her face where she'd crashed into the ladder as she escaped the others. It no longer hurt.

"My bird? Where is he? Could this place mend him?"

But the assistant was already walking away.

"Hey!" Livira gave chase on strengthening legs. "How do I get out of here?"

The assistant paused and pointed. "The east door will take you to a chamber with external access. Follow the wall to the right when you pass through, and it will bring you to the exit."

"Arpix said you assistants never helped."

"Perhaps this Arpix does not know what helping looks like?" The assistant carried on his way, which wasn't in the direction he'd pointed. "We have much to do."

"Wait!" Livira called after him. "I saw an assistant who looked hurt. She was all grey and she wouldn't move, and she had a hole, a dent, here." She touched her temple. "You should help her."

The assistant turned, gazing at her with white eyes. "You asked if the library were here so that you could read. It was, as I said, a big question. Some would answer that the library is here in order that an old war can be fought again and again until the end of time. I thank you for your concern. I have much to do." And he walked away.

Livira continued to shout questions until the assistant was out of sight, and for a while after that. She could have followed him, but she needed to get back. She clutched *Reflections on Solitude* to her and began to run in the direction the assistant had indicated. Lord Algar couldn't be allowed to take this away from her. She had too many questions that needed answers, and the thought of the quiet satisfaction he would take in her eviction ran like acid through her veins.

Keeping to the line the assistant had indicated proved difficult with the aisles running at whatever angle they chose. When she'd had no particular destination in mind it had been less annoying. She ran on, constantly diverted, increasingly sure she'd lost hold of the direction she'd been sent in. This belief was proven incorrect when, probably more by luck than judgement, she broke into the clearing in front of the corridor.

The metal man was where Livira had left him, standing eternal guard. Livira's renewed energy was flagging again, and although seeing a familiar face cheered her up, the featherless skeleton of his wings reminded her that she'd left the Raven for dead without even a goodbye. After a moment to recover her breath, Livira went to stand in front of the frozen guide. She resisted hugging him and instead offered a dignified bow. "I found it!" She held her book aloft and hurried past. When the white door behind him began to dissolve beneath her touch she almost cried with relief. Before it was properly gone, she was through into the final chamber where, still some miles off, the exit lay.

THE CLOSER LIVIRA got to the exit the more she worried about the time. She could have been gone for three days, five, who knew? She certainly needed sleep and food, lots of both. To fail out in the far reaches of a distant chamber was one thing, but to fail with the book in hand, within shouting distance of the exit, would be too much to bear. The idea of handing victory to Lord Algar fed new energy into her legs.

Having reached the first chamber again, she had a path to follow, marked both in memory and on the floor with strategically placed books. With a grim determination Livira ran on.

From the next ladder she scaled she could see the wall looming ahead and make out the white dot that was the final door. Soon she could even pick out the line of the staircase that led up to it. Her legs were already leaden and the idea of climbing that flight of overly large steps made her groan.

Memory brought her stumbling and panting into the aisle that she'd leapt into from the shelf tops. "Arpix? Carlotte?"

Lacking a reply, she reversed course to find a route to the clear space around the base of the stairs. A short while later she broke from the aisles, casting wildly around for signs of the others. She hurried to the start of the index aisle. Nothing. No sign of the mess they'd made. Arpix would have tidied up conscientiously even knowing they'd failed.

Livira started up the stairs, pressing with both hands on her lead knee to try and lever herself up them when her thigh muscles began to fail. The others might be just ahead of her. They might be crossing the cavern as she heaved herself up the stairs with maddening slowness. A laugh burst from her: hysterical tiredness. She'd never imagined the professional librarian needed to be such an athlete.

Finally, she reached the top and collapsed against the door which immediately melted away, offering no support. The next she knew she was being helped to her feet by two library guards.

"Did they come through yet? Have you seen them? My friends?" Livira tried not to let exhaustion slur her words into an unintelligible mumble.

"We came on duty an hour ago." The larger of the two men set Livira on her feet, hands to either side as if checking he'd balanced her correctly. "Haven't seen anyone in or out."

"Hells." Livira started out across the cavern and found herself limping though she'd no memory of hurting her leg. "If they come out after me tell them I was here."

"If who comes out?" the other man called at her back. But Livira was too tired to explain. They'd sort it out. Besides, they were ahead of her, she was sure of it. At least an hour ahead.

LIVIRA DESCENDED THE stairs to the main complex having no idea whether it was day or night. Tiredness washed such thoughts through her head as she limped along the mostly deserted corridors. Night then.

Master Logaris had given no instructions about the handing over of the book. Presumably he intended that they bring it to class. In any event, Livira had no idea where Logaris slept, which was probably a good thing given the temptation to sneak into his bedchamber and leave *Reflections on Solitude* on the pillow, beside his head. Instead, she went to the sleeping quarters, half-drunk with tiredness. Wading through her exhaustion, she reached the rooms at the far end, leaned on a door, and lunged for the bed like a drowning man straining for solid ground. Consciousness abandoned her with a swiftness that seemed no less than when she had hit the floor after falling twenty yards.

LIVIRA FOUND THAT for the second time in a row she'd woken somewhere unexpected. The room looked just like hers, but it belonged to someone else. She rolled from the bed and almost ended up sprawled across the sheepskin rug, so unwilling were her legs to support her weight. She felt as if she were eighty rather than just turned eleven. And she didn't own a rug of any sort, certainly not one so thick and luxuriously white as the one beneath her feet. She noticed that she was still wearing the shoes from Yute's house, having failed to undress to any degree before plunging into the bed. She wanted the shoes off so she could wriggle her bare toes in the rug's softness.

She looked around the room, a huge yawn cracking her jaw. She still felt as if she could sleep another whole day, so why was she awake? Had there been a noise? She looked at the desk, far more orderly than hers and with the books stacked higher around it. Street clothes hung at the far end, not peasant rags but plain and patched. Not the clothes of someone who could afford so fine a rug. Crossing to the desk she picked up the topmost piece of paper. She couldn't read the language, but the quill work spoke clearly enough.

"Arpix." She'd spent the night in Arpix's room. But where was he?

Suddenly she remembered the book. For a heart-stopping moment, as her fingers quested inside the emptiness of her inner pocket, she was convinced that she'd lost it. But a desperate search of the bed found *Reflections on Solitude* resting under the pillow. "I've got to go!"

Livira ran out into the corridor, finding it empty. She glanced into her own room and then hurried to the refectory hall, cursing her stiff and aching legs. By the time she got there only a few librarians and a scattering of support staff were still lingering over their breakfast. The bell hadn't woken her but perhaps the commotion of students outside her door getting ready for lessons had finally dragged Livira from her pit of sleep. She turned on a heel and headed off towards class.

Livira couldn't understand why Arpix hadn't returned to his room. If they'd become lost among the aisles who knew what trouble they might be in? Her mind told her it wasn't her fault if they were lost, but her heart had other opinions. She turned the corner to see the last of Master Logaris's students going through the classroom doorway. The door had closed by the time she got there. Livira barged through into a room that seemed shockingly normal after the strangeness in which she'd spent the past days.

The oldest students, still standing around their desks unloading books, didn't notice her arrival at all. The ones behind them, middle ranking in the hierarchy of Master Logaris's class, pretended not to notice her. Only when the cluster of older children parted to allow her through did Livira find herself greeted by the astonished stares of her four companions at the lowest table.

Arpix and the others looked even worse than she felt. Black circles around their eyes spoke of days without sleep. All of them stood at her arrival, except

Jella who slumped across the table as if some burden had been suddenly taken from her.

The door opened again, and Master Logaris filled the doorway.

"Where in the hells were you?" Arpix hissed, pitching his demand beneath the rapidly quieting chatter.

"I'll tell you later," Livira whispered, taking the chair next to him.

"We spent half our time searching for you," Arpix muttered through clenched teeth. "It's no wonder we didn't find the book!"

"I'm sorry." Livira was rarely properly sorry, but she regretted what the others had gone through.

"What were you thinking?" Arpix hissed. "If you'd stayed, we might—"

Master Logaris loomed over them, his blunt features gathered into an unhappy scowl. "Well, first-years. You've had two full days. Where's my book?"

Jella sat up at that. Carlotte and Meelan studied the table. Arpix began to stutter. "W-we searched the philosophy section in the Rifflean Ordering and the corresponding sections by the west wall and in the Orthodoxy." Livira, waited, expecting him to lay the blame at her feet, as he was perfectly entitled to do. "We wasted a lot of time in the Binary Aisles," Arpix continued. "That was my fault. All of it was my fault really. The rest were following my lead." Livira blinked at him, amazed, still waiting for the hammer to fall. "Then we moved on—"

"It was Arpix who finally thought it might be in the hidden index and got us to start pulling out the books to look behind them." Under the table Livira worked the book out from her robe pocket and thrust it into Arpix's lap. "I'd given up ages before that."

Arpix looked at her in amazement and then glanced down at his lap. He brought the book up to the table in trembling hands. "It's here . . ."

Logaris's laugh was the big and booming thing that Livira had imagined it might be though she had never thought to hear it. He took *Reflections on Solitude* from Arpix's hand and studied it from several angles as if it were something he were considering making an offer on. "Well . . . well . . . well." He shook his head. "The Lost Seam? He sent children to retrieve something from the Lost Seam?" He closed his mouth with a snap, seeming to remember where he was. "You must tell me all about it when you're better rested." He walked to his desk at the front with all eyes on him and locked the book in a top drawer. "But well done. Very well done indeed. All of you"—his eyes found Livira—"have a place in my class for as long as you continue to apply yourselves."

Loss is often remembered in the hands. Fingers recall the feel of a baby's hair. Touch explores the places where they have lain, still hoping to rediscover a child long after the mind and even the heart have surrendered.

A Study of Infant Mortality, *by Tyler Dickerson*

———————

CHAPTER 26

Evar

The girl had vanished into the pool too fast to save, and when he tried to reach in after her the black waters resisted him so that he could barely wet his palm. Snarling with frustration, Evar got up and attempted to push a foot into the water but with similar results. He applied his whole weight and realised that the pool would let him walk across it before it admitted him. The blackness vanished as he was testing his weight, startling him back for a moment, but the change made no difference. He was locked out. Or in.

He circled the pool, staring at the fading ripples that, along with the mark she'd carved into the grass, were the only record he had of the child. Of Livira—that had been her name. He rediscovered the corner of parchment on his first circuit. It was written in a Crunian dialect and seemed to be an account of a battle in the poetic form favoured by Crunian scholars of the fifth Bronze Age. It bore the girl's scent. With a shrug he pushed it into an inner pocket.

After ten more circuits of the pool Evar decided it was time to go. After another ten he said it out loud. After twenty more he finally walked away with muttered apologies. The child had had a certain fire to her, and he was unwilling to abandon the first stranger he'd ever met, even after so brief an acquaintance.

———

EVAR FINALLY SPOTTED the dagger he'd left to mark the pool he arrived by. It had taken him quite a few circuits before he found it, and for a while he'd been working out various spiral search patterns he might have to employ in order to be sure of locating his pool. The degree of relief he experienced on finally registering the distant dot had surprised him. With so many choices did he really care if he couldn't find his way back? Apparently, he did.

"In any case, maybe I don't have any choices at all." Livira's pool had refused him. Maybe all the others would too. Maybe even his pool would reject him, and he'd be left to wander this middle ground until he starved, or some new child popped up out of one of the pools to guide him home.

Evar stopped at a pool no different from any other. He was most of the way back to his own now—only three to go. Standing there, he had no insight into the workings of his own mind. Why had his feet stopped moving at this pool and not the one before or the one after? Starval claimed nothing was truly random. So, had Evar chosen this particular pool? Had it called to him? He didn't know.

First, he tested the water with a toe and then with his whole foot. No resistance. Evar knelt and reached in with his arm. Cold, clear water. He could see his hand and forearm beneath the surface, painted by rippled light. Find her at the bottom? How many would he have to try? As he thought about the nameless woman outlined on the cover of his book, he knew with more certainty than ever before that his years in the Mechanism had been years spent with her. It felt like a missing lifetime. He had loved her with a fierceness that he would never have imagined could be taken from him. He tried to speak her name and tasted it on his tongue. Tasted her.

"I'll try this one." Evar stood, shaking the water from his arm. He didn't have the weight to drag him down, but he had the experience to hold on to—the knowledge that this was more than a pool, its water both more than and less than water. It could take him somewhere else. All that was required was an agreement between them. His conviction and the pool's acceptance.

He looked down into the water, its surface still trembling with the memory of his intrusion, depths obscured. A whole new world beyond each pool? Another part of the same world? Would he end up beneath the same sky as Livira or his family? Were they both the same? Did Livira and the many friends she'd spoken of live their lives just beyond the char wall?

He jumped.

THE DARKNESS THAT had swallowed Evar released him back to his senses in the act of getting to his feet. Crops spread before him in a green arc. He knew the pool lay at his back. The library ceiling was his sky once more, the book stacks his forest. He was back where he'd come from and not even breathless from his plunge. Not even wet.

Evar's profound sense of disappointment hadn't even had time to settle before the next three things he noticed blew it away entirely. "We didn't plant anything like this much!" The melon field ran three, possibly four times further ahead of him than it should. "Where's the wall?" The book wall that Clovis had insisted they build had gone, leaving the stacks themselves as the only perimeter. "Who . . ." And there was a figure moving between the book towers, coming his way. Dressed like him, as tall as Kerrol, but not Kerrol. Not Clovis. Not Starval.

"Gods! There's more of them." Evar stepped back and narrowly avoided falling into the pool.

The three figures approaching didn't seem to have noticed the brief, undignified pinwheel of his arms as he'd fought to keep his balance. Evar no longer cared about the approaching trio. As he'd danced on the pool's edge he'd turned and found that just yards away on the other side a woman was kneeling amidst the wheat rows, bent over some task, so intent upon it that she hadn't even registered his performance. Immediately he tried to call to her, but his voice dried up, his throat contracting around the possibility that this was her, the woman he'd drowned himself to find. The author of his book.

Evar stood lost in wonder. There was something strange about the woman, who was dressed in the same kind of jerkin and trews as he was, sewn together from leather covers. It took him a long, silent moment to work out what was curious about the side view of her face: she was old. Grey in her hair, cheeks withered, deep lines around the corner of her eye.

The woman turned as he stared; she stood and raised her hand in greeting. Evar was so lost in the newness of strangers that for a long moment he made no response, then awkwardly, unsure of himself, he jerked his hand up as she had done.

"You're up early, Arka." The voice came from behind him and Evar spun around to see the three others working their way along a narrow path between the melons and the beans. The speaker was a man who looked almost as old as the woman, two younger women, girls not even Evar's age, came behind him with leather-strap baskets. None of them so much as looked at him.

"Hello . . ." Evar lowered his hand, feeling foolish. "I'm Evar."

"These days my bones get me up before the bell." The old woman grimaced and returned her attention to her work. She seemed to be spreading compost around the roots.

"Hello?" Evar raised his voice. "I came out of the pool. Just now."

The girls started to move among the melon plants, hunched over in the search for ripe fruit, talking together in low voices. The man went to help the woman.

"Can't you hear me?" Evar followed the man in confusion. "Hello!"

He stood over the two of them as they spread the compost. Evar patted himself unconsciously, confirming to himself that he was real, he was there. Could he be dreaming his last dream as he drowned in a pool?

He reached down to touch the man's shoulder, suddenly nervous. His hand sank through leather and flesh without resistance. The feeling was unpleasant, as if he'd reached into a pool just a breath away from freezing. A bone-chilling ache ran up his arm and he pulled his hand back quickly. The man reached up to scratch where Evar had touched him, returning to his work without comment.

Evar stepped back. Not even the crops noticed him, refusing to rustle as he passed through them and as they reciprocated, passing through him in turn. He had read widely enough to understand that in this place he was a ghost. He could move with stealth that even Starval would envy, become the perfect spy. All that was denied to him were the things he truly wanted.

Evar walked away from the pool, habit directing him to avoid the crop even though damaging it was beyond him. It seemed that he was in another world but one quite similar to his own, one where a collection of people of his own race were also trapped within the library. Or maybe in this world they chose to be here. Perhaps whatever lay outside was worse than the sameness of days beneath a stone sky.

There were people everywhere, scores of them, walking together, children playing games, young men and women sitting in circles talking, some working on repairs to clothing or tools, many just sitting in book-walled shelters seeking privacy. A good number of them were reading just like Evar did. With so many of them, access to the Mechanism must be limited, if they even had one.

For an hour or two he simply sat and watched, letting the strangers come and go around him, listening to their conversation, which was mostly filled with chatter about each other, so many names, so many grievances and scandals and romances and intrigues. They talked about stories too, having hunted out seams of fiction and mined them for entertainment. Evar recognised none of the tales that fascinated them.

Even if he hadn't been a ghost, unable to touch anything but the floor, Evar would have felt himself to be in a dream. The strangeness of it all overwhelmed him. At one point he was actually in a crowd. A crowd! More than a dozen people converged around him, drawn by a joke that set one attractive young woman laughing.

Evar found himself instantly tangled in the lives of these strangers, smiling at their banter, following one group and then another, marvelling in their difference and their newness, discovering unexpected characters and fresh faces at every turn. He felt less alone here haunting a people who could neither see nor hear him than he did under the regard of his three siblings back in his own version of the library.

After a while the people began to gather, unsummoned, drifting in from the stacks for some presumably regular meeting. Evar waited, watching, wanting to know how community worked. How people lived together.

Of the hundred and more pairs of eyes, not one so much as flickered his way.

Neither hunger nor thirst seemed to notice him either. He let the trio he'd been following wander off and stood looking out at the less-travelled regions of the stacks marvelling at how familiar and yet how different it all was. A sense of peace and community ran through the place—something he'd never experienced before. With Clovis and Kerrol and Starval it felt as if all they were doing was waiting to die. But here, where children and ancients sat together, it seemed more like a cycle, a living thing that would roll on through the years combining both change and stability.

A child shot out of the stacks as if pursued by half a dozen Escapes, startling Evar despite himself. He watched her thread a path between the book towers, showing her heels in a remarkable turn of speed for such a small girl. He thought of Livira for a moment, though this girl was even younger and sported a mane of red hair where Livira's had been a lustrous black with crimson flashes. Evar had been meaning to wander the stacks for a while longer, but something turned him around. The girl had torn past him in an instant and yet a hook had been sunk in some wordless part of his mind. He followed along the line she'd taken.

Evar found the girl a short while later. A handsome young man was carrying her on his hip and a young woman with a similar mane of red hair walked with them. The woman was laughing at something the man had said. As unfamiliar as he was with the notion of parents Evar understood what he was seeing. His own family were a blur but the scene before him struck a chord that echoed in his chest. This was love. The simple kind that fills you up and wraps you in safety, the kind that gives without demanding and is made of happiness. The sort he'd always felt was locked away behind the Assistant's ivory breast, reaching for them as she raised Evar and his siblings but never able to break free save in a fleeting gesture or rare kind word.

Something about the child fascinated Evar. She seemed familiar in a way that none of the others did, and there was no sense to it. He watched the small family settle to eat. Two boys came running up, breathless and laughing. By the way their mother greeted them he could tell they were her sons, the girl's brothers. Both were older than the girl but just by a few years, neither much past their father's waist. The bigger of the two reached out to snag the last bean-cake as the girl was reaching for it. The father spoke over her wail of protest.

"Break it in half, Cannir. Share with Clovis."

Evar sat down, hard, feeling as if he'd been punched in the stomach. The family continued their meal, oblivious to his astonishment. "It can't be. It's not." Evar moved forward on hands and knees, staring into the girl's face as she munched her cake. "Clovis?" He shook his head. His sister couldn't be the only Clovis in the world. This was just a child who shared her name. And her hair. "Can you hear me?" It had to be coincidence. But she'd been so familiar, right from the first moment. "It's me. Clovis, it's me, Evar!" And there truly *was* something there under the child's soft cheeks and easy smile, the bones of her face spelled out an impossible truth. "Clovis?"

A distant, explosive bang followed by a scream turned all their heads in the same direction. Another agonised cry, a scattering of bangs, and the mother and father were standing, staring at the stacks. More shouting, the sounds of running feet. The mother and the father exchanged uncomprehending looks that turned to horror at the terror and pain in those screams. Screams that instead of stopping were multiplying. The little girl glued herself to her mother's leg. The boys looked bewildered.

"Run!" Evar shouted at them, but they just stood there stupidly. "Run!" None of them had any weapons. He hadn't seen a single knife among the scores he'd followed so far.

"I should help," the father said, though he sounded scared. "Take the children into the stacks." Figures were running through the forest of book towers on all sides, most of them away from the screams and the harsh cries that sounded like attackers.

"Dung on that!" the mother bristled. "You save them. I'll fight!" She snatched up the largest book in reach, part of their shelter, a tome bound in dull red leather and reinforced with iron hinges.

The father opened his mouth to object, but a crimson hole had appeared in his chest, gushing blood. He looked down at it, astonished. Projectiles zipped by and Evar threw himself forward, trying to shield the children even as he failed to gather the boys before him.

"Artur!" Horror fought with rage on the mother's face. Suddenly the attackers were there, racing forward with their unnatural gait—people but not people—swords swinging. The mother swung her book and felled the first of them. A moment later she was overrun. The attackers ran through Evar like cold shadows as he tried to fight them, the violence of their thoughts infecting him. They paid him no more attention than his own people had. It seemed they had formed a perimeter around the locals, good timing or cruel chance allowing a massacre that would have taken far longer had everyone been spread out and able to hide.

Heartbeats later the bulk of them were gone, tightening the noose on those still running from them. Evar stood and stared about him in horror at the wreckage they'd left behind. He fell to his knees, retching, breathless with the hurt of it all. Blood spattered everything in broad scarlet arcs, running down the book towers, dripping from covers, pooling on the floor. One boy lay with his neck half-severed, sightless eyes staring at the ceiling. The other was curled around a fatal wound, choking out his final breaths.

One of the sabbers, an older warrior, grizzled and grey, came stalking through the stacks, driving his blade into the fallen, one after the next after the next.

"Clovis!" Evar, hunting on his hands and knees, found the girl half-hidden under her father's corpse. "Clovis! You've got to move!"

The executioner came ever closer, wrenching his curved sword from yet another body.

"Clovis!" Evar screamed at her. "Get up!" But she lay there, eyes screwed tight, her whole body trembling, all her faith in her father's protection. "He's dead!" Evar roared. The warrior's next thrust would skewer the father and the child beneath it. "You have to r—"

A heavy book came down in an overhead swing on the sabber's helm, sending him sprawling over Artur's body. The mother stood behind the fallen warrior, silent and covered in blood. She dropped onto his back, all her weight behind both knees, and brought the iron-hinged spine of the book down on the sabber's neck with awful force.

"Get up!" An order rasped between crimson teeth as she dragged her daughter clear. "Come on!"

In the next moment they were stumbling away through the stacks, screams on all sides, attackers roaming. Evar followed, ducking pointlessly as a projectile hissed past too fast to see.

Sudden understanding stopped his advance. He stood straight, ignoring the bangs and the zip of projectiles, and stared in the direction the sabbers had attacked from. "The pool? They came from the pool . . ."

All boundaries are challenged by those that neighbour them. Even divides as certain as truth or fiction become fraught on close inspection. The library contains novels written in the style of a historian, leading the unwary down rabbit holes into imaginary pasts wherein sabbers built great cities and dwelt within them, aping the habits of man. Obviously, such flights of fancy are unlikely to mislead any but the most foolish reader, but other variations on the truth may be sufficiently plausible to trick even the most erudite.

Know Your Library, *by Axon Bloom*

CHAPTER 27

Livira

L ivira didn't know what day she'd been born on. The other trainees knew their birthdays and so Livira chose one for herself in order not to be left out. She picked the particular Wodesday when, two years previously, she had been allocated to the library. And it was on the day after her thirteenth birthday that she got to visit the city again—her first time beneath the open sky since Master Yute had escorted her inside the mountain.

As Livira walked towards the entrance she found herself thinking not about her imminent reunion with sunlight and crowds but instead about the strange young man she'd met so briefly in the forest that stood between everywhere. She hoped Evar had found his way. He'd seemed somehow more lost than she had been. She wondered if he'd found the woman he'd been looking for—questing after like a knight in the fairy tales. The love so lost that even her name had been forgotten.

Evar had been two years ago. Livira's first month at the library had been so stuffed with excitement and danger that she'd wondered if she could survive a second one. The dull weeks that followed had at first been a relief, but that relief had turned into a slow disappointment as she began to realise that lightning had struck but would not be returning to strike again. A lord had manoeuvred to get her thrown out. And having failed, seemed to have entirely lost interest in her. Livira wasn't sad about that—but she was puzzled.

The dust had been washed from her skin on her first day through the city gates, but the first year hadn't taken the taste of it from her tongue, and even after a second it still lingered.

She had mastered many arts—reading came easiest, writing a little less so, and Arpix still found fault with her quill work, though he only volunteered an opinion when she asked him to. Languages she found simple enough to understand, and far more difficult to speak. Meelan said her Entragon sounded like Otroosan spoken through a mouthful of toffee, and that when she declined Sappic verbs, rather than using the familiar tone, she just sounded as if she were in pain.

A diet of one book a day on top of her assignments had improved her general knowledge and vision of the wider world beyond recognition. Master Logaris frowned on fiction, and whilst generally disinclined to follow his directions, Livira had thus far confined herself to works of history, natural science, biology, and biography, finding the ocean of them on offer too wide to cross and more than deep enough to drown in despite her unusual capacity.

She had learned less about the mechanics by which people interact than she had about the alchemy of substances both familiar and foreign. She had learned more about the history of the empire than about the workings of the modern metropolis at her doorstep. And more about the dead, both famous and infamous, than about the living. Crath City's inhabitants were almost as much of a mystery to her at thirteen years old as they had been on the day she arrived. But she had deepened her friendships around the table that she'd first been assigned to. Arpix, Meelan, Jella, and Carlotte were brothers and sisters to her now—fair targets for mischief and bickering, but trusted companions whose strengths significantly outnumbered their flaws.

However, what had marked time more significantly than the addition of learning or of height, or the coming of her seasons, was the arrival of new trainees, younger and smaller than herself. That and the changing of tables in the schoolroom. Like flotsam on a wooden river, time was carrying her along the inevitable course from the back of Master Logaris's chamber towards the door through which she would eventually leave for good.

LIVIRA HAD OF course tried to return to the library chamber with the portal in it. Many times. She'd never been able to get back inside, and nobody seemed to believe that she ever had. Even if she could get in, the assistant appeared to have sealed the portal and then died.

She had come to the conclusion that her search for a way back to the Exchange and to Evar had to start among the roots of the library itself. This of course was a mystery of great interest to librarians, and naturally all the books deemed to be important had been hidden long ago within the twists and turns of indexes not shared with mere trainees.

Livira had never been one to be thwarted by rules. She had extended her searches along various tangents, pursuing crumbs of knowledge that others might have overlooked, venturing further out into the extremes of the library than was wise, permitted, or even vaguely sensible. If she could have stolen a horse and knew how to ride, she would have galloped off into the most distant chambers and plucked books at random from strange shelves in the hope of enlightenment.

She could also look for Evar's chamber, of course. But since he, and his people for centuries before him, had been trapped within the room, it must be a forbidden chamber, and if she could open those sorts of doors then she'd have been back to the Exchange long ago. Livira told herself that her main quest was to reach the Exchange, and that alongside such a great achievement the rediscovery of one strange young man would merely be an added benefit. However, despite her own claim, and the certainty that Evar would long ago have left the wood through one of the many portals, her daydreams did constantly return her to the conversation that had been so rudely interrupted. Her imagination had many times brought their discussion to a more civilised conclusion followed by all manner of adventures as they explored the place together.

Livira's searches hadn't been entirely fruitless. There were books, as yet unclaimed, that spoke of the library's origins. Many of them read like my-thology, the ones that didn't read like fiction or plain lies. Though, of course, the truth of a place like the library would probably sound stranger than any fiction, less plausible than a lie.

Her most recent find, from the book drifts of a distant chamber num-bered in the hundreds, was a child's story filled with woodcut illustrations. She had been on the point of discarding it when her eyes found a familiar name: *Jaspeth*. A name Livira had heard only once before, mentioned in passing by Evar among the trees of the Exchange. Instantly, the book had her full attention.

It told the story of two brothers, Jaspeth and Irad, the former depicted as a devil with cloven hooves who stole books from children, the latter shown as an angel showering illuminated pages from the heavens. Irad, it seemed, had built a library in the city his father had founded. The first li-brary, in the first city. And his jealous younger brother was set on tearing it down. Jaspeth would whisper into the ears of sleeping children that knowl-edge was dangerous, a sin, and that he was protecting them. Irad, on the other hand, would answer the questions of even the smallest child with great patience.

On the last page, one child, angry with her own brother and her family who favoured him, came to Irad asking for a way she could punish them.

"Punish who?" Irad asked.

"All of them!"

"Everyone?" Irad asked, his smile serene.

"Every last one of them!"

And Irad had given the child a small box and the key to open it with.

The child took the box to the middle of the city, climbed the tallest tower, and opened it. It wasn't clear from the woodcut image what exactly had flown out from the box. Strange squiggly lines? But what was obvious from the final image was that the squiggles killed everyone and ate the city down to the last stone.

Livira had closed the back cover, blinking at the illustration burned into the leather, showing Irad wearing his brother's horns and Jaspeth wearing his brother's wings. And the book had trembled in Livira's hands.

Quite what message children were intended to take from the text, Livira wasn't sure. But her own conclusion was that there was no reason why this book's take on the origins of the library should be dismissed any more easily than those in any of the other books she'd found thus far.

Although of no help at all, the story of Irad and Jaspeth's war over the library that Irad had built stayed with Livira, and it was Irad, angel-winged and devil-horned, that she pictured when she thought of what stood between her and returning to the Exchange.

Livira shook off the memory and hurried on towards the great outdoors. Today, for the first time since her arrival, she was to escape the library, see the sun, feel the wind, and experience freedom of the body rather than of the mind!

MASTER LOGARIS HAD set a challenge to their table to find as many of the books on a list requested by the laboratory as they could. These days Livira sat at table three, near the middle of the room with Arpix and four older trainees. Meelan and Carlotte, considered less advanced in their studies, sat behind them at table two. Jella worked with the bookbinders now after a brief stint in the scriptorium, copying books that house readers requested. Livira and the rest of that original "first table" sat with Jella at meals and she seemed much happier in her newest role, freed from constant study and examination.

Livira's reward for recovering the most books from the list was to deliver the haul to the laboratory. She chose Arpix to help her despite his lack of muscles. He had been tall and thin when she first met him, and was considerably taller these days but no less thin.

"We'll need to take this slow," Arpix said as they approached the mountainside exit.

"How will that help?" Livira asked. "The faster we get there the less time we'll have to carry this lot for." Her shoulders were already aching where the straps of the two satchels were biting in.

"Our eyes will need some time to adjust to the daylight. It's not the same outside."

Livira shrugged. "I'll squint."

Arpix was right though. It always seemed bright in the library but the sun hammering the mountainside was something else again and shards of its light brought tears to her eyes no matter how tight she screwed them up.

"Careful!" One of the library guards caught her elbow as she passed. "It's steep. Take a moment."

Arpix said nothing. He never did when he was right. It irritated the hell out of Livira because she knew she'd be crowing at this point if their positions were reversed.

"Guess you were right." His silence dragged the reluctant admission from her.

They moved slowly out into the full glare.

"Wind!" Livira exclaimed. "I'd almost forgotten about the wind!" She turned into it, delighted, her hair flowing behind her. "Come on! Let's run!"

"Livira!" Arpix scolded. She called him an old woman, but it paid to listen to him however annoying he was.

Together they walked down the mountain path at a sensible pace, stopping to rest their eyes on distances that even the vast chambers of the library couldn't offer.

"How does it all fit in there?" Livira paused and looked up at the mountain. "I mean, yes, it's huge. It's a mountain. But . . ."

"That's a question we don't ask," Arpix said. "Master Ellis says there's the map he maintains of the library and then there's the map the city cartographers have of the mountain, and the two should never meet."

Livira hadn't seen Master Ellis's map. The librarian was too senior to mix with trainees, his rank on par with Yute's, one of four deputy head librarians. But the layout wasn't really in question. An endless grid of square chambers. Many of the chambers were inaccessible. Of the fifteen chambers you could reach by passing through three or fewer doors, five had no door that would open. One of those five had been accessed by Livira but none of the librarians she'd told appeared to believe her story, especially when the mechanical raven that she claimed had somehow granted her access could not be found following an extensive search centred on the place she claimed to have left it. Abandoned it, some said. Fabricated it, others muttered.

————

FURTHER DOWN THE mountain, as the path broadened into a road, they reached the first houses. Livira's training had not yet extended to dealing with the public in the library foyer where requests could be made, and so her acquaintance with the citizens of Crath remained limited to the brief journey she had made from the gates to the library years earlier. She remembered how they had looked at her, old women spitting in her path, small boys throwing stones and calling her "duster." Often, in the time since, she'd stared for longer than she would care to admit into a mirror borrowed from Carlotte, hunting for whatever it was that marked her. She remembered the sting of that word, *duster*, and wondered if it would be thrown her way again or if the blue robes of a library trainee were sufficient armour.

Livira was so deep in the experience of being outside that she passed Yute's curious tower of a house without realising it.

"I nearly didn't recognise you, child!" A voice from behind her. "Did you think you could just waltz past without a hello?" Salamonda filled the doorway and brandished a wooden spoon in admonishment.

Arpix turned, astonished at being addressed in this manner out on the street.

"I'm so sorry, Salamonda!" Livira started towards the steps then remembered Arpix and dragged him with her. "It's just—I haven't been outside in forever, and the sky . . . isn't it wonderful! And shadows!" She danced, twirling to see her own. "I have a shadow again!"

"And a skinny one it is!" Salamonda frowned. "Your friend could do with an extra meal or two as well." She turned back towards her kitchen. "Come on in."

Livira hesitated. When Yute had dumped her on Master Logaris he'd said that he would come and check on her in a while. She was still waiting. She understood now why the woman who'd nearly hit him with her book trolley had been so shocked. Seeing Yute in the library was a very rare thing indeed. Only the head librarian was more of a mystery. Livira had yet to see her or learn her name.

"Our thanks, ma'am." Arpix spoke for them both. "But we're on urgent library business." He slapped his hands against the heavy satchels at his sides.

"And it's the library asking for your friend upstairs, sonny." Salamonda looked upwards meaningfully. "Who do you think had me looking out for young Livira this morning when I had a million other things to do?"

"Yute asked you to look out for me?" Livira was amazed. She'd convinced herself long ago that the man had lost all interest in her and must be one of those people whose attention is always being drawn into something new only to drop that in turn and move on again.

"Come on." Salamonda went in.

Livira and Arpix followed, taking a few moments for their vision to adjust as they transitioned from blazing sunshine to the relative gloom inside. What struck Livira, before her eyes could see to find the source, was a new and marvellous aroma that filled her mouth with saliva. She still remembered the woman's stew, but this was not that. This was better.

"You go on up, Livira. I'll feed your boyfriend some of my butter biscuits. See if we can put some meat on his bones."

"He's not my— Butter biscuits?"

"We'll save you some. If you're quick. That Yute does like to ramble though. See if you can keep him on track."

Livira fairly flew up the stairs.

She slowed as she approached Yute's door. Suddenly she wanted time to marshal her thoughts. She was angry at him for abandoning her, grateful now for his renewed attention, angry at herself for being grateful.

"Come in." Yute's voice through the door.

Feeling foolish, she went in. Yute sat in the same chair, just as awkwardly as when he'd waited for her to make her choice from his daughter's clothes. She knew about his daughter now. Also a trainee in the library. Lost nearly a decade ago on a book search. Her remains still out there somewhere, still undiscovered.

Wentworth was with Yute, coiled in a furry puddle around both his ankles like a living shackle. It was as if the two of them hadn't moved from the spot since that first day.

Livira glanced around. The clutter that had seemed so mysterious, so alien that she'd had no words for it but "mess," now resolved itself in the light of her learning. For two years she'd crammed her hungry mind with newness until even its vast appetite was sometimes sated. A globe stood with the continents outlined by seas and oceans. A telescope of brass and steel, resting on its stand; an astrolabe; pieces of clockwork in various states of assembly or disassembly, together with other instruments for which she *still* had no name.

"Livira." Pink eyes regarded her as if she might be another of his mechanical puzzles. "So, have you met Wentworth's equal yet?"

This was not one of the many questions she had anticipated on their eventual reunion. "No." She had seen stealthy cats among the aisles stalking equally stealthy rats. But never a monster of Wentworth's dimensions.

"And your studies are going well?"

Livira restrained herself to a nod.

"I hear you opened Chamber Seven with one of the old guides."

Livira said nothing, fearing her own reaction if he laughed at her. None of the other librarians had believed her. She'd been called a liar to her face, and so she had ended her report at the door that they didn't think she'd opened.

Yute nodded for her. "It's the first time one of the forbidden chambers has been accessed." He continued to watch her closely. "Did you know that the further out we go the larger the proportion of chambers that are forbidden becomes? At the extremes we follow corridors of chambers through seas of knowledge that are sealed from us. It's a curious mixture of pride and ignorance that constrains us. And pride in our own ignorance. They don't believe you because to do so would be to admit you were the first into such coveted territory."

"But you believe me?"

Yute said nothing. He reached into his dark-grey robes and when he turned his open hand to her a feather lay across his palm, the blackness of it accentuating the whiteness of his skin. He held it towards her. She took it, finding it heavier than a feather should be.

"Careful," Yute warned. "You can cut yourself on the edges."

She offered it back to him. "Where did you find this?"

"Keep it." Yute raised his palms to her. "I discovered it close to where you said you'd left your mechanical friend. I believe him to be one of the most ancient of the guides. Not part of the library but manufactured by someone with a far deeper understanding of it than ours. He is mentioned in certain books . . . I knew his name once, but I've forgotten it . . . along with many other things."

Livira lifted the feather, marvelling at its blackness. Part of her wanted to tell Yute about the assistant and the Exchange—part of her still wanted it as a secret to keep to herself. She hesitated. Opened her mouth. Closed it. Opened it again . . . but Yute had more to say and filled the pause.

"In any event, you succeeded on your first venture, where generations of the wise failed. Even to concede that you might have stumbled upon the answer by accident hurts my colleagues' pride." He reached for a cup steaming gently on the table beside him, took a sip, and frowned as if the taste were not to his liking. "You should be careful on your venture into the city today, Livira. People can be good or bad one by one. Society is almost always awful. People with your origins are not well liked in Crath." Yute set his cup aside and rose from his chair, dislodging Wentworth. "I have an assignment for you. I want you to see if you can deduce the nature of the library's greatest curse."

"Curse?" Livira frowned. The librarians spoke about the library as humanity's greatest blessing. Everyone did, as far as she knew, though in the city it was the *city's* blessing—the *king's* blessing on the city—and humanity at large could keep their grubby fingers out of it.

"Curse." Yute nodded. "One of several."

Livira said nothing. The library had eaten Yute's daughter. Livira knew the fear that being deep among the aisles could bring. It must have been a lonely death. Why wouldn't he think it a curse after that?

"Let me plant a seed," Yute said, "and when you come back, we'll see what has grown. Consider, although you might not notice it after your brief acquaintance, the city you go down into is not the same as the one you climbed up from two years ago. They say that you can never go back— and that's true. We change and so the places we return to will not seem the same. But here it's the case that the city has grown as much as you have. Ask yourself in the face of the remarkable speed of progress: where did we come from, where are we going, and—most importantly—have we walked this path before?"

Livira didn't know the answer, but she was certain, just by the shape of the question, that Yute had handed her something dangerous. "Why are you telling me this?"

Regret lined Yute's smile. "You listen well for a child who asks so many questions. That's one reason. Some might think it's because you remind me of Yolanda, but that's too shallow an assumption; my daughter was a very different person at your age. Another reason, though it shames me to admit it, is that some truths are hard to bear alone and dangerous to share. In you, Livira, I see a mind that is sharp enough to cut to the facts, and a truth that you have yourself exposed is harder to deny and easier to consider.

"In you I see a spark like no other, and when you're grown, I hope it will become such a light that it will show us a way out." He steepled his pale fingers, then interlaced them. "And make no mistake, child, we are trapped."

Start a tale, just a little tale that should fade and die—take your eye off it for just a moment and when you turn back it's grown big enough to grab you up in its teeth and shake you. That's how it is. All our lives are tales. Some spread, and grow in the telling. Others are just told between us and the gods, muttered back and forth behind our days, but those tales grow too and shake us just as fierce.

Prince of Fools, *by Mark Lawrence*

CHAPTER 28

Livira

Arpix had no complaints about being kept waiting in Salamonda's kitchen, other than that he was now too full to move. He hefted up his share of the load and Livira gathered the rest. The books that needed to be delivered to the laboratory seemed to have grown heavier during their stay. Salamonda waved off Arpix's thanks, telling them both they should stop by more often, as if it hadn't been Arpix's first visit and two years since the only time she'd seen Livira before.

"What did Deputy Yute want?" Arpix lasted two streets before succumbing to his curiosity.

"He was talking about fiction," Livira said.

"Fiction?" Arpix's pace had slowed since leaving Yute's house.

"Stories." Livira had only eaten half as many of Salamonda's butter biscuits and her overfull stomach was slowing her down too. "We never translate it and rarely get requests. But it fills more than half the shelves. A lot more than half. He said everyone should try it. He said to try reading it and writing it."

"A *librarian* said that?" Arpix seemed shocked.

Livira had jumped to the end of her conversation with Yute. She'd known talk of fiction would shock Arpix and that the boy's head would probably explode if she told him that Yute thought the library cursed. The library was a faith which made Yute's talk of curses heresy of the highest order. She was sure of that even if she didn't properly understand what his "seed" might grow into. And Arpix might be passionate on very few subjects but when it came to the library's stated purpose, to bring knowledge freely to the people, he was a fanatic.

"We should read fiction?" Arpix shook his head in amazement. "To learn our languages better?"

"For pleasure."

Arpix blinked. "And write it? What would be the point of that?"

"Yute told me a great writer once said that fiction was easy—all you have to do is sit in front of a blank page and bleed." Livira snorted. "Yute said there was a people who took that literally. They wrote everything in blood, which he felt was trying too hard, but perhaps a good way to conserve paper and make sure you get to the point quickly. Apparently Chamber Eighteen is almost full of just their books!"

"Suffering for their art." Arpix nodded appreciatively. "What else did he—"

"He said a story is a net. It can capture something as large as the spirit of the age or as small as the emotion of a man watching the last leaf fall from a tree, or sometimes both, and make one a reflection of the other."

Arpix nodded and for a moment he was silent, chewing over the librarian's words. Then with a shake of his head, as if throwing off a dream, he tried again. "He couldn't have just wanted to talk about stories. What else did—"

"What's that?" Livira pointed at a smudge on the horizon, grateful for something to distract Arpix from his interrogation.

"Dust storm?"

"Too small. And it doesn't look like one." Arpix knew much more about cities, but Livira considered herself the expert when it came to dust.

"Well . . ." Arpix frowned and glanced around at the nearest mountain peaks to get his bearings. "Tronath is in that direction, thirty miles maybe? It's the nearest city. More of a town really."

"Is it cold there?"

"No." Arpix's frown deepened.

"Why'd they set fire to it then?"

A man bustled past them, pushing a cart on which half a dozen large round cheeses were piled. "Stinkin' sabbers did it."

"Sabbers know how to use fire?" Arpix called at his back, amazed.

"Dog-soldiers." The man nodded and hurried on down the slope, cart bumping over the flagstones. "You didn't hear it from me."

"Why wouldn't they know about fire?" Livira turned to Arpix. "The ones I saw had swords. You need fire to make iron." Over the two years since leaving the Dust Livira's grief had hardened into a cold stone of hate that lodged somewhere between her heart and her stomach. She hoped that Malar's comrades had hunted down every last one of the sabbers who destroyed her settlement. But that didn't mean she would believe belittling stories about them over the truth she'd seen with her own eyes.

Arpix shook his head. "The last book I worked on was being translated from Middle Gargan for the house readers. It says the sabbers breed with dogs and are little more than animals themselves. They probably stole those swords."

"That's not right." Livira stopped to adjust her satchels and turned towards Arpix as he pulled up. "I talked with one. He spoke our language. Animals don't speak."

"What did he say?" Arpix asked.

"'Are you good to eat?'"

Arpix shrugged. "Sounds like what an animal would say if it could talk." He set off again.

Livira watched him for a moment. It hadn't been like that, had it? She thought the sabber had been exercising a rather dry sense of humour. She'd demanded to know if it was going to eat her. It unsettled her how the same words could mean such different things to different people. How it might be possible for two sets of eyes to witness the same events and later give accounts at odds with each other.

LIVIRA FOLLOWED ARPIX through the city, shocked by the crowds and the noise after so long in the library's calm. She scanned the sea of faces for her friends from the settlement and of course saw none of them.

"That's where we're heading." Arpix pointed at the arm of the mountain rising above them. "The laboratory's up there. So the wind carries any fumes away from the city."

Soon after, in the narrow alleys of low town, rooftops sealed away all sight of the laboratory, and Arpix's sense of direction vanished with it.

Livira rolled her aching shoulders under the straps of her book satchels. "Are we lost?"

"Oh, you're more than lost, my dear." A tall man with long, greasy hair and a rank smell to him insinuated himself into their path.

"We're on library busi—"

The glimmer of a knife in the man's hand cut Arpix off. Suddenly the alleyway was very empty. The man's face was unremarkable, mean, bony, but something cold and empty lay in his eyes, the kind of hunger that told Livira this wasn't about theft. The man meant to kill them. The terror that filled her came mixed with a sense of waste—how pointless to die for unknown reasons in a stinking alley, with all the secrets of the library so close at hand and so untouched.

"Run!" Arpix said. But he made no move to run and his courage anchored her. Besides, she could hear the man's accomplice closing from behind.

"On your way, friend." The knifeman raised his gaze to the person behind Livira. Not an accomplice then. "This ain't your business."

"Disagree."

"I ain't alone."

"You weren't. Are now."

The man who pushed between Arpix and Livira stood a head shorter than the knifeman and didn't have a weapon.

"Back off!"

The newcomer continued forward.

The knifeman raised his blade. "Back off! I—"

The exchange was too fast to see. The taller man fell to the ground clutching his chest with crimson fingers.

As the shorter man turned Livira knew him. "Malar?" He looked much the same, perhaps a little greyer, a little more grizzled. The wounds the sabber claws had torn across his face were puckered white seams now.

"Dust-rat." He inclined his head.

"Malar!" Livira couldn't wipe the grin from her face even while the rest of her was still trembling from shock. A sudden frown pushed it away. "Malar?" The city held tens of thousands. "What are the odds . . . ?"

"When I'm being paid to keep an eye on you, they're pretty high." He wiped his dagger on his cloak then returned it to his belt. The man on the ground didn't move or so much as groan. "We're even, dust-rat, don't forget that. Coin's why I'm here. Pure and simple." He turned and walked away. "Come on. And keep your wits about you. The three clowns I put down were paid, same as I was. Probably more of them about."

Malar led them out of the slum and angled them upwards, starting the climb to the laboratory. Livira talked at him, her words running from her like water from a holed bucket. Where the shock had Arpix white-faced and silent, she couldn't keep her mouth shut. She talked about everything, and Malar ignored her until she announced her intention to find her friends from the settlement. She wanted to know they were doing well. She'd been collecting her meagre wage to make sure the little ones could eat. She hadn't imagined it would be two years before she came back out of the library entrance.

"Give me the money. I'll see it gets to this Benth of yours. Your lot are fine though. It's the ones just outside the walls you should worry about."

"The people outside the wall?" Livira asked.

"Folk from the Dust," Malar said. "There's hundreds camped at the base of the wall. The king won't let them in. Says they're thieves and rapists come here because they're too lazy to work their land anymore."

"But why are they here? What do they eat?"

"Running from the sabbers, they say." Malar paused at the base of the long stair leading up to the laboratory and continued in a very different voice as if to make it clear he was pretending. "Of course, that can't be true because the king's armies have scored one glorious victory after another over the bestial foe."

LIVIRA SAVED HER breath for the climb as the streets began to grow steep and the satchels seemed to get heavier by the yard. To distract herself from the pain in her shoulders and memories of a knife glittering in an alley, she focused on what she'd learned since coming down from the library. Frowning furiously and keeping her eyes on the steps, she tried to fit various ideas together, jamming one at the other as if they were poorly designed puzzle pieces that only force of will might fit together. The library was a source of knowledge—the best source anyone knew of. On the pages of ancient books were secrets that unlocked the mysteries of fire and alchemy. The laboratory fed on such secrets, churning out new wonders every year, be they more efficient arrow-sticks, cheaper, brighter lighting, medicines that truly worked, or explosives that could shatter rock. And yet the faith that those successes engendered had allowed King Oanold to sow convenient lies, also underwritten by books from the library.

"With an endless library," Livira muttered, "if you search long enough, you can find a book that agrees with just about any opinion you have . . . And we're the engine of that search. We give the king what he wants to hear, what he wants the people to hear. He doesn't ask the librarians to bring him books about the sabbers—he asks them to bring him books that say '*this*' about sabbers."

"Keep your voice down." Arpix panted up alongside her, though the idea that anyone save him might overhear her was ridiculous. In a barely intelligible whisper he hissed, "Wait till you hear what Bagnus told me when we were hunting down these books."

"What did he tell you?" Bagnus was the oldest on their table by several years and overdue a move to the next.

"Quill search," Arpix panted.

"What's that?" Livira was breathing hard now as they climbed a long flight of stone steps.

"A theory." Arpix shifted his load and heaved more air into his chest. "If the library were really infinite the theory says it would contain every book you could imagine."

"Maybe."

"And if that were true . . . If that were true, then if you know every book is out there somewhere . . ."

"Yes?" Livira was finding all these pauses increasingly irritating though she doubted her ability to speak a whole sentence right now. Malar seemed annoyingly untroubled by the steps but made no offer to help out with the satchels.

"Well," Arpix went on, "wouldn't it be easier to just write the book you're looking for rather than to go and hunt it down?" He wiped sweat from his pale forehead. "Quill search. You use a quill to find the book you want by putting it on the page. And you tell everyone it's a library truth because if the library never ends, then it's in there someplace."

"The library has to end somewhere!"

Arpix shrugged. "Prove it."

Livira was struggling for an answer when her foot came down extra hard, missing a step that wasn't there, and she found they'd reached the top. Malar was sitting close by on a bench in the shade of a wall.

"The laboratory." He waved to an impressive building constructed as if it were some ancient, many-columned temple emerging from the mountainside. Higher up, fissures on the slopes above belched slightly yellowish smoke that the wind stripped away and carried off towards the northern Dust. The air had a sharpness to it that felt like nothing natural and stung Livira's eyes, though she couldn't smell anything in particular.

Livira and Arpix joined Malar in the shade, shrugging off their burdens. Livira, spotting a drinking fountain in an alcove nearby, went to slake her thirst. She drank more than she should and stood, wiping her mouth. She'd never heard of plumbing before she arrived in the city. Now the pipes seemed to be spreading like the roots of some vast plant, reaching into every home. She looked out over the low wall that kept her from a fall into gardens below. The city of Crath lay spread before her. A metropolis of stone and brick and slate and marble, always in the grip of change, as if an invisible fire constantly spread from the library, consuming the old as it demanded a never-ending reconstruction.

Livira wondered how long it had taken the ancients to discover these secrets the first time, not by poring over the pages of learned tomes but uninstructed, through painstaking observation of the universe. She supposed that might depend on quite how many people there were. Perhaps ten billion souls could throw forward a sufficient number of geniuses to unlock the secrets of existence in the same timescale that ten thousand souls might be led through the necessary steps by careful instruction. But the real questions here were Yute's. How many times had it happened before? And why were they back so close to the start of the journey today?

A polite cough from the smartly dressed old man standing by the door drew Livira from her thoughts. She realised she'd crossed the small plaza from the stair and presented herself at the door. "From the library, I assume?"

Before Livira could affirm the obvious, the door began to open and a dark-haired man in a stained white tunic hurried out, glancing their way, leaving the door still swinging wide. The old doorman stared disapprovingly at the man's back. "Who have you come to deliver to?"

"Hiago Abdalla." Livira named one of the three laboratory chiefs who worked under the auspices of the head alchemist. She watched distractedly as the departing man in the stained tunic made a beeline for a richly dressed visitor arriving behind her. He ushered the woman away towards the steps as if she were a stray goat. There seemed to be a sense of suppressed urgency about the man's actions, and the woman's offended dignity wasn't deterring him one iota.

"Something's wr—" The explosion drowned out Malar's suspicions, knocking Livira to the ground as a greenish-yellow cloud belched from the open door to engulf them all.

. . . more popular than the hall of mirrors. The distortions offered by these curved reflectors vary from the comical to the uncanny. Few things have the power to unsettle us as much as a face that is almost, but not quite, right. The lesson of the mirror hall is one of perception. A change of angle, the addition of fresh distortion, or removal of existing distortion, can change entirely our view of someone we thought we knew.

Carnival Entertainments in Southeast Lithgow, *by Mitch Kable*

CHAPTER 29

Evar

Clovis's mother practically dragged her daughter off her feet as they fled among the book towers. Her father and two brothers lay dead behind them, part of the slaughter. The sabbers closed their net about the survivors, coming in from all directions, the numbers in their favour even if they hadn't been the only side to be armed.

Evar gave chase, easily catching up with them as he ran through any obstacle in his way. He soon understood that the mother was aiming for the closest reading room. She still carried the iron-hinged tome with which she'd broken the old warrior's neck.

As they drew closer to the reading-room entrance, with the screams of the dying fading behind them, the mother slowed and began to limp. Evar saw now that she hadn't escaped without injury. Blood ran down over her hip from a puncture wound on her left side, high up between the ribs. Clovis hadn't seen yet, focused as she was on the stacks behind them, watching for any sabber that might be on their trail. It wouldn't be hard to follow. A line of crimson splatters marked the way.

"You're bleeding!" The child's voice held a new kind of horror, something far greater than fear for herself.

"It's nothing." Her mother pulled her on, still lugging the heavy book under one arm. Evar understood her reluctance to surrender it. As a shield and as a weapon, it had served her well despite the odds.

The reading room of Clovis's childhood was much as it was in the adulthood she shared with Evar, a confusion of upturned desks, desk islands, desk walls, the playground of many children. Though if there were any children present when Clovis's mother stumbled in with Clovis and Evar right behind her then they were well hidden.

A man and woman, both young, were hurrying from the Mechanism, making for the corridor. There was something odd about the man: it was as if his skin were smoking, leaving a trail of shadows tainting the air behind him. Like Clovis's mother, he was stumbling, and the young woman was pulling him along.

"What's wrong with him?" Clovis asked.

Her mother drew her aside to make room for the pair to pass. "Hella must have opened the Mechanism to get him out."

Evar knew you should never do that. The Assistant had been very clear on that point. It was something only she should do.

"Don't go out there, Hella!" the mother called to them as they passed. "That's where they are!"

The young woman turned towards them, wide-eyed. "There's more space. I'd rather hide from them out there than in here."

"But . . ." The mother let them go. Neither choice was good. The man left a trail of black smoke that wasn't smoke. Evar glimpsed disturbing shapes in the shadow before it dissipated beneath the library's relentless light.

The mother took them to the grey block of the Mechanism. The door today was a featureless white rectangle that reminded Evar of the Assistant, seemingly made of the same stuff.

"Where is she? The Assistant?" Evar turned to Clovis's mother. "Where's the Soldier?" The Soldier could turn the tide against any number of sabbers. The mother couldn't hear him, of course, and even if she could she had more pressing issues than answering a ghost's questions.

"We need to be quiet." The mother pulled Clovis to the far side of the Mechanism, out of sight of the entrance to the reading room. She looked down and shook her head in dismay. "My blood's going to lead them to us wherever we go . . ." She leaned the book against the Mechanism and inspected her wound gingerly. The same bright crimson that ran from the slot through her leather jerkin now speckled her lips and chin. The weapon had found her lung.

"We can hide," Clovis said. She stared wide-eyed at the corridor. "Can't we, Mama?"

A distant scream pierced her mother's hesitation. Together, Clovis and her mother crouched and edged forward to peer around the corner of the Mechanism. At the far end of the corridor to the main hall a figure moved into view. Then another. And another.

Evar watched his sister, his sister of chance and of opportunity, hardly recognising the soft child before him. A child full of fear, and love. The Clovis he knew, the one who had crawled out of the Mechanism beside him, had been iron from the start, even though she'd worn this young girl's flesh on that first day. She'd been iron ever since, unfaltering in her training, unfaltering in her hatred for the sabbers. With no place for it to go, that hate had washed over all her brothers, a cold thing and all the scarier for its lack of heat. She'd infected them all with her desire for revenge—her need for it—but theirs had been a shadow of what she felt. She had been here when it happened. She remembered. They had been told, but she had seen it, heard it, smelled it. Visions of this last hour must have haunted every quiet moment she'd spent since. Little wonder that she avoided quiet moments.

The only fear Evar had ever seen in his sister had been inside the boundaries of the terrifying dreams that tore her sleep. He understood now what fed those nightmares. That was where she relived these moments, filling her sleep with her father's death, the slaughter of her true brothers, and the horror of waiting here at the Mechanism with her mother bleeding and the sabbers on their trail.

Evar understood now that the Clovis he knew was not the woman this girl would have grown into without this day. She had been forged by the events he'd witnessed, and another Clovis, one he would never know, lay dead with her brothers back among the stacks.

"We'll hide in the Mechanism," Clovis's mother said.

"I thought you had to go in alone?" Clovis looked up at her mother, trembling.

"Two is fine," her mother lied. "The important thing is to run. As soon as we get in, we both run and don't look back. Can you do that for me? Run and not look back? I'll be right behind you."

"But I don't want—"

The swing of her mother's hand slapped the words from Clovis's mouth. "Run and don't look back!" A shout this time. Other shouts came from the corridor: the sabbers were running now.

With bloody hands her mother dragged Clovis to the Mechanism door. "Carry this for me." She thrust the book into Clovis's arms. She set a hand to the door. It should have left a crimson print but instead the white surface simply melted beneath her touch, revealing a grey tunnel.

The sabbers were in the chamber, a score of them, some with blades in hand as they ran, others carrying the metal tubes that spat death over a distance. Evar had read about guns but never thought to see one.

"Go on!" The mother shoved her daughter forward. "I'm with you! Run!"

The instant Clovis passed through the doorway the white surface re-established itself behind her.

"This won't work," Evar muttered, even though he knew that somehow it already had. The sabbers must have seen Clovis going in though. The only protection Clovis had now was that the sabbers might know the dangers of opening the Mechanism from the outside when it was in use. And even if they did, surely they would just wait? Clovis would emerge of her own volition once she understood she was alone.

Clovis's mother pushed herself away from the Mechanism with a snarl, leaving the wall smeared with blood. She hobbled towards the nearest cluster of desks, trying to draw the sabbers with her.

Even as she did so the attackers split, some pursuing her, others closing on the door she'd pushed her daughter through. Evar dropped into a defensive stance before the entrance, knowing it to be useless.

Something was happening to either side of Evar. Something so unexpected that it managed to divert his attention from the sabbers now only thirty yards from him. On both sides of the door grey hands reached out of the Mechanism's walls as if it were thick mud rather than impenetrable stone. Within the space of ten heartbeats two figures tore themselves free, leaving no mark on the wall behind them. The Assistant and the Soldier, just as Evar had always known them, except grey, and not a single uniform grey but shades in motion, darker here, lighter there, swirling like smoke behind glass. Both of them staring at themselves, inspecting their hands as if surprised to find they owned them. The Assistant's palms bore the cut wounds Evar had always known. The Soldier's left hand, all the left side of his body had the part-melted look that he had never explained.

"You've got to stop the sabbers!" Evar shouted.

The Soldier raised his head, fixing Evar with the black eyes of a stranger.

"Soldier!" Evar reached for the Soldier's shoulder to turn him towards the sabbers' charge. Instead, he found himself elbow-deep in the swirling grey of the Soldier's body. In that instant such a wave of violence flooded up his arm that it threw him back to land on the floor, breathless with horror.

The sabbers hurled themselves at the Soldier and the Assistant in the next moment. The Soldier didn't draw his blade. Instead, he disabled his foe with brutal efficiency. His punches lifted sabbers from the ground and hurled them back to land among upturned desks. His elbows broke jaws and sent teeth flying from mouths. A sweep of his leg cut sabbers down like ripe wheat.

Why hadn't the pair emerged even an hour earlier? Why hadn't they saved the people? Evar had never imagined their arrival in these terms. So close to the massacre that it felt now like a sin of omission. They had let so many die . . .

One sabber thrust his blade at the Assistant only to have it slide off her chest. The Soldier shoved him aside with a force that must have broken many ribs. Guns boomed and their projectiles ricocheted from both the Assistant and the Soldier, some injuring nearby sabbers.

The darkness was smoking from both of them, revealing the old ivory of their flesh with occasional grey seams running through it.

"Why are we here?" The Assistant sounded confused, as if she'd woken from a long sleep. "I said we'd wait until the children came back out."

"It's me. Evar." Evar stood, weak and shuddering with the after-effects of his contact with the Soldier. It had been worse than the slaughter of Clovis's people he'd just witnessed. That at least hadn't physically touched him. The memories coursing through his mind now weren't just images but the feel of it, gore coating his arms, the sick pain of wounds, the primal thrill of carving flesh, the hard cold core of survival that selects the least bad option and commits to it with single-minded totality. The Soldier hadn't just killed sabbers in his time, he'd killed people too, with the same savagery. "I'm here. Can you see me?"

The Assistant looked through him. She tilted her head as if she might have seen some faint hint of him. The Soldier meanwhile knocked down the last few sabbers within reach.

"Evar's out here," the Assistant said. "Very close."

"He's still in the Mechanism too," the Soldier grunted. Blood drops beaded his skin, a broader splatter of crimson running from shoulder to hip.

Evar watched the Soldier with faint horror, the echoes of what lay beneath that ivory surface still trembling through him. Training with Clovis was intense. Evar had the skills to take on many opponents. But training was one thing—actually spilling blood, watching the pain you've caused, butchering your foe . . . those were entirely different things. Having tasted them vicariously Evar had no desire for first-hand knowledge. If the same beast that lived in the Soldier also lived in him Evar was fine with never waking it.

The Assistant turned towards the Mechanism door. "It's been used very recently." Her eyes darkened. "Clovis has joined them."

"And your boy?" the Soldier asked.

"Still inside . . . but also outside." She reached out to touch the door. Instead of melting as it did when the Mechanism was empty it resisted the Assistant's touch. "Let me see . . ." She applied more pressure, and her fingers began to sink into the door. A projectile bounced off her shoulder and whined away through the air. "Inside. With the book." It seemed now that rather than pushing through the door she was being pulled into it. She looked back at Evar, seeing him clearly. "There's nothing for you here." The door swallowed her, cutting off any more words.

"Wait!" The Soldier took her trailing hand and tried to pull her back, but the inexorable force drew him in too, and when he refused to release her to the door it swallowed him along with her.

The sabbers approached cautiously, in no rush to help their injured comrades, some groaning on the floor, others insensible, or maybe dead. Evar could see where Clovis's mother fell, her body just another of his ancestors lying curled about their wounds in spreading pools of their own blood.

Suddenly Evar wanted nothing but to be away from this place and to put the sad inevitability of it behind him. The Assistant was right: there wasn't anything for him here. To watch and be able to do nothing as the sabbers hunted down the last survivors was not something he could bring himself to do. Neither would he follow his sister into the Mechanism. Even as a ghost he doubted himself immune to its effects. Just touching the Soldier had plunged him into a world of nightmare whose remnants still clung to him.

Evar wanted the peace and solitude of the wood that lay between this place and that. The wood that lay not only between worlds but between times too. He walked away, slow beneath the burden of what he had seen, aiming for the pool once more.

Trust is the most insidious of poisons, but there are many alternatives that serve almost as well. As with comedy, delivery is a vital component. If the target is aware of the attack, the chances for success are immediately much reduced.

Venom, *by Sister Apple*

CHAPTER 30

Livira

The greenish-yellow cloud that poured from the laboratory to engulf Livira, Arpix, and Malar smelled the way a knife feels. So sharp it felt as if it was skinning her. The poison stung her eyes so badly that she had to screw them shut.

Think. The choices weren't good. Try to get into the building—but that was where the stuff was coming from. Try to find the stairs—but a broken neck from falling down those wouldn't help her situation. Get to the wall at the edge of the courtyard—but the drop to the gardens beneath had looked fatal.

Livira crawled towards the fountain she'd drunk from. Or at least where she thought it was. She could hear an awful choking behind her. She crawled with the breath straining in her lungs and the demand that she replace it growing rapidly. Blind hands found the fountain and she plunged her face into the water, letting it soak her robes. She held the wet cloth over her mouth and nose then risked opening one stinging eye. The wind had kept the worst of the cloud from the wall.

The noises from inside the billowing fumes were truly frightening. It sounded as if people were dying in there. As much as she didn't want to, Livira went back, aiming for the sound of choking. The wet cloth dulled the edge of the poison though the taste of it made her want to vomit and already a slow fire was starting in her lungs. She tripped over someone after half a dozen paces and started to cough as she drew too deep a breath.

Grabbing a handful of their clothing she tried to haul them towards safety. Thankfully whoever it was had enough strength to crawl after her.

"Arpix!" The boy was red-faced, frothing at the mouth, and looked as if he'd been poked in both eyes. Livira flung a double handful of water into his face. "Arpix! Hold this here." She pulled his wet robe up making him keep it over his face then threw more water. "We have to go back for Malar."

Arpix shook his head, gasping, fighting for breath. The cloud was beginning to dissipate but it would still take too long for the wind to take it away. Judging by Arpix's condition, Malar didn't have that long.

"Fine." Livira paused to cough painfully. "I'll go."

The sickly green enfolded her once more. She found the next person with her feet, just as she'd found Arpix, and took hold. She resisted taking the deep breath such effort demanded, then began to haul. At first, she might as well have been pulling a dead horse for all the give she got, but then, somehow, there was movement. A nightmare of straining followed, sucking awful breaths through wet cloth and coughing them out from a chest that seemed to be on fire from the inside.

Gradually the cloud thinned around her, and she realised she had hold of Malar and that Arpix was helping. The soldier was trying to crawl, failing but making it easier to drag him.

The cloud had dissipated long before any of them were able to speak again. Livira felt as if she had coughed up some vital portion of her insides. Certainly, there was blood on her hands.

Alchemists emerged from the laboratory in strange masks, looking out at the world through round glass plates. They checked the old doorman first—he looked dead to Livira—then came to help the trainees and their guardian.

"Inhale this. Quickly!" It sounded like a woman speaking but with the mask Livira couldn't tell. She'd taken two glass vials from the pockets of her protective coat. She poured one into the other and a plume of white vapour hissed up. "Breathe it in. Hold the breath."

Livira did as she was told then lifted Malar's head as they got him to do the same. She didn't feel any immediate relief but had to believe that the alchemists knew what they were doing.

"How . . . H-how did you . . . know?" Arpix gasped beside her. "A-about the wet cloth?"

"I read it in a book." Livira had found time to read an entire book on most days since learning how reading worked. Carlotte accused her of just reading the page numbers, saying Livira flicked through the pages so fast that it was all she could possibly be doing. Livira read every word though and remembered what she read. She often wondered if some other part of her had been sacrificed to make room for the skills she had that others didn't. It worried her, but she was what she was. That had been her Aunt Teela's wisdom on the subject of Livira long before she even knew what books were. She was what she was.

"Fuck . . ." Malar rasped the word past bloody lips and tried to get up. The alchemists pushed him back down, plying him with more of their vapours.

NIGHT WAS APPROACHING outside before the three of them were released from the infirmary within the laboratory and taken to see Hiago Abdalla. Malar had been worst affected and still spoke in a painful rasp between fits of coughing. The alchemist in charge of the infirmary had strongly recommended Malar remain in bed while the trainees completed their delivery. To which Malar had offered the counterargument: "Fuck that." Arpix and Livira had escaped relatively lightly, though both were amused to find that their wet hair had absorbed the gas and been bleached by the resulting solution, leaving them an unnatural shade of blonde. Livira's was darker at the roots and with black streaks here and there where her original colour persisted.

A hefty apprentice alchemist carried all four satchels and led the way through the corridors carved into the mountainside behind the laboratory's elaborate façade. By the time they reached Abdalla's door at the top of a flight of steps Malar was wheezing badly and Livira was having difficulty catching her breath.

Hiago Abdalla looked as if he had once been a large man and had shrivelled through some alchemical process into a small one. He took refuge behind a desk so wide it made him seem to Livira like a wizened doll afloat on an ocean of polished oak. Like the corridors, the room was lit by incandescence trapped within glass balls cradled in copper brackets. Livira didn't understand the workings of the illumination, which seemed quite different from the gas lamps in the streets, but she preferred the library's gentler, more pervasive light.

"Master." The apprentice set the four bags of books on the desk and withdrew.

Master Abdalla studied his visitors with eyes that resembled dull black stones. It seemed that the chemicals he worked with had gnawed away at him over the years, chewing him down to the bone, for he was the most skeletal of men.

"My thanks for delivering texts on the requested subjects." He set a hand to the closest satchel, somehow giving the impression that the contents were both unknown to him and of minimal interest. "It seems you brought more than that with you, however. Accidents are not unheard-of in the laboratory but what happened in the foyer wasn't accidental. Our doorman is dead, an apprentice missing. You delivered a war of some kind onto our doorstep. Clearly you were expecting trouble." His eyes flicked to Malar, who chose that moment to start a lengthy bout of coughing. "To involve the laboratory is unforgivable. We have compounds here that if detonated could bring down this arm of the mountain!"

Livira's anger took control of her tongue. "You're missing an apprentice because he ran away after setting off the reaction that nearly killed us! And Malar here is just a friend who—" Malar's spluttered protest dissolved into more coughing. "A friend who volunteered to escort us after we had trouble with some street thugs on the way. I will be sure to let the head librarian know that an alchemist tried to kill us when delivering books. Let us just hope that your noxious gases haven't damaged the texts. Because if there's one thing that upsets our librarians more than killing trainees . . ."

It was the alchemist's turn to cough and a swift recalibration followed. "Well. Ah ha. Haste is never wise. Our profession teaches us that. I can count on the lost fingers of apprentices the number of times I've said not to add a reagent too swiftly. I will consult with Master Henta on the matter in due course." The casual dropping of the head alchemist's name came as the closing of a heavy cover on the final words of a long story. "But we're all on the same side. The same . . . page, if you like." He allowed himself a dry laugh at his own joke since nobody else cracked a smile. "Progress is the only way we'll outpace these sabbers. Gods know we can't outbreed them." He nodded. "I'll have the boy show you out."

EXCHANGING THE LABORATORY's tainted air for a fresh evening breeze was a blessing that made Livira promise herself to step out from beneath the stone skies of the library at least once a week from now on. The cool air eased the sting that had kept her weeping all the way to and from Master Abdalla's office. She was sure, though, that she couldn't be as bad as Arpix and Malar, whose bloodshot eyes made them look like the monsters in Ella's tales out on the Dust. The ones who crept about in the night in the hope of stealing unattended babies.

"Well"—Arpix stifled a cough—"that was fun."

Livira went to the wall and looked out over the city, already deep in the mountain's shadow. The lamps she had first seen from the Dust as Malar led in a troop of frightened children were coming to life again, more of them now, with a whiter light, picking out streets in a web that spread from many points. She looked up at the black mass of stone to the east where the library waited for their return. Goosebumps prickled across her arms. "Explosives that could bring down the mountain."

"What?" Arpix asked.

"He said they had explosives that could bring the mountain down."

Arpix shrugged. "Sounds like exaggeration to me. But they will do some day. The ancients had such weapons. Mind you, the ancients could fly like birds and reach the moons."

"For a clever kid you—" Malar broke into a coughing fit but recovered himself. "You don't half talk a lot of rubbish. Those are stories for children."

Livira waved his words away. She didn't care about the moons right now. "But what we're agreed on is that there *were* ancients who could work miracles. I mean, we're always hunting books of science for the alchemists or whatever it is the king wants people to believe this week. But there are plenty of histories. We know so much about the past."

"Except how to fit it together," Arpix said.

He was right. There were so many histories and none of them had direct lines connecting "then" to "now." There were few that studied them in these times of feverish progress. "It's a time to look forwards, not back!" King Oanold was fond of saying. The handful who ignored the scorn that Crath's society had for such "time-wasters" argued about where particular civilisations had flourished. There seemed too many of them to fit around the globe, especially when they so seldom appeared to interact.

Malar started towards the steps, keeping a wary eye on the thickening shadows. "Enough flapping your lips. That's twice Algar's tried to have you killed, girl. Let's not give him a third chance before you get back."

It wasn't what Malar said that lit the light of Livira's understanding, it was the way he said it. One chance, two chances, three chances. "What if all those histories didn't happen together in different places, what if they happened in the same places at different times?"

"Then they'd talk about what came before," Arpix said, following Malar, "and it would be obvious. Besides"—he looked around, every bit as suspiciously as the soldier—"that sounds like the Wroxan heresy. You don't want to be talking about it here. Or anywhere really."

Livira's experience had been that things people don't want you to talk about are generally true. This was what Yute had been aiming her at. There were ancients who possessed marvels long ago. With the library's help the people of Crath and of the kingdom beyond had raised themselves from the Dust to commanding incandescent lights, arrow-sticks, and alchemies that might threaten mountains, all in the space of a handful of generations. If the ancients had touched the moons themselves and yet left nothing outside the library but rubble to mark their whole existence, then it made little sense to assume that the people of Crath under the auspices of King Oanold's dynasty were only the second to tread this path.

"It's a cycle." Livira jolted down the first step. "From dust to dust visiting the heights in between." She followed the other two down towards the glowing city. In any good story mankind's hubris would lay him low through the waking of some sleeping evil, some vengeful god jealous of their growing reach. Livira glanced back at the gently smoking vents above the laboratory, lit from below by unseen fires. She thought of Master Abdalla, the little man behind his big desk, feeding on the wisdom the librarians mined from endless shelves. Master Abdalla and his kind, their lives and cleverness given over to the making of ever more deadly weapons with which to fight the foe. Would it really take a vengeful god to bring them all to ruin, or was it simply a case of handing sharp knives to toddlers and waiting for the bleeding to start?

Secrets should never be held too closely, for a secret that is clung to will shape its keeper and in that twisting of their being it will reveal itself. The best-kept secrets are pushed aside, levered to the extremities of the mind, so far from the day's thinking that to press them any further away would be to forget them entirely.
The Truth, and Other Matters of Opinion, *by Gustav Bergmann*

CHAPTER 31

Livira

"What you doing?"

"Research." Livira ignored Jella and kept up her intense scrutiny.

"You're researching the corridor?" Jella continued to rummage around in the leather stores. Her hands, once plump and ink-stained, were strong and calloused these days, always smelling of the glues the binders used. The aroma of leather overwhelmed the glue fragrance here though. The assistants would never allow any of the works Jella and her colleagues produced to be placed on the shelves—such interlopers would be found and destroyed with the same casual wave of a white hand that had once turned Livira's apple to dust and pips. The book copies that Jella and the others produced must, however, appear to have come from the library if they were to be taken seriously in the city, and so their covers were tooled, illuminated, and subsequently aged to convey the necessary gravitas.

"The thing about Master Logaris's training is that he tells us what he thinks we should know when he thinks we should know it," Livira said.

"There's all the books too." Jella laughed. "He doesn't control what you read."

"Yes, but there's too many of them, and he won't point out the ones with the good stuff in." Livira had come to appreciate that an ocean of knowledge is apt to drown you long before it educates you. The art of learning was in selection, and while generations of librarians had ostensibly been cataloguing the collection to make it accessible, they had in fact been turning it into a vast puzzle, a lock whose key was held by those in power. A lock that kept them in power. "I've been reading about espionage. It's widely acknowledged as one of the most effective learning tools."

"Espionage? Isn't that spying?"

"Shhh!" Livira gestured for silence. She had mapped the librarians' complex, and her map showed the junction she'd been watching from the leather store doorway to be one that any of the five most senior librarians had to cross when going from their quarters to the library. Master Ellis who, along with Masters Synoth, Acconite, and Yute, made up the head librarian's four deputies, had just swept by. "Got to go. Tell the others to cover for me!"

"Wait!" Jella started after her, burdened by an armful of hides. "You can't just stalk him!"

"It's called learning!" And Livira was off.

TRAILING THE DEPUTY through the complex was easy enough. The place was always full of librarians, trainees, and support staff going about their duties. The problem would come when Ellis reached the cavern before the library, if he was going to the library—and it seemed that he was.

Livira followed him up the step-filled square spiral that led to the cavern. She trod as quietly as she could, and patted her robes to make sure she had all her treasures with her, her little book of darkness, the Raven's feather, the brass claw, a small collection of coins, and the pouch of dust she carried to remind her where she came from.

On reaching the top of the stair Livira settled to watch Deputy Ellis cross the cavern. The solitude of the library was the main armour for its secrets. If the librarian suspected he might not be alone then his behaviour was likely to change.

Livira had heard rumours of a wonder in the library. One that only the most senior librarians were allowed to visit. Allegedly it was set around with seals forbidding access on pain of expulsion from the ranks, none of which would give her much pause—the main obstacle was simply finding it in the sprawl of chambers. Her hope was that Deputy Ellis would lead her to it. The man had a reputation for delegation and was unlikely to go in search of a book when he could send someone else. So perhaps the reason for this visit was something that needed his personal touch.

Once the guards had let Ellis through the white door into the library, Livira began to cross the cavern at speed. She arrived breathless from the run.

"Livira? It is Livira, isn't it?" The larger of the two guards peered at her through the face guard of his owl-helm. "What have you done to your . . ." He ran a hand over the gleaming steel covering his own hair.

For a moment Livira stared at him in confusion. "Oh!" She understood. "I . . . ah . . . bleached it." The gas attack at the laboratory had turned her wet hair from black to white, though half its length had grown back black in the months since.

"It's an . . . interesting effect," ventured the second guard.

"In a hurry today, Livira," the first man said.

"Always, Mr. Norris." Livira knew the names of all the library guards now. The two men were too busy staring at her hair to pay much attention to Livira's forged library pass. Livira hurried through, thanking them.

Before the door had fully re-formed behind her Livira was at the edge of the platform with an unprotected fifty-yard drop at her toes. She studied the aisles. Almost nothing at floor level was visible save for where a few aisles ran directly away from her. She hadn't expected to see the librarian from up here. Spotting him from the ground would be a hundred times more difficult. Fortunately, she had an alternative that offered a far better chance. A dangerous alternative that nobody she knew would recommend.

Livira started down the stairs, jumping from one to the next with jolts that would have shaken older bones until they rattled. Nearly halfway down she veered sharply to the right and leapt into space.

The jump was one she'd made before and she landed squarely on top of the bookcase, going to one knee and both hands to absorb her momentum. In the next moment she was up and running, glancing from side to side to check the aisles below.

It had taken the best part of a year to, if not conquer her vertigo, put it in a box and store it at the back of her mind. The trick was to fool herself into not understanding the drops and instead see them as familiar but abstract views absent their traditional threat. A hundred yards on, the shelf ended where the aisle folded back on itself. Livira maintained her pace and jumped. This was the most difficult kind of leap to make since she had only the width of the bookcase to tame her speed or be pitched into the fall beyond. She hadn't yet managed not to feel terrified in the instant of landing.

"Still alive!" Livira checked both ways for the librarian then turned to the left and began to run again.

She wasn't silent, of course, and it would be possible that her quarry sighted her before she sighted him, but "up" wasn't a direction many chose to look in the library. Anyone on the hunt for books might be perturbed by the sound of running feet but it wasn't unheard-of, especially in the first chamber, and it was a noise that tended to be associated with the ground.

Livira ran on until she came to the spot she wanted. She turned to look out across the tops of perhaps fifty aisles all running parallel to each other. By jumping from one to the next she would be able to check several hundred thousand square yards of floor space. All it required was fifty eight-foot jumps in a row with a four-foot run up and four feet to land in. Long study of the map—the very map Ellis had worked on for most of his life and which trainees were forbidden from seeing—had shown her that all the quickest routes from the entrance steps to any of the three exits ran through this section she was about to expose.

Livira took a deep breath. "No more falling. No more falling." She repeated it once more for luck. "No more falling." Took two swift paces and leapt.

Ten jumps and one near miss later she spotted him and immediately threw herself flat on the shelf top to ensure it was a one-way transaction. She lay, trembling and breathless with the effort, glad that the search was over since she doubted her ability to make many more successful leaps without a rest.

She waited in silence, listening for Master Ellis's footsteps as he passed beneath her position. She trailed him from on high until she found a ladder, then followed at ground level. She reached the far end of a long aisle and was rewarded by a glimpse of the man turning a corner.

"Got you!" She knew now which door he was headed to. Rather than risk trailing the librarian the whole way, she took off, planning to take an alternative route at speed and wait for him at the exit to the next chamber.

It should have been a simple enough undertaking. The prison of Livira's memory had long ago taken possession of the first chamber's layout, and despite taking her time to find a ladder she was fleet of foot once on the ground.

The problem came at one of the chokes—aisles that if not taken required considerable backtracking to circumvent. Livira was already worried that the delay with the ladder and the longer route she was taking might make the timing tight, so when she skidded around the corner into the choke aisle and saw at the far end a grey-robed figure with long red hair, her heart fell.

Master Jost was one of eight senior librarians in the circle below Yute, Ellis, and the other two deputies. For reasons unknown, but possibly associated with Livira's multiple, unproven break-ins to the sanctum, Jost maintained a very low opinion of her. The sanctum was where Jost and her colleagues carried out research into the fundamentals of the library itself. Naturally it had become the focus for Livira's recently acquired skills in espionage. Jost made trouble for her at every opportunity.

The forged library pass would not withstand Jost's scrutiny. Livira ducked back hurriedly as the librarian turned. "Shit on a stick." Livira liked to blame her brief associations with Malar for her language, but this one was entirely her own. Jost had clearly heard her approach and would be watching to see who it was.

"Can't stop now." Livira fished the small black book from the pocket of her robes. She opened it at a random page and darkness swallowed her.

With the black book open, wrapping her in a lightless bubble, Livira hurried into the aisle. A squeal of fear rewarded Livira's efforts. The rapidly advancing wall of darkness must have looked pretty frightening.

A moment later Livira was past the librarian with the added bonus of having caught her a solid whack with her raised elbow. She ran on but tamed her pace, resolving to maintain the darkness until she reached the distant corner, and not wanting to crash into it at full tilt. Let Master Jost report a mysterious ball of darkness and not include a blue-robed trainee in her account.

———

LIVIRA REACHED THE chamber's left door and waited on the far side. Ellis arrived so late that she was sure he'd outwitted her and turned towards another door. Livira watched from the cover of an aisle, lying with her head at floor level. She was ready to retreat should he come her way, but he chose to head in almost the opposite direction. This was her first good look at him since spotting him from the leather stores back with Jella. She saw now that he had a large travel pack on his shoulder and a good-sized water-skin slung around his chest.

"Sneaky . . ." He must have collected both along the way so that nobody would know he was heading to the library and planning a long trip.

The deputy had a pinched look to his face, which suggested a man who found the world rather unsatisfactory in several departments and expected it to try harder in future.

Livira watched him go, a short figure in his charcoal robes; then, after a suitable delay, she set off in pursuit.

A straight walk from one door to the door opposite it was around two miles. With all the back and forth it was rarely less than four. Something like the labyrinth in Chamber 2 could turn it into a twenty-mile epic. Trailing someone and keeping out of sight just added to the work.

Now that Livira knew about the sustenance circles at the centre of each chamber she could travel endlessly, though after a few days the body began to crave actual food and water even if it didn't appear to need those things to avoid dying. Librarians carried water-skins to satisfy that thirst.

Livira's discovery of the corner circles had been somewhat embarrassing. In each corner was an area about ten yards across where organic matter just disappeared. A process rather like when the assistant had turned Livira's apple to nothing but dust and pips, but significantly slower and more thorough. Standing in the area made your skin prickle but would take some hours to actually evaporate it. With nonliving matter, it was a swifter process. In most corners you would find privies of various designs, built in stone by long-vanished librarians. Anything organic you left there, including wood and bone, would be gone by the time you returned. Books were the sole exception, though with remarkable discrimination the corner would destroy loose pages. Librarians left piles of rags outside the circle. You took a rag in with you and left it there when finished with it.

Allegedly, in the more distant chambers, where restocking the rags proved difficult, a former head librarian had had the works of Enanald Byten stacked close by as a handy alternative. Amazingly, Enanald Byten managed to write 3,210 books in his lifetime, possibly more, but that was the number found so far in the library. Former head librarian Thomas Kensan described them as the most execrable fiction, period, and also as the best argument against learning to read Middle Grethian—a remarkable claim given that the language boasted fourteen tenses and a flexible approach to spelling.

For Livira, though, the most embarrassing part of discovering all this came after having spent nearly two days in the library on her first venture. She had been at lunch the next day with her tablemates when Jella remarked that it was fortunate she'd found out how the corners worked given that she ran off before they'd had a chance to tell her about them.

"There's something special in the corners?" Livira had asked.

"Then how did you . . ." Carlotte's eyes had widened.

"Oh," Jella had said.

In any event, Livira hoped that the journey wouldn't be that long. She didn't relish the prospect of using a corner privy in a great hurry almost immediately after Master Ellis had finished with it.

THE JOURNEY PROVED to be a long one. Master Ellis crossed many chambers, the only saving grace being that he knew reasonably direct routes from one door to the next. Time in the library was a rather personal concept. The place itself hardly acknowledged passing centuries, so the passage of days had nothing to do with the library, and only concerned whoever might be within it. When Master Ellis took a pillow from his backpack along with a blanket to lie on and made camp near the corner of Chamber 36, Livira knew they'd been walking for a whole day. She hoped the others would be both creative and convincing at explaining her absence. Something contagious, explosive, and involving both ends would be best.

Livira now faced the problem that if she slept, Master Ellis might wake before her, and she'd lose him. Fortunately, he'd chosen to sleep near a corner so she could sleep close by and hope that he'd make enough noise when waking to rouse her too.

Livira still had a slight cough from the gas attack and falling asleep proved difficult while all the time struggling to keep quiet. The tickle built relentlessly until she had to crawl away and have a good hack at a safe distance. But no matter how hard she coughed, the tickle would begin to build again. Livira made a mental note to apologise to Neera for every thoughtless remark she'd ever made about how irritating the girl's cough was. In the end she fell asleep wondering about the lives that Neera, Katrin, and the rest of her friends from the Dust now lived. Malar had delivered her money, not to Benth but to Acmar, who swore to use it for the others. Benth, Malar said, had died in a factory accident the year before. Livira thought of Benth, wise beyond his years, Benth who had carried the little ones from the Dust and who had died without knowing what had happened to her, and a tear fell.

Lacking the softness of a blanket between her and the stone floor and having only a large book on economics for a pillow, Livira slept poorly, waking often to blink in the unwavering library light. Even so, she very nearly missed Master Ellis's departure. Some ephemeral thread pulled her from the labyrinth of her dreams and had her peer around the corner at the empty space where the man had been.

"No!" Livira scrambled to her feet in the only direction he could have gone, needing to spot him before facing a choice where she'd have to guess. The visceral wave of relief when she caught a glimpse of him just about to turn a distant corner hit hard enough to make her gasp.

Before the second day was out, Livira had crossed several rooms entirely new to her, including one where whole aisles of books had been perversely shelved spines in, showing only the ends of their pages. That had been surprising, but Chamber 72 astonished her. Her first empty chamber. She was forced to wait and hide while Ellis dwindled into the distance, crossing the echoless emptiness.

"Hells and damn . . ." Livira fought the urge to blatantly trail him out into the open. After so long a chase to just wait while her quarry walked away was infuriating. Worse still, she couldn't even watch since to do so she had to either be in the room or keep the huge door open, providing a far bigger flag for her presence. She waited what she hoped was a quarter of an hour and risked looking again.

She had thought that he might vanish entirely, swallowed by the mile and more between them, allowing her to give chase under the shroud of mutual invisibility. Annoyingly, she could still register him as a tiny speck even though he was nearly all the way to the opposite door.

Livira accepted the risk and hurried into the chamber. She would watch for his departure, hoping to remain hidden at the base of the wall. She took several deep breaths in search of the centre that Arpix was always talking about. She was pretty sure she didn't have a centre. She took a long drink from her half-empty water-skin and sat with her back against the wall, stretching out her legs to rest them.

The empty chamber somehow looked smaller than the ones filled with shelves, as if the mind could not truly believe the walls so far away without the thousands of aisles to measure out the distance piece by piece. She could see the opposite door as a tiny white patch, and the mouths of the corridors to the left and right chambers, along with the corridors to the two reading rooms.

On her first trip through the library, she'd missed the existence of reading rooms entirely, but each chamber had two, built into the thickness of the walls. Many came equipped with thousands of desks as if the ancients had expected the library to be thronged with readers rather than scarcely more than a hundred librarians and their trainees. Livira liked that idea. Do away with the reception desk down near the foot of the mountain and just invite the citizens of Crath to come in and help themselves. So what if they wreaked havoc—or at least what the librarians considered havoc— they would scarcely dent the collection and the unfettered learning that went on would be magnificent.

But it was obvious why neither King Oanold nor the head librarian would favour that option. From Livira's own reading of the histories of lost civilisations, power had a tendency to clump together. Any small concentration of it rapidly drew in more, and it jealously accumulated in any hands that managed to grab a portion. Money did the same and seemed to be, according to Arpix who did not apologise for the pun, another side of the same coin.

Master Ellis crossed the remaining distance with maddening slowness. Livira decided to stay by the wall even though the man would have to be eagle-eyed to spot her with a casual glance at this distance, even out in the open. She reasoned that this chamber might be his safety measure. If he had any sense he would turn at the far door and look for signs of pursuit. Librarians had a reputation for short-sightedness—Arpix, who was somewhat short-sighted himself—said that years of reading soon reeled in your vision, training it to be good at studying the page and poor at everything else. Even so, Livira waited until the opposite door faded from view and rematerialised before beginning her jog across the floor.

It was, she knew, a gamble against long odds. The chances of finding Master Ellis in the next chamber were slim. She had a one-in-three chance of guessing which door he would make for, but even then she would have to beat him there through aisles wholly unknown to her.

LIVIRA ARRIVED AT the opposite door panting and sweaty, her legs leaden. The door melted beneath her touch. Chamber 97—according to the librarians' numbering scheme which radiated from the entrance in a half spiral—proved to be another first for Livira, the first time that she had encountered stone shelving. These behemoths, fashioned from red granite, appeared to reach the ceiling itself and braced against each other with stone arches at various heights. Every couple of yards up the book-face, a stone shelf extended a couple of feet further than the others, providing a ledge along which an intrepid adventurer might walk while perusing the selection.

"Pick a door . . ." Livira chose the left one. She kept close to the wall, not wanting to lose herself in the waiting acres. But since the shelves often came right up to the wall she did need to detour into the interior from time to time.

She'd only been going for a few minutes when she noticed her first ladder. Not a wooden one leaning against the shelves—a ladder that tall would have been far too heavy to move—but stone rungs cut into one of the shelf pillars. Since the aisle she was now following had turned her at right angles to the direction she wanted to pursue, she decided to investigate whether the shelves really did connect with the ceiling. If they didn't then perhaps she could cross over the top and descend another ladder. Besides, tired as she was, curiosity was offering a strong push in the upwards direction.

About ten feet off the ground, she reached for the next rung and discovered she'd thrust her fingers into a mess of grey webbing. She pulled back with a yell of surprise and disgust but found her hand stuck. Something black and owning an unreasonable number of legs scurried out of the niche at speed. Livira threw herself backwards, trying to break free. The stuff proved incredibly adhesive, and it took most of her weight to tear herself loose. Breaking with an audible snap the strands released her into the arms of a fall that took her to the ground with another scream.

She lay winded for a long moment before managing to focus her vision. The first thing she saw was that half a dozen rat bones and a small skull were hanging from the bits of webbing still fixed to her hand. With a fresh cry of disgust, she tried to shake them off but failed. Backing away from the ladder, and glancing nervously all around for the spider, she slowly pulled the bones free and then got to her feet. The left side of her body felt like one big bruise but her outstretched arm had saved her head from the floor. The library had taught her a fair bit about falling.

Limping slightly and picking off bits of web, she hobbled on in search of a different ladder which she vowed to climb with more caution. Where she pulled the web away it took the top layer of her skin with it, leaving raw red patches. The only piece of luck, which really wasn't that lucky at all, was that with the head start he got while she crossed the empty chamber, Ellis must have been too far ahead to have heard her scream as she fell.

Livira chose a new ladder almost out of sight of the last one. It turned out that she didn't need to reach the top—which was good because her arms were soon as tired as her legs. She got about thirty yards off the ground and drew level with the first of several bridging arches. Livira slipped through and found herself on the other side of the shelf, looking down into the next aisle. A ledge allowed her to continue at this elevation until she found either a ladder to take her to another level, or a bridge to cross the aisle. It would have suited a monkey better but with some courage and faith in her sense of balance it offered new freedoms.

Using the ladders, arches, ledges, and bridges, and hoping that Master Ellis was too old or timid to do the same, Livira was able to make swift progress.

And it was from one of these high stone bridges that Livira reacquired her prey. Master Ellis wasn't aiming for a door. He'd just turned down the corridor into one of the chamber's reading rooms, a single book in hand. And had Livira passed by a moment later she would have lost him entirely.

Livira swarmed down the nearest ladder and jogged to follow the deputy into the side room, all the while wondering why an old man would cross so very many miles, and pass by dozens of reading rooms, just to read his book in this particular one.

. . . ginger beer. I say, let's follow him. He seems a bad sort. By God, I think you've
solved it, Fanny. He does look suspicious. Come on, Volente. Such a good dog! Yes,
you are. I dare say we could all do with a jolly good walk and a bracing . . .

Six Go On and On, *by Enanald Byten*

CHAPTER 32

Livira

Abandoning stealth, Livira hurried towards the entrance. The reading rooms were much smaller than the main chambers, measuring about a hundred yards by a hundred yards, with room for perhaps a thousand desks. Peering around the entrance of the corridor leading to the room, Livira could see that, unusually, this one actually had desks, many hundreds of them in ordered rows. It amazed her to find them this far out. But then again, the incredible weight of stone shelving in the chamber behind her was an even greater mystery so far from the entrance. All of it lent credence to the farcical theory that Arpix had once brought to her attention in an old legendarium, namely that once every thousand years, the library chambers shuffled themselves like a pack of cards, or a ballroom full of dancers, each exchanging places with another.

The desks were not the only surprise. The reading room had something she had never seen in one before. At the centre lay what she could best describe as a lump. The grey stuff of the floor rose in a loaf-shaped block, roughly a brick but with rounded edges.

Of Master Ellis there was no sign. Livira wove a path through the desks and approached the structure. At one end, on one of the shorter sides, the lump—which was about twice the height of a man—had a door. A very curious door at odds with the rest of it. It looked for all the world like the door to Livira's bedroom, though where hers bore the number 19, this door had a character from some alphabet or number scheme unknown to her.

If Master Ellis was inside then the safest place to continue her vigil was probably on top of the structure but, having no means of climbing up there, she opted to wait on the far side and listen for the door opening.

Livira set her back to the curious room within a room and waited. It felt worth waiting. This was surely too unusual not to be Ellis's destination. Time passed, punctuated by occasional very faint vibrations that emerged from the grey wall and passed through her shoulder blades. It felt as if something powerful were at work deep inside, something heavy like the grindstone of a mill, driven by an engine where wheels turned within wheels.

She waited and grew hungry, thirsty, and in need of a visit to the corner of the main chamber. She found herself fascinated with what Ellis might be doing in there. Why would he still be inside? If he had come to collect something he would have taken it and left. They were a good dozen miles from the entrance as the crow flies, if crows could fly through solid rock. What was Ellis doing?

Eventually she had slept.

Livira woke, yawning deeply, then jolted into a sitting position. She'd no idea how long she'd slept, but after such a journey it might have been many hours. Perhaps even a whole day. She got to her feet in a stealthy panic, worried that she'd lost her quarry and also worried that she hadn't lost him and that he might hear her. Cursing noiselessly, she crept to the door end. Nothing had changed except that the door now stood ajar by a hand's breadth.

Holding a breath trapped in her lungs, Livira advanced on tiptoe, listening with an intensity that made her quiver. The library's silence refused her, eternal and golden. She came level with the door, ready to spring back at the slightest noise. Nothing.

He's gone. He must be gone.

But what had woken her? Was he really gone? She retreated to the far end without passing the door and circled round to see if Ellis was visible at the side of the structure facing the corridor, or in the corridor itself. He was not.

She returned to the door and cautiously found an angle where she might catch a glimpse of the interior. She saw nothing but grey. She moved in, took hold of the handle, gritted her teeth, and pulled gently, hoping that while this door held many similarities to her own bedroom door, squeaky hinges were not among them.

The door eased open without scarring the silence. Livira peered inside.

A single grey-walled room took up the whole of the interior. An empty room.

"That's it?" Livira knew that couldn't be it. The deputy hadn't trekked across twelve chambers on multiple occasions to stand for hours in a small bare room. There was a wonder here and she needed to see it.

She studied the door. The lack of a keyhole was encouraging. She didn't want to be locked in and die of thirst before the next time someone visited. She was also thankful that Master Ellis hadn't been able to lock the structure up when he left. Though that wasn't the library's style. Whilst some doors might be closed to them, there were no keys that put the power into one particular set of hands. Unless you considered the Raven guide a key, which she supposed he was, but a particularly ill-tempered and capricious key with his own agenda.

She looked inside again at the innocuous grey interior. It didn't feel particularly intimidating, and yet, even so, she was nervous. For some reason the memory of climbing that stone ladder and accidentally sticking her hand into the webbing of a rat-spider returned to her. She shook her head. She hadn't come all this way not to go in.

Livira took off her left shoe and tossed it into the room. It rolled to a halt and just sat there. She took her right shoe and set it so that the door couldn't fully close if it had a mind of its own. Barefooted, she stepped in.

Without transition she was in a world of darkness.

It hadn't merely gone dark. She was in another world, a place where light had never entered. How she knew this she wasn't sure, but the information was just one tiny part of the deluge. Years ago, Malar had pushed her into a horse trough. This felt similar except that instead of water she'd fallen into knowledge, and it was bleeding through her skin, infecting her with new understanding.

She stood on a battlefield. She knew this without seeing it. Above her head hung a stone sky, miles thick. Scalding rivers crossed the immense cavern, descending from a surface where the sun burned so hot as to melt flesh and ignite anything that could burn. The wars that had raged here in the subterranean depths were the passion, the horror, and the shame of the person whose accounts of the events ran through the back of Livira's mind in a many-voiced litany. She had but to ask a question and one voice would rise in answer, drowning out the others and taking her to bear witness to events and deeds that would confirm the speaker's opinion.

Person. Livira had called the speaker a person. But when she tried to see them the impression she got was of something closer to that rat-spider than to someone from the streets of Crath. Her eyes revealed nothing, but the feel of smooth, slim, armoured limbs ran through her fingertips. Here and there a ring of bristles. At one end a bladed hook curving over short, swift, multi-segmented digits. Six limbs.

A primal revulsion shuddered through Livira, something born of shape and expectation rather than based on the creature's thoughts. Its thoughts were those of a scholar, albeit one shadowed by sadness at the events it considered. It wanted to show her these tragic wars, these heroic battles, the waste, the stupidity, the moments of tactical genius.

"The author!" Livira crouched and felt the warm wet rocks beneath her. "This is my dark book!" The book had been in her pocket when she entered—she'd used it on Jost just the day before. She patted for it now and found nothing. "I'm inside my dark book . . ."

She turned slowly, still crouched and blind. Livira stiffened as something small but heavy used its many legs to attach itself to her calf. She stifled a shriek and tried to bat the thing away, but it was already under her robe and clung to her with sharp feet. Something cold and wet touched the back of her knee. The author's thoughts concerning the creature flowed into Livira, drowned beneath her terror. This was worse than the rat-spider. Much worse. A scream erupted from her.

"Help!" Livira couldn't contain her fear—it sprang from somewhere deep in her guts and wrapped her spine, bypassing her intelligence entirely. "Get me out!" If ever she'd needed a guide in the library this was the time. The image of the Raven—her Raven—filled her mind, blacker than the blindness all around her. "Help me!"

And suddenly she was staggering, sobbing, into the light, blinking against its sting as if she had spent a year in darkness rather than minutes at most. "Oh gods!"

Livira spun about, expecting to see darkness and horror tumbling after her through the door. There was nothing but the empty grey room into which she'd stepped shortly before.

The black book was in her right hand, and she dropped it reflexively as if it might bite her. She'd never understood quite how alien it was. She stood, looking at the black rectangle on the floor for quite a while before she noticed that she was clutching something in her left hand too. A black feather. The one Yute had given her.

"SQWARK."

The Raven was perched behind her on top of the building, just above the door.

When a ganar sets the table for a skeer it is important to understand that the more genteel aspects of afternoon tea must be abandoned. Two very different species taking refreshment together must seek to accommodate their sometimes clashing natures. The skeer's preference for dismembering its prey live can, with a positive attitude, coexist alongside the ganar's taste for small but exquisitely decorated cakes.
The Insectoid Who Came to Tea, *by Celcha Arthran*

CHAPTER 33

Evar

Evar clambered from the pool and although he had felt the water and was now dry, the bloody slaughter he'd witnessed still clung to him. Every blood spatter stained him to the bone. He had been wrong to think that being a ghost meant nothing could touch him.

He sat on the grass with elbows on raised knees and head bowed into his hands. For a long time, the warmth and the living silence, so different from the dead silence of the library, enfolded him. The pool became still; the air held its breath; the trees drank. This was a place without time. He knew himself to be the only clock present, his mortality ticking away moments that without him here to count them would refuse to pass.

Clovis. He should think about Clovis. He should see her with new eyes. He should—

"Evar!"

Evar raised his head. A girl was running towards him. A girl or a young woman. She wore a black robe, and trailed a mane of curiously two-tone hair, the bottom half yellow-blonde, the half closest to her skull ink-black. Stranger still, she was grinning as if he were a long-lost friend.

"Evar! You're back! I'm back! I didn't think I'd ever find you again." She reached him as he got to his feet.

After so long remaining unseen within a crowd, to be acknowledged came as a relief. He hadn't liked being a ghost, ignored by the world and unable to touch it. It reminded him too much of his entire life. He had one pressing question, though. "Who are you?"

"Livira!" She seemed insulted. "You've forgotten me?" Then, rallying herself in the face of his confusion, she asked, "Have you found the woman yet? The one you were looking for? Is that why you came back—to find her?"

Evar shook his head. "You're not Livira. She's a small child." He held out a hand to indicate how high. Below this girl's shoulder. "And dirty . . ." He had to admit she could have cleaned herself up in the hours since they first met. "She had a bruised face!" He allowed himself a note of triumph. He could have got her height wrong, but her face wouldn't heal that quickly. "And she was in blue. And her hair wasn't—" He broke off, unsure what this girl's hair *was*. "It was all one colour. Mainly."

"That was years back. Idiot. I'm nearly fourteen now." A self-conscious hand found her hair. "And this got bleached months ago. In an attack . . ." She flashed a grin. "So, where was she?"

Evar shook his head. "You're not making any sense. After you got pulled back into your pool, I tried this one. I've been down there a day at most, watching my sister."

"Pool?" It was Livira's turn to look confused. "Why do you call them pools?"

Evar wondered if this new person claiming to be Livira had been driven mad, or perhaps eaten some of the less toxic kinds of toadstools that Starval had told him about. "I call them pools because . . ." He reached out and splashed the water.

Livira shrugged. "I guess it does look a bit like water when it shimmers. But you know pools are traditionally horizontal, right? To keep the water in."

Evar gave up. "I haven't found her. No. It's only been a day. I've only tried this one pool—"

"Well, if you're just going to lie to me, I'll go and explore by myself." Livira folded her arms crossly. "I'm sorry it took me so long to get back but if you knew how hard it was you wouldn't be being such an arse about it. I couldn't find the Raven, and nobody believed me and without him the door wouldn't open and then I did find him or rather Yute found a feather and he came"—she paused to breathe—"but I had to give him the feather back and I don't know if he'll ever come again. He only came in the first place because I went into this grey room with a book and scared myself half to death."

With the stream of Livira's explanation in full spate Evar was having trouble following her story, but he seized hold of the last thing. "You went into the Mechanism?"

"The what?" She blinked up at him. She'd grown but she was still very short. "Is that what you call it? It took me inside a book that I really didn't want to be in, especially when I wasn't expecting it."

"That's the Mechanism." Evar frowned, remembering that *the* Assistant had turned out to be simply *an* assistant. "*A* mechanism at least. You should be careful with it. There are dangers . . . Anyway, you've done a lot with your day!"

Livira looked to be on the edge of asking a question but instead she clamped her mouth shut, turned away, and began to stalk back in the direction she'd come from.

"Wait!" Evar went after her. "There's something strange going on here. I saw you a day ago, a day at most. I swear it. But you were different. Younger. So, time has been misbehaving for one of us. And it's probably me. I wasn't watching my sister like she is now—I was seeing her childhood. The childhood I wasn't there for. I went into the pool, and I was back home, but decades ago. Watching them like I was a ghost. It was horrible. Sabbers came and killed everyone except Clovis and I couldn't stop them."

Livira turned, frowning. "You really see pools?"

It hadn't been what he expected her to say. "Yes."

"Pools you can paddle in?"

"Well, they're too deep to paddle in, but you can dangle your legs in them. You can drink from them."

"Ah!" She pointed at him accusingly. "Fill my water-skin!" She unslung it from round her shoulder.

Evar shrugged and took it, noting that it was completely empty. He knelt at the nearest pool and held the skin under until the bubbles stopped. "There." He handed it back.

Livira's look of astonishment lasted only long enough for her to get the spout to her lips. After a dozen gulps, she stopped and wiped her mouth. "We're seeing different things! It's amazing. Do you see the tapwoods?"

"Are those trees?"

"Very tall ones."

"I see trees. Lots of them. They're pretty tall. I have to stretch up to reach the lowest branches."

Livira shook her head. "You'd need to be five times as tall to reach a tapwood's branches. Do you even see the birds? The ravens?"

Evar shook his head. He stared at the branches, trying to imagine birds there. "I've never seen a bird. Anywhere." Though he hadn't seen trees before either.

"Why weren't you there when your sister was little?" Livira took him by surprise with a question at right angles to the conversation. "Is she much older than you?"

"Well, that's all pretty complicated." Evar wasn't sure he could properly explain his family.

"Isn't she really your sister?"

"No." Actually it was pretty easy.

"And Starval's not really your brother?"

"No." It seemed like a betrayal to say so. "Wait—how did you know about Starval?"

"You told me." Livira blinked. "Did you forget?"

Evar nodded. He couldn't remember much of what the girl had said when they first met. He'd been more focused on the fact he was talking to a stranger for the first time in his life. "Wait . . . *you* remember our conversation? You said it was years ago!"

"I remember things. It's what I'm best at." Livira made a slow turn. "I think pools would look nicer than doors of light. They'd fit better with the trees."

Evar nodded again, feeling that he was always three steps behind in conversations with Livira. And if he ever caught up, she'd veer off unexpectedly into something new.

"Clovis, Starval, and anyone else?" Livira stopped her rotation with her eyes turned in his direction once more. Eyes that held a magic he'd never encountered before he met her—their gaze made him interesting.

"My other brother—who also isn't really my brother—Kerrol, and the Assistant and the Soldier who are both part of the library. There was Mayland too, but he's gone."

"He found a way out?" Livira asked.

"I think he's dead." Evar guessed that counted as finding a way out.

Livira sat down on the grass. "So, it's you and two boys and a girl? How old are they?"

Evar frowned. He hadn't even kept close track of his own age: he had no idea if his brothers were a year or two older or younger. "We're all about twenty, I guess. If you don't count the time we spent lost in the Mechanism, and we didn't age then."

"Maybe she's the one you're looking for," Livira said. "She's not your sister."

"What?" The suggestion surprised him, even though he had once tried to will it into being true. "Gods no." His laugh sounded forced even to himself. They'd all had the moments of attraction to each other that the Assistant had predicted. Clovis had set her sights on Kerrol for a while after Mayland, but he'd deflected her with such skill that the rejection didn't seem to even sting, let alone leave a scar. For someone so deeply versed in all the levels of intimacy and interaction that people share, Kerrol stood alone among them for never having expressed any interest in the opposite sex or his own. Perhaps after you'd minutely dissected something it was hard to properly engage with it. That might be the price he'd paid for his insights.

"She's the only girl you've ever known, and you're not interested?" Livira allowed herself a disbelieving smile. "I've seen the older trainees after class. They spend longer chasing each other around than they do at their books." She snorted—perhaps a little too hard, as if she might already have begun to feel the same tug herself and was trying to deny it. "Is she pretty?"

"This is your plan to help me find the woman from my book? To tell me she was in front of me the whole time?" Evar would look at Clovis with new eyes following his encounter with her past, but not with that sort of interest again.

"Is she pretty?"

"Yes, she's pretty!" Evar wasn't really sure what pretty was, but Clovis had a strong, symmetrical face, dangerously grey eyes, and a hard body that often gave him restless nights. "I was *interested* in her. Years ago. But it didn't work. And she is definitely not the person who wrote this book." He pulled it out from where he'd stuffed it into his jerkin. "And she's full of . . ." He wanted to say *knives*. That's what it felt like most of the time. "Anger. She's always angry, but it's the cold, murderous kind that's had a long time to settle. All she really cares about is killing sabbers. There's no room for anything else. It's eaten her up inside." He hadn't meant to say so much, but then again, he hadn't ever had anyone to speak to who didn't already know all this.

"I hate the sabbers too." Livira clenched her fists. Something in the twist of her mouth said that the admission didn't please her. "They killed my people like they killed your sister's people. And each year they come closer to the city where I live now. Like they're following me. Malar says they'll be laying siege soon enough."

"Clovis would be pleased about that. She wants to fight them." Evar gazed back at the pool he'd come from. The sabbers were still there, decades back in the past. "She'll be good at it too. Scary good."

"And you?" Livira asked.

"I . . . I used to just want them not to come back. But now quite a big bit of me wants to fight them too. After seeing what I saw. I mean, I probably don't hate them as much as you and Clovis do. But almost as much now, I think. Only . . ." The slaughter stayed with him, and it wasn't the crimson agony of it that saddened him most, but the empty sense of waste. Would it be any different on the winning side? Would it taste different when it was called revenge? He wasn't sure. He looked down. "I'll fight them. Clovis taught me how to, and someone should watch her back."

"Years ago, 'sabber' used to be just another word for 'enemy,'" Livira said. "Like 'foe' or 'opponent.' I guess we were always meant to fight them."

They were both silent for a while then. Evar sat back down not far from Livira, and they watched . . . well . . . whatever it was they both saw. For him it was branches and sky. And . . .

"I see a bird too now!"

"Just one?"

"So far."

"What type?"

"Uh . . . one with wings. I don't know types."

"Now explain how it's complicated with you and these siblings that aren't siblings," Livira said. "I'm good at complicated."

"Well." Evar took a deep breath. "My people lived trapped in one chamber of the library. Hundreds of them. For hundreds of years."

"Wow."

"And every few decades they'd lose a child in the Mechanism, and it wouldn't come back. We have a Mechanism—I think I forgot to say that."

"Wouldn't they just stop putting children in the Mechanism?" Livira asked.

"You'd think so. But, apparently, it's the sort of lesson that can be forgotten in thirty or forty years. Also, I'm told the Mechanism is really exciting—"

"That's one word for it."

"And a great way to learn."

"I learned to be careful what book you take in," Livira said.

"Anyway"—Evar wrestled back control of the conversation—"Mayland, then me, then Kerrol, then Starval were all lost in the Mechanism as young children and decades passed and we didn't come back. In the end sabbers came and killed everyone, except Clovis who was put into the Mechanism by her mother, with a book that turned out to be all about physical combat. And the Mechanism swallowed her too. I think the Assistant made it happen to protect her. More years passed, enough for even the bones of the dead to vanish. And then, for reasons known only to the library, the Mechanism spat out five kids, which were us, and, even though the others say it felt like they'd spent ten years or more wandering inside the book they each took in with them, none of us were much older than seven or eight. And all that was over a decade ago. The Assistant raised us—the Soldier too, I guess. And then I found this book, got the clue about the pool, and now I'm here."

"So how are you going to find her? This clue-giver of yours."

"I don't know. I could just keep jumping into different pools."

"A librarian would suggest you understood the system first. Otherwise, it's like pulling random books off the shelves and hoping you just happen to pick the right one."

"We don't have shelves."

"Oh."

Evar saw that Livira was now lying flat on her back, staring at the sky. He did it too. The sky wasn't the simple blue he'd first thought. It had a depth to it, and the faintest shades, and hints of motion. It bore some study. "So, what's the system here?"

"That depends if it was designed by librarians," Livira said. "Or by sane people."

Everything we see is seen through the lens of our expectation. Our prejudice provides a broad brush, imagination sprinkles detail, some of which may actually be there. We ascribe meaning and intent with a careless disregard for our constant failure at such prediction. One is forced to wonder if the blind man's hands lie to him as eloquently as vision does to the sighted.

Illusion, *by Copper Davidfield*

CHAPTER 34

Livira

Livira studied the sky through the upraised branches of the tapwoods. That lone tapwood out on the Dust was the only tree she had ever seen before coming to the Exchange. She should have been suspicious to find them growing here when it might have been any other kind of tree, or a mix of many sorts. The Mechanism had painted her a blind world using the brush of the author's imagination, laced around facts to bind them into a historical narrative. Perhaps the Exchange had in turn painted her a world using her own imagination, a stolen dream of sorts. Even so it was a good dream. There was a healing peace that shrouded the place. A timelessness that warned should you fall asleep on this grass you might wake in a different century, or perhaps a different life.

"Between us we've visited three of your pools on the same line." Livira spoke into the lazy air above her. "And two of them were your home in different times. And one was my home. If we want to experiment, we should visit a pool that's not on the same line as those three." Reluctantly, she sat up and studied the grid of portals. No pools for her—her portals all still looked the same as the one the grey assistant had been touching as she lay beside it on the floor of the locked chamber.

When the Raven had, at Livira's request, led her back to the portal, it hadn't taken Master Ellis's path. Instead, it had taken her through different chambers, three of which were forbidden, unseen by any librarian or trainee in Crath's history. Livira could only imagine the outrage and scorn she'd meet with if she tried to tell the deputies about it on her return. Once the Raven had taken a longer path through three chambers to bypass one other. Whether that meant there were doors it too couldn't open, or whether it meant that the chamber it had avoided was simply too dangerous, Livira didn't know.

The first of these forbidden chambers, number 94 by the librarians' reckoning, was a literal sea of books. Crossing it Livira hadn't seen a single shelf, just an undulating ocean of books, as if they had rained from the sky and been swept up by unknown weather into drifts higher than houses. Livira had to walk over the covers, constantly hectored by the Raven if she was insufficiently careful.

She'd had to do all this barefoot since the Mechanism, in addition to somehow staining her robe black during her time on the insectoids' battlefield, had also neglected to return the shoe that she had thrown into it. Of the other shoe, the one she'd used to prop the door open, only half remained, lying beside the entrance, as if severed by a sharp blade.

Livira soon discovered that two and a half years of wearing shoes had left her soft. Her feet were starting to get sore by the time she'd crossed the first chamber with eight more to go. And it didn't help that every time a book slid underfoot, sending her tumbling, the Raven treated her to the full force of its ear- and head-splitting condemnation, as if the whole mess were her fault along with the decision to come this way.

The next forbidden chamber, number 67, was the first she'd seen with iron shelves, a planning decision that time had shown to be unwise. The books on the lower four-fifths of every set of shelves had turned orange in the slow but constant rain of rust. Rust also covered the floor to a depth of half an inch and more, crunching unpleasantly beneath her aching feet.

Chamber 46, also forbidden, would have given a heart attack to Master Lapla, who oversaw the team of bookbinders that Jella apprenticed with. It was any librarian's nightmare. In class, Master Logaris had suggested many times that just as the centre of every chamber was an area of sustenance for any human, erasing tiredness, easing hunger and thirst, at least in the short term, the whole of every chamber was an area of sustenance for books. He remarked that under the close attention of Crath's librarians, the books in the trainee library had fared notably less well over the past century and a half than the books in the library proper, despite the rats, cats, spiders, moulds, fungi, lichens, and such that somehow eked out a living among them. In fact, those conditions appeared to have sustained books that were referenced in other books as having been written several thousand years before.

How, then, Chamber 46 contained more book dust than books, Livira couldn't say. It reminded her of an etching of Tneerast after the earthquake, its towers fallen into ruin, its wall toppled, their stones spread before the city. In Chamber 46 most of the shelving had collapsed, leaving a sparse forest of spires from which ancient planks slanted to the floor. The books lay in ruin too, as if the earlier chamber where Livira had crossed book-drifts had been marched over repeatedly by a series of armies in hobnailed boots. Pages were scattered, crumpled, torn. Ancient tomes lay open with only the smallest fraction of their contents still connected to broken spines. And these were the survivors. The greater part of the chamber's contents had long ago been ground to a fine dust, almost evenly distributed across the floor, ranging from ankle-deep to calf-deep. Livira raised a cloud behind her such as she hadn't since she quit her home and entered Crath City's gates. The dreams and wisdom, prejudice and pride of untold millions of authors from many nations and many centuries were now just dust and ruin, making her sneeze and sticking to her feet.

Livira had arrived at the portal in Chamber 7 tired, hungry, and thirsty, despite the boosts from each chamber's healing centre. She was also beginning to worry about the length of her absence. Master Logaris had been known to send junior librarians to check up on sick trainees. Meelan said Logaris only did it because the rooms were hard to clean if you left a corpse in one for too long. But whatever the motivation, the threat was real. Hopefully Carlotte would tell Logaris it was women's problems this time. They'd observed the excuse close down their schoolmaster with startling speed on several occasions, and both of them were of an age now where they could appeal to it.

Livira studied the portal and the fallen assistant. She'd dreamed of this place so often in the years since she'd last been here that the reality of it now seemed fragile. As if at any moment the clanging of the morning bell might shatter the scene before her and replace it with a yawning view of her bedroom ceiling.

The Raven had found a perch and watched with interest as Livira tried to push through the portal. Just as before, it refused her. The assistant lay unmoving, grey and lifeless, her fingers vanishing into the shimmer of light that filled the circle. She'd told Livira on the last occasion that the Exchange was forbidden. Livira had decided that she wasn't satisfied with that state of affairs and always travelled prepared for the eventuality that she might regain access to the chamber.

Livira took the long, thin rope from her pack and knotted one end around the assistant's ankle. It had been hard to acquire all the cords that she threaded and twisted to make it. It had been hard to carry it so far, back and forth across the library. She also had two blankets sewn together. Arpix might have suspected she'd taken his, but he'd never guessed why.

Livira found a ladder in a nearby aisle and hefted it a couple of feet at a time, moving it around a corner and down the long straight stretch until it leaned against the side opposite the assistant. The effort turned her arms to jelly and, she was sure, added several inches in length to both. With her muscles still trembling, she climbed the rungs to the top of the shelves, taking the other end of the rope and the double blanket with her.

Once at the top she laid the blanket flat on the dusty wood and began to pile books from the shelf below onto it. It took a while and she nearly dropped one large tome with what felt like a stone cover. She could only imagine the scolding the Raven would have given her and doubted that her hearing would have escaped without permanent damage.

Eventually, satisfied, she folded the blanket carefully around her collection and gathered the corners together, putting a knot in each. She made a noose of the rope and tightened it around all four knotted corners. Next, she lugged the ladder two yards to the left. Then, gripping the shelf-top's edge, she used both feet to inch the bundle towards the drop on the other side.

Gravity seized the blanket-sack without warning. It fell about ten feet before the rope went taut. Down below the assistant tilted without flexing, as if she really were the statue she appeared to be. She scraped across the floor with the sound of nails being raked down a chalkboard, a sound that Master Logaris occasionally employed to gain the class's attention. Where the assistant's head had lain a silvery sheen caught Livira's eye, as if a puddle of silver blood had pooled there from the injury on her brow. The assistant hit the shelves with a bang and at a leisurely but increasing pace she began to rise, drawn upwards on the rope by the books' descent.

Livira had practically slid down the ladder and was through the circle of light a moment later. Her theory that it was the assistant's touch which kept the portal sealed now confirmed.

"How about that one?" Livira sat up, stood, and pointed to the portal beside the one she'd emerged from earlier. "It's not on the same column as the other three and it's in the same row as mine."

Evar chewed the inside of his cheek and it reminded her of Arpix. Both of them shared a certain studious reluctance to just jump into things. A quality that Livira had to admit was probably in short supply where she was concerned. Even so, after several long moments of thought, Evar nodded.

"I can't think of another way to learn anything here, save for waiting for an assistant to show up."

"I'm not sure waiting works very well here," Livira said. "And they might be called assistants but I'm thinking 'impediments' would be a better name."

Evar seemed to ponder that one. "My Assistant, she . . . well, I think she's constrained by a lot of rules. I think she does what she can." He shrugged. "And what you said about waiting not working. Well, I've wondered about that. I mean. You said you were away for two years?"

"Two and a half."

"Two years, and I'm out of that pool for a few minutes before you turn up. What are the odds of that? And then there's the pool itself. I mean, all right, it took me to Clovis's childhood. That's odd, but let's put it to one side for now. It took me to the day the sabbers came. It took me to within hours of that attack. The most important day of her life. Again, what are the odds?"

"Long?"

Evar nodded. "So, time's more than just odd here. It seems to work to bring us what we want, maybe? Or need? Or what's important to us? I don't know. But whatever it is it's not straightforward." He came to join her beside the portal. "Ready?"

"Ready."

"Let's go!"

THE INSTANT LIVIRA stepped through she knew she'd made a mistake. The air clawed at her eyes and scalded her throat. It was as bad as the cloud that the alchemists had tried to kill her with. She retreated through the portal immediately and fell onto the grass, choking.

It took a while before her lungs allowed her to speak, and her eyes were still streaming. "Evar?" She couldn't see him but then she could hardly see the trees through the blur of her tears. She should have been able to hear him coughing though. "Evar!"

Wheezing, she crawled to the portal again. "Evar?"

He hadn't made it back. He was trapped on the other side, dying. Or dead. Livira had no desire to go back. None whatsoever. Even so she screwed up her courage, dragged a deep breath into her raw lungs, and rushed forward hoping to find him before the poison of that place sealed her eyes. She'd find him and drag him back. She'd—

A large shape heading in the opposite direction collided with her somewhere just inside the portal's shimmering light. She lost the precious breath she'd stored and found herself carried backwards, thrown once more onto the grass of the Exchange.

"Livira!" Evar loomed over her, dark against the sun. "What's wrong?"

It took several minutes before she could answer him with anything but coughing.

"Why could you breathe there, and I couldn't?" Livira wanted to know once she was able to make a whole sentence.

"Maybe ghosts don't need to breathe," Evar said. "It smelled . . . dangerous, but it didn't hurt me."

"You were a ghost there too? I didn't have long enough to find out. But

I guess I must have been myself if it did this to me." She paused to cough and spit, starting to get a bit self-conscious about the drooling, red-eyed mess that she was. "What did you see there?"

"It was the library again. It looked just the same, but the pool was in front of a white door, so I went through. I mean literally through the door. And on the other side was some sort of stone temple built into the side of a mountain. There were . . . creatures . . . there, about half my height but wider and hunched over and covered in shaggy yellowish hair. Just mounds of hair really. With legs. And arms." Evar made a circle with both hands to show arms thicker than Livira's body. "And a kind of single claw from the back of their hands, like a blade."

"A different world," Livira wheezed.

Evar seemed sceptical. "Maybe they have creatures like that somewhere outside the library—just a place you haven't been."

"Maybe. But they don't have different air."

Evar frowned. "The sky was green. I saw it through the pillars at the front. Not like here at all."

Livira laughed, which set her coughing for a while. "I—I would have thought—that was a pretty big clue, even for a ghost."

"Until today I'd never seen a sky," Evar said. "Now I've seen two."

Livira wiped her eyes again. "So, we changed worlds by changing columns, and you changed times by changing rows . . . Which tells us . . ."

"That a little knowledge is a dangerous thing," Evar said. "And as my brother Mayland was fond of saying, that's a law that scales swiftly. A lot of knowledge is a *very* dangerous thing. A man who knows how to sharpen a stick can stab his neighbour to death. That's a little knowledge for you. But Clovis knows about weapons that can level continents and leave nothing save dust. And Mayland knew about wars in which that actually happened."

Livira, who had lived most of her life amid seemingly endless dust, wondered for the first time quite how that dust came to be there, and if its origins might be more sinister than the drying up of a lake. "What's your alternative? Ignorance?"

"Ignorance is bliss—that was another of Mayland's favourite sayings. I think it came from the mythology he liked so much about the foundation of the library. In that creation myth the first woman and first man start in bliss, in a perfect garden, and a single drop of forbidden knowledge spoils everything."

Livira didn't like that idea at all but although her instinct was to say so, she decided to bite her tongue rather than criticise Evar's dead brother. She'd picked up at least a smattering of tact from Arpix and the others over the years, though it still seemed the most difficult of the languages she'd been asked to learn. Instead, she offered a theory. "I think we might be in the same world but at different times. And when you come back in time, you're a ghost because you can't be allowed to change what's already happened. You went through a portal along the column that joins your one to mine, and you were a ghost in your sister's childhood. We both went through a portal off the column and we were in a different world with different air and different sky. But you were a ghost because it's in your past. Move along a row to move back or forward in time, change columns to change worlds. We should go through another portal, one that lies between yours and mine, and try to gather more data.

"But my working hypothesis is that every pool off the line joining our pools connects to a different world. Let's say that line runs south to north. Taking pools off our line, east or west, changes where we are in space. And moving north"—she indicated the line between her pool and Evar's—"changes time. That direction is my future. South is my past. If any of us goes through a pool that leads to our past then we'll be a ghost—because if we could be seen or heard there, or touch anything, we could change what has happened, and that would make no sense." Livira drew a breath. "Your pool connects to a time many years ahead of mine. We live in the same world but at different times. You *will* live in my future. I *lived* in your past."

Even as she said it Livira didn't really want it to be true. It seemed sad to have found a new friend only to learn that they were separated by such an unforgiving barrier. She might be an old woman in his time. Or have been dead for hundreds of years. If Evar were to visit her time he would be a ghost, invisible and untouchable. A sad smile tugged at the corner of her mouth. She had been happier before the idea occurred to her. "Or perhaps ignorance is bliss."

"Which should we choose?" Evar looked along the line.

"You could come to mine. But I think you'd be a ghost there too. I wouldn't be able to see you or even speak to you, just like Clovis couldn't." It seemed unfair.

"You could come to mine," Evar offered. "Maybe we'd both be 'real' there . . ." But even as he spoke, he seemed to regret having said it. He furrowed his brow in a deep frown and Livira felt that he didn't really want her there. Perhaps he wanted to bring someone better back to his siblings, a grown-up at least even if he couldn't find this woman he'd been dreaming about.

Livira decided to let him off the hook and pretend he hadn't made the offer. "Well, if the pools are counting time, like beads on a line, there must be a gap of years between them, each one would be a further step back into the past or into the future. So, choose one that aims at a time you want to visit."

"Years between them?" Evar rubbed at his chin. "But it aimed me at the right day."

"So maybe the fine adjustments are up to you. Maybe you aimed yourself—or could have. We could go and see you as a little boy." Livira grinned. "I'd like to be bigger than you. Stop having to crane my neck for once." She walked slowly to the next portal. If she was correct then it lay in her future, a few decades at most if what Evar said about Clovis was right. "I'd suggest trying to find the woman you're searching for, but you don't have a when or a where. Which leaves the field pretty open!"

"Mayland!" Evar looked up sharply. "I want to see what happened to him. It was only a year ago, so—"

Somewhere, not close by, an inconceivable weight struck the ground. The light in every portal shuddered, ripples moving from the outer edge towards the centre. The trees shook. From high above their heads knife-shaped leaves began to tumble through the air. The light itself flickered.

"What was that?" A stupid question but one that Livira was too shocked to keep from spilling out.

"I don't know." Evar raised his arms as if he might be attacked at any moment and turned slowly, checking all directions. "It reminds me—" The thump came again, setting the light dancing. "Our Mechanism is breaking. Mayland used to say that things didn't wear out in the library, not things that were part of it. He said the library was being attacked. This feels a bit like that."

"Look!" Livira pointed behind him. A black smoke or mist was rising from a distant pool.

"You still have that claw?" Evar asked.

"I do," said Livira, surprised. She always kept the brass claw on her, a memento of her first expedition within the library. She held it out to him. "What are you going to do?"

Shadows or smoke were rising above another two pools closer at hand.

"Use a little knowledge." Evar reached up with both hands, the claw in one of them.

Livira's vision shook and blurred and suddenly the trees were far shorter, their branches reaching out to interlace above her head, dividing the blueness of the sky into innumerable polygons. Evar had cut or torn free a branch that looked too thick to have come free so easily. She would have remarked on his strength but something as black as the Raven had pulled itself from the more distant of the three corrupted pools.

"Pools! I'm seeing pools too!" Somehow the thought seemed more important than the horror drawing itself up to its full height off among the trees. As if changing the course of the conversation might somehow banish the creature to the sidelines.

In two quick motions Evar stripped the branch of the smaller branches it had come with. "Stay behind me."

"What? I can fight too!" She looked for a branch of her own, but they were all out of reach.

"Watch my back. Tell me where the nearest ones are coming from." Evar made four slashes at the end of the branch and suddenly it had a point.

The jet-black creature began to charge, trailing darkness in its wake. It seemed humanoid, with shades of a cratalac in the gangly length of its limbs and the worrying speed of its attack. It was so black that all she really saw was an ever-changing silhouette, though she caught an impression of oversized tusks jutting from a roaring mouth. A roaring mouth that made no sound and felt all the more terrifying for the lack.

The thing was on them before she knew it.

Evar moved faster than thought. He was in the monster's path and then suddenly not. Somehow, he delivered a kick that deflected it headfirst into a tree. The whole thing shuddered, and more leaves started to fall. Before they'd made it even a fraction of the way to the ground Evar had driven his near spear through the creature's back. He wrenched it free as Livira spotted a second attacker closing at speed—this one like a serpent as thick as a man and borne on many thrashing legs. "Evar! Behind you!"

Instead of running, as common sense dictated, Evar threw himself towards the beast. At the last instant he launched himself feet forwards across the intervening ground and contrived to slide beneath his enemy. Livira saw a flash of the claw as Evar dragged it the length of the serpentine body.

Even as its insides fell out in a flood of darkness the beast turned to lunge for Evar with a mouth full of needled teeth. Evar let it impale itself on his spear. He yanked it free, the point blunt and splintered now, and hurried to her side.

"How can you fight like that?" Livira gasped.

"Clovis taught me." Evar grinned and there was more wolf in his grin than Livira had expected. His eyes weren't on her but scanning among the trees instead. "You should see her. She could take ten of me on at once." The grin faded. There were at least half a dozen more monsters closing on them.

"We need to go. There's too many Escapes. You need to go. Back where it's safe." He jerked his head towards her pool, which lay just a yard behind her.

"I want to go with you and find Mayland!"

Something dark and unexpected launched itself from the tree to her left. Evar spun, swinging his spear like a club and the impact of his blow shattered the weapon. The Escape's momentum carried it through into a jolting collision that took Livira down. Despite the surprise she braced instinctively, anticipating the ground. Instead, they kept on falling and after an interval that seemed both a heartbeat and an age, they spilled out between two towering sets of book-lined shelves.

. . . on the third day of the seventh month, Ella reported spotting three ghosts standing at the riverside in full daylight, watching the fishermen land their catch. The astonishment with which the phantoms observed the process matched her own in finding that she alone could see them.

Ghost in the Machine, *by James Watt*

<hr>

CHAPTER 35

Evar

"No!" Evar reached for Livira as she fell. Still entangled with the Escape, she vanished into the same pool that she'd emerged from.

Another Escape came tearing between the trees and for a few frantic moments he was dodging blows. He used his speed to keep the nearest tree between them.

When he'd seen the first one drag itself from its pool with more pools smoking darkness behind, his heart had quailed and he'd tensed to run. At home he'd always had the pool as a place of sanctuary to make for, confident that the Soldier or the others would add their strength to his and make short work of any pursuer.

Here, though, as he'd turned to run, he saw Livira. Perhaps he might have outrun the Escapes but he'd known she wouldn't make it. He'd come from witnessing the massacre of children and, despite the common-sense part of his brain screaming at him to leave, he'd known in an instant that he was going nowhere without her.

The Escape that Clovis had saved him from had been a particularly dangerous one, larger than normal, long limbed, armed with scythes against his knife. These ones hadn't the same reach. These came with tooth and claw. His makeshift spear had given him the advantage.

At home he had been second-best at everything—taught by masters. Seen as second-rate. Dispatching the first Escape with Livira looking on had lit a fire in his blood. He had in that moment understood what Clovis had always been trying to tell him. It had been hard to learn on the losing end of her beatings. But wetting his spear with the black blood of a foe in defence of someone else had unlocked that lesson. And perhaps being washed so recently in the Soldier's bloody experience of real death and real killing had finally put an edge on all Clovis's teaching.

Evar danced to the side. The creature lunged, reaching around the tree with grasping talons. Evar caught the ebony limb lower down, braced his feet against the tree trunk, and hauled his attacker face first into the other side.

With a twist he leapt clear of the next enemy and threw himself after Livira. To his shock, the pool, which had seemed as endlessly deep as all the others, had become a shallow depression. He hit the bottom of the dusty basin hard, barely recovering his breath in time to scramble away as a hulking Escape hurried up to pound him.

Whilst only a small fraction of the pools seemed to be corrupted it still meant that there was a continual and growing stream of enemies converging on Evar's position. They might be less deadly than the last one Clovis killed but it was obvious they would soon overwhelm him. Even so, with a wild cry, half despair, half exhilaration, Evar hurled himself at the thick-limbed Escape that had chased him from the dry pool. He writhed in the air as Clovis had taught him, arching his back to evade the foe's clutches and at the same time trailing one arm wide to drag the razored edge of Livira's brass claw across the Escape's throat.

Evar came to a halt on the dry mud where Livira's pool had been and stood his ground. He couldn't just abandon her—she was the newest of the only four flesh-and-blood people in his life. And perhaps already the one he liked best. He hadn't been able to help young Clovis, and it had hurt him deep inside. How could he walk away from a chance, however slim, to truly save a life?

A circle of Escapes began to build around him, reluctant to advance into the pool, perhaps wary after seeing their brethren dispatched with such economy. Evar twisted and turned, snarling, working to keep any of them from having a clear line of attack from behind.

You'd be a ghost there too.

Livira's words, spoken into the curious quiet of his mind. She'd said he would be a ghost in her world too. Even if there wasn't just baked earth beneath his feet, he would only be able to watch as the Escape killed her. She wouldn't even know he was there. His chance to make a difference had been here—and it was gone.

Evar's snarl turned to one of frustration. His frustration grew as he realised that even if he could break free of the circle of enemies around him, with all his turning he no longer knew the way back to his home pool. On one axis lay different worlds, on the other the past and present stretched off in opposite directions. Cursing, Evar jinked right then darted left into the brief gap that appeared as the Escapes reacted.

He dodged, ducked, and twisted, his feet scarring the turf as he wove a path around his foes. At one point he leapt high, caught a sturdy branch, and swung above two spine-backed Escapes. At each opportunity he looked frantically for the knife he'd stuck point-down into the soil to mark his home pool.

"Missed it!" He must have. He'd come too far. Behind him an ink-black horde boiled after him, more coming between the trees in other directions. "Damnation."

Evar dived headfirst into the next pool.

Evar climbed out of the pool hardly noticing the action. Livira's revelation that she saw doors of light hadn't changed what he saw but it had changed how it felt to use them. He turned immediately and stared at the rippling water, Livira's claw at the ready, jutting between the first two fingers of his fist. All his muscles seemed to tremble, eager to do battle should any of the Escapes follow him.

When at last he was confident there would be no pursuit he backed away slowly and let his attention stray to his surroundings. A library chamber yawned around him, but not his, or at least he didn't think so. There were no crops, and the stacks were barely waist height, reaching for no more than a hundred yards around the pool, except in one direction where they marched off for a considerable way. Everywhere else the floor lay bare, stretching away to the distant walls.

Evar turned and saw the Assistant. "You!" She lifted a book from the pool and added it to a small stack by her feet.

She drew another tome from the waters, perfectly dry. *An* assistant, not the Assistant, Evar had to remind himself. This one was identical to his in every way save she had no blemish where the Assistant had a small, cratered dent on her left temple, no cuts on her palms, no wound on her shoulder. Also, where his Assistant, like the Soldier, was ivory and cream, this one was the white enamel of a perfect tooth, so gleaming and immaculate it seemed unreal.

"Can you see me?" Evar waved a hand at the assistant.

She paused to look at him but said nothing.

"You can. I chose the right direction at least. I'm real here." He reached to press a hand on a book stack just to prove it to himself and stumbled, meeting with no resistance. His sense of balance abandoned him as a rush of images and knowledge ran through him, a swift, confusing mix, changing when his hand moved through different books.

"I *am* a ghost . . . But you can see me!"

The assistant watched him for a moment longer then returned to her work. She appeared to be stocking the entire chamber with books drawn from or via the Exchange. To fill it to the level of Evar's home chamber would require ceaseless labour for decades, even lifetimes.

"Can you hear me?" Evar waved again, loath to touch her after the nightmare visions that contact with the Soldier had sent flooding through him.

Once more the assistant looked at him, said nothing, and returned to her work.

"At least tell me when this is," Evar said. He stared around at the thousands of book stacks and the emptiness all about them. "Is it before or after I was born? Is it before or after I came out of the Mechanism?"

The assistant continued to stack books.

Evar snorted. "Impediment! That's what Livira called you. Good name too." He tried not to think about what had happened to her. "At least tell me the way out. Outside, I mean."

The assistant paused in her work, as if considering, and then, without looking up, extended her arm and one porcelain finger, pointing almost but not quite at the furthest corner.

"Thank you." Evar watched the assistant stack a few more books. There seemed to be no more organisation taking place than in the stacks Evar had lived among all his life. "You're really not going to talk to me, are you?"

After an embarrassingly long pause, Evar set off in the direction indicated, winding a path around the book stacks, letting instinct guide him, rather than passing through them. Part of him worried that if he maintained contact with any particular book too long it might start to change him just as they changed the Escapes. The idea that he might share that in common with the monsters who had attacked him and who had probably killed Livira was not one he wanted to allow space in his head.

As he left the book stacks and headed out onto open floor, Evar looked back and realised that the stacked area, though only a couple of hundred yards wide, was the best part of a mile long.

"She's moving the pool." It was the most obvious explanation for it. As the assistant worked, she was moving the pool—the portal as Livira saw it. In fact, Livira's version made more sense. The pool only made sense if there had been a need for water. Like for irrigating crops to keep hundreds of people eating properly rather than hanging on in the semi-life of the centre circle. After too long depending on the circle for sustenance it felt more like you were being refused permission to die than that you were being given life.

Evar walked on, although he supposed that moving his legs might not be required, given that he was a ghost. When he finally got to the wall he reached into it, tentatively at first, fearing some kind of reaction. It felt like nothing. With a degree of unease, he edged into it until at last he was close enough to dip his face in. The space beyond was black. It scared him. He'd lived his entire life in the light. Even when sleeping he simply needed to open his eyes to see.

If he walked forward, he'd be blind and unsure of what he was even walking *on*. It seemed likely that the outside world, or at least another chamber, lay not too far in the direction the assistant had sent him. But what if it didn't? What if he wandered blind and never found his way out again? Lost forever in darkness. The prospect scared him more than he had thought it would now that he stood a step away from being swallowed by the wall. He'd rather fight another Escape than go inside.

"She wouldn't have sent me if it wasn't safe." Evar wasn't sure that was true, but he repeated it again, as if saying the words out loud would somehow help them to be correct. "There are doors—so there must be something on the other side."

He walked forward, holding tightly to his fear. It was only once inside and having taken twenty or so paces that Evar remembered he'd read somewhere that blindfolded men with nothing to guide them quickly ended up walking in circles no matter how hard they tried to maintain a straight path.

The gasp Evar gave when he unexpectedly stepped out into the light once more was that of a man emerging from deep water after a long struggle beneath the surface. He glanced at the shelves arrayed before him then took the opportunity to begin a map, scratching it with the claw onto the leather of his jerkin.

He crossed fifteen library chambers before he finally emerged from the side of a mountain after a last, much longer, trip through darkness where he had resigned himself to wandering lost for eternity, most of which would be spent broken-minded and insane.

EVAR WON FREE of the rock into a darkness almost as alien to him, but one that, compared to the blindness of the mountain, was alive with light. A cold white twinkling perforated the void above him. Stars, he presumed, though they were nothing like he had imagined they might be. The books had spoken of unimaginably huge spheres of fire wheeling through an emptiness that made even them seem small.

The craggy stone beneath his feet lay too steep for boulders to keep their place. Had gravity been able to set a finger on Evar it would have hauled him down too. But, like the wind that Evar could hear and not feel, it ignored him.

Evar had often read of the wind's moaning, but the texts had never prepared him for the truth of its voice. For the longest time he stood, hunting its source, convinced that some beast must be nearby, hidden in the night, howling its hunger at him. A moment of curiosity saw him take from his pocket the corner of parchment that he'd found at the edge of

Livira's pool on his first visit to the Exchange. He held it out between finger and thumb. Immediately it began to flutter. Its dance grew faster and more wild when he shifted his grip to the very edge—as if it were only a ghost when in his possession and felt the wind most strongly when he had least contact with it. With an unexpected howl the wind tore it from him and in an eye-blink the night had it.

"Damnation . . ." Evar had meant to keep it. He'd lost Livira and now he'd even lost almost the last evidence of her existence. Not wanting to think about his failures, Evar turned his attention to what lay before him.

Far below the mountainside a carpet of pinpoint lights spread itself across a valley. These lights were warmer and more organised than the stars, picking out lines and grids. All around was blackness, save on one side where an even larger area lay covered with tiny dots of light scattered around larger patches whose orange glow danced as if partnering the twinkle in the heavens high above.

Evar crouched, studying the lights below. It took a while to make sense of them.

"It's a city," he muttered into the wind. And outside it a horde waited around countless campfires.

Mayland, with so many histories archived in his mind, and Clovis, with her intimate understanding of endless battlefields, could between them pick apart any conflict and know it better than they knew each other. Evar had only a fraction of their particular expertise, but he hardly needed even a fraction of that to see that this was a city about to be attacked, and by a force far larger than it could hope to withstand.

Few things are worse enemies of civilisation than a corrupt official, but an honest official of corrupt laws is definitely one of them.

Quis Custodiet Ipsos Custodes, *by Juvenal*

CHAPTER 36

Livira

Livira's tumble came to an abrupt halt against a bookcase. She sat with her back against it, half-stunned for a moment, before casting about left and right in search of the Escape that had carried her through the portal.

Nothing.

In fact, there wasn't even a portal. "Evar?"

An ominous cracking sound made her look up. The ceiling falling towards her in pieces would have shocked her less than what she saw. The assistant was dangling above her, very nearly at the top of the shelf, suspended from the rope around her ankle. The grey of her skin had darkened and a few last wisps of black smoke were being drawn into her head through the cratered wound on her temple. She flexed one midnight arm accompanied by another violent cracking noise. More sharp retorts as her head moved, neck craning just like Livira's so that the assistant looked down at her with black eyes invisible in the blackness of her face.

From somewhere high on the opposite shelf came a nervous squawk—the first time that Livira had heard anything but confidence, condemnation, or outrage from the Raven.

"Too . . . late." The assistant's voice came awkwardly from her lips as if she were wrestling with the shape of the words. "I have . . . written myself in."

The assistant turned away, directing her gaze up the bookcase. Slowly, but with less cracking now, and more quietly, like the breaking of brittle stalks, she began to bend, and to reach with one hand for the rope at her ankle.

The Raven descended in a frantic flapping of wings that was half flight and half falling. It landed heavily at Livira's feet and immediately began to hop off down the aisle. Livira hastily crawled away from the spot where the assistant would land if she fell, then scrambled to her feet and hurried after the bird.

A crash behind them. Silence. And then the advance of heavy footsteps. The thud of the assistant's feet sounded as if she were made of iron, though the other assistant, who had saved Livira when she fell, had walked noiselessly.

"What does it want?" Livira scooped up the Raven and ran with him. "You were going too slow," she puffed in response to his squawk of irritation or surprise. The answer to her question seemed fairly obvious—it wanted to kill her. The Escape had somehow infected the assistant, taken her over, and was now using her to hunt down Livira. Frankly, Livira thought the Escape could do a better job on its own but perhaps the ageless and possibly indestructible assistant was too great a prize to leave behind.

Glancing back, she saw the assistant turn the corner into her aisle. She could outrun it for now but something about its pace threatened a degree of untiring relentlessness that would win out in the long run.

Livira made for the door to Chamber 2. Once she'd crossed that chamber into Chamber 1, she would be little more than a mile from the steps and the exit to the librarians' complex. She only had memory to rely on for the route, though, and that was a memory of this single crossing back and forth years ago.

Several times Livira was sure she had taken a wrong turning, only to slowly convince herself that she might be on track after all. The Raven seemed less heavy than on the last journey, but the distant clunk-clunk-clunk of the assistant's advance kept the pressure on. The fact that the assistant seemed to know how to follow Livira, even when out of sight and faced with many choices, was a worrying one.

Livira began to pant so hard that she could no longer hear the assistant's pursuit, which was somehow worse as she might be gaining, especially since Livira was definitely slowing. Sweat ran the length of her body and her sore feet protested every stride. She desperately needed a way to delay the assistant so she could open a big enough lead to get clear of the chamber, and hopefully clear of the library.

When she finally found a ladder, she put the Raven under one arm, ignoring its complaints, and began to climb. Even through the labour of her breathing, as she gained elevation Livira could hear the clunk-clunk-clunk of the assistant's run.

Livira reached the top of the shelves and clambered onto the boards. She set the Raven to one side and, with a grunt of effort, lifted the ladder one rung's worth. It was every bit as heavy as she'd feared. Reaching for the next rung without surrendering what she'd lifted was a matter of speed as she hadn't the strength for it. She hauled up another rung, then another, then another, her arm muscles growing watery already.

Next to her the Raven squawked so loudly that she nearly dropped the ladder. "Gods' teeth! Do you have to do that? If you can't help, then at least—"

At the far end of what was thankfully a very long aisle Livira saw the assistant turn the corner. The additional surge of fear pumped fresh strength into her arms, and she began to lift the ladder rung over rung.

Even with terror driving her, Livira couldn't raise the ladder half of its length before her exhausted muscles turned traitor and the ladder slid from her trembling fingers. Livira lunged for it with a cry of despair and would certainly have been hauled over the edge by it had the ladder's descent not already been arrested. The bottom of the ladder had come to a halt on the tops of the books of an opposite shelf, prompting the Raven to squawk loudly.

The assistant drew level and craned her head to look up at them. The bottom of the ladder was well out of the assistant's reach. Even so, the assistant seemed unwilling to admit defeat and began pulling books out then using the exposed shelves to climb, tossing more books to the floor behind her as she gained height.

The Raven's outrage reached its limit and an astonished croak escaped its wide-open beak. Livira focused her energies on lifting the ladder some more, scraping the bottom of it up the opposite wall of books. It was immediately clear, though, that as slow as the assistant's climbing was, she was heading up faster than Livira could raise her burden.

The Raven began to hop anxiously from foot to foot.

"Still. Not. Helping," Livira managed past gritted teeth. Only half the ladder was above the shelf top.

The assistant reached for the bottom of the ladder, black fingers stretching.

Livira released a shriek of effort and shifted her grip on the rungs to start rotating the ladder in the vertical plane. The bottom moved smoothly to the left, out of the assistant's reach, counterbalanced by the descent of the top as Livira rotated it. When at last the ladder's feet rose above the shelf top, and the whole thing was horizontal, Livira took a step back and let her burden drop from numb fingers onto the planks at her feet.

Black eyes found her. "Jaspeth wants you, child."

Livira froze. It was a name from the child's book about the foundation of the library. Jaspeth, book thief, arsonist, enemy of knowledge.

"Who is Jaspeth?" Livira shouted. "What does he want?"

The assistant's slow but determined climb continued as she plucked books from the shelf above and let them fall, pages fluttering.

"What does he want with me?" Cursing, Livira realised she was wasting time whilst the assistant was closing the hard-won gap. Hastily, she shifted the ladder and began to rotate it—in the horizontal plane this time—with the shelf top supporting the weight. Soon the ladder lay at right angles to the shelf she stood on and stretched out across many shelf tops in both directions. Livira slid it in the direction she wanted to go until only the end remained on her shelf.

With the assistant closing on the top of the opposite shelving, Livira scooped up the Raven and ran as fast as she dared, using the ladder as a bridge, praying she wouldn't end up broken on the ground far below.

Having crossed a few aisles, Livira jumped off onto a shelf top and advanced the ladder before her. Looking back, she saw the assistant gain the top of her unit and clamber awkwardly onto it. Livira held her breath. If the assistant could jump the gaps Livira would have to abandon the ladder and start jumping herself, until exhaustion tripped her up. She'd put all her hope in the assistant lacking the agility required.

"Come on." Livira picked up the Raven again and hurried across the rungs. Four aisles on she stopped again to advance the ladder and to check on the assistant. "Just watching us go." That made Livira feel uneasy, but less so than a chase.

She walked on, taking more care now. She tried to keep her focus on setting one foot safely in front of the other, but her mind kept straying to thoughts of Evar. She'd left him surrounded by those creatures, fragments of a dozen nightmares. He'd fought like a god of war. She felt that even Malar would have been impressed. Evar, she thought, could have given a good account of himself to the sabber who had walked so arrogantly into her settlement and turned her life upside down.

A stumble sent her to her knees. She grabbed the ladder, spilling the Raven out into space. A frantic lunge caught the edge of his outspread wing and she pulled him back. "Sorry! Sorry! Sorry!"

From then on until the door to the second chamber came in sight Livira kept her mind on the business of escaping. The ladder that had served her so well performed one final duty, returning her to floor level. The exit invited her, but the semicircle of clear ground before it gave her a moment's pause. Shaking off her fear, she hurried out from the aisle.

The moment she exposed herself the corrupted assistant broke from the mouth of one of the other aisles forming the perimeter. Livira had no time to question its presence, prescience, or newfound stealth. She ran for all she was worth, barely keeping hold of the Raven. The assistant accelerated, its footfalls once again a clanking thunder.

In a wild flurry of robes and racing legs Livira threw herself at the white expanse of the door. At the Raven's touch the whiteness became mist. Livira kept running, and only at the mouth of the corridor to the next chamber with nothing but silence behind her did she come to a gasping halt. She bent double, panting, watching the door. The portal had refused her, opening only for the mysterious bird in her hands. It seemed that it had refused the assistant too, sensing the corruption within it.

Livira regained her breath and, still trembling, set the Raven on the floor. "Thank you for coming to help me when I was afraid in the Mechanism."

The Raven gave a muted squawk.

"And thank you for letting me get back to the Exchange."

The Raven preened, removing some imaginary speck from the tattered blackness of its wings, possibly from the feather she had returned to it.

"And . . . for just now."

The Raven ignored her.

"I need to go back there. But I think maybe the when isn't as important as it would normally be." Another image of Evar faced by many enemies crossed her mind. "Time works differently there. If he needs my help, maybe that's the time it will be when I arrive." She hoped so. She hoped he was safe.

The Raven looked up, regarding her with the midnight beads of its eyes.

"You don't really care about any of this, do you?"

The Raven gave a non-committal croak.

"I'm going to leave you here," Livira said. "I don't think giving you to the librarians would be a very good way to say thank you. They'd never let you go. And if you didn't do what they wanted they'd start taking you apart to see how you work."

The Raven watched her silently.

"You be careful, bird." Livira backed away. "Don't go near that assistant!" She waved and turned to go. She thought the Raven might offer some form of goodbye, but when she glanced back it was gone, the black dot it had made against the grey floor now erased as if it had never been there.

LIVIRA MADE HER way across Chamber 2 via the labyrinth. Most librarians avoided the labyrinth because it was easy to become lost in it, even with a map, and because most of the books there were works of fiction. The librarians' top interests were the sciences. Crath and all the cities beyond were hungry for progress, not for stories. Fiction ranked below even history which, except where it could be used to back up King Oanold's pronouncements, was a subject of very little interest to a populace with its eyes on the future. What they cared about was the next in the series of developments that was making the staircase they would climb to the heights of the ancients. And, even more importantly, might maintain their edge over the sabber threat, providing ever more deadly weapons to see off the ever greater numbers coming from the east.

Livira had come to like the labyrinth though, not least for the privacy it offered so close to the entrance. Despite her eagerness to get home, Livira's sore feet and general exhaustion prompted her to stop near the heart of the labyrinth and climb a ladder.

Thirty yards up, Livira clambered onto the shelf top and lay on her front, watching the aisle. Stillness was bliss. She lay without motion, letting her heart slow and her muscles relax. She often came to the labyrinth to read. Both fiction, as Master Yute had suggested, and history as well, the latter more out of a sense of duty. The histories were dry, the fiction as if someone had pulled a still-beating heart from its cage of ribs and left it pulsing crimson on the page. Somehow the stories that never happened, ones that merely sprang from the dreaming of some long-dead author, were more true than the histories that might be found on the opposite shelf. The stories, though set free on imagination's wings, had to make some kind of sense to prevent the readers' scoffs. Truth, though, didn't care a whit for making sense and could ride roughshod over people's expectations. Truth, it was often said in the library, was stranger than fiction. Livira also considered it uglier, crueller, and ultimately less satisfying.

For a long time she lay there, picturing Evar as she had last seen him, and wondering how she might save him.

Sometime later she reached out and plucked a book from just beneath her.

Master Yute had said that writing is an exercise in letting your mind wander but making sure that it keeps what it picks up on the way. Livira had decided to follow his advice.

Yute, it had turned out, was something of a rogue librarian, at odds with his three fellow deputies and the head librarian. Quite how he had secured and kept his current rank was a matter of fierce speculation among the trainees. Almost everything about Yute was. His name was pretty much the only thing agreed to be a reliably known fact about him.

In any event, fiction was heavily frowned upon and illegally securing parchment for her own project would have been a risky prospect. If it were discovered that she had stolen supplies from the parchment stores and then adulterated it with mere fiction . . . Livira doubted her feet would have touched the ground on her way out of the library—permanently.

Livira had decided on a different approach rather than adding this particular infraction to the already long list of crimes that the librarians were trying to hang her with.

She understood that the library picked its own books. Unauthorised books were reduced to dust. People like King Oanold had to console themselves with the fact that in the endless aisles of the library there was almost certainly a book that agreed with any ridiculous idea that sprang into their head. Similarly, there would be a text to back up any convenient lie that might allow them to slide past an inconvenient truth in the wider world. All they needed to do was to have the librarians search it out.

Livira had, on many occasions, announced her dissatisfaction with the fact that she couldn't add a book to the shelves. Arpix had laughed and said that it was just the rule. As if that were an end to the discussion. Livira had often felt that the saving grace of rules was how much fun they were to break.

She turned to the front of the book and the blank flyleaf. From her pocket she took one of the new iron quills the trainees had been issued with and a small bottle of ink. She had been writing her thoughts and experiences on the flyleaves of books scattered throughout the labyrinth, ending each page with a cryptic reference to the next book where her tale continued. She made sure to choose works of non-fiction, and boring ones at that, books whose authors she felt would be scandalised and outraged at her vandalism rather than wounded by it. The sheet from *Great Sailing Ships of History* on which she had once scrawled a map of the labyrinth had been the start of it: page one.

Livira wanted to get the events of the last few days down on paper while the emotions were still fresh. Her memory was essentially infallible as far as facts were concerned, but emotion had a tendency to dry like ink and cease to glisten. It needed to be captured as close to the moment as possible. She started to write in the flowing script that Master Logaris criticised as too flamboyant and wasteful of space. His own crabbed handwriting reminded Livira of puzzles where the object is to fit a great number of irregular shapes into a space that seems impossibly small.

Starting at the beginning was another rule Livira liked to break. She
began with a statement, a statement of truth or intent:

> All of us steal our lives. A little here, a little there. Some of it given,
> most of it taken. We wear ourselves like a coat of many patches,
> fraying at the edges, in constant repair. While we shore up one
> belief, we let go another. We are the stories we tell to ourselves.
> Nothing more.

She inked the full stop again, more definitely. This was her life, too large
and too complicated to be contained wholly within her head, spilling out
onto the page. Any book worth its ink must, she thought, have something of
the author held between the lines. There were, she believed, enough parts of
enough people on the library's shelves to repopulate a world many times over,
if only they could be correctly assembled.

It wasn't, she decided, enough to dangle only herself from the scrolling
loops of her handwriting. Evar should be there too. And eventually, perhaps, everyone she knew. But she began with Evar, who, despite his peerless
combat skill, felt to her vulnerable in many ways that she was not. A life
lived with only one girl and three—now two—boys wasn't going to equip
anyone for the casual cruelty of the world or the intricacies of navigating a
society composed of many thousands. Livira herself was still studying the
necessary interactions and trying to understand oddities like Serra Leetar
and Malar. She'd found Evar just as he broke out of his cage for the first
time. In a very real way, he was her—as she was the day after the destruction of the settlement. He was her as she crossed the Dust towards the city.
Only his Dust was the Exchange and his city lay in one of those pools
he saw.

Livira wrote until she approached the end of the page and realised that
she had hardly any room to talk about the Mechanism—that wonder
which Master Ellis and the other deputies kept to themselves. She crammed
in what she could and admitted to herself that perhaps there was some
benefit to Logaris's economical hand over her own sprawling prose. At the
end of the page, she wrote a clue to the name of the book which she had
already scouted out for the next installment.

The fiction would start later. Right now, Evar was a character ready to be set loose on pages to come. Perhaps she would put herself in there and they could share the adventures that the closing of the portal had denied to them.

She wiped her inky hand on her newly black robe and made her way wearily down the ladder, ready to eat some real food and to sleep in her own bed.

War is often described as long periods of boredom, punctuated by moments of terror. A description that is functionally identical to many people's lives.

The Pursuit of Happiness, *by Alfred J. Prooffrock*

CHAPTER 37

Livira

Three years passed and although Livira bent all her cleverness, and all of what many among the librarians might term her wickedness, to the problem of finding Evar Eventari once more, the library continued to defeat her. She applied herself ferociously to the pursuits of learning and research, hoping by such interrogation to force the library to reveal its secrets.

One matter she gave less thought to, and indeed actively avoided, was the "why" of it. Evar, if he had survived the battle she'd left him in, had undoubtedly found this mystery woman he obsessed over. By now they were probably living in a small house on the edge of a forest and had two babies. He would have forgotten the ink-stained girl with her annoying questions. And the truth of that put an ache in her chest that she didn't understand.

Livira told herself that although Evar was her target, her goal was the knowledge that would let her reach him again. However, none of that explained why his face, dappled by the sun and shade of a hidden forest, appeared in quite so many of her dreams. Or why his hesitant smile, unguarded grins, and the fluid way he moved in battle, kept her from sleeping so many nights in the narrow confines of the bed within her trainee cell.

Three years had wrought many changes in Livira and her tablemates, but to the library the time was less than the turning of a single page. Even the librarians remained much the same. Master Logaris sat at the front of the classroom, craggy as a rock, no different from the day Livira arrived, expressing no astonishment as his charges matured at a startling rate.

The city at their gates, however, remained in constant flux. Every year the fruits of the librarians' research rippled down through the streets, placing new wonders in the hands of its citizens and soldiers alike. New colours entered the seamstresses' palettes, new tastes infiltrated the cake-shop shelves, new mechanisms in the toymakers' inventions. Previously unknown chemicals emerged in secure vats from the gates beneath the laboratory's fumaroles.

And across the Dust more sabbers came, one band joining to another. Raids on outlying towns increased. Sightings from the city walls. Seemingly greater numbers every month despite the denials from official proclamations, each war party bolder, or perhaps more desperate, than the last. The stories grew too, stories of a threat in the east, driving the sabbers from their homelands. And though the tales had yet to settle on a single description of this threat, at least they had converged upon a single name. The skeer.

Much of the librarians' efforts were steered towards the search for knowledge that would place in the hands of the king's troops weapons of ever greater deadliness. To compensate for the sabbers' swiftness and strength, arrow-sticks, or in the vernacular just plain 'sticks, were issued to the soldiers. To balance out the unequal numbers, grenades were manufactured. Yet still the sabbers came, lean and hungry, to gaze upon the city walls.

LIVIRA DIDN'T MOVE to the penultimate of Heeth Logaris's tables until her sixteenth birthday. Arpix joined her there just after her seventeenth. Both of them were the youngest trainees at the table by several years. Deputy Ellis had spoken against Livira's advancement. In addition to what amounted to two handfuls of suspicion, he argued that it would create unnecessary friction with the policies being enacted in the city to deal with the "wilds problem." Namely the influx of displaced populations from the Dust and beyond the mountains.

Deputy Ellis had swung the vote of Deputy Acconite against Livira in a meeting of the four deputy head librarians. Livira of course had not been invited, or even told, but librarians like to take notes and Livira took the notes . . . from Master Jost, who had been the one writing them down during the meeting. The deadlock hadn't needed to be broken, since the lack of a majority left the decision in Master Logaris's lap, and he for reasons of his own had decided to keep her. This time.

Smarting from his defeat, Deputy Ellis had set Master Jost to a near-constant watch of Livira's activities outside the classroom. Despite her dogged attention the woman hadn't been able to keep up with Livira in the library chambers. Her watchful eye had, however, slowed down Livira's copying of the Kensan Index, which lay behind only the Helfac Index and the head librarian's own personal index in terms of being both contemporary and comprehensive.

Outside the library, politics and war swept around the roots of the mountain, washing against Crath's walls from opposite sides. Only ripples and echoes of this chaos reached into the complex where Livira laboured over her studies though, the muted cries of a nation in the grip of breakneck progress.

Master Logaris largely left the youngest trainees to sink or swim, placing books in their hands and demands on their shoulders. Those that sank were found other employment, the prizes being either placement within the complex, such as Jella's appointment with the bookbinders, or as house readers out in the city, like Carlotte. Whilst the city exerted a constant pressure for more librarians to meet their need for neatly packaged knowledge, the head librarian resisted and allowed only the very best to take the white robe of a junior librarian. Livira felt that the head librarian appreciated the importance of supply and demand, and in consequence refused the pressure to grow her empire as fast as the king insisted.

With Jella and Carlotte no longer trainees, Arpix, Livira, and Meelan were the only survivors from the first table. Meelan had joined the fifth table, which lay behind Livira's, just after Arpix moved on from it. He was no longer shorter than Livira even though she'd grown like the eponymous weed, and at nearly nineteen he had filled out his skinny frame into that of quite a solid young man. He still looked angry all the time, staring from dark eyes under a wave of black hair, and everything he said still sounded like a death threat. But he'd always been there to help cover up Livira's misdeeds, and where Arpix would tell her off, and Carlotte would encourage her, and Jella would be scandalised, Meelan never offered judgement of any sort.

Lately Livira had been pushing herself hard to discover as much about the library as she could. Visits to the Mechanism with the works of past library scholars had helped—though books about the library itself were fantastically hard to find. Either the library did not like to stock books about itself, or the head librarian had moved all such volumes and only her private index would identify their location. Livira wanted to find another door into the Exchange but even hints of the place's existence were nearly impossible to discover.

But the clock was ticking—literally, since Deputy Ellis had received one of the new mechanical devices from an "inventor" in the city and had it looming in the corner of his office, its pendulum forever swinging. Livira's visit to the Mechanism with a book on lock-picking had paid dividends and the fruits of her spying were a clear picture of the work Ellis was putting in to having her removed. Letters were exchanged between him and Lord Algar with increasing frequency. As a child she had considered Lord Algar's motivation to be personal spite. From her current perspective, and with the correspondence in hand, she saw it to be a matter of policy and politics—though probably with a considerable amount of spite thrown in for good measure.

Livira had even researched Lord Algar himself, an investigation that had required resources outside the library. It seemed that although he was, as Meelan had told her, "old money," Algar's ancestral wealth and standing had been on the decline since his grandfather's time. With this insight, his slavish championing of even the king's most offhand declarations looked more desperate than evil. His co-opting of Serra Leetar from her intended studies to his own department was perhaps an attempt to stamp his authority over the "new money" that she represented, free of aristocratic roots but with growing influence. Livira still didn't like the man, even a little bit, but she found that understanding him at least made him human, replacing the inexplicable villain that her child-self had painted as her nemesis with someone who was in their turn just another cog in the mechanism that was Crath City, subject to their own pressures and goals.

The sabbers' advance had caused unheard-of upheaval and migration of displaced populations. The harshness of King Oanold's response to that crisis rested on the idea that those coming in from the Dust were less than human. Livira's placement in the library might become a rallying cry for those disputing the policy. In any event, it seemed that outside pressure was being exerted to make Deputy Synoth abstain from the next vote, leaving Yute in the minority.

Livira sat with Arpix listening to Master Logaris. The idea that a handful of old men with political and personal axes to grind could see her thrown into the streets, when she already knew more about the library than they did, made her furious. But short of running off into the chambers and living wild among the books, there seemed to be nothing she could do about it.

On her new table Livira had already received more personal instruction from Master Logaris than she had during her time at all the others combined. Today he had broached the subject of the difference between what the library's customers said they wanted and what they actually wanted. He began by inviting the trainees to offer their own opinions, and Arpix walked into the trap.

"Truth?" Master Logaris scoffed at the idea. "We deal in *affirmation*. People don't want truth. They say that they do but what they mean is that they want the truth to agree with them. Take ninety-nine books that say one thing and one that says the opposite. If that opposite was what the customer was hoping to hear, they'll put their stock in the single volume. In this manner we learn more regarding human nature from closed books than from anything that might be written within them."

Logaris went on in this manner for some time, exposing the source of the weary cynicism that seemed to infect most of the senior librarians. It seemed to Livira that there was a message in the way librarians demonstrated their rank with a shade of grey, white for juniors, shading darker with seniority. A symbolism concerning the way the fortress of facts that seemed so dependable, rather than being reinforced by the library's endless knowledge, was in reality eroded by it, a sandcastle before the waves. The black and white of truth blurred into grey under the relentless assault of an infinity of context, interpretation, perspectives, and opinion.

As soon as Master Logaris turned his attention to the final table and the most promising immediate candidates for the white, Arpix picked up his book again. He'd brought it to the table that morning, on a trolley since it was half his height, and had been running his hands over its metallic pages all day, using his fingertips to read the language of bumps and ridges embossed there.

"What's it about?" Livira had avoided asking, having realised that Arpix rarely showed an interest in her own research. But curiosity got the better of her.

"Topology. The mathematics of surfaces and volumes." Arpix didn't look up, even though it was his fingers rather than his eyes doing the reading. "Champart, the inventor—"

"I know who Champart is."

"Well, he's hit a dead end and has requested books focused on certain aspects of topology. Which means I have to know enough about the subject to find what he needs. It's fascinating stuff. Did you know that topologically we're tori? All animals are."

"Ewww." Livira tried to press a disgusted smile from her lips. He was right though. Arpix had a talent for reducing a problem to its essentials. Every animal she knew of was basically a tube with elaborations. Yet such reductions could leave you blind to the world's beauty. Livira rather liked the elaborations. If Arpix really did see her as just another tube, though, it would explain the way he'd looked at her on the few occasions she'd attempted to flirt with him. Before Carlotte had gone to be a house reader for Lord Masefield she'd said she thought that Arpix would end up marrying a book and raising a clutch of papery babies.

Livira was about to ask which animal was most like a torus when the schoolroom door opened without a knock and a frowning, white-robed librarian hurried in.

"You." He pointed at Livira. "You're to come with me immediately."

This was it then. A summons to stand before the deputies and be dismissed. Livira stood, a cold fist of regret clenched in her stomach.

"And . . . which one is Meelan Hosten?" the librarian asked.

Meelan lifted a hand. Everyone knew Livira, though not always for a good reason. Meelan maintained a lower profile in the complex.

"You too, then." The librarian nodded. "Come with me."

Livira couldn't guess why Meelan was involved. Perhaps they had evidence of the many times he'd helped cover for her. But Arpix was just as guilty of that.

Master Logaris raised a bushy eyebrow then shrugged. "Don't beat the boy. It was probably the girl's fault."

Livira followed Meelan out, aware of the many pairs of eyes studying her departure.

The librarian was a man in his mid-twenties named Tubberly, or just Tubby to the trainees, owing to the length of time he spent in the refectory polishing off second, third, and sometimes fourth helpings. He gave Livira an even deeper frown and closed the door behind them.

"You're to present yourself at Master Yute's house within the hour wearing your finest clothes. Don't ask me why. I've no better idea of that than I do of why that man thinks I'm his messenger boy."

"Master Yute?" Livira blinked.

"They do say you've a remarkable memory." Tubberly paused to suck his teeth. "I'm unconvinced. Master Yute, pale fellow, deputy head librarian. Ringing any bells?"

Livira opened her mouth to unleash a hot retort but an elbow in her ribs cut her off. "We'll get ready immediately," Meelan growled.

Tubberly waved them off and turned away. Meelan led the race back to the trainee bedrooms. Livira's head was too full of theories to contest him. And besides, who runs to their execution?

"I DON'T HAVE any finest clothes!" Livira complained.

"Well, make do." Meelan opened the door to his room.

"I'll go as I am," Livira said.

"You can't do that!" Meelan turned back towards her.

"It's my trainee robe or a dirt-coloured dress that I stopped being able to fit into when I was twelve."

"Find someone who'll lend you something," Meelan said.

"Who? They're all in class. And I'm not going back in there to make a fuss. Logaris would have me cataloguing geology books in the stink chamber for a week."

That gave Meelan pause for thought. It was certainly the kind of thing Logaris might do, and the stink chamber was pretty bad. Something to do with the way they'd cured the leather for a fair portion of the books in that section, or the beasts from which the hide was taken. The worst part was that unlike most smells, you didn't get acclimatised to the stink chamber—somehow it got worse hour by hour until you spent half your time retching. And afterwards you brought it home with you on your robe and skin. "Do your best—I'll meet you at the mountain exit," he said.

"They're all mountain exits."

Meelan turned his back on her and went off to his room. Livira went to hers to consider her very limited choices. She made her clothing selection almost immediately, then lingered to ponder the motive behind Yute's summons.

Livira had seen Yute all of three times in the years since she was nearly gassed while delivering books to the laboratory. She'd spoken to him on only one of those occasions. He'd mentioned that he had been getting reports accusing her of extracurricular activities for which the lightest punishment was expulsion. His parting advice had been not to get caught doing it. Much as Livira wanted to ask Yute the questions she'd been hoarding, the ones too dangerous to ask Master Logaris, she couldn't help feeling angry with him for his abandonment of her to the processes of the library. But at the same time she understood that he'd saved her from the low-status jobs in the city that her heritage would have chained her to. So she also felt angry with herself and her own ingratitude.

"What's taking him so long?" Livira asked her question to the wind, and not for the first time. Getting no answer, she went back to chasing her thoughts in Yute-centred circles. Livira had emerged from the complex to find that night had fallen, and the air carried the bite of winter. She'd spent so long poring over books and roaming the shelves that she'd forgotten about things like weather. The mountainside on a winter's night was a rude reminder. She hugged herself, pressed into what little shelter the folds of the cliff face offered, and tried to remember what it had been like climbing to the library's entrance that first time.

"Seriously?" Meelan startled her back into the present. "That's what you're wearing?"

"Gods' teeth, Meelan! Where did you steal that lot from?" She wanted to say it was from Arpix, but while Arpix had a good-quality jacket and trews stashed away in his cupboard they were nothing like the finery Meelan currently sported. "You look like . . ." She wasn't sure what he looked like. A prince? Certainly someone who would ride Crath's streets in a carriage with their own crest.

Meelan waved her words away. "And you look like you've stolen the head librarian's robes! You can't wear that!"

"It's this or my trainee blue. And Yute's summons said 'finest.'" Livira looked down at the black robe. She'd grown three hand widths since the Mechanism had dyed it. She hoped it wasn't noticeably short but her cold ankles suggested otherwise.

Meelan gave a disgusted snort, shook his head, and turned back to the path that wound its way down towards the city. "Come on."

Livira hurried after him and linked her arm in his. "Meelan," she asked teasingly, "are you rich?"

"A bit." He didn't sound very happy about it.

"I've known you nearly half my life. How am I just discovering this?"

Meelan shrugged and untangled himself from Livira—in order, she hoped, to negotiate the dark path more safely. "You're the one who spends her life uncovering secrets. You tell me."

A twinge of guilt ran through Livira at that. The truth was that she dug out the secrets that interested her most, the big ones; the library secrets were the mountain she intended to climb. Meelan knew he was more interested in her than she was in him. Both of them knew it and both of them knew they both knew it. "Why didn't you tell me?" she deflected.

"People look at you differently when they know you're rich." Meelan walked ahead of her, following the path by starlight. "You could give them enough money to change their life, they think—but most lives can swallow any amount and stay the same."

"You can stop them being hungry!" Livira caught him up again but did not attempt to link arms. She'd been a long time in the library, long enough to be surprised by the cold, but not long enough to forget being hungry. Even the library didn't hold enough time for that.

"True." Meelan twisted his mouth. "I wasn't thinking about that kind of poor. I suppose I should have been. But most of the people down there"—he nodded towards the carpet of lights spread out below them—"most of them think money would change who they are, and that's the thing: you take yourself with you wherever you go. Money can't buy a new you. At least that's what I find."

A dark shape loomed behind them. "Rich people talk a lot of bollocks about money. But the bottom line is always that they're keeping hold of it."

"Malar!" Livira whirled around.

Malar took a step backwards. "What's up with your face, girl?"

"What?" Livira pressed both hands to her cheeks, searching, then caught the glint of starlight in Malar's eyes. "It's called smiling, you idiot. I'm pleased to see you!"

"No accounting for taste." Malar shrugged and looked at Meelan. "And this would be Sirrar Meelan. I'm to escort you two to Yute's place, on account of how murdery things tend to get every time Livira leaves the library."

"Once!" Livira protested. "OK, twice, but it was on the same day."

"The only day you've visited." Malar pushed between them and took the lead. "Come on then. I've got a beer waiting."

Whilst it is the first words of a child that often gain notoriety among the family, it's their last words that are more likely to continue to roll down eternity's slope. For those whose path leads to the executioner's stage, this presents the rare opportunity to reach an audience far beyond the picnickers, gawkers, delighted enemies, and misty-eyed lovers who might crowd in upon the day itself.

Always the Bright Side, *by M. P. Thon*

CHAPTER 38

Livira

Livira and Meelan followed the soldier down the mountain road. Livira decided not to mention that she'd escaped the complex on a fairly regular basis over the last few years and got to know the city quite well, all without needing Malar to keep her alive. She'd seen the changes there, month by month, building and rebuilding, better this, better that, reaching for a bright tomorrow. The poor remained though, haunting the narrowest streets on the northside, where you could smell the laboratory fumes on a still afternoon. They were joined by the war-wounded these days. Not that there was an *official* war. But still, more and more of the injured veterans seemed to crowd the corners, rattling their cups for coin. Soldiers who had lost arms, legs, and eyes to the sabbers, but most of all it was their spirit that had been taken from them, snatched away by the sight of too much horror, too much dying.

She kept her experiences to herself, however. It wasn't that she thought Meelan or Malar would tell on her, but secrets always seemed to escape if given space. One person could hold a secret tight to their chest with both hands. When it was two, or three, or four people it was as if that secret had to be tossed back and forth between them, creating many chances to drop it. Instead, she asked, "Why now then? What's so important out in the world that we're risking things getting murdery again?"

Malar pretended she hadn't spoken. "Your friend Yute had thoughts to share on wealth. In his opinion, it's not the gift of money that's the greatest—it's the gift of purpose. He said, and the fancy words are all his: All of us in our secret hearts, in our empty moments of contemplation, stumble into the understanding that nothing matters. There's a cold shock of realisation and, in that moment, we know that nothing at all is of the least consequence. Ultimately, we're all just spinning our wheels, seeking to avoid pain until the clock winds down and our time is spent. To give someone purpose is to free them, however briefly, from the spectre of that knowledge."

Meelan whistled softly. "What did you say to that?"

"That my price was still three silvers and two wouldn't cut it."

Livira snorted laughter. "A good imitation." Malar had caught Yute's gentle, rather distracted tone well, and the fact that he was given to wandering into speeches as if everything still amazed him and he was keen to share each new epiphany. "Still, you remembered what he said. So, he must have made an impression."

The former soldier shot her a narrow look. "You're not the only one with a good memory, girly. And I remember everyone who tries to short me!"

At the next turn Livira paused. "There are a lot of lights out beyond the wall."

"Campfires," Malar said. "There's dead wood out on the Dust if you know where to look."

"Those are the people the king doesn't want to let in?" Livira asked.

Malar shook his head and spat. "The refugees are camped so close to the wall it hides them from here. Also, they haven't got enough fuel to waste on fires like that."

Meelan tried. "Who is it then—"

"Fucking sabbers," Malar snapped. "Too many of them. One's too many, mind. Especially when they get into the city." He tapped the hilt of his sword, as if explaining his presence and the size of his fee.

"They're in the city?" Livira gasped.

"Sometimes. We've had raids." Malar spat again. "You're safer down there than up here though. Been scouting ways over the mountain lately . . . And if they blockade the passes then there's going to be a lot more hungry bellies in Crath. The mountain trails are the only way food's reaching us right now!"

"Why is killing us so important to them?" The old stone of Livira's hatred began to warm in her stomach.

"The king says they're just evil, vicious animals that—"

"Animals aren't evil," Meelan said.

"If you're going to start calling the king out on his nonsense, we'll be here all fucking night." Malar spat to the side. "Me, I think they want what we've got."

"They want to eat us?" Livira frowned. *Are you good to eat?* The sabber's words from that day long ago echoed in her mind.

"What we've got." Malar waved expansively at their surroundings.

"Houses?" Livira frowned again.

"The library?" Meelan snorted. "What would they do with that?"

"Maybe they'd surprise you. They kept on surprising me out there." Malar shrugged and led on. "I do keep hearing one scary rumour though. And it might just be true."

"And?" Livira asked into the following silence.

"They're running from something."

Livira said nothing. She'd heard that one too.

THEY REACHED YUTE's house only a few minutes later and Livira thought that three silvers was an outrageous price for so brief a service.

"I'll watch the street." Malar nodded at the door.

"Gas lights even here . . ." Livira quite liked the effect. The surrounding houses were so tall that their upper storeys vanished into the night while the lower levels basked in the new lighting's warm glow.

"Nothing stays the same for long in Crath City." Malar glanced back the way they'd come. "That's what makes it so dangerous."

Meelan went to knock on the door.

"Go easy on the librarian," Malar told Livira. "It's a bad day for him."

Salamonda had the door open almost as Meelan's knuckles made contact with the wood. "Livira!" She looked past Meelan. "And who's this? You've traded in your last boyfriend for one that's a prince?"

"He's not my boyfriend." Livira hurried up the steps and pushed Meelan past Salamonda.

"You should fix that," Salamonda said in a too-loud whisper as Livira came through. "He's lovely."

Livira scowled at the woman, noting for the first time that there were streaks of grey in the tight bun of her hair.

Salamonda picked up a bowl of biscuits from the kitchen table. "I suppose you're too old for—"

Livira snatched three. "I'll be too old for biscuits when I'm dead." The knot in her stomach had loosened as soon as she entered the kitchen. She nudged Meelan. "What? Afraid of getting crumbs on your lace? Try them!"

"I'm not wearing any lace," Meelan growled. He took a biscuit. "My thanks, madam."

"Salamonda," Salamonda said. "And you're Sirrar Meelan. Yute talks about you all the time."

"About me?" Meelan's eyes widened in astonishment.

"He talks about all the trainees." Salamonda nodded. "Sit! Sit! He'll be down in a moment."

Livira sat at the table, so amazed at the idea of Yute even knowing who was in the trainee class that she forgot to chew.

Salamonda turned away to stir something on the stove. "And that's what you're wearing, is it?"

Livira didn't have to ask to know that Salamonda meant her. "Unless you've got something better upstairs?" Even a mouthful of biscuit didn't take the sharp edge off the words. She'd had enough of being told she was a mess.

"I'm afraid we don't." A voice spoke from the stairs, which hadn't had the decency to creak a warning. "We lost Yolanda when she was about the size you were on your first visit here." Yute came into view in his dark robes, white-faced and sombre.

"I'm sorry," Livira said. And she was. "I wasn't thinking."

Yute forced a smile and lifted a hand to ward off further apology. "It's fine. I'm fine." He paused, thoughtfully, and looked back up the stairs as if he could see all the way to his daughter's room at the top of the house. "Hurts don't stop, but they fade into shadows of what they were. That's sad.

That something so vital, something that bit you so deep, can be eroded by time into a story that almost seems like it happened to someone else. Any hurt. The years have taken away her meaning. It lessens us." He paused, as if realising that his words had carried him away, then shrugged. "It is what it is."

Salamonda watched him, bright-eyed with sympathy. "Yute . . ."

Yute brought his white hands together with a sigh as if trying to wring some warmth out of them. "So, we're ready to depart? Livira's attire will serve."

"You're in robes too!" Livira realised for the first time. She'd only ever seen Yute in robes so the fact that he wasn't dressed up to the nines like Meelan hadn't registered.

"I am." Yute crossed to the street door. "I have an official duty to perform!"

Livira's heart sank again. She wanted to ask the whats and whys, but in the face of Yute's old loss it seemed petty to focus on troubles partly of her own making. She could have kept her head down, played by the rules, waited until she was entitled to know the answers to all those secrets that taunted her. Yute's sombre mood promised nothing good. Deputies Ellis, Synoth, and Acconite would be waiting for him to bring her to the vote.

Once out in the street, Yute began to lead them down into the city. Malar fell in behind them, one hand on the hilt of his sword.

"You haven't got an arrow-stick yet?" Livira resolved to tease the soldier in defiance of her grim mood. Whatever the deputies did to her tonight she was damned if she was going to let them see that it hurt her.

"No good in close quarters on a dark night."

"I heard they use chemical explosives to throw the lead balls these days." Meelan spoke up. "Over great distances." He seemed keen to earn Malar's approval—which surprised Livira more than his up-to-date knowledge of arrow-sticks.

Malar shrugged. "The longer the distance over which you conduct your murders the more likely they are to happen. Not sure that's a good thing. But when it comes to blasting sabbers from the ramparts of the city wall anything that works is fine by me."

"You don't swear as much," Livira said. "You used to swear all the time."

Malar nodded at Yute's back. "Don't want to make an albino blush. Certainly not one who pays a fair wage."

"As long as you're not going soft," Livira teased.

Malar narrowed his eyes at her and for a heartbeat she thought he might actually attack her. "When a dog stops barking, that's when you should be most afraid of its bite."

YUTE LED THEM down the stairs cut into the rock slopes that rose behind the great square. He pointed to some dark entrances in the steepest parts.

"People used to live there. The first homes here weren't built from stones or bricks or sticks, they were caves that just happened to be here. Later people made them bigger. Made more of them." He paused to look at one of them, a doorway or a window, Livira couldn't tell. Yute sighed and led on. "I need new streets to be old on. Walking the same places I walked when things were so different—it makes me forget who I am, when I am."

"Careful there, Master Yute." Malar spoke up unexpectedly. "Nostalgia's a dangerous thing. Especially on steps like these."

Meelan, still more unexpectedly, joined in, quoting from a text Livira had helped him translate from Relquian the week before. "'Nostalgia is the best and the worst feeling—complex—nothing has the ability to so delight and wound us simultaneously, except perhaps for love.'"

Livira watched the three men in the starlight. She expected philosophy from Yute, but the other two? It really did seem that they were descending towards her execution, drawing out each yard as if to wrestle meaning from the grasp of each remaining moment.

Yute, ignoring Malar's warning about the steps, turned to look at Meelan with a mixture of appreciation and amusement. "What does nostalgia mean to a child? An abstraction. A standing stone waiting for them in the mist. Walk a path across some decades, any path you like, and the word will gather weight. It will come to you trailing maybes and might-have-beens. Nostalgia is a drug, a knife. Against young skin it carries a dull edge, but time will teach you that nostalgia cuts—and that it's a blade we cannot keep from applying to our own flesh." His voice carried a measure of pain, as if he felt that edge himself. He stumbled on the next step and both trainees caught him in an awkward clinch that might have seen the three of them pitch to their destruction. Malar said nothing.

They descended in silence after that. Livira turned her gaze towards the rest of the city. Many hundreds of lights burned within the windows of the grand buildings around the great square, and lanterns dotted the plaza itself. Ground-based constellations aping the night's glory.

Yute steered a path around the outer walls of the lesser palace gardens and into the square. It surprised Livira that the library was conducting its business outside the complex. Her reading had led her to believe that nothing undermines a faith so much as exposing the inner workings, and whilst the citizens of Crath might swear allegiance to a hundred different gods, they put their faith in the library.

When they reached the square Livira could immediately tell that the well-dressed crowd was in the grip of a current and that the flow was taking them to the steps of the lesser palace. Yute allowed himself to be carried along.

Livira started to drag her heels and would have fallen back but for Malar taking her elbow.

"People say that murders happen in dark alleys. Really, it's easier in a crowd. A quick stab, and leave before anyone understands what's happened." The way Malar said it made Livira wonder if he'd had personal experience and on which side of the blade.

Yute glanced back and seemed to misunderstand Livira's reluctance as being concern about her attire rather than her fate. He tried to jolly her along, though the tension in his face and in his voice rather undermined the effort. "If anyone asks why Livira's in black we can say she's the new head librarian and has come to assess my performance."

Drawn along in Yute's wake, Livira found herself walking through the palace gates. Malar set a hand briefly to her shoulder and fell back, remaining outside. A score of guards watched on, arrayed around the gateposts in gleaming armour, the scarlet plumes above their helms bobbing in the breeze. Livira doubted their steel breastplates would stop one of the lead balls from the latest arrow-sticks, but they looked impressive.

To her amazement Livira was allowed to follow Yute into the palace itself, climbing marble steps and passing through a doorway as large as a chamber door in the library. Tiers of seating wrapped the huge hall that the doorway gave onto. The gas lamps that had lit the courtyard marched on into the hall, bathing it in a steady light that was kinder than the library's merciless illumination, and had the decency to cast shadows.

Almost all the benches were already crammed with the high and mighty, glittering in diamonds, cloth-of-gold, silks and lace, ornamentation of all manner, a dazzling array that made even Meelan's finest look merely commonplace and rather restrained. There were hundreds of them, some more lordly than others, many merely richly attired but lacking gravitas. Livira struggled to understand what was going on.

"Over here." Yute swerved to the left, aiming towards an empty space in the front and lowest tier.

Livira sat, sandwiched between Meelan and Yute, the former scowling as if he'd rather be translating a page on Galathain economics, the latter as serious as Livira had ever seen him. All around the hall the last few empty places were being filled.

Livira could restrain herself no longer. "What's going on?"

But even as she asked, the hubbub of conversation all around her died away, leaving an expectant silence. Trumpets sounded, a sudden blare that made Livira jolt. People entered at the rear of the hall. More gas lamps ignited, pushing back the shadows there and revealing a throne that Livira had failed to notice while busy gawking at the lords and their families.

A puffy-faced man in long purple robes trimmed with gold came forward, surrounded by attendants. He looked old, though the application of thick paints and a heavy wig full of tightly curled grey hair sought to disguise the path the years had trampled across him. He was overweight but sagging, as if he had once been decidedly heavier and the skin that had stretched to accommodate that bulk now had no purpose but to hang in folds.

The man seated himself on the throne. An attendant in black lowered a heavy golden crown onto the wig. It wasn't until that point that Livira finally realised she was looking at King Oanold. Two guards stepped up to flank the throne. Two large men carrying a new design of arrow-stick.

Ceremonial swords be damned when it came to the serious business of protecting the monarch.

A herald stepped forward in black and vivid shades of red that Livira had never seen before. He began describing the king's many titles and attributes in a voice so booming and exaggerated that Livira had to fight not to let her nervous tension find explosive release in a howl of laughter.

After what seemed an interminable announcement, the herald stated that the diplomatic confirmations would begin, then stepped back, allowing Livira a clear view of the king again. She stared, trying to marry the idea of a ruler of nations who bent truth to his whim with this puffy, painted old man. She was still staring when a growl from Meelan drew her attention to the figures approaching the throne.

"Algar . . ." Livira muttered the man's name under her breath. Lord Algar came in wearing the white robe of his office, his curling powder-grey wig abandoned to reveal thin iron-coloured hair, hanging lank around the contours of his skull. The crimson eyepatch and disc of gold pinned at his chest were the only flashes of colour on him.

A young woman and two young men followed him, all dressed to stand before the king. Serra Leetar showed few signs of the girl who'd entered the Allocation Hall alongside Livira all those years ago. She'd grown into the woman she'd been destined to be, fit to stand among the aristocracy. The flow of her satin dress revealed all the curves that Livira's flat, angular body still lacked.

"King Oanold." Lord Algar made a low bow. "Allow me to present Leetar Hosten on the day of her appointment to junior diplomat in your esteemed service."

"Hosten?" Livira hissed, recognising the name and turning to grab Meelan's arm. "She's your . . ."

"Sister." Meelan spoke past gritted teeth as if the admission pained him.

Details of the two young men also being appointed swept over Livira without registering. She kept looking back and forth between Leetar and Meelan, searching for clues she should have seen long ago. This was why they were here? To see Meelan's sister honoured? Meelan's presence made some sense now. But surely Yute didn't think Livira and Leetar were friends because they'd stood for allocation together?

Lord Algar and his delegation retreated, accompanied by polite applause. Leetar shot a hot-eyed look in Livira's direction, or at her brother, it was hard to tell. Algar's single eye sought Livira out and a small but ugly smile curled his lips as he swept past.

The next delegation advanced into the dregs of the diplomats' applause: Hiago Abdalla from the laboratory wearing formal robes in a rather unpleasant shade of orange—possibly one chosen as the best at hiding chemical stains. He brought two well-dressed young women to be confirmed as alchemists, both older than Leetar—mid-twenties at least, in Livira's opinion. They looked more like the daughters of well-to-do merchants than aristocracy. Perhaps those with less wealth had to wait longer, or maybe the stuff of a trained alchemist just took more time to filter out than that required for a diplomat.

Suddenly it struck Livira that Meelan wasn't here to watch his sister. That same wealth was going to purchase him a librarian's whites today, regardless of what table he sat on. Would Livira's expulsion from the service be equally public? She stared at her knees, seeing only the blackness of her robes. Certainly, the king would appreciate her public censure. Lord Algar would at last have won his bet, and more besides. She imagined the crowd's unrestrained applause at seeing a lowly duster, with ambitions far above her station, put in her proper place. Livira prayed to whatever gods might be listening that Yute would have the backbone to resist such pressure and conduct that part of the night's proceedings in private with the other deputies.

"Come, Livira."

Livira realised that Yute had got to his feet beside her. She looked up at him hopelessly.

"I know you'll miss being a trainee." He made a smile for her, kindness in his pink eyes. "It'll all be over soon enough."

She considered just leaving. Turning her back on the whole thing. But she couldn't do that to Yute. Whatever else had happened down the years, Yute had put his faith in her that day in the Allocation Hall, and she wouldn't disgrace him any more than she had to. She understood the pressures that had driven him to this action. Those she'd identified in intercepted correspondence must be only a fraction of the powerful individuals

who had turned their will to oppose her. With a heavy heart Livira stood
and followed him to where he stopped, five yards before the throne.

"King Oanold." Master Yute made a low bow. "Allow me to present
Livira Page on the day of her appointment to junior librarian in service to
the library."

When the great chimneys of outdated industry are brought to ground it is a spectacle that draws thousands of eyes. The muted explosion, the moment of doubt, the inevitable collapse that seems slow only because of the sheer scale of the structure. When great chimneys are built, the interest is considerably more muted. Perhaps it is just a matter of timing.

Appetite for Destruction, *by Rose L. Axe*

CHAPTER 39

Evar

Evar had read about cities but unlike his siblings, with their frequent use of the Mechanism, he had never seen one, walked its streets, marvelled at its architecture, and looked in awe upon its multitudes.

He descended the mountain slope, discovering a winding stair carved into the rock, and came into the city through a great square surrounded by many-pillared halls. The networks of distant lights that had patterned the night became a constellation through which he moved. Lights that swung from their owners' hands or the wheeled vehicles in which they were drawn; lights that glowed behind elaborate screens set across high windows; lights that burned within glass cowls set to illuminate the streets. And the people. Evar had thought the library of Clovis's youth to be heavily populated but those one or two hundred would be utterly lost among the tens of thousands here.

Evar had never seen a flame before, save the pinprick spread of campfires viewed from the mountain. He followed a carriage trying to see into its lanterns, fascinated by the dancing flames. If he'd been able to, he would have reached out and taken one for closer inspection. He stopped, realising he'd been led deep into the square. People walked on every side of him. Evar turned and turned, trying to watch them all, becoming aware of the wide and amazed smile that was already starting to make his cheeks ache.

It seemed that this city must be in his past, but was it in Livira's past too, or her future, if she had one? Did the same city stand decades or centuries later outside the library in which he and his family-by-association had been trapped their whole lives? Did it lie in ruins? Evar liked to think that it had risen from whatever destruction the army at its gates would visit upon it, and waited for him in even greater glory, filled with people who would welcome his escape.

He thought, on balance, that it must lie in his distant past, centuries even before Livira's time. He had only advanced three pools down the row to visit Clovis's childhood, which had been decades before the time he'd left. To reach the pool that had led him here he had run a considerable distance further down the row, passing dozens of pools after the one that had claimed Livira. Had he strayed from the row, he would, according to Livira's theory, have ended up in a different world entirely.

Evar shook such thoughts away and returned his attention to what lay before him.

The small scale amazed Evar as much as the large. The clothes that people wore! Evar was aware of fashion as a concept, but he had never seen anyone other than Livira wear a garment not made from the repurposed leather of ancient book covers. The variety, the colour, the way the cloth hung, or didn't, the necklaces, brooches, chains: all of it bewitched his eye. It was as if these people had become birds from some steaming jungle and created their own vivid plumage to signal their importance or desirability.

Evar wandered the crowds, trying to avoid collisions that might temporarily immerse him in the thoughts of other people. The wind hushed to a whisper down among the buildings and Evar discovered that whilst it couldn't touch him it could bring him scents. His nose, tuned to detecting small variations in the near-uniform book-must of the library, soon became overwhelmed by the assault of aromas from dire to delicious with everything in between.

This was the life he'd been so long denied. A life of variety and choices. Here he could choose a direction and walk in it for an eternity without ever seeing the same thing twice. He came to a halt at the middle of a street where people crowded along either side, clumping around the glow of stalls selling unknown foods for which Evar's stomach groaned with a passion it had never shown for the pallid bounty of the pool-garden. He spread his arms, looked up at the night sky, and made a slow turn, whirling the stars above him along orbits of his own decree. In Clovis's chamber he had felt alone, ignored by her people, closed out from a family much like his own but larger. Here there wasn't that same cohesion. The populace was so large that each was a stranger to every other person in the street. Here he felt an equality that he hadn't before. Were he as solid and real as those about him they would still pay him little heed.

Evar watched the faces pass. This was a city as it had been hundreds of years before either he or Livira was born. Everyone he could see—and there were so very many of them—was long dead, dust in the wind. The thought made him sad, and he pushed it away. If this was the same city that Livira knew at the foot of the mountain then hers must be an ancient metropolis.

Evar let himself be carried by the flow of people, exploring the night-time city at random, driftwood spinning in the current. Away from the heights of the grand square and the privilege displayed there, he saw tension in the people around him. Here, people walked with swift purpose. Many of the windows were boarded up. The streets were clear of vendors. Men and women shot each other serious looks. He came down through narrowing streets, hemmed in on all sides by tall buildings, every one of them home to families, sleeping children, pets perhaps. From time to time he would think that he'd seen one of his brothers among the sea of worried faces, or Clovis, but it was just that he'd spent so long with only those faces around him, and his mind tried to pattern anything even vaguely similar into the same person.

He saw Starval as a father, leading two small boys by the hands; Clovis as a merchant, selling her wares with a smile for every stranger; Kerrol in a passing carriage, dressed in a jacket with golden buttons, a young beauty by his side; Mayland watching him curiously from a high balcony. He even saw Livira's face for a moment, on a girl passing by as she bit into an apple. He turned to follow her, only to see that it wasn't her after all but someone older, lacking Livira's sharp vitality. Ghosts. Nothing but ghosts of what could have been, seen only by a ghost of what was.

He wandered darker streets, passed the lights and music of taverns, heard laughter spill from the windows. Was she here? The author of his book? If that woman in the doorway were to turn, would he see her face and know her in that instant? Perhaps the pool had brought him here not for the death of a city but to seek her out. If she were here amid so many, would he find her, and would she see him where so many others could not?

Part of him felt foolish, mooning over a lover he couldn't name, whose face still hid among the shadows of his mind. It was foolish. And yet . . . and yet . . . and yet she ran through his veins, and he would know no rest until the world finally returned them to each other. That was the simple truth of it, foolish or not.

Evar came to the city wall without really intending to. Up on the battlements he could see soldiers by the hundreds, their weapons bristling—some sort of projectile device he judged, driven by chemistry rather than tension. It seemed impossible that having just discovered the city it might be taken away within days by the enemy at its gates. The walls were so high, the populace so numerous in their houses of stone. From down among them their numbers and defences felt undefeatable. But the mountain's elevation had offered Evar a different truth. And without guidance it seemed that the pools were likely to deliver travellers to—Evar struggled to put his thoughts into words—times of consequence. Tonight would be a test of that theory.

Evar climbed the steps to stand upon the ramparts. It wasn't until he was up there that he thought to wonder how the steps bore him up when the wall would offer him no resistance if he were to walk into it. He decided to ignore the matter in case the world chose to agree with his logic and the ground swallowed him up.

For some while Evar stood with the soldiers gazing out over the ocean of campfires spread before them. He listened in on their conversation, most of it boasts and jokes. One trooper pointed the barrel of her weapon at the distant enemy.

"I'm not worried. Once they're in range I can take down six of the bastards a minute with this beauty. No problem."

One of her fellows snorted. "I could take more out in less time with my bare hands."

"You're going to have to," said an older man, grizzled and hunched in his uniform. "There's even more coming in from the west. Once that army arrives . . . then we'll see."

The soldiers spoke their words very strangely, drawing on the wrong parts, and sometimes seeming to make up entirely new ones. Evar had never heard an accent before and struggled to make sense of it all at times. He realised that this, as much as his personal lack of substance, might be an indicator of the passage of time between his imprisonment in the library and this city at the foot of the mountain. Just as the language within the library's books drifted from century to century, so did the words spilling from the soldiers' mouths. He was surprised, in fact, to find it so intelligible.

Evar spent most of the night walking among the soldiers on the wall. As much as the city fascinated him, he'd soon felt crowded by it, and preferred to be up where he had more space around him and fewer people at the same time. He sat listening to their bragging, complaints, and worries. The detail of their lives, passed between them in idle conversation, drew him in immediately, although it was of no consequence. It made him feel connected to the vast organism of the city by innumerable invisible lines of strangers' narrative. As if he were back in the Exchange and had started to grow roots that would bind him into the network by which that great forest of trees was joined into one interlinked being of wood and sap.

Evar had never seen a dawn, but he'd read enough about them to understand that the paling stars and the shading towards grey in the eastern sky were heralding its arrival.

"Fire!"

"Where?"

"I see a million of them." Staring at the enemy's camp.

"Fire!" the man repeated, dragging another soldier around to face back into the city.

High on the northern slope, where the city lights stopped and the blackness of the mountain took over, there were fires. Three at least. Large ones.

"The bastards must have come over the ridge."

"But the pass is guarded!"

"Over the ridge. Climbed the cliffs."

"You can't bring an army . . ." But it seemed that they could. Another building began to vomit flame from its roof.

Evar's newfound love of fire started to wane. Even at this distance it looked to be a hungry thing when set loose and allowed to grow. Along the wall, officers began assembling squads to dispatch in order to mount a defence against whatever the dark slopes held.

Evar watched the bands of a dozen soldiers group into larger units and hasten away through the streets. The wind carried the faint strains of distant screaming now.

"Are you mad?" Evar said it to the nearest captain's face and got no acknowledgement whatsoever. "It's a diversion. A large force wouldn't set fires at this stage!" Clovis would have had more to say, but the fraction of her knowledge that had passed to Evar seemingly exceeded that of the officers at the wall. Or perhaps it was just harder to make decisions when it was your people at risk, your soldiers who would live and die by the orders you gave.

The enemy timed their advance almost perfectly. Just as the first reports were coming back from the northern district citing small, swiftly moving bands of arsonists, the huge army beyond the walls surged forwards. The officers screamed for reinforcements. It seemed that the belief the enemy would wait for their second, support army had lulled the city forces into a false sense of security.

Evar stood and looked out at the advance from the parapets. All around him soldiers levelled their projectile weapons.

"Sabbers." Evar said it in a flat voice. The enemy were not people of a different nation—they were a different breed entirely, the same that had wreaked such slaughter among Clovis's family and friends. From the walls they looked tiny, as if he could wade among them laying waste, but Evar knew just how dangerous they were up close.

They came in a horde, running for all they were worth, knowing that they crossed a killing ground. Among them they bore a great number of ladders capable of overreaching the walls. Some carried projectile weapons not unlike those held by the soldiers on the ramparts. As they came closer, and the howl of their battle cries rose above the dusty thunder of their feet, Evar could see that their weapons looked more primitive than those around him, older designs perhaps, and that for every one of them armed in such a manner there were twenty with only spears and bows. Still, their intent was clear. To absorb the soldiers' wrath with their flesh. To run over the bodies of the fallen. To scale the walls. To let their sheer numbers and the tide of their anger carry them into the city and overwhelm everything before them.

Evar looked away, along the line of defenders. He had watched one sabber slaughter already and stood helpless as people died around him. He hadn't the stomach to do it again.

"I'm sorry."

Slowly he walked away.

Popular literature is wont to make considerable song and dance concerning the weight of a crown being greater than the sum of its constituent materials. But this is true of rank in general, of medals in particular, of many words, and especially of names. The word "gift" carries its own weight. Take an item of even moderate value and wrap about it some fraction of an ounce of festival paper—the scales will hardly flutter. Set the word "gift" upon it, and the person who receives it may stagger beneath the added burden.

The Secret to a Successful Saturnalia, by Soton Sloth

CHAPTER 40

Livira

Livira found herself looking side-eyed at Yute rather than ahead at King Oanold, which was a shame since she would have liked to have seen his expression. Yute's was as blank as the statues that lined the path from the gates to the palace steps.

Silence had spread through the hall like blood on an altar stone. The hush had begun to settle as Livira had walked towards the throne and had become absolute in the moment Yute had declared her a librarian. Not a single person in that vast hall had so much as drawn breath since his declaration. Librarians should be used to silence, Livira thought, but this one was beginning to exert such tension that something had to give.

Livira looked at the king. Oanold's mouth hung open, wet-lipped and too astonished for outrage. That changed when Livira's gaze met the king's: something new entered the two pale eyes sitting above the withered bags of his cheeks.

"No."

"Your Majesty?" Yute had been waiting for this. He must have been, given the speed of his response.

"She's a duster!"

Yute inclined his head. "She was born beyond our walls."

"In the Dust."

"As you say, Majesty."

"She's not fit to sweep the library's aisles, let alone wear the white!"

"Her sweeping does leave a lot to be desired." Yute nodded. "I will inform the head librarian of your opinion in the other matter." He placed a hand on Livira's shoulder and began to turn her towards the exit.

"Stop!" King Oanold raised his voice.

"Majesty?" Yute turned back towards him, the hand on Livira keeping her aimed at the doorway which now seemed a thousand miles away rather than a mere hundred yards.

Livira wanted to look but shared Yute's sense that it would further enrage the man who could end their lives with a word. She listened and through the deafening hush could hear what might be the sound of a man chewing over his options. King Oanold owned the city. He owned the mountain and those that rose behind it. He owned the Dust and the cities beyond it. But he did not own the library. He commanded legions but not librarians. Why Yute had chosen to turn this technicality into a stick with which to beat and publicly humble the king, and why the other librarians had allowed him to do it, Livira had no idea. She had similarly little to go on when it came to guessing whether the king would let his pride overrule his common sense and take action. He could easily have them thrown in prison. He could execute them here and now. He could have Livira chained in the sewers where he clearly believed she belonged—though Livira's investigations had revealed that nobody actually worked full-time in the sewers, that was just one of Malar's tales.

The library was a fragile treasure though. Clutch at it too hard and you'd find yourself holding nothing but broken pieces. The librarians and their elaborate, impenetrable indexes kept Oanold from simply seizing what it was he so desired.

In an earlier, bloodier generation, King Oanold's power would have stood upon the might of his sword arm, or his readiness to attack. His forefathers might have carved the path to his current position through the flesh of others, but Crath City was closer to a piece of clockwork than a weapon of war, its gears being political and societal; the aristocracy were the engine's meshing teeth and in turn drove other wheels within wheels, all the way down to the labourers toiling in the streets. This system reached beneath the roofs of new factories in which the crafts once practised in individual shops and homes were carried out in regimented rows where hundreds worked shoulder to shoulder. None of this made the restraint that the king was forced to exercise easy but perhaps it made it inevitable since he could not have maintained his seat of power for so many years without having acknowledged the restrictions under which he ruled.

"Get her out of my sight," Oanold said thickly, his cheeks flushing. "And tell the head librarian she is summoned to the palace in order to discuss this child's future. And yours, Deputy."

Yute made a low bow and Livira hesitatingly turned to follow his example though with far less grace. Once he'd straightened again, Yute began to walk towards the exit which now looked to be about a hundred miles away.

"Don't run." Yute touched her sleeve as she began to pass him. "We're librarians and our office requires a certain dignity."

We're librarians. The idea that she was a librarian was ridiculous. But it seemed that it was true. At least for the time being. "What now?"

"Now we get you back to the library and Malar gets a chance to earn his salary."

"He won't be pleased," Livira said.

"In my experience he never is," Yute replied. "But he was badly in need of a purpose, and between us we've given him a big one."

"I still think he'd prefer money."

"I'm sure he thinks that too," Yute said. "But I doubt he's correct."

A babble of conversation followed in their wake, a growing wave that chased them to the great entrance arch and washed down the steps after them. Livira greeted the cold night air with relief. The stars, scattered in forgotten glory, demanded her attention as if she had no more pressing concerns. She dragged her gaze down to the rank of royal guards still standing before the gates.

"Is the king going to have us killed?"

Yute shook his head. "I very much doubt it. But anyone else who might have been thinking along those lines would view this as the perfect time to do it themselves and win his unofficial favour."

"Meelan!" Livira belatedly remembered her classmate. "We've left him behind!"

"Better that he makes his own way back tomorrow. It will do him good to spend the night with his family."

"His *rich* family." Livira still couldn't believe that her nemesis's assistant, Serra Leetar, was Meelan's . . . Sirrar Meelan's sister. Another secret she'd failed to mine out of her classmates. What next? Carlotte would turn out to be King Oanold's secret love child?

"None of us choose our families," Yute said, still calm but with more feeling than Livira could remember him using on any subject before.

"Yute!" The voice rang out behind them, sharp as a hammer striking stone.

They turned to see Lord Algar at the bottom of the palace steps, poised and elegant as if he hadn't had to scramble from his seat and chase them across the great hall. Behind him, Serra Leetar was still hastening down the stair, robes flapping.

"Algar." Yute inclined his head.

"You can still stop this," Algar said. "Great gods, man, you must know what you're doing, what's at stake here."

Serra Leetar arrived at his side, flustered, her perfect hair no longer quite so perfect. Algar spared her an annoyed glance. For her part, Leetar cast about as if looking for someone she expected to see, presumably having missed the fact that her brother was still inside the palace.

Yute watched the narrow lord as the man stalked closer, torchlight catching on the crimson of his eyepatch.

"The greater good cannot be served by demonising a species, Algar, let alone a race of man. And if the greater good was never truly your goal, then consider that in this instance the same also applies to profit."

"This really is your last chance, librarian." Algar looked away at the illuminated buildings bordering the square. "If you walk away from this then what follows will be on your own head."

Yute turned and led the way past the guards. Livira shot a helpless look at Leetar, who widened her eyes in what might be warning. Before either of them could speak, Algar aimed his singular stare at Livira once more, and under that scrutiny she turned and left the palace grounds. Malar joined them on the other side of the gates.

"You're leaving early," Malar observed.

"I believe we may have displeased the king," Yute replied dryly. "Be on your guard."

Malar looked as if he had something hot to say, but instead offered a curt nod and led the way.

"*You* displeased the king," Livira said. "*I* didn't even know why I was there."

"You displeased him by existing," Yute said.

They crossed the square in silence. The crowds had thinned, probably because most of them were in the king's hall. Livira watched anyone who came near, sharply aware of Malar's warnings concerning the danger when an attack can come from any angle.

"What was that about?" Livira's question only waited long enough to reach the edge of the square. Their path now lay around the back of the lesser palace gardens to where the mountain rose so steeply that stairs were required. "Why provoke him?"

"You didn't want to be a librarian?" Yute enquired mildly.

"All that in there wasn't about what I wanted."

"You deserve the rank. Master Logaris has his opinions, but his assessment is based on how much he's taught you. He doesn't have a proper understanding of quite how much you've taught yourself over the last few years. I doubt that any of us do, but at least I know that it's a lot."

"You were making a point and using me to do it." Livira didn't let herself be sidetracked with praise.

"You see, Malar," Yute said. "I told you she was tenacious."

"Brothel-crabs are tenacious," Malar grunted.

"W—"

"I feel you're undervaluing her." Yute cut off the first of Livira's questions about brothels, crabs, and brothel-crabs.

Malar spat and drew his sword, though there was nothing that Livira could see in the shadowed street ahead of them. "This one is apt to steal your dagger and jump into a dust-bear's mouth with it. She's wasted on the library." He raised his voice, addressing the darkness around them. "She should be doing your job, killer. She'd be a sight better at it."

Nothing but silence. Livira wondered what had caught Malar's attention. Perhaps just the fact that the road was so quiet and so dark. Maybe it was the spot he would have chosen for such business.

"I hope Lord Algar has hired someone decent this time," Malar continued to talk to the night, motioning for Livira to stay with Yute while he advanced. "You're the follow-up to a trio of street bullies. Not a hard act to follow. If you shoot her first—I'll have you. And if you shoot me first— she'll run. But if you come out to play, she'll stay to watch. She won't be able to help herself."

A black-clad figure dropped into the road from the roof of one of the outbuildings behind the bath halls neighbouring the lesser palace. It landed with a grace and unnatural springiness that made Livira think of the sabber's bouncing walk as it had approached her settlement. The figure leaned something long against the wall—an arrow-stick perhaps. Livira saw a faint glow near the thicker end.

The assassin walked towards them, drawing two curving swords, both slightly longer than the soldier's straight blade.

"I normally kill rich people in their sleep." A woman's voice, mildly amused.

"Of course you do," Malar said. "Which one are you?"

"Janacar." The woman rolled her head, flexing her neck. "Who are you?"

"Nobody. Just an old soldier."

The woman pulled away the black cloth covering her face. The starlight caught the angles of her cheekbones and the grim twist of her mouth. "Don't do yourself down, old soldier. You're the man who added a little interest into my dull night. I hope you put up a good show. It would be such a shame to have it all over in a trice. Wham, bam, thank you, ma'am."

"I've yet to have a complaint." Malar didn't move as Janacar closed on him.

The assassin circled to the left. She twitched, then feinted, seeing if she could provoke a response. Suddenly she was on the floor. Malar flicked the blood from his sword.

"Who are you?" The pained whisper of a dying woman.

Malar's only answer was a second thrust of his sword, silencing her for good.

"Come on." He beckoned them forward.

Livira gave the corpse a wide berth.

"Impressive" was Yute's only comment.

"Algar didn't spend enough the first time," Malar said. "Spent too fucking much this time. Everyone's heard of Janacar. She thought I was beneath her. Didn't take me seriously. Should have shot me from the roof."

"Why didn't she?" Livira asked, still aware of the blood dripping from Malar's blade.

Malar shrugged. "Her kind spend most of their spare time training to fight with fancy swords, and most of their employment sneaking about, poisoning drinks, choking old men with wires, that sort of thing. She stepped away from what she does best into what I do best. They've not been in enough fights where they stood a chance of dying to understand you'd have to be an idiot to put yourself in that position just for a bit of fame."

"You did," Livira said. "For money."

"And now I'm a rich idiot instead of a poor idiot."

"But you said they spend ages training at sword fighting . . ." Livira tried to replay the action in her mind, but she'd seen nothing, just a live assassin and then a dead one.

"Training isn't the real thing. Books aren't either. Probably worth remembering that now you're a librarian. Take your nose out of those pages long enough to live some life rather than reading about other people doing it."

Livira stared at Malar. He didn't sound like himself at all. They reached the stair and began climbing. She followed him, with Yute at her back. Something glistened on the steps but the starlight that revealed it also made it hard to work out what she was seeing. She paused and leaned down to set her fingers to a step a few up from hers.

"Blood?" She stared at Malar's back. "You're bleeding?"

"It'll stop," he grunted.

"But . . . you got her!"

"Fucker got me too." He swayed dangerously as he said it, as if the admission had suddenly made the consequences real.

Livira came up on the open side of the steps and got his arm over her shoulders.

"Let me help." Yute hurried up behind her.

"No room." Livira took as much of Malar's weight as she could, thankful that he wasn't a large man. "Besides, you can barely get yourself up these stairs."

GETTING MALAR TO Yute's house left Livira panting with effort and drenched in sweat. She was more scared, far more scared, supporting Malar's rapidly weakening progress through the night than she had been when following him. She had imagined him invincible. Perhaps that was what his warning had been about. She might be the hero of her own story, but real life didn't care about that, and Malar had known it.

"All the gods in heaven!" Salamonda greeted them at the doorway after Yute's knock. "Get him on the table!"

With Malar on the kitchen table, curled about his wound, the ingredients for some or other meal now scattered to the floor, Salamonda dispatched Yute to get a doctor.

"Go hide upstairs." Malar got the words past clenched teeth. Before Livira could protest he added, "I didn't bleed my way here so some fucker could just follow us in and gut you." He looked at Salamonda. "Apologies for my language, madam."

She shook her head. "Any fucker who comes after Livira is going to have me to deal with." She brandished a meat cleaver that Livira hadn't seen her snatch from the table. "Go on up, girl. Anyone tries the stairs without saying who they are—throw Wentworth at them."

Livira nodded, shot Malar what she hoped was a look warning him not to die, and hurried to the stairs. She wasn't sure she could pick up Wentworth, let alone throw him, and thought the cat would probably turn on her in the process. She headed upwards, pausing at each storey to look for a weapon. If there was trouble downstairs, she planned to reappear, appropriately armed.

Yute's house turned out to be woefully lacking in the weapons department and Livira soon came to realise that she had missed her best chance by failing to secure a knife in the kitchen. She picked up an oil lamp from Yute's study and carried it to the top storey. His daughter's room remained unchanged from Livira's last visit. It carried an air, not of neglect but of . . . waiting. It reminded her of the library in a way, though it was the room below that smelled of books rather than this one.

Realising just how tired she was, Livira sat on the bed. Exhaustion from her efforts with Malar trembled through her limbs. She lay back and watched the shadows jitter across the ceiling.

"Livira?"

"I wasn't asleep," Livira lied, sitting up with a jolt. It seemed impossible that she had fallen asleep.

"Yolanda always said that when I woke her." Yute stood at the foot of the bed. A pale ghost. "It's her birthday today. She would have been twenty-six."

Livira didn't have words for that. Suddenly she remembered the night's events. "Malar!"

"Malar should recover. The doctor has stitched his wound."

"He wouldn't *have* a wound if you hadn't made me a librarian. Why did you do that? And don't try to distract me by saying I deserved it."

Yute took the chair. In the lamplight he looked ghostly white, like something apart from the world, as if he weren't part of humanity at all, something closer to an assistant than to a man like Malar. She wondered about that, Yute and the head librarian, recently rumoured to be his equally pale sister. Where had the pair come from? And was Yute's relationship with the library somehow deeper than everyone else's, or were the mysteries around him just the smoke of her own ignorance?

Livira shook the sleep from her head and found that once more he was merely Yute, as tired and as old as the day he found her on the steps of the Allocation Hall. "Why did I do it? I exhausted subtlety. I failed at manipulation and at direct appeal. Challenge was all that remained to me."

"What are you talking about?"

Yute sighed. "If I can't even get the king to see people from the Dust as properly human and deserving of respect . . . If I can't manage to make him see other humans as human, then how can I possibly hope for negotiations with the sabbers?"

Livira's frown deepened. "How can you? I mean why would you? When the sabbers come to our walls they *deserve* to be shot."

Yute leaned back into his chair, shadows devouring his face. "Do you remember when you came to see me here the last time?"

Livira nodded and decided not to argue that she had been merely passing and if not for Salamonda hauling her in they wouldn't have spoken.

"I talked about curses. You'll remember because you remember everything."

Livira nodded again. The passage of years had failed to fully unravel the puzzles that Yute posed her that day.

"Who first built this city?" Yute asked her.

"I don't know." It pained her to admit it with the vastness of the library open to her. "We did. But a long time ago. It wasn't any ancestor of Oanold's. At least not any he can name."

"Why are we where we are?" Yute asked. "If it was so long ago and the library has been here all that time too? Why didn't we take flight to the moons long ago?"

Livira had an answer to this one. "Wars. We keep having wars."

"Wars so devastating that we forget how to make a gas lamp or a clock?"

"I . . . guess so." She tried to imagine what the last one must have been like.

Yute looked grim. "We have wars so devastating that history stops being recorded." He took a small glass jar from his robes and held it before the light. Livira, being from the Dust, could hardly fail to see that the jar's contents had once been all she knew beyond the immediate circle of huts that were her world. "Dust?"

"Cities. Bones. Iron. Cement." Yute turned it over in his white hands. "Wars so devastating that they turned everything people had built into this, and let the wind take it."

"I don't understand . . ." Though maybe she did.

"The library teaches us how to do this. Over and over again it has taught us enough to know how to burn our world to the bedrock, but not enough to stop us from doing so. There's a point that all societies reach. I call it the fire-limit, though whether by 'fire' we mean actual fire or something more deadly depends on the circumstances. Anyway, the fire-limit is when a people become advanced enough to start a fire but lack the resources to put it out when it spreads."

"What happens to them?" Livira asked.

"They burn." Yute replaced the jar. "That is one of the library's curses."

"It sounds like our curse," Livira said.

"The library is our memory. It's all that survives." Yute made a grim smile. "Perhaps it's part of us."

"What are the other curses?" Livira wasn't sure she wanted to know.

"One's enough for tonight," Yute said. "It's been an eventful day."

"What can we do about it?" Livira shook her head. "I mean—it's going to happen again?"

"Slow things down."

"Slow things down? That's it? How will that help?"

"I'm not sure it will." Yute leaned forward, his face illuminated again. "There was a time before the library when these advances must have been made without help. A time when the world was so new and green and full of resource that our population grew so vast it threw up the geniuses needed to unlock one secret after another using nothing but their cleverness. I don't know how long that took, and clearly it ended badly at some point. But without the library and with the numbers we have now it might take ten thousand years to accomplish what has been achieved in the less than two centuries since we started making records again. But you can count these cycles like layers in the rock. Literally as strata in the ground."

Livira thought of the well, cutting down through all those layers. She'd seen it with her own eyes back at the settlement. She'd seen it all before she knew anything at all. "You're slowing things down? Just you?"

Yute shrugged. "I've been recruiting."

Time can stutter, it can drag, crawl, run, race, and, on occasion, fly. But its favourite form of locomotion has always been to skip. Few lives are lived without the punctuation of moments when we realise with sudden shock that a year, two years, maybe two dozen, have got behind us, sneaking by without permission and propelling us into a future we hardly imagined.

From the River to the Sea, *by Mercury Wells*

CHAPTER 41

Livira

The boom of an arrow-stick shook Livira from her walking daydream. She looked up and found herself halfway across the grand plaza, facing the lesser palace where three years earlier she'd been appointed to the rank of full librarian.

All across the great, paved square, Crath City's best-heeled citizens paused in the midst of their distractions and looked up, seeking the source of the blast—not close, but not comfortably distant either.

"Chemical 'stick." Meelan—still a trainee—set down the book satchels burdening him. Nobody called them arrow-sticks anymore, just 'sticks. The newest ones used a chemical explosion to shoot forth a spinning lead cone amid a puff of stinking smoke. The small projectiles looked far less worrying than a long, sharp arrow, but they could put a hole through an inch of oak at a hundred yards.

"You think it's a sabber?" Livira might be pushing twenty but somehow even the mention of sabbers put her back in the middle of the Dust and made her feel ten again. And over the past couple of years their raids had reached over the city walls on a growing number of occasions.

The screams turned her around. A lone sabber tore from the gap between the Allocation Hall and the Palace of Justice. It raced out into the square, long limbed, overtopping even the tallest man by a head. Shouts of pursuit to the rear, terrified men and women scattering before it. The creature's long dark mane streamed behind it. The curved length of a thin sword cut flashes from the sunlight.

Livira became a stranger in her own body. She stood, wrapped in her librarian's whites, unable to move, a child beside the wet mouth of the well once more, that first sabber approaching to turn her world on its head.

"Livira!" Meelan's shouts sounded distant though he had been standing beside her. Now, somehow, he stood between her and the sabber, which, presented with a thousand paths by which it might cross the square, had chosen to run directly at Livira.

Meelan, neither tall nor broad, held his ground, the blue of his trainee robes whipped around him by a sudden wind. She saw in that moment that she would lose him to the sabber as she had lost so much before. Her mind's eye showed her a grey tide following in the sabber's wake, the tens of thousands gathering on the margins of the Dust, the army that would test their walls for only so long before breaking over them in a single, unstoppable wave.

"Run!" Livira could only shout it at Meelan. Her legs rooted her to the flagstones, as if any attempt at evasion would be futile in the face of the sabber's speed. The glitter of the beast's blade hypnotised her, the white glimmer of wolf's teeth in a wide roar.

The final moments came so swiftly that Livira stood imprisoned within them. An explosion, as loud as it was unexpected, barked behind her, and the sabber, in the act of bearing down upon Meelan, became a rag doll tumbling in the grip of its own velocity. It hit the ground, bounced, rolled, scythed Meelan's legs out from beneath him, and came to a tangled halt at Livira's feet, one yellow eye finding her face.

The sabber's sword, a crudely forged length of blood-stained iron, lay against her shins. Freed from her paralysis, she hefted it up in both hands. The sabber watched her without turning its head, crimson teeth exposed in a grin or a snarl or a grimace. Meelan staggered to his feet behind the beast as Livira raised the sword to deliver a death blow. Something unreadable in the sabber's regard stopped her. Was it loss? Resignation? Recognition? Or simply intelligence?

Two soldiers crowded past her, one to either side, 'sticks aimed at the sabber's head.

"It's dead," the first one said.

The second soldier ended the discussion with another percussive blast showering sparks. The bloody result was thankfully hidden behind a cloud of acrid smoke.

Livira stumbled backwards, dropping the sword, and Meelan reached her side.

WHEN MEELAN HAD recovered his book satchels, and Livira had recovered herself, they headed on together, aiming for the library. Neither of them spoke—perhaps because their ears were still ringing from the 'stick shots—though Livira could sense Meelan watching her closely. She realised that the sword hilt had left her hands bloody and tried to wipe them clean on her robe. "I'm fine," she lied in answer to his unasked question.

By the time they reached the road on which Yute's house stood Meelan had actually asked if Livira was all right, and Livira had lied again and said yes. Meelan had not yet called her out on either the first lie or the second.

Salamonda was waiting for them on Yute's steps, watching the street. She intercepted Livira, taking her arm as if everything that had happened was written on her forehead, plain as day. "You come with me, and I'll get you something hot."

Quite what magic Salamonda relied upon for news Livira had never discovered, but she did discover, holding a cup of steaming chai to her lips, that the shock of the sabber still echoed in her fingers, making it hard to sip without spilling.

Salamonda put Livira to shame by noticing Meelan's injury. Blood matted the black hair at the back of Meelan's head and spattered the collar of his robes. Salamonda waved Livira away while she fussed over the trainee with a bowl of warm water and various cloths. "He's upstairs."

Livira found herself marching up the wooden stairs, animated by an anger that hadn't been there until Salamonda aimed her towards Yute.

She found him alone for once, Wentworth no doubt off thinning the rat population. Yute looked up from his book at her purposeful stride.

"This should be on your hands." Livira thrust out her palms, showing the rusty stains left by the sabber's sword hilt. The blood of unknown people. "You're holding us back." The librarian had told her as much years before when he'd tried to recruit her to his cause.

Yute looked up from her reddened fingers to study her face. "It's a question of what I'm holding us back from."

"With the right books the alchemists could arm our soldiers with weapons so powerful that no sabber could ever challenge the city."

"Every new weapon that was first given to the army has ended up killing more humans than sabbers."

"The city will die if we can't help defend it better!" Livira realised she was shouting.

Yute studied his own pale fingers. "My hands were bloody long before you were born, Livira. I've seen cities die before. More often from too much than from too little."

And, as often before, Livira found herself defeated not by Yute's arguments or authority, but by his quiet pain. The unspoken faith he had in her remained a burden. It wasn't even that he believed she would see the rightness of his approach—it was that he still thought she would find a new path where he had not.

She turned on a heel and stalked back down the stairs, having added guilt to her anger. The memory of the sabber's yellow eye haunted her, watching her as it died. It had come to kill her. She hated it. And yet, even as she resolved to deliver to the city, without Yute's help, the weapons it needed to survive, she felt stained by more than blood.

IN HER NEW, professional life Livira swam in the shark-infested waters of library politics, and had neither drowned nor lost a limb, despite being well out of her depth and receiving many nasty nips to her extremities.

In her personal life, she'd flirted with Arpix for sport and in competition with Carlotte, finding amusement in how oblivious the young man was to their overtures. She'd flirted with Meelan with a rather more focused desire to explore uncharted territory. And having explored it, felt bad about her inability to return his stronger feelings.

She'd read an ocean of books on every topic under the sun, sometimes pulling them blind from the shelves, having already sworn herself to reading whatever she took hold of. And still she had hardly read the first letter of the great book of the library, much less turned the first page. She'd pursued the library's secrets with devotion, hungry for knowledge, but all the time the memory of Evar's last words to her ran beneath those efforts: *You need to go. Back where it's safe.* And the image of him, standing to defend her against a sea of nightmare.

Livira didn't want to be safe. She wanted to be there, with Evar, right at the heart of the library's mystery, fighting beside him, if that was what it took. She wondered about him often, about whether he remained frozen in that moment or if his life had moved on. Whether he had found the woman he'd spent so long dreaming about, or perhaps had realised that she stood as a cipher for something unobtainable, and had settled on choices closer to hand. Most of all, though, she wondered how to get back to him. He'd become her unobtainable, and until she found him again she didn't think she would be able to untangle the real person from the myth she'd made of him, or her own emotions from the desire for resolution.

Her rude ejection from the Exchange had never been something that she'd come to terms with. In a strange and unreasonable way, she felt almost as if she were trapped in her current life—despite the privilege and abounding opportunity—much as a dirty child had once felt trapped in a life anchored by a single well within the dryness of the Dust. Only, this time, it was the Exchange and its many pathways that she wanted to escape to, rather than the city and its marvels.

She had tried to live every day, squeeze out of the hours as much progress as she could. And yet, somehow, three years had conspired to get past her and leave her, looking back, amazed to find so many days stacked behind her. She was striding towards her twentieth year, and yet the Exchange and Evar seemed no closer.

LIVIRA'S ELEVATION TO librarian brought with it a surprising number of privileges. She had managed to secure work for both Neera and Katrin within the library, Neera with her quick mind fitted in well among the bookbinders and Jella had taken her under her wing. Katrin, who now had a husband in the city, helped in the kitchens and proved popular with everyone, particularly the young men.

Livira's main official duty was to return books to the shelves, something that rewarded her with ample opportunity for exploration. There were other librarians tasked with recovering books that had not been brought back to the library. Sometimes they went out into the streets flanked by library guards in their owl helms. The borrowing terms were generous, and loans could be renewed repeatedly, stretched out across decades in some cases, but eventually all books had to be returned first to the library and then to the shelves.

Livira enjoyed bringing back the books that had spent longest journeying out in the world. Perhaps a rogue volume passed from friend to friend, home to home, across the city. One story finding root in scores of brains, its characters becoming friends to dozens of readers, discussed in their drawing rooms, thrown into new adventures in the minds of strangers. Or maybe a tome that had waited in one small office all those years, bathed in the same pipe smoke, polished by the same hands, too precious to be returned, simply waiting for its temporary new owner to lose interest or more likely to age and die. Or a journal that had travelled far beyond the walls, sailed seas she would never lay eyes upon, and come to rest in a distant city of spires and spice, or log roofs and relentless snows. They all came back in time.

Returning books to the shelves sometimes took her out to the very extremes of the catalogued space, deep into the loneliness of the library. At such times her mind was wont to return to the assistant in Chamber 7 whose grey flesh had been further corrupted by the Escape that had sought to kill Livira. The idea that it had found its way past the doors that confined it and now haunted the larger library had never left her. When she ventured out to the most distant shelves, the ever-present whisper of fear became an audible mutter, and on occasion, as she turned a blind corner, a shout.

Livira, though, had never been one to let fear confine her. She enjoyed her job and met its challenges with determination. Although she would never admit it to any fellow librarians, Livira liked to sniff the books she carried back into the vastness of the library. Each told a story. It was at such times—despite Yute's talk of how much harm the flow of books might do along with the good—that she felt happiest about her task and about the fact that the library existed.

Returning books was, however, very much an afterthought for Livira, no matter that Master Jost might consider it her sole duty. In truth, Livira's primary occupation was the search for a way back to the Exchange. And day after week after month after year, her failure to make progress ate at her until it poisoned her joy and stole her sleep. She had done it twice, albeit with the Raven's help. And what was the Raven, save for something made by men? Livira had, for her entire life, been built around the asking of questions and the finding of answers. The white doors of the library that would not open for her were questions, the Exchange and every one of its portals were questions, and the need for answers was a hunger, always growing, never fed.

Livira had known hunger of many types. What united them was the lengths to which they would push a person in order that they be satisfied. There were other doors—doors that she shouldn't go through uninvited, but doors that she *could* go through. Doors behind which she suspected answers lay. Each page she turned without solution was a step towards those doors. And the door which loomed largest in her imagination as her third year in the white crawled by was that of the head librarian.

Livira still hadn't seen the head librarian's index, but she did at least now have unfettered access to both the Kensan and Helfac Indexes, Kensan and Helfac being the two most recent head librarians prior to the start of the current incumbent's tenure. A tenure that had seemingly begun long before Livira was even born.

The Kensan Index had led Livira to a fascinating book on library guides, one that even talked about the Raven. It seemed that despite his erratic nature the Raven was held to be one of the most capable of all the known guides, able to open a great number—though far from all—of the otherwise inaccessible chambers. The book had advice on tempting the Raven to show himself and on securing his cooperation but advised that attempts to capture him had ended poorly in the past. The author had dedicated his final chapter to discussion of the library's most powerful guide, one that could allegedly enter any chamber, and which knew the location of so many books that its knowledge rivalled even that of an assistant.

Unfortunately, someone—and Livira suspected the current head librarian—had meticulously blacked out all the lines that might help the reader locate this ultimate guide and persuade it to help. Careful study showed that in one place the censor's pen had failed to entirely black out the guide's name and Livira's best guess was that it started with a "V" or maybe "W." The only other useful piece of information was a final line cautioning against enraging the guide, describing it as what Livira translated from the Arctilan as "red in tooth and claw."

Reading that particular line had put Livira in mind of the claw she had once found among the aisles and that years ago she had given to Evar. She thought of him often now, seeing him as she had left him: tall, lean, athletic, battling a host of nightmare foes, the claw jutting from his fist. The years had frayed her belief that she would find him again. She knew in her heart that he had moved on, found the object of his search, explored a multitude of strange worlds with her. They probably had children. Even so, Livira still dreamed of him sometimes, dreamed that she could find a way back to him, in that same place and time, and somehow save him as he had saved her.

As A FULLY fledged librarian Livira had expected to meet the head librarian soon after donning the white. The woman had, after all, approved her appointment in defiance of the king's wishes. In reality it took three years even to catch sight of her, and it would have taken longer but for the fact that Livira decided to break into her private quarters to steal a book.

All that Livira's new status earned her was the right to know the head librarian's name—Yamala. Requests to see her were politely declined. Written questions pressed into the hands of more senior librarians, even the one Livira entrusted to the gnarled hands of the ancient deputy, Synoth, who had once voted against expelling her, went unanswered. Yute declined to make an introduction. "Yamala is very . . . focused. You need to earn her attention. It's not something I can give to you."

As a librarian, Livira also learned that the politics of the upper echelons, while not literally as cutthroat as the trainees imagined, were complex and often ruthless. Despite the learned nature of all the participants, it was a matter of record that not all transitions from deputy to head librarian were bloodless. Not all head librarians had gracefully retired or died peacefully in post. And even some of those who had died peacefully were thought to have had a little help. In turn, head librarians in the past had been known to wield the Library Guard as a personal weapon, excising any threat they perceived to their position. A year before Livira's arrival a deputy head librarian named Abercroth had failed to return from a trip among the aisles. Abercroth, it was said, had been a particular thorn in Yamala's side, and nobody was saying she didn't have a hand in his demise.

She also had a fearsome reputation for disciplining the junior librarians. Yute said that her logic was that librarians who came up through the ranks knowing they could be tied to a post and beaten for minor infringements of the rules, and summarily dismissed for more serious misdemeanours, were likely to be too scared to plot against her when they rose in station. He didn't sound as if he approved of that particular state of affairs.

In his classroom, Master Logaris, despite being built like an ogre, had doled out only the occasional cuff around the head for inattention. Livira had imagined she was leaving all that behind her on reaching the dignity of higher office. It had alarmed her to learn that she was instead entering a harsher regime. When she had returned to the classroom for the last time to collect her stuff, she had mentioned the matter to her old teacher. Master Logaris had told her with a wan smile that he hoped he'd taught her to follow the rules, and that no librarian deserving of their robes would put themselves in a position where a beating would be necessary. The class had laughed at that, several of the younger ones miming the anticipated thrashings. Livira had left, head held high, followed by sniggering and the image of Arpix's frown.

Yute's advice remained simple and unambiguous. "Don't get caught," he'd cautioned her, without accusing her of any misdemeanour.

Returns might be Livira's official business, but her focus for the three years she'd worn the white had been a very different sort of return: one that brought her back to the Exchange. She saw the place as the key to the whole library. Also, Evar was there.

For the first two years she worked alone, spending all her spare time, and much of the time she was supposed to spend on other missions, on this one quest. In the third year Arpix gained his white robe and she had recruited him to help. Finally, officially allowed to follow his own whims within the library, Arpix also visited the Mechanism, accelerating the pace of his studies considerably. Livira was unsure how many other librarians knew it existed but was certain only a few of the highest ranked shared the secret. Nothing blocked access to the Mechanism save for tight lips and the length of the trek required to find it.

Livira did little to aid Yute in his efforts to slow down the breakneck speed of progress that the library fuelled in the city below and the kingdoms beyond. His arguments had been compelling: there was plenty of evidence of cyclic disaster visited upon mankind by its own hand. However, the current evidence pointed strongly at a different and more immediate doom. The mounting armies of sabbers, drifting in from the east, posed a clear and present threat.

Of late the sabbers had been combining their natural physical advantages with technology stolen from those they'd conquered or had traded for with the foolish nations of the south. Sabbers with arrow-sticks and steam-powered engines of war had even been seen from the walls of Crath.

In the face of such immediate danger Livira couldn't bring herself to deny the people anything that might save them. Her hatred of the sabbers wouldn't let her. If her people had carried arrow-sticks of their own that day the sabbers came to the settlement, then the lone sabber's arrogant advance would have ended very differently!

Yute accepted her decision without rebuke—which had weighed far more heavily on Livira than any rebuke would have. Even so, she kept her resolve. The idea that she might inform on Yute was not one she considered for longer than it took the darkest corner of her mind to whisper it. Each of them, she decided, would have to tread the path dictated by their own conscience.

Yute had been recruiting outside the Allocation Hall for years, ignoring the system in favour of fresh blood, new ideas, and outside perspectives. He'd said he wanted Livira to find her own path, and had the wisdom not to gripe when she chose not to follow the one he'd chosen for himself. For

Yute there was a bigger war than any that the sabbers might bring to Crath's door. A war involving the library and how it bound humanity to a seemingly endless cycle of destruction. The deputy sought to join the battle between abstract figures like the library's mythical founder, Irad, and his brother Jaspeth, both of whom went by many names. But Livira's extended family laboured in the city streets and she cared more about their immediate future than the destiny of races.

AFTER THREE YEARS of dead ends in her search for a way back to the Exchange, Livira came through her own volition to the end of a long corridor and what would have been yet another dead end but for the fact that it held a door. The door to Yamala's quarters. Three years of failure had driven Livira to the corridor. The door before her would, she hoped, open onto a path that would lead her back to the forest that grew between moments, where Evar—trapped like an insect in amber—surely waited for her return.

It had been the tirelessly observant and endlessly methodical Arpix who had found the book. Not a book that revealed how to enter the Exchange, but a book that held lengthy references to another volume that reputedly did exactly that: *The Forest Between*, by Celyn Lewis. It had been Livira who convinced herself that the key to finding this tome must lie within Head Librarian Yamala's personal quarters. Perhaps she might even have an actual copy of it there, for gods knew Livira had searched the library long and hard for it, even using several minor guides who had been both difficult to find and difficult to motivate.

Arpix took the idea that the way forward lay behind Yamala's door as another dead end. Livira took it as a challenge. She hadn't told Arpix about her plan though. At best he would try to stop her. At worst he would insist on helping—thereby exposing himself to the likely ruinous consequences of failure.

THE LOCK ON Yamala's door wasn't a particularly serious one but working on it at the end of a brightly lit corridor, onto which opened the front doors of all the deputies and eight other senior librarians of the second circle, was a logistical nightmare. The unrelenting brightness of the library complex proved to be Yamala's most effective security measure.

Livira had taken various texts on espionage into the Mechanism over the years and with regret had had to skip through the lengthy sections on skulking through shadows given that there were none to be found in the places which most interested her.

Identifying Yamala's door had been easy enough. The deputy heads trekked in through it on regular occasions—all save Yute, who rarely seemed to visit the library—and nobody but the deputies ever came out of it. It seemed that the head librarian must be bed-bound, perhaps because of her great age. Or maybe, as Carlotte had once mischievously speculated, she had died long ago and the deputies had agreed to rule as a team, using her quarters as a convenient meeting spot. "Maybe they killed her! All four of them stabbed her. And her mummified body sits at the head of their meeting table," Carlotte had concluded.

Livira worked her picks, expecting at any moment that one of the librarians would return early from the many and varied tasks which currently occupied them—some of the tasks entirely her doing. She forced herself to calmness and focused on the mechanism. Eventually it surrendered to her ministrations.

Having defeated the lock, Livira eased through the door, silently cursing the ubiquitous brightness that offered as little chance of concealment in the room beyond as in the corridor she'd just left. Thankfully, it was empty and neither her list of feeble excuses nor her sprinting skills were required.

Breaking in had been a huge risk. Livira's heart thundered in her chest, her palms sweat-slick. If she hadn't been banging her head against a solid wall for so long, she would never have gone to such extremes. As far as Livira was concerned, the doors she was now daring were doors that stood between her and the Exchange. Between her and Evar. Whether he needed her or not, it was her duty to find him and learn the answer to that question. He had risked his life to save hers. She would risk her livelihood to see if he still needed saving in turn. She blamed Yute to some degree. She was sure he could help her but, just as on every other occasion, all he would do was steer her with the vaguest of touches, expecting her to discover the truth by herself, applying the same approach to her as to the whole city of Crath.

Livira closed the head librarian's front door behind her. Her only protection from identification was the stolen trainee robes that she now struggled into, raising the hood to shroud her face. The room she'd entered was clearly where the deputies met, a large square chamber with an impressive round table of polished oak at its centre. Carlotte would have been disappointed by the lack of mummified remains. A thick carpet covered the stone floor, a wonder of colour and texture woven in the geometric styles favoured in the western nations. Everything was still and silent.

Each of the four walls had a door set into it. Livira crossed to the one opposite, her feet making no sound on the softness beneath them. At the back of her mind a small, lone voice was screaming that she should turn back now. Screaming that the library had rested its faith on her shoulders. Yamala had appointed her in the face of the king's own decree—she was a representative of all those that came in from the Dust now.

Livira closed her ears to the voice of her conscience and reached for the door handle. She had barely set her hand upon the cold metal when the door began to open.

. . . recommend a three-hundred-gallon barrel. Fill to one-third of its depth with manure. Cows are an excellent source, their ordure being both copious and easy to pour. The remaining volume should be filled with urine. In times of tension, recruit others to the effort. The task will take a single person at least a year, and an additional six months of fermenting before the process of extracting saltpetre can begin.

Brew Your Own War, *by Redding Sharp*

CHAPTER 42

Livira

I f not for playing through scenes like this many times within the Mechanism, Livira would have been caught flat-footed as the door opened. Her game would have been up right there and then, with disastrous consequences.

With no time to spare, Livira managed to veer to her left and position herself against the wall behind the swing of the door. It came perilously close to hitting her. Worse though, it immediately began to swing back. For a split second Livira reached for it, intending to hang on and use it as a shield between her and the other person, delaying the inevitable discovery. She let her reaching hand fall, knowing it was useless.

The door swung shut, revealing the retreating back of someone dressed in a pale green tunic and clutching a book. Where the figure's bare arms showed, the skin was white as bone. Yute's name opened Livira's lips, but she kept it there. This was a woman; she was sure of it. The woman's hair fell in a white river to somewhere between her shoulders and she had a slightness to her that made even Yute's narrowness seem robust.

Livira remained silent, pressed to the stone, certain that she must be seen, if not in this moment, then in the next. But the woman opened the door to the left and went through, shutting it behind her, without once glancing back and noticing the blue-robed Livira against the wall. It took what felt an age before Livira remembered to draw breath again—her heart, which had been beating so hard when she entered the room, had seemed to stop entirely for the duration of the head librarian's passage. It had to be Yamala. There was no one in the library so pale except Yute, and none so pale as the pair of them in the whole city beyond. Livira imagined them both assistants made flesh.

Fighting the urge to turn and run, Livira went to reopen the door through which the head librarian had come with such focused determination.

Locked. The woman hadn't had time to lock it but somehow it was locked. Livira knelt and, with the need to leave trembling in her hands, she set to work once more with her lock picks. The tremble didn't help. The lock refused to surrender. From time to time, Livira would startle from the depths of her concentration and shoot a frightened glance over her shoulder, expecting to see the head librarian standing there watching. She considered abandoning the effort several times. The urge to flee to the safety of her own quarters became overwhelming. She was staking her whole existence on the rumour of a book that Yamala might not even have and, even if she did, might not be behind this door. If she was caught the very least she could expect would be exile to the streets of Crath to pick out a mean existence in its back alleys. She'd probably be beaten to within an inch of her life first. They might accuse Arpix of helping her, or even Meelan, or—

CLICK.

The lock turned. Livira exhaled slowly. Misbehaviour had been much easier when she'd had little to lose, nobody depending on her, and nobody else to bring down. She opened the door and slipped through, closing it quietly behind her. She found herself in a chamber perhaps a quarter of the size of the trainee library, filled with packed shelves.

"A librarian with their own library." Livira began to move between the shelves. "Figures."

Unlike the library proper, where the gems were hidden among legions of the mediocre, irrelevant, and outdated, Yamala's shelves boasted one treasure after another, volumes that a librarian might kill for—and, if the old tales were to be believed, sometimes actually *had* killed for. Almost every book here was a work alluded to in other prized volumes but never to be found despite the competing claims of even the most up-to-date indexes.

Livira longed to just nail the door shut and ensconce herself in this place for however many years it would take to read everything. She was here on a mission though, armed with not only the title and author of a particular book but its full description.

The shelves were set facing the door with access to the gaps between them from either side as they didn't quite reach the walls. Letting her fingers trail book spines, Livira hurried along the first of the aisles, eyes flitting from ceiling to floor in search of the object of her quest. She thought it foolish of Yamala to keep this wealth of books in a place that the king's soldiers could so easily discover. Scattered amongst the near-infinite collection of the library they would be safe and reachable only through the doubtless encrypted index the head librarian maintained. It seemed, though, that Yamala favoured convenience over caution and relied on the city's belief that the only key to such knowledge lay within her head.

It took Livira far longer than she wanted to find the book she was after, but far less time than might reasonably be expected given the size of the collection. Twelve rows in she hefted the locked, iron-bound tome from its place. "Got you!" She shuffled the neighbours together to hide the gap. With the heavy volume filling her book satchel and straining the stitching, she crept towards the exit. Regardless of her load, she felt a weight lifted from her shoulders. Against all the odds and despite her close brush with the head librarian, she was going to make it! In her mind she was already planning her triumphant reveal to Arpix.

She had reached the end of the aisle when a hot prickle at the back of her neck turned her head in a slow dread-laden backwards look. There behind her stood something so black that it seemed to be a silhouette, only its motion revealing hints at structure. Immediately her mind returned to the Exchange and the black nightmares that had assaulted her and Evar. The rest of her body rotated with that same slow fear, facing her towards the creature. It was shorter than her, no taller than her chest, but long, stretching away, filling the aisle, a beast of some kind. Somehow it didn't carry the threat that the Escapes had. No barbs, no talons, no smoking darkness. It was only when it drew in the air with a deep sniff that she suddenly understood what she was looking at.

"You're a dog . . ."

A bigger dog than any she'd ever seen—not that she'd seen many—an enormous hound, impossibly black, drinking in the library's endless light and returning nothing, all detail hidden. It inhaled again, draining her scent from the air.

"You're the guide! The last guide . . . or the first . . ."

Livira was about to reach a hand towards the beast, aware that she could lose fingers or perhaps half her arm to its enormous jaws, when the door through which she'd entered banged open.

"Oh, fuck-me-sideways." Livira claimed to have learned all her curse words from Malar but this outburst was original and born of the moment. She froze, listening intently for the sound of footsteps. She could leave the aisle easily to the left, to go right she would have to clamber over the dog. It seemed, though, that the head librarian had a light step, giving no warning about the direction of her approach. Livira was about to pick a side at random when the dog turned its head as if anticipating its mistress's arrival from the left.

"Blood and hells." If Yamala was coming down this side of the chamber Livira was lost. Trapped at the very end of the aisle, awaiting discovery. Trusting the dog's hearing, she took her courage in both hands and, expecting its jaws to close on the back of her neck at any moment, she began to crawl as quietly as she could between its front legs. Even without violence the creature could thwart her by simply sitting down. Her career and possibly several others could end beneath the backside of a magical hound. Praying to all and any deities, Livira crawled on.

To her amazement she emerged unscathed and impeded by nothing save a tight squeeze and a swishing tail. Livira hurried to the far end, and on tiptoes peered out past the end of the shelves. The walkway that led to the front of the chamber lay empty.

She advanced shelf by shelf, peering around each then darting across the gap to the shelter of the next. With alarm she realised that the dog was padding after her despite having had no room to turn around. Its claws made no sound on the stone floor as it matched her pace. She tried to shoo it back but when she hurried across the next gap the creature advanced too, pointing at her like a black arrow, clearly visible from the other side. Livira hurried on, thankful that at least the beast wasn't barking at her . . . or tearing her into small chunks.

Livira darted past the fourth row where the head librarian was bending to pull out a book. She kept going and reached the exit, sweating, praying that she wouldn't have to pick the lock again. Thankfully there was a latch on the inside and she let herself out, closing the door gently on the face of the dog as it made to follow.

"Open that if you can, doggy." Livira crossed the room, skirting the meeting table.

On reaching the door to the corridor some instinct turned her back towards the private library.

"Oh, gods damn it!" She watched in despair as the dog emerged from the secret library, simply pushing through the two-inch thickness of wood that Livira had secured in its way. The dog padded across to join Livira, leaving the door unscathed. The thing was a ghost, as Evar had said he was when he visited his sister's childhood. Only a ghost you could see . . .

"And touch?" Livira hissed her surprise as her reaching hand found a mass of soft fur and, beneath that, hard-packed muscle. "Sorry." She snatched her hand back when the dog's head turned to sniff at it.

"Stay!" she instructed and opened the corridor door. The beast made to follow her as she left.

"*Volente!*" The faintest of calls from inside the private library.

The dog gave Livira one last sniff and turned obediently to go back. Livira took off running, her nerves too frayed for caution, not even remembering to take off the trainee blues until she was halfway to her own rooms.

LIVIRA ARRIVED AT her quarters still trembling with nerves. She hurried through the front door, only then discovering that amid all her meticulous planning and watchfulness and scheduling she had forgotten the weekly get-together she'd organised long ago with her female friends. She walked into the middle of a conversation in her own reception room. It looked as if they'd been there awhile to judge by the mess.

". . . care about any of that! What's the gossip?" Carlotte lay sprawled on a couch holding a glass of cheap red wine in an alarmingly casual grasp just inches above the expensive blue satin of a dress that looked more suited to a ballroom than to Livira's quarters. Carlotte's visits to the librarians' complex were nominally missions to get the particular books that her house—that of Sir Alad Masefield—had requested. His eldest son and heir had recently been killed in a sabber attack just miles from the city walls, and Sir Alad had been increasingly demanding books on the subject of the afterlife.

Most house readers visited the librarians several times a year. Carlotte seemed to return several times a month and spend the majority of her time chatting with old friends. She glanced across at Jella, seated on a straight-backed chair that appeared rather too delicate to support her ample form. "Well?"

"Gossip? Why are you looking at me?" Jella managed an offended tone. "I just mind my own business."

Neera coughed at that. She coughed all the time but this one was intentional. Whatever the Dust had put into her lungs had stayed with her for the decade since they entered the city, but—unlike in every work of fiction Livira had read, where if someone coughed they were bound to die of it in the next chapter—this seemed merely to be a chronic irritation. Neera had been a thin child, angular, with a sunken chest. The years had done little to fill her out, but she had an unconventional beauty to her despite the alarming blade of her nose: kohl-darkened eyes watched the world with shrewd intelligence from beneath luxuriously long lashes, and the thick, braided length of her oil-black hair was a wonder.

Katrin, the last of Livira's guests, opened her mouth to speak, but whatever she'd had to say was lost under the sudden deluge of gossip that Jella was unable to hold back any longer.

Having drawn nothing but curious glances, Livira sat herself on the arm of the only free chair and perched her book satchel on her knees. She glanced nervously at the door from time to time, wondering if she'd truly got away with it, and also how she could graciously get rid of her visitors.

". . . and Livira still hasn't got a boyfriend," Jella concluded about ten minutes later.

This was hardly news, but Carlotte's eyebrows shot up as if it were a great surprise rather than her favourite subject. "Maybe if we explained it in terms she's familiar with?" She turned towards Livira and put on a fake tone of condescension before continuing. "Men, Livira, are like books—easy enough to read if you know the right tongue. But first you've got to get the cover open."

Jella snorted loudly. "I'd get Meelan's cover off in a heartbeat if I was the one he mooned over."

"He's very handsome," Neera said.

"And rich." Katrin's contribution. She'd married her husband, Jammus, six months earlier; he was also a survivor from the Dust but from another settlement—Livira had yet to meet him. "But Livira likes someone in the library, doesn't she?"

"Fictional men don't count." Carlotte waved the idea away. "The library's stuffed full of stories!" Neither Carlotte nor Katrin were supposed to know about Evar, but Livira had confided in Neera. She'd needed to tell *someone*. And it seemed that Katrin had got hold of at least part of the idea. "Men are *like* books." Carlotte returned to her theme. "But they're not *actually* books, Livira. So you're not going to find one if you're always lost in the aisles." Her tone became scolding. "Arpix is as bad. Locked books, both of you, gathering dust. What's the point of that?"

"I've got a locked book in here!" Livira nodded towards the satchel on her lap in an attempt to change the conversation. "I mean, now I'm going to have to spend an age trying to fiddle the mechanism . . . Who puts locks on books? The whole point of this library is free access, and then they put books like these on the shelves. I bet the assistants could open them if they wanted to or provide a key . . . but no!"

Neera took the bait. "Free access? I'm not allowed into the library. Even Carlotte and Jella aren't allowed in anymore." She ended with a cough.

Livira shook her head. "Yes, but that's just us librarians getting in the way. The library itself doesn't care. Some doors won't open, certainly, but you can wander forever in there and never see the same book twice."

"I say the whole library is a lock," Carlotte said with unexpected passion. "You think it's offering you free access—but to what? Even librarians can only find what they want among a tiny fraction of what's out there.

And that's because they've been working at it for generations. It's a lie. An illusion. I'd like to get hold of one of those assistants, those impediments, and force them to explain themselves. Where's the sense in it?"

"Does it have to make sense?" Katrin spoke quietly into the pause. "The world's never made much sense to me."

Carlotte sat up on the couch and folded her arms, pointing her scrawny intelligence in the direction of the beautiful, kind, but inarguably dim Katrin. "It should make sense. It should make sense because someone built it."

"Didn't the gods build the world?" Katrin's face clouded in confusion. "Some of them anyway. Not Suggoth, because he's more about eating things. That's what Jammus says anyway . . ."

"Well, I don't know about the world," Livira said, "but the library should damn well make sense and I'm not giving up until I find out what's going on, even if I have to pin an assistant to the wall and slap the answers out of them. And until I do that then poor Meelan will have to find someone else to moon over. All my other admirers can form an orderly queue and wait in line too. Because first I need to open this book."

Carlotte took the hint, unusually for her, and stood to go, finishing her wine in one last gulp. She motioned with her fingers for the others to follow suit. "Well, if you manage it, you can come and help me with Arpix next. That boy definitely needs unlocking."

Livira perched on the arm of the chair, too full of nerves to settle, flashing quick smiles and accepting hugs as she waited for the others to slowly take themselves off to their various duties. At last, she closed the door on Katrin's back and slumped against it, sliding to the floor.

She began to ease her prize from the satchel; then, thinking better of it, she got up, slid the bolt in place, and went to her bedroom to examine the book there. She opened the bedroom door, screamed, dropped the satchel, and staggered back.

The black dog was there already. Waiting for her.

It's in the nature of humans to want to belong to a group, to want to be accepted, appreciated, and needed. What is most frightening about their kind are the sacrifices they are prepared to make in order to become part of such a tribe, clique, sect, sewing circle, cult, or book club. Reason and morality are often at the top of the list of what must be surrendered as part of the club fees. Truth becomes a collective property, an adaptable shield used to shelter the in-group from those outside. Dogs, on the other hand, are great.

Training Your Labrador, *by Barbara Timberhut*

CHAPTER 43

Livira

The huge black dog stood facing the door, and although Livira couldn't make out its expression the beast seemed to be giving off a strong air of silent reproach.

"You told her, didn't you?" Her blood ran cold, shock tingling in her cheekbones. This was it. They'd throw her out. Yute had somehow made the whole library defy the king's plainly stated will and had elevated her to stand as the champion and herald of her people—proof that the men and women who came in off the Dust were worth every bit as much as those born within the city walls. She hadn't asked to play that role, but it had come with the robes. And now she'd not only let down Yute but all those for whom she was a beacon of hope. Katrin said some in the city were calling her a hero. Not the ones from her old settlement, except maybe those like Gevin and Breta—who were too young to remember how annoying and troublesome she'd been—but certainly those from other settlements. She'd thrown it all away now, because she couldn't ever play by the rules. She'd made the case for the people who called them dusters and said they were all stupid, lazy thieves. She'd stolen the book, she'd been too lazy to find another way, and too stupid to understand the risks.

The dog just looked at her.

"I'm already ashamed, all right?" Livira threw the satchel onto the bed and stomped past the dog to sit heavily down on the mattress. "Enough with the looking at me." She pulled the book out and scowled at it, then at the dog. The lock was set into an iron plate that entirely covered the ends of the pages and connected with the two hinges that ran from the iron-ridged spine across the width of both covers, making it almost like a box with the only view of the page ends being at the top and bottom.

"It's no use trying to guilt me into taking it back. I'm not throwing myself on anyone's mercy. If she wants it, she'll have to come and drag it out of my hands." Livira took her lock picks out. "Until then . . ." She set to work.

The game was up, but if she could coax the secrets of the Exchange out of the book before her then who knew what options might open up? "You're still staring." Livira worked the picks as fast as she could. The lock's mechanism wasn't making much sense. She glanced up at the hound. "You don't know the Raven, do you? He's annoying too." She had looked for the Raven over the years, pursuing hints and rumours in some of the better hidden works that her new rank had led her to. She'd never found so much as a feather, although several other librarians claimed to have heard its squawks. A mid-ranked librarian named Anderida reported that she'd seen it on a shelf top but that it had vanished by the time she found a ladder and returned. Most frustratingly of all, Arpix had returned from a week-long trainee expedition and recounted with unusual excitement his encounter with a curious bird. It was his failure to take advantage of the situation that prompted Livira into full disclosure of her adventures to him.

Livira very much wanted the Raven's help to enter some of the many sealed chambers. She had summoned him that one time in the Mechanism, but that had been a moment of terror and the bird had come to rescue her. She couldn't abuse that kind of connection, no matter how much she might want the bird's services as a glorified key. Also, he had reclaimed the feather that Yute had given her, and her reading had indicated that without a feather no amount of screaming would summon the Raven.

She needed more than access to Chamber 7 to get to the Exchange. The portal there had gone. Perhaps the Escape-tainted assistant still roamed the aisles there too. Or she might have mastered the doors and have vanished into the vastness of the library. Two years ago, Tubberly, the junior librarian who had summoned Livira and Meelan to Yute's house, had gone missing in the library. His remains hadn't yet been found. Livira often wondered if he'd strayed into the Escape's path.

"Focus!" Livira's jabbing at the lock became more frantic. It wasn't making any sense. She'd specifically sought out information about lockmaking in the empire and time in which the book was written. And the lock still wasn't making sense.

The book had been written in an empire that had washed up around the foot of the mountain she sat in, but of which nothing remained, not worn stones, shards of old pots, or even traces in the main language of Crath. It had been an empire whose calendar and counting of years had no connection to the ones that Livira used. An empire that was an island in history, cut off from those that came before and after it—cut off, if Yute was to be believed, by man's inability to avoid self-destruction. Yute had said that the library allowed men to teach themselves how to light fires long before it taught them how to extinguish them. And the result was that time and again they burned their world down with some cunning new kind of fire.

"Damn it! What's wrong with this thing?" Livira gave the book a shake. At first, she thought the mountain was shifting but then realised that the low rumble she was hearing was the dog's growl. "All right, all right! I'm not hurting it." She stroked the cover to reinforce the point. "What is it with you and the Raven? It's like you're guarding every grain of sand in a desert. I bet there's a million books out there that say much the same thing as this one. It's finding them that's the problem." She continued to grumble as she settled back to her lock-picking.

Livira wasn't sure how long she'd been working at the mechanism. Her eyes were starting to ache. Her fingertips hurt from pressing on the picks. She had four of them in the lock at once now and was attempting a difficult but nonsensical manipulation when the knock came on the door, causing her to spill all the picks into her lap with a curse.

Instantly fear replaced focus. They'd come for her, and she hadn't even opened the damned book, let alone absorbed its mysteries. She squeezed past the dog and hurried to the door.

"Who is it?" She sounded terrified even to herself.

"Are you all right?" Arpix's voice.

"Yes." Livira fought to speak steadily. "Just busy."

"You don't sound all right . . ."

"I'm fine."

"Why are we speaking through this door then?"

"I'm busy."

"New book?"

"Yes—I mean no." He'd never go away if he thought she had a book worth blowing him off for. "Uh. It's women's problems." Genius. If anything was going to get rid of Arpix it was some basic biology. This was a man who preferred to think of all animals, people included, in terms of topology, as tori to be precise.

A long silence.

"Livira?"

"Yes?"

"Are you lying?"

Livira let out a long sigh and unbolted the door. "Don't scream. All right? It's safe. Safe-ish, anyway." She glanced back at the dog and slowly opened the door.

"Why would I scream?" Arpix looked down at her with dark intensity. He'd grown extremely tall. Jella said he looked like a weed, too busy trying to gain height to fill out.

Livira blinked and swivelled back towards her bedroom door. The dog had gone. "It's . . . it's a . . . uh, important book."

"I thought you said you weren't well." Arpix arched a brow at her.

"I thought you already knew I was lying."

"You don't look well," Arpix said as he followed her to the bedroom. "You look very pale and a bit clammy. You— Oh lords above! Is that—is that Lewis's treatise on hidden spaces?"

"I can't open it," Livira said miserably.

"How in the world did you find it?" Arpix knelt on the bed and touched the cover with nervous fingers, as if it were a baby or something equally mysterious.

"It wasn't easy." Livira had become pretty truthful with Arpix, but the truth here would just expose him to more danger.

Arpix sat on her bed, discarding his normal reserve in the excitement of such a find. He hefted the book onto his lap, then with a pained expression reached under his thigh and tugged out one of Livira's picks that must have been sticking into his leg.

"Good luck," Livira said. "I think I'm going to have to borrow a chisel from the bookbinders."

Arpix discarded the pick and frowned at the book. "You can't hack it open. Have you no respect?"

"I've got plenty of respect. What I haven't got plenty of is time."

Arpix lifted the book to eye level and pursed his lips, his frown deepening. "You've forgotten Zackar Gyle?"

"Nobody believes that nonsense." Livira snorted. Though now Arpix mentioned the legend it did give her pause. Zackar Gyle had been a librarian over a hundred years ago and had spent his life in search of one book said to contain the secret of eternal life. In his dotage he'd found the book, locked just as the book in Arpix's hands was. Zackar had struggled with the lock for an age and finally given into his frustration, smashing the clasp with a hammer. Only to find every page blank. The legend claimed that the act of forcing the book had erased all the words within. Most trainees as they progressed through their education came to understand that Zackar had been a victim of a trick rather than of magic, and that the book had always been blank. Livira, though she would never admit it, felt it probably *was* magic and that the old man's act of violence had destroyed the thing he'd sought so long.

Arpix looked up from his inspection. "And why wouldn't you have time? You've all the time in the world. At least until the sabbers come over the walls."

"That's not going to happen. They'll be shot down from the walls like dogs—" Livira stopped, embarrassed at using the dog epithet, firstly because it was one of the king's big lies that the sabbers bred with dogs, and secondly because a black nose had just inched out of the wall behind Arpix.

Arpix thumped the book's spine with the heel of his hand, surprising Livira. His patience normally outlasted hers by at least a factor of ten. The dog's muzzle, followed by its eyes and forehead, emerged from the wall and its growl rumbled through the rock. Arpix glanced around, distractedly. "What in creation is that?"

"Earthquake," Livira said, trying to shoo the dog away without drawing Arpix's attention to it.

"We don't get earthquakes here." Arpix stared at her odd jerking movements and she stopped. He shook his head and his attention returned to the book, striking it again. He started to almost claw at it, digging his fingernails into the edge of the spine. The dog's shoulders emerged and it growled again, the sound so deep that it carried no hint of direction. Arpix stood, looking everywhere except directly behind him and missing the dog by the smallest of margins. "What in the hells is going on?"

"I really don't think you should be hitting the book." Livira moved to try and save it from him. "We're librarians after all. It's our job to preserve—"

"You were just about to take a chisel to the thing!" Arpix accused. He sat back down. "All . . . I need to . . ." He started straining at the book again, pushing at the spine and covers with the flats of his hands. ". . . do is . . . just . . . get . . ." The growl came still louder. The dog was almost half out of the wall now and Livira didn't need to see any detail to know that its mouth was open wide enough to take Arpix's head in one bite. Livira threw herself at the bed to wrest the book from Arpix's grasp. Somehow, they both ended up tumbling backwards together, landing in a heap on the floor.

"What the . . . How?" Livira tried to disentangle herself from Arpix's ridiculously long limbs. The book that had resisted all her efforts lay open, a spray of pages rising between the two covers.

"I thought I saw . . ." Arpix rolled her off him and patted the wall where the dog had been. "It looked like . . . something black."

"Never mind that!" Livira started to leaf through the book in wonder. "How did you open it?"

"Oh." Arpix turned away from the wall, frowning. "It's Al-Athan. They sometimes used to disguise the spine as a lock, and to open the book you need to try the other side and unclip the bit that looks like a spine."

FOR A DAY and a night Livira did nothing except read *The Forest Between*. She sat at her desk with the book in a reading stand before her and stared at each page in turn. Arpix said it looked as if she were trying to burn the words directly into her brain. He stood behind her for a while, reading along, but complained that she was ready to turn each page before he was a quarter of the way through it. In the end he went about his own business, returning periodically with food and drink, and to suggest, then cajole, and finally threaten her into bed for the sleep she so clearly needed.

Livira resisted sleep. Her act of theft could be discovered at any moment and the book taken back. The volume was a collection of fables and stories with varying degrees of connection to the Exchange. The book was a journey, a voyage punctuated by minor secrets, hopefully on the way to a larger truth. One astonishing claim, backing up something Arpix had once said, was that every few centuries the chambers themselves moved, all of them together, as if in some great, slow dance, gradually shuffling the pack. This at least went some way towards explaining why such labours appeared to have been lavished on chambers so far from the entrance.

Another claim was that although Mechanisms were very rare, a search of sufficient length would discover many of them scattered throughout the library's reading rooms.

About the Exchange itself, the book was less direct. An understanding of the place, even the fact of its existence, didn't emerge from the individual stories so much as from the overlap between them. In the common ground that threaded through tales separated by centuries, even millennia, and by distances so vast that Livira's mind could not encompass them, a picture of the Exchange emerged. In truth it didn't add a great deal to what Livira had gathered first-hand. A forest beyond time, in which libraries across time and space were connected. The assistants used the place to bring books from far away and long ago to restock libraries that had room for more.

What Livira wanted was a way to reach it. The stories were at their vaguest when it came to this vital component. Wanderers stumbling through portals, falling into pools, borne there by magic rings or wizard's spells—in one case even an enchanted button!—none of this was of any use to Livira when no specific means of reaching any of these pools, portals, rings, or wizards were mentioned.

Worryingly, Livira was running out of book. The ever-thinning wedge of pages between her current one and the back cover was growing alarmingly slim. Perhaps an answer lay hidden between the lines of what she'd already read. A puzzle waiting to be unpicked. But for a thief, expecting imminent discovery if she didn't manage to return the book undetected, these were not the fruits she'd hoped her larceny would bear.

Suddenly there it was in front of her with fewer than a dozen pages left to go. *A circle drawn with the blood of a white one will open the way to the wood.*

"Huh? What?" Arpix sat up sharply from the bed. "I wasn't asleep."

Livira hadn't even noticed him come back or go into the bedroom. He came through into the office knuckling his eyes and yawning. "I didn't say anything."

"You squealed. Or squeaked. Or shrieked. A bit of all three really."

"'A circle drawn with the blood of a white one will open the way to the wood,'" Livira read out loud.

"You might as well ask for a moon. The assistants are indestructible. Not that I'd want to hurt one anyway." Arpix rubbed the back of his neck and yawned again. "All sounds a bit primitive to me. It's probably just a fairy-tale way of saying that the ability to open portals is in their blood. If they even have blood."

"They do." It was the memory of seeing it that made Livira think that the book had it right. There had been something otherworldly about the shimmer of that blood. Just looking at it had started to rotate her thoughts within her skull. "They do have blood. I've seen it."

Arpix frowned. "Where?"

"In Chamber Seven. When I moved the assistant from where she'd fallen. There was blood under her, from the wound in her temple."

"Great. So, to get to the place you can't get to you need to get to another place you can't get to."

"The Raven can get me in," Livira said. "And I know how to summon it."

"Well, you certainly know how *not* to summon it." Arpix had helped out in a number of Livira's many attempts to call the Raven, the product of months of research, and they'd all failed. The circle of carefully drawn runes interspersed with the skulls of ravens and activated by a long incantation in modern Rillspan had had the most success. After two hours of chanting in a distant corner of the library a bird-shaped shadow had appeared within the circle. But it never became any more solid and Arpix said it was a form of self-hypnotism that had created it rather than some connection to the Raven.

"We need one of its feathers, and we need its name," Livira said.

"Neither of which we have."

Livira put down the book and bit her lip. She stared thoughtfully at the wall. A long moment passed and Arpix looked ready to say something. Livira beat him to it. "Volente."

"What language is that?" Arpix peered at her. "I don't—" Suddenly he threw himself back with a most un-Arpix-like curse.

The black dog walked out of the wall and came to sniff Livira's desk.

"What in all the hells is it?" Arpix asked from the corner he'd pressed himself into.

"A dog." Livira studied the hound.

"I saw it! Before . . . when you pushed me off the bed? That was this!"

"It's a guide. It's here because I know its name. Or maybe because it saw me steal the book. Or both."

"You stole the book?" Arpix gasped. "Who from?"

"Volente, you know the Raven, don't you?"

The dog looked up at her and although she couldn't see its eyes, she could feel their regard.

"Who did you steal the book from?" Arpix repeated his question, advancing from the corner of the room.

"Yamala."

It was Arpix's turn to combine a squeal, shriek, and squeak. He looked as if he was going to hide in the corner again. "And that's her dog? Why isn't it attacking you?"

"I don't know," Livira admitted. "I guess it's built to help." She stared back into the blackness of the hound's face. "Volente, I need to find the Raven."

The dog took a step back and shuddered.

"Volente. I need the Raven. It's urgent."

The dog shuddered again, then coughed, an ugly sound. It coughed again.

"What's wrong with it?" Arpix asked.

It coughed once more, hacking like Wentworth had on Livira's last visit when bringing up hairballs. With a last violent retch, the dog took another two backward steps and there on the ground before it was a black feather.

"He . . . ate . . . the Raven?" Arpix's eyebrows rose.

Livira didn't have an answer for that. Somewhat stunned, she bent to pick up the feather.

"Why do you need the Raven anyway?" Arpix rallied himself. "You've got a guide. Can't he open Chamber Seven?"

"Arpix! You're a genius!" And much to Arpix's surprise Livira flung her arms around him in a fierce hug. "Come on, we're going. I need to see if he'll come to the library when I call him there."

"Now?"

"Now." She tugged him towards the door. "We're going to the Exchange!"

Many objects are an inherent invitation. A sharp edge invites you to cut. A coin wishes to be spent. A sword begs for violence. A door requires that you try to open it.
Temptation: A Novel in Three Parts, *by Summer Applebaum*

CHAPTER 44

Livira

Y ou can't just leave it there!" Arpix protested.

"It's safe enough." Livira tucked *The Forest Between* in among the books on a random shelf in Chamber 1. Arpix had insisted they bring it with them rather than leave it in Livira's room to incriminate her. He'd wanted her to return it before they even went to the library, but Livira wasn't prepared to risk being caught before having an opportunity to use what she'd learned. "Nobody's going to find it by chance."

They were a few hundred yards from the librarians' entrance, out in the criss-crossed network of aisles, and it was time to see if Volente had followed them or would come when called. Livira felt a bit self-conscious calling his name into the silence.

"Volente?" More of a whisper than a cry.

"You could say it a bit louder," Arpix said. "And make it sound less like a question."

"If I shout it someone else might hear," Livira hissed. "And since when were you an expert on dogs?"

"Well." Arpix started to count on his fingers. "Firstly, I said we should go deeper in before we did this. Secondly, I very much doubt that creature has any real dog in it. And thirdly, my family had five dogs that I grew up with, Alpha, Beta, Gamma, Delta, and Jim."

Livira had plenty to say about that, especially on the subject of Jim, but a deep sniff and a black nose poking into view at the end of the aisle dragged her attention to other matters.

"Volente!" Livira hurried over to the hound. She wanted to give it a big hug but restrained herself, not sure how the beast would react to such familiarity. "We need to get into Chamber Seven."

The dog just looked at her.

"That's just information. Make a request," Arpix said.

Livira shot him a narrow look. "Volente, take us to Chamber Seven. Please." Already thoughts of the black assistant had put a nervous tremble in her voice. "Chamber Seven."

The dog tilted its head to the side.

"That's just our arbitrary numbering scheme," Arpix said. "It might not mean anything to him. He could be a thousand years old. More. Also, we know where Chamber Seven is. Let's go there and ask him to open the door."

Livira pinched her lips into a pucker of annoyance. Her excitement had ridden roughshod over her intelligence. "Come on then."

The head librarian's hound had followed them only for the first hundred yards before slipping off on its own explorations. Livira let him go, planning to call him again when needed. She hoped that Volente really would be able to get her back into the forbidden Chamber 7 from which she'd been excluded for so many years. She was more confident that the blood would still be there on the floor at the site of the assistant's accident. The odds were that she hadn't just happened along the day after it was spilled, and that the liquid had defied evaporation for years before her arrival. All that would be needed then was that the promise of the book prove true, and that a circle drawn in the blood really would open a door back to the Exchange.

LIVIRA WAS NOW so familiar with the early chambers that she reached Chamber 7 in under an hour, hot in her robes and rather sweaty, but with plenty of energy left in her.

On reaching their goal Livira hurried down the corridor and slapped her hand on the white door. It resisted her just as it always had, seeming as obdurate as the assistants.

"Volente." She spoke the dog's name.

Arpix looked around expectantly. Nothing happened. "Louder?"

"Volente!" Livira called out into the enfolding silence.

"Hmmm," said Arpix after the slow passage of several long minutes. "Maybe he was only interested in us when we had the book. Or someone else might have called him away. Or—"

"You're the dog expert. You call him."

"Someone might hear." Arpix eyed the encroaching aisles.

Livira pressed her forehead against the door. "I'm past caring. And even if there are librarians or trainees out there—they won't know what it means."

Arpix shrugged. "VOLENTE!"

Livira blinked in surprise. "Wow, that *was* loud!"

"You've got to sound like you mean it with dogs." Arpix looked slightly embarrassed.

A moment later Volente padded into view. He came right up to Arpix, who reached out a hand to ruffle the dog's head, the black fur seeming to consume his fingers.

"I've always liked dogs." Arpix smiled. "They get abused in the city, especially with the way the king keeps talking about the sabbers and . . . well, you know." He stroked his other hand across Volente's shoulder. "Old dogs can teach us new tricks. An old dog shuffles on, relentlessly happy, still interested in the world. Even when they're too worn out to run it's still there—no bitterness, no regret, no looking back, just on to the next thing with amiable confusion. Dogs are nothing but good."

Livira couldn't help but echo his smile. This was a different Arpix. She should tell Carlotte to turn up with a dog next time if she wanted to get under Arpix's covers. "Well, let's see how good this one can be." She turned to address him. "Volente, please take us through that door." She pointed to it.

Volente advanced on the door. Livira and Arpix exchanged glances and followed.

Volente reached the door and walked through it. Livira slowed, reaching out instinctively as she closed on the white surface.

"Damn." Her fingers rested against the door. "Volente!" She backed away.

The dog's head reappeared through the door.

"Can't you open it?"

The dog just looked at her.

"Maybe he helps by fetching books," Arpix suggested. "Dogs are good at fetching things."

"That's not exactly something I can test," Livira grumbled. "I don't know the names of any books in Chamber Seven. And it wouldn't help us anyway."

"Didn't the Raven want you to take a corner of one page back in there? Maybe if you had a whole book from in there it would come after you again?"

Livira didn't think it likely, but now that she thought about it, she had seen the title of one book out of the many millions in the chamber: the title of the book her scrap had come from. At the time she hadn't been able to read Crunian Four, but she could now, and if she could remember the shape of the letters . . . Even for Livira's steel-trap memory it was a big stretch. But she *had* looked at the front cover at the time, all those years ago, and it had mattered to her. She remembered recognising the letters from her scrap.

"Are you all right?" Arpix stepped into her line of sight. "You went quiet."

She raised a hand. "Thinking." Letters and words shuffled around in her mind's eye, some glowing brighter than others, some seeking partners, making clumps, actual words. Volente came back and sat beside her. Time passed. "No." Livira exhaled explosively. "Something about love . . . but that's all I can get." Another idea occurred to her. "Volente, fetch me the Raven!"

The hound quivered, glanced at the wall to the right, then settled down closer to the ground, bowing his great head to rest between his front legs.

"I think that's a no," Arpix said.

Livira furrowed her brow. "How about its name? Can you bring me the Raven's name, Volente?"

The dog looked up at her then stood and began to walk away, slowly. After ten yards it looked back over its shoulder at them. Arpix shrugged. "Let's follow."

Volente led them for two miles, crossing the chamber to the door where the immobile humanoid guide stood. The man's blind eyes still pointed towards a nothing above the shelves, the spars of his ruined wings still rising above him, the brown metal of his body glistening slightly in the directionless light.

Volente went to sniff at the metal man, starting at his feet and seeming to follow a scent up through his leg, stomach, chest.

"What's he doing?" Arpix stared, perplexed.

The dog went up on his hind legs, his front paws on the metal man's shoulders. The bark, if that's what it was, took Livira completely by surprise. A concussive sound that shoved her through the air. She found herself on the ground, surfacing through a thick layer of her own confusion, and feeling as if she'd been punched everywhere. Her ears, on the other hand, whilst ringing slightly, were less impacted than by one of the Raven's scoldings.

She helped Arpix up, or he helped her up—it was hard to tell, what with them both still staggering. She half expected to see flattened shelves and loose pages fluttering down from on high, but the library appeared unchanged. The metal man was still standing in exactly the same position. But now that Livira looked she could see that there was a fire in his eyes that hadn't been there before. With a grating sound he turned his head to look at her. It seemed that Volente's bark had been loud enough to wake the dead.

Tentatively, Livira approached the man, suddenly conscious of his height and the span of his reaching wings. No part of him moved except his eyes and his head.

"Hello?" The metal man had been recorded as immobile in books from two previous eras. He'd made no recorded move in centuries. Livira had no idea how to greet his awakening. Nobody was really even sure that he had been a guide.

The man's lips moved, and his voice rolled out, deep but surprisingly melodic. Livira had no idea what he was saying. She looked at Arpix.

"I don't recognise the language."

The metal man spoke again in a different tongue. Livira didn't recognise this one either, but she was enough of a linguist to know that it was different from the first. The guide tilted his head, his eyes burning slightly more brightly, and uttered a new phrase in a third language. He moved smoothly on into a fourth and a fifth. By the fifteenth repetition—and she felt they were repetitions—Livira was less amazed that the guide knew so many tongues and yet didn't speak hers than she was by the fact there were so many languages that neither she nor Arpix not only didn't speak but couldn't even guess an origin for.

It went on for an age. As time passed, the fire in the guide's eyes began to dim. His voice grew deeper and slower. In the end both of them sat down with the dog beside them and listened with their heads down. When the words finally did make sense Livira was so numbed by the prior flood of incomprehension that it took her a moment to realise it. "Wait!" She got to her feet. "That was . . ." It didn't seem likely but surely had been. "That was sabber-tongue?

"*You speak sabber?*" Livira formed the words slowly. She had taught herself the language from a book and only spoken it with Yute. The text stated that the written form was created by men to teach the spoken language, the new alphabet coined to represent sounds that regular letters couldn't capture. The librarians frowned upon sabber-tongue as a waste of time. Only one book was known to be written in it, a tome filled with love poetry that was believed to have been translated ironically. Livira tried again, making more effort to re-create the inhuman sounds, growling it out: "*You speak sabbertine?*"—literally: "You speak the language of the enemy?"

"*I do.*" The metal man inclined his head, neck joints grating. The fire in his eyes guttered like a candle flame exhausting its wax. "*Why has Volente awakened me?*" The words were sabbertine but put through the mangle. The years had changed it, no doubt, as they changed everything save the library.

Livira shaped her lips for the words she needed. She had learned the language out of stubbornness perhaps, or the desire to take better hold of what had been done to her. The sabbers had murdered and enslaved. They continued to do it. And while they had hidden from her behind their confounding language they had been a mystery, holding yet another kind of power over her. With their tongue on her lips, she might still fail to understand their violence and they might still be a mystery, but at least she had a key with which to unlock them. "*I need to know the Raven's name.*" She held the feather between them.

The guide opened his mouth and for a long moment there was nothing more. Livira feared that the life Volente had put into him had run back out, but just as she was about to say so, he spoke. "Edgarallen."

"And how do I—" But the fire had gone entirely now, and Livira realised she had slipped back into her native tongue.

Livira took a step back. She pulled the Raven's feather from her inner pocket. Name and feather. Could it really be so simple? No circle of runes, no ritual? She held it up.

"Edgarallen!"

"SQUAWK?"

And there he was, hopping down from a nearby shelf top in a clumsy flutter of wings, as if he'd been watching the whole time, just waiting for them to get it right.

WITH THE RAVEN—now sporting an additional feather, having reclaimed the one Livira used to summon him—gaining entrance to Chamber 7 proved easy. Livira's relief at not seeing the corrupted assistant standing there waiting for them was both immediate and huge. She knew it could still be active in the chamber beyond, and steeled herself against the likelihood. Shoulder to shoulder, she and Arpix advanced through the vanishing door. They followed the Raven along the corridor and came to a halt in the clearing at the entrance. Arpix's face was a mask.

"You're stuck between awe at being in a forbidden chamber and disappointment that it looks like most of the rest?"

"Mostly I'm just terrified that one of the monsters you're always meeting is going to kill me."

Dogs, and small children, are well known for showing an interest in the ownership of an object only after another has tried to claim it. Sadly, many adults are too. Not all such struggles are, however, without epiphany. On rare occasions, we realise that while competition may have made us look with new eyes at some familiar thing, we have, unknown to ourselves, always held in our secret hearts the truth that this was precious to us, something holy, and that had it ever been threatened we would have stood in the fire's path to defend it.

Fatherhood, *by Jorg of Ancrath*

CHAPTER 45

Evar

Evar left the city to fall. It burned at his back while he climbed the mountain. It shamed him but he couldn't stand as silent, helpless witness to the slaughter of his people. Not again. This thing had already happened. This was his past. Somewhere in the library would be an account of it, maybe dozens, where a scholar from some other city would have failed to capture the horror of the suffering, failed to tie to the page the screaming that tore the night as fire found flesh. A dry history would record in sterile numbers the toll taken by the concussive blasts as projectile weapons hurled death into the night, as sword edges sought bone, as arrows hissed towards their targets.

This time the blackness and silence of the rock's embrace was welcome. Evar ghosted through the stone, less worried that he might lose his way forever than that he might emerge once more amid the sabbers' carnage.

The library's stillness waited for him, unruffled by the slaughter unfolding less than a mile from its doors. The sabbers would come here too, Evar knew it. With their swords and spears, spilling more blood among the shelves. They would bring their fire too. Animals of their kind would have no regard for learning. He understood the char wall now. Some remnant of his people must have fled to the library chambers and then, chased by fire, they must have built barricades to save themselves. Though why the doors hadn't held back the flames Evar couldn't say.

The horrors of passing through the two-hundred-yard thickness of library walls hardly registered with Evar, so deeply was he wrapped in his thoughts. He came at last to the chamber where the assistant's relentless work to populate the space with new books continued.

"You need to run. The sabbers are coming!" Evar strode towards her. "With fire!"

The assistant didn't even look up.

"You need to run!" Evar shook his head. "Better still—stop them!"

She continued to stack books.

Evar went to the pool. "All this is going to burn!" He frowned, studying her indifference. For him this had all happened. The sabbers had come. Or they hadn't. And yet he was the one passionate about it, while the assistant paid him no attention though he knew she could both hear and see him. "Do something! Do anything!"

Still she stacked books.

It occurred to Evar then that the assistants might hold a very different view of time to his own. He expected this one to act because his past was her "now." But what if, like the library itself, they stood outside time, or at least observed it from a different angle? Maybe to an assistant the present and future were as fixed as the past. Either way, it was clear he couldn't argue her into doing anything other than what she would have done if he had never been here.

With a sigh as deep as the pool before him, Evar dropped into the water.

EVAR CLAMBERED FROM the water's cold into the warmth of the forest. It had been in his mind to hunt immediately for any sign of the Escapes that had pursued him, and to be ready to run. The sight of the woman in white put all that from his mind. She lay in a comfortable sprawl in the grass beside the pool, one arm cushioning her sleeping head, a flood of black hair giving way to the green. A white robe revealed only her uppermost contour, the shape of her shoulder, the gentle hollow of her waist, the swell of her hip. She was barefoot, two shoes lying close by as if they'd been kicked off.

Evar gained his feet slowly, unwilling to wake her. The wood stood just as it had before. In the distance along the row of pools leading ahead of him he could see the tiny black dot that his knife had made at the edge of his home pool.

The sun shone, birds sang, the trees drank. The birds had taken their voices from the night-song that had haunted the darkness beyond the city walls—a beauty sharp with sorrow.

"I make this place," Evar said softly. "It's built from expectations."

He sat with his back to the trunk of a tree, and watched the young woman sleep, letting the slow rise and fall of her chest count away time that might otherwise go nowhere. Had his expectation made her too? He'd come looking for the girl from his forgotten dream, and here with improbable convenience was someone who might fit that very hole in his memory. She seemed somehow familiar too. Doubt seized him. Was she even real? She looked almost too real to be trusted, like the colours that the rich folk had worn in the city: too vivid for an eye that had for decades rested its gaze on the library's dark and tan vistas. Even sleeping, the woman had a vitality to her that seemed to shout, to urge him to his feet.

With a pang of guilt, he remembered Livira. He'd been ready to deal with any Escapes that might be waiting. And after that his plan had been to return to Livira's pool in the hope that the water had re-established itself and that he might follow her to check on her safety, or perhaps to mourn yet another tragedy. On quiet feet he stole away from the sleeper and followed the row of pools in the direction of the future and of his home pool.

Livira's pool had refilled. The ground around its edge still bore the scuffs and scars of Evar's defence. Its unrippled waters reflected the sky through interlocking branches and, glancing up, he found the fractured end of the branch he'd torn away. It looked too thick for him to have wrenched it free. Evar stared down into the lightless depths. Many hours had passed. However the girl's encounter with the Escape had gone, it would be over now. Whether he followed her now or in a short while made little difference.

He turned and started back towards the woman. He didn't want to disturb her sleep, but he did want to talk to her. Even as he glanced her way again, his memory itched with recognition. She *was* familiar to him. He hoped it wasn't in the same way that imagination had patterned his family's faces onto the doomed citizens of the city he'd watched burn. But no— there was more here: somehow even though he couldn't place her, he knew her. Evar's heart began to beat harder, almost painfully so. This was her? In his mind she was the puzzle piece that would complete him, make him whole, like his siblings, like everyone else, not some broken thing limping through life. Even as he approached her, he acknowledged the unreasonable burden he'd heaped upon sleeping shoulders.

Back at the woman's pool Evar stood, unsure. Livira had asked him if Clovis was pretty and he hadn't really been able to answer her. He hadn't known what pretty was. But he had a word for the sleeping face before him. *Beauty*. The quality that made his eyes linger, that gave him joy, that made him want more . . .

"I wasn't sleeping!" The woman sat with a jolt and patted the ground to either side of her, disoriented, as if stumbling from her dreams.

"I—" Evar found his mouth unaccountably dry. "You were doing a remarkably good impression of it."

"Evar!" The woman got to her feet, flustered, hair in disarray. "You're safe!" She stepped towards him, half raising her arms to embrace him, then hesitated and let them fall as if suddenly shy.

"You know me?"

The woman's shyness evaporated in a wave of exasperation. "Not this again! I'm—"

"Livira . . ." What her shyness had hidden her sharpness revealed. He looked at her, amazed. How had that ink-stained child become the woman before him? And yet that child remained if sought for, there in the eyes, there in the line of her jaw. "You've grown!"

"And you're the same," she said wonderingly. "How long has it been for you?"

"A day." Evar shrugged. "Not a good one." He met her gaze. "I'm glad to see you. I tried to follow . . ."

"And I tried to come back." She pressed her lips into a troubled smile.

"We can't keep doing this. I'll be an old woman next time. I'll stagger up to you all grey and wrinkled and you still won't know me . . ." She trailed off, studying his face, growing serious as if seeing something there that worried her. "A bad day? How bad?"

"Sabbers. They burned the city outside the library."

Livira's gaze flitted to the surface of the pool. "You were in there? Your tracks ended here."

Evar nodded. He didn't want her to ask questions. Somehow talking about it might be worse than seeing it happen. The difference between being slashed with a knife and slowly dragging that same blade through your own flesh.

"It must have been centuries before my time. Even more years before yours." She frowned. "History might be going to repeat itself though. They're back again, camping within sight of the walls, raiding across the kingdom. If it wasn't for what the library's taught us, they'd have overrun us already."

"No?" Evar's stomach contracted to a cold fist. The idea of such slaughter being visited on Livira wouldn't fit into his mind. Unbidden images flashed across his thoughts, and he tried to close his imagination against them. "That can't happen." His eyes prickled with unwanted tears, and he looked away from Livira, staring down at the grass between them, ashamed of his weakness.

"I won't ask if you've found her." Livira changed the subject. "If it's only been a day. It's been years for me. Nearly seven years!" Her eyes widened. "Arpix! I forgot Arpix!"

"Who's Arpix?"

"A friend." Livira spun around trying to look in all directions at once. "ARPIX!" The girl could shout.

"I don't see anyone." Evar cast about, more worried that Livira's shouts might summon Escapes than about the whereabouts of her friend.

"We drew a portal," she said. "In Chamber Sixteen, so we wouldn't be trapped if the Raven wandered off while we were gone. And we came through together. Only he wasn't here when I arrived. I went back and he wasn't there either. So then I hunted the wood for him, but he'd just vanished. And so I followed your tracks to this pool. I knew you'd have to come back through it, and I'd have the best chance of finding you if I just waited . . ."

"And then you fell asleep," Evar finished for her.

"I didn't mean to. It's this place." Livira shot him a fierce look.

"You came to the time you wanted to this visit. On your first visit the pool must have somehow chosen the 'when' for you. Maybe the pool—the portal—sent this Arpix to a time that was more important for him?" Evar offered. "And that's why he's not here."

Livira twisted her mouth, seeming a little comforted. "Well, he'd better come back in one piece and the same age, that's all I'm saying. He would never have come except for me. It's my fault if anything happens to him."

"He wouldn't have come except for you?" Evar smiled. "An incurious fellow not to want to see this place."

"It was full of monsters last time I was here," Livira said.

Evar repressed a shiver at the memory. Somehow, the peace of the place had pushed thoughts of the Escapes to the back of his mind. He should be looking for them behind every tree, fearful one might drop out of the foliage. And yet he wasn't. "He must be a very good friend to have come with you."

"He is. I'm worried for him. What if the monsters are where he is? *When* he is."

Evar spread his hands. "What are you going to do?"

"I'm going to go back to the library and use the portal again, but this time I'm going to want to join him. I think if I want it hard enough, I might just get there. Or then."

"That seems . . . sensible." Evar tried to hide the disappointment from his face, but it had taken him by surprise, and he didn't think he'd managed. Probably because it felt closer to panic.

"Oh, I don't have to go now," Livira said. "That's the beauty of it. Time waits for you here."

Evar grinned and returned to his question. "So, what are you going to do *now*?"

Livira looked around. "This is the third time I've been here, and I've never tried any pool on my world line but my own."

"I've tried two and seen more horror than you can imagine." Evar shook his head. He was going home. Even the idea of trying to reach the day that Mayland had vanished on now lacked appeal. He didn't want to see anyone else die. Especially not one of his brothers.

"But you let the portal lead you?" Livira held his gaze. "You didn't say where you wanted to go. You didn't try to influence anything?"

"True. The last time I was running from the Escapes. I just jumped in."

"So, let's go together. We can choose a pool to a time where we'll both be ghosts. And ask to be taken to the day where we'll enjoy ourselves most, or learn most, or would find most interesting."

"I guess it's worth a try." Evar let the words be dragged out of him. He still didn't want to jump into another pool. But on the other hand, he didn't want to leave Livira behind. In fact, now that he'd found her again, grown and changed yet still indisputably Livira, he wasn't sure he ever wanted to leave her side again. Foolishness perhaps, but the idea of leaving her with this undoubtedly suave and charming "Arpix" made his hackles rise. And they couldn't just stand in the wood staring at each other. Actually, he'd be fine with that, but she might think it strange.

"Which one?" Livira crossed her hands behind her back and began to walk the line of pools leading to Evar's own.

Part of him wanted to take her home. But maybe she'd be a ghost there and he'd be real, and they wouldn't be able to see or speak to each other. Also, there were the others to consider. Evar didn't want to share her with them. Not yet. He liked the way she looked at him. And although it was selfish and small, he wanted that to last, not bring her to his brothers and sister who were all so much better than him. In particular, Evar didn't want Kerrol to dissect his feelings—feelings that he hadn't even begun to figure out for himself yet. He'd never met a stranger before. Maybe it was normal to be this unsettled by them. To not be able to look away. It hadn't been the same when she had been a child. He had—

"Come on then!" Livira stood four pools up at the water's edge. She turned towards him, fists on hips, head cocked. "I like this one."

Evar went to stand with her. "Why this one?"

"There was a guinea pig cropping the grass at the edge when I came this way to find you," Livira said.

"A what?"

"Like a rat, only fat and slow with no tail. A sausage on legs. I saw one in a book. This was the first real one."

Evar wasn't sure about the "real" part. "So we're choosing this one because of a lucky rat?"

"Well, not just that. Also because this one reminds me of a well I used to wonder about." For a moment she looked sad.

"But they're all the sa—" Evar looked down to find that she had slipped her hand into his.

"I lost Arpix even though we stepped through at the same time. Maybe if we hold hands we'll stay together." She looked up at him. "Also, we need to think the same thing. Focus on a time when there's no fighting and not going to be any for a while."

Evar nodded. He was still thinking about her hand in his. It had been a very long time since someone had held his hand for anything other than throwing him over their shoulder or hauling him out of danger. The Assistant had taken his hand when he staggered from the Mechanism. He remembered that.

"Ready?" Livira asked.

"No."

"On a count of three. One. Two. Three. Jump!"

She saw them everywhere. She saw them dancing on fence-tops, along old gutters, between the pegs on the washing line. She called them the "dancers," but then "angels" because Mam said that was proper if she couldn't stop talking about them.

"During the Dance," by Mark Lawrence

CHAPTER 46

Livira

Livira's memory had navigated them to the spot where the assistant had lain immobile for untold years and where the portal had stood. Both were gone now but the blood remained, a pearlescent patch covering an area the size of Livira's hand. The surface of it entranced the eye, offering both crimson and silver in a curious, everchanging swirl.

Livira knelt beside it and took the gluing brush she'd lifted from the bookbinder stores on the way out.

"Careful!" Arpix said unhelpfully.

Livira ignored him. She used the brush to soak up or lift as much of the blood as she could. She stood, rotating the brush slowly to prevent drips, and held a worn suede cloth beneath it in case she failed. "Let's go."

They had already decided not to draw the portal in the forbidden chamber. Immediately Livira headed for the chamber's far door. Arpix followed and the Raven hopped along after. The bird had fallen some way behind by the time they reached the door and for several anxious minutes Arpix voiced his concern that they were trapped. Livira worried that he was right, but pointed out that if the blood worked they could leave without needing the door.

"I should have carried him!" Arpix exclaimed and was going to say more when the Raven hopped into sight.

With the door open and with the need to test the blood burning in her,

Livira started to hurry away. The Raven watched them go, uttering a soft squawk. Livira turned. "Thank you. Thank you so much. Can't you come with us?"

But just as Volente had left them at the metal man, Edgarallen seemed decided that his service had also run its course.

They still had a way to go until they reached the place they'd decided to draw the portal. Somewhere where the books were sufficiently dull and obscure that nobody was likely to visit the aisle for years to come.

After what seemed an interminable period of walking, brush twirling, brush twirling, and more walking they reached their destination, standing face to face with the chamber wall. Finally the time to draw the circle had come.

"You should make it smaller." Arpix indicated a circle he could encompass with both arms. "In case there's not enough blood."

Livira frowned. "I don't want to be crawling down a rabbit hole!" But she worried he might be right. If the brush didn't hold enough blood—or paint as she now thought of it—to close the circle, then what would happen? Would it all be wasted? "I'll start off and judge it as I go."

And so, with a trembling hand that felt as clumsy as if she were using her foot instead, Livira began to paint her circle on the wall.

It turned out to be more of a squashed oval, taller than it was wide, and neither wide nor tall. As Livira drew the ever-drier brush to complete the loop at shoulder height, attempting to meet the earlier overambitious strokes, it left an increasingly narrow and patchy line. "Damnation." Her heart pounded more fiercely by the moment. It wasn't as if there were more assistant blood to be had. "You were right. I should have made a rabbit ho—" But the brush re-joined its path, and without pause or ceremony the encircled space lit with a familiar unworldly shimmer.

Not waiting for discussion Livira had bowed her head and stepped through the crude circle. She had emerged almost instantly from one of the Exchange's many pools. The alarm at Arpix's failure to join her, and the failed hunt for him had, after some time, deposited her at the edge of the pool that Evar seemed to have vanished into. And somehow, against all odds, she had slept.

———

Now, REUNITED WITH Evar the pair jumped into their chosen pool, hand in hand. But where her own badly sketched portal had delivered her smoothly to the Exchange, this pool saw her pitched into a tumbling fall through nothingness. She tried to hold to her thought of a time of peace, one in which an unexpected conflict wouldn't spring up to consume everything as it had during Evar's visit to the city.

To keep a focused thought in your mind while falling, a thought other than something concerned with hitting the ground, is difficult. To do it whilst blind and trying to keep a grip on another's hand: harder still. And yet Livira still managed to find room for the worry that perhaps her demand was too taxing, and that in every *when* that the pool might take her to the city was full of death and battle and murder in the alleyways.

The pool she finally crawled out of felt as if it were boiling, though not only with heat but also with emotion and pain. She lay gasping in sunshine so bright that she had to screw her eyes shut against it.

"Evar?" In a panic she realised that she'd lost his hand.

"Here." He was close by and the distracted way he'd spoken that single word told her she was not the centre of his attention.

Livira sat up, blinking. She found herself on the mountainside staring up at the stone head of a roaring wolf-like being, a head so big that its open throat was large enough to drive a wagon through. It wasn't the wolf's head that Evar was staring at, though. Hundreds of assistants, both male and female, stood in rows on the steps leading up into the jaws, arrayed like an audience for Evar and Livira's arrival. Some, however, were departing already, turning back to vanish into the wolf's throat as if the show had already ended and neither Evar nor Livira was worthy of their time.

"I know this place." On her arrival at the library, Yute had told her that the entrance he was taking her towards had once been styled as the head of a roaring god. Now she was seeing it with her own eyes.

"I never thought there could be so many . . ." Evar breathed.

"Me neither." There could be no way this many assistants inhabited the chambers Livira had explored so far.

Livira got to her feet. The wonders didn't stop with the ranks of assistants. There were not one, but two pools set side by side into the stone platform before the library entrance and it seemed that she and Evar had emerged from different ones. Neither pool looked anything like the ones in the Exchange but more like her own recent blood-drawn effort. But where that had been a circle daubed with less than a cupful of the oily silver-red liquid, these looked like the aftermath of two bloody murders. The light within them seemed to bubble and spit, the blood beneath showing through the shimmer here and there, swirling, constantly in motion.

"They're not looking at us," Evar said.

He was right. The assistants' gaze lay upon something more distant. Livira turned and saw below them the city cradled between the mountain's roots.

"Footprints!" She pointed but it hardly took her time in the Mechanism with a book on the subject to see this trail. The footprints led from the pools, one set from each, marked in silvery blood, fading to nothing after a few dozen steps. She set her own foot beside one of them. "Two small children . . ."

"What does it mean?" Evar glanced back at the departing assistants, half of them gone already.

"I have no idea," Livira said. "None at all." She rubbed at her arm as if some residue of the pool were still clinging to her. The turmoil of emotions still churned in her though they weren't hers and were beginning to fade. Sorrow, love too, both the personal and the general. Even as she tried to analyse them, the feelings dissipated like mist before the sun. There had been pain and there had been determination and there had been loss.

Livira's gaze followed the fading trail of bloody footprints down the slope. Two children? Born here amid the bucketing blood of . . . two assistants, before a veritable host of their own kind? If so, where were the parents? What had been the nature of these births?

"Well." Evar stepped off the platform onto the stair that led down to the road. "At least we can see each other. I'd worried we might be ghosts to one another."

Livira shot him a quick smile, glanced back at the thinning crowd of assistants, then followed him down.

"You're sure they can't see us? The assistants?"

"Oh, no. I'm sure they can," Evar said. "And hear us too. At least the one I met could. But she wouldn't talk to me."

"Only, I had questions . . ." Livira glanced back again.

Evar laughed, the first time she'd heard him laugh, a deep, friendly sound that lit him up. "Almost everything about you changes each time I meet you. Your clothes, your hair . . . your height . . . but if you ever stopped the flood of questions, I'd know it wasn't you even if you looked exactly the same."

Livira couldn't help but grin back. They walked on together with a bounce in their step. Livira remembered the many times she'd taken this road, alone, with Yute, with Meelan, with Arpix, never knowing that many hundreds of years before, her ghost had taken the same path.

"I want to see someone. I want to know I'm a ghost for sure. I don't feel like a ghost!"

"How does a ghost feel?" Evar kept close to her as if worried she might fall on the steep trail.

Livira reached out and touched his leather-clad arm and found it solid. "Not like that."

Evar smiled uncertainly. She noticed his hand moving unconsciously to hold his upper arm where she'd briefly laid her fingers. It was, she thought, the reaction of someone unused to being touched, someone unsettled by it, but wanting more. She wondered at the life he'd lived, trapped alone with his brothers and sister. His first venture outside that prison had been to witness carnage in the same spot at a different time. And then his first steps outside the library itself had shown him another slaughter. For all the deadliness he'd demonstrated battling to defend her from Escapes in the Exchange, she didn't think of him as a killer. He might have something of Malar's talent for it, but not the taste. She desperately wanted to show him a better world, a kinder one, with more wonder in it and less horror. No horror, preferably.

"Try picking that up." Evar pointed to a fist-sized rock that lay by the edge of the path.

Livira went to squat beside the stone and reached for it slowly, her fingertips anticipating the roughness beneath them, her mind fascinated with Evar's implied claim that she would be unable to.

"By all the little gods . . ." Her fingers closed on nothing, vanishing within the stone, feeling no more than if it had been just air, or a trick of the light. She looked up at Evar, grinning. "I'm a ghost! An actual ghost!" A sudden thought furrowed her brow. She reached down and pressed her hand through the ground. In fact, no pressing was required. She squatted there, staring at where her wrist terminated against the cobblestones. "But how—"

Evar caught her other arm and drew her rapidly to her feet. "Best you don't ask that question. I don't want to fall to the centre of the world." He started off down the slope. "Come on!"

Livira would have argued with him or at least stayed to conduct further experiments, but she saw at that point that they were little more than two hundred yards from where Yute's house would one day stand. The place was just bare mountainside, but even so she wanted to plant her feet there and imagine the towering storeys of his home rising around her.

"WHERE IS EVERYONE?" Livira sat on the rocky edge of the drop that would, in years to come, sit just beyond the back wall of Yute's house. Evar stood behind her, looking out over the city below.

"I don't know."

"That's not my city," Livira said. "It's where my city is, but it's not mine."

"Perhaps it became the one you know."

Livira shook her head, wonderingly. "Not by just expanding and improving. Those buildings are gone. New ones stand in their place. And not better ones. We've nothing like that tower." She pointed to a delicate structure that seemed impossibly tall. "I still want to know where the people are." She thought back to the twin pools of assistant blood at the library entrance and the two sets of footprints leading from them. Child-sized. She wondered, with a shudder, what might have been born from what could only have been the deaths of two assistants. And why so many of their brethren had watched on, doing nothing to stop it. "There's nobody."

At this distance the citizens would be specks, lost among the houses. But Livira felt she should be able to see some evidence of them in the great square, which lay where it did in her version of Crath City, though now somewhat smaller and surrounded by a different set of grand buildings.

"Maybe they're still in bed?" Evar ventured.

"It's past noon!" Livira got to her feet.

"How can you tell?" Evar frowned and looked up. "Ah, the sun moves." He looked uncertain. "I'm right, aren't I? That's how you knew?"

Livira laughed. "I so rarely meet anyone who spends more time in the library than me." In fact, it was possible that nobody did, except the head librarian. "Yes, the sun moves. The shadows too."

It was Evar's turn to laugh. "I've been trying not to look at mine in case I got too fascinated with it and went head over heels down the mountain." He raised his hand and laughed again as his shadow mimicked the action.

"Head over heels?" Livira pursed her lips, her thoughts returning to the stone she'd been unable to pick up from the roadside. She closed her eyes, spread her arms, and started to spin.

"Careful!" Evar sounded suddenly alarmed. "Livira! You'll fall!"

Livira took three uncertain backwards steps, eyes still closed.

"Livira!"

She felt the rush of him, the iron grip on her forearm arresting her backwards stumble. She opened her eyes and met his, wide, dark, and staring in surprise. She looked at her outstretched arm, his outstretched arm, and at his fingers where they encircled the pale tan of her wrist.

Together they both looked down. The rock face fell away just an inch from his leading foot, stepping rapidly away so that in three steps Livira had put fathoms of empty space beneath her heels.

"Let go," Livira said.

A momentary anguish took possession of Evar's face, as if under any other circumstance he would have snatched the hand back like she'd scalded him. "You'll fall . . ."

"If I weighed anything we would both have fallen already."

Evar slowly let his gaze wander over their improbably balanced bodies. "You're sure? You want me to let go?"

Livira raised an eyebrow.

Evar opened his fingers, hand ready to catch her again, even now. When she didn't plunge to her doom, he somehow regained his balance on the edge with a twist of feline grace. Livira hung where she was, unclaimed by the drop.

"Expectation is what keeps us from falling through the rock," she said.

"You didn't expect to fall?" Evar eyed the distance beneath her doubtfully.

"Not after I'd thought it through. But I decided I should try it with my eyes closed so my mind didn't have a chance to act on reflex."

Evar continued to stare down at the jagged rocks far below, skin paling. "We don't have drops where I'm from. It was dark when I came here before. I'm finding I like drops even less in the daylight."

Livira could see the discomfort etched in the furrows across his forehead. The fear he'd admitted to was just the tip of a much larger terror. And yet he had lunged over the edge to catch her, so far that both of them should have fallen, nothing but her expectation battling his to hold them up. "Try it." She extended both hands towards him, and because she expected to be able to, she moved closer. "I won't let you fall."

Evar swallowed. "You can fly now?"

"Why not? We're ghosts." She held her hands out to him. "Come on. You don't want to miss out on flying, do you?"

Evar looked dubious. "Isn't that just being over a big drop all the time?"

"Well, yes, but you know you're not going to fall." She gestured for him to take her hands.

"Let me try for myself first." Evar waved her away, his shyness overridden by nerves. He reached out over the edge with one foot, patting the air.

"Commit to it! Put your weight on that foot."

Evar favoured her with a look of the sort that madmen must get used to.

"Just don't think about falling!"

Gritting his teeth, he tried it. A moment later he was falling. Somehow, he caught the edge, thumping into it with his chest. A mad scramble, during which his legs seemed to do things legs shouldn't be able to, saw him back on the ledge, panting.

Livira took mercy on him. She flew over him in a delicate arc and landed lightly on his far side. "Maybe we'll save it for later."

"Much later." Evar stood up hastily, trying to recover his dignity.

"Come on." Livira skipped away. "Let's get to the city."

"You're not going to fly?" Evar hurried after her. "Ghost-girl."

"Only if I need to!" And full of a sudden, unexpected joy Livira put on a turn of speed, determined to reach the city first.

Evar answered the challenge, closing the gap with remarkable swiftness. With a squeal of delight, Livira leapt into the air, taking to the skies as the road dipped away. She dived towards the great plaza, arrowing high over the steps where Yute had shown her the mouths of the caves ancient peoples had lived in.

Evar seemed to have shed his fear of heights, or at least of slopes, jumping down the steps with reckless abandon. As Livira took the crow's path over the houses and gardens behind the main square, Evar followed, almost as fast thanks to a breathtaking display of athleticism. He vaulted walls taller than Livira could reach and tore through open spaces like a hurricane.

Even so, Livira was first to the square, landing lightly on her toes. Heartbeats later Evar was there, flushed and panting, a fierce grin showing white teeth.

"I'm impressed!" Livira said. "Especially for someone who's spent their whole life walking the library floor . . ." She remembered her first encounters with slopes and stairs. She'd felt like a baby learning to walk again.

"This feels right." Evar hauled in another breath, exhaled, snatched another, chest rising and falling. "This feels real. I like it."

"Come on." Livira ran, white robes flowing, to the pillared entrance of the largest building. The edifice stood where King Oanold's lesser palace would one day sit, and was grander still.

"What are we going to do?"

Livira clambered up the overlarge steps, stopping halfway to the scrollworked iron doors above. "Teach you to fly, of course." It had occurred to her that a deadly drop wasn't a critical ingredient in the process. "Stand there." She indicated the spot beside her.

Evar joined her and she took his hands again, sensing once more that momentary flinch at what must be unfamiliar contact. He closed his fingers around hers, meeting her gaze with dark intensity.

"Keep your eyes on mine." Livira stared back. "Only on me."

Evar didn't look away. They stood like that for longer than necessary in the building's shadow. Evar's breathing calmed. Livira enjoyed the feel of his hands in hers, the largeness of them, the gentleness of his grip, the heat between him and her. By rights he should be sweaty, but he didn't seem to sweat.

"Stay with me," Livira said, studying his gaze. "Keep your eyes on mine. Step when I do but focus on me."

Long moments passed them by; he held her hands tighter, not painfully so, but affirming the contact.

Livira stepped towards him, he stepped back. "Do you know how to dance?"

"What?" Evar's eyes widened with something like fear. She stepped left. He stepped with her. "No."

"Neither do I." Livira grinned, stepping to the left again. "Maybe we can teach each other."

Evar stepped with her. "Clovis knows some battle dances. But those are to teach parries and counterthrusts."

Livira leaned back, forcing Evar to resist her or be drawn forward, and began to circle.

"Mayland says dance is the oldest form of expression. Older than words. Much older than writing."

"Older than the library then." Livira smiled, leading him into a spin.

"Kerrol says—"

"What do *you* say?" Livira didn't want his brothers or sister interrupting.

"I like it." They rotated between two fluted pillars. And moments later into the sunshine.

"Look where we are!" Livira released his hands with a laugh. The expression on Evar's face when he realised they were more than two yards above the ground made her double up.

It's a rare thing that lives up to expectations. First kisses are rare.
Remembering a Life, *by Methuselah Enochson*

CHAPTER 47

Evar

Livira took off again in a swirl of robes, aimed once more at the sky. This time Evar could follow. He unleashed a cry of delight and gave chase, finding that he was at his swiftest when reaching for the thing he wanted—the person, in this case.

On the ground he'd been the fastest by some considerable margin. In the air, driven forwards by nothing but the mind, speed limited perhaps only by imagination, Livira outpaced him, circling him like some small quicksilver fish might thread its path around his floundering passage underwater.

Evar knew he was out of his element, perhaps out of his depth, or height, but none of that worried him. As if some invisible load had fallen from his shoulders when his feet left the ground, he felt freer than at any point in his life, spiralling through the air, gaining altitude above an ancient city that had vanished long before his birth.

He reached for Livira with both hands and launched himself into the wake of her laughter, finding only empty space.

"Slowcoach!" She hung ten yards above him, barelegged beneath her robe. "Come on!" And in the next moment she was diving towards the distant ground.

Evar found himself less keen about heading down at speed than he was when hurling himself at the blue vaults above. Livira arrowed ahead, her black mane streaming, and landed in front of the steps of the great building where they'd been before. She stood, hands on hips, as if waiting for a tardy child. The sunlight found shades of red in her hair.

While he lingered in the heights a flash of motion deeper within the city caught Evar's attention. Two small figures flitting across a narrow road. Children perhaps, but whiter than any child should be and dressed in white so that it was impossible to see where flesh ended and cloth began, if indeed cloth did begin, for they had seemed almost naked.

Evar shook his head, looked again, saw nothing, and followed Livira to the ground.

"We should go in. Find some people." She turned towards the doors as he floated down to join her.

"All right." He liked the city empty. He realised that he didn't want to share Livira with the citizens of this place any more than he wanted to share her with his siblings, Arpix, or anyone else. Not now at least, not while he could still feel her hands in his.

Livira hurried up the steps ahead of him and waited, staring up at the impressive doors as if wondering how to open them. Evar walked through without hesitation, suppressing his desire to flinch as the last inches between his face and the iron surface narrowed rapidly.

"I forgot about that!" Livira rushed through the door, grinning. A moment later she was gone, having thrown herself back through them. She emerged through the wall heartbeats later, giggling. "We can go *anywhere*!"

Evar would have replied but the surroundings took sudden command of his senses. The hall before them must have taken up the majority of the structure, domed and vaulted to a height that, whilst lower than the ceilings of the library's chambers, somehow managed to make him feel smaller—as if the architects had known exactly what scale to build at in order to evoke maximum awe, a scale where the mind can still just about comprehend what it's seeing, though fail to imagine how such a thing might be built. The details, the marble columns, the carvings, the banding on the dome, the windows of stained glass high above them casting coloured light across the floor: all combined to train and steer the eye, schooling it in the size and wonder of the place.

"It smells of incense," Livira breathed. "A temple of some kind. I can't see any statues though . . ." She stood, craning her neck, studying the decorated ceiling. Animal carvings haunted every corner and the terminus of every pillar, a profusion of species that Evar was unable to name even a fraction of. Lions, deer, fish, serpents. In other places, higher still, the monstrous and divine spread their wings in stone relief.

Unexpectedly Livira's hand worked its way into his once more and together they advanced across the chequerboard floor, their footsteps echoing.

"I like this place." Livira came to a halt beneath the apex of the central dome. She released his hand and stepped back to stare at the heights. Patches of light slid across her, colouring her robes, green here, red there.

"It's incredible." Everything in the library, save the books themselves, had been so utilitarian, free of decoration or any effort at design, vast square warehouses linked together in a possibly never-ending grid, bound to the world only by its edges. Evar had had a taste of something more on his night-time visit to the previous city, but hadn't strayed inside, admiring the buildings only from the streets. It seemed they saved their best efforts for the interiors. Probably because of weather—another thing that Evar had minimal experience of.

Evar stood, drinking it in. Somehow, merely by heaping and shaping stone blocks, the people of this city had made something holy, something with awe resonant through every part of its arching masonry, stained glass, contained space.

This contemplation of the grand scale faltered in the face of still more momentous events on the small scale. Evar became suddenly and desperately aware that Livira was standing beside him. Too close. Someone's feet had closed the distance between them, and she now stood within that circle of space that he alone owned. A space that Clovis might quickly trespass upon with fist or foot but one where nobody lingered . . . until today. Impossibly, he felt the heat of her, as though—like the Assistant—she could raise her temperature sufficient to boil water. But this was a heat that drew him instead of driving him back. More fascinating than his first flame.

He turned to face her, dismayed at the trembling in his hands. Clovis would laugh at him—but, despite their brief intimacies, he and Clovis had never kissed. Kerrol would have balanced both sides of the equation and extrapolated to all solutions. Starval would have stolen the kiss long ago. But Evar was just Evar, and he hadn't the first idea how to go about this.

Livira looked up at him, a question in her dark eyes but just a half smile tugging at her lips.

"Thank you." His dry mouth hunted the words. "For teaching me how to fly."

She kept her eyes on his as she had when he'd been too lost in them to notice there wasn't any ground beneath his feet.

"I . . ." Feeling foolish, he coughed and started to turn away.

"Silly." Livira reached her hand around the back of his neck and pulled him down towards her. There wasn't any time for the anxieties that tried to crowd in. Their mouths met. Tongues met. It was all much simpler than he had imagined. And much better.

There are no perfect lives. Sooner or later, you will bite the apple and see half of a worm. Whether you spit out what you've taken or have a second bite is generally a function of hunger. The worm is, after all, made entirely of apple.

Bush Tucker, *by Ancoo Walkabout*

CHAPTER 48

Livira

Livira broke the kiss. She had started it, so it was hers to finish. Part of her wanted to stay locked in Evar's arms until their lips were sore and their jaws ached. There was a kind of peace to it that reminded her of the wood between now and then, and a thrill that carried the exhilaration of jumping from shelf top to shelf top, and another more primal excitement that made her want to find a private place in which to learn all his secrets and share her own. But, as always, it was a question that demanded the services of Livira's tongue.

"Was that your first kiss?"

"It was that obvious?" Evar's grin faltered.

"No!" She reached for his hand. "It was marvellous. I just wanted to know. That's who I am. I like to know things. That's something *you* should know." She stopped, aware she was babbling.

"It was my first." Evar nodded. "Clovis doesn't kiss. She's more the punching type." His grin returned.

Livira echoed it. It wasn't her first kiss, but it was, by a long way, the one that mattered most to her. Evar might have met her only a couple of days before, but for her it had been ten years. Ten years in which the Exchange and its mysteries had populated her dreams. But gradually it had been Evar himself, not the trees, quiet skies, and endlessly deep pools, that had occupied her thoughts in the quiet moments when she was alone. Evar, every time her many questions left her in peace for long enough to let her mind wander. Evar, trapped in time, a fly in amber, emerging into a world—into many worlds—equipped only with the naivety that the years had stripped from Livira. She'd been the child and he the adult, but she'd grown, learned, a year's study for every few hours that Evar had spent in his snail's crawl through two pools.

He'd fought to save her from monsters. Risked his life for a stranger. Malar had done something similar. She'd told herself she'd wanted to save Evar back, but it had become more than that. Perhaps she'd wanted to save him for herself. Time would tell. A kiss could lead to all sorts of places. Not all of them good. The library's stories had taught her this before practice confirmed it. She had her eyes open about that, she wasn't an idiot, as the majority of girls in the stories seemed to be.

"Livira?"

Livira blinked. "Yes?"

"I thought I'd lost you there. What were you thinking about?"

"Everything." She reached for his hand. "Come on."

"Where are we going?" Evar looked as though anywhere with more kissing would suit him.

"We need to find someone. You don't think it's odd that this whole temple seems to be empty?" More kissing would suit her too, but for once in her life she resolved not to run headlong into something. This felt too important to rush.

Evar frowned and nodded. "It *is* strange."

Livira turned for the doors. Her lips prickled with the memory of his kisses. Strangely, although he was clean-shaven, he had still seemed bristly against her skin. A silly smile took possession of her mouth, remembering how good it had felt to have his arms around her, and how she could have them around her again. She pushed through the great doors, still surprised when they offered no resistance whatsoever. It wasn't until she reached the steps again that another of the many questions swimming in the ocean of her mind surfaced to plague her.

"Expectation . . ." She stopped halfway down the stairs.

"Yes?" Evar asked behind her.

"We built the Exchange ourselves. Or at least we furnished it. You gave it pools, and trees not much taller than you, and no birds."

"I have birds now . . ."

"And I gave it portals, and tapwoods, and ravens." She turned towards him.

Evar nodded.

"And here, the ground kept us up because we expected it to. And when I expected to fly . . . I could. Hells, our footsteps were echoing back in that temple—what sense does that make, except that we expected them to?"

"True."

"So, we might still be in the Exchange for all we know. Seeing what we expect. Or a mix of what we expect and what the Exchange shows us."

Evar licked his teeth. "It's possible."

"And what about me and you?" Livira edged towards her main concern. "We're speaking the same language. What are the odds? Are we even seeing each other, or just what we expect to see?"

"I . . . I don't know." A note of concern entered Evar's voice.

"In Crath City the young women have taken to painting their nails with coloured lacquer—a new creation from the alchemists at the laboratory. A friend of mine located the book that taught them the formula." Livira extended her hand and spread her fingers, concentrating furiously. Her nails turned scarlet, then a poison green, then a deep blue. She held them up. "Do you see it?"

"See what?" Evar stared.

"The colour on my nails?"

". . . no." The admission dragged from unwilling lips as if he didn't like the taste of it. "Wait." Evar held up his own hand in denial. "You were inky when I first saw you. And bruised. I didn't expect either of those things. I didn't expect to see you at all."

"So maybe the Exchange shows us a mix of truth and expectation," Livira said.

"Or just truth!"

"How do I know I'm seeing you? You don't see my blue nails." Livira made a fist and willed them back to normal. "I could make my hair reach my ankles. Or grow a third arm. And you wouldn't see it."

"Those aren't the truth."

Livira ran her fingers across her lips, thoughts churning. Was Evar seeing the real her, and if he wasn't, would he like what he saw when expectation's scales were removed from his eyes?

After a long pause she started back down the stairs. "Let's find some people. I expected to see lots. And that didn't work."

EVAR SUGGESTED THEY try the next great hall along the perimeter of the square.

Livira disagreed. "We should try a house. Houses always have people. It might be some kind of weird holiday where everyone has to stay home, because they're not in the streets and they're not in the temples. Not that one at least."

"Well, they couldn't have got in, even if they wanted to," Evar said.

"What do you mean?"

"You didn't see the bar on the inside? Those doors weren't going to open from outside. I assumed that was why there was nobody there but us ghosts."

And so, at Livira's insistence they took to the air and flew over the city's rooftops, faster than a man can run, and aimed themselves at the clustered housing of low town, down by the great gates to the city.

"There! Do you see it?" Livira had caught a wisp of smoke rising from a chimney and angled herself towards it.

"See what?" Evar chased her.

Rather than answer, Livira landed on the roof beside the terracotta smokestack. "You can smell it now." She'd meant the smoke, but there was something else too.

Evar sniffed. "The whole city smells down here. Of lots of things. But there's one thing in particular. A barbed kind of smell. Gets into your nose . . . You must have caught it too?"

Livira was busy studying the street below. A pool of blood lay across the flagstones, smeared as if the originator of it had hauled themselves away, or been hauled. Two of the front doors she could see hung on their hinges. The houses, like the one they were standing on, were five-storey affairs with many small windows. Lodging houses, she guessed, renting rooms to poor labourers or whole floors to families of rather modest means. Katrin and her husband lived in a similar place, though somewhat smaller and more run-down even than these.

"Blood," Evar said. "I can smell that too, now. Looks like our efforts to arrive when there wasn't going to be any fighting didn't work!"

Livira sniffed but caught nothing save the drifting smoke that had first brought her to the chimney. Evar's sense of smell seemed far more sensitive than hers. "Let's go in." Livira let the sinking feeling that had settled on her carry her down through the roof tiles, through the horsehair mats beneath them, through timbers, boards, and plaster.

"Oh, hells." Evar dropped beside her, stumbling on the bed.

"I didn't think I could hate the sabbers any more than I already did." Livira could smell the sharp chemical stench now, gathered in the room where the wind hadn't yet fully cleared it. It reminded her strongly of the gas that the rogue alchemist had been paid to kill her with. A sweeter, sickly odour ran beneath it. The smell of corruption, of flesh turning bad.

A woman lay on the bed with her baby beside her, tumbled in the blanket. Her body had contorted, every limb at a painful angle, the tendons visible in her neck, foam in her mouth, eyes bulging from their sockets, their lustre dulled by the alkalines that had eaten her lungs and scorched her skin. A sabber lay face down in the doorway, blood leaking from beneath its head.

"The bastards . . ." Livira whispered.

Evar looked confused. "I don't understand what happened here."

Livira shook her head, trying to refuse the sight, but even as she did so she sank through the floor to see what truth lay below.

On the next storey, four sabbers lay dead in the largest room, huddled together. On the stairwell a young man had broken the railings in his death throes.

"The idiots killed themselves with their own weapon!"

On each floor it was the same. All humans, or all sabbers, or a mix of both, all dead. Livira staggered from the house's tall entrance, retching, Evar on her heels. A glance through the doorway of the house opposite revealed the corpses of a woman and a sabber locked together in the hall.

"How far did this reach?" Evar gasped in horror.

"The whole city." Livira understood as she said it. "The whole city. Everyone killed on both sides. That's why the pool brought us here. We wanted somewhere there wouldn't be any fighting . . ."

Understanding dawned slowly across Evar's face. He looked sick. "What kind of demented foe brings a weapon like that into a city? A weapon they clearly lacked the wit to control?"

"They're animals," Livira snarled. If she'd had a sabber before her in that moment, and Malar's skill . . . she would have cut it down.

"The world would be better without them." Evar nodded sadly, his eyes bright with unshed tears. "We should go. There's nothing left for us here."

They walked to the end of the street, each wrapped in their own thoughts, clenched around the horror of what they'd seen.

"We should fly," Evar said. "I don't want to see any more."

Livira nodded. Not to acknowledge the enormity of the crime that had been committed here almost seemed the coward's way out. And yet what was she supposed to do? Enter every house, witness every corpse? Stay until the stench of their rot engulfed the whole city and flies obscured the sky?

"You're right. We should go." She turned for one last look back down the street. It felt like it might be one of many similar roads in her own city. "Wait! There! Look!"

"I don't see it."

There was nothing where Livira's finger was pointing. But there had been, she was sure of it. A white child at the window, bone-white, white face, white hair, gone almost as soon as spotted, taken by the shadows. "A little boy." She started off in the direction she'd pointed.

"Don't." Evar caught her shoulder. "What if it was a boy? We can't help him. We can't comfort him. We can't do anything but watch. All this has happened. We're nothing here."

An unexpected sob racked Livira, convulsing her body.

"Livira . . ." Evar tried to turn her to him, but she couldn't let him, not now. And like an arrow she took to the air.

Livira didn't slow until she reached the twin pools on the platform before the howling wolf god's head. All the assistants were gone, perhaps taking their own portals to return them to the depths of the library unknown weeks or months of travel from the entrance.

"Let's get out of here." Livira stepped towards the nearest pool as Evar landed less gracefully beside her.

"Agreed." He gathered himself to jump.

"Wait." She reached for his hand. "So we both go to the same place." She laced her fingers between his, remembering the kiss that had been forgotten in the horror that followed. It had been a good kiss. More than good. "I'm sorry. It wasn't your fault . . . obviously. I'm just . . ."

"I understand." Evar gave a grim smile and squeezed her hand. "This has been my third nightmare. I'm not sure the past is a land I want to visit again."

She wanted to protest that she was in his past, her pool many places down the row from his, but instead she just nodded. "On three then."

"Three."

They jumped, passing through echoes of the original emotional turmoil, hardly noticed now, burdened as they were with their own. A moment of rushing, passing lights, a sense of swinging around some vast corner, and they were side by side on hands and knees, panting beside a pool in the quiet of the woods.

Livira lifted her head at the sound of a guttural snarl and the pounding of running feet. For a moment she thought another Escape was coming for them. But this was somehow worse. A full-grown sabber with a streaming mane of red fur was charging towards them. A female one.

"Evar!" A scream half of terror, half warning.

But Evar was already gone, tearing across the grass towards the foe. They slammed together at devastating speed about five yards from Livira. Surprise registered on the sabber's face just before the impact but somehow it managed to twist at full sprint, evading Evar whilst simultaneously straight-arming him into the ground. By some miracle, Evar's trailing foot hooked the sabber's ankle and even as it went down with a roar of hate, he was on it.

Again, the thing twisted, its speed and strength breathtaking, reversing their positions, pinning Evar to the ground.

"Evar!" The sabber roared. "What the fuck are you doing? Are you blind? She's a sabber!" The sabber glanced up at Livira, pure hatred in its eyes.

"No, Clovis! No! It's this place. It changes what you see—"

Clovis slammed her forearm into Evar's face, leaving him dazed, then sprang to her feet. "Your eyes, maybe. Not mine."

And Livira, still kneeling by the pool, understood in that moment that the sabber was right.

Kindness is a language in and of itself. In order for it to be understood it requires that both the speaker and the listener be trained in its syntax.
Linguistics: A Study of the Heart, *by Kian Najmechi*

CHAPTER 49

Livira

Evar rolled onto his front and levered himself up, blood trickling from his nose and mouth. Livira could see the sabber in him now, written into every line. The Exchange hadn't hidden him beneath illusion, it was more that somehow her expectations had accentuated what might be taken as human and pushed the rest into the background. With his sister, Clovis, there'd never been any doubt. People were wrong to call them dog-soldiers. There was certainly something of the wolf about them, especially in the mouth, but their movements held something more feline.

Clovis broke the spell that had bound them in the broken moment of realisation. She hurled herself at Livira, only to fall, snarling, as Evar lunged and caught her trailing ankle with both hands. The force of Clovis's heel stamping into his face was sickening.

"Run!" Shouted through a mouth full of blood as Evar hung on to his sister despite the awful punishment.

With a cry of confusion, Livira launched herself towards what she hoped was her own pool, as she did so becoming peripherally aware of something closing on her with awful speed. The rush of that advance filled her ears as she dived for the pool. The waters closed around her and in an instant she was rolling hip over shoulder across the library floor.

She came to a halt on her backside, facing the portal, and scrambled away from it, terrified that the sabber would burst out of it to tear her throat open with its teeth.

Nothing.

Livira realised that even if the sabber had followed her it would be a ghost, unable to harm her, venting its impotent fury unseen and unheard. On any other day Livira might have laughed in relief but now she just fell back, covered her face with both hands, and let her thoughts churn. The black sea of her emotions refused to settle on a reaction. Sorrow, anger, and shock wrestled each other. Hate warred with softer instincts. Time passed: it felt like an age. And at last, with her face still covered and the battle inside her unresolved, Livira let out a single scream that carried all the conflict inside her head out into the silence of the library at a volume that would even have impressed the Raven.

"Livira! You're bleeding!"

Livira sat up sharply. "Arpix! Thank the gods!" Here at least was one good thing. One mistake that had corrected itself. One less thing to feel guilty over.

Arpix fell to his knees at her side. "Where are you injured?"

"I'm not inju— Oh!" The blood had stained the lower part of her robe crimson. Cautiously, she reached for the hem. Her leg had started to hurt . . . or it had been hurting all along and she'd just been too chained in her thoughts to notice? She pulled the robe up. A long ugly wound had been torn down her calf. Clovis had come closer to catching her than she knew. The sabber had laid a single claw on her as she dived into the pool.

Arpix reached for her leg, but Livira flinched away before his long, print-stained fingers made contact.

Evar is a sabber! A horrible thought had twisted its way into her mind. "How do I even know you're you?"

Arpix looked confused. "Don't I look like me?"

"That place is full of lies!" Livira tossed her head at the portal that had spat him out.

"Don't I sound like me?"

"It's not enough." She snarled the words past gritted teeth, the pain pulsing in her calf muscle now. Part of her welcomed the distraction. Anything to keep from thinking about Evar. She pressed him from her mind with a vicious force of will. He didn't exist.

"Livira." Arpix met her eyes. "It's me. Let me help you."

Everyone else she knew would have called her mad or laughed at her or taken offence, or at least tried to argue. She let her head fall and slumped back.

"It's not too deep." Arpix took her leg and turned it slightly. "Needs to be cleaned though. Right now." He released her and started to unsling his water-skin. "This is going to hurt."

Livira winced. "Can't we go to the centre circle and let it do the work?"

"That's our next stop. Otherwise it would need stitching and a week's rest." He spoke gently, not mentioning her strange accusations. She could sense he was aware that something else was wrong but was giving her the space to tell him rather than pressing for answers. "It's a long hobble to the circle, and it's best to clean the wound first. I know the centre's good for physical damage. But does it treat blood poisoning? Let's not gamble on it." He took out a small sharp knife.

"Whoa there, Surgeon Arpix!" Livira backed away. "What are you planning to do with that?"

Arpix rolled his eyes and started to cut away a section of his robe. "I'd use yours but mine is cleaner. Always." He looked at her bare legs again, critically. "How'd you do it anyhow? You tried climbing those trees, didn't you?"

Livira blinked. It actually was the sort of cut you might get falling out of a tree: any jagged edge or thorn might tear your leg on the way down. "Yes . . ."

"Idiot." He started to clean the skin around the wound. "Did you find Evar?"

Evar is a sabber.

Livira considered lying. She didn't want to talk about this. Not now. Not yet. Not ever really. "No. Someone very different."

"Someone else?" Arpix poured half his water slowly over her leg, making her gasp.

Livira nodded and deflected him by describing the crowd of assistants she'd seen outside the wolf's head entrance. Arpix carried on with his work, cutting her off before she could describe the strange pools and the small footprints.

"That's the best I can do. Come on. Let's see if you can stand."

Livira started to get to her feet. "Of course I can stand— Oh! Shit on a stick, that hurts!" She welcomed the pain. *Think about the pain.*

Arpix took her arm. "Lean on me."

Livira did as she was told, easing painfully into a standing position. Was Clovis's ghost watching all this? Revelling in Livira's discomfort, cursing that she'd not been able to inflict more grievous wounds. Fatal ones.

She was doing it already. Thinking about them again. About him. She tried an escape into facts and book learning. "You know what the sabbers call us?"

"No." Arpix gave her a puzzled look, waiting for more.

"The same thing we call them. 'Sabber'—it just means 'enemy.'"

"That's . . . interesting." Arpix positioned her arm around his shoulders and took her weight.

"If you translated a sabber book into our tongue, we'd be the sabbers."

"There are sabber books?" He looked doubtful.

"The sabbers held the city centuries ago. They ran it for years. Decades . . . I don't know. A human army burned them out. Evar saw it."

Arpix looked astonished but didn't contradict her. Instead, he waited.

Livira shook her head. Her throat had grown tight, and tears prickled in her eyes. She didn't want to think about it anymore.

Arpix broke the silence. "Where are your shoes?"

Livira noticed that she was barefoot. Her shoes were still in the Exchange, lying in the grass beside the pool that Evar had visited. Leaning heavily on Arpix, she hobbled around to look back at the portal, noticing that its light had dimmed, as if the power of the blood used to draw it were fading with time, or their transits had consumed some of the vitality that maintained the doorway.

Evar is a—

Livira refused the thought, seeking more distraction to replace it. "What's that lot?" She nodded towards a stack of books just before the gateway. About as many as a man could carry without risk of dropping them.

"Arimistes's *Thesis on Library Time*, Dorgon's *Lost Chambers*, Lady Wentwood's *Memoriam*—"

"What?" Livira swung her head towards Arpix, their noses almost touching. He'd named two of the books at the top of her search list along with one from the top of his own.

"It works!" Arpix grinned. "You can name any book you want, and an assistant will leave it by one of the portals. Ethwin Dorgon's book came from a portal off our world line. It smells a little strange . . ."

It had been on Livira's mind for an age that she might be able to get the books she couldn't find in the library by using the Exchange, just as she'd got hold of *Reflections on Solitude* half a lifetime ago. But both her visits since that first time had been too filled with danger and intrigue to get around to such experimentation. Both had been cut short in dire circumstances too. Arpix, however, had clearly been drawn to a time of peace, one in keeping with his nature, and had come back with a pile of wonders.

"I'll have to leave them behind, of course." Arpix steered her from the books. "We'd be hard pressed to carry them between us even if we were both uninjured."

"Wait! No! I can walk." Livira put her weight on her bad leg and tried to stifle her groan of pain.

"Enough of that." Arpix started to walk her away. "Nobody's going to find them here."

It was true that they'd drawn the portal on a piece of wall at the end of a long aisle of poorly regarded fiction, inaccessible from either side without a ladder. The records suggested that nobody had taken a book off any of the aisle's many shelves since they were catalogued over seventy years previously. In any case, if someone discovered the books then they'd already have uncovered a much greater prize—the portal itself.

As Livira limped towards the centre circle, the distraction provided by Arpix's return and the books he'd brought with him—books that had been the focus of her searching for years—began to fail. Even the pain in her leg proved insufficient to anchor her thoughts in the here and now. Images of Evar began to intrude. They'd shared their hatred of sabbers. But they'd been speaking different languages and the Exchange had translated for them. In the end "sabber" was just another word for "enemy" and the hatred they'd shared had been for each other.

Arpix gently tried to ask her what had happened, but after several deflections the hints of anger and heartache in her voice had cautioned him to patience. They walked on through a silence broken only by the gasps that escaped Livira when she put too much weight on her injured leg.

When she finally spoke, it was without prompting. Her heart was too full to carry. Either she had to tell Arpix—tell someone—or some part of her would burst.

"Evar's a sabber."

"An enemy?" Arpix asked.

"An actual sabber. A murdering dog-soldier."

"Livira." A hint of chiding in his voice. "How is that even possible?"

"The Exchange translates. It colours its world in with what we know or want. Something like that. I'm not sure. He pulled me from the pool, and I saw a friend. He saw someone he wanted to help. I saw him as human; he saw me as a sabber. He told me humans killed his people—I heard sabbers did it. I told him sabbers killed mine—he heard that humans did it. We were tricked."

Arpix squeezed her wrist where he held it over his shoulder. "I'm sorry."

They walked on. A hot tear rolled down Livira's cheek. Another followed. Her thoughts were still in turmoil. "Conflicting emotions" was too tame a description—it was open warfare. The shards of pain shooting up from her torn flesh helped to puncture any warm thought or excuse as it formed. Evar had tricked her. It didn't matter if it wasn't his fault. She'd kissed a sabber. She wanted to spit. To vomit. Her skin recalled the bristles that she couldn't see and the image of that sabber striding into the settlement returned again and again, his declaration of ownership, the words barked from his bristling muzzle, the chaos that had followed. Aunt Teela lost in the dust. Killed then and there or perhaps taken to be eaten later.

Livira navigated the way to the circle. The area that nourished and healed wasn't large and the circles were easy to miss if you didn't know the layout of the aisles. She collapsed into the aura with a sigh of relief, her pain, at least the physical component, immediately becoming more distant. The gash in her leg was recent enough to respond to the circle's power. Several texts speculated that the healing was connected with manipulation of time, a reversal of recent trauma. It fit with Livira's experience. Her broken bones had been swiftly repaired when the assistant brought her to the circle the time she fell from a shelf top. But when her lungs had been scarred by the alchemists' poisons, they had not recovered any more swiftly in the circle than outside it—the damage had been done too long ago by the time she arrived.

Livira set her back to the curved shelves forming the circle's perimeter. She sat watching the torn skin reknit, healing her leg in the opposite direction to which the sabber's claw had cut. She wished that what had happened could similarly be repaired: that the time could be reversed, the harm and heartache undone. But how far back would she have to go? Back past Clovis's attack in the Exchange. Back past that kiss. Back to the moment Evar had pulled her through into the woods, hauling her from the pool. If he'd truly seen her then, what would he have done? Snapped her neck in an instant? But at that point he'd never laid eyes on a human. He'd only heard Clovis's tales. Would he have even known her for what she was? Would he have understood her terror? Or her rage?

Out of habit or duty, or perhaps as another form of healing, she reached for a nearby book, rested it across her knees, and opened it to the flyleaf. Arpix looked on, puzzled, as she withdrew quill and ink from various pockets.

"Livira!" he gasped as she began to fill the blank page with words. "What are you *doing*?"

Since the answer was obvious, Livira ignored the question and continued to write. The scattered pages she'd left isolated in books throughout the labyrinth constituted her own opus in progress. Currently it ranged through scattered—though aligned—short stories, works of fiction but strongly centred on her life and experiences. The people in her life were imported to fill various roles most suited to their true personas.

In all the work so far, nobody but Evar commanded anything like the number of lines Livira did. She'd chased him through the chapters, trying to tease out who he was from the kernel of their handful of encounters. And it seemed that her aim had been very wide of the mark.

Livira shared a dozen adventures with Evar on those pages: might-have-beens, could-have-beens, should-have-beens; places she had wanted to explore with him; things she had wanted to do. Her hand shook and the quill left a glistening blob of ink on the page, ready to run.

Those stories seemed foolish now. He was a sabber. A fucking sabber. How could she look at him and not see his kin walking into her settlement? How could she touch him and not feel that rope which had dragged her from the ruin of her home? She would have to tear those pages out. Rewrite them. Though even as she imagined ripping free those pages and destroying them, she felt an echo of the pain such an act would inflict on her. The tearing of her own skin.

Livira wrote on, her script flowing across the page, a tremble here and there as she painted a new Evar, savage and strange, a killer in disguise. It distracted from the peculiar ache of healing flesh. Overwriting it with something sharper.

And Arpix, reading not the words but what was written on her face, stayed silent, standing guard.

"There, good as new." Livira stamped her foot to prove the point. A faint silvery scar recorded the injury, but the pain had gone.

"Explain it to me again?" Arpix asked, his face serious, perhaps genuinely confused, perhaps knowing that repetition would blunt the edge that had cut her and draw the poison from the wound. "How could Evar be a sabber and you not know it? They say you can tell at a hundred paces."

"One time." Livira nodded and drew a deep breath. "Evar and I understood early on that the Exchange looked different to each of us. He saw pools and short trees and no birds. I saw doorways, giant tapwoods, and ravens. We understood the Exchange was using things we knew to paint variations on the same thing. We didn't question that we were speaking the same language, but we should have. I doubt we were using the same tongue. We didn't question whether the Exchange was only changing how we saw *it*. We should have. It changed how we saw each other. It showed us what we expected. He expected to see someone like him, so he saw me as a sabber. I expected to see someone like me, so I saw a human. We met in the act of helping or saving the other. We expected a friend.

"His sister, Clovis, is clearly more suspicious, looking for trouble. She expected or hoped to find someone to fight. So, the Exchange showed her the real me."

"And when you left the Exchange together?" Arpix asked.

"We were both ghosts; we carried the illusions and the translation with us. I don't know if we really left the Exchange or if it shows us the past like the Mechanism shows the inside of a book."

"So, two angry sabbers could be standing right next to us now? Listening to every word we're saying?" Arpix's eyes flitted left then right.

Livira sighed heavily. "They could."

"Let's get back." Arpix shivered. "And hope they get bored and go away." He started off in the direction of the exit.

"Wait. The books are that way." Livira pointed towards the portal, a mile or so away in almost the opposite direction.

Arpix looked reluctant. "They're safer out here than in our quarters. We can read them by the portal."

Livira gave a slow nod. He had a point. Any other time she would have demanded to stay and start reading right now, but for once in her life the questions she wanted answers for could wait. Repetition hadn't helped. She felt too heavy and sad to read, too broken, too full of sharp edges. Company, even Arpix's, would grate. She wanted her room and darkness and nothing else.

Cain begat Enoch, and Enoch begat Jaspeth and Irad. And Jaspeth, who had his whole life long walked on eggshells around the shame of his grandfather's invention—fratricide—agreed with Irad at an early age that neither would kill the other.

Murder in the Family: A Novel in Six Parts, *by Captain Noah*

CHAPTER 50

Evar

Clovis vanished into the pool, snatching at Livira's trailing leg. Both disappeared without a splash. Evar stumbled after them, trying to shake the daze from a head still echoing with the force of Clovis's blows. He fell into the water and let it take him.

"Clovis! No!"

Evar threw himself at his sister, hauling her off Livira. To his surprise, Clovis let herself be pulled clear. They ended on their backsides, Clovis between Evar's legs, her back to his chest, Evar's arms under hers, his head lowered against the inevitable backwards head-butt.

Clovis, breathing deeply, made no effort to break free. "Why can't I touch her?"

"It looks like you already did," Evar panted.

Livira lay on her back not far from them, both hands over her face. A crimson trail led from the portal to her legs. A fair amount, but not enough blood for a serious wound.

"She'd be dead if I could." The coldness in Clovis's voice belied the intimacy of their position.

Evar slowly released his sister and edged away, tensed for more violence. His face hurt. His mouth especially. The rest of him would probably hurt tomorrow. Clovis wasn't gentle on her best days, and this was not one of those.

He stared at Livira wonderingly. He'd always felt her to be small but this? She was so slight. Clovis could break her in two hands. And yet what he'd seen in her from the very first moment was still there. Even with her face hidden.

A human . . . She didn't look dangerous, but with a weapon in her hand, especially a projectile weapon, her kind could be deadly. In sufficient numbers, even armed with nothing but simple blades, a pack of humans could overrun a city of his people. He had seen it happen. The stink of it had yet to leave his nostrils. The screams still rang in his ears.

And yet . . .

And yet, as Clovis got to her feet Evar rose too, ready to defend the girl.

"Why can't I kill her?" Clovis's fierce eyes pinned him. Not: *Why won't you let me kill her?* She knew she could sweep him from her path. Just: *Why can't I kill her?*

Even so, Evar stood between them. "You can't kill her because she's already dead. You can't kill her because she died centuries before you were born. We're ghosts here. We can't touch anything except each other."

"I made her bleed." Clovis tracked the blood trail from the portal.

Evar shrugged. "It's different in the Exchange. I think . . ."

Behind him Livira let out a scream that made both of them flinch and had Evar spinning around, thinking she must have been attacked.

For a moment Livira remained arched on her back, lifted by the force of the scream. Slowly, she collapsed back to the floor. Evar stood above her, watching, his breath suddenly short, huffed in and out of a chest painfully constricted by unaccustomed emotion. The sort of emotion that rarely entered life in the library and which he'd run from in the massacre and the invasion that he'd been made to witness. He couldn't turn away from this, though. Not from Livira. He fell to his knees beside her.

"Stop!" Clovis commanded him.

Evar shook his head. "I won't."

Livira uncovered her face, eyes screwed shut. Somehow it was the face he'd seen before: the woman sleeping in the grass; the shoeless girl he'd fought the Escapes to protect; the annoying child he'd pulled from the pool. It was the same but different. The beauty that had trapped his eyes before was there but changed. He would never have seen it without the gift the Exchange had given him—the Exchange had fooled his eyes and in doing so had let him understand a new thing, to see beauty where he would have missed it before.

Evar set his hand over Livira's, not touching, but overlapping. The chaos that filled her rocked him back, muscles stiffening, heart accelerating. His arm tried to pull away as though Livira were a fire, but Evar wouldn't allow himself that escape. This was why Clovis let herself be pulled off her. Why she hadn't tried to return.

"What are you doing?" Clovis strode up behind him.

Evar ground his teeth against the pain but still he wouldn't take his hand from Livira's. He was the cause of her hurt. He couldn't take her suffering away but at least he could share it, and maybe there might be some ease for her in that.

Clovis sent him sprawling with a kick to the shoulder. "What's this animal to you? You fought me. Me! To protect . . . this?" She gestured in contempt at the girl by her feet. "This sabber!"

"They're not all evil." Evar stood, rubbing his arm. As he spoke the words, though, he realised that he'd seen hundreds, thousands of sabbers across a span of centuries, and out of all of them only Livira hadn't been murdering his people.

Clovis's hot denial was interrupted as a second sabber appeared, a human as they called themselves according to the books. A taller one, though still short, a male burdened with the stack of books in its arms. It put the pile down carefully, oblivious to Clovis's knife passing through its skull. Finally, seeing Livira as it straightened, the male uttered a cry of distress, one that included Livira's name, and flung itself to its knees beside her. Livira sat up with apparent joy at seeing the newcomer, who in turn seemed more concerned with her injury than what she had to say.

"Arpix," Evar muttered. The lost friend.

"We need to regroup." Clovis jabbed her second knife into Arpix's head with no effect. "You've been bewitched in some manner."

Evar looked at the two humans, Livira's confusions still burning through him. Was it possible that some power of the library had been exerted on him? The Exchange had reached into his mind and taken things from it. Had it put things there too? Livira's feelings ran through him—they felt real and true—but once some liberty had been taken with your perception how were you to trust anything at all?

He spoke slowly, the words unwilling. "Maybe we do need to regroup . . ."

Clovis took his arm and turned him towards the portal. He saw portals now—his ideas infected with Livira's. His sister walked him towards the light. His sister. He'd seen her parents and brothers murdered by sabbers, Livira's kind. His sister who he'd grown with, who had taught him how to fight, a skill that had saved his life. He let himself be led.

"Wait." Evar turned just before the portal. The young human, Arpix, was washing Livira's cut.

"We'll find a way," Clovis said. "We'll come here and destroy them in their lair. Or lure them to us. But later, when we understand the battle-ground. Now we go."

"Wait." Livira's face, twisted in pain, held Evar's gaze. She'd been a child, then a day later a woman. If he left now, he might never see her again. Or, as she'd said, she might be grey and old, hobbled by the years. His mouth remembered her kiss. He felt her hand in his. She had taught him to fly. "Wait!"

But with one fierce push Clovis had him falling into another world.

The art of skipping stones across a lake entails the alignment of many factors: the stillness of the water, the smoothness and symmetry of the stone, the suppleness of the wrist, and the rotation imparted to the projectile at the moment of its release. What is uniformly overlooked by the amateur, however, is the selection of the places where stone touches water. Place your steps wisely in all things. Time especially.

A Mill Pond, *by John Constable*

CHAPTER 51

Livira

He was looking at me!"

Livira woke with a start, the darkness around her complete and unbroken. She reached out, found the book on the bedside table by touch and closed it. The library's light flooded in. Sliding naked into her robe, she hurried from her bedroom, through the reception chamber and out through her front door into the corridor beyond. Her leg felt good. The physical pain had gone. The centre circle had repaired her flesh. Heartache, it could do nothing for.

"Arpix!" His door lay four down from hers on the opposite side. Tubberly had been the previous occupant of the rooms. "Arpix!" The wood reverberated under her fist.

"Livira?" Arpix opened the door in an unbuttoned nightshirt, blinking at her sleepily from his considerable height.

"How is that a question?" She pushed past him. "Close the door."

Arpix followed her into his reception room where she'd already thrown herself down onto his threadbare couch. "All right. Allow me to rephrase: what do you want, Livira?"

"That boy was looking at me!"

"What boy?"

"How could he see me? I was a ghost. Nobody could see us."

Arpix rubbed his eyes and yawned. He blinked again and adjusted his nightshirt.

"Well?" Livira asked.

"I assume you're talking about the pale boy you mentioned seeing in the past iteration of Crath City?"

"Duh."

"Where everyone was dead?"

"Yes."

"So, how did you know they couldn't see you?"

Livira frowned. "Evar said nobody saw him when he went to the city years before that one. And in his sister's past too."

"Maybe this was different?" Arpix suggested.

"We were ghosts. I flew. I walked through walls!"

"And the boy definitely saw you?"

Livira gave Arpix a hard stare. "He was looking right at me."

"Or right down the street?"

Livira bounced up out of the couch. "I don't know why I came here."

Arpix's expression said that he also didn't know, but he kept his lips pressed firmly together.

Livira pulled her robes tight and stalked towards the door.

"You told me that Evar said the assistants could see him when he was a ghost." Arpix said it to her back.

She turned towards him. "I did."

"And that two sets of children's footprints led from pools of assistant blood right in front of where hundreds of them were watching over the city."

"I said that too." Livira nodded. "What does it mean?"

"I have no idea," Arpix said.

"Me neither." Livira went back to her bed.

LIVIRA WOKE EARLY the next morning, having been chased through the night by troubling dreams. She felt that she should have dreamed of Evar and wondered what it meant that she hadn't.

Deputy Synoth had requested her presence in a note delivered during her absence the previous day, doubtless to do further work on his tedious reorganisation of the structural mechanics catalogues. Livira had other plans. Ignoring her duties, breakfast, and the fact that she still needed to somehow secretly return the book she'd stolen from the head librarian, Livira headed for the exit.

In the chilly morning light Livira stood amid the ruin of the wolf's head gate. Some sabber god, she imagined. She could see hints of its form in the larger chunks of rock that still scattered the slopes. She stood for some while, pondering.

"You all right, Livira?" Jash Shuh left his post to approach her, his bushy moustache that had so amused her as a child now tinged with grey. He watched her questioningly from the shadows of his owl helm. The library guards' helms had struck her as funny as a child too. Many things had.

"Things are so easy to see once you've been shown them," Livira said.

"I guess so." The man nodded thoughtfully.

"You can look forever and not find what you're hunting. See something every day and not really see it. And then . . ."

"Isn't that what the library does for us?" Jash asked. "Shows us things so we can see them? Reminds us what we've forgotten?"

Livira nodded and managed a smile, though she felt like crying. "I must be going, Mr. Shuh."

She turned and though she'd set her back to the greatest repository of wisdom and knowledge in creation she felt certain that the answers she needed lay before her. She walked down the path, drawing her robes tight against a slim-fingered wind that carried autumn's touch and a scent of smoke.

It seemed that the path she trod had last been beneath her feet four hundred years ago, and only yesterday. Soon enough she found herself walking between tall houses where she and Evar had seen only bare rock. She climbed the steps to Yute's front door and knocked.

"Livira!" Salamonda opened the door, ladle in hand as if ready to defend her kitchen. "No young man today?"

"Only ghosts, Salamonda."

Salamonda stepped aside and waved her in. "You look as if someone's broken your heart, young lady."

"I think it's just bruised." Livira breathed in the rich aromas of Salamonda's cooking.

Salamonda looked around, distracted despite Livira's news, as if she'd lost something. "A whole turkey gone? A ham yesterday. I swear this kitchen is haunted!"

"Is Yute in?" Livira glanced at the stairs. Wentworth occupied the entirety of the fifth step, spilling onto the fourth, and reaching out with both left legs to the third step to support himself. He appeared to be fast asleep.

"That cat!" Salamonda shook her head and closed the front door. "Yute says they sleep on mountain slopes just the way he's doing there."

"How do you get upstairs?"

"I wait." Salamonda shook her head again. "Or bribe him with a treat. And no, Yute went to the walls very early. He said he wouldn't be gone long."

"The walls?"

"There's a new army come from the west. Sabbers. It's going to be bad this time. Everyone's saying it, but that's not what matters. Yute's saying it too, this time. Wanted to send me to my daughter's in Gunderland."

"Gunderland! That's . . . hundreds of miles. Practically Sambara."

"On the border." Salamonda nodded. "She married a Grekkar oil merchant. I told Yute I'd rather kiss a sabber than spend a night under that man's roof."

Salamonda went on with the cooking, talking endlessly of the many crimes her son-in-law was guilty of, and the general feckless nature of Grekkar men, as if the army on Crath's doorstep was on a par with a change in the weather. She plied Livira with food as she cooked and gossiped, everything from butter biscuits, to buckwheat pancakes laden with spiced tomato paste, to cups of steaming chai sweetened with honey. Livira, who had arrived with no appetite whatsoever, felt as if she were bursting at the seams by the time Yute walked in furling his umbrella.

"Livira." Yute put his sunshade into the rack by the door. "Good to see you again."

"Master Yute." Livira inclined her head. *Good to see you again*. It had been more than a year and the man had breezed in as if they'd met yesterday.

"Let's go upstairs." Yute crossed the room and hauled Wentworth aside. The huge cat eyed him grumpily but let itself be manhandled. "Salamonda, I need you here at the house today. Don't go to the markets."

"But I need parawort, and more cabbage, and Hallamar should be in with the spices from Gondrore by now."

Yute stopped, turned, and went to Salamonda, taking both her meaty pink hands in his narrow white ones. "My dear Salamonda, I would never presume that paying your salary gives me dominion over your time, but for the love that your mother bore me, obey me in this one thing, this one time." He released her and returned to the stairs, following Wentworth's huffy retreat towards the heights.

"He knew your mother?" Livira hissed as she made to follow Yute.

Salamonda, looking pale, dabbed her eyes with her apron. "Took her from the streets and raised her himself." She waved Livira off. "Go. Go! He's been waiting to talk to you."

Livira blinked and hurried after Yute. She'd been sure Salamonda was the older of the pair by a good ten years.

"WHAT DID YOU see at the walls?" Livira asked her question as she entered Yute's dimly lit study, ignoring his nod towards the chair opposite his.

"Nothing I've not seen before." Yute peered at her over his steepled fingers.

"How large is their army?"

"Too big."

Livira shuddered, a chill running through her. She realised that she was scared. Even so, she had her questions. If a sabber were to take her life before nightfall she'd rather die with answers than with questions.

"That day on the Allocation Hall steps," she said. "Was that the first time you saw me?"

"Sit. Please." Yute indicated the chair again, a fine piece covered with dark red leather, deeply buttoned. "You make me nervous with your pacing."

Livira perched in the chair, too tense to settle. "Had you seen me before?"

Instead of answering, Yute removed the silver ring he always wore, his only piece of jewellery. He placed one white finger to the moonstone set into the metal. "Did you know that all the books in all the chambers of the library could be stored in something as small as this stone?"

"That's not possible." Livira had walked a thousand miles in the library. She had passed a weight of books that if sufficient scales could be found would outbalance all the stones in all the buildings in Crath City.

"It's possible." Yute moved his fingertip across the moonstone in a circle and it lit from within. Pages of text appeared across the walls and ceiling, projected there, written by light, one moving over the next as if the pages had been torn loose and scattered across the surface of a pond.

"If that were true then why . . . I don't understand." She hadn't come to ask these questions, but she couldn't help letting Yute distract her from her purpose. "Why have the library?"

"Everything." Yute pressed his hand to his desk, hard. "*Everything* is a compromise. There are no absolutes in life. There is only one absolute, and it lies beyond us." He frowned. "You're familiar with the story of Irad?"

"The first librarian?" Livira had read the story in a book that she was not allowed to read. A book that had been hidden deliberately. "You're not going to tell me that it's true? I'd sooner believe your ring held all the library rather than just a few pages."

Yute offered a wry smile. "Not true, no. Let's say . . . representative. Useful. Irad the first librarian, son of Enoch the first builder of cities, son of Cain the first murderer, son of Adam the first man. None of Adam's descendants were their parents' only child, and all of them were in conflict. It's a defining feature of mankind. Sibling against sibling."

"Not just humans." Livira thought of Clovis pounding her brother's head into the ground in the sabber's attempt to reach her.

"Not just humans." Yute inclined his head. "Cain opposed his brother continuing to live. Enoch's brother opposed his building a city. Irad's brother fought the idea of a library. In that particular mythology the first man and first woman fell from grace by seeking knowledge. Ignorance was their bliss. A devil tempted them into knowledge.

"The first librarian, founder of the great library, had a younger brother, Jaspeth. Jaspeth felt that since their great-grandparents had lost the gods' good graces by foolishly seeking knowledge, it was hardly a good idea that just three generations later Irad was building a great palace to knowledge where all could come and partake of it. Knowledge, he said, was not wisdom. Irad, he said, was continuing the work that the devil had started. They went to war over it. Though neither of them ended up killing their own brother like their grandfather had. Instead, they formed an uneasy peace. A compromise. The library is that compromise. The knowledge—all knowledge—is there for the taking, waiting on a shelf, ready to be picked up. But it must be found. It cannot be summoned effortlessly from a ring and projected onto a wall. Not unless someone puts in the necessary work and cleverness, and then only for as long as that cleverness is preserved. All that knowledge lies there, as agreed, locked behind the letters of ever-changing alphabets in the words of ever-changing languages. It sits there among the lies, mistakes, delusions, and untruths of the unwise. It is, to make a long story shorter, never easy."

"But none of that's true?" Livira's eyes followed the fading traces of the ring's projections.

"All of it is representative of a truth. Truths cast many shadows, some of which are very different when the light shines from one direction than from another. The library is a compromise—that's truth. The library is a battleground. That's also a kind of truth.

"The library is many things from many angles. Both blessing and curse. A razor blade given to a baby; a rope thrown to a drowning man."

Livira raised her hand to stop him. "Enough. Enough with the library. Enough with all the mysteries." Livira knew she was a plain speaker, blunt some might say, rude even, but she'd shocked herself talking to Yute like that. The words had just burst out of her. She'd seen too much. Done too much. Risked too much. Lost too much. "Why," she ploughed on, "why does the head librarian look like you?"

"Like me?" Yute frowned.

"You know what I mean."

Yute gave a slight shrug, a slight smile. "We share a common origin. We were born in the same place."

"Was it far from here?"

"In a manner of speaking. It depends how you measure distance." Yute's pink eyes met Livira's gaze. "Did she look well? I expected you to have news, but I don't think anything else you might have to say could surprise me more than Yamala agreeing to see you."

"I kissed a sabber."

"I stand corrected."

A little knowledge can be a dangerous thing. This old truism becomes more interesting when one considers how it scales. Is a lot of knowledge a very, very dangerous thing? In Figure 46, knowledge is plotted along the X-axis, and danger along the Y-axis. It's immediately obvious from the resulting curve that . . .

Charting the Ephemeral, *by Dr. J. Evans Pilchard, PhD*

CHAPTER 52

Evar

H e *kissed* a sabber?"

Clovis stormed back towards Evar, only the Soldier's intervention stopping her from adding to his already impressive collection of incipient bruises.

"They were intimate. It's written all over him," Kerrol said, tilting his head as if Evar were a page of a book.

"Evar, you dog!" Starval seemed impressed.

"Why would you do that?" Clovis raged. "After all I've told you!"

Clovis had hauled him back through the Exchange and into their pool. They'd emerged to an audience. Evar didn't yet know how Clovis had worked out where he'd gone but, clearly, she'd summoned everyone to watch her attempt to follow him. The Assistant had said nothing yet. The Soldier had only prevented Clovis from beating Evar with her fists and feet and done nothing to protect him from the accusations she delivered with a sharp tongue.

"You think I'm lying?" Clovis shouted over the Soldier's arms. "You think sabbers didn't kill our people?"

"No," Evar said wearily. "I believe you." He looked around at his siblings: Clovis straining to reach him, Kerrol standing too still with his curious stare that somehow always seemed to be fixed on a point five yards behind Evar's chest, no doubt hurriedly adding factors to the equation that represented his brother. Starval was squatting, holding his favourite knife with his fingertip on its pommel and the library floor beneath its point, and flicking it each time its spinning began to slow. "I believe you. But Livira didn't kill your parents, Clovis, or your brothers." Clovis flinched at that. She'd never mentioned her brothers. "Livira hasn't killed anyone. And our people have killed her family, her friends—"

"That's called justice!" Clovis roared. "I'm glad they're dead!"

"It's called revenge." Starval looked up from his spinning blade. "It's what people do."

"It's an understandable response," Kerrol said, though Evar wasn't sure if he was talking about a specific thing one of his siblings had said or everything they'd said and done.

"You!" Clovis broke away from the Soldier and faced the Assistant as if they'd never met before. "How do we get to these sabbers? I couldn't touch her. She couldn't even see me."

The Assistant's eyes glowed a deeper shade of blue. "Your fixation on these historical figures is illogical. They're long dead and nothing you do can change the facts of their lives."

"He!" Clovis pointed an accusing finger at Evar. "He *kissed* her! Are you saying that didn't change the facts of her life?"

"That was an event in the life she led. Past tense. It occurred centuries ago and has been a matter of historical record since before you were born. It was only possible because of Evar's unsanctioned entering of the Exchange. Something I will ensure does not happen again."

Clovis spun away from the Assistant and began to pace. "We need to lure them back into the wood. Or better still, here, the place their crimes were committed." She glanced back. "What would happen to any of them that came here? We could touch them?"

"You could touch them."

Evar shuddered. He knew what Clovis meant by "touch."

"And if some of them escaped? If they got back to their world?" Clovis asked.

"Their world is your world," the Assistant explained again. "But if they came here, they would be part of now and no more able to affect what has already passed than you or Evar are. It's not possible to change the past. If you visit a time ahead of your current one it becomes your now, and everything before it is your past."

"If they tried to go back, they'd be ghosts there too?" Clovis stared intently.

"They would have the same experience as you."

"But we could touch them there—I got hold of Evar when we were both ghosts." Clovis smacked her fist into her palm. "If they come here, they can't escape me again, wherever they go."

Evar tried to state it as clearly as he could. "If someone leaves the Exchange via a pool that leads to their past then they'll be a ghost in the place and time they visit. And a person's past is any time earlier than the 'most forward' time they've visited. So, if Livira visited this chamber, then every time before now would become the past for her?"

"As you say." The Assistant inclined her head. She walked between Evar and Clovis to kneel beside the pool. A moment later it was nothing but a shallow, dusty depression. "I will reinstate the pool at times when water needs to be drawn from it."

"Evar will try to find a way round you," Clovis said. "We should chain him up."

Starval stood. "You're not chaining anyone up, Clovis."

"He's a traitor. He had a sabber at his mercy and what did he do?"

"He showed mercy." Kerrol strode forward to stand by Starval. "What else would you expect? You've met our brother before, yes?"

"I didn't expect him to defend her from me. Me!" Clovis banged her chest. "I didn't expect him to fucking *kiss* the animal! Give him another chance and he'll be fornicating with it . . ." She spat her disgust on the floor and started to stalk away.

"Clovis!" Evar slipped past his brothers and went after her. "It's not what you think. Livira's—" He didn't even see the punch coming. Or the ground after that.

LIVIRA'S DIFFERENT WAS what he had been going to say. Evar sat alone on the books of the fallen tower that had started all this. He had toppled it without meaning to, and his hands had somehow found the book that he shouldn't have been able to read. He'd been going to say that Livira was different—but was she? Livira hated his kind, wished them dead. Now she probably wished him dead too. How was that different?

The falling tower and the found book had started this. They'd aimed him at his missing love and instead of finding her he had misplaced himself. He'd blinded himself with expectation and had lost his heart to a sabber. A creature very different from himself. Once more he'd failed the author of his book, despite her pressing need, and the guilt tore at him.

Livira's different.

Livira *was* different. Evar pressed the heels of his hands to his temples, trying to squeeze some sense into himself. He couldn't do it. The idiocy remained. He could no more squeeze it out than Clovis could punch it out. Even his diversion to the centre circle had only repaired the hurts Clovis had done to his body. His foolishness remained uncorrected.

Livira's fragile beauty filled his mind. He couldn't leave her the way he'd done. Not running from him. Not torn and bloody and raging.

He would return. He would find a way. Whether it took him or her or both of them to their hundredth year, he would place himself before her one more time and accept her judgement. He would speak his mind if she would let him, hand her the words to wound him with, throw dignity aside if that was what was required to place truth between them. And if her fury remained—if hate was all she had for him—he would let that run its course, offer his heart to her dagger in place of those who had injured her. And at last, if his dramatics went unanswered, he would leave, knowing that he had for once taken his shot.

Evar felt a cold knife at his throat.

"Starval. I guess I don't have to ask how you found me." He pushed his brother's blade away.

Starval sheathed the weapon with an apologetic smile. "Got to keep my hand in. And no, you don't have to ask. You leave a trail a mile wide. Despite all my training. Though to be fair, you and I are the only ones here who could spot it."

"What do you want?" Evar tried to sound angry. He'd wanted to be alone, but as soon as he'd got his wish, he'd wanted someone to talk to rather than just lying on a book heap feeling miserable and enduring the headache Clovis had left him with. She'd been gone by the time the Assistant brought him round. Kerrol had warned of concussion. Evar had warned Kerrol to mind his own fucking business and had woven an unsteady path off into the stacks.

"What do I want?" Starval sat on the book heap and stuck his knife into the book cover between his legs. "I want to get you back to this girl, of course!"

"This sabber . . ." Evar hung his head.

"Don't be an idiot. My brother Evar wouldn't be kissing a girl if she wasn't worth kissing. Have you met yourself?"

"You haven't seen what I've seen, Star." Evar kept his eyes on the forest of stacks rising above them, his mind full of the trees he'd seen in the Exchange. He ached for the peace of the place. "I saw them slaughter Clovis's father, her little brothers, her mother. Hundreds of people cut down for no reason. I saw Clovis before the Mechanism took her. She wasn't meant to be this way." He rubbed his aching jaw. "They broke something inside her."

"But—"

"This library is vast. Dozens of chambers, hundreds maybe. Perhaps more. And there's a city outside it. I saw that city full of our people. So many they would fill this chamber, elbow to elbow. And I saw the sabbers sweep over their walls, murder them in the streets, in their beds, rivers of blood. Livira's kind live in that city in her time. They own the library."

Starval tapped the hilt of his dagger, twisting his lips. "People die, brother. That's what I've learned. Life's cheap, easily spent. And if there's any joy to be had it's in the moments between. So, when you find something that makes you happy you take it with both hands, and you hold on to it for as long as you can. It's not going to last. It will be taken from you. But that's not the point. The point is that you took your chance, you drank the wine, you took what good you could from the world, and you gave it yours."

Evar turned to look at his brother. "I'm not sure you're cut out to be a murderer."

Starval shrugged and pulled his dagger free. "I'm good at it though." He threw the weapon, lightning fast, and it sank into the spine of a book in a tower a few yards from where they sat. "You can come out of there, Kerrol. You can't hide for shit."

Kerrol emerged from behind the stack, hands raised in surrender.

"How did *you* know where to find me?" Evar said, exasperated.

"You're very predictable, brother." Kerrol came to join them. He sat on Evar's other side. "Nice spot for sulking."

Evar opened his mouth to say he wasn't sulking but didn't let the lie off his tongue. Instead, he asked, "Why are you here?"

"Same reason as Starval, obviously." Kerrol raised his eyebrows. "Did I teach you nothing?"

"You want to help me get back to Livira as well?"

Kerrol snorted. "I want to get out of here."

Evar stared from one to the other. "I don't understand." He waved at the surrounding chamber. "This is my life. But you two have the Mechanism. You wander different worlds every day."

"One day in three," Starval said.

"One day in four until Mayland vanished," Kerrol added.

"The thing about the Mechanism," Starval said, "is that nothing matters once you leave. No consequences outlast the day. Nothing you do has the least impact on the next world from the next book. This place, however"—he thumped the heaped books—"and the places you can go from this Exchange of yours. They're real. They keep score. They matter."

"I've spent my life learning to study people," Kerrol said. "And all I've got to work with are you three, and an endless supply of authors hiding on the other side of their pages. What you described, Evar . . . observing a multitude of real people. Unseen, with no barriers. It's incredible. The things I'd learn!"

Starval rolled his eyes. "Choose the right pool and we can reach real people. Ones we can touch and talk to. You think you could handle real people who talk back, Kerrol? Better be careful—if there are whole cities full of them you might find one you like!"

"It's agreed then. We . . ." Kerrol trailed off as Evar first raised his hand for silence, then used it to point towards the figure approaching through the book towers.

"Clovis. Let's hear it." Evar sighed. "How did *you* find me?"

"It's where you found that damn book." She strode to the heap that she'd been buried in when the great tower fell. "So, it's decided then? We're going to the Exchange?"

Evar got to his feet. "I'm not letting you back there. You just want to wage war!"

Clovis shrugged. "It doesn't matter that we all want different things. What matters is that none of us can have those things unless we find a way back to that forest. And there are two obstacles in our way. The Soldier and the Assistant."

. . . certainly no fornication! The essence of a library is that new freedom of thought is balanced by new restrictions on behaviour. Voices must be kept low, food is not allowed, running in the aisles is forbidden. And, though it saddens me to have to repeat myself in this matter, certainly no . . .

Library Etiquette: Volume 6, *by Mrs. Emalli Post*

CHAPTER 53

Livira

A nd I thought you disapproved of my ambition for peace between your peoples," Yute said.

"I didn't know he was a sabber when I kissed him." Livira scowled.

"Whilst the similarities outnumber the differences, I would still think it a difficult mistake to make." Yute reached down beside his chair and lifted a large carpetbag onto his lap. "Excuse me while I gather a few things." He reached for his telescope and, having stowed it in the bag, leaned over to pull three books from the nearest shelf.

"Why are you . . . Wait! 'Your peoples'? You said '*Your* peoples.'"

"I did?" Yute frowned and slid the astrolabe from his desk into the bag along with an onyx paperweight in the shape of a portly owl. "A slip of the tongue?"

Livira stood sharply from her chair. "How old are you?"

"A lady doesn't ask, and a gentleman doesn't tell." Yute stood too and began to move around the room putting the occasional oddity into his bag, white fingers hovering over others before reluctantly moving on.

"Damn it, Yute—that was you, wasn't it?"

Yute looked up from his packing. "Without more context the best I can do is 'maybe.'"

"Watching me and Evar in the street?"

Yute put a small dark-wood statuette into the bag then distractedly took it out again. "Maybe."

"When did you—" Livira broke off her question and turned slowly towards the window that overlooked the city. "What's that popping sound?"

"Arrow-sticks, I imagine." Yute came to join her. "The latest ones are very loud close to."

Small puffs of smoke were going up all along the wall accompanied by so many popping noises that it became more of a continuous crackle, rising to a crescendo. Livira had never heard a sound reach the mountain slopes from the walls before. Softened by the considerable distance, the din had been robbed of violence and but for the view from Yute's window she might imagine it to be the pyrotechnics accompanying a celebration.

Livira had more questions but a new series of bangs much closer at hand cut her off. "Someone's hammering on the door!"

"We should go down and see who." Yute bustled past her, burdened by his overfull bag.

"Here, let me." Livira reached out and took it from him. They were of similar height now, but she had a broader frame and young muscles.

Yute made no complaint. He paused on the stairs for a long moment, looking up towards his daughter's room. Then, with a sigh, he led the way down, passing each storey with a lingering glance through the door.

"You're not coming back, are you?" Livira felt suddenly sad, her fear deepening.

"We can never go back. Time doesn't work that way. Not once you've stepped into the current." Yute paused just above the kitchen where people were talking in raised voices. "One of the earliest philosophers told us you can't step into the same river twice. The library taught me you can't read the same book twice either—you're the river." He set a hand to the wall. "This house will always be a part of me, however far I go and whatever ruin comes to it."

"Yute!" Salamonda poked her head through the doorway and peered up the stairs. "Malar's here, and he's brought company!"

"I'm on my way." Yute descended the remaining steps.

Livira followed him into the kitchen. It proved quite a squeeze. At least a dozen people had joined Salamonda, with more on the steps to the street and beyond.

"Malar!" Livira greeted the soldier. "Neera! Katrin! Acmar!" Everywhere she looked were children from her settlement, now grown into adults. Acmar was even balding in his haste to get old, though she'd never point it out. Little Gevin, who Acmar had carried into the city, was taller than Livira now and sported a neat beard like many of Crath's men. There were children too, clinging to parents' legs. A baby's cries reached in from the street. "What is all this?"

Malar, wearing a pitted iron breastplate, with a 'stick slung over his shoulder and a blade at each hip, pushed his way to Yute's side. "I got everyone who'd come. And a group of Livira's folk to stop her running down the mountain after them."

"We'd best go then," Yute said. "We don't have long."

"Go where?" Salamonda elbowed her way between Acmar and Gevin. "I'm not going anywhere. I've got a meal to prepare, and—"

"Ladies and gentlemen." Yute raised one hand and his voice. "It sorrows me to tell you that the end days are upon us. This city will fall before the sun sets, and any that remain will lose their lives to the invaders. I propose to lead those of you that will follow into the sanctuary of the library. To those who would rather remain outside, my advice is to flee northwest across the Terrent Ridge and aim for Harald Pass, thence into the Wilderland of Ost."

A clamour of voices rose as Yute's hand descended and he fell silent. He ignored them all, taking hold of Salamonda's shoulders and steering her towards the door. Using his housekeeper to part the crowd, Yute won his way to the outside, Livira in his wake.

"Can't we fight?" someone called from behind them.

"The king's army will drive the sabbers back. Everyone says so!"

"We can't just leave!"

Livira found herself on the street steps with Malar. Yute was already marching Salamonda up the road. The crowd that Malar had brought to the librarian's house stood arguing, some clearly torn, others adamant it was all nonsense. Behind the house a loose pall of smoke was drifting across the lower city.

A dreadful thought skewered Livira. "Where's Carlotte?" She wasn't here. You didn't lose someone like her in a crowd. She would have been the first person Livira saw. "You didn't bring Carlotte?"

"Who?" Malar frowned.

"Carlotte!" Livira shouted her name in Malar's face before facing down the road. "I have to go and get her."

Malar took her forearm in an iron grip. The same painful grip Aunt Teela had used the day the sabbers came. "If you go down there you won't save her, you'll just die. No ifs or buts. Thinking anything else will happen is like thrusting your hand into a meat grinder and expecting to save all your fingers."

"I have to go." Livira tried to pull away. "She's house reader for Sir Alad Masefield."

"She's got a decent chance then. You know what rich people are good at? Saving themselves. The Masefields will have an escape plan. And who's going to get this lot to go with Yute if you're not here? It was hard enough to get them to his front door, and that's before they knew they weren't coming back."

Livira saw her predicament, caught between impossible choices. "You can't just expect them to follow!" she shouted at Yute's retreating back. She was talking about herself as much as the rest. Yesterday the city was in danger, yes, but it had been in danger before. It wasn't going to fall, surely. Whatever Malar said. Yesterday—threat; today—disaster? She couldn't believe it herself, not emotionally, so how could she expect her friends, her extended family, to act on one man's word when they'd lived more than half their lives in this place, day after day, worked here, become part of the fabric of the city?

"I can threaten them," Malar offered. "Take the fucking lot of them hostage at sword point."

"You really believe Yute then?" Livira asked Malar. None of it seemed real. "The sabbers are going to be over the walls before dark?"

"They're over the walls now," Malar said. "Haven't you listened to anything I've said? Everyone will be dead before the first moon rises. I've seen these bastards' work up close. It was never a question of whether they could take the city. Not for the last five years anyway. Just whether they were prepared to pay the price. Seems like they were. There'll be sabber corpses in drifts down there." He nodded towards the walls and the Dust beyond. "But they're in now and wanting payback. We should hurry, unless you want to fight them right here."

Neera came to join Livira and Malar, followed by a tear-streaked Katrin.

"Jammus won't come," Katrin sobbed, her beautiful face a mess. "He doesn't believe any of it."

Malar raised an eyebrow. "Think you can talk them round?" Behind him the smoke had taken on darker hues. He looked worried. Livira had never seen him worried.

The recurring image of that sabber strolling into the settlement lit the darkness of her mind with more clarity than at any time since the day it happened. She saw its mismatched stare—one eye widened by the seam of an old scar. It was happening again. Right now. "Shit-on-a-fucking-stick," Livira snarled. Malar raised his eyebrows, possibly impressed. She shoved Yute's bag of treasures at the soldier and pushed past him. "Wait here."

Livira took a deep breath, stalked back to the crowd around the steps, and dived into its midst. Several moments later she tore free clutching a squalling baby. "Run!" she screeched and took to her heels after the distant Yute and Salamonda.

True to Livira's expectations, there was something about a stolen baby that made people act without pause for thought. As one, the people outside Yute's house gave chase, followed by those inside. While she panted up the incline, even strangers emerging from their homes joined the mob at her heels. She overtook Yute and kept going, breath labouring in her lungs, all her concentration focused on not tripping or losing hold of the howling bundle in her arms.

She stopped a few dozen yards short of the library entrance, surprised not to have been caught. Still gasping for breath, she set the raging baby down carefully and stepped away from it, though ready to protect it from the threat of trampling.

"It's there! It's there!" Livira pointed to the baby as the first young man came pounding up to them. Thankfully he seemed to know her and rather than grabbing hold of her he went to stand guard over the infant.

The rest of the pursuit began to arrive, Malar towards the front, looking more angry than exhausted.

"I'm too fucking old for running up mountains." He spat and came to stand beside her in case anyone wanted to make an issue out of the abduction. "Fuck me." The view held his attention.

By the time the distraught mother had snatched up her child and the angry father had advanced on Livira, so many people were staring down at the city that both of them turned that way too. They stood with the others, open-mouthed, their complaints forgotten. From this elevation an understanding could be gained that was absent in the view from Yute's house.

An arc of burning buildings marked the battlefront within the city. More accurately, it marked the sabbers' advance, resembling the spread of a water stain in cloth, or the way a glowing leading edge eats its way into a page where an ember has landed, advancing in all directions, leaving the paper black and brittle behind it, and in that blackness hot orange lines flare, advance, and die as the last fuel is consumed leaving only grey ash to fall away. Already a fifth of the city had fallen.

Livira turned away. In her mind's eye, Yute's house was already aflame, fire licking its way up the creaking staircase, Salamonda's kitchen an inferno.

"Malar . . ." She stepped back and grabbed his shoulder.

"What?"

"They're here already." She pointed to where Jash Shuh lay in the shadows among the chunks of the wolf's head entrance. There was no sign of his owl helm, and his grey hair was dark with blood.

"Well." Yute came up between them, breathless from the climb. "That was to be expected, unfortunately. The library is, after all, the only reason they're here."

"Arpix! Meelan! Jella . . ." Livira started to run for the entrance.

Malar caught her arm a few strides into the main corridor. "And if they're in trouble you're going to save them, are you? You're going to take down a sabber raiding party?"

"I—" That was exactly what Livira had been going to do, but saying it out loud would make it seem foolish. "I'm going to warn them!"

"Let's do that together then," Malar said. "Carefully."

"Very carefully." Yute came up beside them.

"Where's Salamonda?" Livira peered past him. "And the others." She realised that in running to the defence of her library friends she had left Neera, Katrin, and the rest out on the mountainside where more sabbers might be closing on them as they spoke.

"I've told her to keep the others together and to wait for me," Yute said. "They're to come in if the attack reaches the slopes beneath them."

"When," Malar corrected.

"*When* the attack reaches the slopes," Yute agreed.

LIVIRA LED THE way towards the refectory, aiming for the trainee chambers beyond, where Meelan had the foremost room now as the senior trainee. The corridors had been empty, so far. Outside Logaris's abandoned classroom three books lay scattered, one fanning its pages, another separated from its cover. To Heeth Logaris it would be more shocking than spilled blood. Further on, when Livira turned right at the kitchens, Yute carried on.

"Where are you going?"

"To Yamala," Yute said.

"She has the Library Guard!" Livira wasn't worried about the head librarian, she was worried what might happen to Meelan, Arpix, and Jella. She paused, frowning. "Who is she to you, this Yamala?"

Yute blinked as if it was obvious. "She's my wife."

The fact that opposites attract is a scientific truth concerning charge and magnetism. One should not expect to extend the same principle to marital relationships with success. And yet . . .

Strange Bedfellows, *by Alexander Cosy*

———————

CHAPTER 54

Livira

Y ou're married to the head librarian?" Livira stared at Yute. His mysterious influence made more sense now. He had swayed Yamala to appoint her as a librarian in the face of King Oanold's wrath.

"I am. I should go to her."

Livira still didn't want him wandering the complex alone. Nobody stood much chance against a sabber, but Yute had always given her the impression that a stubborn six-year-old could wrestle him to submission. "She'll have the Guard around her. And there's Volente!" The books described him as "red in tooth and claw."

"Volente?" Yute shook his head. "He's a big softy." He turned away. "I'll meet you at the library door. Stay safe."

Livira told herself he would be all right. This was his plan, after all. And he knew things. Things she didn't. Even so, she watched him go with a heavy heart, fearing they might not meet again.

MINUTES LATER LIVIRA crashed through Meelan's door and stared around his trainee cell. "He's gone!"

"Let's find the others." Malar had his sword in hand now, eyes on the corridor. In the distance a faint crashing could be heard, as if the kitchen staff were banging their pans together with unusual vigour.

Livira led the way into the service sector. The crashes grew louder with each yard. A body lay at the junction close to the binding halls. The blue robe of a trainee or support staff, black with blood where the back had been shredded. A trainee to judge by their size. Livira glimpsed the victim's face as Malar hustled her past. It was the small woman who had nearly run her book trolley into Yute on the day Livira first arrived. Despite her indelible memory, and the fact she should know it, Livira simply couldn't summon the woman's name to mind. That made it somehow so much worse. Livira hurried on, covering her mouth with one hand.

The crashing grew deafening as Livira approached the final corner. Malar pulled her back and peered round in her place. He held up his left hand, one finger raised.

"One? One sabber?" Livira cried, her question lost in the din.

Without hesitation, Malar slipped into the corridor beyond. Livira replaced him at the corner in time to see that he'd covered most of the distance between him and the second of the binding halls. The door of the first had been staved in and a huge black-maned sabber was hewing at the second door with a sword two yards long that resembled a cleaver. Splinters and shards of wood littered the floor. At least three cracks offered a view into the room beyond, and a whole plank looked ready to come loose with the next blow or two.

Malar should have been able to take it by surprise but somehow the thing was turning before he got there, its oversized weapon hissing in a horizontal arc that would cut the soldier into two roughly equal pieces.

Livira had never understood or been able to follow Malar's quickness. His sword intervened, taking the force of the blow on the flat of the blade, braced at the hilt and with his other hand just below the point. The impact slammed Malar to the side, into the wall, pinning him there behind his weapon. Immediately, Malar slid under the sabber's cleaver, abandoning his sword in the effort. Anyone with the slightest sense would have tried to run at that point, but Malar spun across the floor, drawing a knife and in an exchange too quick to see . . . ended pinned to the floor. The shoulder of Malar's knife-holding arm was trapped under the sabber's foot, on the sabber's leg a shallow cut.

"No!" Livira broke from the corner.

The sabber raised its cleaver. Livira had no time, she was too far away, too slow.

Something jabbed out through one of the cracks in the door, into the sabber's back. It howled, springing away. Malar took the opportunity for a scrambling retreat, grabbing his sword. He gained his feet unsteadily and backed towards Livira.

The sabber, meanwhile, readied itself to finish Malar off, but staggered as it took its first step towards him. Livira and the beast looked down together. Blood was flooding down from a second cut higher than the first, looking no deeper but jetting crimson with every beat of the sabber's heart. In his escape Malar had sliced the creature again, finding the artery his first cut had been seeking.

"Got you that time," Malar growled and drew his second, shorter sword.

The sabber snarled and came on, swinging. Malar leapt forward, throwing himself into the path of his enemy's blade. Livira wasn't sure how the early interception helped but using both swords Malar managed to deflect the sabber's blow into the wall and throw himself back. Livira retreated to give him space.

The sabber came on again, teeth bared, a growl reverberating through it that put Malar's to shame. It looked unsteady, almost slipping in its own blood once, a thick crimson trail behind it. It tried an overhead swing but, perhaps unused to fighting in confined human-sized spaces or losing coordination from blood loss, it struck the ceiling in a shower of rock fragments and sparks.

Malar spun in, slashing at the sabber's face and driving the shorter of his swords up into its chest. The creature collapsed onto him, jaws snapping at his neck. He heaved it to the side. And it lay there, trying to draw breath, the light fading from its eyes.

"Jella!" Livira screamed.

The shattered door jolted, jolted again, and opened with a terrible squeal, large pieces falling away. Jella peered out into the corridor, red-faced and wide-eyed, in her fists a broom handle to which three six-inch needles had been bound, all of them scarlet from when she'd jabbed them into the sabber's back.

"Livira!" Jella threw her broom handle away as if suddenly disgusted by it and rushed to join her friend, half a dozen fellow bookbinders edging out behind her. "They killed Mastri—"

"Mastri, that's her name!" Livira clamped her mouth shut guiltily. In the face of everything that was happening her emotions didn't know what to do, or her mouth what to say. Had she really run up the mountain with a stolen baby?

"There's more dead in the refectory. What's happening?" Jella glanced nervously at the sabber as if noticing it for the first time, though she had just stepped over its legs to reach Livira.

"The sabbers are taking the city. A band of them are here too. I don't know how many. We're meeting the head librarian at the library door."

"The head librarian?" Somehow of all the things Livira had just said this one seemed to impress Jella most. Perhaps, whilst enormous, it still fitted into the parameters of her existence. "I've never even seen her!"

"Well, you will soon. Come on. We're looking for Meelan and Arpix."

WITH JELLA AND six of her colleagues in tow, Livira led the way to the librarians' quarters. She hoped to find Yute still there with the main strength of the Library Guard. Instead, she found the hallway a slaughterhouse. Library guards lay scattered, literally. Arms and heads torn from torsos as often as not, perhaps as few as six dead or maybe as many as a dozen, it was hard to tell. A single sabber corpse sprawled amid the carnage.

Livira turned to prevent Jella from seeing but found herself too late. She pushed her friend back. "Don't let the others past."

Malar went ahead, stepping around the corpses and bits of corpses. All the doors had been staved in—Livira's too. Deputy Ellis lay half out of his doorway, looking smaller and older in death than he had in life, staring in sightless astonishment at the ceiling. Livira's mind refused to make sense of the scene. Her eyes settled on Arpix's broken door and the owl-eyed helm lying on its side amid the splintered planks. It couldn't mean what it meant.

"Arpix!" Livira screamed his name, careless of how many sabbers it might call back to complete their work. "Arpix . . ." The name came out broken the second time.

No reply. No response. Nothing. Livira found she lacked the courage to go in. At her side Jella began to weep.

"What's that noise?" Malar spun around, swords raised. He didn't mean Jella or the shocked whispers behind her. The deep rumbling had been there the whole time, but they'd only noticed it as it grew louder. Loud or not, it admitted no direction, seeming to come from everywhere. Malar cocked his head. "I don't like it . . ."

Livira didn't care about any noise. Jella pushed past her, her face drained of the colour it had held back in the binding hall. She stumbled, grief-stricken, towards Arpix's door. Unable to let her face it alone, Livira followed her through into Arpix's quarters, glancing at the overturned furniture, the bedroom door hanging on a hinge. She frowned, narrowing her eyes at the door. The noise Malar had identified was louder here. A sabber's growl but far too deep.

"Something odd . . ."

"It's dark!" Jella exclaimed. "Dark on the other side!"

Livira rushed over and hauled the bedroom door open. A wall of blackness met her eyes. She stepped forward and the darkness rippled, alive with motion. "Arpix?" The growling sound drowned her out. Another step and it seemed that a fearsome shape momentarily detached itself from the impenetrable night before sinking back into it. Behind her Jella gave a despairing shriek and ran. Malar quickly took her place, swords to the fore.

"Volente!" Livira shouted.

The sound stopped.

"Come here!"

Sheepishly, the great black dog began to emerge from the darkness. Before he got halfway a voice from behind him said, "Livira?"

"Meelan?"

The darkness collapsed and there, holding her black book in one hand and a table knife in the other, was Meelan, kneeling on the bed. Arpix huddled beside him, clutching an oversized book with iron hinges as if it were a shield. Their true shield had been the darkness though, and Volente's growling—something it seemed that even sabbers feared to test.

Livira threw herself at both of them.

Moments later, Malar hauled her from their arms. "We need to go."

Livira let herself be drawn away. "He's right. Come on. Right now!"

Out in the corridor Livira glanced towards the far end where the remains of the head librarian's door littered the floor. She considered investigating then turned away. Either Yute's corpse lay in those chambers, or his living body was waiting for her at the library. If he wasn't there, then she'd know he was dead without the need to see what the sabbers had done to him. His death would undo her, and she needed her focus.

THERE WAS ONLY one more corpse waiting for them on their way to the great cave. Heeth Logaris lay on the stairs that spiralled up from the complex, his neck broken by a blow that had shattered his jaw and cheekbone. Three young trainees, still children, crouched by the body, still in shock.

"He protected us . . ." the eldest of them said as Livira approached, her footsteps slowing.

"How many?" Malar demanded.

"How many sabbers?" Livira repeated, seeing their hesitation.

"Four, librarian. They went that way." The boy pointed up the stairs.

"They . . . they had a man with them," the smallest girl added.

"A prisoner?" Livira frowned.

"I—I don't think so."

"He had a collar on, and dressed like a sabber," the boy said.

"He looked like you." The middle girl—a blonde child with blood spatters on her cheek—pointed at Livira.

Livira set off up the stairs. Crimson footprints made a trail. One or more of the sabbers carried wounds now. "Come on." She glanced back. "Arpix, make sure the trainees come too."

Arpix nodded. He paused then held her book of darkness out. "We came looking for you when there was trouble. You'd left this by your bed. We took it . . ."

"I'm glad you did." She pushed his hand away. "Keep it for me."

As PROMISED, YUTE and Yamala were waiting before the great white door to the library. A small crowd of librarians, trainees, staff, and guards stood with them. Livira picked up speed crossing the cavern floor, practically running across the narrow bridges that spanned the larger fissures.

"You got away," Livira said redundantly as she approached Yute. She was acutely aware of the woman beside him in the black robe, and the pink-eyed stare aimed her way. Yamala looked uncannily like Yute. They might be twins rather than husband and wife. "We went to the librarians' quarters . . . So much blood."

"I'm glad you were able to find other survivors." Yute managed a weary smile.

In the group behind him Livira saw friendly faces, most in shock. Master Jost was there too, wearing her customary scowl. Deputy Synoth also, though Livira would not have bet on the old man to be a survivor.

"Four sabbers came this way," Livira said. "The children saw them climbing the stairs." She indicated the trainees coming up behind her, and suddenly wondered how Yute's party hadn't seen them.

"Lies," Master Jost snarled. "This door opens only for humans." She looked around in an exaggerated search. "So where are these sabbers hiding?"

Livira blinked. In her extensive reading no author had ever made that claim. There did appear to be some confusion as to which chambers were forbidden, but that was normally attributed to mismatched numbering schemes.

"Master Jost is correct," Yute said. "This door will only open to a human. A willing human, moreover. Duress will not succeed. We must find time later to discuss how you came by this information, Master Jost . . ." He gave the woman a sharp glance.

"But . . ." Livira thought furiously. "Does that mean . . ."

"That there are doors which only sabbers can open?" Yute asked. "Indeed. And there are doors that neither humans nor sabbers can open. Every species on this planet that has ever produced a written language has chambers given to them within this structure. Go far enough and you will find doors that can only be opened by the denizens of other worlds."

"They had a man with them," Livira said. "Oh . . ."

"Now you see the curse," Yute said.

"Or the blessing." Yamala even sounded like him. "A library that peace and cooperation will fully open."

"A library that rewards slavery." Livira wanted to ask who the man had been. A child from her settlement? One that the sabbers had escaped with?

In the end, though, did it matter if it was one of Alica's babies, or little Keer who had been holding her hand that day? The fact was that a child from her settlement, or one of those nearby, had been raised among the sabbers to one day become their key to the library. Yute had known this could be done but had kept the knowledge from the public. If he hadn't then King Oanold wouldn't have waited a day before sending his troops to capture sabber babies so that the forbidden chambers might be accessed.

Yamala scanned the cavern. "We've waited long enough. Inside!"

The survivors fell in behind Yamala as she led the way into the first library chamber and down the great stair. Livira walked with Yute, Malar and her friends close behind. She set Meelan to making sure that Salamonda didn't pitch over the side since the woman only had eyes for the endless acres of towering shelving and the silent tonnage of dusty books they held.

"What about Wentworth?" Livira exclaimed halfway down, the thought emerging from the chaos inside her skull.

"Oh, don't worry about him, he'll be fine," Yute said. "The sabbers aren't animals."

"No," said Malar behind them. "Once you get a bunch of them together and make them angry, they're worse than animals, just like humans."

Yute still didn't seem concerned. "Even so, I feel sorry for any of them that get on the wrong side of Wentworth."

Many authorities declare the library to have been Irad's work—but in truth it is the work of Irad and of Jaspeth and of neither of them. The structure that we are familiar with—or at least as familiar as a man may be with a possibly infinite building that reaches into many realities, many worlds, and many times—is something that neither brother would claim as their own. It is both far less than Irad's vision, and far more than Jaspeth would have exist. It is, like every good compromise, displeasing to all parties concerned.

The New New Testament, *by various authors*

CHAPTER 55

Livira

The group of survivors took far longer than Livira would have liked to get to the bottom of the stair. The eclectic group of city folk that Malar had delivered to Yute's door, including nearly a dozen from Livira's settlement, was slowed by their need to gawk at everything. Malar himself was by no means immune. Livira took a certain measure of satisfaction in having shown the soldier something that robbed him of his normal cynicism and left his mouth hanging open. He'd led her into the city half a lifetime ago and she'd stared about her in awe. Now it was his turn.

The business of passing babies and infants down the oversized steps also slowed progress. Even so, Salamonda was the last down, puffing and panting, with Meelan dutifully at her side.

The head librarian returned to the bottom step, seemingly in order to get the altitude she desired to address the company. Instead, however, she looked past them into the mouths of the many aisles leading from the clear area at the stair's base.

Yamala took a small white knife from her robe.

"Don't . . ." Yute reached towards her, stepping forward. But Yamala cut her palm. Livira noticed her other hand was bound with a white bandage, nearly invisible against her skin. The blood that welled up had a pearlescent hue. Yamala closed her fist around it and held her hand high.

"Assistance."

For a long moment nothing happened, and the library's silence held everyone's tongue.

"I am here." An assistant stepped out into the clearing. A male one. Possibly the one that had saved Livira long ago after her fall. She couldn't tell. They all looked the same. The same enamel face devoid of personality, the same vaguely human lines.

"We require protection and a place of safety," Yamala said.

The assistant bowed its head. "Follow me."

Livira fell back to walk with Meelan and Arpix. "She can summon assistants now?"

"Who knows what she can do?" Meelan rumbled. "I've never seen her before. Arpix hasn't either."

"I do know that Yute and some of the other librarians went to her room," Arpix said. "I saw them hurrying past my door just before Meelan arrived. Yute told me to join them. But I went to get the rest of you. I didn't reach the main corridor before Meelan came rushing up with the sabber right behind him—"

"Wait, that was one sabber? One sabber killed all those guards . . . ?" Livira blinked, astonished.

"Anyway, my point is that there's no way any of Yute's group could have got out of there without secret tunnels," Arpix concluded.

"There're no tunnels. Or at least if there are they're still secret." Lastri, a junior librarian that Arpix was friendly with, spoke up behind them. "Yamala cut her hand and drew a circle on the wall with the blood. It was the strangest thing you ever saw. It—"

"Filled with light," Livira said.

"Yes." Lastri looked crestfallen. "It brought us all to the door in one step."

"Couldn't she have taken us where we're going then?" Jella asked, sounding more like Carlotte, which immediately filled Livira with worry for her friend again.

"Maybe she doesn't have an endless supply of blood," Meelan suggested.

———

YAMALA, WITH YUTE now at her side, followed behind the assistant. The rest of the party straggled out for some distance, the aisles allowing no more than two to walk abreast. The continuous tramp of footsteps sounded out of place in the library where Livira had spent almost all her time alone. She was listening to it when she caught something new, a slightly different tempo: clunk-clunk-clunk. There was something worryingly familiar about it. Clunk-clunk-clunk. Louder by the moment.

"Something bad's coming!" Livira shouted. "Get ready to run!" She knew what it was but "bad" covered it more effectively than an explanation.

It came from behind them. The jet-black assistant, corrupted years before by the Escape that had come after Livira from the Exchange. The screaming and pushing began immediately. As the survivors began to squeeze past Yute, Yamala, and the assistant at the front, someone gave a desperate shriek. The black assistant had caught one of the bookbinders around the back of the neck and now lifted the woman from her feet.

"No!" Livira tried to go back but Malar hauled her on.

The sound as the assistant tightened her grip, pulping flesh and shattering bone, made Livira's stomach heave. The corrupt assistant dropped its victim carelessly, letting her fall into a disjointed heap.

In a frenzy of pushing and squeezing, Yamala's band reversed its order. The assistant who had answered her call was left facing its darker twin with the librarians ranked behind it.

The black assistant tilted her head to the side, accompanied by a slight creaking.

"Leave." The guide assistant pointed towards the main door.

By way of answer the black one put her fists together then pulled them apart revealing a sword that had not been there before, a blade as lightless as the rest of her.

The guide stepped towards his opponent, reaching to seize her. The white one was faster, but the black one had the reach, bringing her blade down across the other's face with an awful crack. The white assistant shrugged off the blow and closed his hands around the black one's neck.

The pair went down, locked together. Livira fell to her hands and knees to follow the action through the forest of legs before her.

For several moments the pair struggled, clattering loudly as they rolled across the floor, crashing into the shelves. And then . . . nothing. Both went still. Livira elbowed her way forward for a better view.

"It's not possible," Yamala said.

"What isn't?" But Livira saw it now. The white assistant was turning grey, the pollution colouring his head where the black sword lay against him and tracking down his neck. The black assistant was changing too, paling. Neither of them moved from their position, still locked together on the floor.

In the space of a few more breaths both the assistants and the sword they clutched between them evened to the same uniform grey as Yute's robe, almost indistinguishable from it as he went over to inspect the pair.

Livira shrugged off Malar's hand and went to join Yute.

"Through that wound." Yute pointed to the vertical groove cut down through the guide's eyebrow and cheek. "That's how the corruption got in. Where the sword damaged him."

"The Escapes aren't strong enough to control them both," Livira said. She nudged her toe against the one that had made the sword. "That one was the same grey when I found her. It took another Escape to animate her."

"We should go," Yute said weakly. The head librarian seemed as stunned as her husband by the sight of the two stricken assistants on the ground.

Yamala allowed Yute to lead her away, and the other librarians, staff, and city folk pressed back against the shelves so the pair could pass. Livira fell in behind them. At the next junction the pair paused, neither appearing to have a destination in mind. Eventually Yute turned left, and everyone followed.

"Why did that rogue assistant come for us?" Livira asked. "Why now? Today? After all these years?" For an age after the assistant had first chased her from Chamber 7, Livira had watched the aisles, constantly in fear that a black hand would reach for her. Time had worn that fear down to a whisper.

"Only a pure assistant can open the doors." Yamala spoke without looking back at her. "This one had been trapped in Chamber Seven since it turned."

"The sabbers must have opened Chamber Seven—it was waiting to get out." Livira shook her head, realising how lucky she'd been on her last visit. "Where are they going?"

"Two Hundred and Thirty-Two," Yute said.

"A side chamber." Livira had never been to Chamber 232, but the numbering scheme meant it would be a side chamber, eleven along from the entrance. "Why?"

"It's where the sabber entrance is," Yute said. "Maybe they think there's something in the outer caves that will help them clear a path back to the mountainside, or to show those outside where to start digging."

"And where are we going?"

"Does she always ask so many questions?" Yamala sounded a lot like Yute too, her voice just a fraction higher, several fractions less patient.

"She does," Yute said.

After several more paces Yamala answered. "Safety. We're going to find a safe place and wait."

Livira wanted to ask: *Is that it? Go somewhere safe and wait?* Instead, she made a suggestion. "We could go to the labyrinth. They'll never find us in there and I know how to move through it faster than anyone."

Arpix shook his head. "It's a dead end."

Livira wanted to argue but he had a good point. If they needed to leave the only way out was back to Chamber 1. Chambers 3 and 7 were forbidden.

"We'll go to the labyrinth," Yute said. "Doors aren't going to be a problem."

LIVIRA BROUGHT THEM to one of the two hearts of the labyrinth that occupied almost a thousand acres of Chamber 2. All the librarians knew enough to navigate it, but most avoided the place, uninterested in the well-catalogued fiction dominating its shelves. None knew it as intimately as Livira did. She stood on the stained patch where the Raven, Edgarallen, had first revealed himself to her. A small part of her had been hoping he might be there today. He would have been a comfort and his talent for accessing forbidden chambers an asset.

The group couldn't all fit within the clearing at once. There were forty-six of them in total, about half in the clearing, the remainder resting in the adjacent aisles. The city children had already started to complain of thirst and hunger before they even reached the labyrinth. Their parents had discovered with horror that what little food they'd snatched up during their hasty exodus from Crath had vanished. The assistant Yamala had summoned must have reduced it to dust the moment he arrived.

"How long are we staying here?"

"What are we going to do?"

"What can we eat?"

The questions multiplied, and despite it being a place where answers were stacked higher than houses . . . there were no good ones forthcoming.

TIME PASSED. PEOPLE stopped standing and slumped to the floor, wrapped in their grief and shock, staring at nothing. The children, resilient as weeds, ran back and forth along the aisles, playing tag or hunting through the books, pursued by Master Jost, who twisted ears and whacked the backs of heads in a vain attempt to prevent the unauthorised manhandling of the stock. She was known to despise fiction, but even such a misuse of parchment needed protecting against the sticky-fingered spawn of the city.

Livira took care to ensure all of the children knew to pull out books to record their trail and lead them back.

Librarians discussed the prospects in hushed voices. Yute and Yamala stood stiller than statues, staring not at each other but at the stained floor. Malar brooded, his back to the shelves, swords across his knees.

Soon enough Yamala would gather her strength and summon another assistant. Or Yute would come up with an alternative plan. Knowing that they would not stay long in the labyrinth, Livira resolved to take advantage of the chance offered to her. She seized her moment and slipped away from a gloomy conversation between Meelan, Arpix, and Jella which endlessly circled the same bleak facts, no more able to break free than a drunkard wandering the labyrinth. It hurt her heart to think about their future now.

Arpix in particular seemed ill-suited to change, too delicately woven around his duties to pull free without harm.

Livira moved quietly. For years now she'd been following the advice Yute gave her that day she and Arpix came to his door. She'd been writing, setting her thoughts down here in the endless folds of the labyrinth, covering flyleaf after flyleaf with her overspilling imagination, a story jumping from one book to another, the trail hidden by riddles. It had begun as a diary of her experiences in the forbidden chambers and in the Exchange and grown into might-have-beens instead of what-weres. Evar had started to accompany her across the page, sharing her adventures, following the black line of ink as it convoluted its path into letters, then words, then castles in the sky. They'd stridden hand in hand through chapter upon chapter. The kiss they had shared in the empty city had been auditioned here first, more than once, in more than one place. Evar had ridden dragons with her—so in a sense she had already taught him to fly long before the day she truly did.

Livira climbed the shelves without a ladder, nimble as any monkey. She plucked A. E. Canulus's *Great Sailing Ships of History: An Architectural Comparison* from the highest row and, supporting herself with nothing but an elbow wedged against the vertical support, she plucked out the already detached dedication page. Page one of her incomplete opus. A map on one side, story on the other. Moments later her feet touched the ground, and she was off in search of the next page.

Yamala might disapprove, but the librarians' time was finished. Their rules were in tatters now. The cycle had turned again, and Crath City had new masters. For all that King Oanold had preached that the sabbers were animals, dog-soldiers without intelligence or rights of any kind, they had filled chambers of the library with their learning in centuries past and would once again take control from human hands. The place had not been built by humans or for them, at least not solely for them.

Whatever escape the head librarian had in mind, Livira doubted she would ever return to these chambers, and she was damned if she'd leave her book behind as a puzzle for some scholar a thousand years hence. Besides, she wanted to finish it.

Around the very next corner Livira found evidence of the children's roaming. A thin book pulled from the shelves so roughly that the pages within had separated from the spine and left the plain leather covers lying on the floor a yard or two away like a pair of wings.

On seeing that the book was simply a record of varying salt prices across seventeen provinces for a fifty-year period that ended in a cycle believed to have finished six hundred years previously, Livira opted not to reunite cover with contents. Instead, she pressed her own page one between the worn leather jacket and took it with her. The books she'd chosen for her cuckoo stories had all been of similar size; the pages would fit well between these repurposed covers.

Livira had seen the scale of the disaster outside, and it had floored her. But her world had been torn apart before and, like her namesake, the irrepressible weed, she'd survived, uncoiled beneath a new sun, sunk new roots. She could do it again. The book in her hand—her book—was a statement of faith in the future, not that it would be a good one necessarily, but that she would be there in it. Her fears weren't for herself but for the people she loved, none of whom, save Malar, seemed tough enough to face what was coming.

She had collected all but two of the well over a hundred sheets when a faint cracking sound caught her attention. Something considerably more distant than the muted cries of traumatised children releasing their stress. Livira hastily completed her stack of pages, sandwiched it between the loose covers, and stashed it in her book satchel.

By the time she returned to the clearing she'd heard five or six more of the distant cracks and another flurry accompanied her arrival. Malar was standing in the aisle by which she returned, at a distance from the crowd, his head cocked to the side, eyes down, listening intently.

"'Sticks." Malar looked up at her. "Could be a mile away. A fight by the chamber door, maybe."

They went together to join the others. All of them pensive and watchful now, the children quiet and back with their parents. The backs of Livira's arms prickled with recognition. She'd been here before. On the Dust. She'd been the child. Now she stood in her aunt's shoes, aware of how fragile everything was, how possible the impossible, anchored to this desperately vulnerable collection of people with her whole heart.

"Is it the Library Guard?" Meelan asked. It struck Livira that her friend was no longer rich. His wealth was on fire even now. He probably no longer had parents or a sister though he wouldn't have understood this yet. His only family stood around him.

"It could be the Guard," Arpix said. There were certainly more library guards than the ones Livira had seen dead and the ones with them.

"That's not the Guard." John Norris spoke up behind them and hefted his arrow-stick up as they turned. "We use compressed air and a smaller round. Those are projectile weapons, 'sticks, but chemical ones, explosive rounds like the army use. Louder and much more deadly."

"Could it be more sabbers then?" Livira frowned.

"Someone's shooting at someone," Malar said. "We're not the only ones to have thought of hiding out. Might be soldiers, might be the king himself, fighting a retreat."

Yute pressed his lips into a flat line. "He should have negotiated." His voice as close to anger as Livira had ever heard it.

Livira started to climb the nearest shelves without a ladder. She rolled her eyes at Master Jost's outraged look and wondered how long it would take the woman to understand that the spiderweb of rules in which she'd prowled for so long now hung in shreds. In half a minute Livira was perched on top staring at the distant wall where they'd entered Chamber 2. Something puzzled her. She called down to Mr. Norris in a low voice. "Why don't the Guard have 'sticks like the soldiers?" Surely the Library Guard would have nothing but the best?

The guardsman peered up at her through his visor. "Apt to throw a lot of sparks about, those things, miss. And iffen you shoot too many balls too quickly the barrel gets hotter than hell."

Malar summarised succinctly: "Fire hazard."

As he said the words the first distant coil of smoke rose above the shelves.

There's no one temperature at which a book spontaneously combusts. Books vary as much in their combustion as they do in their contents. But the truth is that any words set upon a flammable substrate have a limited shelf-life, as do the shelves themselves if they are also vulnerable to fire. Flames are ever hungry and will find a path to their food.

Written in the Stars, *by Ekatri Hagsdaughter*

CHAPTER 56

Livira

We need to go." Livira jumped the last ten feet from the shelves, going down on her haunches to absorb the impact, then rising swiftly. "There's a fire."

That set everyone talking at once. They were standing in a flammable maze amid four square miles of parchment, paper, leather, and wood, all dry as the Dust.

"We'll aim for the door to Chamber Seven." Yamala set off without delay.

Several of the librarians raised an eyebrow or two at the idea of entering a forbidden chamber, but Yute had said the door would be no problem.

Master Synoth did more than raise both bushy white brows. "I've been sixty years at this work, man and boy. And you're telling me you could have let us into the locked chambers any time you liked?" He shook his head in slow outrage. "I wouldn't have agreed with taking sabber prisoners to do it. Well . . . certainly not cubs. But if you could open them without the need for all that . . . for gods' sakes, Yute . . ."

Yute walked past the old man, clapping him on the shoulder as he went. "You didn't think you had enough to read already, my friend?"

Synoth managed a wry smile through his beard. "It's always the books you don't have that call to you, you know that. Not the ones already on your shelf. They can wait."

It was Yute's turn to shake his head as he walked away. "Even as a trainee, Synoth, even as a trainee. Always hungry for the next book before you finished the first page of the one before you."

LIVIRA WORKED HER way to the front of the column. She was doubly glad now that she'd saved her story, but the idea that the whole chamber would just burn, the labyrinth gone, millions upon millions of books reduced to ash . . . it just seemed so wrong.

"How can they let it all burn?" she demanded.

"They?" Yute asked.

"Them! The assistants." She waved her arms as if it might help. "You know. Like the one who somehow turned all these people's food to dust by lifting his little finger. They can't stop a fire . . . or just provide fireproof books?"

"Everything is a compromise." Yute raised his hand so she could see over his shoulder the ring whose moonstone he had joked could hold every book in every chamber of the library. "The assistants are Irad's servants. The dark that escapes from between, the blackness that's the library's own blood, is what Jaspeth bends to his will."

Yamala glanced at her husband and tutted, as if she disapproved of such candour. Yute ignored her and carried on. "The library exists on the knife edge between their conflict—their disagreement. It hangs in a web of checks and balances. The library is both the tree and the apple. It offers not knowledge of good and evil but knowledge for good or evil. Of course fire could be forbidden. But one of the compromises that holds back the war—not your little one here, but the big one—is the agreement that if a civilisation is not capable of keeping a book from burning then perhaps it wasn't ready for whatever knowledge was held within."

"So . . . it's all just going to burn then?" Livira couldn't accept it. The idea hurt her inside her chest.

"I'm just glad someone thought to put these corridors and doors in," Malar said behind Livira. "Without firebreaks it wouldn't just be one chamber that went up. Then we'd all be fucking fucked, and no mistake."

Yute did look round at that one. "The doors stop people. They don't stop things."

Malar's face paled. "But there's the corridor too. Two hundred yards."

"When four square miles of books burn, Master Malar," said the head librarian, her eyes firmly to the fore, "those corridors will become throats through which the inferno within will both inhale and exhale. And when it does the latter, flames will vomit into the next chamber further than a man can throw a spear."

"Oh crap," someone said from behind Malar, someone using Jella's voice but obviously not Jella since she had never in her whole life used a crude word. "Can we go a bit faster, please?"

"You're saying the whole library is going to burn?" Livira asked again.

"I don't think you've understood how big the library is," Yute said. "The library is always burning. Somewhere. The assistants restock behind the fires. It's a—"

"A compromise. Don't say it. I know."

"I was going to say an equilibrium," Yute said mildly.

"Well . . . can we outrun it?"

"Not for long." Yute, and more specifically Yamala, had slowed. The head librarian seemed fatigued, though how two cuts to her hands could have left her so drained Livira didn't know.

"We could leave by a side door," Livira said. "Where's the next one after Chamber Two Hundred and Thirty-Two?"

"Chamber Two Thousand Two Hundred and Seventy-Nine."

"Ah . . ." It wasn't as far as it sounded but it was a good forty-six miles past the sabbers' door, which was still some twenty miles off. "Can't Yamala make a portal?"

"Not so soon." Yute glanced at his wife.

"Can't you?" Malar called.

"No."

"Why not?" Malar sounded as un-Malar-like as Jella sounded un-Jella-like. The fear of burning to death had got to both of them in a way that it hadn't yet got to Livira. She was sure that she too would start to unravel, though, once she smelled the smoke and heard the distant roar of flames. "Why can't you do it too? You look the same!"

"That's beneath you, Malar," Yute admonished mildly. "Yamala and I came into this world through acts of sacrifice, a sundering if you like. We both retained different traces of who we were. What we were."

"You were assistants!" Livira exclaimed. She'd harboured a suspicion ever since her journey to the ancient city with Evar, but Yute's earlier deflection and the chaos of the past day had pushed it to the back of her mind. "You made yourselves human." She paused. "Well, humanish. But why?"

"You picked a strange time for this conversation, Livira."

"If we're all going to die then humour me." It actually seemed an ideal time since the portal she had drawn lay in the chamber immediately after the forbidden Chamber 7, and if she were to delay her questions until she'd revealed that fact it might be that Yute would never provide answers.

"I don't think we're *all* going to die. Not in the immediate future."

Livira didn't like the way Yute's voice had dragged its heels across "all." But seeing that, like Yamala, he too was struggling to maintain a decent pace she let him save his breath despite the burning urgency of her question.

"You should tell them, Livira." Arpix spoke quietly but firmly at her right shoulder, just like the voice of conscience he had so often been in the past.

And as so often before Livira had to grudgingly admit that the scribe's son was correct. "I can get us to the Exchange," Livira said, the secret tearing itself unwillingly from her lips. "We can, me and Arpix. We drew it together. A portal. In Chamber Sixteen, closest wall."

Yute and Yamala stopped, causing near collisions to ripple back down the length of the group stretched out between the shelves behind them. They turned their heads to look at each other, pink eyes meeting pink eyes, then slowly turned to face Livira.

"I told you she was a marvel," Yute said to Yamala.

"How," Yamala asked, "would *you* do something like that?" That "you" came freighted with an incredulity which carried unpleasant echoes of the attitude that trickled from King Oanold's lofty throne, down through the likes of Lord Algar and Serra Leetar and continued to follow the social gradients down Crath City's many slopes until it pooled in the gutters of the low town, the prejudice no less ugly for being in the minds of the poor.

Livira met the head librarian's gaze. "I used the blood of an assistant."

Yamala turned away with a shiver and led on.

WITHOUT CLIMBING THE shelves—and nobody was foolish enough to suggest delaying for that—there was no indication of the fire. Livira even persuaded herself that those involved in the fight by the entrance tunnel might have somehow extinguished what they started. It would be the only chance they got, so they'd be fools to waste it.

As the band pressed on through the turns and twists of endless aisles it grew increasingly difficult for Livira to believe in the idea that they were being chased by hungry flames. She'd seen a wisp of smoke rising. Perhaps it merely came from the barrel of one soldier's weapon and had remained confined there. Her mind whispered warnings about the distance. It must have been a lot of smoke, surely? But Livira's unwillingness to believe the worst helped her to ignore such whispering.

It was the breeze that blew away her doubts. A zephyr to start with, no more than a breath. At first it could perhaps have been mistaken for the passage of air over fevered skin created by the swiftness of their advance.

The air that had remained still, yet only slightly stale, for generations, held prisoner between innumerable aisles, began to stir. Only the dust marked these first motions. The aeons-long dance of dust motes, forever lit by the library's omnipresent light, began to shift. Two steps to the right for every step to the left. Then three.

In time the occasional loose leaf, poking provocatively from the mass of its better-behaved brethren, began to tremble in anticipation, to wave for attention, to flutter in a breeze that couldn't be denied. And by this point the once-muted drone of the distant fire, which had until now been drowned beneath the shuffle of scores of feet, the mere buzz of a lazy bee, raised its voice to a level that could no longer be missed, ignored, or wished away. It sounded large. And it sounded hungry. And it sounded closer by the minute.

A loose page rose at the junction ahead, lifted on a spiral of wind before being yanked away behind them, over their heads.

"Fuck." Malar pushed to the front, taking Yute's elbow and propelling him forward with greater speed. "We need to pick up the fucking pace."

———

THE WIND DIED when they were about two-thirds of the way across the chamber. Everything Livira knew about fires said they needed air and would suck it in like a giant lung. But the wind fell from a noticeable breeze to nothing, all in the time it took to take a dozen strides.

"Keep going!" Malar urged.

The stillness that had been the library's trademark for millennia now suddenly seemed uncanny. The calm before a storm.

The distant boom was muffled but spoke of immense power.

"What the fuck is there to explode?" Malar complained. Nobody offered an explanation.

They hurried on, children whimpering, the elderly struggling to keep pace, Salamonda labouring at the rear. Every now and then a shot would ring out behind them. Sometimes a flurry of shots, with faint accompanying screams. The fire's advance was swift, but the people who'd started it were outrunning the flames for now and seemed to be gaining on Yute's party.

BY THE TIME they were approaching the far wall the conflict behind them sounded frighteningly close. A rolling retreat, Malar called it. A spread-out battlefront where small bands fought, fell back, made a new stand. And all with the sabbers advancing as surely as the fire.

As the distance to the wall narrowed, Livira determined to run ahead and use the time before the others arrived to get a look at the situation from the shelf tops. Malar, Arpix, and Meelan followed at her heels. A long sprint brought her breathless to the clearing before the corridor to Chamber 7.

Looking back, she could see the smoke hovering high above the aisles, pooling beneath the ceiling that had always seemed impossibly high. A fierce orange glow lit it from below, a light like nothing ever seen within the library before. Meelan had already found a ladder and swarmed up it while Arpix held it steady.

Livira's fear finally found her. She could imagine nothing more terrifying than the advancing blaze. She was the bug in the hearth, scrambling across kindling as the flames rose. Her legs trembled so fiercely that for a moment they could hardly keep her standing.

She thought of the winged man back at the entrance to the chamber. She'd greeted him when they reached his side and had run her hands over the polished metal of his arms, not knowing it would be for the last time.

"Goodbye, old friend." She was glad that she had got to hear him speak, and glad that he had retreated back to his slumber. She hoped the fire would not wake him and that when it came his end would be a swift one.

"Small fires there, and there." Meelan had climbed onto the shelf top. He pointed left, then right, then left again. "There too." The angle of his arm made them look worryingly close.

"Sparks flying ahead of the main front?" Arpix guessed.

Livira was climbing after Meelan when the second detonation rumbled through the air.

"That's not good," Meelan said above her.

"What isn't?"

"Smoke. Lots of it."

Livira got her head above the shelves and saw for herself. A great rolling cloud of smoke, hundreds of feet thick and filled with flashes of fire, coming their way at speed from the far side of the chamber.

"Oh gods . . ." Meelan's voice faltered.

Livira had seen it too. "Another!" She pointed but it had gone already. A sabber hauling itself over a shelf top little more than a hundred yards away then dropping into the next aisle.

"More!" Meelan pointed further back. Not far ahead of the advancing smoke a score or more sabbers were running the shelf tops, leaping not one but two or even three aisles at once with a natural aptitude that made Livira's hard-won skill look like a toddler's stumblings.

Along an aisle that aimed towards her, closer even than the leading sabbers, Livira glimpsed the gleam of silver 'stick barrels: soldiers running, and civilians too by the look of it.

"Down!" Livira screamed. "Get down!" The sight of it all had paralysed them, wasting precious time. Livira's feet flew over the rungs, barely making contact. She landed heavily beside Arpix and made room for Meelan.

Yute and Yamala broke into the clearing at a pace that was closer to running than walking, the others beginning to pour in behind them.

"We need to go!" Livira seized Yute by both hands, steering him towards the corridor. "Right now!"

Yute, stumbling, protested. "You don't need me. When a chamber's ablaze the doors will open for anyone. The alternative is too cruel."

"Lead them anyway." Livira pushed Yute onwards and turned to help shepherd the rest of the party through. Bodies began to pass her, most too quick for recognition. Katrin hurried by, pale-faced and red-eyed, clutching her husband's hand. A mother carrying the baby that Livira had stolen hours earlier. Library staff. Master Jost, too frightened or distracted for her customary sneer at Livira.

"Have you seen Salamonda?" Livira grabbed the next person to pass her. A man she didn't know. A man spattered with blood across the left side of his face. He pulled free and another man jostled past. Both looked similar. Uniform. "Soldiers!"

"Time to go." Malar took her arm. Soldiers carrying 'sticks were now hurrying from most of the aisles that ended in the clearing. An undisciplined crowd, panic in their faces.

"Salamonda's still out there." Livira shook him off. There could be others too. How many children had passed her? Not all of them, surely? Had she even seen Jella?

The first sabber leapt from a shelf top and landed among them, square in the midst of the clearing. Shouts on all sides, a 'stick boomed, screams went up. And the wave of smoke hit, pouring into the clearing like a waterfall, drowning everything in a hot, choking hell.

The idea that what was needed lay before us the whole time is almost as old as the concept of need. The greenest grass may hide beneath your feet.
"Three Billy Goats Gruff," a postdoctoral thesis by Arnold Grim

---

CHAPTER 57

Evar

E var pondered his three siblings. He needed their help if he was to get back to the Exchange, but he couldn't allow Clovis to go there with him. She'd already spilled Livira's blood and clearly planned to soak the Exchange's grass with the rest of it. Even if Starval could and would put a knife in their sister's back to prevent it, that was too high a price to pay. Better to not go back at all and live with the might-have-beens the rest of his days. Kerrol was the only one of them who could perhaps reach Clovis, but even his talents might not be sufficient to penetrate the scar-tissue around her psyche. Livira was by far the closest Clovis had ever been to exacting the revenge that had been the central column of her life for so many years.

The solution was clearly a plan that ensured Clovis didn't make it through the pool. The problem was finding such a solution.

IN THE THREE days since discovering that the siblings now knew how to reach the Exchange the Assistant had created the pool only once a day. She took it upon herself to fill the drinking buckets, and then to water the crop while the Soldier guarded the gateway. If one of them should interrupt this process, with a question or idle chat, the Assistant would immediately return to the pool and make it vanish before addressing whichever sibling had interjected.

Time would not soften the regime or diminish their watchfulness. Neither of the two felt its flow. Evar was convinced of that now. Only his presence and that of his siblings caused the Assistant and the Soldier to dip into the now, as and when required.

Three days had taught Evar that whatever he told himself about it being better not to go back to the Exchange at all if doing so risked Clovis returning too, he could not remain. The entire time he had spent in Livira's company had occupied just a handful of days, from when he entered the crop pool to when he once again emerged from it, dragged by his sister. But in those days Livira had grown from a child to a young woman who matched his age. She had struggled to reach him time after time, and succeeded though it took her years on each occasion.

His siblings would never understand how he had formed so deep an attachment over such a short span, but where a lifetime of seeking to return had served to sharpen Livira's need, Evar had had her book. He had lived in it for as long as she had hunted him. She was the one he had been seeking, the one who had driven him to his quest to escape the chamber. She might hate him now—him and his kind—but despite what he had seen, and what he knew to be true of her species, he could do nothing but love, need, and want her. Whatever she looked like and whatever crimes her people had wrought, she was Livira, coiled around his heart, woven through his veins.

He would find her again, knowing himself to be vile in her sight, and say his piece. She could reject him, or merely stab him in the chest, but at least there would be an honest parting between them, not one forced by sudden circumstance. And having lived his life within the confines of a library Evar knew that endings were important.

"WHAT WE NEED," said Starval when they had a chance to be out of Kerrol and Clovis's earshot, "is a diversion so urgent that she doesn't close the pool first. Urgent enough for both of them to run immediately to where they're needed."

"There's nothing that important," Evar said. "When have you ever seen either of them run?"

"I saw the Soldier run only the other day, chasing the third of those

Escapes," Starval said. "And I saw the Assistant fly through the air just before that."

"You want an Escape to turn up just after she's created the pool?" Evar asked. "What are the odds of that?"

"Not an Escape. Lots of them. And the odds will be pretty damn good if we make it happen!"

"WE COULD JUST try talking to her." Evar stood in front of the Mechanism, his arms folded defensively across his chest.

"When have you ever changed her mind on anything? Or seen her change it?" Starval looked back across the trail of upturned reading desks that marked the Soldier's run for the main chamber when chasing one of the most recent Escapes.

Evar bit his lip and nodded. Not even Kerrol could change the Assistant's mind. "You really think this is going to work?"

Starval adjusted his armour, which was made from more flexible leathers than Clovis's, all of them black. "It's the same book. If it doesn't work, we'll try something else."

Evar picked the tome in question off the nearest reading desk. A heavy book of indeterminable age, its cover a grey stone-like substance carved in deep relief with a border of vines and grapes. Starval had been secretly investigating Mayland's disappearance, despite his stated belief that their brother's bones would be found beneath a pile of books from one of the many stack collapses. The mystery had been too much temptation for someone who styled themselves as a spy. In addition to searching, Starval had been researching. The book he'd taken into the Mechanism the day that the huge insectoid Escape emerged had been the last book that Mayland had taken in with him.

Evar flipped through the pages. Books like this one, which talked about the library's own history, were the rarest of finds. Mayland's gift from his decades in the Mechanism had been a knowledge of history that would be insulted by the term "encyclopaedic." But about the library's history even Mayland knew little, and most of that was fable and surmise.

"Come on." Starval hauled the book from Evar's hands. "You're not going to get far by actually reading it. Let the Mechanism do the work. Besides, it's in Linear Krol."

Evar frowned. Even Kerrol had struggled to learn Linear Krol, and all of them had complained at being forced to learn it because so few of the chamber's books were written in the language. A memory nagged at him, scratching at the surface of consciousness but from the wrong side, as yet unable to be named.

Starval opened the Mechanism's door, today a humble wooden affair, an untidy collection of planks that reminded Evar of the doors in the lower part of the city beyond the library. "Better get to your position. If it happens like last time we're going to need to move fast."

Evar stared at the grey interior. The last time he'd been in the Mechanism he'd been eight and it had taken away his life. "Let me go instead."

Starval blinked. "You're joking."

Evar reached for the book. "I've got a bad feeling about this. What if it's worse this time?"

"So, I'd let you go instead?" Starval laughed and held the book away from Evar. "Get to the corridor. The timing on this is going to be hard enough as it is."

Evar glanced back towards the chamber. Kerrol was delaying the Assistant but even he couldn't distract her for long. Soon she'd open the pool and they needed the Escapes to make their appearance before she closed it. And all of it had to happen before Clovis returned from whatever wild goose chase Kerrol had set her on. Even so, the thought that had been niggling at him began to surface, to take shape like a body in the mist, a figure in a ball of wind-weed. "You know, the only time I've seen more Escapes than the day you took that book in with you I was in the Exchange."

"And?" Starval was given to patience, but he sounded impatient now.

"You're the one who taught me to look for connections. The key to any mystery is in the threads, however faint, that join its pieces. You said that."

Starval took a breath. "I did."

"Just before the Escapes came—before they started to pour from everywhere—the last name on my lips was Mayland's. I had just said that I was going to use the pools to see what happened to him that last day—to watch where he went. And then they attacked."

"Mayland?" Starval made a face. "I don't think . . ."

The grey space of the Mechanism had grown darker, as if a distant sun had set behind the rain clouds that had hidden it, and only as it vanished could its absence be felt.

"We should run," Evar said.

The Mechanism shuddered and the darkness within began to congeal into nightmare. Starval was already running.

By the time Evar reached the main chamber, Starval's athletics around the maze of reading desks had opened a considerable lead. He stood waiting by the nearest book stacks, a wild grin on his face.

"How many?" Evar managed to gasp as he passed his brother. He didn't dare a backwards glance at the Escapes squeezed from the Mechanism by the mere thought of finding Mayland.

"More than we needed!" Starval kept pace, despite lacking a foot in height on Evar.

The Escapes made a chilling rushing noise behind the pair as they wove through the stacks. A sound like a cold wind through bare branches. Evar stretched his legs, hauling in more air for the effort.

The brothers vaulted the book wall together. The Soldier, thigh-deep in the crop, was already advancing in their direction. The Assistant, by the pool, bucket in hand, turned from Kerrol's remonstrations to see the cause of this new excitement.

"Escapes!" Evar managed.

"Lots!" Starval accelerated past him, trampling bean rows.

The Assistant strode forward, ready to put her body between the boys and the black tide that swept over the wall behind them. A deep pang of guilt tore at Evar but Kerrol simply stepped into the pool and dropped from sight without expression. Starval swerved past the Assistant with a whoop and dived headfirst into the water.

Evar halted at the pool's edge, teetering. The first of a dozen and more Escapes had almost reached the Assistant. The Soldier was moving to join her. And Clovis—who should have been deep among the stacks—was barrelling towards Evar with murder in her eyes.

Evar couldn't let her reach the Exchange. "Soldier! Help! Stop her!"

He didn't expect his desperate cry to be noticed, let alone acted on, but perhaps that note of desperation was what turned the Soldier from his course. The white warrior managed to close the distance against all odds and, just yards from her target, Clovis was sent sprawling among the new cabbages.

With an apologetic look, Evar tipped backwards into the strange waters behind him.

THE QUIET AND stillness of the wood made such a contrast with the scene Evar had just left that he pressed his hands to his ears, wondering if he had water in them, or had somehow gone deaf.

"Brother."

Evar turned. Kerrol had been standing behind him. Starval was further off among the trees, gazing up in wonder at the branches and at the sky above them. He glanced back at the pool. The only one since he now saw all the others as portals. "Clovis found out somehow!"

"She's coming?" Kerrol didn't seem surprised.

"The Soldier stopped her." The pool rippled, perhaps with an echo of the violence occurring on the other side of it.

"And you think this sabber girl of yours will be with us soon?" Despite his apparent coolness, Kerrol's gaze did flicker to the surroundings every so often. Even he must have felt some echo of the awe the place had instilled in Evar on his first visit.

"I think that's what this place does. It brings people together. It brings times and purposes together. There's not really a 'soon' here, only 'now' or 'never.'"

As if to prove him right, the portal to Livira's time shimmered and Livira stumbled out as if pushed, falling to the ground. She looked up, wild-eyed, her white robe smeared with ash.

Evar opened his mouth to call to her but immediately others began to press through. More sabbers, and two white-skinned beings that were neither sabber nor people but seemed somehow familiar even so. More sabbers came, stumbling open-mouthed from the portal, males, females, young, old, some carrying weapons, some bloodied. All of them so stunned by their transition that their eyes slid over the scene without registering the three brothers some sixty yards back among the trees. Only Livira saw them. Her gaze locked with Evar's.

And Evar now saw only Livira.

Truly saw her. Not the strangeness of a sabber's body, but the totality of who she was to him, the way she was: sharp, kind, undisciplined, brilliant, mysterious, funny, passionate, questioning—always questions—changing from one encounter to the next, and he'd let her slip through his fingers too often, lost too many years . . .

"Group dynamics! Fascinating!" Kerrol was already halfway to the sabbers.

Livira had started to walk towards them, an older male at her side, shorter even than the friend Arpix.

Evar shook off whatever spell Livira had put him under. "Kerrol! Stay back!"

Kerrol waved his words away and closed the remaining distance even as Livira faltered. "They're not here to fight. Look at them."

In the next moment Kerrol was on his back. The male sabber had moved with commendable speed as Kerrol had glanced towards his brothers, taking him down with a well-placed kick to the back of the knee then driving him to the turf with a sword blade at his neck.

Evar hastened forward, hands raised, palms out. "He's my brother—don't hurt him."

Livira already had hold of the male's sword arm, shouting at him not to deliver the killing blow. Others among the growing crowd of sabbers were drawing blades. Two of them had iron-barrelled projectile weapons and were bringing them to bear on Evar. He glanced back but Starval was gone—he would be angling in through the trees even now, knives ready. Disaster lay heartbeats away. But violence might still be avoided. If only Evar and Livira could calm their respective—

"YOU!" Clovis burst from the pool in a shower of light, teeth scarlet with what must be her own blood, the largest of her blades glimmering in her clenched fist. She passed Evar, sending him sprawling, unable to stop her. A projectile weapon boomed. The male warrior abandoned Kerrol, flung himself at Clovis to stop her advance, and went down. In the next broken fragment of a second Clovis had her hand around Livira's neck, lifting her one-armed from the ground.

"*Stop.*"

The voice came from everywhere, deep, resonant, larger than the wood.

"*Put the girl down.*"

The male of the white-skinned pair approached Clovis, who, much to Evar's surprise, lowered Livira to the ground and released her neck. The female white had moved away from the sabber group but hung back from Clovis. Both of the creatures had a glow to them that hadn't been there when they arrived. Their skin was no longer merely white but gleamed with whiteness. And suddenly Evar understood why they had seemed so familiar.

. . . very dear friend of mine. Elias, when not consumed with his scientific research, captained his own great vessel out on the Black Sea. He was often wont to speculate on any and all particulars relating to the nature of time. His insights wandered from commentary on the first accurate chronometers that permitted navigation of the oceans, to the vagaries of both arrivals and of meetings, which are, he always claimed, governed by an arithmetic more fundamental than that of particles, planets, or pulsars.

Great Sailing Ships of History: An Architectural Comparison,
by A. E. Canulus

CHAPTER 58

Livira

Livira's feet hit the ground and the rest of her followed, her legs too weak to bear her weight. She tried to breathe through what felt like the narrow straw her throat had become after throttling in Clovis's iron grip. Malar lay nearby, unmoving, and she started to crawl to him as Yute addressed the sabber woman in a voice that had seemed to pulse from the very ground but now drew itself back into his narrow chest.

"Why should I listen to you?" Clovis swaggered. "I've just put one of your kind on his ass. And you're not half of what he is. What are you anyway?" She came level with Yute, peering down at him. "You're not the same at all. You're . . ." She flicked out a hand quicker than thinking. A pearlescent line appeared across Yute's cheekbone. Blood. "You're . . . alive."

Evar arrived, lifting Livira to her feet just as she reached Malar, and pulling her back out of range of Clovis's too-fast hands. People were still pressing through the portal behind Yute. No sign of Arpix or Salamonda or Jella or Meelan, though the great majority were still to come.

"Did your brother tell you about the city he saw?" Yute asked, unmoved by his wound. "The city that existed nine hundred years before your time in the library?"

Clovis sneered. "Yes, he told me. A city of my people. Thousands upon thousands. Invaded by these sabbers"—she glanced at Livira with murder in her eyes—"sabbers who poisoned them in their homes. Men, women, and children choked to death beneath their own roofs."

Evar reached down to help his brother—the one who Malar had felled—hauling him back to his feet. The dark-maned sabber got up with a wince, frowning down at Livira from his great height, even taller than Evar, well over eight feet.

Yute continued to address Clovis. "Did your brother tell you those homes were filled with both races?" There was passion in his voice. It struck Livira hard. She had never heard Yute anything but calm or mildly amused.

"He told me," Clovis spat, "that the sabbers were too stupid to avoid the hell that they'd unleashed."

"Is that what you thought, Livira?" Yute's pink eyes flicked her way.

"I . . . yes . . . well, it never really made much sense." Livira shrugged off the protective cradle of Evar's arms. "Why were they there, room by room, floor by floor?" She looked up over her shoulder, meeting Evar's amber eyes. He had *amber* eyes . . . and the pupils were wrong. She'd never seen him close up before without the Exchange disguising him to suit her expectation. But it was still Evar. Not some animal. Still his kindness looking out at her.

Yute shook his head. "The two races lived in peace for generations. After so many cycles of war, they made their first true peace. Not just a pact to avoid killing each other. They shared the city. They lived in the same buildings. They explored the library together."

"Nonsense!" Lord Algar raised his voice in anger, but he still kept towards the back of the group, flanked by two soldiers with their 'sticks at the ready, and shielding himself with Serra Leetar, his hands on her shoulders as if to keep her in place.

When the smoke had rolled over everything, forestalling the final confrontation between the fleeing troops and pursuing sabbers, chaos reigned for what seemed an age. Yamala had left the door open behind them and Yute's voice had led forward some of those lost in the choking blindness of the smoke. Fire and chaos had chased them across Chamber 7, past the point of exhaustion, a scattered band threading many different routes towards the far exit. Yamala had opened that door too and the dreadful heat had pushed them through into Chamber 16 before any roll call could be taken. Livira led the way to the portal that she and Arpix had drawn on the wall. In the chaos of that final smoke-laden aisle it became clear that Yute's party had changed very significantly in character. He had gained scores, possibly hundreds of the king's troopers and a dozen of Crath's richest citizens, including a bedraggled Lord Algar, and Serra Leetar looking as if she'd just stepped out of a ball for a breath of fresh air.

The encroaching smoke rang with the snarls and cries of sabbers, some sounding as terrified as many in Yute's party, and with the flames chasing at their heels Livira couldn't blame them. Along the length of the aisle, she'd been unable to see Arpix, Salamonda, or many of the others in the original group, and the cries of soldiers believing they'd been led down a dead end swallowed her shouts. In the end, she'd been forced through the portal by the weight of others pressing in behind her, and had spilled out into the Exchange in an ungainly sprawl.

"Nonsense," Lord Algar repeated and rubbed at his crimson eyepatch as if there were an eye itching beneath it. "The people of Crath would never open their doors to these animals. The idea that they would know what to do with books . . . BOOKS, for the gods' sake!"

Yute ignored him. "Both your races lived in harmony. The chemical attack came from members of a third race seeking their own justice. After so many cycles of destruction there was a peace. A way forward that had long been sought. And then suddenly . . . death everywhere. As assistants, we serve Irad, the founder, and our relationship with time is a curious one. Like the Escapes in service to Jaspeth we stand with one foot outside time. We see its entirety and are forbidden from action beyond our tasks—but we *feel* the now. And on seeing the destruction of so rare a peace Yamala and I felt we could no longer stand outside. We did the only thing we could. We shed our immortality and took the frail forms that would allow us to act, to help, to try to nurture a peace and break the cycle. I took a name. I became Yute and embraced time so that I could make a change."

Livira's gaze returned to Malar, who she'd been crawling towards when Evar reached her. The soldier still hadn't moved. She edged closer, trying not to catch Clovis's eye.

"It was hubris. Immersed in the flow of time we found ourselves tangled in the problem we had imagined we might solve. We couldn't even agree on the solution. Yamala still cleaved to Irad's way. Let the library be a perfect memory for endless imperfect intelligences. Let it remember where they forgot. Let it raise them as swiftly from the dust as it is possible to rise. Let nothing be hidden. Everything put into the hands of any who ask for it.

"I found myself in sympathy with Irad's brother. Unlike Jaspeth I didn't want to destroy the library and let the races crawl from increasingly infertile mud at every cycle. But I felt they should be taught to walk before they were given racehorses, chariots, ornithopters to take them to the sky. I felt that knowledge should be earned through wisdom.

"Sadly, my own wisdom has not been equal to the task. I have grown old, and war has overtaken my efforts.

"But the truth is that I traded immortality for the chance to help you. And I gave eternity away because the death of so many Liviras and Evars living together in peace was a moment of shame deep enough to teach sorrow to a being as old as the library itself and with no time for moments." He turned to look at Livira. "And yes, Livira, I was the boy you saw at the window in that poisoned city, and I saw you, and I held the memory of you across the centuries until I saw you once more on the steps of the Allocation Hall."

"You should have worked with me, husband." Yamala's voice amplified through the trees as Yute's had. "If the people of Crath had more advanced weaponry they could have forced a peace and the library would not be burning, yet again."

"If the soldiers on the wall had held in their hands a faster means of killing, the dead would have piled yards-deep at the foot of the wall, and when Evar's people had run, the soldiers would have chased them and killed them in their homes and villages. And he"—Yute extended a white finger towards Lord Algar without looking at him—"would neither deny this fact nor declare it to be anything other than just and reasonable."

"Is it not justice to retaliate when attacked?" Algar spat into the grass. "These *dogs* have driven us from our homes, slaughtered tens of thousands in the streets, and burned the library. All because *you*, Davris Yute, have some delusion of grandeur to excuse your deformity and have in consequence sabotaged the work of the library. You have brought down a king, a capital, and the kingdoms will now topple by the score. No wonder you're all for mercy now. Hear me well, librarian. You will pay for your crimes, and I will find what I need to pay these dogs back for murders too numerous to count. I'll hunt them to the end of the world, slit the throat of every last pup taken from its mother's arms. I'll—"

Clovis raised her hand faster than thought. The knife would have flown from her fingers but for Evar catching her wrist.

"You're going to kill him?" Evar barked. "He's you, Clovis. Those are your words coming out of his mouth. We could kill them all. Hells, you could do it by yourself. And—"

"Don't tell me we'd be making ourselves just as bad as they are." Clovis had Evar by the throat. "Don't try that with me, little brother. Just don't."

Evar tore her hand away from his neck. He bared his teeth and set himself squarely between Clovis and Livira. Livira meantime had gone to her knees and was struggling to roll the unconscious Malar onto his back. Evar took a swift step towards his sister, putting the siblings almost nose to nose. "Do what you will with him then. But hear me on this one thing. You understand me—so you must understand that I will burn *everything* down before I let you hurt her."

A shudder ran through the ground beneath Livira's feet, and she caught the sharp scent of smoke. A mutter of new fear ran through the crowd. A crimson flame flickered up around the trunk of the nearest tree like the tongue of some infernal lizard: Evar's anger given release.

"Help me!" Livira's scream cut the tension. She looked up from Malar's side, both hands dripping with blood from the wound Clovis had put in his belly. "I think he's dying!"

The last words a person speaks are given additional weight. Some legal systems codify that gravitas into the statutes, allowing evidence from the deathbed greater import. But, often as not, the last words to pass our lips do so without the burden of knowing no more will follow. They are a random line from a random page in a novel that believes it will be completed. Just imagine what . . .

In Memoriam: The Things I Remembered to Forget, *by Nicholas Hayes*

CHAPTER 59

Evar

H elp me!"

Livira's cry tore Evar's attention from Clovis and the creature, Yute, who claimed he was once an assistant, part of the fabric of the library.

"I think he's dying!" Livira's hands were red with her companion's blood.

Evar examined the wound. It looked fatal. What else could be expected when a sabber put itself in Clovis's way? The male had been lucky to put Kerrol down, but Clovis was a different matter entirely.

"I . . ." The look on Livira's face made the answer forming on Evar's lips unacceptable, unspeakable. He'd read that love was when the hurts of another became yours, every bit as sharp, even if you didn't understand them. He didn't understand what this man—he would call him a man—was to Livira, but he knew that he had to do something. "The centre circle. It's a new wound. I can get him there."

"The library's on fire." The flames that Evar's anger had brought to the Exchange echoed in Livira's eyes.

"Not my library." Evar scooped the man up in both arms. He was heavier than he looked but not so heavy that Evar couldn't run with him. Whether he could run a mile carrying him he'd have to find out. "Stay here," he told Livira. "There are Escapes where I came from." He hated to say it, hated to leave her with Clovis, with only Yute to talk his sister down. Part of him wished he'd held his tongue and let this nameless sabber die. But he wouldn't have been able to live with that lie of omission any more than he could live with finding Livira gone when he returned, or worse—dead.

Evar glanced back at his sister. He wanted to say that she had trained for war her whole life, but her greatest fight might be not to use the weapon she had become. Even in his mind it sounded too pompous. Instead, he opted for mere honesty. "I saw what they did to you. It hurt me. I wanted to kill them too."

Clovis's eyes widened at that, and although she hid her pain, it twitched in all the small muscles of her face. She tried to speak but couldn't.

"Please wait for me to get back. This doesn't have to end in blood." And with the numbers continuing to mount as armed sabbers carried on stumbling through the portal, stinking of smoke, he was no longer even sure Clovis would win. "Wait for me."

With that he turned and walked towards their pool. Yute was speaking to Clovis, his voice closer to the endlessly patient tones of the Assistant when she had first taken charge of their care. Evar didn't look back at Livira. She was probably relieved to have him go. Her people found his kind repulsive. They thought of them as animals. As dogs. She was probably embarrassed and revolted at the kiss they'd shared before the scales fell from their eyes. The library had played the cruellest of tricks on them.

He stopped at the edge of the pool.

"Shouldn't we be running?"

He turned, startled. Livira was right behind him. "You should be back with your friends."

"I'm coming with you." Dark eyes challenged him. "Besides, most of my friends haven't come through the portal yet." Her voice cracked around this last part, as if she wasn't sure they ever would, and she stepped towards the pool.

Evar moved to block her path. "If you come you can't go back. If you enter our chamber, then in every time before it you'll be a ghost. There's no going back to your life."

"Sabbers burned down my life." She pressed past Evar.

With his arms full, he couldn't stop her falling into the water.

Without hesitation he followed.

———

THE CROPS WERE a mess, trampled, the ground torn and churned, stained black where the Escapes had died. The Assistant and the Soldier had already fallen into their waiting stances, the chamber being empty of their charges. As they turned to greet his arrival, Evar wondered how long they would have remained immobile without him. *One foot outside time*: that was how Yute had put it. Somehow it deepened Evar's affection for the pair—that they had both managed to project some modicum of caring through the barriers that held them back.

Immediately, he set off running, trusting that the Soldier would follow if any Escapes were still lurking among the stacks. Livira caught up with him as he kicked down a portion of the book wall rather than subject the injured man to an awkward clambering over.

"He's called Malar." Livira struggled with the words, her voice thin, the stress on the wrong places. For a few moments Evar thought she was speaking a different language, but with effort he puzzled meaning from the mess.

"Malar," he repeated, and broke loose half a dozen more books with a kick. The realisation hit him suddenly. "You're . . . You never spoke to me before. Not in my tongue. The Exchange translated everything!"

"Lucky I learn!" Livira threw herself at the wall, shoulder first, and knocked out several more books.

Evar stepped over the remains and started to jog. He could outpace Livira but that would leave her vulnerable, and in any case, he couldn't sprint a mile carrying an armoured sabber.

Together they ran through the stacks. The clack of the Soldier's feet behind them was both a comfort, in that they would be protected, and a worrying declaration that danger lurked among the book towers.

"You come back." Livira's pronunciation was even worse when running.

"I came back," Evar agreed.

"Bring sister," Livira said, her diction too bad to carry accusation though it had to be there. "Help you kill me."

"What?" Evar almost dropped Malar. "No!"

"Not need," Livira puffed, "help?"

Evar glanced to the side to see if she was joking, but if there had been a smile it was already gone.

"Whether I'd need help to kill you isn't the issue. I didn't want to. I don't want to." He swerved around a thick stack and set a narrow one toppling as Malar's boots caught it. "Why do you think I'm carrying this idiot?"

"Not idiot. Save life. Many times."

"Not an idiot. I'm sorry. But the reason I'm carrying this very heavy genius who thought he could stop my sister is because he matters to *you*."

Behind them the regular clack-clack-clack of the Soldier's feet faltered. Evar risked a backwards glance but could see no signs of trouble. The Soldier picked up his pace again and the three of them ran on.

Evar arrived at the centre circle's clearing dripping with sweat. He sank to his knees, letting Malar slide from his grasp. His breath was ragged, the fur on his arms crimson where he'd held the man. Livira collapsed beside him a few moments later, gasping for air, retching with the effort it had taken her to keep up. The Soldier came to a halt behind her, untroubled, watching the stacks surrounding them.

The circle's radiance began its work on all of them, slowly reversing the sources of the harm done to them whether by their own efforts or by others'. Evar's strength returned as the circle's power removed the poison of fatigue from his muscles and restored the chemistry of his blood.

Malar's breath came in thin whispers between pale, almost bluish, lips. Not dead then. Evar sat back, almost certain that the circle would draw the man back from death's edge. If he'd passed over then that would surely have been an end to it, but Evar had yet to see an injury the circle couldn't heal. He wondered if the sabbers who had murdered Clovis's people had stood guard around the circle to keep the wounded from it. He looked up from those dark thoughts to see Livira watching him.

"Hello." He made to smile then forced it from his face. What did she see when she looked at him? One of the monsters who had killed her loved ones and dragged her from the ruins of her home? A creature she could no more desire than any other entry in the bestiary? He had never considered how he looked to others before, never cared. His siblings were the same as him, variations on a theme. The idea that he might be ugly, and the shame that accompanied it, were strangers to him. And yet it was the hope that hurt him most, that oh-so-thin sliver that could reach his heart even so. That kiss still burned on his tongue; those moments of closeness, when the space between their bodies had vanished to nothing, remained vital to him, too precious to release entirely. Livira had, in a heartbeat, become his addiction, and however unhealthy that might be he now knew no other way to live.

"Hello," she said, her smile a fragile, careworn thing. She rubbed at her bloodshot eyes and returned her gaze to Malar.

"I . . ." Evar struggled for the words, as if it were he who was the stranger to the language. "Do you . . . I mean—"

Malar drew in a croaking breath and muttered something in the sabber tongue. It strengthened Livira's smile.

Evar frowned and tried to fit his mouth around their language. "What does *fuckme* mean?"

Livira laughed and then to his horror her eyes filled with tears, and she broke into ugly sobbing.

"Livira!" Evar moved to her side, only to find the Soldier there first, leaning forward to place an ivory hand on her shoulder, the skin still bearing the marks of some ancient heat. It was an action so unlike the Soldier that Evar sat back down and stared.

A short while later Malar sat up with a groan and more pained exclamations, including several repeats of *fuckme* and *fuck*. He reached around and released two side buckles. His pitted iron breastplate fell away with a clang. Lifting a blood-stained padded shirt, Malar revealed the stomach wound that had nearly killed him. But for his skill, Clovis would have taken his head off, or at least sliced his throat. But for the armour, Clovis would have stabbed him in the heart. As it was, she'd struck up beneath the lower rim to gut him.

A livid red line was all that recorded the passage of her knife now. Even that was fading to a silvery scar. Evar had always thought that the method by which the circle healed would mean that no scars remained, the flesh returning to before the time of the injury. The library's makers, however, had had different ideas. Perhaps they felt that every wound should leave some record, something to remind the person how short life can be and how disaster stalks us every hour of our lives, waiting its chance.

Evar wondered if there might not be an equivalent cure for injuries of the heart, a way to undo cruel deeds, sharp words, incautious honesty, and roll back each mistake. Perhaps not . . . He wondered where such a cleaning of his own slate might end. Probably at the moment of birth with the freedom to write a whole new story for himself, and to repeat every error he'd ever made.

Malar raised his head and glared at Evar, spitting out more words.

"He says he doesn't like you," Livira supplied. "And that if you so much as look at me sideways he'll end you." She paused while Malar said something else. "And he says thank you for saving his life."

Translation is a powerful art requiring great intellect. It is not a process that can be conducted without bias. The page is regarded through multiple lenses, including those of the author, audience, and translator. Each brings something new to the text. The same sentences, pressed from one language and culture into the language and realm of another, can lead to war or to peace, with the difference sometimes dependent on the slimmest thread of reason.

Babel, *by Josiah Maddie*

CHAPTER 60

Livira

T ell that fucking sabber to eat shit," Malar spat. "And if he lays a hand on you, I'm going to cut it off."

Livira stretched her sabbertine around Malar's instructions.

Malar had more to say. "Tell him if I see that red-maned cunt again I'll cut her heart out."

Livira growled and rumbled. "And he says thank you for saving his life." Sabbertine gave her a sore throat, but she enjoyed the emotive form of the language. The harsher words sounded angry and almost required rage to generate. The softer sentiments were closer to a cat's purring.

"And—"

"He saved your life, Malar. He ran all the way, carrying you. This place is repairing your body. You would have died any other way."

"Huh." Malar made a growl that sounded close to the sabbertine for *excrement.* "Well." He looked around. "We should be getting back . . . to wherever we were . . . from wherever here is. Yute needs us."

"He does." Livira wasn't sure why Yute needed them—he was an ex-assistant who'd lived hundreds of years and could effortlessly open doors she'd spent half her life trying to get through. He could probably have a portal swallow Clovis if she turned violent again. It was far from clear that he needed any of them. But it felt as if he did. In any case, they probably needed him. Also, she'd left friends behind in the Exchange: Neera, Katrin, Acmar . . . Acmar felt like a friend, or at least someone she cared for. She felt a responsibility for him, along with the others from the settlement who had had to carve out lives for themselves in Crath City and now faced a second upheaval of even greater proportions.

Malar struggled to his feet, cursing and clutching his stomach. Evar moved to help him, but Livira's raised hand stopped him. The circle could reknit Malar's flesh—his pride would recover more slowly.

"We need to go back," she told Evar. "Please take us to your pool." She hoped she was getting the tenses right. Also, she had a suspicion she might have used the word for "latrine" instead of "pool." Both were very similar to a human ear.

"Let's make it fast," Malar said, though he looked in no condition to go anywhere at much above medium.

"Actually, the pool tends to take you to the when you want or need to be at. So, there's no need to hurry," Livira said, wanting to spare him.

Malar gave her a narrow-eyed sideways look. "Was that supposed to make any sense at all?"

"Temporally, there's some degree of agency. Even involuntary travel leads to synchronicity." Livira felt that she might have some control over the matter; her desire might guide her in the same sort of way that Evar's anger at Clovis had temporarily imprinted itself on the very fabric of the place. She guessed that the Exchange, intended to be populated only by the impassive assistants, had to work hard to accommodate the raw emotions of beings like humans and sabbers. Sabbers . . . She would have to find another word for them. Perhaps "canith," the sabbertine word for "people." Malar's grunt and his puzzled look recaptured her attention. She tried again: "Time's funny in the Exchange. We'll get back when we need to or want to. That's how it works."

"You should have said that first." Malar sank back down and settled on his side with a groan, holding his stomach. "I'm just going to lie here for a bit longer then . . ." He closed his eyes.

The sword-carrying assistant set off to patrol the perimeter of the centre circle, the book-free clearing being about thirty yards across.

Evar sat back and rested his elbows on raised knees, looking at Livira. "Well," he said. "We're both sabbers, then."

"Yes." Livira felt uncomfortable under the scrutiny of his large, amber eyes, not human but full of humanity. She saw intelligence there, compassion, things she already associated with Evar, and other far more complicated feelings too. His gaze made her self-conscious, but she didn't want him to look away.

"I didn't mean to trick you," he rumbled.

"I didn't mean it either." Livira wondered how she must look to him. Small, frail, perhaps cold or bald, lacking as she did the small fine hairs that covered his limbs. "Will you tell her?"

"Who?" A frown.

"The woman in your book. When you find her." Livira imagined the two of them laughing over Evar's mistake. The time he kissed a human.

Evar gave her a curious look, as if waiting for her to confess something. After a moment's silence he shrugged and reached into his leathers. "I'm thinking I should just read it." He tugged the slim volume out. "I mean, she tells me not to. On the very first page. It's basically all she says. But . . ." He ran a finger over the ends of the pages. Livira noticed for the first time since one had arrived at her settlement many years ago, that sabbers—canith—only had three fingers on each hand, a blunt black claw at the end of each. Clovis had nearly killed her with just one of her claws. ". . . but I think maybe I'm past being told what to do."

"Wait." The cover design caught Livira's attention, faint lines endlessly coiling back on themselves within the bounds of a circle, a figure emerging as a trick of the light where the threads crossed each other most densely. It reminded her of Ella's wind-weed sculpture. The one she'd given Livira on the day the sabbers came, half-finished, a boy hinted at in its depths. "Wait . . ."

Evar waited and Livira realised that she didn't have a reason. She shrugged her satchel into her lap and unbuckled it. "I've been . . ." She pulled out the stolen cover into which she'd collected all her stolen pages. ". . . writing."

Evar's face went still, his eyes wide and brilliant. Slowly he held out his book. It had always looked small in his grip. But he was very big.

The backs of Livira's arms tingled as she held her book out. Apart from the faint design on the cover of his . . . they were the same book. The same book in two very different hands. Very different but both trembling.

When the books touched there was no implosion, no shudder that passed out through the world rearranging every atom. It was more as if a god had turned the last page of a story they'd been reading since time started. Livira found her breath escaping and being replaced in short, aching pants, tears were falling from eyes that had cried too much already, and she couldn't say why.

There was only one book, held in both their hands, fingers interlaced.

"What does it mean?" Livira managed in a faint voice. She knew what it meant but hearing him say it might make her understand it.

Evar shook his head wonderingly, surrendering the book to her keeping. "I remember it . . . I remember. It's coming back . . ."

Livira held the book to her chest. She'd written her heart into it. She'd let her pen wander the pages through adventure after adventure, imagination unchained. And through it all Evar had walked beside her, run beside her, flown to the moons, dived to the darkest depths the seas contained. She had written it. He had lived it. With her.

Malar coughed and sat up. "Fucked if a man can sleep with all that growling and grunting. Let's go."

And Livira and Evar—without requiring translation but needing the space to absorb this revelation—agreed.

THE FOUR OF them—the sword-bearing assistant, the sabber . . . canith, the librarian, and the soldier—made a much slower return. Livira studied the book columns, considering how annoying it must be if the book you wanted was at the bottom. She tried to place the chamber in the library map she carried in her mind. Evar said they had a Mechanism, and she knew of only one chamber with a reading room that boasted a Mechanism. This one bore no resemblance to that one—the other had had granite shelves and the closest that this chamber came to granite was a red grittiness to its dust—but a lot of things can change in a few centuries, even if they rarely did in the library.

"And you've been trapped here all your life?" Livira rumbled and snarled in the language of the canith.

"For generations."

"I learned something today—"

"What are you saying to him?" Malar interrupted. "He's the enemy, remember."

Livira sighed. "I know." She pictured the bodies scattered along her corridor. One of them would have been hers if she'd been in her rooms. If Yute hadn't summoned her to his house. "It's literally what we call them. Sabber."

"What's he saying?" Suspicion tinged Evar's voice. Livira's skill with the language should have been too basic to detect such nuance but she supposed that her ears had been hearing him speak all the time they'd spent together while the Exchange put his meaning into her mind. It was a level of schooling that Heeth Logaris would die for. If the sabbers hadn't killed him only half a day ago.

"I learned something today," Livira repeated. "There are doors in the library I can't open—no human can—but that will open for any of your people. And there are doors that your kind, the canith, can't open but that will open for any human. And there are other doors that neither of us can open."

"Do you think . . ."

"I don't know. But it's worth trying, isn't it?"

Evar adjusted his course, leading them into a glade where the books were stacked only five or six high in single columns, the tops giving the impression of a gently undulating surface.

Livira turned her head to look at the sword-bearing assistant walking beside her. Unlike the pure assistants she'd seen in great numbers, this one and the one they'd left behind at the pool weren't the gleaming enamel-white of a new tooth, or the grey or black of an assistant corrupted by Escapes. Instead, the pair were off-white, ivory and cream, almost yellowing in places, shot through here and there with faint grey seams.

The side it presented to her had a buckled, melted texture to it, as if it had been exposed to some great heat. "Assistants don't carry swords."

"I do." The assistant kept its eyes forward, ever watchful.

"Why?" She remembered that she had seen one assistant with a sword.

The black one that had escaped from Chamber 7 had made itself a sword to strike down the assistant that Yamala had summoned to guide them.

The assistant ignored her.

Livira remembered that the corrupted assistant had given Yamala's assistant a wound down across its eyebrow and cheek. A wound that had allowed it too to be corrupted. "Look at me."

The assistant turned his face to her. The same wound marked it.

Livira stopped walking and took a step back. "Evar. Do you trust this assistant?"

Evar turned. "I do." He set a hand to the assistant's shoulder. "You should too. If the Soldier wanted us dead, we'd all be dead. Even Clovis can't beat him." Evar looked between them, unsmiling. "Besides, I think he likes you."

The assistant said nothing, merely returning to watching the lines along which danger might approach.

"Come on." Evar led off, avoiding Livira's eyes. "I want to see if you can open the door."

THEY APPROACHED THE huge white door along a hundred yards of corridor set into the vast expanse of the chamber wall. There had been two doors in Chamber 97 that Livira could not open. Based on the location of Evar's Mechanism, this was a different exit. By rights she should be able to open it.

Livira craned her neck, looking up at the door's height. Behind her, Malar, the assistant, and Evar waited in a row. Livira was glad to have something to focus on. Evar couldn't hide his disappointment. He seemed hardly able to look at her, lost in his own thoughts. He'd spent his life waiting to find his mystery woman, this marvel who had somehow defined him, given him meaning in a bleak existence. He'd expected some fierce, glorious creature like his sister, but wise and loving and full of poise and wisdom. And got . . . a skinny duster, not even his own species, despised by most of her own, one full of questions and sharp angles and an inability to settle or do what was expected of her. The white expanse of the door brought her back to the moment.

Livira glanced back at the assistant—the Soldier, Evar called him. "You could have opened this door any time you wanted to. Why didn't you? Is there something we should know?"

"It's not my place to open doors. The doors serve as intended."

"But you *can* open them?" Livira remembered Yute had said a corrupt assistant couldn't open doors.

The assistant made no reply.

"Have you been on the other side?"

"Yes."

"Recently?"

"Define recen—"

"In the last fifty years."

"No."

"Is it safe to open?"

"Nothing is safe."

Malar moved in front of the Soldier, who was about the same height as him, and leaned into whatever personal space the creature had, until their foreheads were nearly touching. "I may not like your boyfriend much, but this fucker . . ."

Livira turned away, reaching towards the door. For a moment she thought it would resist her but instead her fingers met only mist, dissipating in all directions. Evar's gasp behind her sounded as if it had been held within his chest since the day he was born.

It is often said that there's always a bigger fish. The universe, however, prefers cycles to stretches. There is in fact a biggest fish. What is true is that there is always something that will feast upon the feaster. The biggest of fish are ultimately devoured by many small ones.

An Angler's Companion, by J. R. Hartley

CHAPTER 61

Evar

E var had waded to the door rather than walked. The flood of memory threatened to drown him. Something new every step, each thread he pulled pulling on a dozen more, books tumbling from a tilting shelf, each a story in and of itself, each a world, enough to consume him, bouncing off, too much to absorb, but rather than falling away they circled him, waiting their moment to invade. Every time he glanced at Livira the flood increased in ferocity, images of lives he didn't lead pressing on his vision until it was hard to see. The sensation left him dizzy, weak, and a little nauseous. Throwing up in front of the woman whose ghost had filled his dreams for so long would hardly raise her opinion of him from the floor, and so he turned away.

They reached the north door and although he'd thought of little but escape for his whole life Evar could hardly keep his mind on the moment. More memories rose from the scar in his mind. Journeys he and Livira had taken but never taken, jungles explored, seas crossed, kisses stolen under strange skies. But these must have been kisses before she knew he was the enemy, a sabber, before she'd seen his strangeness, the brute ugliness of him compared to her fragile beauty.

Livira was talking to the Soldier who replied in the human's chirping birdsong tongue. It almost made sense, as if real words were being strung together in an unending chain and pulled rapidly past his ears.

The exchange carried on and Evar was sure he recognised words here and there. Then the warrior, Malar, stepped up as if to challenge the Soldier.

"... not like ... your boyfriend ... this fucker ..."

Evar raised his head to regard Malar. He was definitely understanding the man. It was the language he'd read on the first page of Livira's book. The same tongue she'd spoken to him in the Exchange and in all those years within the Mechanism. He opened his mouth to see if he could shape the words himself, but as he did so the great white wall that had always blocked his escape melted away to nothing.

Three creatures waited for them. Three identical creatures that must have been standing with their faces all but pressed against the opposite side of the door. They stood, immobile, one by the wall on either side, and one dead centre, close enough to reach out and touch. They reminded Evar of the Escape with the scythe hands that had caught him at the book fort, though these were considerably more robust creatures, a head taller than him but much more solid, insectoids covered in armour plates that were a curious combination of a creamy, almost yellowish white along the grooves and plates, shading to black or deepest blue on the prominences. The projections that reminded him of scythe hands were more by way of shards of armour plate jutting out from their right arms, extending their reach by over a yard. Their heads were blunt exo-skulls swept back and beaded with half a dozen black eyes set deep in armoured wells.

"Are they guides?" Livira stared up at the one in front of her, dwarfed by its bulk.

The only answer was a high whining. Evar hunted the source of the noise. Small holes lined the seams of the creatures' armour. Spiracles. The word came to him: spiracles. The vents through which the insect draws in air to feed the parts of its body that require it.

"It's taking a breath." Evar caught Livira's shoulder and pulled her back.

Over Livira's cry of protest a rapid series of clicks snapped the air, loud enough to be the shots of projectile weapons. The creature's whole body flexed and shuddered; an untold weight of sleep being shrugged off in moments. It took one step forward on four of six limbs and, with disturbing speed, thrust its spike on a trajectory that would have skewered first Livira and then Evar.

The Soldier intercepted the thrust, deflecting it by throwing his body against the spike's side as it came forward. Malar attacked with a rapidity that Evar had not previously associated with humans. His swords did little damage, glancing off the beast's armour.

"Run!" the Soldier shouted.

A glance to either side showed that both the creature's companions were closing on the conflict. Evar was loath to run from a fight if it meant leaving someone behind, but his faith in the Soldier ran deep. The assistant was near-indestructible and deadly. Livira on the other hand was highly destructible, and Malar might be an able killer, but experience had shown he'd take on opponents too deadly even for him and get himself slain.

The Soldier spun inside the insectoid's reach and drove his sword into a joint of its leg armour. The wounded insectoid unleashed a horrendous cry that seemed to emanate from its whole body, a shrill whistling from its breathing holes, a deep penetrating throb from its abdomen. The sort of sound that could carry for miles in the stillness of the library.

The Soldier, using all his weight, twisted his blade, grinding it inside the joint and splintering armour. One of the creature's other three supporting limbs—heavily armoured legs—reached up like an arm, grabbed the Soldier and slammed him into the floor with a sick-making crunch. The Soldier's white blade flashed, and toe-like appendages flew into the air. "Run!" he shouted again, spinning back onto his feet.

Evar picked Livira up under one arm and ran for it. Her screaming was the most convincing argument he could put to Malar, certainly the most effective. In fact, she only screamed once and it had more outrage in it than fear, but it was enough to set Malar sprinting after them.

A quick look back towards the chamber showed that none of the creatures had given chase, instead choosing to combine their efforts to take the Soldier down. One hit him from the side, and he staggered. After that Evar could see only flashes of white as the three hulking insectoids came at the Soldier from all sides.

For a moment Evar hesitated. The huge Escape had cracked the Assistant. She had always seemed indestructible, but she wasn't. The Soldier too bore wounds and would have his breaking point.

Between Evar and the fight Malar slowed too, seeing Evar turn.

"Don't let him fight them," Livira said from under Evar's arm. "He'll die."

Evar nodded. "Follow!" He shouted it in the human tongue and ran for the pool.

EVAR WAS ABLE to put Livira down at the chamber entrance and let her run unassisted. He kept to a pace the two humans could manage, bringing them breathless to the pool. The Assistant came to meet them at the book wall.

"Creatures are attacking the Soldier," Evar told her. "Real creatures, not Escapes, insectoids. Big ones. Three of them." He stretched his arms to show their width.

"You opened the door." The Assistant looked at Livira, a red glow in her eyes that Evar had never seen before.

"You kept them trapped in here," Livira shot back. "For hundreds of years. Prisoners!"

"I am unable to open the doors," the Assistant said, the glow fading. "I am impure."

Impure? The Assistant was the purest thing in Evar's life. "Wait! Where are you going?"

"To fight beside the Soldier against the skeer." The Assistant vaulted the wall, landing more lightly than the Soldier would. "Return the humans to the Exchange."

"I can help." Evar looked between the Assistant and Livira. "Wait!"

"I cannot." The Assistant began to run towards the corridor. Evar realised that he had never seen her run before.

He started after her. "Wait! Please!" He faltered and looked back at Livira. Both of them held a piece of his heart, though he hadn't ever understood how much the Assistant owned. She had taken her real estate in his soul fraction by fraction over the years, advancing her claim with such slow stealth that he had never noticed. The others might say that her patience and devotion were part of her nature and that the span of their lives was nothing to her, a flicker in the eternity of her existence. Evar might have agreed with them, but the depths of him disagreed.

Livira's claim was different, manifold, and growing with each passing moment, though the memories that were chaining him to her were memories not of the woman before him but of the ghost of her that the Mechanism made from her writing to entertain him and lead him through the landscape of her imagination.

What decided him was his belief that the Assistant would not be harmed whereas something as small as a scratch from his sister could almost kill Livira. One needed his help. The other was the one he went to *for* help.

"We need to go." He reached for Livira's hand and started to lead her towards the pool.

"Will they be all right?" Livira looked after the Assistant, her brow furrowed.

"Yes." Evar had seen the Assistant take on bigger bugs than these skeer. Livira allowed herself to be led. Malar followed.

They reached the pool and stood amid the ruined crops. Evar eyed the trampled kale he had been tending since planting it some months earlier. For no reason that he could pinpoint it brought tears to his eyes. It was silly. They were just plants. More could be grown.

"Come on." He was still holding Livira's hand. The heat generated between them had little to do with body temperature.

They jumped and the pool claimed them.

You can't go back. Time is a river and there's no swimming against it. You can't go back. Yesterday does not wait for you. The past is on fire. What you find when you return to it will be ashes.

The School Reunion, *by Ian Evans*

CHAPTER 62

Evar & Livira

Evar clambered out of the pool, Livira beside him. The scene in the wood had hardly changed, as if the hour and more spent with Malar and Livira in the chamber had occupied none of the Exchange's time. Clovis still glowered at Yute. The human refugees still clustered by the portal through which they were still arriving. Yamala still stood to one side, observing her fellow "fallen" assistant. Kerrol watched fascinated as if seeing every conflict within Clovis's skull written in the twitches of her face as she struggled to deny Yute's words. If this rationale had come from any source other than an assistant, or something close to one, she would have disembowelled them before they'd got through their opening argument.

Evar had never thought to see someone stand between Clovis and her war, let alone a frail creature like Yute. But his calm logic seemed to be inflicting a death of a thousand cuts on Clovis's desire to murder anyone from the species that had destroyed her life. Even so, violence trembled in the air and the balance that Yute had miraculously established could easily fall to either side of the knife's edge. The Exchange's insistence on translation could sink them in an instant if the one-eyed human with the ugly mind opened his cruel mouth again to stain the air with more of his opinions.

Livira ran ahead of Evar and Malar, swinging her head as if looking for someone. Malar muttered an oath and gave chase. The pair gave Clovis a wide berth. Evar, following, saw the swift glance exchanged between Malar and Clovis—killer to killer, though in truth Malar was the closest Clovis had ever come to taking a life, assuming that neither Escapes nor the creations of the Mechanism were properly alive.

Two girls with anxious expressions broke from the group of refugees to greet Livira. Evar's arrival behind Livira caused the pair to startle back from their hugging and handholding with cries of fright. A young male with shaking hands came forward to protect one of the females. Others among the crowd—males close to the one-eyed trouble-causer—levelled the steel barrels of projectile weapons at him.

"No!" Livira interposed herself between them, though she could hardly shield all of him with her slight frame. "He saved Malar's life!" It seemed enough—for now. The weapons were lowered slightly. Turning to her two friends, she started to introduce them. "This is Evar Eventari, Neera."

The girl, with what humans must consider a mane of black hair, looked up at him with a nervous cough.

"Evar, this is Neera, one of my oldest friends. And Katrin." Livira pointed to the broader girl with browner hair who had continued to edge away in the arms of her mate. "And . . . there are others coming. Soon." She looked with concern at the humans stumbling from the portal, all of them coughing and stinking of smoke. "Katrin and Neera grew up with me before . . . before—"

"Before my kind drove you from your homes." Evar bowed his head. "As Master Yute is explaining to my sister that you are not the humans who murdered her family, I hope you will accept my sympathy and sorrow and accept that I share nothing save my shape with those who came against your people."

WHILE EVAR ADDRESSED her friends, Livira's gaze kept straying to the fading portal where any moment now Arpix, Jella, Meelan, and Salamonda must surely arrive. She caught Serra Leetar's eye in the small crowd behind them. Leetar had broken away from Lord Algar's side and seemed to be struggling with conflicting emotions while she watched the portal, looking for her brother among the thinning stream of people. The doorway's light was guttering now, like a flame at the limit of its fuel. Livira stepped past Neera, brushed by Katrin and Jammus, and approached the diplomat.

"Was Meelan with you?" Leetar demanded. "Have you seen him?"

"I . . ." A smoke-blackened man collapsed through the portal, his skin red, clothes smouldering. He fell to the grass choking as others tried to help him. Livira's voice broke. "He was with me. Meelan and the others. I don't understand. They were right behind me. Right behind me."

Livira met Leetar's eyes and found them full of tears. Their hands hovered, inches apart, then met, each trying to wring the strength they needed from the other.

"They . . . they might escape," Leetar said hopelessly.

It was true that they might have lost their way but still have escaped the smoke and still be ahead of the flames, but they couldn't outpace the inferno in the long run. And they wouldn't be coming through the portal Livira had drawn. Even if there were enough power left in it after the passage of so many people, the aisles had been thick with smoke when she left. Nobody could cross that chamber now. It would be as bad as the other-world library Livira and Evar had once stepped into where the air had begun to kill Livira's lungs on her very first breath.

"It didn't hurt you though . . ." Livira turned back towards Evar.

"What didn't?" He looked confused.

"The air in that other world. The one where I was poisoned."

"I was a ghost."

Livira shifted her stare to Malar. "We'll all be ghosts if we go back through there." She pointed at the portal. "You, me, and Evar."

It was Malar's turn to look confused.

Evar shook his head. "I'll come of course. But if you go back, all you can do is find their corpses, or worse, watch them die. You can't help them." His face showed only sympathy, and a wince of pain as if imagining what she would feel.

"At least I would know!" Livira had raised her voice unintentionally and now became aware that Yute, Clovis, all of them really, had stopped talking and were looking at her. She looked at Yute and understood in that moment the sorrow which had walked with him since the first day she had known him and for long before. His daughter had vanished in the library. She wouldn't ask him if seeing her body would have been better than all those long years of not knowing. It was too cruel a question and she already knew the answer. "At least I would know . . ."

Livira went to Yute, careless of the red-maned canith looming over him. She took his cool, white hands in hers, shocking both of them. Yute had never been one for touching.

"I'm going after Arpix and Salamonda and the others," she said. "I can make it so that when I come back, you'll still be here, can't I?"

"You can." He nodded. "In this wood you can't go back to what has already been, but you can slow time's march to the flow of resin down a tree's trunk."

"I won't ask you to wait for me then." Livira managed a smile. "I'll make you wait."

Yute's answering smile was smaller and sadder. "I see you followed my advice."

She followed his gaze to the book poking from her satchel where she'd stuffed it as Neera and Katrin had rushed at her. "How did you know? It could be any book I picked up."

"Books in the library are my speciality." No smile this time. "That one is perhaps the strangest of all of them for its story is woven through the Exchange, a place where creatures in time's flow were never intended to tread. Guard it well, Livira." He paused then squeezed her hands in a most un-Yute-like gesture. "It has been an honour."

Livira gave him a puzzled smile. "I'll be back. You won't even know we're gone." He looked so solemn that she felt an odd compulsion to cheer him up. "I'll be a ghost. Nothing can hurt me. And I'll have Malar with me."

She backed away, letting his hands fall from hers. Passing Yamala, she shot the woman a glance and spoke in a quiet voice. "Look after him for me. He seems sad."

Yamala didn't smile either. "We stepped into time's fire but even as we burn, we still see an echo of what's coming at us through the flames."

Livira shook her head. She'd have time for the couple's curious melo-drama when she came back. She wouldn't let a single breath pass their lips before her return.

"Come on!" And beckoning Malar and Evar, she elbowed a path through the refugees towards the portal. And, as she went, she realised that the wood was packed with them, soldiers greatly outnumbering civilians. She was glad that Evar would be with her. It seemed that the only thing stopping the soldiers from taking out their anger on Clovis and the other canith was not knowing quite how many more of their kind this enchanted forest might hold.

Ghosts surround us. We swim through their currents, breathe them in, perform our lives before their audience. And yet, they remain unseen, not only by us but by each other. A multitude of loneliness, a crowding silence full of screams.

The Haunting of Crath City, *by Olidan Ancrath*

CHAPTER 63

Livira

S
moke hung so thick in the aisle before Livira that she couldn't see the shelves much beyond the reach of her arms. The feeble light of the portal she had just stepped through barely reached her, and for a moment she panicked that if Arpix and the others did come here they would find she had squandered the doorway's last power to look for them. They would choke to death within touching distance of salvation. But the idea that anyone could navigate the chamber now was too far-fetched for her guilt to survive long.

"Looks hot." Malar emerged beside her. "Why can't I feel it?"

"You can't feel anything here." Evar stepped out on her other side. He passed a hand through the nearest books, then shuddered. "Except bad writing."

It did look hot. An orange light stained the ever-present glow of the library that lit the smoke from within. Flakes of ash fell in a gentle rain.

"How can you possibly hope to find them in this?" Malar squinted down the aisle. "Even if it wasn't burning, you could never find someone in this place. It's a maze. Before today I had no idea it was this big."

Livira had been focused on this very problem and the solution had occurred to her before she made the decision to return.

"Volente!" She made it both a shout and a command, adopting Arpix's tone.

Evar and Malar looked at her with wide eyes.

Nothing happened. "Volente!" She shouted it more loudly, realising for the first time that the dog might not be able to hear a ghost's voice.

"What are you doing?" Evar asked.

"Trying . . ." Livira couldn't keep the sudden despair from her voice. She looked around, hoping to see Volente's black muzzle nosing through the shelves. "Volente! Please come. It's for Arpix. You liked him!"

Perhaps the dog would have come anyway, or maybe it was good memories of being fussed over by Arpix that made him brave the burning library. Either way, the enormous hound bounded through the nearest shelves, causing both Malar and Evar to leap back and raise their blades.

"He's a friend!" Livira waved Malar away as he advanced to protect her. "He's going to find Arpix for us."

"He's a guide?" Evar peered at Volente. "I've read about those. Don't they only find books?"

Livira nodded. "They do. But I happen to know that Arpix or Meelan is carrying a certain book." She reached a hand to pat Volente, finding him solid. Seeing her fingers swallowed by his utterly black fur was slightly unnerving. A new terror flattened the brief-lived relief which had followed the terror that Volente would not come. If she named the book and Volente didn't start leading them down the aisle it would mean that it had burned, and that almost certainly her friends had been consumed in the same fire. In a trembling voice she asked, "Volente, take me to *A History of the Gratatack Cavern Wars, Volume Six*, by Sscythic Twenty-Nine."

Volente raised his head. He sniffed the air. He knew where books should be. Sscythic's book should be on a shelf in Chamber 7 near to where the injured assistant had lain for untold years before the Escape possessed her. Did the dog know where books *were* though? Could he track a moving one?

Volente sniffed once more, rumbled deep in his chest, and led off.

Livira, able to breathe again, hauled in a great breath, and then, wondering if ghosts actually needed to breathe and why the smoke didn't make her cough, she followed.

THE DOG LED them out across Chamber 16, aiming for the door to Chamber 29. The first time they came to a dead end and Volente sauntered through it, Livira threw up her hands and called for him to come back. It took Evar to remind her that they too could walk through walls. Malar, who had been deeply unsettled by the dog's size and blackness, remained similarly unnerved by its ability to pass through solid objects. When encouraged to do so himself he recoiled from the idea, seeming more worried by the concept than he would by the prospect of taking on an armed man.

"Do it quickly," Livira told him. "At a rush. You don't want to spend time overlapping with books. It's very unsettling."

"Can't we go round?" Malar peered back along the hazy aisle.

"No! Just do it! What kind of soldier are you who can't follow orders?" Livira felt her temper slipping.

"A retired one who doesn't see any fucking officers here," Malar snarled. "You want me to put my head through a solid wall."

"It's just wood!" Livira tried to calm herself. Malar wasn't like this. He wasn't used to being frightened and it showed.

"Is that supposed to help? *It's just wood*?"

"We could wait for it to burn down if you like." Livira's good intentions suddenly gave way to sarcasm. "Then you can walk over the pile of ashes!"

Evar took a more pragmatic approach. Quick as thinking, he grabbed Malar's arm and shoulder, propelling him forward. The soldier vanished through the shelving. "After you." Evar gestured for Livira to follow the sound of swearing.

The ability to plot a straight line through the chamber made a huge reduction to the distance needing to be walked. It also allowed them to open some space between themselves and the blaze.

Volente led them deeper into the library, chamber by chamber. The smoke thinned for a while. Just before entering Chamber 29, Livira climbed a ladder. Or rather, she flew up the ladder but close enough to it not to further shake Malar's confidence.

From the shelf tops Livira could see naked flames gouting from the distant entrance to Chamber 17, the shelving deflecting the flames upwards, licking dozens of yards into the air. The glow to the east told her that the shelves around the portal must be ablaze. The books she'd sought for years and that Arpix had stacked in that aisle would be ashes. The thought hurt her heart.

Volente led them through the tunnel to Chamber 29. It seemed that whilst he recognised their ability to follow him through shelves, he either wasn't able to pass through the library walls or didn't trust Livira's ability to trail him blind through such a thickness of stone.

Livira began to wonder where Meelan—if it was Meelan who still had the book—was heading. She prayed to any god that would listen for her friends to be together. She prayed that Meelan or Arpix had found Salamonda and Jella and brought them to safety, or as much safety as could be found. Volente was leading them towards 46, or the Chamber of Ruin as Livira called it. Her friends wouldn't be there and couldn't have come this way, for the chamber was forbidden, but that didn't mean it wasn't the best route to catch up with them.

With each passing mile the smoke thinned, eventually to nothing, and Livira felt much happier knowing they had, for now, outpaced the fire.

"This should slow it down," Malar said on seeing the Chamber of Ruin. Dust dunes undulated away from them in all directions, decorated with the remains of tattered pages, loose covers, and scattered books with broken spines. Here and there a damaged shelf still managed to stand upright, or more often just the main supports, leaning at drunken angles.

"Hard to say . . ." Evar eyed the desolation. If the destruction of so many books upset him Livira could see no sign of it on his face, though she supposed that far more books were being destroyed behind her with every passing hour. "Dust and fire can be an explosive mix, I've heard."

Malar frowned and would perhaps have been happier remaining ignorant of such facts, but the language barrier that had existed in Evar's chamber had been absent in the Exchange and remained absent here in the past. They were citizens of the future now, and as far as their bodies were concerned, this fire had run its course long ago.

Something caught Evar's eye. "Over there." He pointed.

From her childhood before meeting Malar, Livira knew how to judge the dust clouds raised by feet. "More than twenty of them." The band was headed north, towards Chamber 47.

"Let's go!" Evar set off with Volente at his heels.

Malar followed, before glancing back at Livira. "Come on! Shouldn't you be looking happy? These are your boys!"

Livira caught them up. The dust drifts didn't slow them down, and they raised no trail. As ghosts, it seemed that they could run without tiring or even having to breathe faster. Also as ghosts, they had walked through the door rather than opening it. She shared her fears. "This is a forbidden chamber." Arpix and the others could neither have ghosted through the door nor removed it by touch.

They closed on the band of travellers a quarter of a mile before the door. Evar led them to the side so they wouldn't come on the group through the clouds of book dust they'd raised. Volente gave them a still-wider berth, moving through the deepest drifts of books and book dust without disturbing even a mote.

Livira angled in. There were thirty of them, all sabbers. All canith, she corrected herself. These were the canith who had stormed the city, fought King Oanold's retreating soldiers within the library, and brought fire to the aisles. But they still deserved a better name than just "enemy." She found it hard to push her hatred down, though. The blood that spattered some of them might belong to librarians. The arrow-sticks they carried might have started the blaze. Certainly, they'd been close to it: even from her current remove, Livira could see that several were blackened, some bore livid burns where the flame had seared away the short hair from their limbs and shrivelled the skin beneath.

Livira moved ahead of the group and stood her ground as they came closer.

"Get back!" Malar, still not confident in the business of being a ghost, tried to pull her away. Even for a unit of cavalry a hundred strong, thirty canith would be an encounter best avoided.

Livira shrugged him off. "They could walk right through us and never know."

Evar came to join them. "It's not nice when that happens, so I wouldn't advise it. And they wouldn't know what had happened, but they'd know *something* had happened. I think it's like cold fingers down your spine. They'd shiver—like someone walked across their grave." He frowned at the approaching canith and put a hand on Livira's shoulder. "Come on, let's find your friends."

"I need to see," Livira said quietly. "They might have prisoners. They might have . . ." She wanted to say *trophies*. Something that could tell her they'd killed one or more of her friends.

Evar sighed. A complicated noise. Not a happy one. "I understand."

The canith drew closer. And closer, until Livira could smell the death on them and the chemical stink of their weapons. And then they stopped, just ten yards shy of her. A shorter, older canith growled a warning and raised her staff. Unlike the others she bore no weapon save her stick, which was as thick as her arm and which ended in a twist of polished roots hung with cratalac claws. Her greying mane had been cleverly braided and each braid ended in a ball of brass or lead, the latter perhaps the projectiles fired from Crath's walls.

Livira froze, staring at the priest before her. Impossibly, she had seen this canith before. Long ago on the Dust this sabber had walked beside a line of children all roped together. Livira's wrists still bore the scars of that rope. An old anger trembled in her hands. These ones deserved the fire and she couldn't help hoping that it found them.

She glanced left and right, hunting for the sabber she had first seen from beside the well. The one that had walked into the settlement wrapped in his own arrogance, bringing with him death and violence. He could still be with this priest—one of her warriors. *There!* In the first rank! The old scar still pulling one eye wider than the other.

"Livira!" A warning shout from Malar.

Livira realised with shock that the priest appeared to be looking directly at her. The canith was staring in that squinting kind of way adopted when trying to figure out if what you've seen is real or just some trick of the eye.

"She can see us!" Malar, sounding both scared and vindicated, started to pull Livira back.

Livira twisted out of his grasp and ran to the side. The canith's eyes tracked her and she levelled her staff in Livira's direction, steering the eyes of the warriors to either side of her.

"She can see *me*!" Livira said.

Evar lifted into the air, provoking a startled curse from Malar. "Why just you?" he called down. "It's not like they've seen someone fly before."

Livira understood that Evar was trying to draw attention away from her but none of the canith so much as glanced in his direction. The canith to either side of the old female were staring at her too now, with less certainty, as if where she saw a shadow they saw only a flicker, or some curious twisting of the light. "Why me?" Livira could only echo Evar's question.

One of the canith swung her 'stick to point in Livira's direction, though with insufficient aim to hit her target. Malar shouted at her to run, and did the opposite himself, coming forward to shield her. The old one slapped the weapon down with her staff. Clearly, they'd learned a lesson about starting fires.

Evar swooped to hover above the greying priest. He clenched his jaw and reached a hand briefly into her head.

"A book!" He jerked his hand back and shuddered. The priest shivered too and looked sharply around herself as though buzzed by a deadwasp. "A book . . ." He flew higher. "She sees a book . . ."

Livira blinked in surprise, reached around, and drew out her collection of stories. "This?"

The canith erupted in snarls and yips of surprise, some throwing themselves back, others raising their blades in defence. Dust began to rise all around them. An arrow-stick boomed and something zipped past Livira's head.

"They see you!" Malar roared and charged the front line, swords raised.

"Drop it! DROP IT!" Evar swooped down from on high towards her.

Livira, paralysed in the moment, couldn't release the book. It seemed bonded to her. Her fingers wouldn't let go. Her heart didn't want them to. She had poured herself upon those pages more surely than if she had spilled her lifeblood over them.

"Livira?" A small voice amid the shouts and snarls and blasts.

Evar crashed into her before she could locate the source, and for a moment both of them held the book.

Those who have ventured inside one of the library's mechanisms will understand what is really meant when a book is described as unputdownable. Many claim to have been captivated by a novel, but only in the mechanisms' embrace is a person truly captured by one, imprisoned firmly between two covers. It is vital, when entering a book in this manner, to maintain a clear path to the exit.

Immersive Reading, *by M. Phelps*

CHAPTER 64

Evar

I've fallen into this book before.

Evar woke with a start. The sky above him held the same shade of blue that forever does. The leaves silhouetted against its brightness moved in the lazy way that's more the speed of the trees than of any wind. It seemed to Evar that he had fallen from a vast height and that the softness of the grass had saved him just a moment before his eyes jolted open. It also seemed to him that he had lain exactly in this spot for as long as it took the trees to grow around him. Both things felt true, and their incongruence didn't trouble him as perhaps it should.

He turned his head to find that Livira, lying beside him, their shoulders touching, had turned hers at the same time. Evar sat up. Just beyond his feet a pool of dark water reflected the sky and the leaves and the branches. Trees marched in all directions, not in orderly rows but in nature's chaos, though well spaced as if still remembering some ancient gardener's care. It felt to Evar that he too had something to remember, something urgent, though the forest held no place for urgency to take root.

"Only one pool?" Evar frowned at it. Shouldn't there be more?

Livira sat up beside him. She wore a simple white dress and her hair had been somewhat tamed, coiling around her face, flowing over her bare shoulders. "I think there's only one pool. One's all that's really needed. The rest were more of a training guide."

"Is this the Exchange?" Evar looked around.

"You should remember." Livira smiled.

"Remember?" That word again, pulsing through him. "This is a memory?" Memories had been flooding his mind ever since his book touched Livira's and they became the same thing, completing a circle: the book she had written and that he had carried into the Mechanism. The memories of his time in the Mechanism, for all their newness, felt no different from those of his childhood outside it. Both were a dream of the past. "This isn't real. It's just something you made up. Something you wrote down."

Livira blinked and got to her feet, features sharpening towards that wickedly combative intelligence he knew of old. A different kind of beauty to that she'd first presented as they lay together by the pool. "Perhaps it's something we're making up now? How do you know I've even written it yet? Isn't that a bit presumptuous on the basis of one kiss, Evar Eventari?" She turned away in a swirl of white.

"I didn't mean . . ." He rose and stepped towards her, then stopped. "I mean, how can I be remembering something that hasn't happened yet? How could I have read stories you're going to write but haven't?"

Livira walked away, skirts swaying, looking up into the branches, and everywhere she looked birds alighted, and where she walked butterflies lifted. Their colours put to shame every other colour Evar had ever seen, so vibrant he could almost taste them, so vivid that they might at any moment ignite. Livira glanced back at him through a swirl of indigo wings. "Well, that's the mystery of the Exchange, isn't it? That's probably why we're not allowed to go there." She turned and carried on among the trees.

"Where are you going?"

"To break some more rules." Livira tossed her head. "Coming?"

Evar followed. He couldn't not follow. In fact, even though she had been a child when they first met, and when grown remained both frail and unsuited to the hostile environments they'd found themselves in, and even though she was without the least command of weapon skills, despite all this Evar felt that Livira had been two steps ahead of him the whole time. As he caught up with her, she reached for his hand.

"I wrote a lot of stories in my book." Her fingers laced his. "And if you want the honest truth, you weren't in very many of them at all. They were about me. Or rather, about parts of me, woven into other ideas, stuck together with bits of dreams. The library's a good place for that sort of stuff."

"I remember all kinds of adventures . . ." Evar was sure he'd been in every story from the front cover to the back. "We sailed oceans, visited strange cities . . ."

"A good book invites the reader in," Livira said. "The writer's only half the equation. So of course you were with me. I just don't want you thinking I sat around mooning about you, filling page after page with accurate devotions. I'm writing this book for me."

"Oh, no. I never—"

"Good." She smiled up at him. "You're my only reader so far, and I'm glad the stories were there to keep you company when you were lost."

The forest thinned, giving way to fields before the shores of a lake so vast that the far side was little more than a suggestion. A lake on which the sun sparkled and sailing boats plied their trade. Not far off, a jetty reached out into the blue, stilted on weathered timbers, smaller boats moored along its length.

"How's your rowing?" Livira grinned at him.

"Uh . . . I've seen an illustration—"

"Oarful, then."

"Was that a joke?"

"Hush. I'll row."

"Didn't you come from a place called the Dust? When did you learn to row boats?"

"I expect I'll manage." They were coming nearer to the jetty now and Evar could see that the half a dozen figures sitting along its edges with fishing rods in hand comprised both humans and canith.

Livira led the way along the far end of the rickety structure, the sun-bleached planks creaking beneath her bare feet. A small rowing boat was tied to the last support and bobbed minutely on waves that were more like ripples. Livira released his hand and clambered down into the boat, swaying dangerously for a moment before finding her seat. She looked expectantly up at Evar.

He hesitated. His hand felt too empty—wrong without hers within it. He glanced at the perfect sky, the glimmering beauty of the lake, the girl beneath him, suddenly achingly precious to him, and yet he forced his unwanted doubt into words. "I think there's something else we should be doing . . ."

Livira frowned. "I don't think I would have written that. I think I'd have you jump gallantly into the boat and row us out to the island with strong, sure strokes."

"What island?" But Evar saw it now, a green jewel out in the midst of the lake, white limestone cliffs on one side, a ruined tower close to the edge, mobbed by trees, either trying to save it or push it to its doom. On the other side the island shelved down to a pristine beach. Evar got into the boat and, finding it larger than he imagined, he sat beside Livira on the bench with his back to the prow.

"Can you swim?" Livira asked as she untied the rope.

"I can 'not sink'—I guess you could call it swimming." Evar shivered. "The Assistant made sure of it." It might have been her first lesson.

"Let's not row." Already the boat had drifted from the jetty. Livira stretched out in the sunshine. It was warm, unlike the library which was only ever . . . sufficient.

"Is this still the Exchange?"

"Or the Mechanism," Livira said. "Or my mind. Or yours. Does it matter?"

"I don't even know what language we're speaking." Evar tried to listen to his voice.

"Maybe it's mind to mind," Livira said, closing her eyes, head back. "And the words are just decoration. Maybe we can't even lie!" She opened her eyes briefly to give him a wicked look.

"I think that would be dangerous," Evar said truthfully. He'd been thinking of their kiss for most of the walk from the forest. For most of the time since it had happened, in fact. Technically, for centuries. It didn't seem real anymore. The desire to repeat it felt ridiculously strong. As strong, perhaps, as the addictions that drugs could breed. The idea that Livira might see his need—how shallow he was, how dependent on her beauty— was not one he felt comfortable with. "Unwise at the very least."

"Why?" Livira wrinkled her nose and answered her own question without giving him time to respond. "It would be inconvenient when it came to misbehaving. That's certainly true. Lies are a necessary part of the diplomat's toolkit—that's what Meelan told me—his sister said it. You can't negotiate if you're too honest, she says."

"Starval says oversharing is the best cover for secrets. If people believe you could no more hold a secret than a hot stone, then they won't pry." Evar had from his siblings the views of an assassin, a tactician, and a psychologist on lies: each viewed them as weapons or tools. Evar didn't disagree, but his current fear was simply that a language without lies would leave him open to being hurt. "I wasn't thinking about misbehaving when I said not being able to lie would be dangerous. I had a different reason." Evar felt mildly horrified that he'd admitted even that much.

"You don't think I have the same one?" She answered as if he'd spoken his heart rather than just let the edge of its shadow fall upon her.

The shore had dwindled in the distance, the jetty a narrow line, though it seemed their drifting had been as languid as a leaf on a millpond. "We're getting . . ." He was going to say they were close to the island, but it seemed just as far away as when they started.

A cloud moved in front of the sun and the day dimmed. Livira looked up at him. "I worry that the Exchange tricked you into liking me." She raised a tanned arm, looked at it, let it fall. "I think that when you saw me truly your stomach turned. That I'm ugly to your eyes. I tell myself that if you were someone I should be interested in then you wouldn't care what I looked like. You'd care who I am."

Evar couldn't help the laugh that barked from him. "You really are reading my mind!" The wounded look in her dark eyes as she sat up suddenly, rocking the boat, made him scramble to explain. "No! I didn't mean that I think those things! I meant those are my thoughts, my fears, *mine.*" The words were out. He'd handed her a knife to gut him with. She hadn't said any of it wasn't true. Just that she thought the same of him.

Across the bow a storm cloud could be seen moving in their direction, small, black, trailing veils of rain across the surface of the lake. The island seemed no closer, the shore just as distant. Evar glanced back to find Livira watching him.

"I don't know how long we have." She held the side of the boat as a small wave rocked them, then stood up.

Evar hesitated, surfacing once more from the belief that the place had bred into him, like a dreamer understanding that they were dreaming. He stood up too, a cool breeze riffling through his mane. "Are we in your book, or am I in my memory of it? Have you even written this part yet? Are you even you, or just the story you're telling about yourself?"

"We're all the story we tell about ourselves, silly." Another wave rocked them. "That's all anyone ever is—the story they tell, and the stories told about them. Fiction captures more than facts do. That's why the library keeps it. It's the most important part of our memories."

The boat jolted and water slopped over the oarlocks. Evar stumbled against her, unused to the instability of the planks beneath his feet. Livira caught hold of him, stronger than she looked. The closeness of her against him felt like something he'd needed all his life and never known he was without. A breath drawn after a life of suffocation.

The breeze grew colder but carried the taint of smoke.

"The library's burning." Livira looked up at him and he could almost see the flames reflected in her eyes. She lowered her head and rested her face against his chest.

"I'd forgotten." The weight of loss was all around them. It had been there in the forest when he woke, but now he understood it. The library was burning. "I . . ."

"I've lost too much," Livira finished for him. "And I don't want . . ."

"To lose you too," Evar said.

Livira raised her head again and this time she didn't need to reach up to pull his mouth to hers.

I've fallen out of this book before.

The main comfort in maintaining a journal is not that those who come after you may read through the progress of your life. Nor is it that, however faded, flexible, and fallible your memory may become as the tide of years washes over it, you will have this record to look back upon. It lies primarily in the illusion that were you only to press on at the end of this Tuesday and write your way into Wednesday, you would become the master of your life, subject to no bounds save those of imagination.

The Journals of Samantha Peeps, *by Samantha Peeps*

CHAPTER 65

Livira

Livira stumbled, caught for a moment between the conviction that she was falling from a boat and the certainty that she'd been held in the warmth of Evar's kiss for hours. Neither turned out to be true. Evar, who'd crashed into her, fell away, losing his grip on the book he'd been trying to pull from her hands. Livira felt the leather covers pulled from between her fingers, the book sliding from her grasp. It fell a couple of feet into the dust drift she'd been standing in. The loose pages almost came free, several of them half out of the covers. Another boom sounded and a muffled cracking rang out behind her—a projectile penetrating the dust and hitting the library floor. If she'd still been holding the book—still been solid and visible—there might be a hole through her now. A wave of snarling canith came forward in a rush and dust engulfed everything.

For a hellish moment Livira was back in the settlement on the day her life changed. Lost in a dust cloud. Sabbers on every side. Holding her aunt's hand as if it were her chance to escape the madness—only to have it torn from her grasp.

This time her hand was empty from the start, and in the blindness someone's fingers found hers. Before she could cry out, Livira was hauled skywards. A heartbeat later she emerged into the light again, flying with Evar just as they had centuries before above a city where canith and human lived in peace.

For a moment two Evars held her: one the stranger who so swiftly became a friend and then her love; the other a stranger still, a savage beast, kin to those beneath them, the same sabbers who had smashed her childhood apart and slaughtered her family.

"Livira!" Evar seemed frantic, patting her all over, turning her in the air. Below them the shouting and chaos continued as the canith fought to tell friend from foe amid the dust. "Are you hit? Are you hit?"

"I don't think so . . ." Livira pushed him gently back as his concern bled the anger from her. She looked down at herself. "It would hurt, wouldn't it?"

"Sometimes not at first." Evar calmed. "That's what Clovis says, anyway."

Livira pressed her hands to her face. They'd been kissing. Again. She couldn't tell if Evar had shared it with her, or whether it had all flowed from her imagination and hers alone. She felt she should be able to tell by looking at him, but she couldn't.

"It was the book," Livira said wonderingly. "It's real here. It made me real too. A little bit when I had it next to me. A lot when I touched it. I sank into the dust when I held it. Look." The lower part of her robes was dusty. Nothing had touched them before, not solid objects, not dust, not smoke. "Yute said it was special. It's got the future wrapped into it."

"It has?" Evar looked confused. Did he look happy too? She couldn't tell. He'd seemed happy. In the boat. In her arms. Or was that just what she was going to write?

"You took it into the Mechanism." Livira met his eyes. "Maybe you've read stories I haven't even written yet. Or stories we could write together . . ." There! She saw it! Something in his eyes, the twitch of a smile. "You were there! I know you were. In the boat. Don't lie!"

He gave a wolfish grin.

Livira turned away primly. "In any case, I know what you read on the first page isn't there yet."

Evar flew back into her line of view. He looked confused again. "But why would you write for me not to turn the page?"

Livira thought hard, then frowned, then grinned. "Well . . . you didn't, did you? So, I had better write it to stop you . . . or none of this would make sense. And gods know what would happen then. It might be like tugging on a loose thread and having a whole tapestry unravel, only the tapestry would be time. That sounds like a bad idea."

"It might be why the assistants don't let us go to the Exchange." Worry replaced Evar's confusion.

Below them the shouting had died down, and Malar's voice emerged above the canith's, calling for Livira.

"We're up here!" she shouted back. "Let's go to him." She swooped down towards the thinning dust cloud.

Malar tried to hide his relief behind a scowl as Livira landed beside him. "We're birds now too? Can I fly as well, or is it a secret?"

Livira nodded. "You can fly. Just jump up and don't fall back. It's all about believing it."

Malar sheathed his swords. "Well, I've never had much luck with faith. Or falling, come to that. Broke both ankles stealing apples from the Masefield estate when I was a sprat."

Half the canith were in search mode now, the warriors moving out in a spiral pattern, slow enough not to obscure their own vision, thrusting at the deeper dust dunes with swords and spears in search of the young woman they'd seen. None of them looked Livira's way, not even the priest who stood exactly where she'd been the whole time, gazing around with eyes like black stones. She'd slung her staff across her back, and in both hands, clasped tight to her chest, she held Livira's book.

Something else bothered Livira, though. Malar tried to lead her away, but she shook her head, raising a hand to silence his objections. "When they all saw me . . ."

"When you nearly fucking died, yes—what about it?" Malar growled.

Evar landed beside them.

"When they all saw me," Livira said, "you both shouted at me."

"We did." Evar nodded.

"But you didn't use my name." Livira closed her eyes, summoning the memory back.

"If you say so," Evar said.

"Someone did though . . ." Livira walked towards the priest and the dozen or more canith who remained with her. Her old anger flared again, a bitter heat trying to own her mind. She pushed it down and set her jaw. She circled the enemy, trying to see within the group. "There!" In amongst them, dwarfed by their height, was a figure wrapped in a grey blanket, hooded by it. At the bottom of the blanket, almost lost in the foot-deep book dust, Livira caught a glimpse of soiled blue fabric, the folds of an expensive dress. Quickly she wove a path between the wary canith until she could see—

"Carlotte!" She held herself back from throwing her arms around her friend. They would just pass through her. "Malar! It's Carlotte!"

"Who?"

Livira tried to position herself so that she was staring directly into Carlotte's eyes, which were red with smoke and tears. The girl didn't so much as twitch. "She can't see me."

Evar came to stand just outside the canith group. "This is why I didn't want you to come back here." There was no triumph in his voice, only sadness. "We can't do anything for her. Even if we weren't ghosts, we couldn't get her away from this war band. And even if we could, the portal's in the fire now."

"I . . . I could set Volente on them!"

"I don't think he'd see them as the enemy. But if he did they'd fight him. In any case, is she better off alone? They could probably run from the fire faster carrying her than she could by herself. And they've got her to open doors they can't. They won't abandon her."

That rang true. The sabbers had taken Livira long ago, intending to use her. It now seemed likely that this priest was the one who had understood that humans raised as slaves, treated as part of the tribe, would open the library doors for them. It had been a far-sighted plan, long in the execution. They had fought to keep her, they would fight to keep Carlotte, and for at least as long as they navigated the library they would keep her safe.

"She has to be willing in order to open doors," Livira said. "Properly willing. Of your own volition. You can't torture someone into it. Yute said so."

"I think the fire will make her properly willing." Malar joined them, eyeing the canith warily since they were little more than a spear's reach away. "That's not something the sabbers are doing to her. It's happening to them all."

Livira nodded. Not bothering to point out that if the chamber was actually on fire then the doors would open for anyone.

Malar looked away. "We need to go, girl. There's no use dwelling over this stuff. It'll eat you up. I've lost friends, fast and slow. Every time it was slow, we all wished it was fast, me and them."

"We could grab the book!"

"And get cut into small pieces a moment later. This lot just sliced their way through the streets of Crath." Malar shook his head slowly as if trying to convince himself as much as Livira.

"Evar could do it. Talk to them."

Malar answered for Evar. "And tell them what? I mean if he survives long enough to tell them anything. Sneaking up on frightened warriors isn't a sensible tactic. And what could he say that's going to change what they do? She's alive. They're going to keep her that way, at least until they're sure they can get out of here. Or . . ."

Or the fire gets them. Livira knew what he was going to say before he thought better of it. "We should go." The first tear ran down her face.

Evar started to reach towards her but let his arm fall. "I could try to grab the book and run with—"

"No." Livira walked away, aiming for Volente, head bowed. "They'd shoot you in the back. And besides, this way Volente can always find them again."

There is a wood that stands between all worlds and all whens. A woodcutter walks its rows. Time is the echo of his axe. Once one has mastered the navigation of this place, there is no destination beyond reach, be it Chorley or Charn. Similarly, any date upon the calendar and beyond is yours for the taking. Simply remember that you cannot go back, and you need never fear the woodcutter.

Larking About, *by Lionel Witch*

CHAPTER 66

Evar

S eeing Livira walk helplessly away from her friend put an ache in Evar's chest. Livira might have a librarian's seemingly endless vocabulary but until today he sensed that "defeat" had never been a word she understood. The sadness in him was an echo of hers, but with it came the extra burden of seeing something precious crushed before you and having no means to defend it.

Volente led them into the chamber Livira called 47, still on the trail of the book in Arpix's possession. Evar was surprised to see dense black smoke advancing through the chamber from the east.

"It's not spreading evenly." Malar frowned, looking up at the cloud rising to spill across the ceiling.

Evar guessed the speed of the fire's advance depended on all manner of things: the nature and spacing of the shelving, the type of books in its path. Perhaps some races had fashioned their books out of materials not given to burning. Those chambers would slow the conflagration, while in other places the flames would leap along shelves, spanning a chamber in minutes. In this chamber the books seemed to produce an alarming amount of smoke whilst the fire remained quite subdued—at least Evar could neither see nor hear it.

Volente led towards the door to Chamber 68, putting the smoke to their right, racing them to their destination. The dog plotted a straight line, passing through shelf after shelf. Evar and Livira took an arm each and hoisted Malar into the air so they could fly above the shelf tops, avoiding the frequent disconcerting encounters with books whose contents tried to stake some claim on each of them as they passed through.

The race to the chamber door remained close, though the smoke held no real fear for Evar: even the hidden flames wouldn't touch him. As they closed on the door, the black wall rolling towards them lay less than two hundred yards behind, swallowing row after row of shelves.

A faint, unexpected sound caught Evar's attention. There it was again, overriding the eerie silence of the rapidly advancing smoke and the crackle of distant flame.

Clunk. Clunk. Clunk.

"Are you hearing that?" he asked.

"Hearing what?" Malar tilted his head then shook it.

"I can now." Livira paled.

Clunk-clunk-clunk.

"What is it?"

Livira gained height, towing Malar and Evar towards the ceiling. Her eyes scanned the aisles below, then seeing something, she dived towards it, eliciting a high-pitched protest from Malar.

Below their feet an assistant broke from the smoke, outpacing it. A jet-black assistant. Clunk-clunk-clunk, maintaining a decent speed but without the grace of the assistants Evar had seen before. It almost reached the tunnel then collapsed as if a rope had been strung across the aisle at ankle height, hitting the ground with a bang. As Evar watched, the blackness seemed to drain from it, at least partially, leaving it ash grey while a shadow—an Escape—flitted back along the aisle and straight into the smoke.

"What's that about?" Malar asked, staring down past his own dangling feet.

"It's the assistant from Chamber Seven," Livira said. "The one the Escape took over."

"Escapes," Evar said. "It's still grey. Corrupted. It must take more than one Escape to control it."

Clunk-clunk-clunk. More footsteps from the same direction, lost inside the smoke. Clunk-clunk-clunk. The swirling cloud was nearly on them now. A second black assistant, this one bearing a black sword, emerged and collapsed beside the first just as the smoke rolled over the pair. Evar pulled the others down towards Volente, who waited patiently in the clearing before the corridor. As they landed, just ahead of the smoke, the sound of running started again.

"The Escapes are trying to hold on to them both," Livira said, following Volente down the corridor. "Keeping them out of the fire. But they can only move one of them at a time."

"They're saving them?" Malar asked.

"For their own purposes. Greed maybe. Or for whatever master they serve, so they can fill both with Escapes."

"Jaspeth," Evar said.

"What?"

"Jaspeth. Irad's brother. That's what your Yute said. Irad made the library and the assistants to tend it for him. Jaspeth opposes the library, and the Escapes are his servants, trying to tear it down."

"Do they really need to?" Malar asked. "It's burning, in case you didn't notice."

"It's always burning somewhere," Livira pointed out. "Yute said that too. But it's just the books that burn. And the shelves. The assistants restock, and people like us, creatures like us, rebuild. That was the compromise to stop the war—the library's vulnerable, difficult, inconvenient, but eternal."

CHAMBER 68 LOOKED so much like the chamber they'd just come from that it hardly seemed they were making progress.

"We need to speed this up. There's no reason we can't go faster." Livira scowled down at her feet as if they were the problem.

"We just need to believe it?" Malar raised an eyebrow that suggested he hadn't forgiven either of them for the flying yet. "What about the dog? We can't go faster than our guide."

"They can't be far, surely?" Evar wasn't certain on the timings but there didn't seem to be a way for Arpix and the others to have outdistanced the canith by much more than they already had. There was a limit to the advantage that knowledge of the layout would give them.

"Go on, Volente." Livira waved the dog on and, steeling herself, plunged after him through the next bookshelf.

Evar clenched himself against the unpleasant feel of passing through dozens of books and followed. It turned out that every time they tried to overtake Volente, he sped up, and when they sped up, he accelerated again. Evar had never run so fast. He found it both exhilarating, a release after the tensions of the day, and frightening. However often he reminded himself he was a ghost, his brain told him that running flat out with almost no forward vision was bound to end in disaster.

The process ended abruptly. The pursuit of Volente's fleeing hindquarters through a blur of shelves suddenly became a solo journey. Evar willed himself to stop and came to a halt in an anonymous aisle. Some way off behind him a mix of screams and exclamations drew his attention.

"Volente!" Someone was excitedly calling the hound's name.

"That sounds like Arpix!" Livira emerged through the nearest wall of shelves. "Except for the excitement."

Evar followed Livira as she ran towards the voices, passing through shelf after shelf with a shuddering thrill until they broke into the chamber's centre circle.

Livira fell to her knees, laughter and tears bursting from her, trampling each other in the fight to get out.

"They're all here?"

Livira nodded, breathless with emotion, reaching for Evar's arm as she stood again. "All of them. That's Arpix hugging Volente. Meelan right beside him." She pointed out two females of solid build sprawled exhausted on the floor. "Jella and Salamonda. The rest are other library staff, bookbinders mostly." She pointed out two older males. "Mika and Regg are cleaners." Finally, she swung her finger towards a robed female whose vibrant orangey hair in glorious disarray somewhat reminded Evar of Clovis's red mane. "And that's Master Jost." Livira's voice suggested a measure of distaste for the woman staring in disbelief at the newly arrived giant dog.

With uncharacteristic restraint, Livira didn't throw herself at her friends. Instead, she joined in the general praising of Volente, who at least could be touched by ghosts and people alike. Evar held back, looking for

Malar, who stumbled through the nearest shelf moments later, shivering and wiping at his arms as if spiderwebs were clinging to him.

"What now?" The warrior looked up at Evar, his eyes haunted by the concern they both had: that Livira would be forced to abandon her friends or watch as the fire caught them.

"We could steer them to safety with Volente," Evar said. "He's the link. If we can get him to go, they'll follow. But is anywhere safe?" In order to begin to answer his own question Evar took to the air. Hopefully the fire hadn't reached the chamber yet, but they knew smoke was pouring in from 47.

"What can you see?" Malar jumped after Evar and fell back with an oath.

"Nothing good . . ." Evar made a full rotation. It didn't seem possible but there were smoke clouds around all four entrances to the chamber. "Is someone spreading it?"

"Which way out?" Malar called.

Evar dropped down to join him. He couldn't bring himself to speak. It seemed answer enough for Malar.

"Fuck it all to hell." Malar threw both swords down. The clatter made no impression on Arpix and the others, but Livira looked up from hugging Volente.

"What is it?"

Evar shook his head, fearing to tell her.

"Could you possess one of them?" Malar asked. "That's what the soldiers who went to Durn said. They said in the marshes there's spirits that'll take hold of a man and make him do their bidding. Some'll walk you into the sucking pools, but others'll take your mouth and speak in dead languages."

Livira said nothing but flew up. The cry that escaped her a few heartbeats later would have made Evar think she'd been wounded if he didn't know better. He'd heard the same from the mouths of men on Crath's walls as they took an arrow to the guts. She fell back down, making no effort to resist gravity. Still unspeaking, she went to stand behind Arpix, her hands reaching out to either side of his head.

"Don't . . ." Evar couldn't see what good it would do. They would know that they were trapped soon enough.

Livira froze, arms trembling, then let them drop. "It might hurt him. Twist him up in time. Like my book."

Malar exchanged a quick look with Evar. A look that said the fire would soon undo any problems of that sort.

"You couldn't tell him anything that would help." Evar went to stand as close as her tension would allow. "He already knows you'd burn yourself to save them if you could. All your friends do."

Livira's chest hitched as a sob tried to break free. She pressed her hands to the sides of her head as if trying to crush an answer out, and Evar braced himself for the inevitable scream. It didn't come. She whirled on Malar with fierce eyes, her face tear-streaked and determined.

"Are you ready for the fight of your life? Are you ready to bleed?"

"Fuck, yes."

"Follow me."

"We're not our bodies, Simon."

"We're not not our bodies. You can't pretend we're some sort of angelic intelligence tied unfairly to our flesh. We are our flesh—it shapes our needs, our desires, our hunger—"

Sam conceded the point by silencing him with a kiss.

Fireman 6: Lust in the Ashes, *by Miranda Lovegood*

CHAPTER 67

Livira

L ivira ran. She stormed headfirst through shelf after shelf, trailing the stories of a hundred authors behind her, shaking off the temples to logic built by philosophers, the scientists' careful arguments, the inventors' instructions, the laments of historians. She ran until the smoke's black wall loomed above her like one of the rolling storms that the Dust had thrown up so often, blanketing her childhood in silence, darkness, and fear.

Evar and Malar drew up at her shoulder. The aisle led away ahead of them, the advancing smoke a hundred yards off, the flames' hunger an unknown distance behind.

"What are we—"

Livira silenced Evar with a raised hand. "Listen."

Nothing.

Malar moved his lips but thought better about it and kept silent.

At first it might be imagination. Hope even. Hope can be cruel like that. Clunk-clunk-clunk. Louder now, definite, a promise. Clunk-clunk-clunk. It even sounded as if Livira had picked exactly the right aisle.

Malar raised his swords. Livira hadn't seen him pick them up but maybe ghosts didn't need to.

"Whichever one comes out first is yours," she told him. "I'll go in after the other."

"You can't touch them . . ." Evar said, frowning.

"It's Malar's idea. We're ghosts. We're going in," Livira said. "We just need to wait until the Escape in charge leaves one to go to the other. Then we take possession."

"How do we do that?" Malar's turn to frown. He looked at his swords as if he might cut a way in.

"I don't know. We're just going to have to try. Putting yourself in the same space should do most of it. Just remember there'll be Escapes still in there. Maybe one, maybe more. Enough to keep the assistants immobilised." The footfalls grew louder, almost on them. "Take control. Fight. Bring the body back to the others at the centre circle." She turned to Malar. "You can do this. You're a warrior. You know how to fight."

"What am I?" Evar demanded, outraged. "I can fight."

"They're our friends. Not yours." *And I don't want you to die,* she would have said if it wouldn't have strengthened his objections. The warmth of his arms still wrapped her and whatever happened she wanted him to survive. She wanted him to escape his chamber through the door she'd opened, or go with Yute, anywhere so long as he was free to leave, and to live the life he'd been denied so long. "Besides"—she forced a smile—"you're too big to fit."

Evar opened his mouth to argue but in that moment the male assistant with the cut face broke from the smoke, took ten more heavy steps, and fell to his hands and knees.

"Wait." Livira held Malar's shoulder.

The Escape, surely the one that had pursued her from the Exchange and then hunted her through Chamber 7, slithered from the assistant, an inky serpent drawing darkness from the assistant's wound, coiling down beneath his face, then weaving its path swiftly towards the advancing smoke.

"Now." Livira released the soldier. "Expect to win. Use your anger." She didn't know if it was the right advice, but it *felt* right. Without his swords, Malar's anger would be his sharpest weapon. It was probably his sharpest weapon even when he was holding them.

"I win. It's what I fucking do." Malar surged forward.

Livira accelerated past him, arrowing after the Escape.

Visibility within the cloud was next to zero, even with the library's light illuminating it from within. Livira sensed rather than saw the Escape as she overtook it. She might have missed the fallen assistant but for the guiding walls of books to either side, and the fact that as she ran into it the corruption within the assistant immediately tried to kill her.

The first thing Livira understood as the Escape within the assistant sank its talons into her was that this was a fight she needed to win before the other returned. Two would be too many. One was already too many.

The second realisation was that this business of black and white signified only division. The Escapes and the assistants were both creations of singular purpose, set to opposite tasks, but one side wasn't good and the other evil. The Escape trying to overwhelm her had been brought into being in order to oppose the library, just as the assistants had been made to preserve it. In fact, both were made from the stuff of the library, the assistants from its body, the Escapes from its blood. Tools turned to different ends. The two represented differing extremes of an argument in which two parties, each believing itself correct, sought to plot a path for intelligence to circumvent its self-destructive nature. And as a consequence, in perhaps the primal irony, intelligence fought intelligence.

Within the body of the assistant, with ghost battling Escape for rights to such prime territory, there were no punches thrown, no teeth seeking flesh. The talons that had been sunk into Livira were merely the connection between her and her opponent. The Escape sought to gut her. It drew out her memories, sucking the meaning from them, trying to wear her like an old coat. Livira felt herself fraying, the fabric of her being unwinding. She was smoke dissipating across the face of the water, ashes on the wind. Without malice or care the Escape plucked one precious moment after another from her. With invisible claws it hollowed her, cored her, picking away until even the letters of her name began to come loose like the teeth of some old skull abandoned out on the Dust, finally drawn from their sockets by the patience of the rattling wind.

The Escape took everything, leaving nothing but a husk. And, in the empty darkness of that husk, Livira, who had throughout her life been defined by the steel trap of her memory, opened her eyes and took it all back. "I don't forget."

The swiftness of Livira's reclamation turned the Escape inside out and its remnants drifted from the assistant's head wound to join the smoke.

"No." Livira slapped an ivory hand down on the second Escape as it reached the assistant's body. This Escape, the one she had outpaced on her way here, proved easier to battle given that she was now in charge of the assistant and the Escape was stuck outside. She wrung the phantom between both hands as she stood the assistant up. The Escape fell apart and she tossed its shreds behind her.

She leaned down to seize the discarded sword, then ran. She found that Evar was running beside her, having followed her and having perhaps delayed the second Escape to buy her time. They broke free of the smoke before finding the other assistant. The old ivory of its skin told them immediately who had won the fight within it. Livira and Malar were still pollutants within the assistants and neither body was its proper gleaming white, but both were closer to what they should be than the grey that showed an Escape lay within.

"It ran away," Malar grunted as they reached them. "Tried to mess with my head—I think what it found scared it. My nightmares are a hundred times worse than that horror, and that's on a good night."

"Keep up," Livira said as she passed him. She handed him the sword, white now. "There's still the bleeding to do."

ENTERING THE CENTRE circle, Livira broke into an atmosphere of terror that hadn't been there when she left. Arpix and the others had discovered what Evar found when he flew above them. They knew that the fire had them trapped. Meelan was locked into an argument with one of the near-hysterical bookbinders, their voices so loud that nobody heard Livira's approach. All their attention was either on Meelan's attempts to stop the hefty red-faced man leading his colleagues towards the least smoky exit, or on the black wall looming high above them from the east, the one rolling up behind Livira.

"Oh, thank Croma!" Arpix was the first to notice her standing at the mouth of one of the thirty or so aisles that terminated at the circle's perimeter. Normally if he appealed to the gods, it was a generic net cast across as many of the heavenly host as might listen. The imminent prospect of choking or burning to death appeared to have focused him on one in particular: Croma, a favourite among librarians, goddess of learning and wisdom in the Fatra pantheon.

Livira strode forward. She knew something was wrong with her. She'd known it ever since she ejected the Escape and took possession of the assistant. She felt distant, wrapped in blankets that somehow insulated her from emotion. The excitement that should have filled her like the crackle of a lightning bolt merely prickled. The compassion that Jella's tears or Meelan's misplaced anger should have evoked still stirred her but didn't shake her as it should. The spreading relief on the ten faces before her was simply scenery.

Malar arrived and followed her into the circle. Evar ghosted after them. Arpix was talking, Master Jost demanding, the large bookbinder pleading. It slid off her: discordant noise. She turned to face Malar, anchored by her purpose. She wanted to open a portal, to send her friends to safety. An assistant should be able to do that at will, but whilst she retained more control of her host than the Escapes had, such powers did not appear to be hers to command. She held her hand out. "Cut me." She had to struggle to say the words and struggle to hold her arm out. Only assistants were permitted to visit the Exchange. She knew that. What she was doing was forbidden. And after a life spent breaking rules with reckless abandon, suddenly she was finding it hard to do.

Malar raised his sword so that it pointed towards her.

"Quickly." Livira raised her palm towards the sword's point. She would have been scared if it were her own hand. Even in a different body she wanted to snatch her hand back. She could feel the floor through her feet—she would feel his blade cutting the skin she didn't own.

"It . . . it's . . . forbidden." Malar shook his head as if he didn't understand, or rather he shook the head of the assistant he'd possessed.

Livira wanted to argue, but she couldn't. It *was* forbidden. Access to the Exchange for any creature still locked into time could have unforeseen consequences. Disastrous ones. Livira had taken possession of the assistant but, unlike the Escapes, her kind lived in time's flow, carried along by it relentlessly from cradle to grave. Putting herself inside the assistant had set her apart. It had started to sever the bonds that attached her to passing days. She might have taken possession of the assistant, but in another very real sense, it had taken possession of her.

"It's against the rules." Malar started to lower his blade.

It had been Livira's memory that had defeated the Escape and some among her fellow librarians might have called that stranglehold on the past her defining characteristic. But only the ones who didn't know her well. Livira—the weed—always found a way past; she lived to break rules.

"It's against the rules," Malar repeated.

"Good." Livira seized the sword's end and drove her palm against its point. The pain was intense, bringing her to her knees. She reached out, smeared her hand across the library floor, and shuffled in a full rotation to draw a circle around herself. Light shimmered across it, and she fell through.

The greatest puzzle is one not understood until the final piece is set in place. Life, appropriately, can be like that, all the pieces tumbling together in a slow dance until in one last joining of hands epiphany strikes.

A History of the Jigsaw, *by Icarus Salt*

CHAPTER 68

Evar

E var hadn't seen what he should have seen when the first assistant had burst from the smoke and fallen to his knees.

One of the Escapes inside it had emerged and shot off into the advancing smoke. Malar had aimed himself at the fallen assistant and Livira had plunged into the smoke, aiming to beat the Escape to the second assistant somewhere back there in the swirling blindness.

It wasn't until later when Livira finally broke free of the smoke, now wearing the second assistant's body, and Malar followed behind her, that Evar found himself with the Soldier to one side of him and the Assistant to the other. Not just nameless, identical assistants from the unknown numbers that served the library, but the Soldier and the Assistant: the ones that had raised him. The ones he'd left alone to fight the skeer.

Running before the fire he had little time to wrestle with the enormity of what had happened. If he paused to consider it for only a moment he felt that the weight of epiphany might pin him to the ground. In one moment his whole life had been inverted, and he'd been left spinning. He tried to focus on the now: Livira's friends needed saving or they would burn.

When they reached the centre circle, Evar immediately knew something was wrong. Well, everything was wrong. Livira's friends were trapped and facing horrific deaths. He still had trouble seeing a group of humans as anything but sabbers, but individually he knew they were every bit as important to someone as Livira was to him. And even sabbers couldn't be left to burn. Everything was wrong, but something specific was wrong with Livira and with Malar. The man, usually so free with his foul mouth, and so cautious in his movements, ready for anything, was silent and still. Livira didn't greet her friends, didn't rejoice at finally being seen, albeit in a borrowed body. Instead, she ignored them. Ignored him.

"Cut me," she said, hardly seeming to see the humans crowding around her, not hearing their pleas or their questions. "Quickly."

"Livira? Can you hear me?" Evar braced himself as he passed through one of the humans and stood directly between the Assistant and the Soldier. "Livira?"

"It . . . it's . . . forbidden." Malar seemed to be struggling. There was colour in his eyes, the same darkness that Evar had only ever seen once before in those blank white orbs. "It's against the rules."

Evar had seen those eyes darken just the one time—in front of the char wall when Evar had been considering digging. What had the Soldier said . . . ?

I've lost her. I've lost myself . . .

And then the threat, the only time the Soldier had ever spoken with true passion: *Know this . . . if you hurt her, no army will save you from me.*

"It's against the rules."

"Good." Livira snatched the Soldier's sword and stabbed it into her palm. She collapsed to her knees with a cry of pain, and with three sweeps of her bloody hand she had sketched a circle about herself.

"No!" Evar reached for her. He was fast enough this time, faster than he'd been when the pool had reclaimed her in the Exchange that first time. Faster than when the Escape had crashed into her and carried her into the pool the second time. Faster perhaps than he had ever been. But he was a ghost and fast as he was Evar couldn't catch her. In a broken moment she was gone.

Livira fell away from him into the portal that her own blood had written.

Evar plunged in after her.

He rolled from the far side of the portal, coming to his feet amid the wood that had always waited for him. The Exchange, normally both empty of people and full of peace, was, for once, crowded and noisy—at least around the portal he'd emerged from, a portal that now burned at his back, radiating a heat that singed his fur. He'd been brought back to the scene he'd left. Perhaps a few minutes had passed in this place since he was last here.

Evar had left the refugee humans led by Yute and Yamala being confronted by Clovis, with Kerrol a fascinated onlooker. Now, though, Yute was in the process of ushering the refugees through a portal that lay between Livira's time and Evar's. That was a good thing, since there were many more soldiers than he remembered. Well over a hundred of them. Hopefully, Yute could continue to siphon them away before they decided to replay the battle they were running from.

Clovis watched the exodus with Kerrol, the desire for violence twitching through her limbs but restrained, at least for now. He doubted the numbers held her back. Perhaps the goodness that he had always hoped resided at her core was keeping her from the fight that would doubtless end her and her family, albeit at the cost of scores of human lives.

Yamala watched from the other side of the proceedings. Of Livira there was no sign.

"Livira!" Evar roared her name, causing everyone to look his way, a dozen gleaming 'sticks starting to rise. Evar didn't care. All he cared about was Livira. The forest could catch fire and it wouldn't distract him from the singularity of his purpose. Nothing could. Except when it did. "Liv—"

Mayland's sudden appearance from a portal just behind Yamala took Livira's name from Evar's tongue. Evar, who just moments ago had actually been a ghost, stood stunned, as if he were seeing a real one for the first time.

In three quick strides Mayland came up behind Yamala and put his arm around her neck in the chokehold that Clovis had taught them all. Clovis and Kerrol stared at him open-mouthed. The humans noticing this new arrival, a hostile canith, backed away, more 'sticks being lifted among the soldiers' ranks. Several of the owl-helmed ones actually stepped forward, clutching their 'sticks like drowning men clinging to silver ropes.

"Stay back, please," Mayland instructed pleasantly. "And Kerrol, though I've missed your voice, I must ask you to stay silent or I'll snap this one's spine and be on my way."

"Mayland?" Evar balanced simultaneously on the edges of elation, horror, and total confusion. For a moment he wondered if he'd been mistaken, and this was some other canith. In the ancient city he'd seen Mayland in the crowds, but not just Mayland, his imagination and lack of experience with faces had painted his siblings' features onto anyone that looked even vaguely similar. But it *was* Mayland. Older, thinner, a ragged scar down the left side of his face, but Mayland nonetheless. The others saw it too. Those grey-green eyes, a little too far apart. The slight stoop in his back. That crooked mouth always hinting at a smile, rarely giving one.

"What are you doing?" Had Evar believed his brother to be alive then he would have put Mayland top of the list of his siblings least likely to resort to such methods. Ahead of Kerrol and then himself. Kerrol he always suspected of being bottled too tight to not one day explode, but Mayland surely knew more history than any ten historians and the lesson of many centuries had always been that violence breeds violence. "Let her go—she's called Yamala—she was an assistant . . ."

It should have been enough to set her free, but Mayland simply tightened his grip.

Evar tried again. "She was an immortal servant of Irad. And she gave it up to save us."

Mayland glanced to either side, ensuring nobody was sneaking up on him.

It didn't work. Starval could sneak up on someone with eyes in the back of their head.

"Evar asked a good question." Starval kept his knife at Mayland's throat. "What *are* you doing, brother?"

Mayland smiled. "Fighting the sabbers."

"She's not one of them any more than she's one of us," Starval said.

"'Sabber,' dear brother, means 'enemy.' The library is our true enemy. It always has been. He sees it. Him over there." Mayland directed his gaze towards Yute, who hadn't moved a muscle since his wife had been seized. "Two assistants graced us with their presence, dipped their toes in time's currents. And what did they end up doing? *Working for the library.* What vision, what imagination! They married each other and ran the human portal to the library. And this one—this one decided Irad had it right all along. She kept on feeding the poison to the children at her doors. Yute, on the other hand, had his doubts. There was trouble in paradise, separate beds, compromises, a semi-truce. Irad and Jaspeth in microcosm. One of them seeking to return to the fold, the other heading in the other direction, perhaps about to stage his own escape."

Behind Yute, soldiers and civilians continued to escape through the distant portal, wanting no part of the magical forest or whatever this conflict was. Yute stepped forward, moving between his owl-helmed guards, lowering the barrels of their weapons with his pale hands. "Please let her go."

"Why?" Mayland seemed unaware of the blade at his neck. "You don't love her anymore."

"I care about her deeply." Yute was looking at his wife rather than Mayland.

"She stands for everything you're against."

"She has a different view."

"You should fight for yours," Mayland said. "You believe it. More than that: you *know* it to be true."

"Compromises can be made. Compromises *must* be made." Yute stepped out from between his guards, both hands open and raised before him.

"What do you think, Starval?" Mayland acknowledged the brother at his back. "Are there compromises in the business of slitting throats? Or is it all or nothing?" He reached up and took hold of Starval's wrist, pulling it slowly but firmly away from his throat before returning his hand to the lock he had around Yamala's neck. "My particular study is history, Master Yute. I know all about these cycles of destruction, the rise and fall of civilisations, the fire-limit—yes, I read about that in your own work. And what do you think I've learned from the untold numbers of books to pass before me, in themselves an infinitesimal fraction of what the library has to say on the subject?"

"I don't know. Please release Yamala and tell me about it."

"I learned that there's only one history of any consequence, and that's the library's own. I learned that compromise"—he broke Yamala's neck with a sudden motion—"is the cancer that consumes us." Cries went up; weapons were raised again, Yute's arms dropped like cut strings. "Jaspeth is right. Raze the library to the ground, dig out all traces of its legacy, and let the world run its course at its own speed untrammelled by memory. This"—he raised his arms and let Yamala's corpse fall—"experiment is over."

Somehow, in the face of Mayland's confidence, only one of the guards made to fire. Starval's arm snapped out and his knife blossomed from the man's face. All around them portals started turning black, and Escapes began to clamber from them.

Evar's gaze fixed upon his home pool, the only exit still to look the way it had the first day he came to the Exchange. The madness of the last few minutes had somehow pushed Livira from his mind but now she was the only thing on it. The only thing that made sense amid the chaos. Livira who had become trapped in the Assistant. Livira, the woman he'd been hunting all this time, who had haunted the edges of his dreaming since the day he had crawled from the Mechanism. And the woman who had been standing before him that whole while, lost in time, trapped in the ageless body she had stolen, caring for him day after day, while whatever love she might have for him stayed bottled up inside that ivory chest.

Evar tore across the grass, passing portal after portal. Nothing mattered except reaching the pool. Not the humans' screams, not his "dead" brother's plans, not the Escapes trying to block his path. He leapt at one, landing both feet against its face, carrying it to the ground and leaving it in his wake. Livira who he'd left alone to fight an unknown enemy, the skeer, just three of which had managed to put the Soldier on the ground.

"I left her." He said the words as he dived for the pool. He couldn't believe it. He had left her.

. . . irony or paradox?

> *To truly understand something you must see it whole. You must step outside the thing, outside the world that holds it, outside the time that counts its measure. Only when you stand outside the object of your interrogation and set God's eye upon it will you understand that to know it properly you should never have left.*
>
> Within and Without, *by Larry Mote*

CHAPTER 69

Livira

L ivira stepped into the Exchange, finding it quiet, ordered, and strangely comprehensible, as if its mechanics were integral to her now, another part of her skin. She turned around to face the sphere of radiance out of which she'd just stepped. Humans were forbidden in the Exchange, so she redirected the gateway she had used, aiming it at a place and time.

A memory of the Exchange haunted her, but in it the Exchange had presented a different face, suited to her understanding as it was then. There were no pools or portals here, just the nexus, and only one nexus was required. It had been placed in a forest long ago once Irad understood that his library cast many shadows and had acted to connect them. To reach any particular world or time required only direction. The rows and columns that Livira and Evar had seen with other eyes were merely a projection, helping simpler brains to make sense of something occupying more dimensions than their thinking.

Since the nexus connected all parts of the library across worlds and time, the battle for the athenaeum's soul lay written across its surface. The veins of Jaspeth's influence pulsed like black lightning through the sphere's light.

Within the Assistant, Livira counted as corruption, similar to Jaspeth's pollution, though considered less hostile. More like a fever than a cancer. Even so, few of the Assistant's abilities were at her disposal, and as she progressively lost her grip on time so all of Livira's wants, desires, ambitions, loves, and friendships began to erode, sandcastles before the tide.

Livira reached for one of the few levers she could pull. Communication. She placed both white hands so that their palms touched the nexus, and she spoke to her fellow assistants, who were, in a manner of thinking, all shadows of the same original as herself. She asked for a service. And, since it involved only the moving of books, she hoped that they would not enquire too deeply or suspect her of being compromised by the human taint.

As the words left her mind, borne to countless assistants scattered across achingly large distances, so did her purpose. Images of people she could no longer name faded from her thoughts. Urgent tasks slipped away, her white fingers making no attempt to snatch them back. She drifted on a deep sea. As if she were a needle drawn by the lodestone's pull, she turned to contemplate the perfection of the forest. Even in the darkness, with a chill wind questing through the leafless branches, it held a peace that seduced the mind. She could have stood there forever within the stolen moments that Irad had stitched together to make the Exchange. She could have stood, watching the shadows shift in the nexus's glow, while years stole past behind her back unnoticed. But somewhere, somewhen, a book wasn't burning.

Harboured in the assistant's flesh, Livira knew all about books. She knew the location, disposition, and contents of so many books that, were they to be gathered in one place, the forces of gravity would fashion a sphere from them. She knew that the vast majority of those books were not on fire, and that was well. She knew that a small fraction, constituting an enormous number, were on fire, and that was part of the accord, the compromise that had avoided a Ragnarök and instead plunged the library into its state of eternal cold war. Undesirable but acceptable. And she knew that amid all those oceans of the written word there was just one book that should by rights be burning, and yet was refusing the flames.

Somehow the flames that should have been consuming those uncooperative pages were burning her instead, a fierce heat building inside her. So, instead of contemplating the darkness of the forest until the end of time, she turned to face the nexus once more and stepped back into it.

———

LIVIRA CLAMBERED OUT of the pool of her own blood into the centre circle of the chamber she had bled in. Flames were dancing above the shelves to the south, their hunger drawing in the air as fast as the centre circle created it. The resulting draught had thinned the smoke to the point where she could see that the humans and the construct—Volente—were gone. And for reasons beyond her reach that created contentment inside her.

The Soldier had gone too. The circle lay empty of everything but smoke. Livira gazed once more at the fading portal she'd made then set off towards the book that wouldn't burn.

She crossed two chambers before needing to enter the conflagration. The roar of the fire within the confines of the chamber overwhelmed all other sounds. When the aisles ahead of the fire's advance burst spontaneously into flames, with such force that some books literally shot from the higher shelves and exploded into brilliant comets as their pages spread, Livira heard nothing but the roar. When shelving units two hundred yards long and taller than trees fell, disgorging their burning contents, Livira heard nothing but the roar.

The fire's glow and heat reflected from the ceiling and glimmered across her skin. She entered the burning aisles, walking paths that lay hotter than the smith's furnace where iron bends, and drips, and runs. Livira wasn't immune to the inferno's touch. The assistant's enamel might have shrugged off temperature just as it let time slide away without leaving a mark, but Livira had alloyed her own spirit with the assistant's substance, and it wasn't an alloy that retained the full strength of the original. She felt pain. She felt the need to retreat. And yet above the fire's roar she heard the call of the book that wouldn't burn, and above the pain she felt the need to reach it.

In time she passed through the inferno's heart and moved on through the devastation it left behind. She waded through waist-deep embers glowing the bright orange with which a furnace answers the bellows' call. She strode through crackling ashes where the air shimmered and rippled as it baked. She walked on and came in time to a black mound no higher than her hip, and began to dig into it with her hands.

The Soldier lay beneath a yard of scalding cinder, as black as soot. She brushed away at the last inch still covering him. The side of his body that he had presented to the fire was still the yellowed ivory of before, streaked here and there with grey, but the kiln that the chamber had become had left a melted look to that half of him.

Without speaking, the Soldier levered himself up. Underneath him Livira's book, which should be charcoal, lay unmarked.

"It can't burn," Livira said. "It exists in the future."

"It can burn," the Soldier corrected her. "But the future would burn with it."

The Soldier picked the book up with fingers hot enough to melt glass and handed it to her.

For several heartbeats Livira was in two places at once. And then only one.

"WHO LIVES IN the tower?" Evar reached down to pick it up.

Livira slapped his wrist. "Don't! You'll break it."

"I thought we were gods." But Evar pulled his hand back.

"We are. For now."

"Gods can't pick up towers without breaking them?" Evar eyed her doubtfully, kicking at the ocean around his ankles.

"Don't do that either! You'll drown some sailors or squash a whale or something."

Evar rolled his eyes.

"And of course we can pick up towers without breaking them. It's just that there are more elegant ways of doing things." Livira pointed at the tower and immediately both of them were shrinking and drawing closer to it. Where moments before they had needed to stoop to see below the clouds, now they both fitted on the windowsill of a room at the tower's top, nestled below a tiled conical roof. Livira peered through the diamond-shaped pane in front of her. It stood as tall as she did and was one of scores leaded together to fill the window frame. Evar leaned in with her.

"So, this is what it's like to be you?"

Livira elbowed him. "I'm not *this* small."

"Who is she?" Evar stared at the beautiful girl on the bed at the centre of the small room. She lay on an embroidered cover in the light of a dozen candles, and her hair was a black river, wine-dark, braided into a rope thicker than her arms. It coiled beside her bed in a heap as big as a man.

"A girl I read about in a folk tale, but I've made her into my friend Neera as well."

The girl coughed.

"I thought about taking away her cough—it can be a bit annoying— but it's part of Neera now and you can't just go about erasing bits of people to please yourself, or even them. It's not honest."

"What's up with her hair?" Evar paused. "And why did she look like you just now as I started to glance away?"

"She's being held prisoner by a witch, but she's grown her hair to use as a rope to escape."

"Uh-huh."

Livira glanced at Evar, who was giving her a look that told her he wasn't going to let the other thing go.

"And she looked like me just then because really the story's about me now. Happy?"

"I'll be happy when I see her climb down, get to the foot of the tower, and find she's anchored to her bed by her hair."

"She cuts it off then, idiot, and she's free. That's the purpose of the story. To say that you can escape from somewhere but you're always going to leave part of yourself there."

"All right . . . Then who's he?" Evar turned and pointed to the brow of the nearest hill where a figure in shining armour had just crested the rise on a black stallion.

"He's the knight who climbs up her hair every night and . . . you know . . . gets to know her."

"Why doesn't he kill the witch?" Evar stared at the approaching horse-man. "Looks like he's got a really big sword."

"He does that too." Livira waved the question away.

"So, he's the knight in shining armour who comes to save the princess?" Evar sat down and dangled his legs over the windowsill's edge.

The knight brought his horse to a halt in the courtyard below them, looked up at the window, and raised his visor.

"That's me!" Evar exclaimed. "I'm the knight who saves you."

"That's not it at all," Livira explained crossly. "You think I'd fill my book with nonsense like that?"

"Weren't you twelve when you started it?"

"Ten, but that's not the point. I was a very advanced ten-year-old."

"What *is* it about then?" Evar glanced at the knight then gave her some doubtful side-eye.

"Yute told me it's not the gift of money that's the greatest—it's the gift of purpose. In this story I gave you purpose. It got you out of the castle you were imprisoned in and away from your awful family. By allowing you to save me I gave you the purpose that unlocked the whole world for you. Also, we had a lot of fun every night." She felt herself flush and pressed on hurriedly before he asked questions. "It ends sadly though."

Evar raised both brows in alarm. "What happens?"

"The princess climbs down from her window, using her hair, but the witch cuts it when she's halfway down. The princess falls to her death and the prince arrives too late and finds her broken on the ground."

"But you said the prince killed the witch!" Evar protested.

"He does, then."

"Well, I don't like that. I don't like it at all!"

"It's a teaching story," Livira said. "It tells us that often things don't work out for the best. People die. Things get broken and can't be repaired. It doesn't matter how brave the prince is or how shiny his armour. It doesn't matter how plucky the princess is or how unusual her hair might be. The fire comes and there's no fighting it."

"I don't like it." Evar shook his head. "There are blank pages left in your book—the Assistant told me—so there's more we can do. We're gods, aren't we? We can fix this!"

"We're gods in here." Livira took his hand in hers. "We can't fix the world, though. Nobody knows how to. We just have to do our best. Move on. Rebuild."

"What are you telling me?" Evar looked ashen now, as if this fairy tale had suddenly become the whole of his heart. "I don't arrive too late. I'm not going to. You've seen how fast I am."

But Livira, who had no more than her fingertips still touching time's flow, knew better than that. She saw the future stamped upon the face of the past, two sides of an ever-spinning coin. She understood the gift of purpose, the distraction it provided from the awful completeness of the circle. She knew the knight would find her broken no matter how fast he rode.

She squeezed his hand, blinded by tears. "Thank you for trying to save me, my love. But don't forget to save yourself."

THE ASSISTANT BLINKED and looked down at the book in her hand. She glanced up briefly at the Soldier. He held his silence but nodded. The Assistant opened the book and wrote with her finger across the middle of the sheet.

> Evar! Don't turn the page. I'm in the Exchange. Find me at the bottom

That done, she handed the book to the Soldier before the tendrils of story reaching from it could find new purchase and drag her into more heartbreak. "Come on."

There was one more thing to do, and as so often before, a book would lead her to it. She had thought it would be *this* book, but the person who took it had discarded it, perhaps thinking it cursed.

The Assistant and the Soldier ran, chasing a new book. They were swift and tireless. They passed through the ferocity of the fire once more and got ahead of it. The Assistant couldn't say why she pursued this particular book through the expanse of the library. A tawdry piece of fiction, a steamy romance written in a week by an author with a thousand titles to their name. But something drove her, and finding books was her business, so she didn't fight it.

THEY FOUND THE book many hours later. It lay in the possession of a terrified young human female who in turn appeared to be the possession of a band of exhausted canith only half a chamber ahead of the fire and losing ground.

The canith—who had held stewardship of this corner of the library for at least as many years as the humans had down the millennia—saw the Assistant and the Soldier as a blessing rather than a threat. They fell to their knees, hands raised in supplication. Their priest broke her staff and offered her life for the part they had played in bringing fire to the library. They came, she said, not in anger against the humans, though King Oanold's ancestors had driven hers from the city. They came because a foe harried them in the east. Sabbers against whom there could be no victory without the knowledge held here. The skeer, she said, were like no other, numberless and deadly. She cast down the pieces of her staff and begged the Assistant to save those with her.

"I will try." The Assistant spoke above the roar of the approaching fire and inclined her head.

Quite what the priest imagined the pair might do against the hellscape rushing after them the Assistant couldn't say. She doubted that any of them would ever have predicted her solution, even with a million years of guessing.

The Assistant advanced unopposed to the girl.

"Carlotte."

The young woman, who had seemed stunned by the Assistant's arrival, looked still more shocked at hearing her name on the Assistant's lips. She stood as if paralysed while the Assistant reached into her elegant but tattered evening jacket and withdrew *The Marquis and the House Reader's Daughter*, by Babran Cartlode.

Handing the book to the Soldier, the Assistant walked away from the girl. "Follow me."

WHILST VERY FEW chambers held a Mechanism, the Assistant knew that there were an endless number of them throughout the library. The one closest to the human door on this world lay in a reading room in the chamber just ahead of them.

As they approached the corridor, with the Assistant and the Soldier in the lead with the canith party straggling behind them, the Assistant could see that her request had been acted upon. She could no longer remember why she had asked that the chamber be cleared, and all the books be stacked within the four access corridors, completely blocking them from wall to wall and floor to ceiling. It was not part of her timeless purpose. Merely some temporary thing. An eddy in the flow, there and then gone.

Hundreds of assistants had clearly been at work for many weeks, if not months. As requested, a narrow tunnel, barely big enough for a canith to crawl through, had been left along one side of the southern corridor. It was to this small entrance that the Assistant led the war band. The chamber behind them was half-aflame, orange tongues of fire reaching the ceiling, the flames in other places dark crimson and even blue, tainted by the chemicals in the books they devoured. The awful heat singeing the canith's fur was perhaps all that kept them moving. Carlotte had passed out sometime previously and lay cradled in the Soldier's arms.

"Go in." The Assistant pointed for the Soldier to go first. She addressed the canith next. "The rest of you will need to block this tunnel as soon as you're through. Fill it in completely or the fire will find a way past." She dropped to the ground and began to crawl into the tunnel after the Soldier.

THE ASSISTANTS HAD taken their instruction literally. The chamber lay empty. Empty of books, empty of everything. Of the granite shelves that had filled the chamber floor to ceiling, only scatterings of gritty reddish dust remained, the stone removed with a wave of a white hand.

While the canith laboured to fill the tunnel, the Assistant helped Carlotte out into the chamber. They walked for several hundred yards.

"How long will we be here? What will we eat?" Carlotte asked weakly. "We can't live off the centre circle forever." She shuddered, as anyone who has had to use the circles for any length of time would. They were intended to prevent starvation, but only just, they were not intended to encourage habitation.

The Assistant looked at the Soldier. Both were thinking that the first thing the canith would eat would be Carlotte.

"Cut me." The Assistant held her hand towards the Soldier again.

"It is not permitted."

For a time, both stared at the other in silence. Long enough for the canith to make progress on blocking the tunnel. Long enough for Carlotte to sit down beside them, put her head into her hands, and weep. Long enough even for the Assistant to lower her hand.

An image rose within the Assistant from a place she didn't own. The image of a hand holding an apple, and then, in the next instant, holding only a scattering of apple pips. "I'm not sending her to the Exchange. It's to bring water, so they can irrigate their crops."

"They don't have any crops." The Soldier kept his sword at his side, as much a prisoner of the body he'd invaded as she was.

"They're not going to have any without water."

"How will water help?"

"You destroyed their rations, correct?" the Assistant asked.

The Soldier nodded. It was the rules. No food could be brought into the library.

"Then they will have seeds remaining. Which require water."

"No food is allow—"

"Allowed to be brought into the library. This food will be grown here, not brought in." She held her uninjured hand out to the Soldier.

The Soldier cut her.

The Assistant drew a perfect circle, from the outside this time, and shimmering light filled it as she stood up from her task.

She looked at Carlotte, sitting close by. "Don't fall."

"What?"

"Carlotte . . ."

"How do you know my name?" The girl stood uncertainly, meeting the Assistant's eyes.

The Assistant felt something stir deep inside her, something timely, fluttering against the timeless barriers that held it trapped. Her eyes filled with blue light that felt like tears, though she had never known tears. Confusion trembled through her.

She made a shooing gesture, hiding it with her body so that the Soldier couldn't see. She didn't know why but it seemed as if it was something they shared, this girl and her. She looked meaningfully towards the circle of light. "Don't fall in, Carlotte."

Carlotte's eyes widened. She stepped closer to the circle, staring at the

Assistant as if seeing something new but only half believing it. Not even half.

The Soldier swivelled his head. "Remain where you are, human. Assistant, summon the water."

Carlotte jumped. The Soldier was fast, but not as fast perhaps as he normally was. The girl vanished in a flutter of silk skirts and all that remained of her was a scrap of blue fabric in the Soldier's hand.

"Bring the water," he repeated with more conviction.

Whatever strangeness had steered the Assistant subsided within her, leaving her exhausted, drawn down to still greater depths. Left to her own devices, the Assistant knelt and completed the task. The portal she had drawn connected to the forest where the Exchange lay. Besides the nexus, it contained all manner of superfluity. Trees, for one thing. Pools, streams, brambles, squirrels, rabbits, foxes, a tumbledown wall . . . all manner of things. The Assistant connected her portal to one of the pools. She adjusted a few parameters and stood up.

In time, books would be delivered. It was an empty chamber. It would need books. The Assistant and the Soldier would set them out around the room. She would set out the books and perhaps write some more of the one she held in her hand. The rest was for whoever came by to deal with. Maybe the canith would show an interest. Eventually she would be needed again. But until that time she and the Soldier would rest within the Mechanism. In the meantime, there was little to do but wait. And she was good at waiting.

Sometimes being too slow is the whole of a nightmare.
                    Dreams of the Eldest, *by Gaim Menneal*

CHAPTER 70

Evar

Evar shot from the pool, an arrow loosed from a bow. He was home. No longer a ghost, the laws of the world snared him in a web of limits bound in such things as traction and acceleration, but he pushed against them until they tore, or he did. He carved a straight path through the crop, leaving greenery twisting in the air behind him. He leapt the boundary wall as if it weren't there.

It won't be too late.

Livira had been trapped within the Assistant for his whole life and many lives before. She'd been watching him from the other side of time, powerless to reach him, faint echoes of her love lapping against his shore, realised as the efficient care of a tireless guardian.

I can make it.

Evar ran as he had run in this place many times before, when what was inside him felt impossible to contain. He had sprinted through this ancient prison a thousand times, pursued not by Escapes but by his own demons, finding release in the sudden, extravagant expenditure of energy. He had run always knowing what he would find—another wall.

Now he ran with hope and horror pounding through his veins in equal measure.

Away to his right book towers were tumbling. Through the forest of remaining stacks Evar glimpsed skeer, a trio of them, moving through the chamber. They turned his way, the black globes of their eyes tracking his progress.

"Livira!" Evar shouted her name as he skidded around the corner, into the mouth of the corridor.

The door remained open. The hundred yards of corridor lay scattered with skeer dead, dozens of them. It didn't seem possible that so many had been close enough to be summoned by the cries of the trio waiting in some kind of stasis at the door.

"LIVIRA!" Evar leapt three corpses, piled almost taller than he was. He swerved around the Soldier's body, the top half at least, the lower portion gone. He'd died with his fingers in a skeer's eye sockets and his arm down its throat.

"Livira . . ." Her name fell from his mouth as broken as she was. Her white body lay shattered as if she had fallen from the tower in her story. Dead skeer were heaped around her, though whether slain by her own hands, or in the Soldier's last extravagant defence of her, Evar couldn't say.

"Livira." Evar fell to his knees beside her. He reached for her, but the courage left him and his arms dropped to his sides. Touching her would make it true.

Her face lay turned to one side, lips parted as if in some final word, her eyes blank and white. He could see her there, somehow; beneath the Assistant's smooth, detail-free features he could see the lines of Livira's face.

"Oh . . ." A sob broke from him. He was too lost for anger. ". . . my sweet girl."

And at last, his fingers found the curve of her cheek and tears began to fall. And in the nature of his kind, he raised his head to howl his sorrow to the unseen moons.

"WHAT'S HE DOING?" Malar asked.

"Grieving."

"It's a bit much, isn't it?"

"He loves me, you idiot." Livira wiped her eyes.

"I love you too, but you wouldn't catch me howling like a . . . like that. I'd

be sorting out that fucker holding the door. Or better still, getting ready for those three coming up behind." Malar shook his head. "Damn . . . didn't think I'd left so many standing." He drew his sword. "And why the fuck are we still ghosts?"

"I don't know." Livira knelt beside Evar, next to the ruins of her old prison. The tower she'd locked herself into so long ago, although it only seemed like yesterday. She guessed that in the tale she was both the witch and the princess.

She steeled herself, focused her thoughts, and reached out to touch Evar lightly on the shoulder. "Get up, you. I still need saving."

SOMETHING DEEPER THAN the self-preservation that his grief had swept away forced Evar to his feet and turned him to face the trio of skeer that had appeared at the far end of the corridor. Whatever it had been, the sudden impulse saved him. He might not be able to fight these monsters, but he could certainly run from them.

"What's he doing?"

Evar reached for his knife. He'd seen three of these creatures land blows on the Soldier that would have destroyed any canith. The Soldier wasn't just tougher than a suit of armour, he was swift as well, and far more skilled at reading a fight than Evar was. He'd had a sword too. Evar wondered if he had time to grab the blade.

"Why isn't he running?"

Evar bared his teeth and held his ground. He didn't know where the sword had ended up and he'd trained far more with his knife—his knife would do. He raised a hand, growled deep in his throat, and beckoned them on. He had no illusions about his chance of survival but dying in the defence of Livira's last remains felt right.

"Why isn't he running?"

"Because he's a fucking idiot"—despite his words, Malar sounded as though he approved—"also he thinks you're dead."

The skeer came on, clambering six-legged over the corpses of their brethren, clearly unsure how much threat he posed. The black streaks on the largest of them bled a dark blue into the milky-white plates of its armour. It was oddly beautiful. Evar knew he was going to die, and it seemed that his mind was going to snatch at every last thing of wonder while his heart still beat.

A glance back revealed one more skeer in the doorway. Neither canith nor skeer could open the chamber's doors, but once open, a door wouldn't close while an intelligence occupied the space.

Evar wondered where death would take him. He wouldn't be a ghost—that was to do with time, not death. He hoped it would be somewhere peaceful. Like the forest between. And that Livira would be there.

The skeer began to close the last ten yards. With a sigh Evar raised his knife.

Clovis came from behind like a whirlwind, silent until she struck. She leapt onto the back of the middle skeer, and the Soldier's white blade burst out between its eyes. She moved before the strength left the creature's legs and was on the nearest of the remaining pair before Evar properly understood that she was there.

Evar had never seen a blend of grace and fury so deadly or so frightening. Clovis understood the skeers' range and power. She had probably absorbed a dozen books dedicated to close combat with just this species. She kept close, clambering over them, swinging on their appendages, acrobatic, cutting at everything that could be cut, seeking every chink in their white armour.

She moved between the pair, letting them impede each other. The second skeer died from a score of joint wounds, pouring its creamy ichor onto the floor and the dead alike.

Evar didn't see the blow that took Clovis to the ground. She couldn't have taken the full force of it, or half her bones would be broken. Instead, she rolled until she came to rest against another skeer corpse. She held the Soldier's blade out in front of her but seemed unable to rise.

The thrust of the spear-like shard that the skeer aimed at Evar nearly took him from the air as he leapt at the insectoid. He followed Clovis's example and used one of the creature's hind legs to climb it. To his surprise he found Kerrol arriving on the skeer's back just as he got there. His brother, scarcely trained in combat, clutched the skeer with one hand and both knees, stabbing wildly and largely ineffectively at its back plates. Evar kept his balance, turned, and came up behind the insectoid's head. He reached over, found an armoured eyelet, and drove his blade into the eye within.

Both brothers went flying as the skeer convulsed. Evar landed badly, Kerrol much worse. Remarkably, a knife blade in the brain only seemed to anger the thing. It turned on Evar as he tried to ready himself. The skeer had its spear shard drawn back, primed for the thrust. Evar knew he couldn't dodge it. Part of him was ready. Livira was gone. He wanted to follow.

Clovis came in from the right in a blur and slammed the Soldier's sword through the skeer's head. She swung from the hilt, twisting the blade, and the creature died, folding its legs beneath it.

Evar fell back and lay against the corpse he'd been thrown into. He watched his sister yank the sword clear and flick the ichor from its length. She offered him a fierce grin then came across and took his hand, pulling him to his feet. She didn't say anything. She didn't have to. Clovis had her war at last.

"Oh gods. I'm in so much pain." Kerrol hauled himself up, using a skeer body for support. He spotted the skeer in the doorway and forgot his discomfort. "Remarkable. It's really just going to sit there?"

"It's waiting for the rest of them." Clovis eyed it appreciatively. "It doesn't think I'll kill it."

"Why the hell not?" Evar asked.

"Because then one of us might have to hold the door open." Clovis thrust her sword through her belt. "These sabbers don't lose. They're smart, dangerous, relentless, and they want everything."

Evar walked back to the Assistant's remains and stood, looking down at them. He didn't want everything, he didn't want this war, he wanted one thing, and she was gone.

"Where's the book?" Kerrol came to stand beside him.

"How do you know about the book?" Even in his heartbreak Evar managed to be both amazed with and annoyed at Kerrol.

"It was written all over you," Kerrol said. "Excuse the pun. An undistinguished old book and it meant *everything* to you. Every line of your body said so the day you brought it back. A little deduction and I knew it must have been the book you got lost in when the Mechanism snatched you."

"I don't know where it is. I mean, she had it, then I had it, then she had it. I think it's a kind of circle. A circle through time. Only it's in the past now."

"Hmmm . . ." Kerrol rubbed his chin. "Didn't the Assistant tell you that half the book was still blank?"

"How . . ." Evar looked up at his studious, too-tall brother. "Is there nothing you don't hear?"

Kerrol shrugged. "You lot can be very entertaining."

Evar's grief shuddered through him and he returned his gaze to the Assistant's broken body. "She didn't finish it. What does it matter now?"

Kerrol put a hand on Evar's shoulder. "I'm sorry for your heartache, brother. I truly am. But you've been missing the bigger picture all your life. You thought Mayland was dead—"

"You didn't?" Evar looked at Kerrol sharply.

"Of course not." Kerrol shook his head as if it were a silly question. He waved his knife at the skeer in the doorway. "These creatures may be tenacious, and they may want everything, but frankly they've met their match in this family. The biggest mistake any of them has ever made is leaving that door open." Kerrol took his hand from Evar's shoulder, brushed off a relatively small skeer claw that had become stuck in his leathers, and sheathed his blade. With that he began to walk towards the open door without so much as a backwards glance.

"W . . ." Clovis exchanged a confused look with Evar. "Kerrol, wait! Where are you going?"

"To find your war, dear sister."

Clovis frowned, gave Evar a punch of sympathy in the upper arm, and walked off after their brother.

"You should come too, Evar," Kerrol called back. "I know where to find your girl."

ACKNOWLEDGEMENTS

As always, I'm very grateful to Agnes Meszaros for her continued help and feedback. She's never shy to challenge me when she thinks something can be improved or I'm being a little lazy. At the same time her passion and enthusiasm made working on the story even more enjoyable.

I should also thank, as ever, all the staff at Ace for their support, especially Jessica Wade, Jessica Plummer, Stephanie Felty, and Gabbie Pachon. And of course my agent, Ian Drury, and the team at Sheil Land.

Photo by Nick Williams

Mark Lawrence was born in Champaign-Urbana, Illinois, to British parents but moved to the UK at the age of one. After earning a PhD in mathematics at Imperial College London, he went back to the US to work on a variety of research projects, including the "Star Wars" missile-defense program. Since returning to the UK, he has worked mainly on image processing and decision/reasoning theory. He never had any ambition to be a writer, so he was very surprised when a half-hearted attempt to find an agent turned into a global publishing deal overnight. His first trilogy, The Broken Empire, has been universally acclaimed as a groundbreaking work of fantasy, and both *Emperor of Thorns* and *The Liar's Key* have won the David Gemmell Legend Award for best fantasy novel. Mark is married, with four children, and lives in Bristol.

Visit Mark Lawrence Online

MarkLawrence.buzz
 MarkLawrenceBooks
 Mark__Lawrence

Ready to find
your next great read?

Let us help.

Visit prh.com/nextread

Penguin
Random
House